First published in Great Britain by Macmillan Publishers, 1987
This edition first published by Simon & Schuster UK Ltd, 2012
A CBS COMPANY

The r... of ... Park to be ... ...ork
ha... ... in accordance with sections 77 a...
... the Copyright, Designs and Patents Act, 1988.

Simon & Schuster Australia
Sydney

Simon & Schuster India
New Delhi

www.simonandschuster.co.uk

A CIP catalogue record for this book
is available from the British Library

B Format ISBN 978-1-47110-024-6
Trade Paperback ISBN 978-1-47110-025-3
Ebook ISBN 978-1-47110-026-0

Printed and bound by CPI Group (UK) Ltd, Croydon, CR0 4YY

Lynda La Plante

THE LEGACY

**SIMON &
SCHUSTER**

London · New York · Sydney · Toronto · New Delhi

A CBS COMPANY

For Suzanne Baboneau, for her constant support
and encouragement throughout my career as
a novelist. My sincere thanks, too, to
Simon & Schuster for this exciting republication
of my first and most favourite novel.

Remember me when I am gone away, Gone far
away into the silent land; When you can no more
hold me by the hand, Nor I half turn to go yet
turning stay. Remember me when no more day by
day You tell me of our future that you planned:
Only remember me; you understand It will be late
to council then or pray.

Yet if you should forget me for a while And
afterwards remember, do not grieve: For if the
darkness and corruption leave A vestige of the
thoughts that once I had, Better by far you should
forget and smile Than that you should remember
and be sad.

Christina Rossetti (1830–94)

Prologue

Evelyne Jones sat at the kitchen table, the tip of her tongue pressed to her top lip as she concentrated on her handwriting. The house was silent, everyone asleep, and the kitchen was lit only by firelight. She wore an old shirt of her Da's, and her long, skinny body was hunched over her work, her bare feet one on top of the other for warmth. Evelyne's waist-length thick red hair was braided into a single plait down her back. Small wisps of curls clung to her forehead.

She yawned, stretching her arms above her head like a ballet dancer. Her thin frame, without an ounce of fat, was more like a young boy's, and she was so tall, too tall for her age, head and shoulders above the rest of the girls in her class at school.

Hugh Jones, Evelyne's father, caught his breath. She hadn't heard him come down the stairs to stand in the darkness, watching her. Everyone said that poor Evie Jones was no beauty – so tall and thin – her best feature was her wondrous hair. Some had even said it should be ironed, it was like the fan of a concertina. But at that moment Hugh thought she was the most exquisite creature he had ever set eyes on; he couldn't move, she held him mesmerized by some magic.

Slowly Evelyne became aware of him, and she turned to give him the sweetest of smiles.

'Oh, Da, I love the family so, I love you all so much.'

'Ay, well, that may be right, but you should be abed . . . get yourself up, gel, now.'

She brushed past him and gave him a tickle in the ribs, and he caught her to him, held her tight. He could smell the soap on her face and neck, and kissed the white, white skin. His voice was muffled with emotion.

'We all love you, too, gel, with all our hearts.'

Slipping past him she went up to bed, but he remained standing, unable to move. His Evie, his darling child, had been untouchable for that single moment. He was so used to seeing her in her worn clothes, doing the household chores. She was just a little girl, like the other girls in the village, but that moment struck like a warning bell, telling him that Evelyne, his daughter, was different.

BOOK ONE

Chapter 1

Doris Evans looked through the compositions handed in by her class. They were, as usual, grubby, the cheap exercise books food-stained and dog-eared. Coal dust from the small hands made the texture of the paper gritty. Page after page of misspelt, blotched, childish dreams. Their subject was, 'Choose a character from history, one you would like to have been.'

The stories were similar – in many cases too similar – and Doris suspected that Lizzie-Ann Griffiths had been making herself a few halfpennies. Ninety per cent of the girls from her class fancied being Gaiety Girls, but they all spelt it 'Gayity'. Doris sighed and corrected the scrawled lines. So much for history.

Doris saved Evelyne Jones' composition until the very last. Neat, meticulous handwriting on clean, flat pages – the girl kept her notebook in a brown paper bag. At the top of the page Evelyne had printed the date, February 10th 1909, and the title: 'I am Christina Georgina Rossetti'. Then in the same perfect handwriting the composition followed. The young girl discussed her love for her brothers, Dante Gabriel and William Michael, but what was so remarkable was that Evelyne had interwoven her feelings for her own brothers around her fictional self. She compared her own family's education to that of the Rossettis. It caught the teacher's imagination. Doris was taken aback at the depth of feeling and Evelyne's sophisticated use of the English language. She wrote about what it was like to be part of the Pre-Raphaelite movement. Evelyne was ten years old.

Doris was so fascinated she didn't even correct the spelling. She turned page after page, until the final paragraph moved her to tears. Evelyne had copied down two lines from one of Christina Rossetti's poems: Remember me when I am gone away, Gone far away into the silent land, followed by a few lines in which she said that, for many in her village, there would be no distant land, just the blackness of the mine, the blackness of death hanging over them. The blackness never stopped the laughter, the love, but so many lives were lost, and too easily forgotten.

From the schoolroom window, Doris stared down into the village. It was growing dark, and the few streetlights twinkled. In the half-light Doris could see the groups of miners gathering and moving towards the pithead for the night shift.

A hawker led his pony and cart through the village, crying that his apples were cheap, just threepence a pound. Grey house crouched close to grey house, each opening directly on to the street; there were no gardens, no colours to relieve the grey. Doris sighed. Even the leaves were grey, never green, and the berries black before they were red.

Doris hugged her brown coat around her, closed up the school and walked down to the village. It was strange to think that only a few hundred yards from here was that wondrous valley sheltered by mountains, their lower slopes covered with the darker greenness of trees, the upper by the lighter mountain grasses and ferns which seemed to reach up to meet the sky. Then there was the river, curving across the width of the valley, coursing slowly along the ten miles that separated the village from the sea at Swansea. Doris' heart often ached to have all that beauty so close, and yet their houses huddled, cramped together with the massive furnaces, the coal slags and trams looming above them, the colliery dominating and overpowering the village.

The miners felt differently. To them, God had been extra kind, because just below all this beauty He had placed seams of coal, anything from eighteen inches to eighteen feet wide, and beds of fireclay and iron ore. But for Doris, man had come and defiled the beauty. Man had blackened nature with his meddling, and she hated the coal. She hated the constant threats of pneumoconiosis, 'black lungs', and nystagmus, the wandering eyes, that the men lived under, their poor, bent knees and 'beat' elbows. Doris had good reason to hate the mines – she had been widowed by them. Her treasured wedding gown was still kept in tissue paper. Her neat house was scrubbed every day and the gleaming brass in the rarely used kitchen dazzled the eye. The brass candlesticks, the strip of brass on the mantel, even the brass rod above the grate shone. The tiny, immaculate house seemed held in suspense, waiting for the warmth of a family, waiting to come alive, for life to breathe through the flower-papered walls. The big tub hung at the kitchen door ready for her man, even his tools were cleaned and polished, but Walter Evans was never coming home. The house remained a glittering monument.

Doris threaded her way through the dark streets, hearing the odd murmur of greeting from the young men who remembered her teaching. She kept her head down, her nose wrinkled against the slight wind that stirred the coal dust. In some of the back yards she could see washing still hanging. The kind of household that left its washing out was the kind that didn't care. Only on certain days could the washing be done, for unless the wind blew from the north-east it would quickly be covered in coal dust. Windows were always closed unless the north-east wind blew. The cries of the miners' wives were often heard as they belted their daughters either for not putting out the washing in time or for not bringing it in.

The men were coming off from the day shift. As Doris passed them she could hardly tell one from another. With their blackened faces and clothes they looked much like the coal they mined. Many would need to get the dust from their throats with a few pints before departing homeward for their baths. Doris made a small detour around the pub to avoid the ones who had already downed a few too many.

Doris knew them all, and as she passed they called and smiled. Mrs Griffiths, Lizzie-Ann's mother, yelled to Doris, her raucous voice grating on Doris' ears as she asked how her brood were coming along. Doris nodded to her, said that they were doing well, knowing Mrs Griffiths had already decided that they would leave the following term. Over the years Doris had tired of trying to make them understand how a few more years of education would benefit the boys. It had always proved pointless. They just followed their fathers into the mines as soon as they had enough education to sit the qualifying test, usually by the age of thirteen or fourteen. Some slipped in even younger.

The Legacy

The village women never tired of discussing Doris Evans, who even after thirty years was still an outsider, and always referred to as 'poor thing'. Some of the women, too young to remember, thought it was because she was widowed and without children, still living alone after all these years. Many whispered that, unlike everyone else in the village, Doris never took in lodgers although she had four rooms. Little Evelyne Jones had been right, oh so right, thought Doris. Memories fade fast. Heartbreak surrounded the village, every family was touched by it, so why should they remember hers?

The bakehouse smelt wonderful and Doris, who had left her tin of dough there in the morning, now collected her fresh bread. She paid her penny and carefully folded the linen over the bread tin. The short distance from the bakehouse to her front door could ruin the bread, covering it with coal dust so that it tasted gritty. She noticed that already her hands and coat had a fine film of dust on them. She blew her hands clean, then hurried on down the dark street.

Halfway down her street Doris met John Prosser, Tom Clapham, Rees Griffiths and Danny Tanner carrying Jack Carlick between them. Jack's blackened face was screwed up with pain, and he moaned softly. Doris pressed herself against the wall. She had taught so many of these boys and so many of their names were listed on the church walls, for explosions and fires down the mine were an annual occurrence. When the men moved on, she found the back of her coat smudged with soot from the wall.

A group of small children, clutching their farthings, were clustered around Ernesco Melardi's ice-cream cart. They should have been tucked up in bed, it was almost six, and Doris tut-tutted at them hanging around playing tic-tac. They saw her and waved, and Doris gave a sharp nod of her head. She could hear the children sniggering and whispering behind her but she didn't turn back. 'Droopy-Drawers Doris' was their favourite name for her this week.

It was the sound of a child's screeching voice that made Doris catch her breath. It was sweeping over her again, and she only just managed to open her front door before her head began to thud with one of the blinding headaches that beset her so often. Doris was back in Clydach Vale again, her head thudding, her ears filled with the sound of the rushing water. She clung to the edge of the polished kitchen table. Twelve years ago, and yet it was as if it were happening at that very moment . . .

Again she heard the children's voices, the screaming hooter as the warning went out. The school had been flooded with water from an abandoned coal level. Doris had waded through the slime, searching, calling out the children's names. Three tiny bodies had been found in the playground, and then little Ned Jones was found curled up like a baby in the corner. Further on the boy's mother cradled her six-month-old baby girl in her arms, her pitiful body covered in mud. It had been so long ago, but Doris' vision of the children never dimmed. She stumbled to the rocking chair by the fire, and closed her eyes. It usually began with the memory of the children, then Doris would hear again the sound of clogs clattering on the street, the high-pitched voices calling, 'Mrs Evans! Mrs Evans!' Doris rocked herself back and forth, the clogs came closer . . . oh, so much closer . . . The fists banged on her door. The smell of the brass polish made her nostrils flare, her eyes water, and the memories swept over her, like the tears that rolled down her face.

They had been married only days, their honeymoon just a weekend in Swansea, and then Walter had returned to the mines. They said he had been in good voice, they'd heard him singing as the cage came up, then he had collapsed and no one could revive him. The doctor said the work had drawn all the moisture from his body and because it was not replaced he had died of dehydration, just like five others that same year.

The rocking chair creaked, Doris sighed, and the pain in her head began to fade, her thin lips moved as she smiled to herself and sweet memories now eased the pain.

Doris' father was an inspector for the Cardiff Railway Company, and often at weekends he would get tickets for his family to travel around and see the countryside. He was proud of his eldest daughter; Doris was going to Cardiff University to study English. She was artistic and shy and loved to do quick charcoal sketches as the train puffed and chuffed its way across the valley.

On one of her sketching trips she had met Walter and fallen in love. Her father did not approve of the friendship. He considered the illiterate miner to be far beneath his clever daughter. However, when her father fell ill, Doris had no option but to leave the university to take care of him. Her mother had died when she was a child and there was no one else.

Once Walter had travelled all the way to Cardiff to see her, but he had been refused entry to the house by her elder brother. He, like his father, felt Walter was not good enough for her. It was not until Doris' father died that she was free to marry the patient miner. By this time her brother had qualified as a doctor and had met a well-connected girl. After a terrible argument, Doris had packed a bag and travelled to the village. She knew she would never be happy living with her brother and his snooty bride-to-be. She had wasted no time telling them, had even said that they had aspirations above their station. Doris chuckled, she could still hear herself . . .

'Father only worked the railways, he was nothing special, my Walter's good enough for me,' and off she had marched with the small legacy her father had left her, determined to marry her man.

It was the legacy which had enabled Doris and Walter to set up straightaway in their own home, which was unheard of in the village. They did not need to live in Walter's parents' house as so many newly-weds had to. They chose carefully every bit of furniture, each piece of linen, discussed the crockery, the glasses. Walter's family became hers.

She went to Swansea to choose her wedding dress. It was one of the finest the village had ever seen, cream lace-covered satin with lace cuffs and frills at the neck, the veil and train stretching a good six feet behind her. It was decorated with small seed pearls, and she had embroidered shoes to match. Walter had helped her choose the dress. The gossips had whispered that it was unlucky and it was.

Three days later Walter was dead, and Doris was alone in the immaculate house. The wedding dress lay spread out across the bed. She hated her father, blamed him for not letting them marry earlier, at least she would have had those few precious years with her beloved husband. Nor did she ever forgive her brother and his wife. Dr Collins, as he now was, never even sent a wreath. The letter had been short and written by his wife: 'Perhaps it is for the best, he was never good enough for you and we could, I am sure, accommodate you for a while until you find a place of your own here in Cardiff . . . ' Doris never replied. Dr Collins, for all his snobbishness, still lived in the old family house. Half of it had been left to Doris and she had every right to move back, but she didn't.

The memory of those two full days and nights were all she had to last her a lifetime. And, sadly, they had lasted. Doris had begun to teach in the village school a year after Walter's death. Her sweetheart, her husband, was with her in every corner of the house, and she needed no one else . . . 'poor thing'.

Chapter 2

Evelyne had not been still since she had returned from school. She had slipped a pinafore over her skirt and rolled up her cardigan sleeves. Her thin arms were red raw from the cold, and yet she was sweating. Her pale face shone, her red hair clung in tight curls around her neck and the long braid down her back was loose. She tucked the wildly curling strands back and picked up the heavy buckets, puffing with the effort. As she tipped the water into the pans and the kettle, it splashed out, soaking her, drenching her bare feet which were filthy from the coal-dust-filled streets. She carried the empty buckets outside and waited in line to refill them as she did every day, every week, every month. Come five o'clock the line of village girls and women was always a hive of chatter as they met to collect water for their menfolk's baths. All their families worked in the mines and every night was bath night.

Lizzie-Ann wiped her button nose on the sleeve of her threadbare cardigan. She grinned at Evelyne.

'You back again? Well, well, Evie Jones, you'll make a fine wife.'

She wrinkled her face and pointed to her black eye, a real

shiner that made her wide pansy-coloured eyes appear ever larger. Lizzie-Ann was the prettiest girl in the village, and she knew it, she was a holy terror. Laughing, she said, 'Is it any blacker? Me Mam hit me so hard I near fell off me feet. "Oh," she said, "you little bugger, not brought in the washing, and Lord love me it's covered in coal dust. "'

Evelyne smiled shyly and moved a step closer to the tap. She loved to hear Lizzie-Ann's prattle, and knew they'd all be laughing in a minute.

"'I'll be leaving your coal dust, Ma," I says, "because I'm going to London to join me auntie, ohhh I'm following in father's footsteps, I'm following my dear old dad."'

She swished her skirts and danced up and down, her piping voice off key, but everyone began to giggle. Seeing she had an audience she began to do the can-can.

'Come on, Evie, kick yer legs up, come on gel . . .'

'Will you really be going to London, Lizzie?'

'Didn't I just say I wuz? Oh, look, there's Dirty Jed, I'll bet a farthing I'll get a lemon sherbert outta him for showing me knickers.'

Evelyne poured the water from the buckets into a big iron pan balanced on the coal fire. Will grinned at his little sister as he stripped off his working clothes and she ducked under his arm to fill the tin bath. She loved bath time – loved the laughs and the warmth of the big old kitchen. Will was a strapping lad with curly, dark auburn hair, and black as his face was it still couldn't hide his rosy cheeks. He had a tooth missing where he had fallen down in the pit and it gave him a cheeky little-boy look, but he was a devil when it came to teasing her.

'Look at her stick legs, Mike,' Will said to his younger brother, 'it's a wonder they don't snap.'

Evelyne slapped him with the newspaper she was laying on the floor. Clouds of coal dust filled the air as the boys dropped their work clothes into the box and Evelyne pushed it under the table. Mike gave her a friendly pat on the bottom.

'An' she hasn't got a bum either, but I love 'er, I love 'er.'

Mike always tried to be like his brother Will, but in truth he was as reserved and shy as Evelyne. Today had been his first day down the pit, and he was so tired she had to hold his hand to help him step into the bath. He moaned as he squatted in the water.

'Give us a yell, gel, when he's through. I'll be out in the yard.'

'Won't you help me get Mike clean, Will? You'll have time before supper to go a-courting.'

They all knew that Will was stuck on Lizzie-Ann, but, good-natured as ever, Will nodded, picked up the old sheet and ripped a piece off. He touched Mike's back, which was raw from rubbing against the coal surface, and noticed that his elbows were bleeding and there were lumps on each side of his head.

'You did well, our Mike, now get yerself clean. Do it this way.'

He twisted the piece of sheet into a point, dipped it in the water.

'We do our faces first, mind, roll the corner into a point, wet it, and stuff it into yer eyes, then yer nose and ears . . . always do this first, while the sheet's clean.'

Mike prodded and sneezed and coughed, his skin felt as if it was crawling.

'Aw, put yer back into it, lad, or you'll not get the muck off ... Evie, give him a hand, he's so tired out he's lost his strength.'

When she had helped Mike get clean, Evelyne rushed out to refill the buckets. The kitchen was steaming and five times she went to the tap. She never blushed to see her naked brothers, nor were they shy at her scrubbing their backs with a pumice stone. They bawled at her for being too rough, splashed her when she was too gentle. She had seen her Ma bathe her Da since she was able to toddle, and had shared bathtime duties since she was strong enough to carry a bucket of water.

Mike stood up, dripping, and held out his arms for the sheet that served as a towel. She wrapped it around him and held his warm body for a moment. He was much younger than her other brothers, and his face puckered as he stepped out of the tub. Blood was running down his legs in rivulets from his knobbly knees, and Evelyne looked up into his face.

'You all right, Mike? Shall I get the disinfectant?'

'No, I can't stand the stinging.'

Sighing, Will eased his body into the water.

'My God it feels good, don't it, Mike? Ahhh, this makes it all worthwhile, will you soap me back, gel?'

As she rubbed his back, she could feel the scars under her fingers. Mike sat huddled by the fire and watched her, and she gave him one of their secret, intimate smiles. He looked down, his long eyelashes looked as if they were resting on his cheeks.

'Did Lizzie-Ann ask about me?'

Evelyne scrubbed and soaped, her skirt sopping.

'She did mention that she couldn't sleep for thinking about

17

a certain person with no front tooth. Could that be you, our Will?'

'Is that the truth, gel? Aw, yer having me on, but if you get the chance tell her what a fine-looking man I am naked.'

With a mock gasp of shock, Evelyne slapped him. He stood up and took the towel from her, wrapping it around his waist. He was indeed a fine-looking boy, even with the tooth missing.

Evelyne busied herself setting the table and pouring away the dirty bath water. Will brushed his hair, saying he would just parade on the front doorstep for a while.

'Will you get dressed, Mike, lovey, you don't want to catch cold now?'

Mike looked furtively around to see if Will had left the room then turned back to the fire. His voice was soft, lilting.

'It's so black, Evie, it's indescribable. You push your hand out to feel it, and it goes right through the solid blackness. There is no gleam of light, no shadow. It is so black – like a massive weight on you, all around you as hard on the eyes as bright light.'

He was worn out, and afraid, she could feel it, but it was unspoken. He did not look at her, knowing that she knew. He was only three years older than Evelyne.

'Will, Will, supper's on the table now, come on.'

Evelyne set down the steaming bowls of stew, the big chunks of fresh bread. The two boys ate hungrily, washing the food down with gulps of scalding tea. There was a jug of ale, too, and that went down fast, but the dust stayed deep in their lungs. They were still eating when there was a rap on the back door.

'I were just passin' an' wondered how yer Mike got along on his first day?'

Old Peg-Leg Thomas hobbled in, grinning a toothless smile, his hand already out for a mug of tea. He gasped and heaved for breath, but he rolled a cigarette as soon as he had sunk into the most comfortable fireside chair.

'Who's yer butty-mum?'

Mike wiped his mouth and told him it was Danny Williams.

'Ahhh, now there's a good butty-mum ... yer know, if yer get allocated a butty that don't know the ropes then yer can spend maybe two years learning what should've been taught yer in the first week, an' there's the truth. Good butty, Danny Williams, knows what's what, you got a good lad ter teach yer ... is there another drop of tea fer me?'

Evelyne wiped her plate with some bread, washed it, and refilled it from the stewpan. She poured a fresh mug of tea and loaded a small tin tray.

Her mother, Mary, was lying in the big double bed. Hanging from the ceiling and all around the room were sheets drying and the men's work clothes washed for the following day. The bedroom was above the kitchen, so the big fire kept the room hot and stuffy. Mary was dozing, her thick black hair loose, her cheeks flushed, and Evelyne saw she was sweating. Softly, she put the tray down, and went to the washstand, rinsed a cloth and crept quietly to Mary's side. Evelyne mopped her mother's brow as gently as she could, but Mary stirred, opened her eyes and smiled. Evelyne helped her to sit up.

Mary was in her ninth month, and very ungainly. The baby made a huge mound in the centre of the bed, a mound that didn't seem to belong to the woman who carried it. Mary's once-strong arms were thin, her hands bony, as was the rest of her body apart from her belly. It was as if all her strength and energy had been drawn from her and given to the unborn child. Evelyne propped up the pillows behind her Ma, and Mary leaned back. As Evelyne put the tray carefully on the bed, she noticed the tea and bread she had brought earlier had not been touched.

'How's our Mike, he get on all right, Evie?'

Evelyne nodded and began to tidy the room, patted the drying sheets.

'Are you feeling any better, Ma? You not been sick?'

She watched as Mary used both hands to lift the mug of tea.

'You eat the stew if you can, Ma, you need your strength.'

'Get along with you, Evie Jones, treating me like I was a baby.' Mary lifted the spoon and tried to eat but couldn't, she felt too exhausted. 'Spend some time with Mike tonight, it's always bad on their first day. I'll maybe finish my supper later . . . have you been into see little Davey?'

'I'll go to him now. You try and eat, Ma, there's not too much salt is there?'

Mary put her hand out to take her daughter's, gripped it tight. 'You're a good daughter, and the stew's just perfect . . . I'll have a little rest now.'

She felt so weary, and her eyes closed. She was more than worried, she'd not felt as bad as this even with little Davey.

Little Davey was in his cot, his nappy wet, his shining face red and blotchy. He banged his rattle against the sides of the cot. Evelyne picked him up. The sheets were sodden, she'd have to wash them out in the morning. She put Davey on the floor while she changed the bedding and grabbed him just before he crawled out of the door, laid him on her knee and took off his wet things. The little fellow lolled in her lap, sucked her arm. She held him close, smelling his baby smell, his soft, downy hair. Little Davey was always happy, gurgling away, but his lolling head and drooping mouth revealed that he was spastic. The full extent of his problem was not yet defined, old Doc Clock putting it down to Davey being just that bit backward. Davey was three years old, but he could not walk by himself or say more than 'Da–da–dada' . . .

By the time Evelyne had cleared the table and washed the dishes, filled the kettle for the tea caddies in the morning, it was nine o'clock. She made sandwiches for her brothers, packing them in their tins. The mines were plagued with rats so all food had to be carefully packed. She then washed the rest of her brothers' clothes. They had already gone to bed as they had to be up at four for the five o'clock shift. Their beds would be taken by their Da and their eldest brother Dicken when they came home from the night shift.

It was after ten before Evelyne had a moment to sit alone by the big kitchen fire. Her eyes were red-rimmed from tiredness, she could hardly see her school books. She read by the firelight, careful not to get dust on the books that Doris Evans had lent her. This was Evelyne's favourite time, the only time of the day or night when she could be alone. She treasured it, hungered for it, and used it. This was when she did her writing, when she could dream her dreams.

Mary woke and tried to ease her bulk into a more comfortable position. She sighed, this was one she could well do without, especially with Davey as he was. As she turned she saw Evelyne standing by the bedroom window. She said nothing, just lay and watched her daughter brushing her hair.

'You awake, Mama?'

'I am, lovely, I was just looking at you. Like a mermaid you are.'

Evelyne slipped into the big bed beside her mother.

'It won't be too long then I'll be back on my feet.'

Evelyne snuggled closer, loving the smell of her mother. She kissed Mary's neck then looked up anxiously.

'I'm not too close, am I? I don't want to make you uncomfortable . . . can I feel your belly?'

Mary laid her daughter's hand on her stomach, so she might feel the baby kick.

'Can you feel him? He's a big one.'

Gently, Evelyne ran her small hand over the swollen belly, then she yawned and her eyes began to droop.

'Goodnight, Mama, sleep tight, mind the bugs don't bite.'

Mary eased her body into a more comfortable position and Evelyne's hand slipped away as she fell into exhausted sleep. Mary stared at the ceiling, imagining mermaids reaching to her from beneath crystal-clear water.

'I've never even seen the sea.'

Her own voice startled her, as if she had spoken to herself from the grave, and she was enveloped by an overpowering sense of loss. She sighed a deep, shuddering sigh, and two tears, like dew on a flower petal, slipped down her gaunt cheeks.

In the cold light of dawn Mary could just make out the fading photograph of herself. She was not alone, she was standing arm-in-arm with Hugh Jones on their wedding day. The love she still felt for Hugh couldn't warm her. Her whole body felt as if it was growing colder and colder. 'Where did I go?' she wondered. 'When was I last just Mary? Not Ma, not wife, but Mary.' She couldn't remember, and the harder she tried the deeper became her sense of loss. She wept because she couldn't remember herself, could hardly remember a time when she wasn't tired, when she wasn't carrying or worrying about one child or another. Had her whole life just been rearing children? Cooking, washing, baking? When was the last time she had been up the mountain?

The pieces fell together in her mind like a jagged jigsaw puzzle. The blazing colours, the flowers . . . Mary remembered, oh, the mountains . . . the green fields, the clear, ice-cold water. Havod, the wondrous gardens at Havod, the peacocks. Then, like a picture postcard she saw herself as she had been before all these worn years. She was so free, so carefree, and she was laughing . . . her big, blown-up body felt light . . . she was running like a hare, running on long, strong legs, a bunch of wild flowers in her hand, throwing them up into the bright, warm, blue sky, they were cornflowers . . .

Then there was Hughie Jones. She saw him as he had been all those years ago, so tall and golden they had nicknamed him 'The Lion'. Hugh was the one she had set her sights on, although he was a real lady-killer with all the girls chasing him. But Mary had been the one, the only one, to give him not so much as the bat of an eye in church. She had felt his eyes on her, and when they all congregated outside the Salvation Army Hall she had turned to her friend and in a voice just loud enough for Hugh to hear she said, 'Well, I'm going for a walk, going up the mountain.' No one had wanted to join her, they talked of going to play the piano and have a sing-song. So Mary had gone to the mountain alone. She knew he was following her, way behind and below, but she behaved as if she was completely alone. She found a secluded spot, bathed in warm sunshine, and lay down with the flowers around her, the blue sky and bright sun above. He was close, she could feel him coming closer, but she kept her eyes tight shut. She knew when he sat down only a few feet away, but still she kept her eyes closed. It seemed an age, and when eventually she opened them he had made a crown of cornflowers, and handed it to her. She slipped it on her head and they looked into each other's eyes.

It was not done for a girl to make the first move, or even be out for too long a time with a young man, a young man who hadn't even been courting her, a young man who had hardly said two words to her, let alone one with the reputation of Hugh Jones. They said not a word – he just sat there and she lay back with the crown of cornflowers on her head. Her hands were at her sides and she could feel the cool grass between her fingers. She began to wonder if he would speak at all, or if he would just get up and walk away. When she opened her eyes he was leaning up on one elbow, staring into her face.

She smiled, but he continued to stare as he slowly threaded his fingers through hers. Still keeping his distance from her, his huge hand covered hers completely ... then he lay back and closed his eyes, holding her hand tight. Mary raised herself on her elbow and looked at his handsome face. His hair was a thick, curly mane, blond, yet his eyelashes were almost black. She bent closer and closer, and in one sudden move he pulled her on top of him, held her face and kissed her. She had expected him to be rough, to kiss her like Joe Scuttles had when he grabbed her

24

on New Year's Eve. Hugh's kiss was sweeter, and so gentle her body ached to pull him tighter to her. He laughed, his eyes twinkled, and the dimple in his chin deepened. Then he stood up, scooping her in his arms and carried her to the steep drop of the mountainside and she clung to him. She knew he was teasing, but he took her closer and closer to the precipice.

'Marry me, Mary, or I'll throw you over the mountainside, because if you don't I'll not let another man touch thee. You belong to me.'

Mary clung to him, burying her face in his big, broad shoulder and kissed his neck. There had been no need to speak of love, no courtship, no arguments with the families. They were destined for each other.

The village said that Mary had tamed the wild lion. Stories of what Hugh Jones had been up to, and with whom, were passed around and several girls wept themselves into puffy, red-eyed misery. The prize had been caught by Mary, the quiet one – a dark horse if ever there was one, with her big brown eyes and lanky legs. She'd never even said as much as two words to the lad. The truth was there'd been no 'taming', simply a mutual recognition that they belonged together. Everyone said it wouldn't last without even a few weeks' courtship for them to get to know each other. Of course, some said she had to get married – the wild one must have got her in the family way – but that wasn't true either.

Eventually even the most sceptical had to button her mouth, because the couple seemed so contented, so happy, with no need of the social life of the village. They kept themselves to themselves, and were the envy of many other couples. Hugh Jones never stopped off at the pub on his way home from the mine with the other lads. He would be up and out of the cage faster than anyone else as soon as the hooter sounded the shift's end. At home he would be building, sawing, painting, and if anyone so much as hinted that he would go back to his old ways, Hugh's temper would flare up and no one in his right mind ever wanted that. Memories of Hugh with his shirt sleeves rolled up, taking on any comer at fist fighting, even the gypsy travellers, were as clear as day. Hugh had been the source of much gossip in his wild days, but the gypsy fight was the one the village remembered best.

No one could recall the reason, it had been so long ago. It was a blazing hot day in August when, as Peg-Leg Thomas remembered, three gypsies had called on Hugh's invalid father. They had come to exact some kind of vengeance and they weren't just any old travellers, they were from the Romany clan that sold the pit ponies to the mine. They would arrive in midsummer every other year, with their wagons and trailers and roped lines of ponies. Once they had set up camp the women would go from house to house selling pegs and ribbons. Some, with their bright skirts and headbands, would be invited in to read the tea leaves or the worn, red palms of the miners' wives.

It was always an occasion, and if they were there on a Sunday, they would set up a small fair. The children were warned not to go too near to the camp or the gypsies, as no one could ever really trust them. On this particular Sunday, according to Peg-Leg, three gypsies, all wearing their smart suits and brightly coloured neckerchiefs, walked down Elspeth Street. Their arms were linked and they knocked any passer-by out of the way with a shrug. It was whispered that the man in the middle was descended from the Romany king himself. Proud, their black eyes expressionless, they were the real *Rom-antishels*. They seemed almost to skip, their steps as light as if walking on air. Peg-Leg said you could always tell a gyppo by the spring in his walk.

It was typical of the Jones family, no one could get out of them the real reason for the visit of the three cocksure, high stepping men. All they did know was that Hugh was taken from his house, not exactly held between the men, but walked by them up to their camp. A few of the village boys followed, but kept well back because they could see trouble brewing, like a small cloud in the air.

They saw Hugh Jones being led to one of the very ornate caravans, taken inside and then brought out again. All the gypsy men formed a circle around him, and the one who had walked in the middle of the threesome took off his jacket. Hugh threw his own worn jacket to the ground and adopted a boxer's stance. Quite a few of the older men from the village had joined the watching boys. They all had to admire Hugh. He seemed fear-less with his fists up, his face grim, and yet he could have been no more than sixteen or seventeen. For all his youth, Hugh was a lot taller than his opponent who was a grown man and, by the firmness of his muscular body, also a fit one.

The villagers watched Hugh Jones take one hell of a thrash-ing. Time and time again he was knocked to the ground, but every time he got up again, although his nose was bleeding and his eyes cut. Nor did his opponent fight clean – there were kicks, and Peg-Leg swore he saw the gypsy snarling and snapping as if he was trying to bite Hugh's ear off. There was no outright winner; the fight went on for a full hour until both men sank to their knees in exhaustion. Hugh had been picked up by two youths and flung out of the camp. His pals slunk down and helped him up, and only when they had put a safe distance between them and the camp were there raised fists and defiant yells, before they hurried away with the bleeding Hugh. And, by God, Hugh was at the pithead that night, bloody nose and all. They tried to wheedle out of Hugh why he had taken such punishment, but he wouldn't say a word. A couple of the boys even tried bribes, but he shook his head. It was a private matter.

The gypsies moved on and soon the incident was forgotten, unless Peg-Leg was in one of his story-telling moods or had a few beers too many. Of course, Hugh Jones always came out as the champion, taking on five men − sometimes six or seven − which only built up his legend as a great boxer. It was always murmured in the ear of anyone who crossed Hugh, 'Eh, watch it, remember the gyppos.'

So when Hugh had insisted on staying by Mary's side for the birth of their first child, the account of the fight Hugh had with Doc Clock brought out all the old stories again, and Peg-Leg drank quite a few free pints down the pub. Hugh's workmates shook their heads in amazement. 'Imagine wanting to be there at a birth,' they muttered, 'dear Lord, what was the world coming to . . .'

Hugh had been at Mary's side for the birth of his eldest three sons: Dicken, the first, then Will and Mike, but for Evelyne's and little Davey's births he had been on the night shift so he had missed their deliveries. The neighbours whispered that perhaps if Hugh had been there when Davey was born, he wouldn't be the way he was.

Hugh Jones, Mary's man, lover, husband; the crown of

cornflowers had married them on top of the mountain. The taste of that sweet kiss had long since gone, but now the memory of it filled her with a new strength, and she was fifteen again. She knew he'd find her, would come running to her with his big strong arms open wide, to scoop up her tired body and hold her close to his chest. The lioness was exhausted, her brood grown, but the lionheart wouldn't fail her.

Evelyne woke from a deep sleep, sat up and felt for the warmth of her mother.

'Ma?'

She wrapped a blanket around her and crept down the stairs. As she pushed open the kitchen door she almost cried out. Mary was dressed, pulling on Hugh's heavy coat, wrapping a long, woollen scarf around her neck.

'Ma, where you going? Is it time? Shall I go call Nurse Thomas?'

Evelyne rushed over to her mother, but when Mary turned round her face was so flushed and her eyes so bright that Evelyne drew back.

'I'm going to see the mountains, Evie, I have to go up to the mountains before it's too late. Don't try to stop me, don't call the boys, I beg you ... I'll be back soon, you'll see.'

Evelyne ran back upstairs to get into her clothes, and she heard the door slam. She ran to the window. She was frightened. Something was wrong and she knew it. From the bedroom window she could see her mother's bundled figure as she hurried up the street, helping herself up the hill with her hands against the brick walls of the houses. Evelyne woke Will, shaking him, shouting that their Ma had gone out.

Will sat up and rubbed his head. Evelyne was already shaking Mike awake, and the boys scrambled out of their bunks and ran to the window. Mary was way up the street now.

'What's all the fuss, our Evie? Ma's all right ...'

The hooter sounded for the end of the night shift, and it was only minutes before the sounds of the men returning home would fill the street. Evelyne ran to the pithead looking for her father. She knew something was wrong – knew it but didn't know what to do. As the cages full of black-faced men were cranked up Evelyne ran from one group to the next. Dai Thomas pointed over to Hugh, and Evelyne ran towards him. He was well over six foot two with broad, strong shoulders, and he stood out from the rest of the men. His back had never buckled over, he still stood upright, and with his shock of greying red-blond hair he looked more the grizzled lion than ever.

With Hugh was his eldest son Dicken, tall as his father. They were just climbing out of one of the cages when Hugh saw Evelyne running towards him. He thought automatically that Mary was having the new babe and waved to her, his mouth and gums glowing pink in the blackness of his face.

'Da, come quick, Ma's gone up the mountains, and she's too near her time, she was strange, she shouldn't have gone walking, not now, not at this time.'

Hugh and Dicken began to run, and the word spread quickly. Soon they were joined by Shoni 'Bully' Thomas, Rees Jones, and Willie 'Black Pipe' Keenan. Still black-faced, covered in dust, they ran down the street. The day-shift men were leaving home and as word sped through the street, several of them dropped their tools and went to join the search. This meant a lot, for the day men would lose out on a day's wages if they didn't turn up at the pithead on time. Dicken, Will and Mike followed their father, all of them running out of the village towards the mountain.

In the early morning the mist had been thick over the mountain-top, but the sun began to cut through and it slowly lifted. Echoes of the men's voices rang round and round as they called out for Mary. It was a strange sight, the searching, black-faced men calling to Mary as the clear, beautiful day began.

'Oh Christ, man, where is she? *Mary*!'

Hugh Jones was beside himself. He thrashed at the bramble bushes, calling his wife's name, his face streaked with sweat. He turned to the men, told them to go back, not to lose a day's work because of him; he and his boys would find her. The men eventually turned back to their work or their beds.

The whole village was agog. What on earth was Mary Jones thinking of – a woman in her condition going up the mountain – she must have lost her mind. They discussed it avidly at the water taps, over the clanking of the buckets. They would occasionally look up beyond the village, not that they could see anything, but Mary was up there somewhere. Their menfolk down the pit talked about it and, like their wives, they were only too ready to recall stories of people lost up in the mountains, men who had run wild up there after being too long underground.

Hugh Jones was exhausted. He sat on a rock, his sons around him. They had never seen their father so distraught: he clung to Dicken and began to weep. The boys were scared. Why had Ma suddenly upped and left them in that condition? It was so strange. Their safe, strong Ma, where was she?

Evelyne kept on searching and calling, climbing higher and

higher. Surely Ma could not have got this far, she must be below, they must have missed her. Evelyne looked down and could see her Da and her brothers way below like small black dots . . .

'Ma . . . *Mama* . . . *Ma!*'

Evelyne's voice echoed round the mountain. Mary was standing staring down at the river. There was a puff of smoke where a train had just passed below a bridge, a little train chugging on down the valley.

Evelyne called down to the men that she had found her mother, and they climbed up the mountainside towards her. Mary stood frozen, eyes staring vacantly into space. Hugh reached his daughter's side and Evelyne pointed to her mother, his wife . . . His face was almost clean of soot, whether from sweat or tears she couldn't make out. He edged towards Mary, speaking her name, so softly the children could hardly hear him. They watched, bewildered, as the huge man moved closer and closer, saw him take hold of his wife, rocking her gently in his arms.

'Gave us a proper scare, you did, Mary. Had the whole village out looking for you. Did you not hear us calling you?'

He turned back to his children, told the younger boys to go to the pithead and see if they could still get on the shift, the others to go home.

They began to wander down the mountainside, turning to look back up at their parents. They saw their father still holding their mother tight, so tight as if he was afraid she would throw her swollen body over the precipice. As they went further down the slopes, the two figures on the mountainside sat down, their arms around each other, their heads close, like young lovers.

Dicken could see his little sister getting anxious so he made light of it.

'You know our Ma, Evie, she's just wanting to have Da to herself.'

Evelyne smiled, then went and sat on the front doorstep and waited for hours. She saw Mr Williams' dog wander past with his shopping bag and little leather purse, saw him trot into the butcher's and collect the meat. Clever little dog, went by the main street there, but round by the back cobbles when he'd got the meat. That way he was sure none of the other dogs would steal his owner's chops.

At midday Evelyne woke little Davey and fed him, then sat and played with him on the doorstep, and still her mother and father had not returned.

Dr Jones came by, with his gold watch chain. Doc Jones only had the chain, no one could recall him ever having a watch on the end of it. So he very rarely knew the time and was known as Doc Clock because of it. He'd heard about Mary, and said to tell them he'd drop by to see if everything was all right.

Along the street net curtains twitched aside. Hugh and Mary, entwined in each other's arms, walked slowly down the narrow, cobbled road. They were like young lovers – twice Hugh stopped and cupped his wife's face in his big hands and kissed her upturned face.

Evelyne saw her big Da carrying her mother up the stairs. Mary was weak, and her cheeks were flushed bright pink. When Hugh came down again his daughter had already filled the tub with water for him. He said nothing, but began slowly to wash his face and hands, soap his hair. He bent his head as Evelyne scrubbed his back, and when he stood up from the tub his massive, muscular body looked like a warrior's; there were deep scars and gashes across his back, arms and thighs. His body was still as strong as a young man's, his thick grey hair stuck up in waves like a mane.

Evelyne kissed his back softly and he squeezed her hand. Oh, how she loved him. He was not a man of many words, never had been, but he had held them all together. The boys, all of them, adored him.

'Your Ma wanted to go up on the mountains, that's where we used to do our courting. She's all right now, just very tired. Take her some hot tea, there's a good girl.'

Evelyne prepared the tea, and just as she was about to take it up her father stopped her, took from the pocket of his old work coat a tiny wild flower, and stuck it in her hair.

'Stay a while with her, until I'm home. That woman up there is part of me, understand, child? We just found a bit of our yesterdays ... you get so you forget she was a rare beauty. Today she was just as beautiful again, I had almost forgot.'

Mary lay in the bed, her eyes closed. Evelyne placed the tea beside her and lay down close to her mother, took her hand and kissed it. Mary turned her huge, swollen body to face Evelyne. They smiled at each other as if they had an intimate secret. Mary looked into her daughter's face, traced her high, strong cheekbones with her worn, rough hands.

'You're a good girl, Evie, I'm sorry to frighten you all so, I didn't mean to, but I just had to go up there one more time.'

As young as she was, Evelyne seemed to understand. Mary

held her daughter's hand and whispered to her, made her promise on God's Holy Bible . . .

'Don't let the mines take your youth. You get away from here, Evie, don't stay too long. It'll soon be time for you to go, find yourself someone from outside, promise me, Evie?'

Evelyne promised, but she was unsure exactly what her mother meant.

She left her mother sleeping and went downstairs to give her brothers their dinner. They had just come back from the day shift. Will was laughing and shoving Mike . . . it seemed that Lizzie-Ann had said 'yes', and she and Will were going to be married. Only half listening, Evelyne gathered that Will planned for Lizzie-Ann to move in with them until they saved enough money for a small house of their own. So much for Lizzie-Ann and London.

Mike's back was worse, the cuts deeper, and he said it was his own fault because the rocks were jagged and he couldn't remember to keep his body crouched. His knees were in a terrible state, and his clothes were sodden.

Evelyne washed the boys, fed them, washed their clothes, washed out little Davey's sheets. It was night again, and she was so tired her arms ached, too tired to get her school books out. She sat in her mother's rocking-chair, close to the big, blazing fire. Evelyne and Mike were left alone. Mike subdued, his eyes red-rimmed, unused to the coal dust. His hands and nails were already becoming ingrained with black. Evelyne sat and listened to him, he needed so badly to talk to someone – not the lads, they already knew what he was saying, they had all been through it, but for Mike it was all new, all disturbing.

'My legs were cramped all day, Evie, I got no skin left on the backs of my hands. An' with the dust in your lungs you can't stop coughing, an' it's burning inside your eyes. My skin is smartin', flying bits of coal cut into your face ... see, I'm in one of the lower surfaces, an' I got to shovel on my belly.'

Evelyne listened like an old woman, nodding, darning the men's socks. All the while she was alert for sounds from Davey or her mother. Mike started to tell Evelyne about the pit ponies. Mike had always loved the outdoor life, running up the mountain to school, and he loved animals, especially horses. Mike continued in his low, lilting sweet voice, like a musical whisper, telling Evelyne about how the horses were treated in the pits.

'Poor devils, Evie, they work sixteen hours or more straight, they often have no water. One dropped this mornin' from exhaustion – just dropped, Evie. I mean, it's not all the men's fault, sometimes you've got to take a horse out again right after it's been workin', so the poor bastard's dead on his feet before you start your shift. You got to whip him to make him work.'

Mike went on about the conditions, and Evelyne listened quietly and continued her sewing. Mike was in tears as he told her how some of the horses had to work in tunnels that were too low and, like him, they couldn't remember to keep themselves bent down, so they ripped their backs open on the jagged rocks. But they were whipped into such a frenzy that they kept on opening up the old wounds.

'After the first time through the squeeze the horse knows it's cut him, so next time he's forced through he wants to go fast, but if he goes too fast and the handler loses control, the tram full of coal can tilt and spill out its contents ... so the men put chains through the horse's mouth to pull him back ... and there he is, poor little bastard, with his back ripped open, his mouth chained, tortured . . .'

Evelyne looked up. Mike was on his feet, tears smarting in his eyes. He was talking about the pit ponies, but it was himself he was really talking about. And the more he talked, the more he upset himself. He ended up clinging to Evelyne and crying like a child.

'I can't go back, Evie, I can't, I hate it, I hate it, I'm scared all the time, Evie, I'm scared, and they keep on tellin' me terrible stories.'

Evelyne heard little Davey cry out, and she had to pry Mike's arms from her and scramble up the stairs to look after the boy . . . she heard the scream from Mary's bedroom as she reached the child's door. It was Mary's time. Hugh had already left for his night shift, he would miss this birth too.

They always said buy yourself a good dark suit, you'll need it, and every man did have one good dark suit besides his working clothes. The dark suit was necessary because there were so many funerals.

Will, Mike and Dicken were all dressed and ready. They sat in the kitchen waiting for Evelyne to come down. Mrs Pugh had taken Davey until they came back from the service.

There was only one coffin for mother and child, and flowers around the simple wooden box were from all the villagers. The family had asked them to pick wild flowers – cornflowers. Two horses pulled the hearse through the streets, and the grieving family walked slowly behind up to the church. It was a good turnout, everyone spruced up and wearing their Sunday best.

Funerals usually took place on Sundays, as the mines were closed and no one lost a shift.

Mary Evelyne Jones and her son were buried where they could always see the mountain.

Evelyne had been a calming influence throughout. A rock, as they all said, astounding for one so young. There was quite simply no one else to run the house. No time even to grieve, and she wept into her pillow at night, quietly so as not to wake anyone. Evelyne would never forget her father's face as he watched the cornflower-strewn coffin lowered into the ground. He had been so silent, so isolated that no one dared interrupt his solitude. But there at the graveside he had roared out his grief, like a wild animal. The cry echoed round the mountain and chilled those standing at the graveside. Evelyne had held on to his hand, held it so tightly her nails cut into his palm.

That night his sons had taken him down to the pub and they had all got so drunk that Evelyne had to put each one to bed. Her father's head lolled, his eyes unfocused, as she helped him to undress. Sadly, the drunkenness persisted. Mike and Will would come straight home as usual from the mines, but Hugh would remain in the pub until closing time. Dicken waited to help him home, help put him to bed. No one tried to stop him: it was as if they knew he was trying to ease the pain, the agonizing pain of life without his darling Mary.

Chapter 3

Six months passed and Evelyne did not return to school. There was always so much to do at home. Little Davey was dependent on Evelyne and the menfolk had to be cooked, washed and cared for. Lizzie-Ann had married Will and moved in until they could afford a place of their own. Evelyne put away her school books; her Christina Rossetti days were over.

Doris Evans had never been one to poke her nose into anyone's business. She had once, she'd gone to see Mrs Reece Mogg, wanting their youngest son to stay on at school. She'd been shown the door so fast, so the story went, she'd left her brown lace-up shoes behind. However, she had thought about it for a good few weeks, and she had decided she would try one more time, this time with Evelyne Jones.

Doris dressed very carefully, in her brown hat, her brown skirt, and matching coat, set off by a nice cream blouse. She also put on her coral crêpe blouse, but felt the cream more suitable.

Doris stood on the Jones' front door step, thought it looked quite clean considering. She lifted the brass knocker, thinking it could do with a good polish, and tapped lightly, then rapped louder. She could feel inquisitive eyes boring into her back, net curtains flicked aside across the street. Her mouth went dry, her carefully rehearsed speech of introduction slipped away from her. She was about to leave when the front door was inched open.

'Evelyne, is that you? It's Mrs Evans, from the school.'

Evelyne had little Davey balanced on her hip, a duster in one hand, and her face was streaked with dust. Doris flushed a bright pink.

'Do you think I could step inside for a minute? If it's not convenient I can come back.'

The door edged open wider, and Evelyne coughed as she swallowed backwards. Her eyes watered, and Doris had to pat her on the back.

'Would you mind coming into the kitchen, Mrs Evans, only I was just feeding little Davey?'

Doris followed her along the corridor. The smell of stale beer, cigarettes and cabbage made her nose wrinkle with distaste. Davey gurgled and threw a soggy, nasty-looking crust of bread at Doris' head. A lot had changed since Mary's death, and gossip about the Jones family was rife. Mike, the youngest boy, had run off to join the army, and Will, so rumour had it, had got Lizzie-Ann in the family way so they'd had to marry. The house was bursting at the seams.

'Er, well, Evelyne, you certainly seem to have your hands full. Should I come back another day?'

With her free hand, Evelyne lifted the kettle and put in on the fire.

'Will you have a cup of tea, Mrs Evans?'

Side-stepping a teddy bear, Doris picked it up and turned to put it on the dirty table, cluttered with crockery.

'Oh, I don't want to put you out.'

Evelyne smiled and went to sit Davey on a chair, looked around the room, then at Doris.

'Would you mind just holding him while I make the tea?'

Poor Doris could hardly stand the smell of the child, and his nappy was sopping wet, but she held on to him and perched on the edge of a chair. It was a mistake, she knew it, and the girl looked terrible. She'd aged years in a matter of months, if that was possible. Her once clean, shining hair was dull and uncombed, and her face was so pale she looked ill. Evelyne was all thumbs, dropping the tea caddy; and she was so aware of the filthy state the kitchen was in that she tried to clear everything into the big stone sink.

'I won't bother with tea, Evelyne, but don't you think he should have a clean nappy on?'

Evelyne flushed and grabbed Davey, so embarrassed she was near tears. Always a sensitive woman, Doris was just as embarrassed and made things worse by sitting awkwardly, perched like a brown crow.

Evelyne laid Davey over her knee and removed the dirty nappy, dropping it in a bucket. He gurgled and laughed, drooling as she washed his bottom. And all the while Doris coughed dry little coughs, and kept opening and shutting her mouth. Her hand was sticky and she took a small lace handkerchief from her handbag.

'My Mama died, and I . . . well, I've been meaning to come and see you.'

Doris looked at her as she sat with her feet neatly crossed, her knees red and her bare feet so filthy Doris wondered when the girl had last bathed.

'Yes, I know. Did you get my note?'

'I should have written, I'm sorry, Mrs Evans.'

Doris stood up and straightened her hat. 'It's about your writing that I've come, Evie ... Evelyne. Your last composition was good, more than good, I still read it. And the reason I'm here is to see if it would be possible for you to return to school.'

Evelyne tugged at a loose strand of hair. 'I can't do that, I've no time to come to school.'

'But you are more than good, child, it's a sin not to finish your education.'

At that moment Davey put a piece of coal in his mouth, sucking it. Evelyne bent down and took it from him, threw it on the fire and picked him up. She buried her face in the small boy's neck and to Doris' consternation her thin shoulders began to shake. Doris realized she was crying.

Although never one to show her feelings, Doris suddenly rose to her feet and wrapped her bony arms around Evelyne. Doris smelt of mothballs and her pale eyes were wet with tears.

'I understand, I understand, you have the boy to care for, and the menfolk, but ... here, don't cry, child, here ...'

She handed Evelyne her tiny handkerchief, and didn't even mind when Evelyne blew her nose on it. She poured the tea and handed it to Evelyne, patted her head, and it all came out in a gush.

'I know times are hard, but what I've been thinking is that if you have a few hours of an evening, when the little boy is sleeping, then you could come over to my house. It's quiet, and all my books are there, and if you would like ... well, what I'm saying is that I would be prepared to give you private tuition, I don't want paying for it, but I would like it if you could manage just a few hours.'

She felt her hand gripped tightly, and the girl kissed it hard.

'Oh, Mrs Evans, I would like that so much.'

'Well, then it's settled, whenever you say – when it's convenient to you.'

With little Davey in her arms, Evelyne walked Doris to the door. Doris was excited, she chucked the baby under his chin and laughed when he tried to bite her, a strange, high-pitched squeak. Then she was gone.

Evelyne had to shake her father awake, Dicken was waiting to go on shift.

'Da, Mrs Evans came by today and said I could have private lessons.'

Hugh swayed and stumbled as she helped him dress. He hadn't even bathed the night before, he had got so drunk coming back from work.

'You do as you wish, Evie ... where's Dicken? *Dicken*?'

Hugh left the house with his eldest son. Evelyne went back and began to clear up the kitchen, the broken beer bottles. The new lodger arrived back from his night shift, looked in for only a moment, then went into Dicken's bed in what used to be Davey's room, the little lad now sleeping with Evelyne. They'd had to take a lodger as lately the household was always short of money – the tin on the mantel always empty. Evelyne owed money at the baker's, the pie shop, the hardware store. Things had most certainly changed. The Jones family had never been in debt before. With them being such a big family, and mostly men, there had always been wages coming in.

Hugh still worked the mines along with Dicken and Will, but Will needed his wages for Lizzie-Ann, and they were saving as best they could. But Hugh was getting a bad reputation as a drunkard. Poor Dicken not only did his own job of shovelling, but he hacked the coal face too, his father's job. Hugh was perpetually drunk, but Dicken never confronted him – he worked without a word of complaint. He went to the pub with his father, watched him waste the hard-earned money that rightly belonged to Dicken, but he could say nothing. The Old Lion was losing his roar, his shoulders were bent and his face was always filthy. At night he staggered home, leaning on his eldest son for support.

Dicken was worn to a frazzle, and he knew the managers were beginning to talk. The 'measurers' had been round – the men who counted the coal trams and picked over the contents to see if there were any stones or clay clods making up extra weight. The miners were paid by the tram-load so if the loads were down so were the wages. The wage for boys under fifteen was one shilling and sixpence a day, and over fifteen it climbed up by a few pennies a day. A twenty-one-year-old boy, even when married like Will, still only received three shillings a day.

The miners' wages were scaled according to the job. There were truck-weighers, coal tram-weighers, engineers, stokers, tenders, strikers, lampmen, cogmen, banksmiths, rubbish-tippers, greasers, screeners, trimmers, labourers, small-coal pickers, doorboys, hitchers, hauliers, firemen . . . but the élite, who worked the big veins of the mines, were the colliers, the men who hacked and chipped away at the coal. They worked in teams of two, and were completely dependent on each other. One hacked and chipped, one shovelled and filled the trams behind them, as they burrowed like moles deeper and deeper into the face. If the shoveller sat down, too lazy or too tired, then the chipper would have to lay off too. Dicken had been working for both himself and his Da. He knew it would be found out and could not continue. That night, as they came up from the cradle, the manager called them over. They went into the office and stood, caps in hand, like guilty schoolboys. The manager, Benjamin Howells, was sorry – he didn't like doing what he was going to do. He had known Hugh Jones since he was a boy, he'd been at Dicken's christening in the chapel.

Ben spoke in Welsh – maybe he thought it would soften the blow – but it hammered down anyway. Hugh was given his employment cards and Dicken, of course, stood by his father and wanted his. Ben tried to reason with him, but Dicken was adamant so Ben handed them their cards and the week's wages kept in hand, and the two men walked out. Ben sighed. What a waste to see a man like Hugh go to pieces; it was tragic. And the worst of it was, it looked like he was dragging that fine boy down with him.

Dicken and his Da were both getting drunk, drowning their sorrows. They called for drinks all round, banging on the bar for their pints. Dicken rose to his feet, weaving, and began to sing. He had a clear, high tenor, and stood with legs apart, eyes closed, while his beautiful voice soared.

Mike pushed open the bar door and stood framed in the

doorway, looked first at his brother then his father. His boots were so highly polished you could see your face in them. He swung his haversack down and Dicken lurched into his arms.

'Mike, is it you, lad? Mike . . . Da, will you look who's back, an' all togged out in his fine uniform.'

Hugh fell off his stool and climbed up, gripping the edge of the bar for support.

'A drink, get a drink for my lad, the soldier boy.'

Mike could smell Hugh's breath – he reeked and his clothes were stained and filthy. He shook his head and looked at Dicken.

'Mun, he's drunk out of his mind.'

Mike soon discovered that since his Ma's death their father had rarely been sober.

Evelyne checked the stew and left the pan half on the stove. She knew they would be late again. She had hoped to go and see Doris, but she had not had even a minute to herself for weeks. Lizzie-Ann was no help in the house; if there was work to do she swooned.

'Oh God, I can't, Evie, not in my condition. A woman in my condition should not lift nothing heavy, I don't want to have a baby like little Davey, now do I?'

While poor Evelyne washed and scrubbed, Lizzie-Ann sat with her feet up. It was true she made Evelyne laugh, especially when she put flour over her face and blacked her eyelids and lips like Theda Bara. She could do endless movie-star imper-sonations.

'You know, soon as I've had this baby, I'm going to London,' she would say.

The lodger, a coloured gentleman, fascinated Lizzie-Ann. She would ask him to turn his palms over and then shriek with delight at the pinkness of them. Josh Walker was a kind-hearted man whose family lived in Leeds, like many coloureds who had arrived in the village. There was hardly a house left in the village without a lodger of some kind, Italian, Indian, black ... well, there was one house. Doris Evans kept her four rooms to herself. The war, everyone said, was taking their men and replacing them with outsiders.

That night Dicken and Mike carried their Da home between them. Evelyne was so happy to see her brother that she forgot about going to see Doris. Somehow she made the stew go round, pushed her worries away. Tomorrow was another day and she'd manage to get a little meat from the butcher.

'Evie, want to walk awhile with me?'

Mike smiled, slipping their mother's old shawl around his sister's shoulders.

'I'll be gone by morning, going to France. I'll write to you, and send you pretty things ... oh, Evie, Evie, come here.'

She went into his arms and held him tight. She loved him so, she thought her heart would break.

'Dicken's coming with me. Now shush, it has to be, they lost their jobs at the mine, this way he'll be able to send money home, and me too ... but what of you? You're so thin, and I swear you look older, older than you should ... ' Mike could not say how he really felt, how sad he was to see his sister so gaunt, so pale. It was obvious to him that she was working herself into an early grave.

'It'll be for the best, Evie. With me and Dicken gone it

should ease the burden on you. You have a lad? Someone that's courting you?'

She hung her head as she walked alongside him, flushing bright red. 'Be off with you, Mike, there's no boy interested in me, an' I'm too young yet even to be looking.'

Mike pulled her to him and kissed the top of her head.

'You are special, Evie. Tell you what I'll do, I'll bring a handsome soldier home for you on my next leave.'

The two boys were dressed and ready. Evelyne slipped into the kitchen, afraid they would go without saying goodbye. Dicken ruffled her hair, but he was close to tears. 'Take care of Da for us, we'll be back.'

Mike smiled and blew her a kiss, as hand-in-hand with Dicken she walked them to the door. 'Evie, think about seeing that schoolteacher. You'll have more time now, promise me?'

She smiled but couldn't speak, she was too close to tears.

'Goodbye, darlin', and God bless you.'

She watched her two brothers walk down the cobbled street, their arms about each other's shoulders. Will came and stood behind her, put his arms around her, 'So they've gone. Da was too drunk to understand last night; I'll tell him.'

Deep down he knew his own days at home were numbered, he could be called up at any time.

Six months had passed since the school teacher's visit, and Evelyne popped a note through Doris' door. She had worked out how many hours a week she would be able to spend with Doris, although it had not been easy to arrange. Lizzie-Ann refused to take charge of little Davey so Mrs Pugh had promised to look after him.

'I don't know why you bother learning, Evie. Find yourself a boy, that's what you should be doing.'

Evelyne looked at Lizzie-Ann. She was wearing only her bloomers with one of Will's shirts over the top, her belly sticking out.

'I've no interest in boys, Lizzie-Ann ... if you could turn your charms on at the bakery I'd be grateful, we've no bread.'

'I'll do me Theda Bara for that old bugger ... well, go on, if yer going.'

A plate of sweet, home-made biscuits and a glass of warm milk were waiting for Evelyne, and Doris had been back and forth to the window to see if she was really coming. All her precious books were laid out neatly on the table with a clean notebook, ready for work to begin.

Evelyne tapped the polished door knocker. She was acutely self-conscious about her appearance; her hair needed washing, her cardigan was darned and threadbare, even her skirt was torn at the hem. She wore a pair of her mother's shoes, three sizes too large, and she went pink with shame when she noticed that her heels were black with soot.

'Well, dear, better late than never. Now come in, wipe your feet on the mat.'

She stepped on to the gleaming linoleum in the narrow hall, her heart pounding, hardly able to say a word. She had never seen such lovely, gleaming furniture. There was a sofa covered in velvet with crocheted white cloths on the head rests, and there was a lovely rug in front of the fire.

'You could eat your dinner off your floor, Mrs Evans.'

They sat at opposite sides of the table and gradually became more relaxed. Evelyne soon forgot her shyness and turned the pages eagerly, clapping her hands when she discovered a word she had not heard of before. She thumbed through Doris' heavy dictionary.

'And how, Evelyne, would you spell chameleon? Look it up ... now remember, it might not begin with a "k", it could be a "ch", so search for the word ...'

The wall clock chimed nine and Evelyne looked crestfallen.

'Never mind, dear, we can continue next time.'

Evelyne found herself watching the clock in the kitchen waiting for Mrs Pugh to take little Davey, and then she was off, running as fast as her legs would carry her. Doris was always ready, standing at the door, biscuits and milk waiting on the table. She would dearly have loved to open her thin, bony arms and hug the child. Evelyne delighted her so, but she was too shy.

'Oh listen, Mrs Evans, I know it by heart now. All night I practised just as you told me ... "From her celestial car the Fairy Queen descended, and thrice she waved her wand, circled with wreaths of amaranth. Her thin and misty form moved with the moving air, and the clear silver tones as thus she spoke, were such as are unheard by all but the gifted ear".'

Doris watched as Evelyne stood with her arms held up, her wondrous red hair wild from running, her cheeks flushed.

'That was very good, dear, now drink your milk, and remember descend is "s" before "c".'

She nibbled her thin lips, watching Evelyne eagerly thumbing through the dictionary. She had received a letter from her brother more than two weeks ago, and had spent sleepless nights over it. His wife had died – not that that had disturbed Doris in any way, far from it – but he had invited Doris to stay. He had said it was time they forgot their old wounds. And she did, after all, own part of the house.

'Evie . . . Evelyne dear, I'm going to Cardiff.'

Seeing the desperate, haunted look on her young pupil's face made her swallow hard.

'Oh, will you be gone long, Mrs Evans?' The child's thin hands clenched and unclenched. She was fighting back the tears at the thought of losing her precious lessons.

'Not long, but I was wondering if your father would give his permission . . . of course, I would pay your train fare and any expenses . . . would you like to come with me? Just a weekend trip? We could see the museums. Would you like to come?'

Evelyne was up and out of her chair, hugging Doris so tightly that she could hardly catch her breath. Evelyne's kiss was frantic, but then she raised her fist and bit her knuckles. 'I don't think it would be possible, but thank you ever so.'

Doris had confused herself, she had not really intended asking the child. Yet now it seemed imperative that she should go. The life flooding through her tired, empty shell was turning Doris into a new woman.

'Well, I won't take no for an answer, and here, look, I've a few things put by for you.'

Rushing into her immaculate bedroom, Doris pulled open a drawer, even pushing aside her wedding dress as she searched through her neatly folded clothes and wrapped a selection in brown paper. Knowing the child possessed only the poor things she stood up in, she told Evelyne she had no need for them any more.

*

Evelyne carried the brown paper parcel up to her room and inspected the skirt, cardigan and blouse Doris had given her. They were nearly new and smelt of mothballs. There was not a single darn or hole and even though they were old-fashioned and not a very flattering colour, Evelyne thought they were fit for a queen.

'Well, will you look at her, Will, if she doesn't look a lady! Now, don't you worry, Evie love, we'll take care of everything, and if you don't hurry you'll miss the train.'

Evelyne kissed everyone, checked that Lizzie-Ann knew what to do for little Davey, and gave her so many instructions that they almost got into a fight. Doris wouldn't come in, but stood on the doorstep with her overnight case. As the two went down the street Lizzie-Ann stared after them, then slammed the door. She turned on Will.

'There'll be no livin' with her when she gets back. Wish to God I'd never got meself married, I'd be in London by now, and that's where I'm going, you mark my words.'

Good-natured as ever, Will said nothing, didn't even mention that he'd received his call-up papers that morning.

Chapter 4

Doris had packed a small picnic for the train, and they shared it as the train puffed its way across the valley. Evelyne was more like a child of six than a fourteen-year-old, pointing out of the window, moving from one side of the carriage to the other, unable to keep still for excitement. She smoothed her skirt with her hands, mimicking everything Doris did, acting the lady.

'Now, Evelyne, pack everything neat and tidy, don't leave any rubbish on the train. We'll put it in a bin when we get to Cardiff.'

Evelyne would have eaten the brown paper wrappings if Doris had asked her, she was so thrilled. She grew quieter as the train slowed its pace and moved into the siding at Cardiff Central Station. In clipped tones fit for a sergeant major in the Salvation Army, Doris barked orders to Evelyne.

'Tickets, handbag, case, exit up ahead, keep close by me ... now then, we have to get a tram to Clifton Street.'

When they were seated on the top of the tram, Evelyne turned her head this way and that, her heart thudding in her chest.

'Oh, Mrs Evans, look at the castle, it is just beautiful, and the grass, is it not greener than at home? Oh, look, look at the motor vehicles!'

Some of the passengers sniggered as she shouted in excitement.

'Evelyne, dear, you don't need to shout, I am right next to you, not in an open field . . . speak softly, child, it's not ladylike to shout.'

As they got off the tram Evelyne clung tightly to Doris' hand and almost got them run over, she was so unused to the traffic.

'Taxi . . . Taxi . . .'

Evelyne clapped her hand over her mouth to stop herself shouting out. She had never seen a taxi like it. It had red leather seats, and the driver wore a peaked cap. They got into the back seat and Doris rapped on the glass partition with her umbrella.

'Clifton Villas, number thirty.'

The taxi drew up outside one of a row of bow-fronted, Victorian houses, with white steps leading up to the front door and more steps leading down to the servants' entrance behind the basement railings. Evelyne followed Doris like a lamb, waiting quietly as she lifted the ornate brass knocker. A maid in a black dress with a frilly white apron and cap ushered them through a dark hallway leading to what looked to Evelyne like a palace. There were paintings and china everywhere, chiming clocks, and the drawing-room furniture was covered in velvet, everything in rusty, autumn colours.

'Doris dear, how good to see you, come in, come in.'

Doris kissed the pale lips, identical to her own, and the dapper little Dr Collins gave Evelyne a formal bow and adjusted his pince-nez as he ushered them in. He spoke so quietly that

Evelyne could not catch everything he said, but he was so clean and fresh in his starched white collar. It was obvious he and Doris were brother and sister, Dr Collins was so like her, but Evelyne watched Doris change in front of her eyes. She became stiff and formal, and after their initial greetings they appeared to have nothing to say to each other.

'Would the gel like tea, Doris ?'

Evelyne stood rooted to the spot, staring down at the rose-patterned carpet. The house was carpeted everywhere, she couldn't believe it. Her feet sank into the pile, into two dusty pink roses.

'Sit down, Evelyne, and say hello to Dr Collins.'

Evelyne perched gingerly on the edge of a velvet sofa, feeling its softness beneath her hands. She swallowed, about to say, 'How do you do', but he went over to the fireplace and rang a bell beside it. Evelyne noticed the pretty rose-patterned tiles around the fireplace.

'You keeping well then, Doris ? Tea, Minnie, straightaway.'

Minnie bobbed a small curtsey and scuttled out, leaving the door ajar.

'Your practice well, is it, dear?'

'Well, it keeps me on my toes, ya know ... glad you could come, makes a nice change, and young David will be pleased to make your acquaintance. He's a fine chap, fine boy ... ah, good, tea.'

The tea was wheeled in on a trolley. There were small cucumber sandwiches, little cup cakes, and a big currant cake with a frilled collar. The maid poured the tea and handed plates and napkins. Evelyne found it very difficult to balance her plate, napkin, teacup and saucer, and looked to Doris for help.

'Get the gel a side table, Minnie.'

Minnie brought a small table to Evelyne's side then picked up the sugar bowl.

'You take sugar, Miss?'

Evelyne nodded and waited, then realized that the maid was waiting for her to help herself. She was all thumbs and picked up what she thought was a spoon, but it seemed to be two spoons in one.

'Use the tongs, child, don't use your fingers.'

Just as she had her mouth full the Doctor spoke.

'So this is your young protégé. And how do you find Cardiff, Evelyne?'

Evelyne swallowed and gulped and spluttered as the sandwich went down the wrong way. Doris moved quickly to her and patted her on the back, concerned.

'You must never speak with your mouth full, dear.'

Dr Collins consulted his fob watch and stood up, saying he had to make his rounds. Evelyne couldn't help but think how much Doc Clock would have liked that watch.

'Ahh, this sounds like David ... yes, he's here,' the Doctor beamed with pride, standing at the bay window. 'He's got some high-society friends now, Doris, he's at the university. Oh, I wrote, yes, I remember I told you, well-connected people, be good for his profession, going to be a lawyer, did I tell you? Ah, yes, I suppose I did ... yes, his mother would have been proud of him, God rest her soul.'

Doris crossed herself, and Evelyne looked from one to the other. She had not thought the doctor could ever have been married or have a son.

There was a bellow from the hall.

'Minnie ... *Minnie*! *Minnie*! Anyone call for me while I was out?'

They heard laughter, then the double doors of the drawing-room were flung open. David Collins made his entrance like an actor. His blond hair shone like silk, his perfectly tailored grey suit hugged his tall, slender frame. He was very self-assured, his ice-blue eyes twinkled. 'Aunt Doris, well I never, Pa mentioned you would be arriving, do forgive me for not being here to welcome you.'

Unaware that her mouth had dropped open, Evelyne stared. He could have been a prince, she had never in her life seen a man so handsome. He bowed over Doris' outstretched hand and kissed it, then turned his attention to Evelyne. He had no trace of a Welsh accent.

'And you must be Elaine, how do you do?'

As Evelyne half stood, her plate in one hand and cup and saucer in the other her cake rolled off the plate and landed by his highly polished grey kid boots.

'Absolutely the place for Mrs Darwin's cakes, my dear. *Minnie*! Come along, gel, and bring a dustpan and brush ... now, Pa, can I get you more tea? Aunt?'

David dominated the room – lifted the mood as if the sun had suddenly shone in through the windows. He wore a delicate perfume, like lilies, that filled the air.

Doris rose from her chair. 'Well, if you'll excuse us I think we'll have a little sightseeing tour, and a wash and change before dinner. Evelyne, dear, have you finished?'

Flushing, Evelyne put her china down on the tray, and stood with head bowed, so tongue-tied it made her desperate to visit the bathroom. Doris took her arm and pulled her towards the door. David watched them leave, waiting until the door closed behind them, then looked at his father with raised eyebrows.

'Are they staying long?'

Dr Collins dabbed at his mouth with his napkin, 'Just the weekend, just the weekend.' David flipped his silk handkerchief out of his pocket and flicked a cake crumb from his boot.

'Is the skinny child an orphan? Smells quite dreadful, and one couldn't really say she was frightfully clean.'

After ringing again for Minnie to clear away, Dr Collins went towards the door.

'Couldn't spare a fiver, Pa? Bit short, only I have to take a couple of chaps to dinner this evening.'

'I would like it if you dined at home. Doris hasn't been here for many years. It would show a bit of respect.'

David whistled, irritated, then sprang to his feet.

'Okie dokie, but between you and me, it's no wonder Mother kept her at arm's length, what?'

At times Dr Collins loathed his son's supercilious attitude, but then he could be so charming the doctor gave him whatever he wanted, as did everyone else.

David turned abruptly, moving like a dancer, swept out of the room and bounded up the stairs two or three at a time. Evelyne was standing at the top, on her way to the bathroom, carrying a fresh white towel. They almost collided.

'Sorry, Elaine, bathroom's second door on your right.'

She didn't have the nerve to correct him, just blushed and scuttled past. At the bottom of the stairs Mrs Darwin stood smiling, her big red face glowing.

'Now then, Master David, will you be having dinner at home?'

'I will, Mrs Darwin, light of my life ... oh, Mrs D, will you make sure my shirts are not folded, just put on the hangers, can't stand the creases ... thanks awfully.'

Mrs Darwin shrugged her shoulders and plodded back down to the basement, passing Minnie.

'Prince Edward himself wants his shirts not folded, he'll be wanting me to press his socks next.'

The marble bathroom was like a wonderland. Evelyne touched the white bath, the washbasin, and gasped with delight as she turned on the taps. Hot and cold water!

What would Lizzie-Ann have to say, hot and cold, and a toilet of their own with a cord that flushed it.

'Evelyne, dear, have you run your bath? Don't be too long, we won't have too much time for sightseeing.'

In his room, David sighed. 'Sightseeing' ... dear God, he hoped none of his friends would show up during his aunt's stay.

Doris and Evelyne spent the rest of the afternoon in the museums and wandering around the castle. Everything was a wonder to Evelyne. They were both tired when they returned so Doris suggested they take a little nap before dinner. Evelyne was loving every minute of it. Her small single bed with its crisp white sheets was heaven, and she dozed blissfully. She was still snoozing at dinner-time, and Doris woke her. She was embarrassed to see that Doris had changed. She had only one clean blouse.

'Shall I wear my other blouse, Mrs Evans?'

'I don't think so, dear, the gong has already rung, and you'll need it for tomorrow . . . just give your hair a brush, would you like me to do it for you?'

Doris had never brushed a girl's hair before, and she was not much good at plaiting it. At the end of all her hard work it looked as if it still needed brushing.

'Thank you, Mrs Evans.'

Doris gave her a small, tight smile, patted her and then straightened her cardigan.

'Well, shall we go down? Don't eat too fast, dear, don't speak with your mouth full, and keep your voice lowered, no need to shout, all right?'

The meal was an agony of uncertainty for Evelyne, and she spoke not a word, terrified she would choke or be caught with her mouth full. Her bread crumbled so much that she kept glancing at Doris and picking up each crumb from round her place setting. She watched Doris coping with the lukewarm soup, moving her spoon away from her and then sipping from the side of it, and followed suit. It tasted like her mother's gravy.

'So, Aunt, how is village life? Do you not miss Cardiff?'

'I don't, David . . . Evelyne, have you finished your soup?'

The main course consisted of roast beef, carrots, peas, and small, crisp roast potatoes.

'Do start, dear, don't want it getting cold.'

Evelyne began to eat and felt David's half-amused stare making her go hot and cold. She could feel her legs sticking together.

'You are to be a lawyer, David?' Doris asked her nephew. 'Congratulations.'

'Well, I will no doubt be called up. Bit of a nuisance really, in the middle of studies, but then one has to do one's bit. Wretched business, this war.'

The pudding was served, a chocolate sponge with thick, bright yellow custard.

'You know, I really must go to the valleys one day. Spent last vacs in London, met some of Mother's relatives there, jolly nice people.'

'She was a good woman, miss her you know, Doris,' put in Dr Collins. 'She ran the house like clockwork, didn't she, David?'

'So, Elaine, tell me how you like Cardiff?'

'Her name's Evelyne, and she's a very clever girl, my best pupil.'

Evelyne couldn't meet his blue eyes. She bit her lip, loving the sound of his voice.

'I do apologize, you should have corrected me before, Evelyne ... so, Ev-e-lyne, you are still at school?'

Every time Evelyne opened her mouth to speak Doris butted in until David laughed, a lovely, chuckling laugh.

'Good God, Aunt, can't the gel speak for herself?'

'Mrs Evans is teaching me private.'

'Oh, I see ... oh I say, Pa, did I tell you I'm playing polo? Charlie Withers said I could use one of his ponies, rather chuffed about it, actually. You know Freddy Carlton's always said I should try my hand ... did you know Lord and Lady Carlton, Auntie?'

Doris pursed her lips, dabbed them with the napkin.

'No, when I was a girl I didn't mix in those exalted circles, but I have seen pictures of their estate. Your grandfather did their gardens, when he retired from the railway.'

Doris' quiet reproach to her nephew went over Evelyne's head. She was happy to listen to him talk, and when his attention was directed to his aunt or his father it gave her the opportunity to study him. He had a habit of running his fingers through his silky hair, then tossing his head slightly. He wore a large gold ring on his little finger. Evelyne had still not spoken more than two sentences when everyone rose and went into a small sitting room. It was cosy and informal with a huge, round bowl of fresh roses on the table. The maid wheeled in the trolley with coffee and small, round peppermints covered in dark, home-made chocolate. Evelyne slipped one into her pocket for little Davey, and tucked her worn shoes as far out of sight beneath her skirt as she could.

The fire was stacked as high as it could be and made the small room hot and stuffy, but it was a pleasant stuffiness. Doris sat next to her brother and talked with him in whispers. Evelyne had never tasted coffee before and she found it bitter but nice, like a cross between hot chocolate and very strong tea. She nearly spilled it as she sensed David standing beside her. Evelyne was too shy to look up, and all she could see was his grey trouser-leg and soft leather boot. Her blush was even worse than at supper.

'Would you care for another?'

David held out the peppermints and smiled. Evelyne was sure he had seen her pocket one, so she shook her head and felt her hair begin to come loose from its braid. She tried frantically to push it back, but the harder she tried the more the strands worked loose.

David picked up the family photograph album and carried it to the table, moving the roses aside and laying it on the crushed velvet cloth. He gave Evelyne a look to join him. She sat next to him with her hands clasped tightly in her lap, knowing her hair was all over the place and feeling her rough skin above the worn shoes, but she never once turned her face towards him, seeing only his hands with their long, tapering fingers, and the immaculate cuffs of his shirt. The village boys seemed so rough and unkempt in comparison. David wore his hair slightly long, whereas they had to keep theirs short because of the coal dust, and Evelyne had never seen hair with such a sheen on it, even on a girl.

At bedtime Evelyne scrubbed her face, neck and arms, then spent a long time washing the face cloth so it wouldn't look grey. She unfolded her mother's old, greyish nightgown that had once been white and pulled it over her head, then folded all her clothes neatly, and unlocked the door.

She tiptoed along the corridor and heard Doris below saying goodnight to her brother. About to enter her bedroom she caught sight of David's half-open door opposite. She couldn't help herself, she stared. David was sitting on the side of his bed wearing only his grey trousers and boots, nothing on the top at all. He was leaning forward, reading a book, and running his fingers through his hair. Evelyne knew she shouldn't be standing there, but she couldn't move, she wanted to touch his soft, clean white skin. She had never felt like this in her life before. She was used to seeing and touching male skin from bathing her menfolk, but this was somehow different, she didn't know quite why, but she had a pain in the pit of her tummy, and her whole body felt hot.

There were footsteps on the stairs, and she turned quickly,

dropping a shoe. Mortified, she grabbed it and heard David's door close as she scurried into her room. Oh, dear Lord, had he seen her watching him?

Evelyne pretended she was asleep as Doris crept around the room and then slipped out to the bathroom. The darkness was lovely, lying between clean sheets with clean smells all around her. She snuggled down into the bed but couldn't sleep, because David's face kept floating in front of her eyes. Oh, she had so much to tell Lizzie-Ann!

Evelyne did not see David again. Their visit had passed quickly, and they were about to depart for the railway station. Evelyne stood with clasped hands as Dr Collins handed Doris a parcel, saying it contained a few things that had belonged to his wife that he would like her to have.

As Dr Collins waved them on their way, David came down the stairs, yawned and asked if they had gone.

'I think you should have made the effort to come down, not good enough, you know.'

David shrugged, 'I doubt if we'll be seeing her again, and even if we do I hope she won't bring that dreadful child with her. I mean, what on earth possessed her to bring the girl?'

The Doctor studied his fob watch, 'Doris was always one for picking up waifs and strays – look at that chap she married. Illiterate, you know, broke up the family. Now I must be off on my rounds, will you be home for supper?'

David was always irritated by his father, the way his father referred to dinner as supper, it wasn't done.

'I'll be dining out at the Carltons'.'

'You know, son, it's all very well you mixing with these

chaps, but you must never forget your roots, don't get above yourself.'

David swiped the top off his egg so hard it shot across the table. 'Don't get above yourself . . . ' David had every intention of getting above himself, out of his dreadful house, away from his father's penny-pinching ways.

'Goodbye, Father, have an enjoyable day,' he muttered.

When they were on the tram, heading home across the mountains, Doris opened the small parcel. She sighed, knowing she would never wear the dead woman's bits and pieces of jewellery. There were also a couple of woollen cardigans and a shawl.

'You know, I never got on with my sister-in-law. Her name was Eleanor, and she was cruel to my dear husband, mocking him. I always said I would never visit while she was still alive, and now . . . well, did you enjoy it, Evelyne?'

'Oh, yes, Mrs Evans, I loved every single minute of it, and I'll never be able to thank you enough.'

Rewrapping the parcel, Doris murmured that she would give the clothes to the poor. Evelyne half hoped that Doris would give them to her.

'Could you make use of these ribbons?'

'Oh, yes, thank you Mrs Evans, thank you very much.'

Doris sighed and looked out of the window. The break had done her the world of good. She looked back at Evelyne who was carefully winding the ribbons round her finger.

'We'll make it a habit, I think, yes, I think it would be good for you to spend more time at the museums. Perhaps we can even go to the theatre.'

Evelyne grabbed Doris' hand and kissed it.

'Oh, thank you, thank you, Mrs Evans.'

Her whole slender body trembled with pleasure. Just think, she would be going back to that palace of a house and, even better, she would see him again – she would see David.

Evelyne knew there was something amiss the moment she let herself into the house. It was dark, cold and silent. The kitchen fire was almost out, and she stoked it quickly, disappointed to find no one at home, and worried.

'Da, I'm home ... Da?'

She ran up the stairs, bursting to tell her news, pushed open the door.

'Oh, Da, I had such a time, such a wonderful time.'

Hugh was lying on the bed, holding Davey's small, well-chewed teddy bear. He raised himself on to his elbow. He looked ill, his eyes were red-rimmed, but he was sober.

'Has Lizzie-Ann not been looking after you?' Evelyne asked, 'I dunno, I leave you for no more than two days ... does Mrs Pugh have little Davey, I'll go and pick him up, I've built up the fire ...'

Hugh moaned and lay down, put his arm across his face, and his body shook.

'What is it? Has something happened? Da?'

He gripped the small toy and his face crumpled. He sobbed.

'Aw, Christ, gel, I was drunk, I was drunk ... he was up here, an' I heard his hollerin' and I went to bring him down, down to the fire ... he was in my arms ... halfway down I fell.'

Evelyne was on the bed, pulling at his arm, 'Where is he, Da? Where is he? I'll go to him, I'll go to him.'

Hugh reached out and pulled her down to lie beside him.

'I fell, Evie, I fell . . . I fell on the little chap, and God help me, I've killed him.'

She moved away, staring, her eyes bright with tears.

'Ah, no, you didn't . . . you didn't . . . *Davey, Davey!*'

Hugh couldn't stop her, he sobbed as he heard her running through the rooms calling out the little boy's name. She gripped the side of his empty cot and called for him, all she could remember was his funny, fuzzy head, his drooling, soft mouth . . . and he was always so happy . . .

Lizzie-Ann, her belly even bigger, stood at the door.

'Oh, Lizzie, Lizzie, poor little Davey.'

Lizzie-Ann's face puckered, a child carrying a child herself, 'Maybe it was God's doin', he wasn't right in the head.'

Evelyne wiped her tears with the back of her hand. All her stories, all the things she'd wanted to tell Lizzie-Ann meant nothing now. She could even detect the envy, see it in the puffy, pretty face, the huge, searching pansy eyes. Little Davey was far from her thoughts. 'You have a good time?'

'No, not really . . . I brought you back some ribbons, they're on the kitchen table.'

Lizzie-Ann whooped and rushed to the kitchen, leaving Evelyne standing by the empty cot. She touched the chewed, sucked sides, and thought it could be put to use for Lizzie-Ann's baby.

Later that night Hugh was heard thudding up the stairs. He was drunk as he had been on the night he had fallen and killed his little boy. He was struggling out of his filthy old working jacket, stumbling against the bed. Evelyne slipped into the room and he straightened up while she took his clothes off him. The bed smelt terrible, the sheets and pillows stained with beer and vomit. The huge man was so broken, so pitiful . . . he held out his massive, gnarled hand to her, she slipped her own into it, although she didn't want to stay in the squalid room. Poor little Davey, his whole life just a few silly words, Da da–da–daaaa . . .

The next Sunday they buried Davey. Only a few villagers turned out to follow the sad, small family to the churchyard. They couldn't even afford a hearse. Hugh was sober, and he carried the tiny coffin in his arms as if it was a precious box of eggs that would smash if he jolted it.

Over the tiny grave Hugh swore he would never touch another drop, so help him, and as the rain started the big man went down on his knees and wept. There were no cornflowers this time, as it was winter.

Evelyne was drained, but she knew her Da depended on her and didn't give in. She stood, straight-backed, her arm ready for Hugh to lean on. Will wouldn't meet her gaze, he was ashamed, like his father. The little boy who had been left in their care now lay alongside their Ma and the baby with no name.

Chapter 5

The birth of Lizzie-Ann's daughter was a noisy affair. Red-faced, bawling her lungs out from the very beginning, she started as she meant to go on. She was christened Rosie.

They now had two lodgers, and Evelyne worked part-time in the bakery. They paid her a proportion of her wages in bread. Will still worked in the mines. It was 1916, and the fear of conscription hung over every household. Every day saw another boy leave for the Front, and lorry-loads of workers were brought to the mines, which caused ill-feeling and fights among the men. Uniformed soldiers were a common sight, some on leave and some new recruits. The village was being torn apart.

Doris had taken Evelyne to Cardiff three times. She treasured these trips, but she rarely discussed them at home as she knew Lizzie-Ann was secretly jealous. Fussing with the baby, she would make snide remarks, 'Oh, off again, are we? Well it's all right fer some, others have more important things to be doing than traipsin' to Cardiff. What ya do there that's so special?'

Evelyne would quietly continue with the housework.

'We just go round the museums, spend time in the library.'

'Very borin' if you ask me. Are there nice young men there? You should be thinking of looking, you know, being so tall you won't find it easy.'

Evelyne never mentioned David, but then she had not seen him since her first visit, and it was not until her fourth trip that she saw him again. He strode into the lounge. He was now a captain in the Artillery, and wore his gold-buttoned uniform with dashing flair, his greatcoat slung round his shoulders and his riding boots highly polished. 'Well, my dear aunt, oh, and your little friend, well, what a surprise.'

If David was aware of her infatuation he gave no sign, and spoke to her as if she was a child. Alone with his father he was less than enthusiastic.

'Good God Pa, I've only got a few weeks at home and *they're* here. That girl positively reeks of carbolic.'

David was enjoying his new status, as he had his time in France. He had not as yet seen any fighting, but the social life was exhilarating, and he did cut an exceptionally elegant figure. He was determined to flirt with all and sundry, setting about it like a military campaign, and was extremely annoyed when his father suggested he give Evelyne a tour of Cardiff.

'All right, Pa, but then I've done my bit, I *am* on leave, you know.'

Evelyne gasped as David carefully tucked the blanket around her knees. She had never been in a private motorcar before, only in a taxi and on a tram, and here she was in David's sports car. He wore goggles and drove carefully, but to Evelyne it seemed very

fast, nearly thirty miles an hour. Whenever anyone got in the
way, David would hoot at them. He even let Evelyne squeeze
the large, squashy rubber bulb of the trumpet-shaped horn, it
was wonderful. Evelyne was like a child. The wind had brought
a lovely colour to her cheeks and her hairpins had slipped out
as usual. She wore no scarf, and her hair tumbled down, blowing in the wind. At first she held on to it, but then she laughed
and let it fly free. In spite of himself, David enjoyed the little
trip, and found 'Carbolic', as he called her, quite sweet in her
gawky way. Occasionally he pointed out features of the city to
Evelyne.

When they arrived home David removed the blanket from
around Evelyne's knees, folded it and helped her out of the car.
Her face was flushed, and she smiled, it had been the happiest
day of her life. His gentle grip on her elbow thrilled her right
through and made her head buzz. She wasn't sure why he felt
he had to help her through doors and up stairs – she wasn't frail
or anything – but she liked it.

'Care for a glass of sherry?' He handed it to her with a flourish. 'Drive did you the world of good, got some colour into
your cheeks.'

Evelyne was so nervous that she spilt her sherry. The thim-
ble-shaped glass was so small and she had difficulty in raising it
to her lips.

'Here, allow me.' He handed her his handkerchief and she
dabbed at her mouth. 'If you will excuse me, I must bathe and
change.'

David swept out, leaving Evelyne to finish her sherry and
look forward to dinner when she would see him again, but the
sight of the two places set at the table made her heart drop like

a stone. David was dining out, murmured the Doctor, who then spent the remainder of the meal reading the *Cardiff Gazette*.

Later, Evelyne slipped in between the cool sheets and lay listening to the night sounds. From beneath the pillow she drew out the handkerchief with his initials, the one he had given her when she spilt her sherry. She would keep it as a memento, a keepsake of her love.

At breakfast David fairly glowed. He stood up smartly when Evelyne entered, sat down again and whacked the top off his egg. Doris was too ill to come down, in fact she felt so bad she had decided she couldn't return to the valley until the following day. Evelyne wanted to sing with joy, another whole day here with her love. David noticed that she was wearing exactly the same clothes as on the previous day, and there was a piece of newspaper sticking up from her shoes.

David ate ravenously, and more and more toast was brought in in a silver toast rack. He swamped it with thick butter and marmalade, and Evelyne couldn't believe her eyes. He took so much that sometimes he even left some on the edge of his plate. He poured tea, munched and chatted, then laughed as he noticed that Evelyne could eat just as fast as he could. In fact he reckoned she had wolfed down two more slices than he had, and joked that she must have been at the Front along with his men. Evelyne flushed with embarrassment, making a mental note not to eat so fast.

David excused himself and walked out to the hall, and Evelyne heard him pick up the telephone. He caught her staring and closed the dining room door, but she could hear the low murmur of his voice and then his laugh. The door swung open and he lolled against the jamb, smiling. 'Care for another little drive?'

All Evelyne could do to stop herself bursting into song was to pinch herself. She had never known such delight, and being tucked up in the motor, feeling his hand brush her thigh even though it was covered by at least three or four layers, made her shiver. David smiled into her upturned face, then cupped her chin in his immaculate, white-gloved hand.

'Comfortable? Think we'll have a spin in the country.'

David had arranged to meet a friend, Captain Ridgely, at a small country inn. The inn was frequented by officers on leave, and a number of rooms had been set aside for their private use. Captain Ridgely had assured David he would enjoy himself, and that he had two exquisite creatures for him to meet. Desperate to ingratiate himself with the social set, David accepted, believing he would be meeting acquaintances of Ridgely's. Evelyne, of course, had no idea she was being used to cover any potential gossip.

David drove Evelyne out past the castle and into the country, and they had to shout above the roar of the engine. They passed the railway station, leaving the town behind them, and headed along narrow lanes between the fields.

Evelyne sat smiling, taking sidelong glances at her beloved's beautiful face. Eventually they drew up at an inn with small tables covered with checkered cloths under the shade of a huge oak tree. Again he helped her out, and guided her to a secluded table. He snapped his fingers at a rotund man wearing a big white apron, turned to Evelyne, 'Sherry? Or would you prefer something else?'

Evelyne sat with her sherry under the tree. David excused himself and entered the inn; just like the men from her village, they always left their womenfolk out-side. Making sure she would be able to see David if he came out, Evelyne went for a short stroll.

The fields smelt wonderful, the sun was warm and lovely . . . she sniffed, stretched, twirled, and up bubbled a laugh of perfect happiness. It took her by surprise and she wanted to shout out. Why was it she never had anyone near when she had things to tell them? She walked on across the fields then turned to stroll behind the inn. It was part of a farm complex and she could see the cows being led into the milking sheds. How little Davey would have liked to see these cows, big fat ones, browns and blacks . . .

A car similar to David's roared through the farmyard at the back of the inn. Evelyne stared down the hill as a uniformed officer, accompanied by two women, entered the inn. The women were laughing and clinging to the soldier's arm. Evelyne was so busy watching the car that she didn't see the big cow pat right in front of her. Splosh! In went her shoe, and it was such a shock that she slid forwards, lost her balance and slithered down the embankment. Evelyne had cow dung on her skirt, her knees, and her left hand – and her right shoe, the one with the newspaper inside, was covered in it. The silk scarf had slipped from her hair and was mucky too. Almost in tears she squelched towards the brook that circled the field. She took off her skirt and, dipping the hem into the icy water, rinsed it out. Then she put the whole of her shoe in. It was stinking so she picked up a stick and scraped the muck off. She smelt her hands, noticed that the cuffs of her blouse, the one Doris had given her, were covered too, so off it came ... she was trying to clean her shoe, her skirt and blouse all at the same time, and it was disastrous. The next thing she knew she had toppled over and was sitting waist-deep in the brook.

David had already downed half a bottle of wine, and was growing impatient. The room was stuffy and smelt of stale beer and cigarettes. He was about to leave when the door opened and there stood Ridgely, with a wicked smile and a blonde on either arm. 'Now, gels, I want you to meet a *very* dear friend, and more than that, I want you to make him feel very special – after all, he *is* on leave, so let's not waste any time, eh?'

David had to turn away to conceal his astonishment. The blondes wore nothing but lacy panties and stockings beneath their coats. Ridgely came to his side and nudged him in the ribs.

'Get what you pay for? Nothing like these two in France, I assure you ... this one's on me, old chap.'

David took another covert look at the two girls who had sat down and were casually sipping wine, waiting.

'Which one is mine?'

'Both, I'll be back in an hour.'

Flamboyantly, Ridgely kissed each girl, then with elaborate winks and gestures he left them. David gulped his wine and before he had put his glass down one of the girls was unbuttoning his uniform.

Ridgely tiptoed into the adjoining room, locked the door behind him, and crept to the dividing wall. Moving a picture aside he peeked through the spyhole. He would have a jolly story to tell the lads at the barracks tonight.

Evelyne had spread her skirt out flat in the sun, her blouse on a thorn bush. Her left shoe was all right, but the right one was very squashy and still smelt dreadful. She crept to the hedge and peeked over, looking for David, and sighed with relief that he was not there. Dear God, please don't let him find me this way, not in my mother's old shift and a cut-down vest of my father's. Please, dear Lord, I'd do anything, but don't let him find me this way. Make the sun hot to dry out my skirt and Doris' hand-me-down blouse or I will kill myself. The square silk headscarf David had given her was drying on the grass, but it was full of wrinkles. Evelyne's hair had tumbled down, all the pins flung everywhere in her panic to wash her clothes free of the cow dung. She wished she'd at least brought a comb with her. The water had made her hair curl and frizz, it was sticking out like a bush and she knew it. Her nails were full of dirt and her knees were scratched.

Freedom Beshaley Stubbs approached the field where his stallion was. It was his own *gry*. The farmer had allowed Freedom to field him separately from the ponies. The *gry* was a wild one, with a temper, but Freedom believed he was a racer and intended to keep him, not sell him with the rest of the pack. The camp was six miles from the farm, and they were moving on. Freedom didn't want his stallion broken in yet. Any travellers seeing him might try for him, the horse was a rare one. This way, keeping him wild, only Freedom could handle him and would break him when he was ready.

Apples and crusts bulged in Freedom's jacket pocket, and as he came close to the gate he saw the great beast toss his head, his black eyes flashing. In one movement Freedom legged it on to the gate, and sat on the top bar. He called the stallion 'Kaulo', the Romany word for black, and black he was. The horse pawed the ground, snorting.

'*Choom, choom*', Freedom whispered, meaning 'kiss, kiss', and the stallion moved slowly towards his master, tossing his powerful head. He nuzzled Freedom's open palm, got his apple and crust of bread, and then as if playing a game he backed away. Freedom was too fast for him, he grabbed the flowing mane and jumped, heeled his beauty forwards and they galloped around the wide, open field.

Evelyne lay back, the brook bubbled and gurgled, and she looked up into the bright clear sky. The sound of horse's hooves seemed to come from beneath her, underground. She sat up, waded across the brook and stood on tiptoe to look into the distant field.

The black-haired boy and the stallion galloped round and round and, bareback, the boy seemed to be part of the horse, his hair as black as the stallion's gleaming coat. The boy wore a red neckerchief and an old striped flannel shirt. Evelyne knew at first glance that he was a gypsy – she had seen them come to the village often enough with their ponies to sell to the pits. She and her brothers had never been allowed near the camp, their Da decreeing that his children would not mix with the gypsies ever. No matter how they had pleaded with him they were not allowed even to go to the fairs. They had cried bitter tears because all the other village children had been allowed to go, but on this one subject Hugh Jones was adamant.

Evelyne shaded her eyes, watching the boy riding, and tutted like a little old maid. Those wild gypsy boys would never come to anything. Maybe her Da was right, they were a bad lot and always thieving, so everyone said. She closed her eyes – oh, how very different her David was, now *there* was a gentleman.

She waded back across the brook and felt her clothes, they were almost dry. She began to think about David, he had certainly been inside the inn a long time. She stared over the hedge, saw the black car drive away. Funny, there in the field was that gleaming black horse, and down below in the yard by the inn the gleaming black motor. Evelyne mused, she'd prefer the motor if ever given the choice.

Her sodden shoe had shrunk, it fitted her now, but still smelt quite terrible. She stood up and stamped her foot, then bent down to pick up her skirt. She turned, looked back again – it had disappeared. She scratched her head, then walked round the bush to see if it had slipped down the other side.

Freedom was stunned. It was her hair, he had never seen a colour like it. She was the palest *manushi* he had ever seen, with hair of *sonnikey*. He gaped, then swallowed hard. She was looking at him, staring, and she had the eyes of a sea witch. They stood for a moment, frozen, his dark eyes brooding, his olive skin clear, not swarthy, his high cheekbones giving him a look of arrogance. His mouth was wide, and just as Evelyne was about to scream he smiled, showing the most perfect strong, white teeth. She was no longer afraid when he smiled, but she was still in her drawers, so she covered herself with her hands.

'Are you not chilled swimmin', gel?'

Evelyne put her hands on her hips and pursed her lips with anger. This common gyppo was standing on her skirt. All thought of behaving in a ladylike fashion left her.

'I am not swimming. I was ... excuse me, would you mind leaving? I am not dressed.'

Freedom chuckled, but made no move to leave. He cocked his head to one side, looking her up and down which made her blush and grow so hot she didn't know what to do. But she couldn't just leave because he was still standing on her skirt.

'That's my *gry*, yonder, the stallion.'

'What?'

'I said that's my stallion yonder. I've a right to be in the field, are thee from this part?'

'No, I'm not, would you please go away?'

Freedom gave her a twinkling smile.

'I shall scream, please go away.'

But still he stood on her skirt.

'Get off my skirt, please, you are standing on my skirt.'

He hopped away, then with deliberate movements he picked up the skirt and shook it, held it out by the waistband as though for her to step into it.

'It's best thee dress yerself, gel, there's many a-wandering around these parts ... here, give me your hand.'

Angrily, she took his hand and stepped into the skirt, then moved back sharply and began to do up the small buttons.

'Thank you.'

'It's my pleasure.'

David's voice echoed up from the inn's courtyard, calling her name. She backed away from Freedom but still he made no effort to leave. He lolled against the trunk of a tree, his eyes never straying from her face for an instant.

'Evelyne . . . ? Evelyne . . . ? *Evelyne?*'

She turned and ran a few yards, stopped to look back. He was still there. He cocked his head to one side and kissed the tips of his fingers. He repeated her name, and she tossed her head, glaring, her golden-red hair swirled around her, and then she was gone. Like a monkey, Freedom climbed the tree until he was perched high up in the branches. He watched her running down the courtyard and could see the uniformed figure pacing up and down impatiently.

By the time Evelyne, out of breath, reached David, he was irate. He could not believe the state she had managed to get herself into. Her hair was loose, her clothes, dreadful to start with, were creased and damp. As he inhaled angrily he caught the stench of cow dung. He gestured for her to climb into the passenger seat, not even bothering to open the door for her, then slammed the car into gear with a crashing, grinding noise. The car jolted forward so fast that Evelyne was pressed back against the seat.

Hearing a peal of laughter, Evelyne turned, looked back at the inn to see a blonde girl standing at one of the top windows. She was in her underwear, and even from this distance Evelyne could see her thickly painted red lips.

'Coooeeee, David . . . cooooee, lovey . . . David . . .'

David looked up at the window, and to Evelyne's horror the girl blatantly bared her breast, flicked her tongue out at David and shrieked with raucous laughter. Evelyne couldn't believe her eyes – she looked at David, then back at the inn. An officer in uniform was now standing behind the blonde woman, and he too was roaring with laughter.

'Who's that, David? Who is that terrible woman?'

David snapped, his face furious, 'That is a cheap whore, a paid woman, a prostitute, a tart, a common slag . . .'

'But why was she calling you?'

'How the hell do I know? Shut up, I don't want to talk about it.'

He ground his teeth, his mouth set in a thin, tight line. He felt dirty, the women had wanted more money, although he knew Ridgely had paid them already, and it annoyed him. They were just like the whores in France, out for every cent they could get. He felt unclean, used, and wanted to get home for a bath as fast as he could. He hadn't really enjoyed himself, it was all bravado – the Ridgelys of this world, rich as Croesus, loved the tarts, the whores, but David didn't. He made up his mind he wouldn't go with another. They were all the same. Worse was the humiliation, because Ridgely had told him he'd been watching his performance, and it would be all round the barracks in no time.

'I saw a gypsy boy . . .'

David looked at her, through her, and muttered something inaudible as he swerved the car round the gatepost of the inn.

Freedom remained high up in the tree. He whistled softly, then watched the sports car bouncing across the cobbled courtyard. He screeched like a bird, high-pitched . . . Evelyne saw him just as he swung down from the tree and raised his arm, waving to her. She turned away quickly, annoyed at herself for wanting to take another look. David swung the car along a track running beside a field, then out into a narrow lane.

'Do we have to go so fast?'

David said nothing, but he slowed down. The weeds and brambles on either side of the lane scratched against the sides of the open car, and Evelyne held her hands up to protect her face. When she took them down again she saw Freedom on his stallion, galloping through the fields alongside them. He rode bareback, clinging to the horse's mane, urging it forward and jumping the hedgerows, keeping up with the car, he was going so fast . . . Evelyne stared, it frightened her, the black horse, the boy so dark, his shoulder-length hair streaming out behind him. She gasped, clung to the windscreen – ahead of the horse and rider was a high, fenced hedge. He would never make it, he couldn't, it was too high. She screamed.

Freedom urged the *gry* on, felt the muscles straining beneath him, and then they were flying through the air. He let rip with a shout of sheer exhilaration, pure joy . . .

'*Stop! David, stop . . . stop!*'

The car screeched to a halt, almost in a ditch.

'What is it, what?'

But horse and rider had disappeared, there wasn't even the sound of hooves.

'Evelyne, for God's sake what's the matter? Did we hit something?'

'No, no, it was nothing, it was no one.'

Freedom stood with his arms wrapped around his stallion's neck, their lungs heaving as though they were one. The horse tossed his magnificent head, snorting, and Freedom laughed.

'Did thee see her, Kaulo?' Isn't she *rinkeney*, eh boy?'

*

82

Minnie the housemaid had run a steaming bath and was hovering at the bathroom door. She had been given instructions by the doctor himself to clean the girl up because she smelt so much. Minnie felt sorry for her, and even more so when Evelyne had stripped off – she was like a skeleton, and her ribs could be seen clearly. As for her undergarments, they were not even fit to clean the brass with.

Doris still lay in the darkened room with an icepack on her forehead. She had not touched her food, even the slightest noise seemed to pain her. Dr Collins sat with her for a while, taking her temperature. He was not too worried, saying it was just a migraine.

'But I feel so ill, and sometimes I just go dizzy, like a fainting fit, and the pain moves from one side of my head to the other.'

The Doctor pursed his lips, hissed softly and looked, as always, at his fob watch. 'Well, you rest up, don't worry about the young gel, perhaps if you could eat a small meal . . . I'll get Minnie to bring you something on a tray.'

Doris murmured that she didn't feel well enough to eat, and the strain of talking made her head worse as if thousands of tiny hammers were beating against her eyes.

Evelyne slipped into the hot, soapy water, her face pink with embarrassment at seeing Minnie pick up her clothes as if she had fleas, and holding them from her at arm's length.

'I fell in a cow pat, but I washed them.'

Minnie murmured that judging by the smell, she'd brought the cows home with her. The problem was that Evelyne had no change of clothes and even if Minnie washed them, they'd never be dry before dinner. Minnie soaped Evelyne's back and bony shoulders, then went to the door, locked it tight, and leant over the bathtub, speaking in a whisper.

'I'll bring you some things, but don't say nothin' about where I got 'em from, all right lovey?'

She nipped out of the bathroom and was back within minutes with a neat pile of fresh white underwear. There was a camisole with a small frill round the neck, a pair of satin bloomers with elastic at the knees, and a petticoat.

'They was the Mistress's, but he don't know what's in the wardrobe. Me an' cook have delved in there a few times, see, everything's just left in the drawers, terrible waste.'

Evelyne blushed with shame at Minnie stealing from the Doctor's dead wife.

Unlike the rest of the house, there was warmth and friendliness in the big basement kitchen. Mrs Darwin, the cook, was a round, fat woman who bellowed with laughter when she saw Evelyne in the huge bloomers, and gave her a wet, motherly kiss. Evelyne's hand-me-downs were steaming on the fireguard and an iron sat on the burner ready to press them.

The front doorbell chimed and Minnie rushed out. They had visitors and the Doctor asked for tea to be served right away. Evelyne watched the fat Mrs Darwin move like lightning, setting the tea tray, wrapping a gold frill around the cake, cutting tiny cucumber sandwiches, everything done fast and efficiently.

Evelyne, not wanting to get in the way, sat quietly by the fireside, taking it all in.

'He wants you in for tea, lovely, he's asking where you are.' Mrs Darwin threw up her hands in despair. How could the girl go up in her bloomers, her skirt wasn't ironed yet. Minnie fetched the ironing cloths, laid them on the edge of the kitchen table and began to press the skirt. Mrs Darwin tried to tidy Evelyne's hair, but she'd never before had to cope with such length and such thickness, and in the end decided to put it in a long braid down her back, whipping out the ribbon from the frilled camisole and tying it in a bow. At the same time Minnie helped Evelyne into the freshly-pressed skirt, and banged the iron over the blouse.

'Shoes, where's the girl's shoes, for heaven's sake, Minnie?'

Evelyne was painfully self-conscious, Minnie's shoes were too tight and made high-pitched squeaking noises as she entered the drawing-room. Dr Collins rose to his feet and introduced Evelyne to the two guests who were sitting, straight-backed, on the velvet sofa.

'This is the young girl I was telling you about, this is Evelyne ... Lady Sybil Warner, and her daughter, Heather.'

The pair looked so regal, Evelyne wondered if she should curtsey. Lady Warner shimmered with rows and rows of multi-coloured beads, amber and ivory, draped across her ample bosom. Her daughter, dressed in oyster silk with a matching hat, had unfortunate buck teeth, which made her appear to smirk. Evelyne shook the outstretched, beringed hand, then squeaked her way to a chair.

'Lady Sybil has very kindly invited you to a soirée this evening, Evelyne, and as Doris is no better, I er ... well, I ...'

Evelyne had not the slightest notion what a soirée was. She gave the Doctor a perplexed look as Lady Sybil spoke in a very high-pitched warbling tone, as if savouring each trill and tremor.

'We all have to do our part for the war effort, and I am sure you will enjoy yourself. Some of the boys are from the hospital, some are on leave, always good to have a new dancing partner . . . Heather?'

Heather blinked, startled.

'Come along, dear, we must be on our way.' Lady Sybil rose majestically to her feet, 'Thank you so much for your advice, I will make sure Heather remains on your diet . . . so nice to meet you, *Eevaleen*.'

Heather gave Evelyne a doleful look as she followed her mother. Just as Lady Sybil and Dr Collins reached the hall, David arrived home. He removed his hat with a sweeping gesture.

'Lady Sybil, I must apologize for my lateness, but I was held up at the barracks.'

'Don't apologize, David dear, quite understandable, and we shall be seeing you both this evening. Heather, say hello to David. Thank you again, Dr Collins, come along, Heather.'

Evelyne craned forward to see them depart and then went over to the window. A Rolls-Royce was parked outside, with a uniformed chauffeur holding the door open. She could hear David and his father talking in the hall.

'Don't tell me, Pa, you are actually socializing this evening?'

'No, no, I'm on duty, but Lady Sybil kindly invited Evelyne.'

'What?'

'Yes, most kind, Doris isn't well enough to travel, it'll be a nice outing for the girl.'

'Outing? Outing? Father, it's a dance, really, you might have discussed it with me.'

'You weren't here . . . where are you going? David?'

David looked into the drawing-room and met Evelyne's startled gaze. He cocked his head to one side.

'Well, it appears Cinderella's been invited to the ball.'

The next moment David was running up the stairs calling for Minnie to run his bath. Soirée, dance, now a ball – Evelyne couldn't make out what on earth they were talking about. Dr Collins walked in and caught her bewildered expression. He felt sorry for her. 'Pay him no attention, you'd like to go, wouldn't you?'

Evelyne chewed her lip. Just thinking of spending an evening with David made her so excited she couldn't speak. The Doctor opened his wallet and coughed, a nervous, ticklish cough.

'Don't suppose you brought a party frock with you, so, Minnie . . . ?'

Minnie was just rushing up the stairs after David.

'I'm just going to run Master David's bath, he's already had one today so I don't know how hot the water will be.'

'Minnie, will you take Evelyne out and get her a frock to wear for a dance?'

The Doctor handed Minnie a folded note and then glanced at his fob watch, murmured that he must be off and scuttled out. Minnie looked at the five-pound note and her jaw dropped.

'Lord love us, look how much he give me! Get your coat, lovely, I'll be two minutes.'

Evelyne hadn't even had time to thank Dr Collins, it had all happened so quickly. She squeaked up the stairs after Minnie, who disappeared into the bathroom to run David's bath.

Evelyne was buttoning her coat when she saw David coming out of his room, barefoot and wrapping his dressing gown around him.

'Well, well, appears we are going out together tonight.'

Evelyne swallowed, unable to look into his teasing, smiling face. As she passed him he quickly tugged her hair. She stopped, but he continued down the corridor to the bathroom.

Minnie was waiting for Evelyne at the foot of the stairs.

'Come on, hurry, I don't want to be caught by Mrs Darwin, she'll find something for me to do and we need all the time we can get. Come on, we'll go out the front way.'

Evelyne followed her out and as the door closed behind them, Minnie snorted.

'I never known a man take so many baths, ever so particular, isn't he?'

David was actually in rather a good mood. The chaps had ribbed him quite a lot about his afternoon at the inn, but he was now very much 'in' with the 'in' set, and everyone had been impressed with Ridgely's account of David's prowess with the two ladies.

He lay in the perfumed, soapy water. His skin tingled as he scrubbed himself hard with the loofah, worried that he may have picked up some disease from the tarts. He shivered with revulsion, remembering their bodies: he couldn't understand why on earth Ridgely and the other officers enjoyed these prostitutes. They revolted him, but the improvement in his reputation made it worthwhile. He set about scrubbing himself with renewed vigour, perhaps he would find someone more to his liking at the Warners' dance.

Evelyne and Minnie took the tram into the centre of Cardiff. They didn't go to any of the big stores with the elegant models in the windows – they went down a back lane into a small second-hand shop run by a Jewish family. Minnie assured Evelyne that this was where all the posh people who had fallen on hard times sold off their dresses, and they were sure to find something at half the price they would pay in any of the fashion houses. The added bonus of this arrangement was that, as Minnie knew one of the shop assistants, maybe they would get a few shillings off their purchases.

Jeremiah Goldstein's tailoring establishment and pawn shop was a back street hovel. Rows and rows of suits hung on racks, and there were shirts stacked to the ceiling. Minnie knew everyone in the shop, and Evelyne wondered how many of the doctor's wife's clothes had found their way here.

Minnie's friend was named Clara. They kissed and joked with each other, then Clara opened up an Aladdin's cave of ball gowns, feather boas and sequins. There was a smell of body odour in the room, of stale perfume clinging to the garments. Clara walked around Evelyne, looking her up and down.

'She's a right bugger to fit, our Minnie, she's all skin and bone for one, and then there's her height. She's not a dainty one, that's for sure.'

Gown after gown was taken down from the rails. Whether they were too short or too long they all looked dreadful. Clara disappeared and came back with her arms full of bridal gowns.

'Eh, she's not getting married, our Clara, they won't do. For Gawd's sake, she just wants a dancing dress, a lovely frock that swings when she moves . . .'

Clara ignored Minnie and held up a cream satin. She pulled the dress over Evelyne's head, at the same time giving Minnie instructions to go to her cousin Bertha 'what does all the ladies' hair in the salon in the main street'.

The bride must have been as tall as Evelyne, the dress was the first one that was the right length. None of them had any thought about what fashion was now in, they wanted something long and swirling. Clara was snipping round the back with a large pair of scissors, then she whipped out a box of pins. She snipped some silk orchids off a peachy-coloured dress and started pinning them round the neck.

'Have to hide her salt cellars, you could balance a teacup on those bones . . .'

Evelyne was covered in pins, and still trying on shoe after shoe. Eventually, buried beneath a pile of feather boas, they found a pair of cream satin shoes with lavatory-shaped heels. They made Evelyne that much taller, but Clara assured her the hem would drop a bit anyway.

By five-thirty Evelyne was so tired she wanted to go to sleep, but there was no rest for her. She was bathed and perfumed, keeping the noise down all the while so as not to disturb Doris. Minnie said Evelyne would not have time to eat, she would need all the time until eight o'clock to get herself dressed up.

Bertha, her mouth full of hairpins, brushed and braided, twisted and curled the mass of golden-red hair.

By seven-thirty Evelyne's hair was still not quite ready, but the dress hung waiting for her to slip into it. Mrs Darwin had whitened the shoes slightly, as you could tell they had been worn. Minnie suddenly jumped up, panic-stricken, they'd forgotten to get Evelyne a cloak, how could she travel there in an open motor without a cloak, she'd freeze to death.

Minnie disappeared to poor, dead Mrs Collins' wardrobe, which was becoming remarkably sparse. She returned with a glum face saying there was only the black mourning cloak Mrs Collins had worn for funerals. Mrs Darwin told her to fetch it, it wasn't the wrapping that counted, it was what was inside, and no one would notice, they'd whip some of the black ribbons off it.

Finally, Evelyne was ready, and Minnie, Bertha and Mrs Darwin stared. It was a shame, there wasn't one item of jewellery on the girl, but they'd done it, she was ready, and she could be taken for a lady any day of the week. Evelyne looked at her reflection and her mouth trembled. This wasn't, couldn't be, Evelyne Jones . . .

Bertha sat on Minnie's bed, picking up hairpins and tiny ribbons. Minnie came in and ran to the window.

'She's going now.'

Bertha joined her at the window and they stared out, watching the car slowly draw away from the dark pavement.

Doris clung to the window-frame watching her sweet Evie leave the house. She looked so beautiful, and Doris felt so proud. Weak and tired out, she held on to the furniture as she made her way back to bed, replaced the icepack on her brow and sighed. She began to daydream of her wedding day, of her beloved Walter. That was what Evelyne had looked like, a bride.

There was a sweeping gravel driveway, and several other cars already parked by the house. Evelyne's head was spinning, she had never seen such comings and goings. The mansion was white, with pillars and huge trees on either side. Lamps illuminated the garden and the lake, and on the velvety lawns the bushes were thread with tiny glass candleholders all indifferent colours. She had to pinch herself to believe she wasn't dreaming.

David waited at the bottom of the steps with a look of irritation on his handsome face as Evelyne stumbled out of the car. He sighed, knowing this was a mistake. She'd almost fallen flat on her face and they weren't even inside yet. Together they walked up the steps to the main entrance. The double doors stood wide to reveal a marble hallway with more footmen and guests milling about. Music drifted from a ballroom with gilt-edged glass doors, flowers arranged on pedestals at least four feet high exuded their perfume into the air, vying with the fragrances of the laughing, chattering ladies. The sights, the smells, textures and ambience of wealth overpowered Evelyne. Her heart seemed to jump in her chest, her breath came in short gasps, and tremors shook her body. Only the gentle touch of David's hand on her elbow gave her the assurance that this was real, not a dream from which she would soon awaken. But her over-riding emotion was terror. Behind the masks of smiles, the bows of the footmen, the fleeting glances from the other guests, Evelyne felt they could see right through her – they could see she didn't belong, she was an outsider.

A small, sweet, white-haired woman was taking care of the guests' cloaks. She darted forward to help Evelyne with hers, then with a tiny wave of her hand she directed her to a powder room with a row of gilt-edged mirrors and small velvet piano stools. At least, that was what they looked like to Evelyne. Several girls sat or stood around chattering and powdering their faces, touching the flowers in their hair, dabbing themselves with chiffon hankies dipped in crystal bottles of cologne. Their bracelets jangled and their diamonds glittered. They greeted each other in squealing voices, flinging their arms around each other. Kisses were exchanged, and admiring remarks about each other's frocks.

One of the stools became vacant, and Evelyne sat down and mimicked the actions of the girl next to her. She was like a tiny china doll, with pale blonde, curly hair, wide blue eyes and rosy cheeks. She wore the palest pink gown, and her tiny feet were encased in satin shoes. She turned for a moment, giving Evelyne an icy stare that swept from the top of her head to the scrubbed, second-hand shoes. She continued talking to her friends as she stared, then turned back, leaned slightly forward and cupped her hands to her tiny rosebud mouth. Her friends tittered and two other girls leaned back slightly to stare at Evelyne.

David hovered outside, waiting for her. He saw everyone coming out and wondered what on earth Evelyne could be doing in there. Then his look of impatience changed. Leaving the powder room was an angel. Lady Primrose Boyd-Carpenter couldn't help but notice David, who was one of the most handsome men she had ever seen. As she passed him she gave him a tiny smile. David's heart lurched in his chest and, forgetting Evelyne, he turned and followed the vision in the floating pink. She appeared to be very well-known, everyone acknowledged her. Officers kissed her hand as she made her way slowly towards the ballroom. Twice she turned back, aware that David was following, then she was surrounded by a chattering party of people. David caught the arm of his closest friend, Captain Freddy Carlton.

'Freddy, who is she, who is she?'

Freddy laughed, raised his eyebrows.

'Not for you, old chap, she's already taken, that is Lady Primrose Boyd-Carpenter.'

'Introduce me, you have to introduce me, I'm in love.'

Freddy beamed, his round, good-natured face glowed above his solid frame.

'So am I, and I was there before you, she's mine, so don't you dare move in. I've been after her for months.'

David leaned against the wall, watching Freddy, full of himself, easing his way through the crowd to Lady Primrose's side. She turned her heart-shaped, perfect face to smile up at Freddy, then stood on tiptoe to kiss his cheek, slipping his hand through his arm. David could have sworn she flicked a knowing look at him as she began to introduce Freddy to her party of friends. The titles rolled, Lady this, the Honourable that, and again David could have sworn that her wicked, twinkling smile was for him alone. He was besotted.

Captain Ridgely, already flushed with champagne, breezed up to David. 'Lovely little thing, isn't she, but I'm here to tell you it's a kiss on the cheek from that quarter. Place your hand on that type of gel's knee and all hell gets let loose.'

David pointed towards Lady Primrose, 'Line me up there, Ridgely, and you'll be my friend for life.'

Ridgely snorted. 'You must be joking, that's Lady Primmy, old boy, her family owns most of the mines in these parts. Besides, Freddy Carlton's got a pash for her, look at the drooling idiot. Her family no doubt already has it arranged, ya know, titles and money always marry each other . . . you, having neither, don't stand a chance . . . oh, I say, this is more my line, look what's hovering yonder.'

David turned to see poor Evelyne standing awkwardly at the powder-room door. Angry at Ridgely's insinuation that Lady Primrose wouldn't even consider him, he snapped.

'That's unfortunately with me, some wretched charge of my aunt's, if you want her, for goodness' sake take her . . .'

At that moment a fuzzy blonde swept into Ridgely's arms and demanded a dance. He departed, giving David a lewd wink.

'Another time, what?'

David sighed and walked across to Evelyne. Begrudgingly, he gave her his arm and led her towards the ballroom.

The next disaster was the dancing. It had never occurred to Evelyne that at this sort of dance they didn't do jigs, and gallop around like they did in the Salvation Army Hall. David led her to a small couch and told her to sit there while he fetched her a glass of champagne. He then disappeared into the throng of dancers. Most of the young men were in uniform, and everyone seemed to know everyone else, calling out, waving, and whizzing past on the dance floor.

Evelyne sat waiting, looking and waiting, and eventually David came back to her side with champagne in a delicate, fluted glass.

'Don't gulp it, Flamehead, just sip.'

Lady Primrose danced past, giving David another flickering, darting glance, and he turned and gazed after her pink, floating figure. Then he moved away without another word, and Evelyne wrinkled her nose as the champagne bubbles fizzed, but she quite liked the taste. It was sharper than lemonade, and icy cold, and she drained the glass and sat twiddling the stem.

*

David danced past with Heather Warner. The girl was sweating, swathed in tulle and net, and while she looked like a powder puff, David made her feel like the most important girl at the dance. He leaned close, feeling her plump, jelly-like body quiver.

'Tell me, Heather, that girl in pink, is it Lady Primrose? Only I am sure I know her family . . .'

Heather trod on his foot as she peered round, then blinked up into his handsome face.

'Yes, Lady Primrose Boyd-Carpenter. She's very pretty, isn't she?'

David smiled into the buck teeth and held Heather closer, placed his cheek against hers. She sighed, her frustrated passion mounting. 'Oh, she's all right . . . I must say, you're very light on your feet, Heather.'

The poor girl nearly swooned, unaware that David was slowly manoeuvring her closer and closer to Lady Primrose, until she was forced to introduce him.

'Primrose, this is David Collins, David, Lady Primrose Boyd-Carpenter.'

David bowed, kissing the delicate, white-gloved hand, and asked if he would be permitted a dance. Lady Primmy excused herself to Freddy, who was glowering at David, and they moved off to the centre of the floor. She was so fragile, so delicate, and he held her as if she were precious glass, he couldn't take his eyes off her. She smelt so fresh, her hair shone and her wondrous eyes sparkled, and dancing with her was like twirling a feather. Neither of them spoke, they just looked into one another's eyes, then smiled as Freddy huffed and puffed past, pushing Heather around as if she were a wheelbarrow.

*

A butler approached Evelyne with a large silver tray, and bent low towards her. She wasn't sure what he wanted, and she looked, licked her lips and placed her empty glass on the tray. He still waited, so she took another full one and smiled her thanks.

At the far end of the dance floor sat a group of uniformed soldiers. Two of them wore arm bandages, one had a large pad on one eye. Another sat in a wheelchair. They seemed out of place, holding the fluted glasses with care, afraid to drop them or snap them in their big fists, as they watched the dancers gliding past. Evelyne could tell they were as uncomfortable as she was.

Lady Sybil Warner looked over at Evelyne then searched the ballroom for David. The poor girl was still sitting alone on the sofa. Lady Sybil weaved her way towards Evelyne. More beads and feathers than ever floated around her, she was like a ship in full sail. 'Now, dear, are you enjoying yourself? Come along, come along, let me introduce you to some young men, can't have you sitting all alone, now can we? Follow me, come along.'

She introduced Evelyne to the young soldiers. Her feathers tickled their noses and she got everyone's names wrong, but they were all so nervous they didn't like to correct her. Evelyne sat and tried to think of something interesting to say, but nothing would break through her headful of pins and bows.

'Would you like to dance, Miss?'

Evelyne bit her lip, then hedged, and finally admitted it – she actually couldn't dance. The soldier boy laughed, throwing back his head.

'We all thought you was a duchess sittin' over yonder, too good for the likes of us. Yer can't dance, girl, is that true?'

Evelyne nodded. These lads weren't the same as the young officers on the dance floor, they were her own kind, like her brothers.

'Well, I've never done this fancy two-and-two-step, but can you polka?'

Evelyne nodded, she could do a polka all right. Lizzie-Ann had taught her that. So they waited for a polka and now they were talking freely to her and asking questions. They came from different parts, but they all had families working the mines.

As the boys talked Evelyne's eyes kept straying to the dancers. David was dancing yet again with Lady Primrose, they looked perfect together. Heather appeared with small beads of sweat along her upper lip, her dress stained at the armpits.

'Are you enjoying yourselves? Food will be served in a moment.'

'Would you like to dance, miss?'

'Pardon?'

'Dance, you want a dance?'

Heather licked her rabbit teeth, nonplussed, and stuck out her arms. The young soldier, wearing heavy boots, guided her on to the floor. All the boys sniggered and whispered about her teeth.

'Always the way, ain't it, eh? All this money an' she got a face like a buckin' bronco, she looks like she's been eatin' too many of these toffees her family makes.'

Evelyne knew she shouldn't but she couldn't help laughing with the lads.

One boy, the boy in the wheelchair, didn't smile, he sat staring into the dancers as if they weren't there. His eyes were glazed, dead, empty. Evelyne moved to the seat next to him.

The boy seemed hardly aware of her. A red-haired soldier with bright red cheeks moved along to sit beside Evelyne.

'He'll not talk, he's shell-shocked, he don't know where he is, been like it for two days since they brought him home.'

Four more soldiers pulled their chairs closer, forming a protective circle with the vacant-eyed boy in the centre. They started to talk as if they needed to, the dancing and the champagne were all very well, but they had seen things, terrible things, and none of them wanted to go back. Their stories gushed out like rivers in flood, and Evelyne listened. She wanted to hold them in her arms, she felt their fear and confusion, and thought of Dicken and her darling brother Mike; they had gone off to a war she knew nothing about. The more the lads talked about what they were up against, the more Evelyne feared for her brothers. War was a long way from this elegant house, the orchestra, the young, dashing men in their cavalry uniforms. Evelyne realized that many of the so-called officers had never been to the Front. They were all show, like peacocks, in their braid and polished boots.

'Wait 'til they see what the Germans are like, lot of them won't be dancin' then, be lucky if they still got their legs.'

The tight group was suddenly aware that couples were drifting into a large side room where a long trestle table had been laid out, the weight of the food bending the legs. Food! The lads rose in unison, then they remembered they were with a lady and turned back, but she grinned at them. She stood up and moved to the silent one, bent over him, touched his face. The lads moved off towards the food and Evelyne took hold of the silent boy's hand.

'Would you like something to eat, lad?'

The vacant eyes stared towards her – so empty they frightened her. Slowly the boy lifted his hand. It was a strange move, his hand wavered, moving to her face. Then she felt his rough hand touch her cheek. She held his hand and kissed his fingers. The sad-eyed boy was so helpless, so cut off from reality, and his mouth moved, he was trying to speak. She moved her head closer.

'Mama ... ?'

Evelyne piled up a plate with chicken and ham, sweet rolled things with bacon wrapped around them, and tiny sausages on wooden sticks. The plate was so full, she dared not heap on any more. She was unaware of anyone watching her, of the nudges and the smiles or of David's eyes, bright and angry. He was ashamed, it looked as though the girl had never eaten in her life. Lady Primrose at his side ate with delicate, bird-like movements. She smiled up at him with her rosebud mouth.

'Do tell me, David, who on earth is that creature, and where exactly did you find her?'

David was very angry and flushed with embarrassment, he glared at Evelyne and then turned his back on her.

'My aunt works in a school in one of the mining villages, she's some sort of orphan, one has to do one's bit.'

Lady Primrose muttered, 'Poor thing', and her sweet voice trilled, agreeing that of course one simply had to do one's bit.

Several of the guests watched the tall girl in the flowing gown as she walked straight back to the sad, vacant-eyed boy in his wheelchair. They watched her place the napkin across his knee. Then she sat next to him and gently fed the boy with her own hands.

If anyone felt guilty they didn't admit it, but they remembered then the reason for the dance. It was not for flirting and courting, it was to give the boys who had come from the Front a night to remember. They were aware that the number of boys actually from the Front was exceedingly small, but then they knew mostly young officers anyway. Lady Primrose murmured, and it was hastily passed on, that Evelyne was a poor orphaned soul and all the gels there would react the same way if the officers they danced with came home wounded.

The ballroom had become very hot, the hundreds of candles and the great chandelier in the centre of the room shimmered and cigar smoke hung in a haze from the small smoking room. David seemed to have disappeared. The red-haired soldier pressed his face up against the window and rubbed the condensation clear as he gazed out into the garden.

'Eh, there's a big bird yonder with a long feathered tail!'

Two more of the boys scrambled up to stare out of the windows. They were becoming a trifle rowdy, having discovered that there were spirits to drink. Evelyne excused herself, she could feel her dress sticking to her body and could hardly breathe in the heat of the room.

There were several couples standing outside the gilded doors that opened on to a flower-strewn balcony overlooking the gardens with steps that led down either side to the velvet lawns. Evelyne was grateful for the cool night air and breathed deeply; no smoke, no soot here, the air was fresh and clean. She wandered down the garden, bending to smell the perfume of the roses, pure sweet fragrances in comparison to the ladies' scents.

The peacock screamed and it made Evelyne jump, then the bird swung its head and turned. As if dancing for her, it spread its tail, the colours shining in the twinkling lamplight. She laughed, thrilled by the sheer beauty of the bird, and moved closer and closer, and was suddenly knocked right off her feet by the most enormous dog she had ever seen. She sprawled face down, and the dog licked her cheek.

A small, rotund gentleman in rather ill-fitting evening clothes came rushing round the rosebushes. Red-faced, puffing with exertion, he made a grab for the dog's trailing lead and landed with a thud next to Evelyne.

'I apologize profusely, Madam . . .'

The dog stood over him and licked his face, making the gentleman's snow-white hair stand on end. Evelyne was on her feet first, and helped the gentleman to his feet. He bowed, and with one hand holding the dog's lead he apologized again, but his eyes twinkled and his arm was jerked back and forth. He whispered that he was just giving his friend a spot of exercise before he had to parade like the peacock he'd just scared off.

The gentleman's manner was so warm and friendly that Evelyne found herself automatically linking arms with him, and together they walked around the wonderful gardens. He pointed out various flowers to her, he knew almost every one by name. He asked her name, repeated it, and then wanted to know all about her and where she came from. Evelyne told him, and when she started to explain about her gown, and Bertha and Minnie, the laughter shook his whole body, his right arm still constantly being jerked by the massive St Bernard.

'But you *can* polka, is that right? Well then, may I ask you to give me the honour of a polka, or would you like me to give you the fastest dancing lesson? I'm not what you might call a light one on my feet, but by God I can and would love to waltz with you.'

There on the lawn, with his dog tied to a privet hedge and instructed to sit, the white-haired gentleman began to teach Evelyne the simplest one-two-three waltz step. He kept up a funny commentary about 'Now you move back, now you come forward, not on my foot, young lady, turn yourself around, that's a girl, by God you're light on your feet, just like a fawn ... round you go again ...'

The strains of the orchestra drifted down to the lawn as they danced, the old gentleman with his head full of white hair, and the tall skinny girl in the old-fashioned gown.

The St Bernard was then dragged off, and Evelyne returned to the house. She examined her face in the powder-room mirror. Her skin was shining, her cheeks rosy from the fresh night air, and Bertha's coiffure about to tumble down from its hundreds of pins. The orchestra stopped playing, and two girls rushed out of the room. The attendant peeked around the door.

'He's here, he's here himself, be quick or you'll miss him.'

Evelyne rushed to the door, not really knowing who it was she might miss.

A crowd had gathered at the ballroom doors. Sybil Warner was on the bandstand, and to thunderous applause she introduced Lloyd George himself. Evelyne could just see his shock of white hair above the heads of the group listening by the door. He gave a short, rousing speech, thanked Sybil for her efforts, and toasted 'The Boys in Uniform', wishing them God's luck and telling them to enjoy themselves while they could. Then he turned to the waiting orchestra, and in his enormous, mellifluous voice, demanded to know if they could play a polka, he was exceedingly fond of the polka . . .

Lloyd George stepped down from the bandstand, and searched the faces of the guests. He caught sight of Evelyne and gave her a bow, held his hand out to her as the orchestra struck up a polka. He led the blushing Evelyne to the centre of the ballroom, whispered to her that she was doing just fine, and they danced. For the first few bars they danced alone on the huge floor, then other couples joined them. Lady Sybil complained to David, her nose completely out of joint, that she should have opened the dancing with Lloyd George, it was outrageous. David didn't seem to hear her, he just stared at Evelyne. How in God's name had *that* come about? Captain Ridgely passed David and whispered to him from the side of his mouth.

'Old boy certainly can pick 'em, what? Stunning-looking gel.'

David glanced at Evelyne and raised one eyebrow slightly.

'Takes all tastes, old chap, but then he is notorious for his rough side, gel's an orphan from the valleys.'

Captain Ridgely murmured that Lloyd George wasn't the only one who liked a bit of rough. He nudged David and winked.

'I did a good turn for you, what you say you arrange something for me with that delicious redhead, is it a deal? What you say?'

David glanced at Evelyne; she made no impression on him whatever, the common touch left him cold. However, David wanted to keep on the right side of Ridgely, and he gave him an equally lewd wink and returned the nudge.

David could see Lady Primrose talking quietly with Freddy Carlton. Now there was someone who really interested him. Not only was she virginal, beautiful and wealthy but, to add icing to the already delicious cake, she was titled. David leaned close to Ridgely and whispered. They both glanced at Evelyne and then put their heads together again.

The dance seemed to end all too quickly, and Lloyd George moved off towards the soldiers, sat with them and talked and listened earnestly. As he got up to leave he touched the top of the sad-eyed boy's head. He didn't look back at Evelyne until he reached the main doors, then he smiled to her, and with a wave of his hand he was gone.

The orchestra began to move out of their seats, and a band of colourful gypsy men and women entered the ballroom. The women wore bright skirts and headbands, and were decked out in gold jewellery. They smiled and 'entertained' their audience, but their eyes were unfathomable. Smiling lips, friendly gestures, and yet there was an untouchable air to them. They remained aloof, distant.

The fiddlers played well, walking around the room while waiters served tea and brandy. Some guests were already departing, others sat talking. A large group, mostly women, moved into the card-room, where two gypsy women prepared to read fortunes from palms and Tarot cards. There was no need to cross their palms with silver, as Sybil had settled an overall price with them before their arrival. The soldiers were leaving, returning to their barracks, hospitals and rest homes.

Evelyne searched in vain for David, and strolled out on to the balcony. It was very late now, almost eleven-thirty. She was tired, and her mind was full of the events of the evening. She kept biting her lip to stop herself smiling. She had danced with Lloyd George himself! In actual fact, Evelyne had not the slightest idea who he was but she, the outsider, had been the centre of attention for one moment ... she wished Lizzie-Ann or her Da could have seen her. There was so much to tell them, they wouldn't believe it. She wondered if she would be allowed to keep her frock. If so, she'd give it to Lizzie-Ann. Evelyne just knew it was her style, she'd just die for it.

Evelyne didn't notice the boy, she hadn't heard his step, and he scared her. He was staring up at her from the grass below, head to one side, and he didn't look away when she looked down. He kept his eyes on her face. Black, cold eyes ... then he smiled, and she remembered him, it was the gypsy boy from the field.

Freedom moved up to the balcony steps, stealthily like a cat, his back to the white stone. His hair gleamed black as his eyes, and they never left her face. His gaze was magnetic, she could feel him, closer, closer, and his eyes were drawing her to him. He stopped two steps below her, and then he whispered, 'One two three, one two three ...'

For a moment Evelyne didn't know what he meant, then he rocked his body as if dancing, and she knew he must have watched her practising on the lawn. He climbed higher and there was now only one step between them. He lifted his hand towards her, his eyes still staring intently into hers. 'Read your palm ...'

Evelyne leaned forward slightly, her hand towards him, palm up. He lowered his head, keeping his eyes raised to hers, and kissed the centre of her palm. She curled her fingers and tried to draw her hand away, but he caught it and held it tight.

A woman seemed to spring from the darkness. Her head was swathed in a shawl, partially hiding her face, and she wore a long, dark skirt and heavy gold necklace. Her voice was soft, but sharp.

'Freedom ... Freedom ...'

He turned to the woman, gave her a hard look, almost vicious. Releasing Evelyne's arm, he glanced at her briefly, then turned and moved lightly down the steps, following the woman into the darkness of the bushes. But before he was out of earshot he heard a voice call.

'Evelyne!'

David stood at the balcony doors, his face set with anger. He had seen the incident. He moved to Evelyne's side and gripped her elbow tightly.

'I've been searching for you everywhere. Come inside, we're leaving.'

Lady Sybil joined them as they entered the ballroom. Patting David's arm she asked if they had both enjoyed themselves, surely they were not going to leave before the last waltz.

'I insist that you stay for just a little while longer, dear boy, your charge will just adore the fortune-tellers ... come along and sit with me ... Heather, dear, see if you can get the waiters to bring us coffee.'

David gave Evelyne a curt nod, and she went to join the girls waiting inline by the gypsy woman's table.

David could see Lady Primrose and her party leaving. She didn't even turn to look at him, hadn't even said goodbye.

The gypsy musicians were packing their fiddles into their old, worn cases. They had done their allotted time and wanted to leave. They still smiled and their manners were perfect, but they were like trained animals on display. The older of the two gypsy women looked at one of the fiddlers, and he gave a tiny sign with his hand to tell her their time was up. Two of the girls moaned that they had been waiting for ages, surely they wouldn't disappoint them now. Paying not the slightest attention, the women packed up their cards, slipping them into their worn packets, and, folding their shawls around them, they started to leave. The younger woman brushed past Evelyne, then stopped and turned back. Her skin was dark and tawny, her eyes the same as the young boy's, the boy called Freedom. She stared into Evelyne's face, touched her hair. Her hands were rough, the fingernails cut short and straight across. With a quick look at her menfolk she wavered, seemed nervous. The men waited impatiently, but she remained at Evelyne's side. One of the disappointed girls pushed forward, her hand held out, but the woman ignored it, brushed it from her as she would a buzzing fly. She pulled Evelyne's hand, unfurled the fingers and stared into the palm, the same palm the gypsy boy had kissed. The gnarled finger traced along the thin lines, and she could feel the roughness of this 'lady's' hand. She looked up into frightened eyes, eyes the colour of the cold northern seas, and for a moment she hesitated, about to speak. Then she turned and joined her menfolk.

The ballroom was virtually empty now, the servants were clearing the debris, collecting the glasses. The sweet-faced powder-room attendant slipped the black mourning cloak around Evelyne's shoulders.

'This'll be a night you won't forget, child. God bless you.'

*

Mrs Darwin heard the front door open into the darkened hall-way. She wondered if Minnie had stayed awake to see to the couple. The stairs creaked and she lay back. They must be going straight to their rooms.

David walked ahead of Evelyne up the stairs, then put his finger to his lips and pointed down, creeping on tiptoe and gesturing for her to follow him into the dark drawing room. She tiptoed after him, and they bumped in the doorway. After shutting the door David lit the gas lamp with a taper from the still-glowing fire. His face twisted into a snide smile.

'Well, my little Flame, didn't you do well? Polka with Lloyd George, kissed by the riff-raff gypsy boy, and we never had one dance together . . .'

He opened the drinks cabinet, careful not to make a noise, and took out a bottle of brandy and a glass. Evelyne's heart thudded, this was the moment she had dreamed of, alone with David, did he know she loved him, was he going to learn?

He poured a measure of brandy with care and sipped it, rolling it around his mouth, then looked at her over the rim of his glass, 'You made a great impression on a friend of mine, Captain Ridgely.' He didn't even offer her a drink. 'Yes, he was really taken with you. Comes from a good family, lots of loot . . . well, to cut a long story short, he wants to see you.'

Evelyne was puzzled. She asked who Ridgely was as she couldn't recall meeting him.

'I doubt if you will be going home tomorrow, so I said perhaps you could meet him at tea time, it'll be up to you what you want to arrange with him.'

'I don't understand, what arrangements?'

David sighed. God, he thought, she really is stupid.

'He likes you, I don't want to get involved, it will be entirely up to you whether you go to meet him or not. I think you'd be throwing away a good opportunity, he's very rich, could set you up in a little place of your own ... and he's not a bad chap, you should be flattered, girl like you won't get many opportunities, especially if you have to stay in the valley all your life.'

Evelyne still stared, dumbfounded.

'Good God, do I have to spell it out, you could earn money, he'd keep you if you pleased him enough ...'

Evelyne's hand swung out and slapped David hard across the face.

'Christ, what did you do that for?'

Evelyne was hurt and shaking with anger. He was suggesting she sell herself, and to one of his friends.

'Now, come along, I didn't mean any harm, no need to get yourself all upset, you don't have to go if you don't want to, all I said was I would ask you.'

Still Evelyne was speechless, staring at him, shocked, wide-eyed.

'You stupid little girl, this was an opportunity for you, I'm sorry I even bothered with you.' He walked out, leaving her confused and bewildered by all he had said, by his manner towards her. She could not remember the last time she had cried for herself – little Davey, Ma, that was different. She caught her breath as the sobs rose inside her. She wept for herself, for her stupidity, for the dream that had just been shattered. Her foolishness in believing, even for a moment, that she could be part of David Collins' life filled her with shame. She ran up the stairs to her room, remembering to creep the last few steps so she would not waken Doris.

David's bedroom door was ajar, and he was watching her as she tiptoed along the landing. Evelyne turned, caught him staring, and he gave her a strange, apologetic smile, then closed his door. The smile made it all the worse, his handsome, perfect face so far from her reach. All she wanted was to go home, home to her own people, her own class.

She cried herself to sleep, her face buried in the pillow, afraid to waken Doris. No one must know, ever, of her humiliation. Suddenly she remembered that dreadful painted woman at the window of the inn, just like Nellie Lanigan from the village, she knew the men paid money to go with her. Evelyne sobbed into the handkerchief David had once given her, and even through her tears she could smell him, his faint lavender perfume.

Chapter 6

The two brothers died with their arms around each other, Mike and Will, but the cable Benjamin Rees brought didn't mention that, simply the dreaded words, 'killed in action'. Dicken wrote a letter from the front dated March 1917 – it took four months to reach the village, and that was when they learned how the two brothers had died.

The Old Lion seemed to bend under the weight of their loss. The drinking had stopped when little Davey had been buried, and Hugh had found work in a small colliery. When the news of the boys' death came he went straight back to work a double shift. Every morning he rose at dawn and, wrapped in his great-coat and carrying his tea caddie, sandwiches and tools, he donned his cloth cap and silently left the house. Money was very short and there were now three lodgers who worked in the mine with Hugh.

Lizzie-Ann had been very brave. Rosie was now almost eighteen months old, a pretty little girl with rosy cheeks and curly hair. Lizzie-Ann had made considerable progress as far as house-keeping and cleaning were concerned. She was skinny again, and spent hours chalking and polishing the front step. Often she had a faraway look in her eyes, daydreaming, but she never talked about London now. She was grown up, a widow with a daughter to look after, a widow and still only just eighteen.

Evelyne worked at the local brick factory, tough, hard labour from six-thirty in the morning until three o'clock. In the afternoon she went to the schoolhouse to help the new teachers. Doris Evans was still at the school, but she taught the senior girls and boys. The only house without a lodger was Doris' —she was still able to keep her four neat rooms to herself.

Poverty was everywhere in the village. The children scavenged for coal chips on the slag heaps, the men no longer sat eating their packed lunches together, laughing at what the missus had landed them with this time. They all knew they had the same, bread and dripping and tea.

Evelyne trudged up the hill to the schoolhouse. The rain was bucketing down, and she'd got soaked earlier in the day on the way to the brick factory. Her hands were raw and blistered, and she was as thin as ever. She had grown even taller, reaching five feet nine and a half inches. She was Hugh Jones' daughter all right.

The schoolhouse was cold, the small fire banked low, and the children huddled in their overcoats to keep out the freezing draughts. Evelyne helped in the junior class and also cleaned the school.

Mr Matthews, the new headmaster, was elderly, and had actually retired, but he had come to take the place of the original headmaster who had joined up. He called Evelyne in.

'Mrs Evans has not been in for the past two days, Miss Jones, will you look in on her?'

Evelyne pushed open the polished front door and called out. When she got no reply she began to worry, and went along the passage into the kitchen. It was neat and clean as ever, but empty and very cold. She hurried into the tiny living room. There were books on the table as always, but no sign of Doris. Eventually Evelyne found her lying in her clean bed with the starched white sheets. She was extremely pale and as Evelyne pushed open the door she asked, with a strange look on her face, 'Walter, is that you?' Doris didn't seem to recognize Evelyne at all as she bent over the frail, thin woman and rubbed her icy hands. She pulled more blankets from the wardrobe and laid them on top of Doris.

The coal bunker was piled high, and Evelyne took the full bucket back into the bedroom, laid the fire and lit it. Then she found vegetables in heir neat trays beneath the kitchen sink and made some broth. She held the frail woman in her arms, the skinny frame wrapped in the blankets, and gently spooned the hot soup into her. Slowly, Doris seemed to come to herself, and gave Evelyne such a heart-rending look that Evelyne said: 'I'll not leave you tonight, Doris, I'll stay with you.'

She sat by the fire and read Dante's *Inferno* until Doris slept, then she banked the fire, pulled a rug over herself and went to sleep.

The following morning Doc Clock came and examined Doris, muttering that she was not taking care of herself – and with her money! He stuck a thermometer into Doris' bird-like mouth, and fumbled for the watch that wasn't there, as usual. Doc Clock, the village said, would stick a thermometer into a dead man's mouth and pronounce him perfectly fit.

Doris went very fast and as quietly as she had lived. Doc Clock said she had a brain tumour, must have had it for years. Lizzie-Ann, who always got everything wrong, told everyone that Doris had died from a brain *rumour*, and that she'd had it for years. Evelyne wrote to Dr Collins, taking the penny postage money from Doris' little leather purse. The money was needed, but there was no reply to her letter.

Evelyne had to arrange for the coffin and the funeral, since there was no one else to do it. All the while she still worked at the brick factory and up at the school. She made sure Doris' house was locked up tight, because already the coal bunker was empty and with things the way they were it was a wonder the furniture was still intact. Evelyne would shiver as she checked the house, knowing Doris was lying upstairs, cold and stiff.

Doris was buried beside her husband, Walter, in a simple ceremony attended only by Evelyne and a few villagers. In her neat handwriting, Evelyne noted down all the expenses she had paid out from the money she had found in the house, and how much was left, and sent the list to Dr Collins. Still she heard nothing back and often villagers passing the cold house would mutter, 'What a waste', the four rooms could easily be let and be making someone a few bob a week.

Lizzie-Ann ran from the post office with Dicken's letter. All the women went every day and asked old Ben Rees if there was any news from the Front. Ben used to get angry, swearing that he did his three rounds a day with the post, and if there was a letter or any news they would be the first to know, but it still didn't stop the women popping in and asking.

The pub would be lit up and the piano wheeled out when any of the boys came home on leave, only to be wheeled back again when they had to go again after too short a time. Then there would be the tears at the station and the Sunday prayers that the boys would come home.

Hugh and Rosie were sitting by the fire, playing with a bat and ball. Lizzie-Ann had gone on a date with a boy who had been invalided out of the army. He was a good-hearted boy with a bad limp, and Lizzie-Ann seemed to have some of her old sparkle back.

'Will you not find yerself a lad then, Evie?'

Evelyne laughed, and carried the washing out to dry. Over her shoulder she told him she had no time to spare for lads. As she hung out the cold, worn trousers, she remembered the night she had danced with Lloyd George. She pictured David's face and sighed. She still thought of him, almost every night and prayed every Sunday that he would be safe and unharmed. It was strange that she had received no word from David's father in Cardiff, maybe they felt it best simply to forget poor Doris.

Summer was coming on and the war still raged. The villagers found it hard to picture their menfolk fighting in another country somewhere, even harder to understand what they were fighting for. The old boys sitting in the pub said they were after the bastard Germans, and that the Tommies would 'wipe 'em off the face of the earth'– their lads could do it, it was as if only Welsh lads were over there.

Lizzie-Ann had decided to marry her young man with the limp. Evelyne made Jim feel welcome, even though it meant an extra mouth to feed in the house. He was good-hearted, and made Lizzie-Ann smile again. The wedding was a simple affair, and Lizzie-Ann wore the dress Evelyne had brought home from Cardiff. The couple had no honeymoon, they just took over the front room, and life went on as usual. At least the house (unlike so many others) throbbed with life now, a bit too much at times as they still had four lodgers. Lizzie-Ann dropped numerous hints about how awful it was that they could be so cramped while Doris Evans' house stood empty. It had been more than six months since Doris had been buried, and still no word from Dr Collins.

Evelyne hurried home from the brick factory. It had been boiling hot in there, and working right next to the kilns made you sweat your guts out. She wanted a good wash before going up to the school. Already they called her a schoolmistress, although she wasn't actually qualified, but she liked it and got on well with the two proper teachers.

Ben Rees was standing by the door, his bike propped up by the wall. He had one of the dreaded yellow telegrams in his hand.

'No, Ben . . . Ah, don't say it's for us, no, please . . . no.'

Dicken was gone, and two days after the telegram arrived they got his last letter, telling them how well he was doing, and that he might make sergeant within the month.

Hugh seemed unable to take any more pain, his whole body sagged as if the wind had been punched from his huge frame. He still struggled up every morning and went off to work, but he was so silent, so empty, it was as if his soul had already slipped from his body.

As she had done all her life, Evelyne held the last tenuous threads of the family together. She had to keep on working, she had to keep going up to the school, but she no longer went to church, she couldn't, and she didn't care what wrath He sent down on her. How could there be a God who would take each and every one of her brothers, and leave them with nothing?

In August, one of the hottest Augusts ever, Evelyne prepared for another burning day in the factory. She noticed her Da had gone off to work without his tea caddie. She sighed, he'd be dying of thirst by twelve, she'd just have to be late. The sun blazed in the cloudless sky, birds sang, the grass smelt good and all over the hedgerows the flowers were blooming. The further up the mountain she walked the cleaner the air was. The raspberries hung thick and ripe, and she ate them as she walked, thinking that on the way back she would fill her skirt with them to make a tart.

She walked down the further slope of the mountain, crossed two streams and a field of cows. Her legs were getting tired, and she realized just how strong a man her father must be to take this long trek day in and day out. The winter months must have frozen him, the rain soaked him, and then he spent all those hours down the mine. When she reached the small pithead she asked for Hugh Jones, and was directed to a shaft at ground level. Black-faced men called 'hello', and five women sitting in the sun called to her and waved. This new mine took quite a few women at the pithead to sort the coal. They were as black as the menfolk, but they were laughing and joking and soaking up the sunshine.

Evelyne edged along the coal seam. She had to bend almost double, and the blackness was just as Mike had described, so thick she couldn't even see a shadow. She called out, directing her voice towards the sound of hammering and the click–click-clicking of the pickaxes.

She passed two trams being pushed out by Dai Roberts, who grinned at her and said to keep on walking, and to watch her step as it sloped steeply. The air was getting so thick she was gasping for breath as she inched her way along the tunnel – her hands were her only guide.

'Hugh Jones. *Hugh Jones!*'

She could barely draw breath and the blackness was so heavy she didn't know whether to turn back or go on . . .

'*Hugh! Hugh Jones . . .*'

As Evelyne turned a bend in the tunnel she saw her father, lit up by the flame of a single candle. His face was stricken, his eyes stared into the blackness as in a nightmare. Evelyne ran to him, knowing what must be in his mind, that he must have thought there was some other tragedy, could there be another? She was quick to shout that she'd brought his tea caddie.

Hugh held his blackened arms out to her and she clung to him. With barely enough air to keep the candle flame flickering, with no more than four feet of space to work in, the massive man had to hunch himself nearly double to chip away at the face.

Evelyne felt his powerful arms holding her as he had when she was a little girl. In the blackness the grief that filled both of them was released, and they cried together, their tears mingling with the coal dust that dominated their lives.

*

The war was over, and home-made paper chains were strung across the streets, trestle tables were erected on the cobbles and from God knew where came buns, cakes, biscuits and lemonade for the kids.

There was hardly a family in the village that had not lost a loved one in the mines or in the mighty war that had raged across the Channel. Now the lads who had survived were coming home, and their families went crazy. They sang in the streets, they belted out the old tunes on the piano and they held hands and sang 'God Save the King . . .'

Evelyne rushed around handing out cakes, and handmade crackers with no *bang*! in the middle, but containing little gifts made by some of the old women for the children. It was a wonderful day, and everyone crowded into Mrs Morgan's to drink her home-brewed wine.

Evelyne was standing well to the back of the crowd as the home-brewed wine took effect, and the singing reached a raucous level . . . Evelyne left the stuffy house. Some older women, well inebriated, grouped on a corner, looked at her with pitying faces as she walked on up the cobbled street.

'Ah, poor thing, she'll never get herself a lad now, left it too late . . . or maybe with her being so tall she'll get one who's injured, disabled, you never know.'

Evelyne Jones was twenty-one, that was all, but her eyes mirrored the anguish she had experienced. Hugh Jones could see her striding up the hill, her lean, tough body, high cheekbones and flame red hair, her strong legs like an athlete's . . . he closed his eyes, dear God, how he wished she was one of his boys come home.

*

Lizzie-Ann could have given herself a miscarriage, she ran so fast. The thick bundle of letters all addressed to Evelyne Jones was in a brown paper parcel, and she had to sign for them at the post office. She signed after a hell of a row with Ben Rees, who was livid because he hadn't had a chance to snoop through them. He'd dropped his bike in fury – that bloody girl was always a little bugger, and her with another kid on the way when she was no better than one herself. Ben picked up his red bike and threatened to strangle Alfred Moggs' illegitimate grandson, half coloured he was, with black, curly hair. The little bugger had already let the air out of Ben's tyres once this morning.

Evelyne took the thick brown envelope with the red line across it and started to open it, with the entire class of nosy children peering through the glass door, the headmistress looking on, and Lizzie-Ann gasping. Before Evelyne had a chance to examine the contents, Lizzie-Ann's waters broke, and the children sniggered that she'd wet herself. The headmistress, a flat-footed woman in her late sixties, took over the class while Evelyne ran for Doc Clock.

The Doctor now had the only privately owned motor vehicle in the village. This was patted, polished, and sat in by the Doc but in the driver's seat he was absolutely hopeless. More than once he had been found still sitting in the car as it teetered on the edge of a ditch, his face concerned and puzzled, his specs dangling from one ear.

'Christ almighty, there's something wrong with it again, it turned right when I wanted to go left.'

Doc Clock arrived just in time as Lizzie-Ann gave birth in

the school kitchen. He shouted that it was a boy, but when he put his glasses on he realized it was a girl.

'No, it's a girl, it's a girl.'

Lizzie-Ann, sweating and exhausted, screamed.

'Oh, Christ Almighty, I haven't got twins, have I?'

Evelyne held her hand and stroked her head, saying it was all right, it was just the one.

The Doc huffed and puffed and dropped them all home. The trip in his car made Lizzie-Ann forget the letters for a moment, but she was soon reminded when Evelyne eventually opened the package and gasped, then fainted, out cold, in the kitchen.

Doris Evans had named Evelyne Jones as her heir, leaving her the little four-roomed house, which no one had realized she'd owned outright, and two hundred pounds. The news went round faster than Mrs Morgan's radio could have blasted it. In the first version, Evelyne had had a heart attack and a daughter at the same time, but eventually the news filtered through that she had received a legacy.

When it got straightened out and the story told in the right order, there was a strange calm. The villagers whispered, spread the story from house to house, pub to pub. Suddenly the Jones family's cramped house had an aura to it. Evelyne Jones had a legacy and overnight, out of the blue, the tall schoolmistress became extremely eligible. She had money, she owned Doris Evans' house, actually *owned* it. She was now a woman of property – more than the village realized, because Doris had not only left Evelyne her house in the village, but also her half-share in the Cardiff house. There were, of course, the gossips in the washhouses that said no good would come of it, but they all secretly wished they had been a little more friendly to poor old Doris.

There was no word from David in the lawyer's letter, just a stiff, formal note from the doctor thanking Evelyne for coping with all the arrangements for Doris' funeral, and that was all.

Lizzie-Ann had cried and Rosie had howled, though not really understanding why everyone in the house was so emotional. Evelyne insisted they move into Doris' house. There was no question of rent, it would be theirs for as long as they wanted it.

She stood and watched the couple running in and out of each room, hugging each other, then they would kiss Evelyne and thank her for the thousandth time. Evelyne took very little from the house, just Doris' books and pens, a silver-framed photo of Doris and Walter on their wedding day, and two pairs of linen sheets and pillowcases, a set for her own small bed and another for her father's.

Evelyne's first purchase with her legacy was a wireless, which was installed in the kitchen. Hugh moaned and muttered that he wouldn't go near the infernal noise machine. The house was quiet now, no lodgers. Evelyne and her father were alone, and spent long evenings sitting by the blazing fire. He still rose before dawn to go to the mines, and she still prepared his tea caddy and sandwiches. Evelyne couldn't help but smile as Hugh rushed in from work and turned on the wireless. He listened intently and would talk back to the speakers. On one occasion when she was late home from school she found him standing, fist clenched, shouting back at the radio that the man was talking rubbish, let him spend some time down the mines before making these rules and regulations. Unemployment was out of control, the blasted politicians were talking out of their arses.

Hugh was so irate that Evelyne thought he would put his fist through her precious radio, but he grabbed up his cap to go out. If no other bugger in the village was going to stand up for his rights, then he would. Three sons lost in the war, and for what? He banged out of the house and marched to the pithead.

The Old Lion roared, and the men listened. It was as if new life had been breathed into him. Meetings were held in their front room. The radio became a focal point for many of the meetings, the men clustered around listening, listening to their fate, but until now not actually going out and doing anything about it . . . until now they hadn't had a leader. Hugh Jones had become that leader, and his new-found energy gave him back the respect he had lost.

The men listened to him, and gradually his work with the union became a full-time occupation. He was at the pitheads, he was in the managers' office, discussing safety precautions, he popped up everywhere, he was unstoppable. The men began to turn to him with their problems, their insurance claims, and he turned no one away. The house throbbed with life, and Hugh would stand with his back to the fire, testing out his speeches on his daughter.

Evelyne appeared contented, often at her father's side handing out leaflets. She, too, got up on the small platform and spoke for women's rights in the brick factory, the bakeries, even for the women working in the mines. They wanted better conditions, overtime, holiday pay, insurance. She worked all day at school and at night she would read, discussing the campaign with her father. They became close, a unit. After church the pair would hold meetings, gathered in the small church hall. It was after one of these that Hugh stood and looked up at the mountains, then turned to his daughter and held out his hand.

'It's a fair day, we'll walk awhile.'

They walked in silence, the climb taking their breath away. They climbed higher and higher until eventually they sat, side by side, looking down into the valley. Hugh had never been a great man with words, not intimate words, and Evelyne could tell by the way he kept on coughing and starting to speak, then closing his mouth tightly, that he wanted to talk but just couldn't get around to it.

Evelyne lay back in the warm sun. She could smell the sweet, fresh grass. Hugh lay down beside her, coughed a few more times and then leant on his elbow and looked into her face. He loved her passionately, and he wished he could find the right words to tell her so. Hugh had never referred to Evelyne's legacy, never asked her what she intended doing with it. He looked down at her face, framed by the thick red hair coiled in braids and clipped tightly to her head. He had not seen her with her hair loose for a long time. With his big, rough hand he gently traced her chin, her cheekbones. She kept her eyes closed, not ever having had such a quiet, intimate moment with her father before. Almost afraid to open her eyes in case the moment slipped away, she kissed his hand softly.

'You're a fine-looking woman, Evie, you know that?' Still she said nothing. 'You're also intelligent, a clever girl, and a good daughter, no man could ask for a better lass. Do you not think of marrying? Or having children, gel?'

He turned to her and knelt down. His body was still muscular, his shoulders wide, not an ounce of fat on him. He could have been a young man but for the grey hair, the heavy lines in his face, that gave his age away.

'I'd like to hear the sound of a boy's voice in our house, Evie, a grandson. Lizzie-Ann's pair are real sweethearts, but I'd like a grandson. Is there no boy takes your fancy? ... fine-looking woman like you, Evie, could take your pick, it's not natural for you to be with me so much of your time.'

Evelyne had never told anyone of David, of her time in Cardiff, and there on the mountain top it all poured forth, as if she was sixteen again. The hurt, the shame, and at long last she whispered of her obsessive love of David.

'I loved him since that first time, Da, and no one seems to come up to him. I know I don't mean anything to him, he's more than likely forgotten I even exist but I see his face every night.'

Hugh was nonplussed. All the years she had kept her secret to herself, and more than that, her shame. He turned to start down into the village. He struck his fist against his thigh.

'Go back to him, then, girl, you must get the lad out of your system, or you'll start to be like Doris herself. Go to Cardiff, but by Christ, this time you'll go wearing the finest. You have the legacy, then spend it, go and see this David ...'

Hugh held out his hand and hauled Evelyne to her feet. He roared with laughter ... it echoed round the mountain.

'Did you really dance with Lloyd George himself?'

Hugh brought in some pages from a magazine that he had found in Doc Clock's waiting room. He had gone with one of the men to try to get the Doc to sign a medical claim, and had torn the pages out. Evelyne laughed, they were plastered all over the table, the latest fashions. She kissed Hugh, and looked at the crumpled pages. The magazine was only eight years out of date, and the skirts were being worn almost up to the calf now. 'See, gel, dove grey is the latest colour, now get yourself decked out in that and this David won't be able to say no.'

He took out of his pocket a return ticket to Cardiff, bought, he hastened to add, with his own money, so it was not to be wasted, and she was not to hang on to her cash like an old miser but go up to Cardiff and get herself done up.

Hugh held out the ticket as proud as Punch. She went into his arms and hugged him tight.

'Oh, Da, I love you so, I love you more than I ever tell you.'

Hugh held her at arm's length, and his face shone with love for her.

'An' I get so full of love for you, girl, all I want is for you to be happy . . .'

Evelyne delayed her journey to Cardiff until the Easter holidays, then she had no excuse. Hugh marched her off to the steam train. She took a small overnight bag and her post office savings book. Hugh had got her a list of bed and breakfast hotels for her to choose from. They were so close, so loving, and his pride in her shone out of his eyes. Some said it wasn't natural, the two being together so much, and Wally Hampton said he saw them kissing like lovers on the station platform.

'Right, gel, you go and get this David and bring him back . . .'

She could see him standing, waving his big red handkerchief from the platform . . . he remained waving until the train chuffed round the mountain.

*

Evelyne was scared, but realized she was happier than she had felt for years. Perhaps Hugh was right, she was becoming an old maid up at the school. She began to make out a list of all the things she would buy on her first shopping spree.

David's blond hair, his smile, his sweet lavender smell. Would he still be at the same house? Her mouth went dry, what if he hadn't returned from the war – what if he'd moved. Evelyne counted the months, the years she had been away. Time had gone fast, and with trepidation she realized her foolishness. Over four years had gone by, he could be dead, killed like her brothers, her letters to Dr Collins had not been answered. By the time the train had chuffed into Cardiff Central station she was as nervous as on her very first journey all those years ago with Doris.

'Think positively,' she told herself, and set her shoulders back as she walked along the platform, her face determined, almost haughty.

Evelyne booked into the 'Rosemount', a bed and breakfast hotel. The house had a view of the castle, it was clean, and the landlady was a kindly woman named Violet Pugh.

By teatime Evelyne had been in every single women's wear shop, and her feet ached. Millinery, shoes, gloves, suits, every item had been jotted down and priced. She was stunned at the cost of clothes, and she had by no means calculated for such extravagance. That night she made a list in readiness for her next day's shopping expedition.

The saleswoman at 'Chic fashions' sighed. God, that wretched woman was back, she wished the other assistant was free. The woman had tried on every single outfit in the shop the previous day, and bought nothing. Nor was she an easy one to dress, being so tall, and then she was thin with it — a lot of the new fashions looked dreadful on her. She forced a smile between her 'Lush Red' lips, and hovered. Out came the list and Evelyne, with a look of determination on her face, asked to try on the dove-grey pleated skirt with the matching white-collared jacket.

The shop assistant stared at Evelyne as she emerged from the changing room. She muttered to herself. 'Just shows you, you never know. Girl like that looked more like she should be sweeping the place out, never mind buying anything.'

The shoes Evelyne had set her mind on did not match the outfit. She was shown the new, fashionable high heel.

'Don't you think I'm too tall to wear two-inch heels?' she asked.

The sales assistant showed how perfectly the two-toned shoes matched her outfit.

'I'll take them, thank you, and the matching handbag.'

It was a rash decision, but having made it she felt tickled to death, she was going to look so elegant.

Her next stop was a small milliner's in a side-street, 'Paris Designers'. The hat was a problem, the small cloche hats were very fashionable now, but none of them would fit over Evelyne's thickly coiled hair. The sales assistant pondered and sat back, took a peek inside the bag from the well-known fashion shop that contained the suit, and rifled through the tissue paper. That exquisite dove-grey ... to her mind it was a trifle ageing for such a young woman. She scurried into the back of the shop and returned with three large hatboxes, new stock not yet on display. She sat Evelyne down before the mirror in a cubicle. She was a tiny, grey-haired woman dressed neatly in black, her name, 'Miss Freda', written on a tag pinned to her dress. She had a strange accent and was very apologetic, yet not cloying in any way. She could see the girl's big, red hands, and just by looking at her worn clothes she knew she must have some very special occasion in mind, perhaps even a wedding. She brought a magazine to Evelyne's side, flicked through it, her small, neat white hands moving fast. She stopped at a page. The fashionable bobbed hair was very much in vogue, but then perhaps for someone as tall as Evelyne the bobbed style would not be flattering enough.

'If Madame would allow me . . .'

Evelyne chewed her lip as Miss Freda worked quickly and deftly, her nimble fingers fluttering around Evelyne's head. Down came the coiled braids, flick, flick, they were undone: a silver-handled brush was retrieved from the drawer of the dressing-table. Miss Freda, her mouth full of hairgrips, tossed and wound the hair into an ornate bun, low on the nape of Evelyne's neck. She then studied Evelyne in the mirror, her head cocked to one side, then the other, and satisfied, she opened up a large hatbox. The tissue rustled and she held up a white cloche hat with a small spray of embroidered white daises along one side of the brim. As Miss Freda held the hat to the side of Evelyne's face, the doorbell rang and a very elegantly dressed couple entered.

'Freda, my dear, I am quite desperate. I have to go to the races, and you know that darling little rose-flowered hat we had from Paris, well, Poochie here has eaten it.'

Evelyne peeked out as the woman held out a fluffy dog with

an awful turned-up nose and popping eyes. Miss Freda almost curtsied and ushered the couple into another cubicle. She still held the daisy hat in her hand. 'Oh, that is a little darling, Freda, do let me try it.'

Miss Freda popped back into Evelyne's cubicle and drew the curtains, and whispered, 'She is much too old to wear this, but if it is not suitable for you, Madam, well ... ' Freda had a delightful tinkling laugh. As she spoke she placed the hat gently onto Evelyne's head, tilted the daises a little lower, stood back and beamed. Evelyne stared at her reflection. She turned to right and left as Freda held a small silver mirror behind her so she could get the full effect.

'I shall leave you to make your decision, Madame, but believe me, you look stunning.'

As Freda slipped out between the curtains, she put the price tag face down on the dressing-table.

Evelyne turned the price tag over. One pound fifteen shillings. It was far too much, she simply couldn't. One pound was almost half a week's earnings for the girls at the brick factory. She sighed, wondered if she could keep her hair in this lovely knot – that would mean saving a little on the hairdresser, at least three-and-six. She stared, perplexed, at her reflection, she adored the hat, but the price ... it really was too much.

Miss Freda passed to and fro, discussing the weather with her clients. Evelyne heard the yap-yap of the dog, the *ping* of the doorbell and then swish of her curtains. Evelyne turned to Miss Freda, and swallowed.

'I'll take the hat, thank you.'

Miss Freda beamed and gently lifted the hat from Evelyne's head as though it were precious crystal, and laid it in the box.

Out of the corner of her eye she noticed Evelyne lift the mirror, studying her new hairstyle, her fingers tracing the coils.

'It is a very simple hairstyle, no? I can show you in two minutes how to do it. The hairdressers here have no idea, all they do is snip, snip, everyone's head looks the same, or they frizz, frizz with the perms.'

Freda turned the small 'open' notice on the door to 'closed', and clapped her hands in delight as she moved towards Evelyne.

'Come, we have some coffee, some croissants, unless you are in a hurry? Come, darling, then I show you, it is very simple.'

Miss Freda's back room was piled ceiling-high with hatboxes. On a small work-table were laid out roses and ribbons and nets indifferent shades. Evelyne sat watching the bird-like woman as she chattered away and made up a hat right in front of her eyes.

'I come from Vienna, but I tell everyone I am French, I sell only Paris creations. As you can see this is a long way from France, no?'

From a small drawer she took a box of labels and waved them at Evelyne.

'I print them specially, but I don't think it is a lie because my hats are copies from French magazines, only the price is French.'

She covered her face like a small child as she twittered with laughter, then still talking fast she began sewing and serving coffee all at the same time. It tasted different from the coffee she had been served at David's house, stronger, thicker and sweeter with no milk.

Miss Freda taught Evelyne how to do her hair, then she brought out a small velvet box filled with tiny jars and fluffy powder puffs. She showed Evelyne how to whiten her hands, instructed her to cream them every night until they were soft. Then she tipped Evelyne's chin up, stared into her face, and searched through her box, bringing out a tiny pot. She opened the lid carefully and, with the tip of her little finger, dabbed a very soft, pale-pink over Evelyne's lips ... she sat back and clucked and nodded, then, 'Oh, là là.'

Apparently quite unconcerned about the shop being closed, Miss Freda insisted on plucking Evelyne's eyebrows, careful not to make them too arched as was the fashion, just, in her words, 'tidying them up a little'. After every move she sat back, her tiny head bobbing up and down like a bird, constantly repeating, 'Oh, là là ... ' She even painted Evelyne's square-cut fingernails with clear polish. Then she carefully packed the daisy hat and tied the box with ribbon.

'For you, darling, I will charge fifteen shillings.'

Evelyne tried to argue, without much enthusiasm, as even fifteen shillings for a hat that did not really come from Paris, France, was terribly expensive.

'Will you come and see me again? I would like it, I don't have many friends, you see, I came over *many* years ago as a lady's maid.'

She whispered as if afraid someone would overhear.

'First I was in Liverpool, then we travelled to Wales and I was just so unhappy that I left and ... *voilà*, here I am, *chérie* ... so you must go, but come and see me again.'

Miss Freda locked up her shop, bolting the door, and sat studying her accounts. She looked at her face in the mirror, how she hated to bow and scrape with her 'oh, là là's ...' she sighed. If she didn't get more business there would be no shop, and she would have to go back to being a waitress, but never the other thing. She would never do that, and looking at herself she knew that not many men would want her now anyway. She put one of her specials on her frizzy head, lifted her chin and decided she was not that bad, not that old, thirty-eight wasn't old at all ... then she sat at her sewing machine, surrounded by net and roses.

The boarders looked up briefly, but went back to slurping their soup. Mrs Pugh did notice the difference, and remarked to her reflection in the spotless hall mirror that the rest was obviously doing wonders for the girl. Catching sight of a spot of dust she flicked it with her finger.

'Something most definitely is ...'

As she came out of the dining room, Evelyne passed Mrs Pugh in the hall.

'Are you not having pudding, Miss Jones? It's semolina with jam.'

Evelyne smiled and said she was too full, then went up the stairs to her room. Mrs Pugh stared after her, pursing her lips. The girl had done her hair differently, that was what it was. She hoped it didn't mean she had any funny ideas, any fancy men ... then she marched back into the dining room.

'It's semolina, with strawberry jam,' she announced.

The two elderly boarders were fast asleep at the table.

Evelyne had a dress rehearsal in her rented room. First she practised her new hairstyle, then she sat for over an hour in just her camisole and bloomers with the hat on. She watched herself smiling ... she had never been so preoccupied with her face or her body and she wasn't as sure about her appearance as Miss Freda was, but she certainly did look quite nice.

*

The following morning, Evelyne was dressed and ready when Mrs Pugh called to her that there was a car waiting for her, and she slowly descended the stairs from her rented room as Mrs Pugh stared, open-mouthed. She was dumbstruck, the girl moving slowly, slightly unsteadily down the stairs *couldn't* be Miss Jones ... but there she was, looking as if she had stepped straight off the front of a French fashion magazine. Mrs Pugh looked up into the girl's face as she passed in a cloud of sweet perfume, immaculate from head to toe. 'My God,' she thought, 'the girl must have a fancy man, and a rich one at that.' Well, any funny business and she'd pack the girl's bags, she couldn't afford any gossip, not just as she'd got her two regulars installed, and for life, judging by their ages.

The hired car had been Hugh's idea. He'd told her, 'Don't go up in a ruddy horse-drawn carriage, they're old-fashioned. Hire yourself one of the new-fangled motors with a uniformed driver'. It had cost her one pound ten shillings, and she had the car for eight hours. Now as she stepped out of Mrs Pugh's front door she knew it was right. The chauffeur moved smartly to open the door, and even gave her a tiny bow.

Mrs Pugh almost pulled her net curtain down from the window, she was so eager to see everything that was going on. All the nets along the road flicked. Mrs Pugh could see her nosy neighbours, and tutted to herself, they were always at their windows, she couldn't understand why. That she was doing exactly the same thing never even occurred to her. The car moved slowly off and Evelyne sat back, savouring the smell of the leather upholstery and her perfume. So far so good. They drove slowly along the kerb as the chauffeur searched for the right house. Evelyne was so tense she sat forward on the edge of her seat. She knew exactly which house, it was printed indelibly on her mind, but she was taken slightly aback. The house didn't look as grand as she remembered. The brass didn't gleam as bright as hers back in the village.

She pressed back against the leather as the chauffeur walked up the path, rang the bell and waited. Her heart was beating rapidly and her lips felt dry. She licked them and tasted her rose-coloured lipstick. Her heart lurched as the door opened and Mrs Darwin stood framed in the doorway. She was nodding and speaking to the chauffeur. The years hadn't been kind to her either, she was much fatter and more flushed than Evelyne remembered her. Her chins wobbled as she nodded her head up and down, and she looked past the chauffeur towards the car. She was trying to see inside, and Evelyne pressed even further back against the seat.

The chauffeur gave Evelyne no hint of what had been said as he walked back to the car and opened the passenger door.

'The housekeeper said for you to go straight in, Miss.'

Evelyne was grateful for the chauffeur's firm, white-gloved grip on her elbow. She walked slowly to the door. It had been left ajar, but Mrs Darwin had vanished from sight. There was no sign of Minnie either. The comforting grip on her arm withdrew as the chauffeur returned to the car. She was alone, and instead of being full of confidence she could feel her body trembling.

Mrs Darwin stood at the bottom of the stairs. She gave a small bob and gestured for Evelyne to enter the drawing room. The smell of the house – the strange mixture of polish and medical spirits – sent a shudder through Evelyne, and she was again the gawky girl who had come here with Doris Evans. Mrs Darwin didn't recognize her.

'It's me, Mrs Darwin, it's Evelyne, don't you remember me?'

The big woman squinted, stared at her, and then her jaw dropped and she slapped her hands to her fat cheeks in total amazement. She went to give Evelyne a hug, then stopped, flustered. She flapped her apron, stared, turned away and stared again, and then her huge face crumpled into a strange, half-laughing cry.

'Lord above, oh God Almighty, gel, if you don't look like visiting royalty, then . . . can I kiss you?'

It was all right suddenly, and Evelyne bent right down and felt the plump, wet lips kiss her cheek.

Mrs Darwin ushered her into the drawing room. From below stairs came a terrible clatter, and Evelyne turned.

'Is Minnie here?'

Mrs Darwin shook her head and laughed. Minnie now had three little ones and lived over in Carlisle Road. She turned and thudded out, yelling at the top of her voice to someone called Muriel.

Evelyne stared around the room. It was just the same, but smaller, not so overpowering. There was even a bowl of roses exactly as there had always been, except that they were dead, the petals fallen around the bowl. She went to the bookcase and looked at the titles; she had read all these books in the years since she had last been here, while Doris was alive.

Mrs Darwin came back in, carrying a tray with cake and biscuits.

'Will you be moving in, Miss Evelyne? Only, we don't know what to do, like? Not since he passed on.'

Evelyne, turned afraid.

'What did you say?'

Mrs Darwin busied herself laying out the teacups.

'The Doctor, miss, terrible it was, him a doctor and to be so poorly, couldn't do a thing for himself at the end, you know, shocking. We had to make up a bed down here for him, I mean, I couldn't carry him up and down them stairs, even though he was all skin and bone.'

Evelyne had to sit down, for a terrible moment she had thought it could possibly be David.

'When did he pass on?'

'Oh, it must be a year or more ... now, I'll just get that ruddy girl downstairs to bring up the tea. Shocking time you know, now, can't get a good girl. Mind you, we've not been paid our wages, not a penny for months now, I was getting to me wit's end, I was. I really was.'

When she had gone out, Evelyne looked at the tea tray. The biscuits were stale, soft, and a slice had been cut off the cake where it had gone mouldy. She heard the basement door slam and went to the window. She could see Mrs Darwin hurrying down the road, wrapping her shawl around her fat shoulders. Evelyne jumped as a thin, dreadfully scruffy girl stood in the doorway and sniffed.

'I've mashed the tea. Mrs Darwin says she won't be long.'

She hovered, watched as Evelyne poured the tea.

'You bein' here, does that mean we'll have our wages?'

Evelyne stirred sugar into her cup.

'I don't know – Muriel, isn't it? I'll obviously have a lot of things to arrange.'

'I'll be downstairs if you want me, the bell don't work so you'll have to holler.'

Evelyne wanted to ask about David, but she couldn't get the words out. She began to wander from room to room. The house smelt musty, dank, and there was a thick film of dust on everything. Ghosts of the past crept with her as she quietly looked into each of the ground-floor rooms. Then she mounted the stairs. They creaked, and even the banister was dusty. On all the walls were dark, empty spaces where pictures had been. The house had been stripped of every valuable ornament and there was an air of desolation to the place.

She went into the silent room she had shared with Doris. Nothing had changed but the mounting dust. She closed the door and went on to the bathroom, the memories flooding through her. Then she was standing on the landing looking towards David's room. She remembered his half-naked body, bending over to untie his boots, remembered his silky hair. There was even now a faint smell of lavender ...

Downstairs, David walked into the hall with Mrs Darwin. She took his arm, whispered.

'Her name's Evelyne.'

David nodded, looked up the stairs. He rested his arm on the banister rail and shouted.

'Evelyne ... *Evelyne, come down!*'

Evelyne dropped her comb and ran to the top of the stairs. She stood staring down at him, he hadn't changed, he looked just the same if not even more handsome ... and he was smiling up at her.

David thought she was lovely, just lovely. Turning to Mrs Darwin he gave a slight shake of his head, and she looked sadly up at Evelyne. Then David leapt up the stairs two at a time.

'Evelyne ... Evelyne, how are you?' Catching her in his arms he swung her up in the air. Close to she could see that he had grown a small moustache and he was much thinner, but his hair, oh, his lovely, silky blond hair was just the same.

'You remembered me? Oh, David, you remembered me?'

Taking her hand he bowed and led her down the stairs.

'And who could forget such a beautiful gel? Come along, I refuse to let you out of my grasp ... my hat, Mrs Darwin.'

Mrs Darwin held out his brown bowler.

'Sir, don't you think you should tell her ...'

'Now, Mrs Darwin, not another word.'

'It's little Evelyne, Doris' girl from the valley.'

David tossed his bowler in the air, ducked, and it landed right on his head. He gestured with both hands like an acrobat.

'Can I take her away from you for a while, you great, fat, horrible woman, eh? I want to show this creature off ... come along, dear heart, your chariot awaits.'

Bursting with happiness, Evelyne was ushered outside while Mrs Darwin blinked back her tears. For a moment David's face changed as he looked at Mrs Darwin, hard.

'Not a word.'

Her fat face wobbled as she nodded. 'She danced with Lloyd George at the Warners' ball, sir, when Miss Doris was here.'

David snapped, his face looked pinched.

'Yes, yes, you said, we won't be long.'

Evelyne stood on the steps as David danced down them two at a time, took off his bowler hat and bowed low, opening the door of his sports car, bright red with snazzy upholstery. After helping her in, he tucked a rug round her knees just the way he used to, then he leant over her, his face so close she gasped.

'You smell like a fresh mountain flower, and so you should, I mean *you* are the girl who danced with Lloyd George, no wonder, m'dear, it'll be the Prince of Wales next.'

David shouted to her as they careered round corners, they would have a celebration, this was a wonderful surprise. She laughed, and the sound of her laughter shocked her, it was so infrequent, the sound triggered the release of all the tensions and she didn't want it to stop.

As they drove through the city centre, David tooted the horn and waved and called out to many people driving past. He seemed to know everyone. He appeared elated, as happy as Evelyne. They headed out towards the country.

'You'll meet some of my very best friends, we'll be in time for the last race.'

The car roared up to the special enclosure at the race meeting. Everything was happening so fast, and there was a craziness to the whole afternoon. Evelyne was introduced to so many new faces, and everyone was friendly. She was accepted as part of the group; in fact, as the champagne flowed, several of David's friends showed more interest in her than in the racing. Not that David allowed his prize to be taken from him more than a few moments, he wanted to introduce her to everyone. He told them all she was an old friend, and they smiled and proffered drinks. Evelyne remembered Freddy Carlton, older, redder in the face, but he was delighted to meet again the girl who had taken everyone's heart at the midsummer dance.

David darted around, the centre of attention, especially with his strange, beautiful girl in tow. The women with their cute, bobbed hairstyles and short skirts seemed hell-bent on enjoying themselves, and when the last race was over no one seemed inclined to leave the private enclosure. Someone brought out a gramophone and couples danced on the grass or sat watching.

Having never danced to this kind of music, Evelyne remained slightly aloof, which only added to her attraction. She was also watchful of her new clothes; there was champagne flying around, sprayed from bottles all over people, so Evelyne moved further and further to the fringe of the crowd.

David stood on the roof of one of the long, shiny cars.

'Everyone, listen, listen . . . we'll all dine at Bianco's, the party must go on, I'm in love . . . ' He tap-danced, jumping from one car to the next, tossing his bowler up and catching it on his head. 'Who's out of champers? Come along now, glasses at the ready, chaps.'

Evelyne felt as if she and David were royals; everyone followed him, and accepted her as being with him. They proceeded to get into their cars.

'I say, look at the posters, be a jolly good wheeze, why don't we go?'

The posters, in crude, bright red letters, were stuck to the walls on the stand. 'FREEDOM STUBBS VERSUS DAI "HAMMER" THOMAS'.

There was a rough sketch beneath the lettering of two boxers, fists up, about to fight each other. David immediately began charging around with his fists up, dodging, and tapping his friends with mock punches.

'What say we all go to the fight, it's a gyppo fair, chaps, should be jolly?'

Evelyne smiled with the rest of David's crazy antics. She felt a tap on her shoulder and turned. A face loomed from the past – Captain Ridgely.

'Well, well, hello there, I don't remember meeting you deah gel, do tell me where he found you? Captain Ridgely at your command, at your feet, deah, lovely lady.'

David bellowed across the grass.

'*Ridgelyyyyy . . . Get off her, she's mine!*'

David leapt to Evelyne's side and put a protective arm around her shoulders.

'She's mine, you no-good rascal . . . now, Evelyne, we are all waiting on your decision. Do we or don't we go to the fight? What do you say, eh?'

Evelyne saw that everyone was waiting, and shrugged, smiling.

'Whatever you say.'

'It's the fight, everyone, *meet at Bianco's first . . .*'

The cars began to roar out, cheering passengers shouting to each other and waving their arms and champagne bottles. David got into his car.

He leaned back, slithering lower in his seat, and closed his eyes for a few moments. Then he turned his head, still resting on the back of the seat. 'Where in God's name have you been all my life, Flamehead, especially when I needed you? Why have you taken so long to come back, my gazelle, my strange, wonderful lady from nowhere?'

The kiss she had dreamed of had not been so hard or brutal. She could feel his teeth, then his tongue pushing open her lips and licking them, then thrusting inside her mouth. She actually felt disgusted, the taste of champagne and cigar smoke was so strong. His hand began slowly to unbutton her dove-grey jacket with the white collar, her lovely Vogue suit, and he was pushing her against the side of the car ... and her hat? He was crushing her hat! She pushed him away, and he lolled against the opposite door. He turned his face away, slapped the steering wheel with his hand, and when he looked back he frightened her. His eyes were blazing, staring straight through her, and again he hit the steering wheel with his fist. He was muttering, swearing, a jumble of words. Evelyne didn't know what to do. David began to rock backwards and forwards, banging his head on the steering wheel. His actions, behaviour frightened her, was he drunk?

'David, stop it please, don't ... *David*! *Don't. Stop*!'

Freddy ran to the car and cupped David's chin in his hands.

'You okay ... *David*? All right, old chap, eh? All right, are we?'

David shrugged Freddy's hands away. Freddy gave Evelyne a grin and then ran back to his motor. 'Everyone follow me!'

David pulled himself together, crashed the gears, then the sports car spun round and followed Freddy's car, way up in front. Evelyne clung to her daisy hat, terrified it would blow away. David was relaxed again, smiling to himself as though nothing had happened. Evelyne glanced at him and he caught it, winked at her. Everything was all right again, and she felt better when he reached for her hand, held it to his lips and whispered quietly, gently, 'Sorry Flame ... make it all up to you.'

The kiss she held in her memory now didn't seem so bad, and if he kissed her again she would open her own mouth.

'I love you, I love you, I love you ... ' but David didn't hear because it was all inside her bursting head, besides, he was singing at the top of his voice as he swung the car this way and that in a zig-zag across the road. His craziness was contagious and soon she was joining in with him, standing with one arm raised, the other holding on to her hat.

'My Lili Marlene ... Ahhh ... my Lili Marleeeeeeeeene ...'

The tiny, elegant restaurant was almost entirely filled by David's party, the tables, covered in checked cloths, placed close together. A pianola played at full blast. Steaming bowls of spaghetti and chilli were promptly served and wolfed down by all, while they drank themselves into a loud, drunken state with more champagne and red wine.

The proprietor, a good-natured, roly-poly Italian, served the food, opened bottles and turned a blind eye to the damage. They would pay – this young set always did – and he could feel their madness, their desperation for fun. The men were all officers and he knew they had seen sights that had left them scarred – he knew because often they were too drunk to leave. He had sat with many of them crying drunkenly for their comrades, spilling out their nightmares to him, a stranger, a nobody.

Captain Ridgely stood up on a table, glass in hand. 'Here's to unemployment ... here's to us, *to us, the ones who made it home ... Cheers!*'

They sang, 'It's a long way to Tipperareeee, it's a long way to go ... ' At first glance this party of beautiful young people seemed not to have a care in the world. It was only when one looked close that one could detect their lostness. Seemingly hell-bent on living life to the full, in reality they despaired for those they knew had no life left.

Evelyne looked hard at the women, as outrageous as their men, dancing on the tables holding their skirts high, garters flashing. One girl named Tulip had stripped off her dress and was dancing in her shift. She had bobbed hair and was very pretty.

One young chap with a lady's garter around his head seemed to be having a great time, waving a walking stick in the air. Evelyne craned her neck to see over the table then sat back quickly – he was in a wheelchair, he had no legs. As she looked around the dark, music-filled restaurant she could see that several of the boys were minus one or two limbs. The crazy atmosphere began to change, it became hotter and hotter, and Evelyne wanted to leave. David sat staring sullenly into space. She tapped his arm. 'David, I think we should go.'

He turned and stared at her as if he didn't know her for a moment, then he smiled his wonderful smile and cocked his head to one side.

'Whatever you say, darling one.'

He jumped up on to the table and yelled at the top of his voice that it was time to go. 'Come on, come on or we'll miss the fight, we can have our fortunes read, *everybody, let's rollll . . .*'

From beneath a table Tulip emerged, her lipstick smeared, pulling down her undershirt. She searched for her dress and spotted one of the boys dancing round in it. She gave chase with squealing laughs.

'Tulip, you naughty girl, come along and get your knickers on.'

She turned, and pursed her smeared, cupid's bow lips.

'I would, duckie, but I can't find 'em.'

At the reception desk Freddy Carlton swayed, a large cigar in his mouth, holding his open wallet. Tulip leaned on his arm.

'Give me some too, Freddy, I want to make a bet on the boxers, ohhh, Freddy, who's a booful boy!'

'I say, Bunny, are we splitting this or what, it's jolly expensive, ya know ... *Bunny?*'

Bunny waved as he slithered down the wall, and Freddy handed over all he had and tossed the empty wallet over his shoulder.

Evelyne caught David's hand as he led her back to his car. He stopped, holding her at arm's length.

'What a lovely creature you are.'

Evelyne's heart was pounding. He pulled her to him, cupping her face in his hands, and gently kissed her. She moaned with pleasure, and he kissed her neck, her ear. Then he whispered.

'Where are you staying? Back at the house?'

She touched his silky hair, said she was in a small hotel. He caught her in his arms, swung her round.

'We'll go back to the house later, would you like that, my lovely?'

Choked with tears, all Evelyne could do was nod in agreement. She felt as if she would explode with happiness. David tooted the horn.

'To the fair, to the fair.'

The car roared off, leaving a trail of blue smoke in the clear night air.

Chapter 7

Freedom Stubbs sat in the back of the covered wagon as it jolted its way to the match. He sat quietly, bandaging his right hand, intent on getting the bandages tight the way he liked them. His left fist would be done by Kaulo Woods. Kaulo sat opposite Freedom and looked out of the canvas flap of the wagon, then turned to Freedom.

'I *kair'd* a lot of *wongar acoi*, I *chopped* my *vardo* for another, maybe I'll *dock'd to rardi*.' (I made a deal of money here, I exchanged my van for another, let's hope I do it tonight.)

Kaulo leant over and began to bandage Freedom's left hand. He shot a slanted look up at Freedom who was leaning back against the side of the wagon, his eyes closed. He looked as if he was going for a moonlight stroll rather than a heavy fight. His breathing was as regular as if he was sleeping. Kaulo could weigh the big hand, Freedom was so relaxed, letting Kaulo bandage between his fingers and across the knuckles.

Freedom looked at the small, skinny, elderly man hunched on his left, smiled at him, nodded and rested his head again on the side of the jolting wagon. The old man finished the bandaging, picked up his fiddle and began to play, singing softly.

148

Can you *rokka* Romany,
Can you play the *bosh*,
Can you *jal adrey the staripen*,
Can you *chin the cosh* . . .

Freedom clenched his fists, nodded to Kaulo that all was fine, all the while tapping his foot to the rhythm of the old gypsy's fiddle.

Two other fighters were further up the wagon, their hands, like Freedom's, bandaged and ready. They were smaller in build, dark and swarthy, and they sat hunched on the benches facing each other. Freedom always sat apart. He stood apart from them anyway, because he was six foot four. This was tall for anyone – never mind a Romany – but then it was known that his blood wasn't pure. Freedom was a half-caste. His mother, Romalla, was the daughter of a Romany king, and Freedom's birth had brought shame to the family. His mother was dishonoured, an outcast, and she had been forced to join another, non-élitist, Romany camp. Her father had refused to have anything to do with her and hadn't spoken to her since, nor had any member of her family.

Romalla was a catch to have in any camp. She was not only a princess of pure blood, but she carried the powers with her. That made her a valuable asset as a money-earner. Freedom had inherited her powers, but he didn't use them; it wasn't done for a male Romany to read hands. However, he had proved to be of royal blood even though half-caste, and was accepted by the lower ranks as a prince. This made him acceptable, and he roamed from camp to camp, even as a child, taken into many families and treated with respect. The stigma of the words *posh ta posh* – bastard – having no effect on him, at least outwardly.

Romalla was rumoured to have had many lovers, and who Freedom's blood father was no one ever discovered. Or if anyone knew they kept quiet, not wanting to earn Freedom's *tippoty*, or wrath. He was both respected and feared, and although still only twenty-four it was likely that he would become a clan leader. Romalla had died three summers ago of a heart attack. The news was brought to Freedom by a courier carrying the charred back wheel of her caravan, all her goods having been burnt with her body. The wheel was proof she had gone and it was handed to him to roll his fortune further. Romalla had died without revealing who Freedom's father had been. All she had ever said was that he was a 'lion of a man' and one she was proud to have bedded, always implying that the man had been her choice, and one she knew would dishonour her.

Freedom was now becoming famous as a heavyweight boxer and had already made a lot of money for the travellers. The wagon entered the field where the fair was being held and the big tent for the boxing match had already been erected. A beautiful young girl was sitting on a low wall at the entrance. As the wagon rumbled through she jumped down and ran to it, directing the horses to the space allocated for the wagon. It was the best place near the exit; the best was always reserved for Freedom.

When the wagon was in position, Rawnie pulled back the canvas flap. She was a stunning Romany *dukkerin*, and she would make good money at the side shows tonight. She was decked out in all her finery, her red silk shawl wrapped around her head, her hair in two long braids down to her waist. There were gold studs in her ears with loops of gold coins dangling from them. She wore rings and bangles, and even a ruby stud on the side of her nose. Coal dust enhanced the blackness of her slanting eyes, and she would bite her full lips until they shone as red as the ruby in her nose.

She jumped aboard the wagon, pulling behind her a heavy wooden box of food and drink for the men. She always served Freedom first, she was his *manushi*, and although all the men were after her she had eyes only for Freedom. As the men ate the cooked rabbit with chunks of bread and steaming, sweet tea, Mr Beshaley came aboard.

Mr Beshaley was dressed in a smart suit with a waistcoat; it was only the scarf around his neck in place of a collar and tie that made him look different from a well-dressed city gent. He wore a gold fob watch on a chain, gold cuff links, and a gold looped earring in his right ear. His once jet-black hair was now iron-grey, but straight, not a wave in sight.

All the Romany men's hair was black, even Freedom's, coal-black and shining. They all had the same dark, tilted eyes with strange black pupils, high cheekbones and full, wide lips. Freedom differed only in his size. In every other way he looked like a pure-blood Romany.

Mr Beshaley seated himself on the bench. He opened his leather wallet and took out a wad of notes for the betting. Although he himself would not be allowed to place bets as Freedom's manager, there were many of the clan around the match who would place bets for the team. First Beshaley turned to the two fighters at the front of the wagon and discussed their impending fights with them, how they thought they would fare, even asked outright if they would win or lose. Joe shrugged, he felt that the miner pitted against him being that much heavier might sway the odds, but he wasn't going to get himself badly hurt, because he had another bout coming up the following Saturday at a fair in Glamorgan. Beshaley nodded, so they would place bets on the miner for that bout. He turned to the second, a young boy, and asked him what his chances were. Then he told them to go out and get some fresh air into their lungs. It added to the cash flow, because on their walk about the site they would keep their eyes and ears open and report back to the guv'nor. Occasionally they would also feed back bits of gossip for Rawnie to use; it was pointless using her powers in a place like this, it was too much effort.

Freedom stayed behind and listened to Beshaley, and the meeting became serious. Freedom could be up against it as his was the main event. Beshaley talked in detail about his opponent's moves in previous bouts. The man was a good stone heavier than Freedom and a dirty fighter who butted with his head. Hammer also had a habit of not shaving before an event and would get his opponent into stranglehold and rub his thick stubble hard into the man's eyes. The referee they had for this fight would probably give way to the miner and not break up the holds as he should. There were many miners in the audience to support their man, and the referee was also a collier. Three trams of miners had arrived from Llanerch Colliery and they were already drunk and causing havoc. Beshaley knew it was going to be one hell of a night.

Freedom gave no hint of how he was thinking or feeling. Beshaley drew neat little diagrams and made Hammer Thomas sound more and more like a nightmare. He certainly sounded so to Rawnie who sat silently listening and watching Freedom with her dark heavy eyes. Her heart reached out to him. She wanted to sit close, tucked in the crook of his arm the way they did when they were travelling.

'Now the last bout I watched Hammer close, he gave some heavy hits, using a kind of weaving style, half round body blows. Hammer goes for body punches rather than the face, he's a good five inches shorter than you, lad, so he can hurt, you'll have to try and take him fast.'

Out of Beshaley's pocket came a crumpled scrap of paper, and he read out a doctor's report that said Hammer had been badly cut over his left eye, the skin was still very tender . . .

'Go for the left eye, Freedom, get him blinded by his own blood, then try and bring him down before the fourth. You'll have nearly a hundred riding on you, lad, so do your best.'

Beshaley stood up and straightened his checked waistcoat. His own face showed he had been in the ring many times, his nose was flattened, and he had a scar across his left eye. He touched it for a moment and laughed, showing cigar-stained teeth, then he stepped down.

Freedom had said not a word. He clenched his huge fists and leaned back against the canvas with a sigh. Sometimes, Rawnie thought, looking at his handsome face, he doesn't even know I exist. At that precise moment Freedom turned to her and smiled, his whole face softened and a twinkle came into his big, dark eyes, and he winked . . . as if he knew what she was thinking.

It was expected they would marry, she was already nineteen and he was twenty-four, but he had never brought the subject up. They walked together often, but he had never made a serious approach to her. Once, just once, he had kissed her and she would have given herself to him, but he had turned her pressing body from him with that enigmatic smile of his, and then given her bottom a hard smack.

Rawnie knew that Freedom had been with women, all the old'uns told her so – often told her with toothless nudges and winks that it was better to have a man who knew what was what before they were joined for life to a wife.

Rawnie would wait. She knew she was beautiful, had known it from the days when she was just a little *dosha*. When they found out she had the powers handed down to her from her grandmother, she had become important in the camp and was now the main *dukkerin* (fortune-teller), and the palefaces came to her regularly with their pieces of gold. The strange thing for Rawnie was that, although she could read the hands of others, she couldn't foretell her own destiny. But she knew what she wanted – simply Freedom.

In the wagon, Freedom got up, but he had to crouch so as not to hit his head, then he jumped to the ground. He stretched his huge frame like an animal and then turned to help Rawnie down the wooden step. She felt the rough bandages and wanted to kiss his hands, but he was already walking off towards the big tent.

Crowds were gathering and a number of gypsy vans had pulled in to sell their wares. There were artificial flowers made of wood chippings, fern baskets, bottles with wooden crosses built inside, sets of doll's furniture, pegs, heather brooms and rush whips, bouquets of reed flowers, all made by the old women of the camps. Some wandered around with their heavy baskets calling out their wares, while others sold directly from outside their wagons.

Freedom walked among them and they tipped their caps and wished him luck. They had all placed their hard-earned pennies on the prince and Freedom knew it. He picked up a couple of tiny *doshas* and gave them a kiss and a pat on the head. He was waved at by members of many different clans, and he gave them his flashing smile before he disappeared into the tent to prepare for the match.

Rawnie was set up in a small booth, and already had clients waiting inline. She always had one of the lads standing by in case anyone got troublesome, but she was tough and capable of looking after herself. Rarely did she tell anyone the truth, because sometimes she saw such sadness and heartbreak in people's hands she knew it was best not to say. They only ever wanted to hear good fortune was coming their way and that they were lucky.

But this was not the case with her own people. They always wanted the truth. And if she saw sadness, loss or great pain she told them so and they would be ready to face it, but then her people were different from these palefaces. The palefaces always wanted happiness ahead and Rawnie didn't look on what she told them as lies: she contended they were no more than the white lies the palefaces would tell a sick relative, 'Oh, my, you look better today', knowing they were drawing their last breath.

The crowds were getting thicker, and above the clamour could be heard the voices of a group of Romany girls singing. The singing was very seductive, whether it was due to the witchery of their slant-eyed glances or the strange, slow body movements, turning their hands with all the clinking bracelets slowly in the air. Groups of boys stood around with gaping mouths, nudging each other. The gypsy girls were sexy all right. They would lay their hats on the ground while they danced for the crowds, and as coins chinked against each other their dancing would get wilder and wilder, like a tarantella with no accompaniment but their seductive chanting. The lamps threw shadows and caught the colours of the kerchiefs, yellow or bright red, the brilliantly coloured skirts, necklaces, gold chains and red beads; the girls were magical, captivating, their swarthy skins even darker in the lamplight, their eyes flashing, eyes that belonged only to the Romany.

Few among the crowds ever detected anything but fairground atmosphere at the gypsy gatherings. They missed the undercurrent of arrogance, or apartness. The gypsies were a naturally hostile group, it was inherent in them all and made them completely unapproachable. But years of concealing their true feelings just to earn enough to live, to eat, gave the Romany eyes a strange blankness. Tonight they appeared to want nothing more than to delight the gathering crowd, but this was their work.

From the top of the hill the fair looked more like a circus, the big tent for the boxing in the middle with the booths and caravans lined up in a circle around it. Lights twinkled and there was music playing. There were many vehicles and two opentopped buses parked in the field. David's car bounced and rocked over the churned-up grass. He hauled the brake on and a loud cheer rose up from the tent. He looked over, swore, and was out, running towards the entrance. Evelyne fumbled with the catch on the door and ran after him. He shouted for her to hurry, the rest had already gone inside. Evelyne had never been to a fair in her whole life, she would have liked to stop and look at the booths and the gypsy wares but David didn't hesitate. Another roar went up, then cheers. David turned and held out his hand for her, paid the entrance fees and pulled her inside.

The place was packed. Some people were sitting on tiered benches around the ring which was six feet off the ground and had a bright canvas around it to hide the wooden stilts. Others milled around and some even sat on other people's shoulders. Big, bright torches lit the whole area and smoke drifted up into the tent top. It was stiflingly hot, and the air was thick with smoke from cigarettes and cigars as well as from the torches. Scuffles were breaking out, fists flying, and the noise was deafening. Car horns sounded, whistles blew – the whole place was in an uproar. A man in an unbelievably loud checked suit, holding a loud hailer, stood in the centre of the ring. Behind him men were taking bets, money was being passed over heads, under arms, and two men sitting on ladders at a blackboard constantly wiped and wrote up new rows of figures in chalk.

David elbowed his way forward, and Evelyne lost her grip on his hand twice and had to push her way to his side. Her hat was knocked off and she had to scrabble for it. The daisies were looking a little ragged now, but she crammed the hat back on her head. David caught sight of Freddy and the others huddled up close to the ringside. A fight was breaking out as people at the back couldn't see over the heads of the people standing on the front benches.

David eventually fought his way through to the group. How on earth Freddy had managed to capture half a bench was beyond Evelyne, but David sprang up on to it and helped her up, flinging his arm around her waist. 'Can you see? We're just in time.'

Evelyne almost fell over, but a small man behind her propped her up, and then toppled over himself as he tried to retrieve the cloth cap he had dropped. A woman hit him with her handbag and called him a dirty little bugger. He countered this with a furious glare and lewd remark about her bum being too big for his liking anyway.

The check-suited man's face looked ready to burst, the sweat running down his cheeks, 'Ladies and gentlemen, the main event of the evening!'

This was greeted by a roar of approval, and he had to wait for it to die down before he could speak again.

'In the right corner, Hammer ...'

Hammer paraded around the ring, bowing, waving, kissing his huge, gloved hands, and eventually went to his corner where three burly men stood with towels and a large bucket. A small milking stool was placed in the corner for Hammer to sit on, but he refused, and stood pulling at the ropes which provoked more cheering and yelling.

There was obviously some problem getting Hammer's opponent into the ring. Fists were flying at the other side of the tent, men were being hauled off each other, and the screams of the man in the checked suit through his loud hailer were accompanied by howls from the crowd.

'Freedom, the Romany gypsy prince ... FREEDOM!'

Again no one could hear any details over the crowd's bellowing, and cries of 'Boooo ... Booooo ...' swamped the tent as Freedom appeared. He bent low, entered the ring, and went straight to his corner. He stood head and shoulders above the men in his corner until he sat on his little stool, and then they closed ranks round him and he couldn't be seen.

A burly man in a white shirt entered the ring with a white towel over his arm. He held up the towel in one hand, a stop-watch in the other. The man in the checked suit collapsed out of the ring to sit, hugging his loud hailer, in a state of total exhaustion.

The referee waved his towel a few more times, then turned gesturing to both boxers to come out of their corners. Hammer bounced off the ropes and up went his gloved hands as he waved to the crowd. The roars of approval and disapproval came in ear-shattering waves. The referee gestured to Freedom to come forward, and as he walked slowly towards Hammer the boos and hisses grew even louder. The two men touched gloves, and whatever the referee said went unheard as the boxers returned to their corners.

Hammer hung on the ropes again, screaming that he would take the gyppo out in three rounds, '*Three, three, not-a-one, not-a-two, but three . . .* ' The crowd roared back, '*Three, three, three.*' The tent felt as if it would collapse as they stamped their feet in unison.

The betting rose to fever pitch before the fight could commence, and more money passed over more heads in cloth caps. The fight was held up again as someone removed a passing cloth cap and tried to take the cash, provoking yet another fight.

A small, balding man fought his way to the ringside and held up a large school bell, which he rang once at Hammer and then once at Freedom. Holding the bell high above the head for the spectators to see, he clanged it again and the fight began. The crowd went quiet as the two fighters moved closer, their corners slipping out of the ring to hang on the corner ropes. High up in the tent two men had crawled like monkeys along the ropes to get a better view.

Rawnie could hear the cheers and boos, and she packed up her little card table. All the gypsies were packing. They knew better than to stay because if their man Freedom won, they would be the target of fighting-mad miners. They moved quickly and quietly, counting their money and collecting their children so that they were ready to move out.

Jesse Blackton lounged in his booth and jingled the money he had made. He was twenty-two years old, and with a *stardo* of petty thieving already mounting up. He had the longest coal-black eyelashes, as black as his hair which he wore in a long braid down his back. He also wore his mother's earring, a long loop, in his left ear. He was very slim, and some said that was why he was such a good thief – his tiny hands could slip into a woman's *putsi* like a small child's. His family didn't approve of his thieving and he was constantly brought before the elders. But Jesse was *Tatchey Romany*, very pure-blooded, and because of that he had been forgiven many times and taken back into the fold. Jesse hated Freedom, partly because he was a *posh ta posh* and yet took the position of a prince. Among the clans Freedom was held up as an example to the children, who were told that one day, according to the readings, Freedom would be rich and successful; he would one day be the king and lead them. Jesse had always felt that to be *his* prerogative. He could trace his ancestry on both sides back to royal blood, and his many *beebees* and *cocos* were scattered from Scotland to the East End of London and beyond to Devon and Cornwall. Jesse could travel anywhere and be greeted with respect and open arms, but he remained with the Welsh family because of his desire to make Rawnie his *manushi*, his woman. He had been after her since he had joined her clan two years ago, but she would never even give him the time of day.

Rawnie knew Jesse was after her, and often she played him along a little. She knew he was royal but, in her opinion, he didn't come anywhere near her man Freedom. As it was, Jesse stood only five foot seven, but she had to admit he was a looker and she saw the effect he had on the younger girls.

'Well,' said Jesse as he leaned casually against the tiny booth, 'did you have much *bokht* tonight?'

Rawnie jingled her purse and smiled, and asked if Jesse had done well. He said nothing, just lifted his long, silky eyelashes, and gave her a cheeky grin.

A roar from the crowds inside made them both turn. That was a roar of approval, and it meant that Freedom must be hurt. Jesse turned back to see Rawnie's frightened face. He kicked at the floor, tossed a stone on to the top of his boot and flicked it away.

'Dinna worry, he's no *lang gry*. Freedom has to have the taste of blood in his mouth before he gets his temper up.'

There was a massive swell of shouts and boos, and Jesse grinned.

'See what I mean, that'll be a few *dands* gone. Maybe he won't look so handsome after this, but he can *cour* for a *diddicoy*.'

Jesse's use of the word *diddicoy*, or outcast, made Rawnie slap him hard, but Jesse just laughed and shook his head which must have been stinging. He ambled off, turning as he went to say, 'I'll wait for you, Rawnie. You'll come to me one day.'

Another huge cheer from the tent made Rawnie shiver and she packed her belongings fast, hauling them into the wagon and then, knowing she shouldn't, she made her way towards the big tent.

She couldn't even see the ring from the back of the tent so she shoved and pushed her way closer, ducking under the sweating arms, narrowly missed by clenched fists that were boxing on behalf of Hammer. She dodged men who were so absorbed in the fight they were giving blow-by-blow accounts of it to themselves. She could hear the thudding, cheering and yelling but could still see nothing. She didn't know how the fight was going, but her little, wiry body wriggled through until she could glimpse the corner of the ring through a tiny gap in the crowd.

Suddenly Rawnie could see Freedom as he sat on his stool, drinking from a bottle of water like a baby, then turning to spit into the bucket. The sweat was dripping from his hair like tears as he leant back against the post. He was rubbed down with a white towel, water was splashed on his face, and then grease was plastered over his eyes. His face looked red, but she could see no cuts, just deep, red marks, and deeper red ones on his chest and shoulders. Then her view was blocked by a screaming fan as the school bell rang for another round.

Rawnie didn't even know which round they were fighting or who was ahead on points, so she began to burrow her way closer until she stood behind a bench. 'The bloody palefaces, typical,' she thought, 'they are standing right up close to the ring, no wonder the lads at the back are jumping up and down just to get a glimpse.'

*

Hammer was hammering blows to Freedom's upper body while Freedom ducked and weaved but seemed unable to find a break in Hammer's defence. Hammer lowered his head, almost as if he were looking at the floor, but kept his fists up and jabbed, jabbed, then he swung. Three times his heavy blows had connected, but Freedom had taken it and not gone down. Hammer was heaving for breath, hissing between his teeth, and like an old ram he thundered body blows at Freedom, but the bastard just kept on taking them.

This was the hardest fight Freedom had faced to date, and he was at a loss as to how he could get at the man at all, never mind hit him hard enough to floor him. Freedom couldn't break through Hammer's defence – his guard – his jabbing fists, like an oncoming tank.

Hammer was huge and overweight, and his punches hurt. One had nearly winded Freedom and if it hadn't been for the bell he might have gone down. Hammer was judging his man, knew he'd got him foxed, now he needed to close in, but Freedom's reach held him back. The gyppo, Hammer knew, would go for any advantage he could find. He hadn't expected the fight to go this far and he'd already lost on the betting that he'd have Freedom down in three. The lad looked as though he could go the distance. But Hammer's age was against him. He had to get the boy out because there was no way Hammer could go the full fifteen rounds at this pace. He decided to open up a little, let the boy think he'd found a chink in his defences, then he'd use his famous right uppercut.

The crowd was getting restless. They weren't getting enough action, and Hammer acted on his decision to open up. It was a fatal mistake; he had misjudged the power of Freedom's punches, and he felt his left eyebrow split open like an orange. The blood streamed down and he tossed his head like a crazed bull, trying to cut the boy up with his famous Hammerhead, when another sharp blow to his streaming left eye blinded him on that side. He couldn't see the punches coming, and as he fought on he couldn't feel them either. They were coming fast, bang bang, one after the other – there was no let-up. The crowd's boos and hisses were telling Hammer he was losing, but he struggled on, hunched up and tried to get Freedom hemmed into the corner. He knew his eye had to be attended to, the blood was splashing over Freedom's body. He hung on, leaning his weight on Freedom, hoping to tire him and praying the bell would ring – only the bell would save his neck. But Freedom couldn't be cornered, and he couldn't be stopped.

Hammer lurched at Freedom, felt the big arms trying to push him away, but he clung on. The white towel of the referee flicked – it was now spotted with blood, Hammer's blood, and then the ref. was between them, trying to break Hammer's hold.

'Break ... *Break* ... *Come on, break!*'

The referee hauled Hammer off Freedom and gave him a warning against holding, which caused more loud boos and yells from the crowd. Hammer swayed and gave a quick glance to the man with the bell. He was sure it was time. That look was his downfall, he felt the left side of his face blow apart. He was reeling backwards, he stumbled, and the blows kept on coming and coming, then it was black, black on black; Hammer was going down, down into the mines. He was shouting for his Da to help him up, there was heavy, black, thick smoke everywhere. He couldn't breathe, his chest heaved and he screamed again for his

Da, screaming that the roof was caving in. He was falling, falling down a black shaft, no light, no sound, just silence.

The huge crowd in the tent was ominously quiet, they stared in disbelief as their magnificent Hammer crawled along the canvas floor. He seemed to be crying and his knees were gone, he couldn't get himself up.

Then his body crashed, face down, the spray of blood and sweat drenching the first row of the audience.

Evelyne gasped as the red spray splashed across her suit, and she put her hands up to cover the nightmare in front of her. The huge man crying like a baby, his head split open and the cheering, screaming crowds. She heard herself shouting, and the next moment the place was in an uproar as the men clinging to the ropes high up in the tent fell, landing in the crowd. The benches started toppling as they were pushed from behind, spilling their occupants forwards on to the people in front. Bench after bench went over, trapping people underneath, screaming, fighting, writhing bodies everywhere, a mass of struggling arms and legs.

Freedom and his crew ran from the ring, pushing the avenging, clawing miners back. They were spat at, insulted, accused of cheating, rigging the match. This had happened once before at a boxing match and the gypsies knew they had to get out fast, move their wagons. The touts would collect the money and bring it to the camp; the main thing was to save themselves from the mob.

Hammer's trainer and corners were still trying desperately to revive him, shoving the crowds out of the ring. It was pandemonium as a sprawling mass of bodies fought to get out of the crush. The apparently lifeless body of Hammer was passed over heads and outstretched arms to give him air, get him out of the tent.

Evelyne clawed her way up over bodies and finally stood, screaming for David, searching frantically for him. She saw Freddy dragging benches aside and he shouted for help. It looked as though David had broken his leg.

Rawnie pushed and shoved, trying to follow Freedom, and felt her scarf being yanked off her head by an irate miner, who held it in the air.

'Here's one of the bloody gypos!'

Hands were all over her, pawing at her, ripping at her clothes. Dear God, why hadn't she listened, why hadn't she done as she'd been told? Rawnie scratched at the leering sweating faces.

With the help of two of the others, Evelyne and Freddy finally managed to get David outside. He was bent double in agony, teeth clenched. Freddy tried to calm him, giving orders to the hysterical women. The rest of their friends were gathering, calling out to each other, thankful they were safe. There was so much shouting and screaming going on that their voices were drowned.

Freedom jumped aboard the wagon where the waiting boys patted his shoulder and cheered. There were two men up front, and one of them flipped the horses' reins and the wagon made for the exit. Motor horns were blaring, and now above the yells could be heard the distinctive bells of police cars as they approached the field. The horses kicked and rolled their eyes, and Freedom climbed up front to take the reins.

The guv'nor, Mr Beshaley, ran to the wagon, his face flushed.

'Get out, get out fast, past the law, he's dead, Hammer's not come round, they think he's dead – I'll sort out the cash here, see you back at the camp.'

Beshaley saw Freedom immediately draw the horses back as if to get down. He banged on the side of the wagon.

'Get out of here, all of you ... *Go go go!*'

The horses were skittish because of the running, shouting people and the sound of the police bells. A crowd of miners was heading for the wagons, shouting to each other. They were going to overturn the gyppos' carts. The wagon moved forward, cutting through the mob. Suddenly Jesse was running wildly towards them, waving his arms and pointing back at the tent. Freedom stood between the horses, heaving them back by their collars, handed the reins to one of the other men and jumped to the ground. Jesse's panic-stricken face was streaked with dirt from the clods of earth the miners had started hurling at them.

'She's still in there, Rawnie, she went back in there, in the tent!'

Freedom looked back in horror. The boys tried to hold him back, but he just brushed them aside and took off with Jesse running at his heels, shouting as he went, 'Get out, all of you, we'll use Rawnie's cart. ... go, go, move.'

The wagon hurtled forwards, knocking three burly miners off their feet. They stepped out of Freedom's way, wary of him as he raised his huge fists.

Freddy managed to lay David down on the back seat of his car, then ran to the driving seat. Evelyne held on to his arm.

'He must go to the hospital, get him to a hospital.'

Freddy released her hand, 'Get a lift home with one of the others, you can't come with us, I'm taking him home, for God's sake.'

Evelyne didn't understand, and she was almost knocked over as Freddy drove the car out of the field. She stared after them. The rest of their group was already moving out, their cars heading for the exits, and Evelyne ran towards an oncoming car with Tulip clinging to the running-board. The car drove straight past, leaving her standing there.

Freedom kept on the move, and when any miner approached him with clenched fists and abuse he growled like a mad dog, baring his teeth and snarling, and they stepped back.

'*Fix* . . . bloody fix, man, you cheatin' bastard!'

With one hand Freedom grabbed the man, hauled him up and threw him against a pole in the side of the tent.

'You want to take over the fight, man?'

The man's false teeth rattled in his mouth, and he held his hands over his face, terrified.

'Anyone else? Anyone else . . .?'

They backed off and let him pass. Jesse was waiting at the torn tent flap and together they went inside.

Chapter 8

Evelyne searched the ground for her handbag. She put her hands to her head in despair. Her hat? She'd lost her new hat! At first she felt tearful, then her temper flared and she turned back. She'd not paid fifteen shillings for a new hat to lose it, never mind her handbag. Her hair had come down from the bun, tumbling around her shoulders, and she was being shoved from all sides, but she gave as good as she got. She stood taller than a lot of the lads she battled through. Having been brought up with three older brothers and having Hugh for a father helped. She rolled up the sleeves of her new suit, it was like the old days out in the yard of a Sunday when she was no more than nine years old. Dicken, Will and Mike were always fighting, and she'd joined in. Now she was as good as any man around her, and she punched and kicked her way through into the tent.

Jesse searched the dispersing crowd without luck, then he jumped up on Freedom's shoulders, looking for the familiar red scarf, and saw it being waved around by a group of men by the side of the ring. He urged Freedom forward like a stallion.

*

Evelyne felt her hair pulled from behind, and swung her fist round, belting the gormless young boy on the nose.

'Christ almighty, there's a bloody Amazon in there, bach.'

The police had imposed some sort of order now, and they gathered around Hammer's body with their notebooks out. His manager and trainer stood by, helpless. They kept looking at each other and then down at the massive bulk of Hammer at their feet.

The crowds were thinning out faster than before because the police were there and no one wanted to get booked. Hammer was carried to an ambulance and its crew worked desperately, massaging his heart and trying to resuscitate him. Eventually they were rewarded by a slight flutter of his chest, and he drew a faint breath.

Evelyne searched among the benches, lifting them up. She didn't care about her suit, it was ruined anyway, but she wanted her handbag. It had more than three pounds and sixteen shillings in it, a new comb and mirror. Evelyne suddenly felt faint, oh God, she thought, my post office savings book! She didn't care who saw her, she lifted her skirt and felt inside her bloomers, then she sighed with relief. Her precious savings – her legacy – was safe. Then her temper rose again as she remembered that her return ticket was also in the handbag.

She was now close to the ring. Its platform was on stilts, some six feet off the ground and was swathed in tarpaulins. Could her handbag have slithered beneath the ring? She pulled the fabric aside.

Underneath the ring, three lads held Rawnie down, her skirts around her head. A fourth was on top of her with his trousers round his ankles, while the others leered and encouraged him. Her face was scratched and bleeding, her mouth bruised and a tooth missing. She lay half-conscious mewing like a small, drowning kitten.

Evelyne let the tarpaulins fall back into place. 'Go away,' she told herself, 'don't get involved, get out of here, never mind the handbag, just get out, Evelyne Jones, and for God's sake do it *now*!' At the same time as the voice in her head was talking to her, someone else not Evelyne, she was sure, but another person entirely grabbed one of the broken bench legs and was under the boxing ring like a wildcat.

The lad on top of Rawnie had his head cracked by the bench leg, felt his hair being torn out by the roots, heard a scream like a tiger. Two of the others tried to grab Evelyne; one caught her by the hair, but she was kicking, biting, spitting, and punching with all her strength. The other tried to pull her off his mate and suddenly they all turned, open-mouthed. Light flooded beneath the ring as Freedom, his muscles straining, lifted the platform bodily upwards and tossed it aside.

Jesse took on one of the lads and Freedom, panther-like, moved towards the other three. He grabbed two of them by their necks, bashing their heads together, and knocked out the other with one punch. The boy's nose split in two and blood streamed down his face.

'You're all right now, love, it's all right, you're safe, we'll take you right now, nobody's going to hurt you any more, it's all right.'

Evelyne held the terrified, raped and beaten girl in her arms, covering her body with her own jacket. Rawnie moaned and clung to Evelyne like a child, her body heaving as she sobbed.

Her small body jerked and shuddered, and Evelyne stroked her hair.

Evelyne talked non-stop, saying anything that came into her mind to try and calm the terrified girl. Wood splintered around them, cries of 'Fire! *Fire! Fire!*' went up. The tent was aflame.

Jesse repeated the cry as smoke began to billow from one side of the tent, the lanterns having fallen when Freedom moved the boxing ring. He called again, but Freedom was searching one of the boy's pockets. Jesse pulled Freedom's sleeve, urging him to get out, the police were inside the tent arresting everyone insight. Freedom still grasped the terrified boy with one hand and shook him, his feet off the ground, until his teeth rattled in his head.

'Remember me, because I'll be coming after you, each and every one of you, this is not the end of it.'

Jesse turned and gestured for them to hurry.

'Bejesus, Freedom, it'll be us in the clink if you don't get a move on.'

Freedom picked up Rawnie in one arm as if she were no more than a rag doll, and with his other hand he guided Evelyne out. They kept moving, Evelyne crouching down as she ran along behind a row of chairs. Half of her felt she had no need to flee like a *criminal*, but the flames were spreading behind her and the boy she had walloped with the bench leg was shouting after them, pointing at her. The smoke billowed back and masked their escape, Jesse slicing through the side of the tent with his knife.

They made it to Rawnie's wagon and Freedom helped Evelyne aboard. He laid Rawnie gently down, and the wagon jolted off, Jesse whipping up the horse. Evelyne had now lost her hat, her handbag and one shoe, her hair was loose, her stockings laddered and one sleeve was torn right out of her jacket and soaked with Rawnie's blood.

As the wagon made its way across the fields, keeping off the roads and away from the police, one of the youths was telling a detective sergeant that he had seen with his own eyes an Amazon woman with a sword, and she was beating everybody up. It was she who had given him the bloody nose, he'd not touched a soul. The youth was thrown into a police wagon and taken away to be charged with disorderly conduct. He maintained his innocence in the wagon, still persisted with his story at the police station. There had been this enormous bloody woman, like an Amazon he had seen at the local cinema. She had red hair down to her waist and was screaming like a crazy horse. One of the other boys, with his head cut open, was put into the next cell. He said nothing, but by God he'd remember that wildcat as long as he lived. Nearly broken his skull, she had.

The Amazon sat hunched in the wagon, having no idea where she was going or with whom. She watched as the big fighter they called Freedom rocked the poor girl in his arms. He talked quietly, intimately, close to Rawnie, and his soothing voice and quiet strength calmed her. She lay with her face turned away from Evelyne and began to weep softly, and all the time Freedom talked in a language Evelyne couldn't understand. She had never seen a man so gentle; it was hard to reconcile him with the fierce man she had seen fighting in the ring.

They travelled for about thirty minutes and then Jesse pulled up the horses. They were by a stream and Rawnie would want to wash. Freedom bent to lift her down.

'*Acoi Rawnie, chies so betie*, you'll wash here you're so *chiklo*, an' Jesse mun, we'll leave *gav*, the *gav mush* will be after us.'

Evelyne did not understand what they were saying. She saw Freedom lift Rawnie in his arms and then Jesse grabbed him.

To Evelyne's astonishment the men argued, the poor girl between them. Rawnie clung to Freedom's neck as Jesse tried to pull her out of his arms.

'She's ma woman, raped mun, we take revenge.'

Freedom snarled angrily, his voice hissing, '*Kek, kek.*'

Evelyne stood up and hit her head hard on the roof of the wagon. She saw stars before her eyes and slumped down again.

'Will you stop your arguing, the girl should be washed.'

They carried Rawnie to the water and she was silent, head bowed.

'Leave her with me, go, the pair of you, and let me help her.'

Jesse gave her a foul, snarling look and Freedom held him back.

'Thank ye for this, woman.'

Freedom filled a pail with water and placed it beside Evelyne. Then he took off his shirt and ripped it in two, throwing her the pieces to use as washcloths. The two men went back to the wagon, still arguing.

Rawnie sat staring, stunned, and Evelyne wet the cloths and washed the girl's face and neck, then sat down and eased the girl's skirt back to wash her thighs, and was horrified. Her legs were crusted with blood and bruised, deep blue and red marks where the boys had forced her thighs apart.

'Oh God help you, God help you.'

As Evelyne washed her gently, the girl laid her head on Evelyne's shoulder.

When it was done Evelyne whispered to her that there was no trace left, she was clean. She dried Rawnie with the remainder of Freedom's shirt and called out that they were ready. It was Jesse who gently scooped Rawnie into his arms and helped her up the wooden steps of the wagon.

Evelyne went to empty the pail of water. Her foot slipped and she ended up standing in the stream. Freedom appeared on the bank and held out his hand to her, and as she reached for it she slid down the bank again, ending up sitting in cold water to her waist. Freedom hauled her out with one jerk of his strong arm, but her new suit was now soaked.

'Ye'd best come back to camp and dry off by the fires.'

Evelyne hesitated, and he cocked his head to one side and waited. Then she gave a brief nod and was helped aboard. Well, she couldn't really arrive back at Mrs Pugh's in this dishevelled condition.

As the wagon rumbled and bumped its way along the rutted lanes, Rawnie sat staring into space, her hands plucking at her brightly coloured skirt. The bracelets tinkled and jangled, but she stared straight ahead, her beautiful face scratched, her lips puffy and bruised. She was calm now, her eyes impassive and distant. Evelyne supported herself on the wooden frame of the wagon as it jolted and swayed. She tried to remember what she had in her handbag, maybe the return ticket was on the dressing table at Mrs Pugh's, but she knew in her heart that it wasn't. How much money? The more she tried to remember the more she felt like weeping. Her lovely hat, oh God, fifteen shillings gone. She sat as far from the fighter as possible, aware that he kept staring at her. She felt no fear, she wasn't afraid of them, just extremely worried about her purse and the waste of money, bag, hat and shoes. She bit her lip to force back the tears, then felt disgusted with herself – that poor girl raped and all she was worried about was her outfit.

At long last the wagon stopped, and Jesse opened the flap. They helped Rawnie down, she wouldn't be lifted but stepped down, her head high, even her dark eyes were proud, her face a mask. Caravans and wagons formed a semicircle with large tents and the site was lit up by a huge, blazing fire in the centre. Women sat on caravan steps, while cooking pots on stands around the fire sizzled and boiled.

The gypsies had done well that night and they were celebrating. Four girls danced around, flashing their skirts. In the firelight they glittered with gold and their red underskirts flashed as they clicked their heels. A fiddler started to play and an old woman beat her fists against a ribboned tambourine. As Freedom stepped down from the wagon, they cheered and a group of small children clustered around him. Jesse took Rawnie's hand and led her towards a painted wooden caravan, its shafts laid flat on the grass.

Evelyne hovered at the door of the wagon, and felt the whole camp grow still and silent as they all stared towards her, their expressionless eyes taking her in, then turning to Freedom for an answer. Freedom guided Evelyne into the glare of the fire, and she was very conscious of her appearance. She knew she must look very strange to the gathered people. Her hair was loose, her skirt filthy, she wore no stockings and her jacket had only one and a half sleeves. On top of that she was covered in mud and blood, even her face was streaked with dirt.

Freedom held her hand, guiding her firmly forward, and

spoke sharply to two old women who whispered to each other. Evelyne couldn't understand him, he spoke in his strange language. Whatever he said made one of the old women step towards Evelyne and take her hand, tugging at her to follow. Evelyne was a little afraid to let go of Freedom's strong hand, but he nodded that it would be all right and to go with the old crone.

She was let into a rounded tent. Inside she could see the carved willow hoops that supported the canvas, shaped like a ribcage. The tent was large, and inside were four cot-like beds. Cooking utensils and household equipment were stacked in one corner and the floor was strewn with rushes. The tent was warm and cosy, and the old woman tugged at Evelyne's sleeve for her to follow. Opening a wooden box, the woman chatted away, although Evelyne couldn't understand a word. Out of the box came a cardigan, an old skirt and a white petticoat. Again the woman plucked at Evelyne's sleeve, gesturing for her to take off her skirt. There was a strange, musky smell to the clothes, but at least they were dry, and she began to feel a little warmer.

Evelyne could see the women scrubbing her clothes and she sighed; they looked as if they were trying to get the oil stain out, but she knew they were rubbing too hard. They should have used vinegar and brown paper, but she didn't like to move out of the tent, in fact she wasn't too sure exactly what she should do. She had no idea of the time or where she was.

Jesse was all for driving into town and finding the boys. He constantly flicked his knife, it was razor sharp and his intentions were obvious. Freedom strove to keep the peace.

'Jesse, I know, mun, what was done to her, but for us all to ride into town is madness.'

Jesse hurled the knife at a tree. It whizzed through the air.

'I'll not move out of camp until I take revenge, you saw nothin'— you did not see what they done. It scarred her mind, not just her body, mun.'

'Jesse, the men will pay for what they done.'

'Oh, yeah, you tell me how much? Go on, an' tell me how? By us going to the police when you know what they would do, clap every one of us into jail so much as look at us. We all go in *now*. We ride in, take them bastards one by one and then we ride out.'

'You go in tonight, Jesse, and they will arrest you.'

Jesse put up his fists and struck out at Freedom. He was crazy with rage.

'It's you, *mush*, they want you, the law want you for tonight's fight.'

The other men stepped in and held Jesse back. Their prince, their great warrior, made them more money than Jesse, they needed him and they needed his fights.

'He's our fighter, *mush*, so listen to what he says. It was fair, no fault of his if that bastard dies.'

Freedom gripped the furious, blazing Jesse. 'Trust me, *mush*, we'll get each one.'

Jesse wanted to weep, always they turned against him in favour of Freedom. He removed his knife from the tree.

'So be it, but I want each man dead, I want their hearts.'

Mr Beshaley rode up on his sweating horse. He shouted to the men to collect their winnings, and make it fast.

'Hammer's still alive, but the law want to question one and all, so pack up and get out, move fast, we've made good money . . . head for Scotland.'

Never one to ride with them, Beshaley heeled his horse and galloped away. He looked back once to Freedom and shouted that he would arrange a fight come next month, then he was gone.

The men occupied themselves with counting their winnings, and Rawnie's plight was forgotten for the moment. Freedom took Jesse aside and told him to get everyone prepared to move out by morning. Everyone except himself and Jesse who would repay the men who had raped Rawnie.

'How will ye do it, man, punch every miner we cross?'

Freedom smiled, and took out the wallet he had taken from one of the boys. Find one and they could get the names of the others. Jesse was so eager to use his knife – he would soon have the opportunity.

Jesse seethed inside. It was as if Freedom was always one step ahead of him, but he had to concede that it made sense. Already the men were preparing to move out, quietly taking down the tents and bringing the horses from the fields.

Freedom went to the tent where Evelyne was and stood at the opening. He could see Evelyne fast asleep, her mass of hair sprayed out across the pillow. Her white skin seemed translucent, and the soft violet shade of her eyelids fascinated him. He moved closer to the bed, and stood for a while looking down into the strange, beautiful face. He touched her hair gently – golden hair, it felt soft to his touch, and then he looked again. There was something in the back of his mind, a long-forgotten memory. Evelyne woke to see his face looming above her, and started. As she sat up he smiled at her and said she had no need to fear him.

Her clothes were dry but wrinkled, and when she was left alone to change she discovered that they had shrunk. So much for expensive French labels! She went to the tent flap and opened it a fraction. Freedom was waiting, as if on guard, outside.

'I can't get into my skirt, it's shrunk.'

He turned and looked at her and then laughed, said for her to keep what she had been given. Wearing the petticoat and brown sack skirt, with her own blouse and the jacket that now had only one sleeve, she opened the tent flap. There was a blackened area where the fire had been, and all the tents had been packed away. Most of the camp had already moved on, there were just a few caravans left in line with the horses being backed into the shafts.

The last caravan in the line, with red curtains, was brightly painted, and the blues, reds and greens merged into a strange pattern all over the wagon itself.

'Rawnie wants to see you, then we will take you back to town.'

Evelyne was led over to the caravan, and she mounted the steps and tapped on the door. Jesse opened it, and with a curt nod jumped down and gestured for her to go inside.

Jesse joined Freedom, who was dismantling the tent Evelyne had used. He jerked his head in the direction of Rawnie's caravan.

'By God she's a big'un, you see the way she fought, like a wildcat . . .'

Freedom made no reply but continued to pull down the canvas.

The caravan inside was as bright as the outside, full of colours and wonderful paintings. Each panel bore a different scene, and the wooden ceiling was dark blue with moons and stars, and lanterns dangling. The brass was sparkling, polished like mirrors. Bright skirts and blouses were strewn around, and the heavy, sweet smell of musk was everywhere. Aside table attached to the wall of the caravan was crammed with pots of cream and rouge. Hanging on hooks were bracelets and bangles and hundreds of beaded necklaces, mostly of bright red beads mixed with gold coins. There were boxes of gold earrings, hair slides, strange, diamond-cut stones, and amber, quaint and oriental. There was malachite and silver, and wonderful, rich, matte yellow gold, a treasure-chest of coral and jet. Evelyne gasped: there were so many colours and sparkling ornaments, it took her completely by surprise.

Rawnie sat curled up on a couch. She was dressed in a bright red skirt with layers and layers of ribboned petticoats. Her hair glistened with oils, her arms covered with bracelets, and she wore a shawl with embroidered roses. She gestured for Evelyne to sit, and seemed pleased with the effect her home had on the strange girl with the funny hair.

Evelyne had to bend slightly, the ceiling was so low, and she sat down next to Rawnie. The girl took Evelyne's hand and kissed her palm, then she removed her heavy gold earrings and handed them to Evelyne.

'No, no, I can't, please, you don't have to ... take them back.' Rawnie frowned, took back the earrings and reached for some beads. She held them out, and Evelyne again shook her head.

'You don't like them? What is it you want?'

Evelyne smiled and said she wanted nothing.

Rawnie's eyes filled with tears. She lowered her head, and her voice was so soft Evelyne could only just hear.

'Will you take him when you go?'

Evelyne did not understand. She looked puzzled and reached for Rawnie's hand, but Rawnie cowered back against the cushions.

'What is it, Rawnie? That's your name, isn't it? Are you afraid of me? I am ashamed for what happened to you, and I will help you in any way ... if you want the police informed ...'

Rawnie grasped Evelyne's arm and shook her head, said there were to be no police, they had their own ways of taking care of their people. She had to give her thanks, and Evelyne had refused her gifts; was she ashamed to take them? They were not stolen, they had been handed down to Rawnie from her mother ... Evelyne accepted a tiny pair of hooped earrings, and as she bent to kiss Rawnie again, the girl shrank away. There seemed nothing more to say and Evelyne prepared to leave. She could hear the men moving, putting a horse between the shafts of the caravan.

She was aware of Rawnie's dark eyes staring at her, as if she could see inside her head. Then Rawnie took Evelyne's hand, her own in comparison were dark-skinned, tiny. The girl's touch was delicate, as she slowly traced the head line, the life line, her dark eyes seeming even darker as the feather-light touch traced the heart line. Three times she traced the heart line and murmured, 'Mercury, Apollo, Saturn, Jupiter ... venus,

venus, venus ... the venus.' She reached over for a lighted candle, brought it closer, and as Evelyne tried to withdraw her hand, her grip tightened. She began to drip the wax slowly into Evelyne's upturned palm until it was covered in the warm wax. Her black eyes held Evelyne as she began to spread her hand down, pressing hard, palm to palm.

Freedom looked in at the caravan door, glanced at the two women and closed the door again. Rawnie was distant, her eyes expressionless, dark pools. They held Evelyne's like a snake and then Rawnie lifted her hand away together with the imprint of Evelyne's in the wax, like a shell. She held it up against the candle flames and stared at the strange, delicate imprint.

The sides of the wagon were banged and Jesse's voice called out that they must be on their way. Evelyne stood up, nearly knocking her head on the ceiling but remembering just in time. Rawnie still held the paper-thin waxen palm to the candle flame. Evelyne was opening the door to go outside when Rawnie spoke, her low, husky voice as hypnotic as her eyes, 'He will give you two sons, strong, healthy sons, and you will lose him when the sky is full of black ... dark birds. They fill the sky. Beware of the big dark birds, my friend ...'

Rawnie was crying soundlessly, tears streaming down her face. She could not read her own destiny, but the faces of the palefaced woman's two sons mirrored Freedom's. She might not know it now, but one day he would be the paleface's *rommando*: she would have his heart, she already had his soul.

Evelyne turned back, but Rawnie did not look up. She was melting the wax palm in the candle flame, the tears on her cheeks like wax drops, clear, heavy drops.

Chapter 9

The caravans moved out. As the *dukkerin*, Rawnie travelled last. Roped to the wagon shafts was their herd of wild ponies. Rawnie stood at the door of her wagon and heard from up front the boy yelping and clicking his tongue to move her horse forward over the field.

In the distance she could still see Freedom, Jesse and the paleface woman sitting on top of the rag-and-bone cart. She sighed, so be it, she would marry Jesse, the Black Prince, if he would have her. She closed the door and flicked open the knife Jesse had given her, similar to his own. He had carved her name on the shaft. She ran her finger along the blade, then opened her palm and slit the mound beneath her thumb. The blood oozed out, became a fine trickle. Although the wagon rocked and jolted, she was able to stand still as if by magic, unaware of the movement ... suddenly she opened her eyes wide and screamed, cursing like a witch, and the blade sang through the air to land poised in the wood of her caravan wall, twanging.

*

Sitting on top of the cart, Evelyne clung on for dear life. Jesse led the donkey, pulling on the reins and glowering, muttering to himself. Freedom walked casually alongside, occasionally looking up at her and smiling. Twice she had almost slipped off, but each time he had been there, hand out to help her regain her balance. He had a way, this fighter, of always being there.

Jesse hit the donkey with a stick and the beast veered to the right, tipping Evelyne over. Freedom made Jesse stop the cart for a moment and got up beside her. Jesse flipped him the rein and walked on, swishing the hedges with his stick. Casually, Freedom slipped an arm loosely around Evelyne's waist and clicked his tongue for the donkey to move on. She sniffed, there was a musky, sweet smell, and at first she thought it came from the hedgerow, maybe a flower, but as she turned her head she realized it came from Freedom, that he must be using a perfume on his hair, or oil. He caught her looking at him and smiled, showing his perfect white teeth.

As soon as they entered town Evelyne jumped down, insisting she would be all right. Without a word Jesse hopped up on to the cart and took the reins again, flipped them and whacked the donkey with his stick at the same time. The cart rattled off.

'Rags, bones ... bring out yer rags ...'

As Jesse shouted, Freedom turned back to stare at Evelyne. He gave her a small wave and then turned to face ahead.

Not having the slightest idea where she was, Evelyne kept walking. She had not a penny to her name, and wondered if there might be a post office, then remembered it was Sunday. She sighed, no train ticket home, no handbag, and what did she look like? She was filthy, her skirt was wrinkled, her blouse torn, her beautiful suit completely ruined. She walked on until her feet ached, heading towards the centre of town.

Miss Freda stepped out of her shop, neat as ever and wearing one of her hats. She always walked past the Grand Hotel on a Sunday, showing off her creations as a means of advertising.

'Miss Freda, oh, Miss Freda ... I've found you.'

She squinted in a short-sighted fashion and looked in the direction of the voice, then her mouth dropped open.

'Oh, oh, what happened to you, child?'

'Could I possibly borrow my bus fare, it's a threepenny ride from the terminal, only I lost my bag and ...'

To Freda's horror Evelyne burst into tears. She looked around to see if anyone was watching, ashamed to be seen with the girl, and hustled her towards a shop doorway. Wiping her nose on Miss Freda's little lace handkerchief, Evelyne promised to come to the shop next day and repay the three pennies. Freda opened her purse and counted out the money, snapped it shut again and said she had to be on her way as she had a very important business meeting and couldn't stop to talk. From the doorway, Evelyne watched her hurry away down the street.

By the time Evelyne arrived at Dr Collins' house her heels were blistered and red raw. Mrs Darwin opened the basement door to her.

'Gawd love me, what have you been doing? Come on in, lovey.'

She ushered Evelyne into the kitchen where the maid was slumped in a chair by the fire.

Kicking the maid out of the chair Mrs Darwin settled Evelyne down with a steaming cup of tea. As Evelyne drew breath to launch into an explanation of her appearance, Mrs Darwin began to cry, wiping her nose on her apron.

'I'd have left long ago, but I've not had me wages and Master David's taken everything of value, and what *he* left that bugger Morgan's made off with. It's a shocking state of affairs . . .'

Evelyne felt the tea warming her chilled body.

'Is David at home, Mrs Darwin?'

Mrs Darwin looked at Evelyne, her jaw dropped open.

'We went to a fair last night, there was a terrible to-do afterwards, all the benches fell down and David hurt his leg. Did he come home, or is he in hospital?'

Mrs Darwin glanced at Muriel then back to Evelyne. 'He doesn't live here, not any more.' She could see the confusion in Evelyne's face and she bit her lip, concerned. 'He only stays here occasionally, see, he wants to sell this place but he can't, not without your permission, and then what with all his debts, well, the place is not what it was. He's sold off everything that wasn't nailed down. We've not been paid . . .'

Evelyne interrupted her, saying she had already said that she would see about the wages as soon as things were settled.

'Where is David living, then?'

'Well, with his wife of course. Then if he's not there he's with his friend Freddy Carlton, spends a lot of . . .'

Mrs Darwin didn't finish. Evelyne's body shook and she had to put her teacup down.

'Wife? Is David married?'

'Oh, yes; he's married all right, not that you'd know by his manner, and he's got a little boy too ... Lady Primrose, he married Her Ladyship – oh, what would it be – three, almost four years ago.'

Evelyne couldn't stop herself shaking, her whole body trembled. Mrs Darwin stood up and bent over her. 'Are you all right, lovey? You've gone ever so pale.'

Unable to speak, Evelyne bit her lip hard, forcing herself not to faint, not to cry out, scream his name. Mrs Darwin held her close, patted her head.

'I can see by your face, lovey, something is terribly wrong. What did he do to you? Oh, dear God, what did he do?'

Mrs Darwin blew her nose on her apron and, shaking her fat head, slumped into her chair.

'We've had a terrible time with him, he killed his father, you know. Oh, it was shocking the way he carried on when he came home. See, he didn't know who he was – sometimes he would be gone for days on end and we'd have to send the police out looking for him. Her Ladyship had a shocking time of it, it's memory loss, they say, but it's terrible to see. He don't know who he is, where he is, and he never recognized his father. Broke his heart, it did, killed him as sure as I'm sitting here, shocking, terrible, shocking time.'

Evelyne's heart was hammering inside her chest and Mrs Darwin's voice droning on made it worse. She put her hands over her ears.

'Stop it, stop it.'

'But it's the truth, if it wasn't for Lord Carlton he'd be in a mental home, isn't that right, Muriel?'

Evelyne stood up and clenched her fists.

'But he knew me, he recognized me. You saw the way he ran

to me. He knew who I was ... he called my name, he did, he called me ... he called my name!'

She sobbed, and Mrs Darwin rocked her in her arms.

'No, lovey, I went to fetch him, tell him you was here; you see, they say perhaps something from his past'll make him remember, sparking something off, like. I told him, *I* told him who you were ... but he didn't recognize you – he didn't know you.'

Evelyne felt again the sweet kisses, his gentle kisses on her neck, her face, her lips ... she wouldn't believe it. She shook her head fiercely, and Mrs Darwin sighed.

'Did he have his way with you?'

Evelyne turned away.

'Oh, lovey, I wish it was different, but what can I say, he used this place like a whorehouse, always bringing terrible women back here, some of them so filthy I'd have to burn the sheet afterwards. He don't know what he's doing ... and him what used to have two baths a day.'

Evelyne downed her tea and carefully placed the rose-patterned cup back on its saucer. Always able to fight her emotions, she was suddenly icy calm, controlled, 'I'll need to see him, see about signing over my part of the house. We'll have to sell it to give you both your wages ... Do you – do you have a telephone number where I could call him?'

Mrs Darwin nodded and led Evelyne to the hall. 'There'll be his own home, Lady Primrose's, it's her family house they live in. They had a shocking war, she lost her brother and her father, you know ...'

Evelyne snapped, her voice hard. 'What is the telephone number?'

Mrs Darwin dialled the operator and waited for an answer. The waiting was painful. David was not at home, and a servant suggested they try Lord Carlton's home. Mrs Darwin called the operator again . . .

'Do you remember Lord Carlton, he was in the army with Master David? He married Lady Warner's daughter, poor bugger, Lord love us, what a lump . . . an' 'im such a nice looker and titled as well. Still, he's sitting in clover, lot of money and the factory's going strong. Major Warner, his Lordship, never came back neither. Some say he was killed in action, but there's those who say he stayed away, out of Lady Sybil's reach . . . hello? Hello? Here you are, lovey, you're through to the house.'

In the marble hallway, the butler held out the telephone to Freddy. 'It's Mr Collins' housekeeper, sir.'

Freddy sighed and took the receiver. 'Hello? Speaking . . . who is this? Mrs Darwin? Oh, yes, yes of course, I remember. Well, I'm afraid David's still rather poorly . . . Yes, he's here, resting. I don't really think that would be very convenient.'

Evelyne gripped the telephone tightly.

'Would you please tell Mr Collins that Miss Evelyne Jones will be calling to see him. Thank you.'

Evelyne put the ear-piece back so hard Mrs Darwin thought she'd snapped the hook off.

'Now I would like to take a bath, then I'll go straight to the Warners'.'

Mrs Darwin nodded, even said, 'Yes, ma'am'. Suddenly Evelyne frightened the life out of her.

*

Heather opened the drawing room doors. Freddy was standing staring at the telephone, his thoughts miles away.

'Who was that, dearest? Mummy said she thought she heard the phone ring.'

She stood staring like an owl, waiting, and Freddy sighed.

'Just someone for David, nothing.'

'Primmy's due at any moment. She called earlier to say she would be driving up from London.'

'Yes, yes I know, I'll go and tell him.'

Heather watched her husband climb the stairs. She sighed. David really played such an important part in their lives. If they weren't chasing around Cardiff looking for him, Freddy was staying at David's house or he at theirs. They had virtually made over to him one of their best front bedrooms, he stayed so often. Not that Heather ever said anything against it; far from it. It was not in her nature ever to disagree with anything Freddy wanted to do.

Just as she was about to close the door, the children's nanny appeared, dragging their twin daughters along. The little girls were very like their mother, even down to the buck teeth. They were both crying because Clarence had kicked one of them. Clarence was David's little boy and, like his father, he spent more time at Freddy and Heather's home than his own.

'Tell Clarence, Nanny, that if he doesn't behave I shall tell his mother, she will be here at any moment.'

The nanny hauled the howling children up the stairs. Trailing behind was the little golden-haired boy, his silky hair just like David's. Clarence began to shout that he wanted his mother, and was pulled away up to the nursery.

*

'David? You awake, old man? Just had a call from that gel Evelyne whatsit.'

David lay in the large double bed with its frills and canopy, his injured leg propped up on pillows. 'Oh, Christ, that one from last night, I thought we'd got rid of her ... I say, want a game of cards? Double or quits?'

Freddy sighed. There David sat, looking as angelic as ever, bathed, his hair shining, almost sparkling, his complexion fresh.

'Just that it could be a trifle embarrassing, Primmy called and she's on her way here. Don't think it's a frightfully good idea for them to meet, do you? You were making a bit of a meal of her, you know ... David?'

Unconcerned, David shuffled his pack of cards. 'Can't you get rid of her for me? You know how I hate to upset Primmy ... what on earth does she want, did she say?'

Freddy scratched his head and shrugged, muttered that it was something to do with the house, David's old home.

'You think you could sneak her up the back way so no one will know? See what she wants?'

Freddy nodded. He always did what David wanted, always had. Deep down he knew why. He would do anything to be near Lady Primrose, even if it meant taking care of her husband.

Evelyne stood at the iron gates and peered through them, up the gravel drive to the big white manor house. Without the twinkling fairy lights the drive seemed longer, and the house had lost its fairy-tale aspect. The sweeping lawns were devoid of peacocks, but the flowerbeds and the hedges were as immaculate as ever.

Freddy met her in the drive, as if he had been looking out for here. He seemed ill at ease, nervous of her, and cleared his throat. 'Would you come this way, just follow me.'

They followed a path leading away from the front of the manor, around to the back of the house that had been part of his dreams for so many years, and in by the servants' entrance.

Heather flicked the velvet curtains back into place. She was spying, she knew it. David was obviously up to his old tricks again. The girl looked positively wretched.

She went back to reviewing the firm's accounts. She now ran the family business, Freddy paying not the slightest attention to it, although he dipped into their joint account freely. Heather never rebuked him, never questioned what he did with all the 'spending money'. She was frightened that he might tell her the truth. What she didn't know couldn't hurt her.

Lady Sybil sat by the fire wrapped in a thick woollen rug. She appeared weighed down by her treasured array of beads.

'Who was that outside? I heard the gravel crunch.'

'No one, Mother, just the gardener.'

The clock chimed three.

Evelyne could hear the chimes as she and Freddy climbed the back stairs. He had said not a word, simply gesturing to her to follow him. As they crossed the landing towards David's bedroom, Clarence ran from the nursery, being chased by Nanny.

'Watch it, Clarence, don't fall over and hurt yourself,' she warned.

The little boy ran on, disappearing from view with the nanny calling after him. Freddy tapped on the bedroom door and opened it. 'Here's your visitor, old chap, don't make it too long.'

Freddy turned to Evelyne. 'I hope you'll keep quiet about the boxing match should anyone ask you, you know there was a frightful rumpus afterwards. Police were called in to keep the rabble quiet, and David and I think it best you don't mention our presence there to anyone, all right?'

Evelyne nodded her head, and Freddy went into the bedroom. He laughed at something David must have said, then opened the door wide for Evelyne to enter.

The room was vast, and the ornate four-poster bed had a frilled and flounced canopy with more flounces round the base. A huge tallboy with a mirror on top flanked by carved angels dominated the room. A dressing-table swathed in the same fabric as the bed was covered in little silver pots, brushes, a hand-mirror, and shaving equipment in a silver rack. There were clothes draped across the back of a velvet chair, and a large tray of half-eaten food rested on a stand.

David lay back on a mound of pillows, the embroidered frills matching those on the sheet. He was wearing monogrammed silk pyjamas, and he looked as handsome as ever, just a fraction paler.

'Well, hello, Flame, come in and sit down. Have you had some tea?'

Unaware that Evelyne could see him in the mirror, David raised his eyebrows questioningly at Freddy.

'S'all right, old man, I've briefed her, she won't let the cat out of the bag . . . be back in about ten minutes, toodle-oo.'

He closed the door, and Evelyne was left standing awkwardly in the centre of the room.

'Well sit down, girl, here, next to me, but gently, the leg's really painful.'

Evelyne perched on the end of the bed and took a deep breath, hardly able to meet his smiling blue eyes.

'Suppose you met his wife? Dreadful-looking, isn't she? But then poor Freddy had to take what was available, needed the cash. They run a chocolate factory you know, absolutely loaded. Still, I must say I'm eternally grateful, got me back here in no time . . .'

He had the grace to blush slightly, aware that they must have abandoned her at the boxing match. He reached over and poured himself a glass of whisky from a cut-glass decanter.

Evelyne blurted out, 'You didn't remember me at all, did you? What did Mrs Darwin tell you about me?'

David downed the drink in one and shrugged, then he told her Mrs Darwin was a drunkard, she'd just said that there was a beautiful girl waiting at the house. He gazed at the ceiling, frowned. 'They tell you about me? They treat me rather like a loony you know, because I can't remember my past. Well, my father did. If it weren't for Freddy I'd probably have been put into some kind of home. I'm all right, though, and maybe it's for the best. God knows what's hidden in the recesses of my mind, God knows.'

Evelyne twisted her hands and mumbled that she was the girl Doris had brought to the house. She bit hard on her lip, but couldn't stop the tears. David picked up her hand and pulled, making her move closer until she could smell his lavender perfume, then drew her fingers to his lips and kissed them. She moaned softly, then withdrew her hand.

'You're married, you should have told me.'

David cocked his head to one side and asked, 'Why?' He wanted to know what on earth it had to do with her. She moved off and paced the room, and slowly, bit by bit, she told him everything, even down to buying her outfit, hiring the chauffeur-driven car. He listened, put a cigarette into a holder and lit it, breathing out the smoke. He was staring into space, and suddenly, out of the blue, he spoke, not to Evelyne but to the wall, 'Did you know that the average life expectancy of a subaltern on arrival in the trenches was little more than three weeks?'

His face crumpled, like a child's, a puzzled furrow on his brow. He touched his forehead with one finger, pressing hard, and then took another drift of smoke into his lungs and turned his clear, ice-blue eyes to her. 'I'm sorry, what did you say?'

'I love you, and I've been in love with you since I was fourteen years of age.'

There, it was out, she'd said it, said everything she had intended to say, and at the finish she felt drained, empty.

'I'm very flattered, sweet girl, but tell me what did you intend me to do with this love of yours? Oh Christ, did I make a play for you yesterday? I was drunk, you know that, surely?'

Evelyne stared at him. He flicked the ash off the end of his cigarette and looked enquiringly at her. She couldn't meet his gaze. He vaguely remembered what had happened last night, and he remembered Evelyne. But he had been drunk, he excused himself. Looking at her now he couldn't believe he had made a pass at her, and all she had just told him meant nothing to him. He had absolutely no idea who this woman Doris was. His eyes narrowed, he leaned back and stared. After a moment he asked in a clipped, cold tone, 'What do you want? Well, what do you want?'

Evelyne twisted her hands, swallowed hard, and said, 'Half of your father's house is mine, Mrs Darwin said her wages have not been paid.'

'She's a liar, absolute lies, pay her every month, ask Freddy.'

'She says neither she nor Muriel has been paid. Now, maybe they have or they haven't, I don't know, but I need to know what you want to do with the house. It's in an appalling condition. Are you going to sell it? If so, then do you need my signature?'

David yawned and said that he had not the slightest idea. Evelyne's temper was rising, her fists were clenched at her sides.

'Well, maybe the money is of no interest to you, it is to me, and I could well do with it. How much is the house worth?'

'Is that what you've come here for, money? Christ, you are all the same, money, money ... do what you like with the house, sell it, live in it, I don't care ... I don't care.'

Evelyne sprang to her feet.

'Maybe you don't care, but I spent money on my clothes, they were ruined, I spent money on a train ticket, my handbag, all lost at the fair *you* took me to. I own half that house, now it may mean nothing to you, but ... I want to be paid, no more than is my right.'

David's mouth turned down like a child's. He reached for his jacket and took out his wallet, throwing it across the room.

'Take whatever you want ... money is all your kind ever think of.'

That was it. Evelyne turned to face him, eyes blazing.

'What do you mean by that? What do you mean by "my kind"? *What is my kind? Poor, is that my kind, poor?*'

She frightened him, confused him, and he sat back in the bed, pressing himself against the pillows. He was as helpless as a child, and she knew it. She opened his wallet. There were three five-pound notes and two ten-pound notes. She held each one up as she took it out, showing him exactly what she was taking.

'Two five-pound notes, David, and one ten-pound note, I've taken twenty pounds.'

He turned away, staring out of the window. His voice was soft, hardly audible.

'Please go away, you make my head ache ... take anything you want, I don't know what you are talking about, I really don't.'

Evelyne folded the money and told David that if he needed any papers signed he could send them to her. He turned to her, his eyes wide, frightened, childlike. He held up his arms, his beautiful face pleading. She sat down on the bed, gently so as not to hurt his legs, and he wrapped his arms around her. His silky head was close to hers, she could feel his soft skin, his sweet perfume was in her nostrils. She thought he whispered, 'Sorry', but she couldn't tell. She didn't want to hold him, but her arms lifted and she hugged him. His warm mouth kissed her innocently, then his arms tightened and his kiss became sexual, forceful.

The door opened and Freddy stood there. 'I think you had better leave ... Come along ... David, straighten the bed, your wife's arrived. I'll show her out.'

He stood there impatient, then stepped forward and picked up David's wallet where it had fallen. He opened it, checked inside and then looked at Evelyne. She flushed, knowing he didn't understand, and tried to explain.

'I own part of David's house, his Aunt Doris ...'

Freddy paid no attention, he was straightening David's bed. Then he hurried to the door, pulling her by the arm.

As they reached the landing, Evelyne heard the soft, laughing voice of Lady Primrose as she caught her son in her arms.

'Clarence, yes, it's Mummy ... it's Mummy ... Oh, what a big boy you are, shall we go and say hello to Daddy? Yes? Come on, you show me the way.'

Freddy pushed Evelyne along the corridor towards the back staircase. Lady Primrose, beautiful as ever, appeared at the top of the stairs, Clarence pulling at her hand. She was swathed in furs and wearing a pale pink suit.

'Hello, Freddy, I got here sooner than I expected ... all right, Clarence, Mummy is coming.'

Standing behind Freddy, Evelyne knew she had been seen. Lady Primrose gave her a cold stare, her blue eyes flickered.

'Oh, I'm sorry, I didn't know you had company. Is David alone?'

Freddy murmured that David was waiting, and that he himself would be back in a moment. Primrose called out to David as she headed for his room.

'My darling, are you all right, I drove down as soon as I got Freddy's call.'

She entered the room and shut the door behind her. Evelyne stood with Freddy in the dark little corridor and shook, her teeth chattering in her head.

'It's all right, she didn't know you, not that she would have minded, I'm sure. I'll see you out.'

He moved quickly ahead of her, guiding her down the stairs.

*

Lady Primrose fussed and patted the bedclothes down around David. She'd seen the girl leaving, thought maybe she was a housemaid, but she knew there would be more to it than that, there always was. She poured David's usual measure of laudanum into a glass and topped it up with water. She held it out to him, and he drank it like a good boy. Clarence sat on the end of the bed, kept on asking what she had brought him from London, until he got a sharp smack. He started to howl, so Primrose had to kiss and cuddle him.

David held up his arm for her to go to him and she sat beside him and kissed his neck and his brow, petting him just like she had Clarence.

'There, there, darling, shusssh now, you get some sleep and in the morning we'll all go home ... Oh, who was that girl I saw a moment ago?'

David shrugged and said that Mrs Darwin had done her usual trick, told him that his aunt had brought the girl to the house before the war. She was the poor little orphan girl he'd brought to the dance when they'd first met. Primrose nodded, she remembered her vaguely, a strange, tall girl with red hair, the girl who danced with Lloyd George. She recalled that dance very clearly because it was there she had met David. They were married on his next leave, and she later became pregnant on their three-day honeymoon. A year later she had David home for good, but he wasn't the same and they said he never would be. Basically, Primrose had two children on her hands, little Clarence and her husband. Sometimes, most times, she wished she'd married Freddy, never left him for David.

'Did you remember her, darling? Did you remember the poor little orphan girl at all?'

David's eyes dropped and he shook his head, he hardly seemed to notice Primrose take Clarence's hand and lead him out of the room. As the doors closed behind them, he began to drift into a drugged sleep and all he could see in front of his eyes was an old pair of boots with newspaper sticking out of them. Suddenly, in brilliant, flashing colours he saw the dining room, Doris sitting upright with a teacup in her hand, and then a clear picture of Evelyne.

'Primmy? Primmy?'

The panic started, the terrible feeling of being on fire, the boom, boom of guns was deafening. The nightmare began again and he put his hands over his ears, began to shout, 'No … no … *No, no, no!*'

Evelyne tried hard to explain to Freddy about the house, but he was so concerned with getting rid of her that he didn't listen. He instructed a housemaid to take Evelyne out through the kitchens and the servants' entrance. In a way he felt sorry for the big, awkward girl, but then he heard the awful screams echoing down from David's room. He knew he would have to go to him, and he blamed Evelyne.

'Don't come back, this is your doing, listen to him … I think you got what you came for, didn't you? Go on, get out.'

Lady Primrose rushed into the drawing room. Heather and Lady Sybil could hear David's screams. Heather shut the door and put her arms around Primrose.

'It's all right, dearest, Freddy will see to him, really it's all right.'

Lady Sybil, eating tea and crumpets, muttered:

'Should be in a home, not right in the head.'

Heather gave her mother a stern look and tossed her the evening paper to read, then sat Primrose down and poured tea. The shouts and screams from David's room slowly subsided.

Freddy returned to the drawing room, giving Primrose an intimate smile. He said David was sleeping, the laudanum had taken effect.

'That girl, Freddy, apparently Mrs Darwin suggested she visit David. I think, as it obviously upsets him so, that we really should watch out for him, don't you think?'

Freddy blushed. Just meeting her eyes made him want her. He nodded.

'Perhaps we shouldn't try any more, I'm sorry.'

Primrose gave him a sad, helpless look. Freddy made no mention of David's wallet or the night spent at the gypsy fair. He nearly dropped his teacup when Lady Sybil read aloud from the evening newspaper.

'"Riot at boxing match" . . . have you read this, Freddy? Says here a gypsy fighter nearly killed his opponent, a miner. Look, read for yourself. Says the man was almost murdered. Caused a riot, tent burnt down, dreadful to-do. Riff-raff shouldn't be allowed in the country, none of them fought in the war. If Reggie were alive he would take his twelve-bore and shoot them down.'

Freddy took the paper and agreed with Lady Sybil that they were riff-raff, he couldn't understand why anyone would want to watch them fight, *he* most certainly wouldn't. Heather smiled at him and patted his knee. He left the room, and no one noticed that he took the paper with him.

*

Evelyne never went back to Mrs Pugh's, not because she didn't want to pay but because she couldn't face her. The few belongings she had left there she could do without. All she wanted was to go home and forget everything that had happened. All the way home, above the noise of the steam engine chug-chug-chugging, she could hear the strains of those high-pitched voices, those posh, upper-crust voices, their secret looks and nudges, their self-satisfaction, their money. She opened her bag and counted out the notes she had taken from David's wallet, then sat back against the seat and closed her eyes. Even after everything he had done, if he wanted her she would go to him she knew it, and she was angry with herself. 'You are a bloody fool, Evelyne Jones, forget him, take the money and forget him, he's not worth it. They treated you like dirt, you only took what was rightly yours. He owed you that money, it was yours to take.'

Her heartache slowly turned to anger. She twisted her hands in her lap, folded and refolded the money. All her love slowly turned to bitterness, turned sour, and her mouth took on a thin, hard line, her face tight. By the time the train stopped at her station she was composed, her anger and pain under control. At least, she said to herself, she hadn't lost any money on this trip, in fact she'd made it.

Chapter 10

Evelyne let herself into the house and changed her clothes, bundling up the ones she had been wearing and burning them.

'Well, how did it go, lovey?'

'It didn't work out, Da ... Now, I'd best hurry and get to the school.'

Hugh said nothing, saddened for a moment that she didn't confide in him, but he had become so busy of late that he soon forgot all about it.

Evelyne was stunned to be told at the school that a new teacher with proper qualifications would be coming for the next term. The school governors had visited during her absence and, although they appreciated the work she had done in the past, they had to have someone with proper qualifications. There was no work to be had at the brick factory, or at the coal face. Come Easter she would be unemployed, but that was Easter, and until then she would continue at the school. Her heart was no longer in it, though, and the children noticed and called her 'Miss Stick'.

Hugh was going from strength to strength within the union. Twice he travelled to other mines to give talks to the men, and returned jubilant that they were solidly on his side, and if the mine owners didn't bow to their demands for better wages and safety regulations, they would strike. The small house was full every evening with groups of men who would bring their problems to Hugh. Evelyne had once been pleased to be part of this, but now she withdrew upstairs to her mother's old room, where she would read until her eyes hurt.

Hugh was in good spirits. Dai Thomas had brought the local newspaper and on page three there was Hugh, wearing his cloth cap, standing rigidly straight and glaring into the camera.

As he went up the stairs, he saw the gas lamp still glowing in Evelyne's room. He tapped, and popped his head round the door. Evelyne was lying on top of her bed, wearing just a white shift, her waist-length hair brushed and gleaming. 'My God,' thought Hugh, 'if any of those buggers was to see her now they wouldn't be calling her "Miss Stick".' She looked like a mermaid. 'I got a few copies, see . . . it's me in the main photo, not a bad likeness, gel, wouldn't you say? Told me not to smile, see, so I'd look fierce, look like I know what I'm talking about.'

'It's good, Da, and you look no more than thirty, real fit and strong.'

Hugh laughed and twisted his cap round on his head, pulling a funny face. She handed the paper back to him, but he whipped out another two copies from his pocket. 'Keep it, Dai's gonna bring us a frame.'

He wanted to talk, but she put the paper down and picked up the book she was reading. He went out, then came back again.

'Now don't start, just let me say something to you, I love you more than my own life, an' I can't stand to see you wastin' yourself, sitting up here every night, goin' up to the school every day, gettin' more an' more like an old maid, like Doris.'

Evelyne shrugged, tossed her hair and said, tight-lipped, that he had no need to worry, she wouldn't be going up to the school much longer, they were replacing her with a proper teacher. As soon as he had left Evelyne felt dreadful. She loved him so much. Why hadn't she talked with him like they used to, why had she shut him out lately? She picked up the paper and looked at the photograph, his stern face glaring into the camera. She kissed the photo and took some scissors out of a drawer.

As she snipped around the photo she couldn't help but notice the lead article on the next page, 'Police investigate two revenge murders'.

She carried the paper over to the lamp and sat down. The article stated that the two boys had been found with their throats slit open, their hands tied behind their backs. At first, they believed the motive had been robbery, but then a third boy had given himself up to the local constabulary. He admitted that he and his friends had made advances to a gypsy girl and one of the gypsy men, Freedom Stubbs, had warned them that they would take their revenge. The article requested anyone knowing of Freedom Stubbs' whereabouts to come forward.

From then on Evelyne kept every article she found, carefully hidden in her bedroom. She never mentioned the article to her father, not that she saw that much of him to talk to. He spent most evenings in a room above the pub holding meetings for the local miners. Evelyne worked at the school during the day and studied for her examinations in the evenings. Hugh no longer even needed her to help out at the meetings, taking notes and writing letters and so forth. Gladys Turtle had taken over that side of things.

'No need for you to interrupt your studies, love.'

'I don't mind, Da, really I don't.'

'Well, lass, as a matter o' fact we've got a sort of committee secretary, Gladys Turtle, from Lower North Road, nice woman, a widow.'

Although slightly put out, Evelyne said nothing. She watched from her window as Hugh met up with the 'merry widow', as Gladys was known in the village. Not that she was particularly merry, just that she had overindulged in the sweet sherry at her late husband's funeral and passed out. She was a small, neat, white-haired woman with a shelf-like bosom, and a habit of wearing crocheted flowers on her hats or pinned to her coat collar.

Gladys had found a new lease on her boring, mundane life, working with Hugh. She had always had an eye for him, even when he was a youngster, but of course he would never have looked at her – she was no beauty like his Mary. Gladys reckoned that the way to a man's heart was through his stomach, and she cooked stews and casseroles for Hugh to take home in small pots. He would sneak into the house with them, as if embarrassed, and Evelyne would watch him heating them up. Then he would wink at her and wolf the food down.

Gladys had passed by earlier, walking with Hugh – he always took her home after meetings. 'I've just walked our Gladys back, do you fancy one of her scones?'

Shaking her head, Evelyne closed her books.

'She's got a young nephew staying, nice young fella, Willie, looking for work like the rest of us. He had a good job over at Glamorgan, beats me why he gave it up. Word is, he may have got a young girl in the family way.'

Hugh coughed and stuck his finger down his starched collar.

'I was wonderin', like, maybe as she's so nice with all these scones and stews, perhaps it would be neighbourly like if we had her and this young Willie come to tea Sunday?'

'Why not, if that is what you would like, Da?'

He stood up, beaming, and shoved his hands in his pockets.

'Ay, it is, good, well, I'll leave it with you, shall I?'

Evelyne collected their supper from the fish and chip shop, and carried it home wrapped in newspaper. As she left the shop she bumped into Gladys, and cordially invited her and her nephew to tea on Sunday.

'Oh, that's lovely, I'll look forward to it.'

Not wanting Evelyne to see that she also frequented the fish and chip shop, Gladys waited until Evelyne had walked the length of the street before she went in. From behind the counter the sweating Nellie gave her a toothless smile.

'Eh, she's a right stuck-up one, that, ever since she got that wireless, come with her legacy . . . two cod, Gladys, is it?'

As she unwrapped the fish and chips a grease-stained headline caught Evelyne's eye, 'Third Murder Victim'. She pulled at the paper, spilling chips on the table.

'Police step up their search for Freedom Stubbs. They now

believe the murders to be revenge killings, all committed by the same hand. Each victim has died in the same circumstances, their hands tied behind their backs and their throats slit. In each killing it seems the murderer knew where his victim lived and worked.'

Sunday was chapel day which meant choir practice, and Hugh went off in his Sunday suit, leaving Evelyne to prepare tea for Gladys and Willie. She baked some scones and, of course, just when she would have liked them to be the best batch she had ever made, they went flat and hard as a rock. Then she slipped down to the newspaper shop to buy a Sunday paper.

Walking back, searching through the paper to see if there was any more news of the murders, she passed a poster advertising the Easter fair. As usual the gypsies would set up their fair on the mountainside. It was always a big occasion, and being a Bank Holiday the men had an extra day off work. There would be coconut shies, hoop-la, and sometimes they built a giant see-saw for the children.

Evelyne stopped. There was a small item on the second page which simply stated that the police were no further along with their investigation. She hurried on, then stopped again. Even from the street she could smell her bread burning. She ran in with a scream of fury, but it was burnt to a cinder. As she opened the windows to get rid of the terrible smell, she saw Hugh outside with a group of miners on their way back from choir practice.

There was a hell of a row going on, Hugh standing in the centre of the crowd thumping his fist in his palm. The men were shaking their fists at him, all shouting at once.

'You bastard, Hugh Jones, we go out on strike you tell me who's gonna feed my ten kids.'

Hugh shouted back and waved his arms, 'We'll all chip in, if we don't stand united then we fall. You said yerself, mun, you not got enough money to feed yer babies now, an' yer workin', don't you understand that's what we're striking for, a living wage, mun! *We strike!*'

Some of them started to walk home, and Evelyne was about to turn back to her studies when she saw a figure on the edge of the crowd around Hugh. It was Freedom Stubbs, large as life, leaning against the wall with a half-smile on his face. Evelyne clapped her hand over her mouth and turned away from the window.

'Oh, God, it couldn't be him, not here, not in our village.'

When she looked again he had gone, as if he had vanished into thin air.

'Evie! *Evie!* Is tea ready, they'll be here by half past three lass, and the table's not laid.'

She ran downstairs to the kitchen where Hugh was already shaking out a clean tablecloth.

'Da, the gypsy fair, they're not setting it up yet, are they?'

Hugh reached down the best crockery. 'Oh, they start early for Easter, lovey. It's their big time. An' then they'll be arranging a fight as usual, Devil's Rock.'

There was a tap on the door, and Hugh gave Evelyne a startled look.

'They're here early, are we all set?'

Before Evelyne had time to answer he was opening the front door and ushering Gladys along the passage.

'Come in, Gladys, and you, Willie. Welcome, welcome.'

'Is something on fire, Hugh love? I can smell burning.'

With a frosty smile Evelyne turned to greet them.

'Here they are, Evie, Gladys you know, and this is Willie, her nephew.'

Evelyne dropped the plate of solid scones on the flagged floor and the plate smashed in two. Immediately Willie pushed forward and bent to pick up the scones.

''Fraid yer plate's broken, but the scones are none the worse.'

Hugh laughed and said it was more than likely the scones that had crashed through the plate.

Evelyne stared at Willie as he held the chair out for his aunt. She knew it was him, had known at first glance. So this was why he had left Glamorgan, given up his job, Willie Thomas was the boy she had seen on top of Rawnie, this was the lad who had torn her hair out by the roots and who Evelyne had virtually knocked unconscious with the bench leg. She wondered if he recognized her and could hardly bear to look in his direction.

'Auntie tells me you're a schoolteacher, that right, Evie?'

She busied herself passing the jam, and murmured that it was quite right. Her mind was racing. He wouldn't know her now, surely he wouldn't ... she looked up to meet his gaze. He gave Evelyne a wink. His familiarity, calling her Evie when he had only just met her, made her temper rise. It was definitely him, the red neck, the horrid, bright red hair.

Gladys simpered coyly and looked up at Hugh, then spoke to Evelyne, 'We thought you might get uppity, another woman in your kitchen, but you've made us very welcome, Evie.'

Evelyne looked down at her plate. The scones were terrible, she could hardly get her teeth through hers. Hugh coughed.

'Ah well, I've not actually told her, we'll announce it in chapel next week, but we are unofficially engaged to be married, that right, Gladys?'

Somehow Evelyne found her voice and said stiffly that she was very happy for them. The soft, powdered cheek brushed Evelyne's, and she got a close-up view of the silly crochet work on Gladys' hat. Evelyne wanted to cry out. How could her Da want this silly woman?

Gladys insisted on staying with Hugh to wash the dishes, and Evelyne showed Willie into the front room. Willie sat on the sofa and gave her a wide smile. 'She's a good woman, Aunt Glad . . . Evie, will you sit beside me?'

'My name's Evelyne . . . so, you're here looking for work, is that right? You'll not find any, and there's the strike coming, you should go back to Glamorgan, or Cardiff even.'

He shrugged, took out a packet of cigarettes and lit one, blowing out the smoke and crossing his legs.

'Do you know Cardiff then, Willie?'

She caught his sly glance, and noticed that he flicked his ash on to her polished lino.

'I've been there, but I prefer it here.'

She was one hundred per cent sure it was him, any doubts had disappeared and she boiled with anger at what he had done.

Hugh interrupted the tense moment. 'Right, Evie, will you be at the meeting? They'll be arriving any moment, Gladys is setting out the books . . . an' you too, Willie, it's important tonight.'

*

Hugh stood before the fire with his trousers almost sizzling.

'No man's takin' these decisions lightly, for Lord's sake, mun. You think I for one dunno what hardships we're all headin' for?'

Harry Jones jabbed the air with his finger and demanded to know if Hugh could face starving women, never mind starving kids. Hugh sighed and rubbed his hair until it stood on end. 'Jesus Christ, mun, I know that even the most tenacious strikers are giving way, but . . .'

Hugh had heard the word 'tenacious' on the wireless and now used it at every opportunity. The others stopped arguing for a moment as he explained what he meant. Harry muttered that he didn't give a bugger who was 'tenacled' or not, all he knew was his kids were starving, and he had to work to put a crust into their mouths. Hugh banged his fist against the mantel. Intensive union activity had taken its toll not only on him but on four others who were blacklisted. Again his voice rose as he told the men that there were some working with their union badges sewn into their collars for fear of the managers knowing they were members.

Taffy Rawlins twisted his cap and blurted out, 'Lot o' men tried workin' in other collieries. Soon as it was discovered they was union men, none of 'em could get taken on.'

Harry Jones rose to his feet, jabbing the air with a stubby finger. 'Ay, an' rumour 'as it, any man what's a member has 'is name circ'lated from the union roster. They'll never get work, not now the strike is on, not when it's over.'

Taffy was at it again, waving his cap. 'I believe, Hugh Jones, an' there's many that says I'm right, your union is bloody destroying a man's right ta work.'

Dramatically, Hugh tore off his threepenny-piece-sized union badge and held it up above his head.

'If we don't join this union now, if we don't pull together, you'll all be no better than the pit ponies left down the mines to rot. The managers, the owners, don't give a hang whether a man dies or not, they're more worried about losing a dram than they are about any man.' Hugh's voice was earshattering in the hot, stuffy, confined kitchen. 'You lose a dram o'coal, mun, and what happens? The buggers make you pay for it. But when have *they* paid for a man's life? The proprietors know the men are weak, that they have no organization so they can do what the hell they like. The pit manager can sack when he pleases, and the poor bugger can do nothing about it, and they'd hardly pay him a penny ... *Am I right, tell me?*'

Throughout the meeting Gladys took copious notes for the minutes. Willie paid little attention, picking his teeth with a match and yawning. Evelyne kept feeling his eyes on her but refused to return his stare.

At last the meeting broke up and Evelyne packed what food was left over from tea and slipped it to Taffy for his kids. Hugh walked Gladys home, still arguing with Harry. Willie made no move to leave with his aunt, sitting in Hugh's chair by the fire. 'I just seen there's a good film at the pictures, Evie, last show's at nine, fancy an outing?'

Evelyne folded her arms. 'My name's Evelyne to you, son, or Miss Jones. And if you want some advice I'd clear out.'

Willie looked completely unabashed. He propped his feet on the fireguard.

'That's none too friendly, considerin' we'll be related soon.'

Evelyne would have liked to swipe his gloating face.

'I've no intention of makin' a friend of you, none at all, and I don't want you in this house again, now out ... go on, hop it.'

His piggy eyes glinted, and he slowly removed his feet from the fireguard. He looked at her, and she could almost see the wheels churning round in his flushed head.

'Way I hear it, you should think yourself lucky bein' asked out, there's not many lads left in the village. There's plenty of young girls panting to go to the pictures so don't put yourself out, Miss Schoolteacher.'

Evelyne watched the cocky boy saunter out, and she restrained herself from aiming a blow at the back of his stocky, flushed neck. As the door closed behind him, Evelyne went to fetch her heavy coat. She wrapped a scarf around her neck and slipped out the back way. She didn't want anyone to see her, to know where she was going.

The gypsies were just setting up their camp, the wagons and trailers drawn up in a semicircle, a group of men erecting the big, round living tents. A fire blazed in the centre of the ring, and a few children were hanging round, wearing cotton dresses and thin, threadbare woollies. Although barefooted they seemed hardly to notice the cold, but they noticed Evelyne striding up the hill. She'd opened up her coat as she was warm from the long walk, and her cheeks flushed pink from the evening air.

A runny-nosed little boy with huge, dark eyes watched her, a brooding look on his tiny face, then he put out his hand.

'Give us a penny, come on missus, just a copper, we're starvin' hungry.'

Evelyne looked down at the tiny boy already adept at begging, and showed him her empty pockets.

'Is Freedom with you, boy? I need to talk with Freedom.'

At that moment a woman with a shawl wrapped around her appeared from behind the bushes. She grabbed the child by the hair and walloped him, with a cold, angry look at Evelyne.

'There's no one of that name here.'

The children ran like hell away from the sharp-tongued woman, the little boy looking back at Evelyne. She went nearer to the camp, and now the men turned and stared with the expressionless, unnerving faces. She stood looking around, then spoke loudly, her voice echoing.

'I need to speak with Freedom, is he here with you?'

They made no reply, just turned their backs and continued working. Women passed hooded looks to one another and she saw two men talking together in sign language.

'I know he's with you and I have to talk with him.'

A grey-haired man, wearing clothes fit for a scarecrow, shuffled towards her. He came within about six feet of her and showed his toothless, shiny gums as he spoke.

'There's no one by that name here, wench. Git out of it. Listen to what I say, go away from here.'

Evelyne turned and walked out of the field and headed down the steep path, thinking to herself that at least she'd tried. She stuffed her hands into her pockets and felt the newspaper clippings, paused, looking back, and then walked on. She took the narrow path round the mountainside, beginning to think herself stupid for risking walking out this late, and so close to the gypsy camp. All her father's old warnings came back to her and she quickened her pace.

Freedom had watched her walk into the camp, seen the way she stamped her foot angrily, turned on her heel and marched out. She had snapped a dead branch off a tree and was whacking the hedges as she walked along. He sat up in the fork of a tree, watching her with his dark eyes, amused, smiling. She was an odd one, that was for sure. As Evelyne walked beneath his tree he dropped down, and she shrieked with terror. When she saw it was him, she put her hands on her hips and let him have it.

'That's a fine thing to do! You nearly gave me heart failure, you did!'

With a mocking bow, but without saying a word, Freedom began to walk along beside her. Evelyne took the newspaper cuttings from her pocket.

'I suppose you've read all these? You *can* read?'

Freedom cocked his head to one side, smiling. She only came up to his shoulder and had to look up into his face. His hair had grown longer and he had tied it back with a leather thong. He now wore a gold earring in his right ear.

'I've come to tell you to leave, the police will be here, that's what I've come all this way to say.'

With one quick hop Freedom was in front of her, walking backwards.

Still walking, she continued, 'You can't just go around killing people, even if what they did was a terrible thing. The law must know the boy's here, and with the fair being here too, they're bound to come around asking questions.'

Freedom halted and she walked straight into him. He gripped her arm, hurting her. Evelyne looked into his face, she wasn't afraid, she never had been afraid of him, but he hurt her wrist and she jerked her hand free. 'I said the fourth boy's here in the village, and you know it, *that's* why you're here.'

Freedom took the tree branch from her hand and swiped at the bushes in anger.

'I'm here to fight at Devil's Pit, nothing more.'

Evelyne fell into step beside him, told him he was crazy, the police wanted to question him about the murders. If he came out in the open to fight, they would certainly arrest him. They had even put his name in the papers.

'So, Evelyne, you came to warn me, is that it?'

She tripped over a stone and he caught her, but she moved quickly out of reach. Flippantly, she said she was amazed that he remembered her name.

'You remembered mine, I heard you asking for me, and I thank you.'

They walked on and she asked after Rawnie. Freedom told her that she was now Jesse's woman and would be at the camp. As they walked she became aware of his familiar but strange, musky perfume, and even more aware of his cat-like litheness. He seemed hardly to make a sound as he walked, his step surprisingly light for his size.

'Have you got yourself a man yet then, Evelyne?'

She flushed and bit her lip, and he laughed softly with his little lopsided smile and slightly raised eyebrows.

'Did you ever go to an inn close by Cydwinath Farm? When we last met I thought I'd seen you before, a long time ago.'

Evelyne shook her head.

'Oh, it wasn't you, huh? See, first I saw this girl in a field – like a mermaid she was, and dressed in naught but her shift – and then I saw her again, a big society dance, it was.' He gave her his strange half-smile, his eyes twinkling, 'I was standing in the dark and it was as if she was lit up by the moon, like a moment of magic. It was a mermaid again, only, only this time she was a princess in a flowing gown, and she was dancing with an old fella with white hair, there on the lawn with not a soul to see but me.'

Evelyne stopped and bit her lip so hard her teeth almost went straight through. He looked down into her face and cupped her chin in his hand.

'I was never at a dance, and most certainly not at any farm in my shift, and I find it very ungentlemanly of you even to suggest it.'

Again he laughed, and he did a small jig then bowed low. She knew he was laughing at her, and she almost – just almost – laughed at herself.

They were coming closer and closer to the edge of the village and could see the lights twinkling from the houses. The track was smoother here and soon they would be on the cobbles leading to the main street. Freedom still walked at her side. All she needed now was for someone to see her – pray God it would not be Mrs Morgan or it would be all round the village by ten o'clock next morning. As if he could read her thoughts he stopped, bowed again, and without another word made to move away. This time Evelyne caught hold of his arm. 'Don't be a fool, mun, don't fight, don't let them arrest you, get away from here.'

Freedom's eyes went darker than dark, and his voice was soft but cutting, 'My people depend on the fight for their living. Money is scarce all round, but no scarcer than with us travellers.'

Evelyne told him angrily that his people would be a lot worse off if he were put in prison, which would certainly happen if the people arrested him. He turned on his heel, swishing at the air with the stick. 'They'll have to find me first.'

*

Evelyne let herself in by the back door. She was greeted by an irate Hugh who was worried stiff about her being so late and not letting him know where she was, and they had an argument for the first time in years. She accused him of not letting her know about his friendship with Gladys, a stupid, simpering woman if ever there was one. The stinging slap from Hugh shocked her and she lifted her fist to go for him, but he held her too tight.

'You'll take that back, you'll not say those things about her, it's jealous you are, girl, jealous, you who's too bound up in your books and readin' to find yourself a decent lad. They're all laughin' at you an' callin' you Doris behind your back. And by God, girl, you've got like her, with your mouth always turned down and your nose never out of paper!'

Evelyne countered this by telling Hugh he was behaving like a foolish eighteen-year-old, and making himself the laughing stock of the village with that Gladys. And as for her nephew! He was a pig-eyed, sweaty, revolting youth, it ran in the family. Wallop! She got another stinging blow and she backed away, scared; she had not seen Hugh so angry for such a long time.

Hugh started on about David – all that show about her going to Cardiff to find the boy she loved, the boy of her dreams. It must have been all fantasy because she came back with a face like a nun's, and a tongue so sharp no one could speak to her.

'What happened, Evie? Did he turn you down? Can you blame him, look at you, you act like an old woman ... dear God, gel, what are we doing, what are we saying? Come here, for the Lord's sake, come here.'

Evelyne went into her father's arms as if he were a long-lost lover. He held her, rocking her, kissing her hair, her neck, and saying sweet, soft things, taking back everything he had just said. She found herself kissing him back, she was so in need of love, so in need of physical contact that she was bursting inside. They were held suspended, staring into one another's eyes.

The crash of the door-knocker brought them round, and Gladys' voice, high-pitched and hysterical. Hugh let her in. It was Willie, he'd not been home since tea, and now it was one in the morning and she was worried stiff. No one seemed to know where he was.

On hearing that Willie was missing, Evelyne said that he had gone to the picture house to see the jazz film. 'Perhaps he met a girl there, Da? Wait, I'll come with you.'

She ran down the street after Hugh and Gladys, who were calling out Willie's name along the way. Lights were coming on in the houses, heads popped out of windows. Soon there was a trail of people behind them, like the children following the Pied Piper, everyone looking for Willie. Evelyne's heart hammered in her chest ... 'Dear God,' she prayed, 'let him have met someone and gone walking.' Anything but what she dreaded.

Gladys began to shiver with cold and Evelyne took off her greatcoat and slipped it round Gladys' shoulders, forgetting the newspaper clippings in the pocket.

By the time they reached the picture house the village bobby was wobbling along beside them on his bike. Evan Evans asked over and over what the fuss was about and slowly pieced the story together in his thick brain. 'The lad's missing, is that so? We'll get a search party out.'

'What the hell do you think this is, mun? That's what we're doing.'

The manager of the cinema, Billy Jones, lived in the house next to it. They woke him by hammering on his door.

'All right, I'm comin', I'm comin' ... ' He stood on the doorstep in his dressing-gown as they explained the problem to him, then fetched a torch and a huge bunch of keys. With everyone rushing him he had trouble finding the right keys to open the door. He took so long that Hugh wanted to belt him.

'There was not a soul left in the theatre, I'm telling you, unless he went to the gents'.'

Gladys, panicking now, wanted to know if Billy had definitely seen Willie.

'Yes I did, he was here nine o'clock just before the start of the film, *It's the Jazz, Man* – best houses I've had for weeks.'

Eventually he got the door open and they spilled into the auditorium, calling for Willie.

'Now, everyone, keep back, this is police work.'

Ignoring Evan Evans, Hugh bellowed for Willie, while Billy tried to light the gas lamps.

'Which bugger's got me torch? I can't see to light the lamps.'

As they walked around peering along the rows of seats, the lights came on. Billy, up on a ladder, looked down and screamed hysterically, pointing. Hugh pushed his way through to where Billy was pointing, looked for a moment and then turned, 'Stay back, Gladys, Evie. Don't come up here, any of you ... Evan, get the doctor.'

Gladys screamed and screamed, then fainted in a heap at Evan's feet. Evelyne moved cautiously between the seats.

'Aw, Christ almighty ... Holy Mother of God ...'

Willie lay between the seats. Blood from an open wound on his neck had formed a thick, dark pool which had already congealed. It was obvious from his open, staring eyes that he was dead.

Next morning the village was in an uproar. There'd not been a murder since 1905 when Taffy Ryse hammered his mother's head in, but then he was funny upstairs. Who would have wanted to kill Willie? They could all understand why Taffy had beaten his mother to death, she had been a right bitch, but Willie?

Doc Clock was limping badly from yet another car accident, and he was also getting old. He examined Willie's body and muttered that he was dead all right, which got everybody shouting at once that they'd already told the soft bugger he was dead – what they wanted to know was when it had happened. Doc Clock shrugged.

'How the bloody hell do I know – I've not been to the pictures since last year.'

Evan Evans was buzzing around with his notebook and a blunt pencil which he had to keep on licking. Doc Clock said he would give himself lead poisoning if he carried on. Poor Evan was out of his depth and was very swiftly pushed aside when a motor vehicle arrived with three uniformed police and a plain-clothes officer from the main station in Cardiff. They were all banned from the cinema and poor Billy was beside himself. He'd only got the film on lease and he had to send it back; if he couldn't let his customers in then how was he going to run his business?

The police searched for the murder weapon and drew chalk marks around the body before it was removed. They began questioning everybody who was known to have been in the picture house the previous night, and put out a request for any person not on their list who had been in the cinema or in the vicinity to come forward. A lot of folk, who were interested in the proceedings rather than having anything useful to say, couldn't wait to be interviewed. One of the harassed police officers was heard shouting, 'No, no, we're not interested in the week *before* the murder – just if you were in the picture house itself on that specific night or if you happened to pass it.'

Billy hovered and moaned as they closed the cinema, and begged to be allowed to open up before he went bankrupt. The police eventually conceded, and Billy opened up with a broad, white ribbon carefully hooked around five seats in two rows. He had never done such business in the whole time the place had been open. He played three shows a day with a Charlie Chaplin short in between for half-price. Not that anyone was watching the film, they were all agog at the blood-stained seat and took turns to sit close, whispering and pointing out to each other the bloodstains and the chalk marks around the spot where the body had lain. Mabel Hitchins, the pianist, drummed her fingers to the bone playing along with the films. Her neck was at a permanent angle from twisting round to tell the kids to leave the ribbons alone, they were police property.

For the three days that the murder investigation was centred in the village, Evelyne stayed indoors. She knew the police had questioned the gypsy men, and in fact seemed to have talked to everyone in the village. They mentioned nothing about the murder being one of the 'revenge killings', but there was an undercurrent of emotion among the villagers and the blame was laid on the 'gyppos'. The police were very firm, warning that there must be no vendetta between the miners and the gypsies. The law would handle the case, and once they had completed certain inquiries they would return to the village.

Hugh came home with the local newspaper and read aloud to Evelyne while she darned his socks. 'It's the gyppos, the police have been over the camp, got to be one of them, must be, police say there'll be an arrest any time now.'

The paper also stated that the murder had to have taken place during the second half of the last showing of the picture. This was because Mrs Dobson remembered selling Willie a toffee-apple. She remembered Willie very clearly because he had demanded his money back as the apple under the toffee had been rotten. The police placed the killing between nine thirty-five and ten fifteen. They also believed the weapon was similar to the one used to kill the boys in Cardiff: a thin blade, perhaps even a cut-throat razor. The gypsy camp had been searched, but they had found nothing.

Hugh shook his head and grunted, 'Be one of them vermin, sure as I'm sitting here.' He continued to read aloud from the paper, where it stated that no one at the picture house recalled seeing a gypsy at the box office. Nor had they seen any in line for Mrs Dobson's toffee-apples and coconut slices. This was also verified by Billy. Hugh jabbed the air with his finger. 'Too right, he said he wouldn't allow the buggers in his picture house anyways, not that many went in by the front door. Ask me, most of the audience slipped in the back way.'

He frowned, looking at the paper. Evelyne finished one of his socks and looked up. 'You'd think if anyone did see the killer they would come forward. It's common knowledge that most never pay at poor Billy's, though, so if they did speak up they'd have to admit they'd slipped in the back door too.'

Hugh sniffed, spat into the fire and jabbed his big finger at the paper. 'Says here they given orders for the gyppos to stay put until the police had finished accumulatin' their evidence, the way those lazy so-and-sos go about it I'm surprised they ever catch anyone. An' wouldn't you know there's not one man up at that camp who can't vouch for the others being up there all night, the bastards – killers, bastards!'

Evelyne had nightmares. She kept waking up sweating, going over and over the time she went from the house up to the camp. She was sure it was after nine. She remembered Gladys telling old Evan, the policeman, that Hugh had returned quickly because he wanted to hear something on the wireless at nine. The walk up the mountain would have taken her at least three-quarters of an hour. Freedom was there, she could see him clearly, dropping from the tree with that smile of his on his face. Could he really have slit that lad's throat and then laughed and joked with her? Walked almost into the village, right up past the picture house itself? The more she turned the evidence over in her mind the more she knew deep down that Freedom could not have killed Willie. Freedom couldn't because the time wasn't right, but what of Jesse? He had been at the camp, but she had not seen him. Had Jesse killed Willie? Freedom had told her Rawnie was now

Jesse's woman. She knew she should go to the police – knew it, but then she would have to go through all the questions about how she knew Freedom, how she knew about the rape, why she hadn't come forward before. Even worse would be the questions about the other lads' deaths. Why hadn't Evelyne said anything before? Told the police what she knew? No matter which way she looked at it, silence was the only way out, but it was giving her sleepless nights. She prayed for the fair to be over, for the gypsies to leave, and for the village to return to normal.

The terrible scandal began to die down and the Cardiff Constabulary returned to their station, leaving the 'Super Sleuth', Evan Evans, pedalling around the village with his notebook and pencil at the ready. They had found no murder weapon, and no evidence against anyone in the village or at the gypsy camp. Willie's body was sent back to Cardiff for burial, and without his corpse the Easter festivities began to pick up in earnest.

Life was so harsh that any reason for a moment's relief was grasped with both hands. The band marched through the streets and the choir sang their hearts out at Sunday service. Easter Monday came, and the Bank Holiday gave the village even more of a festive atmosphere; they were still poverty stricken, but the gaunt, grey, worried faces relaxed, if only for a few days. Children's money-boxes had been raided by their parents, and somehow the odd few coppers had been found for the Sunday fair.

The gypsy men were no fools, they knew they would be targets. Freedom warned them all to keep out of harm's way. Don't start anything, just let the folk spend their few coppers, read their palms. There was to be no fighting, they were in trouble enough as it was. He didn't have to say why; the hooded looks and downcast eyes were enough. The revenge was complete now.

Freedom wondered if Evelyne would come. He doubted it, but he was sure she had kept her mouth shut, but then he had known she would. He had even sworn as much to the men and women of the camp. The paleface woman was their friend, and they could trust her as they did him.

As the villagers prepared for the fair, the travellers got out their gladrags, set up their booths and tables, brought out all their wares to sell. The older women made doll's house furniture and small, carved flowers from wood chippings, which were painted bright colours. There were goldfish for prizes and headscarves hand-sewn with beads and embroidery.

The streets were filling up with families on their way up the hill to the fair. Evelyne closed her window and went down to make herself a cup of tea. She boiled a big pan of water and had an all-over wash, scrubbing her skin until it hurt, then brushed and brushed her hair. Then she went back upstairs and lay on her bed, listening to the sounds of the fair drifting down, the music, the laughter. Her mouth went tight, and she wondered if they would all be having such a good time if they knew what she knew.

Hugh had gone off to a meeting in another village, and Gladys said she would wait for him to return. She couldn't think of going to the fair, not after the terrible tragedy.

'Yes, lovey, you can, it'll do you good. When I've finished my meeting I'll come and collect you, walk you up the hill, just for a while.'

Gladys was dressed and ready. She fetched the coat she had borrowed from Evelyne and hung it in the hallway to give to Hugh. Noticing a mud stain on the hem, she tut-tutted and carried it into the kitchen to clean it. Humming to herself she wet a sponge and rubbed at the mud. As she turned the coat round she felt a bulge in one of the pockets, slipped her hand into see what it was and brought out all the newspaper cuttings Evelyne had kept so carefully. Laying them on the table she took out her glasses and began to read.

By the time she finished the last article her hands were shaking. Something was wrong, terribly wrong, and she had to have a glass of sherry to calm herself. Why, she kept asking herself, why had Evelyne cut these articles out of the papers, some were more than a year and a half old? She'd get Hugh to talk to Evelyne and ask her to her face just what was the meaning of it. Evelyne knew something, she was hiding something, and Gladys would find out what it was.

Chapter 11

M r Beshaley felt the train was going slow on purpose.
Twice he got up and looked out of the window, nearly
getting his head chopped off. He checked his gold watch and
drummed his fingers on the sill. A very elderly gent sat opposite him, staring into space with a pipe in his mouth. 'They
dinna go as fast as they used ta, it's the strike, see, fuel shortage,
it's slowin' everythin' up.' The old boy nodded, as if he had satisfied Beshaley as to the slowness of the train, and stared out of
the window.

Mr Beshaley had been in London, and had not seen Freedom
for nearly eighteen months. He hoped to God that Freedom
had kept himself in shape, the fight this evening was very important – more important than any other fight that Beshaley had
organized before.

He had been up in Scotland arranging a lightweight bout
with three of his men when he had been approached by a tall,
elegant man. Sir Charles Wheeler, with his cloak and cane, cut
a sharp figure in the new, fashionable double-breasted suit and
a brown slouch hat. He was a member of the British Board of
Boxing. A gentleman boxer himself in his youth, Sir Charles

financed professional boxing bouts all over England, searching out talent, and rumour had it that he paid big money when he wanted a man for his own team. He had acquired a gymnasium in London, filled it with all the finest equipment, and he recruited trainers and managers from all over England and America.

Beshaley had asked for an introduction, but it had proved unnecessary, because Sir Charles had come to Scotland with the sole purpose of meeting Beshaley. Sir Charles had seen Freedom Stubbs fight and thought the boy showed remarkable promise. More than that, he believed Freedom was a possible contender for the British Heavyweight Championship. Beshaley and Sir Charles discussed the forthcoming event at Devil's Pit, where Sir Charles could see Freedom fight again. Beshaley said he owned the boy, and he too believed him to be a rare boxer. He implied that he had spent considerable sums training Freedom and that he couldn't part with him without a contract that included himself – unless, of course, he was paid enough to release the boy.

Sir Charles had known immediately that Beshaley was lying and that he no more had a contract with the boxer than Sir Charles himself had. However, Sir Charles intended to rectify that.

While Beshaley was on his way to the railway station Sir Charles' automobile had cruised past. Through the open window he had smiled at him. 'No doubt we'll catch you at the fight?'

Beshaley wanted to run after the motor and demand a lift. He swore blue murder as he paced the platform, waiting for the train. He had to get to Freedom first and sign him before Sir Charles could approach him. The damned train was so slow he feared Sir Charles and his party would get there first, before he got the chance to make Freedom sign on the dotted line. They could be difficult these gypsy boys. Even though Beshaley was part Romany himself, he belonged to no clan; in his own terms he was an entrepreneur. Far from helping Freedom further his career, if anything he had stayed clear of him since the fight with Hammer. But he had overheard Sir Charles describing to one of his men how Freedom had brought a man down with a single body punch. 'Man punches like the Devil, and he's light on his feet, best I've seen for years', and Beshaley knew it was true and could kick himself for not having signed Freedom.

The train ground to a halt and he pushed open the window.

'There'll be a blockage on the line now, sir, mark me words. Some bastard'll have laid a log on the track. It's the strikers.'

Two guards walked through the compartment and when Mr Beshaley approached them, they told him curtly that there was engine trouble and they would be on their way as soon as possible. Beshaley gave one of the men a shilling to see if they could hurry things along, he had an important appointment. The guard could hardly believe his luck, and assured Mr Beshaley he'd get the train moving within minutes.

Sir Charles adjusted his driving goggles and tried to make sense of the road map. His two companions were hunched against the wind, wearing heavy coats and goggles, their hats pulled down low. Ed Meadows was a huge man with an ex-boxer's face, his nose broken so many times it had remained flat after his last bout, the bridge pulverized. He looked up at the sign-post and shook his head. They'd passed it three times to his knowledge.

'You sure you know this place, guv? Only, we been past this post three times now, an' wiv the night comin' on – I don't fancy us drivin' round all night.'

Sir Charles turned and put big Ed in his place with his upper-crust English voice.

'You'll find this lad's worth it when you see him, Ed. Now come along, chaps, let's have a good gander at the road map again.'

Ed shivered and hunched further into his greatcoat. In his twanging, cockney voice he told Sir Charles to stop at the next village and ask – it was the only way round these parts. There was more than one Devil's Pit, and they could get the wrong one.

Dewhurst, Sir Charles's valet and butler, sat stiffly next to his master in the front seat. He turned his pink face to stare up at the signpost.

'There's a village two and a half miles further on according to this, sir, perhaps it would be better to ask there.'

Ed threw up his hands in despair, 'That's wot I just suggested, but nobody listens to me. I said stop at a village, these ruddy Welsh signs don't mean nuffink.'

Sir Charles pulled his goggles down, started the motor, and they headed for the village. They were actually close, within ten miles, but the winding paths around the mountains were mis-leading. There was only fifteen minutes before the match was due to start.

*

233

The afternoon over, many of the villagers made their way home, clutching their small token prizes. The children began to whine, they didn't want to leave the fair and yet they were so tired they could hardly keep their eyes open. The men hung around the camp, still playing on the coconut shy and throwing 'six darts for a ha'penny'. The see-saw had done a great trade and the teenage boys were now, as the dusk fell, shoving and pushing each other to have a go for a farthing a time.

The atmosphere was becoming tense, the groups of lads hanging around and knots of older men hunched in corners, smoking. The gypsies' eyes were everywhere, and some of the men nodded to their women to pack up and get ready to put the tables away. A fortune-teller's booth swathed in canvas like a Turkish tent had been doing a roaring trade, but now only a few boys hung around outside, their hands stuffed into their pockets.

Freedom's opponent, Taffy Brown, had arrived at the camp-site two hours earlier. With his two aides he had wandered around and had a few goes on the coconut shy, but he was so strong that one of the balls had not only knocked the coconut off its stand but split the stand in two. This had raised cheers from the spectators and disgruntled moans from the gypsies. The balls, bright reds and yellows, had been 'lifted' from snooker tables, and quite a few pubs would be missing them.

The younger lads drifted over to the shy, cheering Taffy on, nudging each other as, enjoying the attention, he rolled up his sleeves. His muscular arms bulged, and he moved further and further away, then went for the stall at a loping run, throwing the ball overarm as if playing cricket. The ball ripped through the canvas amid even more cheers.

Two gypsies, knowing there could be trouble, yelled that the fight was due to start at any time in Devil's Pit, which made Taffy turn and roar, arms up in the air, for his opponent to show himself.

'He's waitin' for you, Taffy, he's waitin' at Devil's Pit, mun.'

The gypsies were relieved when the miners began to drift off towards the fight.

Devil's Pit, which lay a couple of miles from the campsite, was so called because the mountain curved out in a huge arm, enclosing the dark, flat earth in jagged rocks. Not even grass would grow there. Below the pit tumbled a waterfall, the water making strange moaning sounds which all added to the eeriness of the place, as if a soul bound in the earth was trying to get out.

Some of the men from the camp had gone ahead with a wagon to prepare the site. The ring was simply marked out in the dirt with ropes hanging from crude posts at the corners. They were raking the ground flat and pulling benches from the wagon to place around the ring.

The men formed a line outside the rocky entrance. An entry fee of threepence was charged, and for this the men got a single sheet of paper which announced forthcoming events in London at the famous Premierland. It also gave details of Taffy Brown's previous bouts. Taffy had a good record, and had so far never been knocked off his feet. His manager was sure he was world champion material, but he knew Taffy had to have more experience before going to London. This match against the man who had almost killed the famous Hammer was perfect for him.

Taffy's men looked around for Freedom, but he was nowhere to be seen. They presumed he was in the covered wagon parked at one side of the dirt ring, more than likely shaking with nerves. They took Taffy back to the car and he sat with his trainer, talking tactics. Taffy wanted to know more about this gyppo, and his trainer gave him details of the three bouts he had seen Freedom fight. Two he had lost, but then it looked like a fix. The third was Hammer and the rest was history. Taffy wiped his nose with the back of his hand. 'Not quite, mun. Gimme the rounds one by one. I seen Hammer fight, he was a big bastard, this lad must have a lot of weight behind his punch. Was it a body or a head punch that floored him?'

'The lad's good, Taff, but that's not the reason we're a bit on the edgy side. We've heard Sir Charles Wheeler is goin' ter show, and we want you to be part of his stable. You know how we feel, we know you can go to the top, but we need backing, we need money. It took all we had to get these leaflets printed. We even need the few bob from this bout, but if Sir Charles sees your potential then we'll all of us be in clover.'

Taffy had heard of Sir Charles, the 'gent of boxing'– everyone on the circuit had – but to think he was coming up here to this godforsaken place was beyond Taffy's comprehension. Roberts could see him hesitate, understood why, and put his arm around Taffy's shoulders. 'Wipe him out, Taffy, that's what you're here for. The lad's got the press writin' about him, because of those murders. You drop him on the canvas and it'll be *you* they'll be writin' about, and next stop it'll be the belt. That's what you've dreamed of, isn't it?'

Taffy had more than dreamed of it – it was his one goal in

life. They saw him straighten up, clench his fists, and they knew they'd have the fight they wanted.

As if on cue, the roar of a car's engine coughing its way up the hillside heralded the arrival of Sir Charles himself. He pulled on the brake and looked around the pit, shaking his head. He'd certainly been in some out-of-way places looking for fighters, but never halfway up a mountain before.

'Gor blimey, guv, you sure they're not bringing the dogs up 'ere, don't look like a boxin' match to me.' Ed sniffed and hugged his coat closer. 'Bloody cold fer Easter, ain't it?'

As debonair as ever, Sir Charles seemed entirely unruffled by his long journey. He opened his brandy flask and drained it. Already he could see the line growing at the entrance, and below them men were heading up the mountainside in force. He passed his flask to his valet who nipped round to the boot of the car to refill it. The men crowding around were uncouth, shouting and carrying beer bottles.

'I think, sir, if you don't mind, I will stay inside the vehicle. I'm sure someone will try to remove your cases.'

Sir Charles laughed, then pushed his way through the crowds to look over the ring. He was pleased to note that there was no sign of the wretched man Beshaley. It would be difficult to miss that loud checked suit.

The crowds cleared a path for Sir Charles and nudged each other, nodding to 'the toff'. Sir Charles gave Taffy a courteous nod. Taffy watched him and grunted, he'd give him his money's worth.

Freedom sat in the wagon, his bound fists ready, arguing with Jesse. Freedom was angry that he was still around, having told him to leave days ago. But Jesse had disobeyed and returned for the fight. Jesse grinned, he would steal a few wallets tonight, and one from the gent in the big motorcar. Not that he mentioned it to Freedom, he just said they needed all the hands the camp could provide – and anyway the law had left the village. The crowds were bigger than expected and the takings had to be counted. Jesse rubbed his hands with glee – money, money.

Twice a boy from the entrance came with a sack of coins, tipped them into a box and rushed out again.

'Where's Rawnie, Jesse, I told you to keep her out of this.'

Jesse opened the flap of the wagon and hopped down, reassuring Freedom that Rawnie was safe, back at the camp. No one but their own had seen them return, there was nothing to fear. Freedom sighed. Jesse was a madman, he knew it, to kill the boy here in the village, in the picture house, was an act of utter madness. The police had searched every wagon, every trailer, and Freedom knew it would not end there. The law would follow them from town to town, searching, questioning. He clenched his fists, the fight far from his thoughts, preoccupied with Jesse and Rawnie. She had changed profoundly since that night at Cardiff, not that anyone could blame her after what she had been through. Freedom had detected a cold hardness in her, she would no longer come near him, curl up beside him. If anything, she would turn away if she saw him.

Rawnie and Jesse were inseparable, as if they had secrets between them, their eyes constantly gliding to each other's, giving sly, soft giggles, their hands entwined. Freedom found them unnerving when they were together. True, he had tracked the boys down for Jesse, but then he had stepped aside because, as Jesse said, it was no longer his business. It was Jesse who was exacting vengeance. He had tried to reason with Jesse and the results had caused friction within the camps. Freedom chose to move on, and joined up with various other bands. Some whispered it was because he was scared, others murmured that it was Freedom's name that was connected to the revenge killings and it was right that he should protect himself.

The Easter fair was a big money-earner for the travellers, and as there was a fight going they sent for Freedom to rejoin them. That was the only reason he was here, but it had angered him when Rawnie and Jesse appeared. He watched Jesse through the flap. He strutted around the makeshift ring, arrogant, cocksure, and the miners stepped aside. Behind his back Freedom saw them give the sign of the fist. Freedom knew the signs, and was sure there would be more than one fight tonight.

The miners already outnumbered the gypsies by ten to one, and a restless murmur was growing as they began to take their seats. It was gone six o'clock, and still the fight had not begun. The referee jumped up into the wagon, a pleasant-faced man from Glamorgan who had refereed many bouts between the gypsies and the miners. 'Now lad, keep it clean, I want no head-buttin' and no kicks, any punches below the belt an' I'll disqualify you. Make it a good fight, there's someone out there from the professional circuits watchin', so don't let's make a monkey of this, understand me?'

Freedom smiled, nodded briefly and asked if the ref. was giving the same lecture to the miner – any head-butting usually came from that side, not the gyppos. The referee checked Freedom's fists and gloves, and spoke a few words to the young lads with his bucket and stool.

'Thirteen rounds, lads, three minutes per round. When the bell goes you get into the ring, and not before.'

The crowd was now very restless, and torches were lit to illuminate the arena. The beer was being swilled down, and a couple of men who had brought a crate of beer were doing a fair trade selling bottles. It was home-brewed, tasted like stewed apples, and had a hell of a kick to it, but no one minded, they were getting thirsty from shouting for the match to begin.

Hugh read the newspaper cuttings about the killings in Cardiff. Gladys was distraught, and angry.

'She knows something, Hugh. All this time she's known something and not said a word to anyone. When was she in Cardiff? Remember that time she went away and came back here like she'd seen someone die? It's the same time, Hugh, look, read for yourself.'

Like an omen, the roar of the crowds echoed down from Devil's Pit.

Evelyne was surprised to see Hugh when he burst in through the back door.

'Hello, Da, I wasn't expecting you back so soon.'

Hugh threw her big overcoat on to the kitchen table, then dragged the newspaper cuttings out of his pocket. He waved them in front of her nose. 'Come on, out with it, gel, what's all this? An' don't tell me it's just morbid curiosity, there's more to this than meets the eye, isn't there? And by God I want it, all of it! Poor Gladys is at her wits' end. This Freedom fella's fighting up at Devil's Pit right now, an' if he's the one murdered our poor Willie . . .'

Evelyne let rip. ' *"Our . . . ?" What do you mean, "Our"?* That little bugger wasn't ours, Da, he wasn't worth the worry we all had, he had it coming to him!'

Hugh stared in horror as she faced him, arms folded, with such a look of fury on her face he was astounded. He threw the papers at her. 'The lad had his throat cut by those vermin and that's all you can say about it, he had it coming to him? What kind of woman are you?'

Evelyne turned away from him and he walked out, slamming the door so hard the house shook. Why hadn't she told Hugh the whole story, why hadn't she told him now? She knew it was because of Gladys, and she felt guilty. She went up to her room and from the window she could see Hugh and Gladys running up the road. If she cut across the fields as fast as she could and up the other side of the mountain, she could get to Freedom before them.

The crowd roared. The two boxers were well-matched, and both around the same weight. Even though Freedom was five inches taller, Taffy had the extra inches in muscle, his solid body straining and sweating as he threw punch after punch. Freedom was up to his old dancing tricks, as light on his feet as a woman. He seemed to be running rings round Taffy.

'Git the bugger to sit still, Taffy lad!'

They were already into five rounds, with neither boxer giving points away. They were even and both looked strong enough to go to the distance. The bell clanged and they split up, heading back to their corners. They were both filthy from the earth and coal dust they kicked up as they fought. Taffy panted and gulped at the water, spat it out and looked at Roberts.

'He's the toughest I've had yet, you buggers, he's like a ruddy fly dancing around me.'

Roberts rubbed Taffy down and he kept up a steady flow of instructions. 'Tire him, let him dance his feet off, he'll soon slow down, but don't stop the punches hitting home.'

'What d'ye mean, don't stop 'em, I'm trying hard enough and can't get at him, he's clobbered me twice.'

Roberts could see that Freedom's punch had caught Taffy's right eye, which was swelling up like a tangerine.

Throughout the break the crowd yelled, 'Tafffyyyyyyyyy ... Taffyyyyyy ... ' No one shouted for Freedom, the gypsies sat silent and watchful. They were acutely aware of the growing drunkenness on the far side of the ring, and the echo of the men's voices combined with the gurgle of the waterfall made a horrible, rumbling, guttural noise. Like animals they were baying for blood.

Sir Charles sipped from his brandy flask, gazing at the black-haired gypsy through half-closed eyes. He watched the lean body swerving, dodging, the strong legs keeping up the strange dance steps, and wondered how long the man could keep up such a movement. He didn't seem to tire in the least, but one look at his opponent told him the big Taffy Brown was starting to tire. Sir Charles knew that the lad was waiting for an opening – knew Freedom was merely toying with the Welshman – and he was excited, grinding his teeth, a habit he had had since childhood. The lad was even better than he had been told, like a wild animal. But the most important thing about him was his intelligence. He was playing for time ... an intelligent boxer? Unheard of!

Trying to predict when Freedom would knock Taffy out, Sir Charles turned to Ed and saw the same dazzled look on his friend's face. 'What do you think of him?'

'Gawd help us, he's beautiful, just beautiful, what I wouldn't do to get me 'ands on 'im, work wiv 'im.' 'E's world-class material guv, look at 'im, dancing round like 'e was fresh as a daisy.'

Evelyne raced up the path, her breath heaving in her chest. She cut her hand on the brambles as she jumped the stream, but kept on running.

Rawnie was washing out Jesse's clothes. There was no visible sign of anyone but she could hear the sound of running foot-steps. She straightened up, her hackles rising. It was clearer now, someone running, and running fast ... there was fear, and Rawnie's dark eyes flashed around the dark mountainside.

Evelyne gasped for breath and rounded the curved pathway, with still a good mile to go. She paused as another massive roar echoed down from Devil's Pit. The next moment her heart lurched as a scrawny hand gripped her hair from behind and a razor-sharp knife pricked her throat. Her legs went from under her as a hard kick from hobnailed boots cut into the backs of her knees. She fell forward, and felt her hair torn out by the roots. Screaming with agony and fear, she rolled over and found her-self looking straight into Rawnie's face.

Rawnie's eyes blazed, the knife held high, and Evelyne shouted 'Rawnie! Rawnie!' As if a cloud had lifted from her face, Rawnie relaxed and backed away from Evelyne.

'Remember me, Rawnie, it's Evelyne ... Rawnie, it's me, the girl with the red hair, look, I wear your earring, see?'

She pushed back her hair and showed Rawnie the gold hoop earring. Rawnie stared, and Evelyne saw the small, clenched hand loosen its grip on the knife, and then Rawnie sat back on her heels and smiled.

'*O lelled thee for a jal a moskeying, an you as almost mullo mas.*'

Evelyne didn't understand and Rawnie explained, 'I thought you were a spy, you were almost dead meat.'

Evelyne got to her feet, still panting for breath. She had to find Freedom, had to speak to him. Rawnie pointed up to the mountain. Freedom was still fighting, the roars of the crowd echoed down.

It was very difficult to explain to Rawnie, but Evelyne told her of the newspaper cuttings and how they were discovered in her pocket. She didn't mention the possibility that her father could cause trouble, just that the men might turn nasty. She wanted to warn Freedom – warn the whole camp that they should leave. Rawnie laughed and asked what the papers said about the killings.

'This is hardly the time to discuss it – the fact is the villagers will believe Freedom guilty.'

Rawnie looked closely at Evelyne and then turned away, her voice soft and quiet, strange. 'Thee don't believe this to be true, but the *gav mush* do, is that so?'

Evelyne looked puzzled, and Rawnie told her that *gav mush* was the law, then she spat on the ground. She had changed so much, there was something chilling about her. Still as beautiful, but there was a nasty, sarcastic edge to everything she said. Her eyes were expressionless, then mocking, and she waded into the stream to prevent Jesse's shirt from floating away. She slapped it on to the bank, and lifted her skirts high.

'Thee washed me down that night, thee saw the marks on my body, what you say should be done to those that had their way with me? What you say, paleface? Let the *gav mush* smack their filthy hands that pawed and prodded into my body? Smack their hands and say, "She was only a gyppo whore"?'

Evelyne shook her head as the cheers carried down from Devil's Pit, and they could have been back in Cardiff inside that nightmare tent. Rawnie rolled Jesse's shirt and laid it on a rock, banged it, twisted it. She seemed in no hurry to help Freedom.

'I'm Jesse's *manushi* now, he made me *romms* him to show he didn't care what those vermin had done to my body. I wear his ring now, I'm Jesse's woman.'

Satisfied the shirt was clean, Rawnie shook the wet material and then in a strange movement wrapped the wet shirtsleeves round her waist and gave Evelyne a slant-eyed look. Rawnie moved closer and closer to Evelyne, her eyes hypnotic, just like the time she had read Evelyne's palm.

'I'll tell you the *tatcho*, paleface, only you'll know, and I can see in your *yocks* ye'll not betray me, *mande mui*.'

Closer and closer she came until her hands traced Evelyne's face. 'We done each one – one by one – an' Jesse let me have their throats, look into their eyes before the blade was drawn across.'

Evelyne stepped back, afraid of her.

'The best was the last, sucking on his toffee-apple, and I was right behind him, just a small move and . . .'

Rawnie flicked open the razor-sharp knife and cut through the air. She laughed delightedly at Evelyne's shocked face, then she turned in one sweeping move, her voice trilled '*Kushti rardi*, Evelyne', and she was gone.

Evelyne called after her, but the girl didn't turn back. She heard another roar of men's voices, cheering in unison and ran towards Devil's Pit, hoping to God she could get there before her father.

Gladys hammered on the post office door, looking up at the windows and calling for Ben Rees, the postman. His wife opened a window and called down that they were all at the fair, Gladys shouted that she had to use their telephone to call the police. Hysterical, she screamed that the killer, Freedom Stubbs, was up at Devil's Pit.

By the time Gladys had got through to the police a group of women had gathered outside the post office. In murmurs and whispers they passed the name of Freedom Stubbs among them. Lizzie-Ann, always one to be in on anything going on, came rushing up. The garbled story gained detail. Evelyne Jones knew the killer, he was one of the gyppos, and he was boxing up at Devil's Pit.

'Let's get up there and warn the menfolk. We'll get the bugger even if the law can't.'

Rolling pins were hastily collected, and one woman who had armed herself with a heavy frying pan swung it around, saying she'd take first crack at the vermin. Lizzie-Ann fuelled their rising tempers, telling them that Evelyne Jones knew more than she let on. Schoolmistress she may be, but why hadn't she shown anyone what the newspapers said? She'd concealed evidence, that's what she'd done. Half the women were illiterate and would never have read the papers anyway, but, egged on by

Lizzie-Ann's bitterness towards Evelyne, they went on the march, fists clenched and rolling pins at the ready, heading for the Devil's Pit.

Mr Beshaley was beside himself, there was not a soul at the station, even to collect his ticket. There wasn't a horse or a cart, nothing insight, and Devil's Pit was a good five miles up the mountainside.

Doc Clock chugged by in his precious motor. He'd been up at Mrs Morgan's on an emergency call, only to discover it was her dog that was ailing. The poor animal was very old and couldn't understand that with the strike on Mrs Morgan didn't have the money to put in the purse for him to take to the butcher. He was turning nasty, hanging on like grim death to the shopping bag and biting anyone who tried to take it from him. Doc Clock's thumb was bandaged to prove it.

As if that wasn't enough, the Doc was confronted by a lunatic in a dreadful suit who demanded to be driven to Devil's Pit. Beshaley took out his fob watch and looked in desperation at the Doc. 'The fight, I've got to get up there to see the fight,' he said, 'I'll pay you whatever you ask – anything – it's a matter of extreme urgency, sir, I beg you.'

Doc Clock tooted his horn as he rounded a curve on the narrow mountain track, and smiled to himself. At long last he'd got a watch on the end of his chain. Beshaley held on grimly as the old motor bounced and swerved along the unlit track. Twice he thought they'd go over the edge, but the motor somehow weaved its way back to the centre. They could hear the cheering and shouting, and Beshaley stood up, banging on the windscreen, and bellowed for the Doc to go faster.

Evelyne stood on tiptoe at the back of the screaming crowd, but she couldn't even see the men fighting. She pushed her way through the crowd and, spotting Jesse, made her way towards him.

'Jesse . . . Jesse? Do you remember me? . . . Jesse?'

He shrank away from her, wondering if she'd seen him lift the man's wallet. His eyes narrowed and he turned to dart back into the crowd, but Evelyne caught his sleeve, and then he recognized her by her red hair tumbling down from her schoolmistress's bun. She was Freedom's paleface friend. Jesse could barely hear what she had to say over the roar of the crowd, but when he understood they weaved and elbowed their way through the men to the opposite side of the makeshift boxing ring where the gypsy men watched the fight together. He squeezed his way among them, cupping his hand to their ears and whispering, and they passed the message on.

Evelyne looked at the ring and shuddered. Freedom and Taffy were in the centre, Taffy bleeding badly from a cut below his eye. Jesse moved like a dart, in and out between the men, then he returned to her side. 'The wagon's yonder, git outta here.'

He slipped away so fast that Evelyne had no time to grab his arm, and the gypsies were quietly leaving, one by one. The combined noise of the waterfall and the men's voices was deafening, and across the ring she could see fists raised as the miners yelled, 'Take the man out, Taffy!' Over their heads she could see her father, way over on the far side, shoving his way towards the ring. His face was set, he looked vicious, and he too was shouting, but she couldn't make out the words.

The bell clanged for the end of the round, and Freedom walked abruptly to his corner and sat down, snorting through his gumshield. He was surprised Jimmy One-Eye didn't take it out of his mouth, and where was the water? Then Jimmy leaned over and cupped his hand to Freedom's ear. 'Go down, mun, first punch go down, they know who you are, all hell's gonna be let loose – police'll be here, we're gonna have to do a runner.'

Hugh was close to the side of the ring, pointing at Freedom and yelling at the top of his voice, '*Killer! Killer!*'

The men around him tried to hear what he was saying and Evelyne could see him making gestures, slicing his hand across his throat and pointing again to Freedom.

Taffy's corner men worked hard, rubbing the big man down, plastering Vaseline over his swelling face. Taffy was heaving for breath and trying to listen to his trainer's instructions. He gasped with pain as they painted his cut then flapped their hands and blew to dry the paint. It was smarting so badly his eyes were watering, but he could have been weeping. His hopes of the Heavyweight Championship were dimming – he couldn't even get near the bastard.

The bell clanged, and Freedom was up on his feet before the clapper was still. He looked fresh, his breathing under control but his body glistening with sweat. Taffy lumbered into the centre and hunched up, somehow he knew he was going to get it, that was it, he knew it was coming, but he wasn't going to let the gyppo get him down easily.

Freedom opened up his defences and looked as if he'd walked into the right uppercut. Over he went, falling back against the ropes, which sagged under him. The crowd went berserk and Taffy gazed in astonishment at the slumped body, the ref. bending over him, counting and waving his arms. The crowd joined in as he counted.

'One ... two ... three ... four ...'

Beshaley ran from the Doc's car just in time to see Freedom take the final punch. He slumped against the rocks, feeling as if he himself had been hit, winded. Through the celebrating crowd he could make out the tall figure of Sir Charles and was about to push forward to talk to him when he saw Taffy's manager. Sir Charles was shaking his hand, congratulating him.

Doc Clock panted over to Beshaley, muttering that nobody had told him about any fight. Beshaley had paled visibly, and the Doc was concerned, but he was bodily moved aside by a group of women. 'Dear God,' he thought, 'what is the world coming to when women are watching boxing matches?' He was walloped on the back with a frying pan, and spun round.

'Oh, sorry, bach, didn't recognize you!' said the woman.

Taffy was riding high on the shoulders of two miners, and the make-shift ring was swarming with men, dancing and yelling, while Hugh Jones stood in the centre, screaming for quiet, his arms waving and his face bright red with fury. *'Quiet ... Quiet ... Listen to me, will you listen to me!'*

Freedom went inside the wagon while Jesse organized the hitching of the horses. Outside the wagon the noise of the men was diminishing, and one voice was raised high above the rest, a voice screaming, 'Murderer! Murderer!' The wagon rocked as the horse was backed into the shafts. Hugh Jones was slowly getting the men to listen, despite the added din of the high-pitched screams of the women who had just arrived. 'The police couldn't find him and they been lookin', we got him right here, here amongst us ... Freedom Stubbs killed Willie, slit his throat, are we gonna let him get away with it?'

Evelyne put her hands over her ears to shut out her father's voice. She wanted to turn and run – run away from the madness echoing round the mountain like the Devil himself. She stood up and tried to get to her father's side.

'Turn the wagon over, get him out, get him out!'

Evelyne was within feet of her father, screaming at him to stop, but a clod of earth flew through the air, narrowly missing her head.

'Tell us what you know, Bitch! *Bitch*!'

Frying pans and rolling pins thudded down on heads, the women were screaming and pointing at Evelyne. A man grabbed Evelyne from behind and held her arms. 'This is the one, she's known all along ...'

Now Hugh was fighting to get to his daughter. Evelyne pulled her arms free and lashed out at her father with her fist.

Miners swarmed around the heavy wagon, heaving together to overturn it. The horse reared and kicked, striking a man on the side of his head. The wagon rolled forward, heading directly into the crowd around Hugh and Evelyne, and the men and women sprang away in fear for their lives.

Jesse whipped up the horse and lashed out at a man who tried to bring him down from the wagon. As they careered through the crowd, Freedom leaned out of the back and grabbed Evelyne by the waist. She tried to fight him off, but she was lifted off her feet and hauled on board as the wagon bounced and rumbled through the crowd.

251

Chapter 12

Hugh stood in the ring, or what was left of it, the ropes trailing on the ground. His initial fury had subsided, he knew he had been wrong, but he couldn't understand his daughter – his own daughter had raised her fist to him in front of the whole village. He stood still, shaking. What in God's name had got into her? Suddenly he took off after the mob chasing the wagon.

Evelyne clung for dear life to the side of the wagon, terrified. Behind them the mob followed, running down the mountain. Freedom yelled to Jesse to keep clear of the camp, lead the madmen away from their people, take to the main roads. Evelyne wept, begged to be let out, but Freedom ignored her and clambered up beside Jesse. The wagon rolled from side to side as the dirt track wound and curved. The running figures were now a good distance behind them. They passed the entrance to the campsite, and Jesse handed the reins to Freedom. He jumped down as Freedom whipped the horse faster, leading the mob away from the camp. They could see that the camp was already packed up, the caravans in line, set to move out. Alone in the back of the wagon, Evelyne was bruised and battered against the sides, and still she held on.

The sound of the wheels clattering on cobbles told Evelyne they had arrived in the village. The horse slowed its frantic pace and stopped.

'Stop in the name of the law, now get down, hands above your head, come on, you vermin, do like we say, get down.'

The wagon's flap was pulled open and a policeman who looked inside shouted that there was a woman on board. At the same time Evelyne heard a voice asking, 'You the gyppo they call Freedom Stubbs?'

They were already putting the handcuffs on him by the time she stepped down. He made no effort to escape, did nothing to stop them handcuffing him, and said not one word. They hauled him roughly towards the police van, and even though he made no effort to evade arrest, one of the policemen brought his truncheon down hard on the back of his neck. He slumped forward, and they dragged him like an animal into the cage at the back of the van, locking and bolting it just in time as the mob appeared at the top of the village street.

The men and women were quieter now and, seeing the uniformed police encircling the van with truncheons at the ready, they kept their distance. 'Keep on walking now, come along, get back to your homes, the show's over. Come along now, keep walking, everybody keep walking.'

Slowly, they moved in groups past the police van, their interest directed first at the van, then at Evelyne. The women shot foul looks at her, then turned their faces away.

Hugh walked to his daughter's side and laid his hand on her arm.

'Don't touch me, this is your doing, this is down to you, Hugh Jones, I'd have thought you had more sense.'

Lizzie-Ann passed by and heard Evelyne's words, and muttered an abusive, bitter, 'gyppo lover'. The other women nearby picked up the phrase, murmuring quietly but clearly as they passed the wagon, 'gyppo woman, gyppo lover.'

Hugh stood still, head bowed, and Gladys whimpered and slunk to his side. The police van was cranked up and the engine chugged into life; then it headed for the police station with Evan Evans, flushed and apologetic, hurrying alongside.

Evelyne walked, head held high, back to Aldergrove Street. She knew they were all looking at her, talking about her, and she kept her eyes straight ahead. She was comforted by the thought that behind them all the caravans would be silently moving out, at least they had not torn the campsite apart.

Hugh wanted Gladys gone; he wanted to talk in private with Evelyne, but Gladys clung to his arm. He sat her down, then folded his arms, staring hard at Evelyne. She met his gaze head on, defiant.

'Now, Evie, out with it, we have a right to know.'

In a quiet, dead voice, Evelyne told them the truth. 'I was at a boxing match in Cardiff, remember, Da, the time I went by myself? I don't want to go into the details of how I got there, but I went to a boxing fair. There was a riot, and I was leaving, but I had to go back inside the tent for my bag, I'd lost my handbag.'

Gladys stood up and demanded to know what on earth this had to do with Willie's murder. Evelyne pushed her down and leaned over her.

'Because when I went back I saw a poor gypsy girl being raped, not by one but by four lads. An' they'd worse than raped her, they'd taken a bench leg to her.'

Gladys screeched at the top of her voice, 'You sayin' Willie had something to do with it?'

'*I saw him, he was on top of the girl* . . . it was me that pulled him off by his hair, and I'd swear to it on the Bible, you want me to swear it on the Bible?'

Gladys shook her head, repeating over and over that she couldn't believe it – not that boy, not her sister's boy, he wouldn't do a thing like that.

'He did it, Gladys, he was one of those lads, the poor girl. I'll never forget her face.'

Hugh brushed Evelyne aside. 'That's enough now, come on, Gladys, I'll walk you home.'

He helped Gladys to the door, and just as he went out he gave Evelyne a heart-broken look. She couldn't meet his eyes, the look was filled with so much hurt, why hadn't she told him?

Freedom sat in the small village gaol that had only ever housed the poor lunatic who had bashed his mother's head in. Evan Evans ponderously filled in all the forms. His prisoner was to be taken directly to Cardiff to answer the charges there. Evans had to endorse the charge-sheet accusing Freedom of the murder of Willie Thomas.

*

Doc Clock, very irate, appeared to report the theft of a gold fob watch. He was insistent, never mind the ruddy gypsy, his new gold fob watch had been stolen right off the chain he had just put it on. Evans took down all the particulars, and waited until the Doc left, before he tore up the description of the fob watch. 'He's not had a watch attached to that chain for more'n fifteen years. We should have a word with the Medical Board, he's past it, the silly old fool.'

Mr Beshaley sat in Rawnie's wagon. He swung his gold watch on its chain, fingered it and replaced it in the pocket of the checked waistcoat that matched his suit. He had used that watch to bribe people on several occasions, but he had always been able to steal it back. 'Ye think he got himself away then, do ye?'

Jesse shrugged and put his feet up on the shelf, Freedom would be all right, he murmured. Mr Beshaley pursed his lips, what a wasted night it had been, all this way and for what, to be almost mobbed. He had never even got a chance to talk with Sir Charles Wheeler – maybe to get him interested in one of his other boxers.

Rawnie, with her skirts hitched up over her bare knees, smoked a hand-rolled cigarette clenched between her teeth. Perched up on the boards she held the reins loosely between her fingers, clucking for the horses to move on, then flicked a whip across their backs. She began to sing, low, husky, as if she had not a care in the world.

> Mande went to poov the gry, all around the stiggur sty,
> Mush off to Mande, I takes off my chuvvel,
> I dels him in the per,
> So ope me duvvel dancin Mande cours well.

Inside Rawnie's caravan Jesse was held by her husky voice, he smiled at Beshaley, and lowered his thick, black eyelashes.

'Freedom always was a loser, tonight he proved it.'

He joined in singing with Rawnie, their voices as soft as each other's. Beshaley shivered, they seemed so close, these two, and he felt like an intruder. He couldn't wait to get to Swansea. The pair of them unnerved him.

Hugh climbed the stairs, heavy-hearted. He could see the gaslight beneath Evelyne's door. Before he reached the door she opened it and stood, hands on hips. 'Well, what have you heard?'

Hugh shifted his weight and mumbled that they'd taken the gypsy to Cardiff, and the word was he'd be hanged.

'What if I was to tell you he didn't do the killings, none of them, it wasn't him?'

Hugh said that was for the courts to decide. Evan Evans was in the pub telling everyone that the gypsy had said not one word, which in Evans' eyes proved that he was guilty.

'If what you said about Willie is true, then so help me God I'm for the gel, but that's no reason to slit a man's throat – *more* than one.'

Evelyne snapped that more than one boy had raped Rawnie, and turned to go back into her bedroom. Hugh caught her arm. 'Tell me how you know so much, miss? Why you had the papers, why you showed your fist to your father in front of the whole village?'

Evelyne pulled her arm free and pushed past him, back into her bedroom snapping that he'd no need to worry, she'd not been touched by any of them.

'Where you goin'? Evie?'

She kicked the door to behind her, shouting that she was going to Cardiff. Hugh kicked the door back open again, his temper rising. 'Like hell you are, you stay out of this, you've done enough as it is.'

Evelyne was pulling clothes out of a drawer and throwing them on her bed. 'It's you who's done it, Da, you, you're power-mad since you got into that union. They hang him and they'll hang an innocent man.'

As fast as Evelyne took out her clothes, Hugh stuffed them back in the drawers, his temper mounting, and he shouted that she was not to leave the house.

'I was with him, Da, the night Willie was killed, I was with him, and I'm going to say so, he couldn't have done it.'

Hugh pulled her roughly to him, his hand raised to strike her, and she stared at him, stony-faced. 'Go on, hit me if it'll make you feel better, I was with him but not in the way you think. God help me, I went up there to warn him.'

Hugh slumped down on to the bed. He couldn't understand her. He shook his head and rumpled his hair. She still opened and closed the drawers, taking out what she needed. She brought a cardboard box out from under the bed.

'Don't get involved, gel, trust me, leave it be ... unless ... does this lad take your fancy, is that it?'

Evelyne threw up her hands in despair. 'No, I just know he didn't do it, and I can't live with myself knowing what I know ... Oh, Da, I should have told you before, everything, but I just couldn't, I just couldn't.'

He patted the bed beside him and she sat close to him, resting her head on his shoulder. Slowly, piece by piece, she told him about the night in the boxing tent in Cardiff. The terrible humiliation she had suffered, the money she had taken from David, money she'd been so ashamed of, and at last her bitterness came to the surface. She made no sound, but he knew she was crying and he cradled her in his arms.

'Being poor, Evie, is nothing to be ashamed of, one does things in a life that're much worse.'

She looked up into his sad face and asked if he was thinking of little Davey, and he nodded his head. He still held his big arm around her shoulders, but he stared vacantly ahead. After a moment he rose and walked to the window, drawing back the curtains to look out into the dark night.

'I was quite a lad, you know, when I was a youngster. Easter fair was always a night out for the lads. She was telling fortunes in a small booth – not like they have now, it was decorated with painted canvas, sort of draped – and you paid a ha'penny for a palm reading. By God, Evie, she was a beauty, not like your ma, different, exciting to young bloods, and we was all after her. See, we couldn't lay a finger on the local gels, not without their mothers coming around with their rolling pins ... Anyways, I set out to capture the little dark-eyed wench, all the while cocksure of myself, telling the lads I'd have her. She said I was to come back at midnight, she'd leave the caravan door ajar. Well, I had my night with her, and the next day three of 'em came prancing down the street, seems she wasn't no ordinary gyppo, but one of high blood. They dragged me out and up to their fields and all of them set on me, even the old man threw in a few punches. I was handy with me fists so I gave as good as I got, but me pals hadda carry me home.

'Next morning, black-eyed and aching all over, I made my

way to the pithead, an' she was there, waitin' with a small bundle under her arm. Seemed the family threw her out, see, an' there she was waitin' for me with her bangles and beads and the little bundle tied up with string.'

Hugh turned from the dark window. He seemed heavy, sluggish, and eased his body down on to the bed and lay flat, his eyes closed. 'Maybe if the lads hadn't been gathered around I'd have acted different. I just laughed at her, Evie, told her to be on her way with the rest of her vermin.'

He leaned up on his elbow and fingered Evelyne's slip which was lying across the bed. 'Her eyes went black, like a cat's, and she lifted her hand and gave me some kind of sign, she didn't scream or shout, it was husky, her voice, that's what made it worse, the strange softness of her words . . . She cursed me, Evie, said I'd have no sons to bury me.' He put his arm across his face and his whole body shuddered as he wept, his voice muffled. 'By Christ she was right, I've seen them buried. God help me, Evie, she was right.'

Now it was Evelyne's turn to hold her father gently, wipe his tear-stained face. She said that maybe it was fate, fate that made her cross the path of the gypsies.

'I'll leave for Cardiff on the first train, Da, all right?'

The mist clung to the top of the mountain, the grey rain drizzled, making grey, cobbled streets shine. As Evelyne turned at the corner to wave to Hugh at the bedroom window, he felt a terrible sense of loss, as if he would never see her again.

Evelyne passed three women standing at the water taps. They turned their backs to her and whispered. Evelyne held her head high and walked on.

'You'll not be teaching my kids, Evelyne Jones, you dirty gyppo lover.'

A group of men leaving their house for the early shift called to her and raised their fists. 'You should know better, Evelyne Jones. Our lads not good enough for you, eh?'

Their laughter echoed down the wet street, and she hunched her shoulders as if to defend herself from their malice. She crossed the street so she wouldn't have to face another group of women who stood waiting for the post office to open. They, too, stared at her then turned and whispered to each other. She gave them a frosty smile and almost bumped into Lizzie-Ann dragging the two kids and a pramful of laundry.

Evelyne stopped, and Lizzie-Ann had the grace to blush – she had, after all, thrown a clod of earth at Evelyne the night before. 'Well, where you off to at this hour, thought a woman of leisure like you would have a lie-in of a wet morning?'

Evelyne murmured that she was on her way to Cardiff.

'Going to see your boyfriend, are you? Better make it fast before they hang him.'

Evelyne looked into Lizzie-Ann's face. Her hair hung in rat's tails, her coat was stained, her legs bare and her shoes so worn that her heels, red and raw, were showing.

'That's right, go on, take a good look at me, Evelyne Jones, nothing a few pounds wouldn't put right, but then you're such a tight bitch, you'd not a give a beggar a farthing.'

Evelyne banged her cardboard box on top of the pram and pulled Lizzie-Ann to her by the lapels of her coat.

'What have I ever done to you, Lizzie-Ann, to make you talk like this? Tell me now, I don't deserve it and you know it.'

Lizzie-Ann pushed Evelyne away, her voice rising hysterically.

'You've always been too good, haven't you? You give me a roof over me head but begrudge a shilling for food, you're a hard one, Evelyne Jones, you always were . . .'

Evelyne felt sick. She couldn't fight Lizzie-Ann, there was nothing to say. She picked up her cardboard box and turned away.

'Don't you turn your back on me, Evelyne . . . *Evelyne* . . . *Evie!*'

There was such desperation in Lizzie-Ann's voice, it made Evelyne turn. Old before her years, beaten, roughened, the prettiest girl in the village had gone, and in the big, pansy eyes was a terrible, heart-breaking desperation. For a fleeting moment Evelyne wanted to hold her, but the accusing voice persisted, 'Where you going? Cardiff is it? Oh, well, all right for some, go on, there'll be more than one person pleased. You should stay there, your poor Da can't get up the courage to tell you he wants to get married, go on, you won't be missed.'

A few of the women joined in, chipping in their farthing's-worth.

Evelyne was already walking away, knowing Lizzie-Ann was trailing behind.

'Take the deeds to Doris' house, take them, just like you took everything, without a thank you.'

Head high, she strode off, clutching her cardboard box in front of her. Lizzie-Ann broke down, propping her swollen, sagging body against a filthy brick wall. She cried out, but her voice was distorted with tears, 'Oh, I wanted to go to London . . . oh God, I wanted to go to London.'

*

Somewhere out of the past Evelyne heard the soft, sweet voice of her mother repeating, 'Get out of the valley, Evie, don't let it drag you down,' well, she *would* get out, and she would never come back, there was nothing left for her here.

As she paid for her ticket, her mouth trembled, and she had to bite her lip until it bled to stop herself from crying. She had only one goodbye to say, it cried in her throat, the sound of the train's steam hissing and the 'chunt, chunt' of the engine drowned her words, 'Goodbye, Da, goodbye, Da.'

BOOK TWO

Chapter 13

Evelyne walked up the stone steps of the police station in Cardiff and stood at the high counter. The sergeant on duty gave her a pleasant smile. 'What can I be doing for you, ma'am?

Taking a deep breath, Evelyne coughed. 'I have information regarding the murders of the four boys. I would like to make a statement, and I am prepared to go to any court and swear on oath that what I have to say is God's truth.'

The sergeant rubbed his head and leant on the desk. 'And what murders would these be, young lady?'

'The gypsy revenge killings ... my name is Evelyne Jones. I want to make a statement.'

Half an hour later, after she had related everything to the sergeant, she was taken to meet the detective chief inspector. The sergeant held the door open for her and placed a stack of forms on the inspector's desk.

'I think you'd better listen to what this lady has to say, sir.'

The inspector listened attentively to every word, nodding his head and refilling his pipe. He puffed and stared at a spot on the wall just above Evelyne's head.

'And that, sir, is the truth. I was with Freedom Stubbs the night he is supposed to have killed Willie Thomas, and I'll stand up in court and say so.'

The inspector tapped his pipe and began to scrape at the bowl. He chose his words carefully, because asking this tall, stiff young woman if she was 'familiar' with the gypsy was a delicate matter.

'I know him only as someone who helped me on the night of the rape, that is all.'

The inspector felt she was withholding something, she knew more than she admitted, but he had to take her statement and pass it to his superiors. The statement took an hour and fifteen minutes to complete, and Evelyne's meticulous handwriting and perfect spelling impressed everyone.

'I see you've put no address down, Miss Jones, where are you residing in Cardiff?'

Unable to think of where she would stay, Evelyne bit her lip. A large poster behind the inspector caught her eye – it was an advertisement for a charity ball at the Grand Hotel.

'I'll be at the Grand, Sir.'

He looked at her for a moment then carefully wrote down the name of the hotel.

'Will Mr Stubbs be released now?'

Evelyne's innocent question made them laugh, it wasn't as simple as that. The man was charged with murder and one statement was not good enough. There were, after all, three more murders with Freedom Stubbs the main suspect in each case.

'Will I be allowed to see him?'

The men flicked sly glances at each other and then back to

Evelyne, looking at her from top to toe. One of the uniformed men said it could possibly be arranged.

'Thank you for coming in, Miss Jones, and we will contact you at the Grand Hotel if we feel it is necessary.'

As Evelyne walked out of the office, she heard a chuckle behind her and the inspector speaking to one of the officers, 'I'm sure Miss Jones will be at the Grand, lads, I'm sure.'

She felt humiliated, and realized she had accomplished nothing, and they were laughing at her behind her back. She took a deep breath, decided she would have a good breakfast and think about what she should do next. She would have breakfast at the Grand, and book a room there.

When she reached the Grand Hotel she realized why the inspector had been cynical about her staying there; it certainly lived up to its name. Even the steps up to the lobby were covered with thick-pile red carpet, and there was so much braid on the uniformed doorman's jacket he looked in danger of being tied up in it permanently. He inclined his head to her, haughtily, and swung open the big brass doors with 'The Grand' painted on the glass in gold.

Once inside, Evelyne felt even more overpowered by the ornate building. The lobby was busy with residents and porters everywhere, and a bellhop loudly calling a name, trying to deliver a telegram. The head clerk Mr Jeffrey, wearing an immaculate black jacket and pin-striped trousers, looked up sharply as Evelyne tentatively rang the bell on the desk.

Evelyne almost dropped the cardboard suitcase when she saw the prices of the rooms. A heavy smell of perfume wafted past her nose, and a woman with two tiny parcels tied up with

ribbon held her hand out languidly for her key. The clerk grov-
elled and bowed, placed a key into the kid-gloved hand and gave
Evelyne a sidelong look.

'Room twenty-nine, Lady Southwell.'

Evelyne glanced down at the brochure and noted that her
Ladyship had a suite on the third floor.

'Do you have a room vacant on the third floor?'

'The third floor is suites only, modom.'

Evelyne was getting hot, a flush creeping up from her toes.

'I'll have a suite, then.'

The suite was decorated in different shades of pink, the twin
beds draped and canopied with tiny, fluffy pink mats beside
them. The bathroom was huge, marbled, and more luxurious
than any she'd ever seen in a magazine. Bath salts, courtesy of
the hotel, stood in a neat row. The water smelt lovely and she
stayed in the warm, scented bath until her skin wrinkled.

Her scrubbed face shining, Evelyne walked through the lobby,
aware of Mr Jeffrey's scrutiny. She gave him a small, prim nod
and nearly walked into a palm tree. A painted board on an
easel announced the opening hours of the various dining-
rooms.

'The Grand Hotel is pleased to offer guests the choice of
three dining rooms . . .'

Evelyne chose the tearoom. The small tables were painted
white and laid with white linen cloths, the upholstered chairs
also in white, and there were potted palms scattered around the
room. A trio played on a corner stand, and the few customers
spoke in whispers.

The Legacy

Evelyne selected a table at the far side which gave her a good view of the whole tearoom and the lobby from behind one of the palms. A waitress in a neat black dress with a frilled white cap, pinafore and cuffs promptly placed a menu in front of her. The toasted teacakes and pot of tea tasted better than anything she had ever made at home, with jams in tiny individual pots. Hot water was brought to freshen Evelyne's teapot without her even asking, and she ordered another round of teacakes. She was loading butter on the hot bun when she heard a familiar voice.

'My darling, forgive me, I'm late, but I simply couldn't get away earlier, children's wretched teaparty – have you ordered?'

Evelyne peeked around the large potted palm to her right and saw Freddy Carlton just about to sit down at the next table. He seemed to have aged. His neat moustache was waxed at the ends, and he wore a pale blue shirt with a stiff white collar and narrow black tie with his brown pin-striped suit. She could just see a tiny gloved hand as Freddy raised it to his lips and kissed it as he sat down. Parting the thick leaves of the palm tree, Evelyne peered through.

'We don't have long, dearest, I have some shopping to do. I've ordered tea, are you hungry?'

Evelyne let go of the palm. Lady Primrose laughed softly, and Evelyne saw Freddy lean closer to her. She was sure Freddy kissed her, and in public!

'Is it you? I saw you from the staff door, is it you, Evelyne?'

This time Evelyne was so startled that she yelped. There in front of her was Miss Freda with a large tray of toasted scones.

'Shush, not too loud, yes it's me, Miss Freda.'

Freda beamed at Evelyne, her frizzy hair trapped beneath a frilled white cap.

'I work here now, I'm not supposed to talk to the customers, but I will bring you over some cakes . . . shusssh . . . then maybe we can meet and talk, yes?'

'That would be nice.'

Evelyne was thrilled to see Freda, but a little worried about Freddy and Lady Primrose, at the next table. Freda gave her a little wink and scurried to her customer's table, getting a stern look from a stout woman with an enormous bosom who was taking up her position at the pay desk.

While Evelyne eavesdropped on the conversation between Freddy and Lady Primrose, several waitresses passed her table, each depositing a cake in front of her with a wink. She ate her way through a piece of strawberry gateau, a cherry pie, and a large white meringue filled with fresh cream, and still they kept coming.

Rising to his feet, Freddy leaned once more across the table.

'Can we meet this afternoon? I can't bear being apart from you, it's been three whole days, will you call me and I'll arrange a room?'

'You'd better leave, darling, they'll be arriving . . . I'll call you, I promise.'

Evelyne hid behind her napkin as Freddy walked past her table. One of the waitresses blocked him from view as she laid a paper bag by Evelyne's plate.

'Freda says for you to put the ones you can't eat into this, but careful, she's got eyes in the back of her head.'

Evelyne looked at the woman behind the pay desk while the waitress cleared Freddy's teacup. She slipped three cakes into her paper bag and put it beneath the table. As she raised her head she found the woman with the huge bosom looming over her.

'Your bill, madam.'

Had she been spotted? Evelyne flushed, but the woman pivoted on her heel and made her way around the room, depositing more of the little pink slips on other tables.

Freda sidled over to Evelyne. 'Where are you staying?'

'I'm here, room twenty-seven ... I mean, suite.'

'Here? You are staying *here*? Well, I'll see you later.'

She whizzed away through the swinging kitchen door, thinking to herself that Miss Evelyne certainly must have more money than she knew what to do with.

Holding her bag of cakes close to her side, Evelyne gave two shillings to the stern-faced woman with the bosom, and her sixpence change clattered down a chute. She struggled to get it out with one hand, afraid to lift the other to reveal the bag of illicit cakes.

'Do come again.'

Turning quickly away she bumped into Sir Charles Wheeler, who stepped aside and apologized then surveyed the room from behind his monocle. The cashier beamed and led him to a small booth, murmuring that she felt sure Sir Charles would find it suitable. He sat with his back to the room and opened a copy of *The Times*.

Evelyne pressed the lift button and waited. The brass was so highly polished it was like a mirror, and she adjusted a stray curl of hair ... then her heart stopped.

David Collins strode in to the hotel, paused to smile at the manager, flicked his gloves off and walked towards the tearoom. He looked handsomer than ever, wearing the latest Prince of

Wales single-breasted suit, a tie with a Windsor knot, and carrying a brown trilby. With an ingratiating smile the fawning cashier directed him to Lady Primrose's table.

The lift gates clanked open.

'Do you want to go up? Madam, *up*?'

The snooty bellhop doubled as lift attendant during teatime. 'Third floor.'

Evelyne stepped out of the lift and the boy nearly caught her coat as he slammed the gates shut behind her. On the carpet outside her room lay a newspaper, and looking up and down the corridor she saw that there was one outside each door. At least something was included in the price of the suite.

The headline ran in big, black print: 'Gypsy to stand trial for killings.' Ed Meadows paid his twopence and opened the paper as he made his way to the tearoom.

'Yes, have you booked a table?'

Ed stared around the room then pointed to Sir Charles' table. The cashier was aghast, the man looked dreadful in a shabby suit and down-at-heel shoes. She was about to stop him when Sir Charles laid down his newspaper, turned, and gestured for the new arrival to join him.

'Well, guv, that's the gyppo up the spout, you seen the 'eadlines, they got 'im not fer one murder but free . . . I dunno, what a bleedin' waste.'

Freda stood by the table as Ed looked over the menu. 'You got eggs an' bacon, somefink like that, eh?'

Sir Charles raised his eyebrows and turned to Freda. 'Welsh rarebit, for two please, and a pot of coffee.'

Her legs aching, Freda moved off, jotting down the order as

she went. She was tired and wanted to sit down, but she had hours to go yet.

Ed leaned across the table. 'I just come from Taffy and his manager's place, the man was cut bad an' I'd say it'll open up again first bout he has, be at least five weeks before he's healed up, an' he's pudgy, you know, not in good nick at all.'

Sir Charles frowned. 'You think the knockout was fixed, what?'

Ed spread his chubby hands and sighed. 'Guv, that gyppo could've 'ad 'im in round one, what a fighter, it's tragic – it's bloody tragic. Far as I could make out old Taffy was bleedin' surprised to floor the gyppo 'imself. Now, 'is manager was givin' me the old story, yer know, about Taffy's bein' famous for 'is left uppercut, but I said, I said, do me a favour, mate, the punch was a wide, open-'anded right, couldn't 'ave floored a flyweight wiv it, never mind a big'un like Stubbs.'

Sir Charles mused, fiddling with his cutlery. 'So . . . we forget about Taffy, what? He may be useful as a sparring partner, but I doubt anything else.'

'You ask me, guv, 'e's ready fer the knacker's yard. I got a theory, see the 'eadlines? Now, yer know the police was after 'im – what if he got tipped off and done a runner, like? *Hadda* go down 'cause 'e knew the law was on to 'im? That's the way I sees it.'

'Either way, old chap, we come out the losers. Pity, really felt that fellow Stubbs was champion material, damned shame, but then these gyppo fellows are not to be trusted . . . Ah, jolly good, breakfast!'

Freda placed the Welsh rarebits in front of them. Ed stared in horror. 'Gor blimey, what in hell's name is this?'

Freda put down the coffee-pot and a jug of hot milk.

'Will that be all, sir?'

Sir Charles nodded, picking up his knife and fork. 'Try it, Ed, it's quite tasty.'

Ed poked at his plate, then sighed. 'Fair breaks me 'eart. What a fighter, they'll 'ang 'im ... We goin' back ter London then, guv?'

Sir Charles carefully cut through his toast. Yes, they would return first thing in the morning, he had some relatives he might call on. Ed looked at the orchestra and began to hum along, 'Tea for two ... ' Then he took an enormous mouthful of rarebit, chewed and pulled a face.

'Sooner the better, I've 'ad enough of Wales, Welsh rabbits an' all ... can't taste any meat in this, more like cheese ter me.'

During her lunch break Freda went to Evelyne's suite. She took a great interest in the furnishings, then flopped down on one of the single beds, exhausted. To Evelyne she seemed happy-go-lucky as she related, with little shrugs, the story of her business failing and the fact that she was working to save for another shop. Secretly, Freda wondered where Evelyne was getting the money to stay at the Grand. Perhaps she had some cash to spare and they could go into partnership together.

'So why are you here, Miss Evelyne? Ah, I know, you are getting married, is that it?'

Evelyne laughed. 'Far from it.' She explained at length why she had come back to Cardiff, while Freda lay with her eyes closed, listening. She didn't mention Jesse and Rawnie by name, just the basic facts of Willie's murder.

'I'm a witness you see, Freda, that's why I'm here, I know he didn't kill that boy. Freedom is innocent, and I want to help him.'

Rolling over on the bed, Freda propped her frizzy head on her hands and scrutinized Evelyne. 'But it is not just one killing, is it darling? Perhaps he did not kill this Willie boy in your village, but what of the three murdered here in Cardiff? Goodness, I've read terrible things, such scandal, everyone has been frighted, it's like Jack the Ripper.'

Freedom Stubbs was no Jack the Ripper, Evelyne told her.

Recovering some of her energy, Freda sat up and swung her legs over the side of the bed. They didn't reach the floor.

'We shall go to see him, that is what we must do. But first, and I hope you don't mind me saying this, your dress is very drab, you must look smart, not like a schoolteacher, really smart . . . do you have the money for some clothes?'

Evelyne answered evasively, not that sort of money, and studied her reflection in the mirror. Freda looked her up and down, she was so thin and had grown even taller. For a small price, she suggested, she could alter Evelyne's clothes, perhaps they could buy some secondhand things.

'You will feel more confident, and I can do it very cheaply, what do you say?'

Smiling sweetly as Evelyne agreed, Freda took out a tape measure, saying that she never went anywhere without it. She departed with two pounds ten shillings of Evelyne's money, assuring her she could do wonders with it.

When she had left, Evelyne counted her remaining money. She had been 'paid' with two five-pound notes last time she had been in Cardiff, and now she was putting them to good use. As Freda had taken most of her few clothes to alter she couldn't go out, so she lingered in yet another soapy bath, her thoughts on David. She wondered if he knew what was so obviously going on between his wife and his best friend Freddy.

The following morning Evelyne was astonished at how fast Freda had worked. Her hemlines were up, and the new buttons on her old coat made it look quite nice.

'I will have a dress ready soon, your skirt and blouse will do for now, and perhaps if you can give me a few more shillings you can have a nice new hat.'

The desk sergeant remembered Evelyne, but refused her permission to see Freedom. Miss Freda launched into a furious speech about citizens' rights, and said that if he didn't allow Miss Jones to visit the prisoner, she would write to all the newspapers. After that they were kept waiting for half an hour, but permission was granted. They were sent to another building, where again they were kept waiting, until a tall prison warder with a set of big keys on a waist-chain approached them.

'Miss Evelyne Jones, please?'

He led her to a bare room where Freedom was sitting at a wooden table, handcuffed, an officer standing beside the door. Another officer stood outside, where he could see into the room through a small window set in the door for that purpose. Freedom had no idea why he had been brought out of his cell and sat, head bowed, staring at his hands. His hair was unruly, uncombed, and his face already dark with stubble.

As the officer left he locked the door behind him, after informing Evelyne coldly that she had ten minutes. Freedom was stunned and made to rise, but was immediately pushed back into his chair by the officer. Evelyne sat in an identical chair opposite Freedom. Now that she was here she didn't know what to say to him and could see that he was dumbstruck by her appearance. She could smell him, his heavy body odour, for the man had not been allowed to bathe since his arrest.

His shoulder-length hair was greasy and hung limp, and when he lifted his hands to move it back from his face she could see his handcuffs.

The presence of the police officer loomed over them both, and for a good two minutes neither said a word. Evelyne placed her hands, with the neat, square, shining nails, on to the table. 'I have come to say you were with me the night Willie was in the picture house. They say in the papers that you'll be standing trial for all the killings and that you'll hang.'

Freedom looked into her eyes, and then turned to look at the prison officer. His voice was so quiet, she had to lean forward to hear. 'So be it, and I thank thee for coming, God bless you.'

Evelyne leant even further across to him, trying to make him look into her face, but his head remained bowed. 'You can't just accept it, you can't, because I know you didn't . . .'

Freedom looked up, his face was hard, and now his voice was firm, though still not loud. 'You know nothing, go back to your village, *manushi*, go back, this is not your business. Forget what you know – she must never be mentioned, understand me?'

She knew he meant Rawnie, and she leant back against the wooden chair. He was prepared to say nothing, prepared to hang . . . she couldn't believe it.

'Will you do nothing? Freedom . . . ' His name sounded hollow and foolish, and he turned to the officer and jerked his head for the door to be opened. The officer banged on the door with his wooden baton and it was unlocked from outside. With a hesitant look at the officer, Freedom waited to be allowed to stand.

'Do you have proof that you were not in Cardiff for the other killings? Freedom? Where were you? Freedom?'

Standing, Freedom dwarfed the prison officer who only came up to his shoulders. He didn't look back but walked straight to the door, and it was not until he bent his head to avoid the doorframe that he turned to look back at her.

His dark eyes were expressionless, black, his powerful arms bound by the handcuffs. He was like a magnificent wild beast trapped by man, unbowed and undaunted. He gave Evelyne a quick, unfathomable smile, then he was gone.

Miss Freda linked arms with Evelyne as they walked away from the prison. The girl was silent, her body stiff, her hands cold to Freda's touch. One of the prison officers had walked through the waiting room and mentioned to another that the gyppo killer had not said a word during his time in the jail.

'That his woman in there with him, is it? She'll do no good, he's for the rope and he knows it.'

Miss Freda still did not know the truth behind Evelyne's visit, surely it could not just be because she believed the lad innocent, there must be more than that.

In the middle of the street Evelyne suddenly stopped, her face angry, eyes blazing.

'They'll not hang him, Freda, I won't let them, he's like a child in there, a foolish, stubborn child.'

*

Together they returned to Freda's small lodgings. The room was cluttered with hatboxes, and in pride of position in the centre of the room was Freda's sewing machine. From the garret window Evelyne could see a long line of men waiting for the dole, and there were children begging in the street.

'I won't let them hang him, he's innocent, I'm going back, and I'll *keep* going back until they take me seriously and do something about it.'

Freda patted her arm soothingly and at the same time tried to measure her for a sleeve.

'I don't want a new dress, Freda, I'm sorry, I'm not going to walk away from him, I'm going to make him see sense, I have to.'

Frightened that Evelyne would ask for her money back, Freda wanted to weep. She was so short of cash that she'd already spent the two pounds ten on back rent. 'You seem so sure he is innocent – I know, don't get angry . . . I know you say you were with him, he could not have killed that boy in your village, but Evie, what of the others?'

Evelyne still stared down at the growing line of poverty-stricken, unemployed men. 'He's killed no one, I know it, there are things I can't speak of . . . but I will, I'll make him let me.'

Back at the prison, at first the warder was most unhelpful. Evelyne refused to budge, she had to see Freedom Stubbs, and it was her right. The prisoner was entitled to a lawyer. She opened her purse and took out a shilling. 'And you'll have another after I've seen him.'

She was taken to the visiting room and told to wait. At long last, after two hours, she heard the footsteps of the warder returning.

'You got two minutes and then he has to go back, I'll lose me job, ma'am, I'm trusting you to behave yourself.'

Evelyne clenched her fists, nodded her head. Another fifteen minutes passed before she heard the sound of keys turning, iron doors opening and closing, and then heavy footfalls. Freedom was ushered in, head bowed, lips tight.

'He didn't want to see you, ma'am, so much for all your trouble . . . now, *you*, sit down, I'll be right outside the door.'

They were alone, and she sat opposite him.

'We've got two minutes, so let's not waste it. Will you listen to me, Mr Stubbs? If you won't help yourself then I am going to do it, whether you like it or not.'

His teeth were so tightly clenched she could see a muscle twitching at the side of his mouth. He refused to look up.

'Now then, I have the time of the murder at the picture house, and I know for certain I was with you. Now where were you on the other occasions? I'll check out your whereabouts and try to prove you were not in Cardiff when the other lads were killed. Are you listening to me? Will you not stand up and fight? Fight for your own life?'

Still he was silent and she could feel his anger. She leaned forward, whispered, 'I'll give you my word I'll not mention Rawnie, or Jesse, I'll not ever say their names, and that's God's truth.'

Her face was close to his, her hands on the table, and he moved so fast it shocked her. His shackled hands reached over and grabbed her wrists hard, hurting her, and she was frightened.

'Woman, go away, you've no business here.'

For the first time he looked into her frightened face, and then he moaned, rubbed her wrist softly.

'I didn't mean to frighten you, girl, I'll not hurt you.'

She swallowed, he was still holding her wrists, she could see where the handcuffs had cut into his skin. She eased her hands away.

'Do you not understand? They'll say you're a gyppo lover, just like I heard them screaming at you when I was inside the wagon. You'll be treated like dirt – you'll get no respect, they'll drag your name in the muck alongside mine.'

She slapped the table between them. 'I don't care, I want to help you, can't you understand that, I *need* to help you?'

He cocked his head to one side and looked at her, repeating the word 'need' as a question. Evelyne bit her lip and felt the tears welling up. She sniffed. 'Oh, you won't understand, but I never see things through, you know? I've not even taken my examinations, I'm not a qualified schoolteacher, and then, well, last time I was here . . . I've never had the fight in me, not for myself. I'll fight for *you*, I want to see you released, I want to give you your name, Freedom.'

A tear trickled down each of her cheeks, and he lifted his hands to wipe them away, but she recoiled. 'I don't know what I'm crying for. It's you that should be weeping, will you not stand up for yourself, man? I'll stand alongside you, I give you my word, and I've got a bit of money for a lawyer.'

The key turned in the lock, and Freedom stood up. He was walking to the door of his own free will. At the door he stopped, his back to her, and his voice was so soft she could only just hear it.

'Take your fight, *manushi*, take it for yourself, there's naught ye can do fer me. Don't come back, I don't want to see you again, I won't see you . . . walk away if you know what's best, and get your teaching qualifications.'

He was gone, the visiting-room door stood open and the warder was looking at her. 'All the same, ungrateful animals, you wasted your time. Go on, love, go home.'

She handed him his shilling, and he looked at it, then looked her up and down. He shook his head. 'Keep your money, lovey, you look as if you could do with a good meal inside you, now go on, go home.'

Freda watched as the coppers, the shillings and a half-crown tumbled out on to the sewing-machine table. 'You love this man, Evelyne, is that what it is?'

Evelyne was stunned, her mouth dropped open. She had never thought of that. 'Good heavens no, he's a gypsy, Freda, but that doesn't mean he has no right to a fair trial . . . Oh, I feel so good, elated, you know. I'm doing something really worth-while, and what's more I'm going to see it through . . . I'll be at the hotel, I'll leave the dresses and things to you, just make sure you make me look like a real lady.'

Freda was rendered speechless. She wondered if Evelyne was one of those suffragettes she'd read about, they were always going on about people's rights.

'Remember, Freda, if I look good in court then people'll want to know where I got the clothes from, you'll be back in business, what do you say?'

Freda picked up the money and was already delving into her pattern book as Evelyne ran down the wooden staircase.

Ping! went the desk bell, and Mr Jeffrey whipped round, picked up the key to suite twenty-seven and banged it on the desk.

'Will you want a table reserved for dinner, Miss Jones?'

Evelyne turned to him, and for the first time she wasn't in any way ashamed or embarrassed. 'Not at those prices I won't, thank you.'

She was off to the lift before Mr Jeffrey could close his open jaw. Good God, she's got herself a suite and now she was acting up like she was a duchess.

The lift-boy was about to clang the lift shut on Evelyne's coat when she turned and gave him a look. 'Just you try it, lad, an' you'll get the back of my hand. Time you learnt some manners.'

Ed Meadows was tapping on Sir Charles Wheeler's door when he overheard Evelyne's remark. He turned to her and grinned.

'Good on yer, gel, cheeky little blighter, ain't 'e?'

Evelyne smiled, picked up her evening newspaper and put her key in the door.

'You from round these parts, are you?'

Evelyne had already opened her door and gave him a rather frosty look. Being friendly was one thing, but he was a little too chatty. 'I'm from the valleys, good evening to you.'

Getting no reply from knocking on His Lordship's door, Ed waddled towards Evelyne.

'I'm from London, suppose you can tell by me accent I'm not Welsh, I'm up 'ere wiv me guv'nor, name's Meadows, Ed Meadows.'

He brandished a rather dog-eared card at Evelyne.

'Boxing promotor and trainer, 'Ackney, London.'

Evelyne took the card and gave a curt nod, then realized she was behaving a little rudely.

'Evelyne Jones.'

As they shook hands, Sir Charles appeared at the door of his suite. He was dressed in a plum-velvet smoking jacket. Ed Meadows turned, then stepped back and introduced Sir Charles to Evelyne. Very debonair, Sir Charles strode up to Evelyne and kissed her hand. 'Charmed to meet you, are you staying long?'

He wasn't frightfully interested whether she was or not, and was already heading back towards his open door. Ed beamed at Evelyne and followed the guv'nor, telling him before Evelyne could open her mouth that she was from the valleys. About to enter his suite, Sir Charles smiled. 'What a coincidence, we were there only the other night. Well, nice to meet you, good evening.'

The door closed behind them and Evelyne entered her own suite. She bumped the door closed with her behind and tossed the keys on to the bed. Typical Londoners, think there's only one valley . . . and then she pulled up, and Sir Charles' words click-click-clicked in her brain. Surely that titled gent couldn't have been to her valley . . . but it would make sense, that man . . . Evelyne fished in her pocket for Ed's crumpled card, bit her lip, and then before she could change her mind she strode out of the suite and along the corridor.

Dewhurst opened the door to Sir Charles' rooms, and stiffly enquired if she had an appointment. Behind him Ed Meadows bellowed, 'Who is it?'

Sir Charles was sitting at a small desk. There was a big fire in the grate and there were so many doors leading off the main room that for a moment Evelyne thought she had got confused, perhaps he lived at the hotel, surely he wouldn't have all this space just for one person? He fixed his monocle into his left eye and looked at Evelyne. 'Ah, yes, now what can I do for you?'

Evelyne's nerve almost deserted her, but she blurted it out as fast as she could. Had they been to the Freedom Stubbs fight? She was a friend of his and he was in prison, but he wasn't guilty and she wondered if they could advise her what she could do. Her knees buckled slightly as she finished, she could feel the flush creeping up her cheeks.

Sir Charles leaned back in his chair and his monocle popped out. He swung it on the end of the black ribbon round his neck.

'Dewhurst, bring the young lady in. I'm sorry, please forgive me, I didn't catch your name ... ? Ah, Evelyne, yes, yes of course, a drink, dear? What would you care for?'

Evelyne said sherry because it was the first thing that came into her head, and Dewhurst placed a chair for her close to the desk and backed out of the room. Ed Meadows moved to stand behind Sir Charles, and asked Evelyne what she knew of the gypsy and how was she involved. 'They say he's killed four lads and you say different, that right?'

Sitting in the cosy, firelit room, Evelyne told them what she knew, took them right back to the first time when she had seen Freedom fight Dai 'Hammer' Thomas. She was taken aback because Ed Meadows kept interrupting her, asking all sorts of questions about other fights she knew of, had she seen him fight anywhere else in Wales? Did she know about the knock-out in the ring the other night? Sir Charles eventually put his hand on Ed's arm and, looking directly at Evelyne and speaking very slowly, asked again why, exactly why, she had come to see him.

'Because he's innocent and I can prove it. I've offered to go into court, and I just don't think they're going to pay any attention to what I have to say, but I *know* he didn't do those murders.'

Sir Charles listened intently to Evelyne's story, then excused himself, leaving her alone with Ed.

''E's a bit of a toff, but 'e's a real gent, know what I mean, a true blue, an' take it from me I know what I'm talkin' about, nothin' he don't know about the game, he's even bin to America, United States of America, you know, oh yeah, 'is Lordship's a real pro, was a fighter 'imself, see.'

They both turned to the closed doors, and Ed, without stopping except to swallow gulps of his frothing black Guinness, continued. 'Nineteen-o-eight there was the Aussie fella, Jack Johnson, Gawd almighty what a fighter 'e was, saw that big'un with Jim Jefferson, nineteen-ten, July fourth, you heard of the Great White Hope? I was there for that wiv 'im, 'e took us both over. But yer fighter knockin' 'em all into the corners is Dempsey, the man's a joy ter watch, a joy ter watch, I was there, an' guess who was sittin' not two rows in front of me? Special cordoned-off area – Ethel Barrymore, yes, on my life Ethel Barrymore, the famous actress, was watching Dempsey fight, bloody marvellous . . . pardon the language, miss.'

Behind closed doors Sir Charles gave quiet instructions for Dewhurst to go down to reception and ask about this Miss Jones, find out how long she'd been staying, et cetera. When he returned to the drawing room Ed beamed at him. 'My God, this gel knows about fighting, your Lordship.'

Evelyne hadn't actually said a word, but she smiled, looking into her sherry glass. Sir Charles replaced his monocle and with his long fingers he drummed on the top of the inlaid writing desk. 'Tell me, dearie, this Freedom fella, what is your relationship with him?'

She placed the glass on top of the desk and sat up very straight. 'There is no relationship, sir, not even a friendship, I simply do not want to see an innocent man hang.'

She could feel Sir Charles' eyes carefully noting everything about her from the top of her hair to the scuffed shoes. She was glad Miss Freda had altered her clothes, at least she looked respectable, if not fashionable.

'You say you are prepared to go into the witness box? He is a Romany gypsy, isn't he?'

Evelyne nodded, bit her lip. She knew he was trying to imply that there was something between the two of them, and it made her angry.

'I don't wish to sound rude, dearie, but, well, you don't look, if you will excuse my saying so, you don't really look like most of the clientele in this establishment. I was wondering if you will excuse my rudeness for asking, how you are able to stay at the Grand?'

Evelyne stood up sharply, her hands gripped at her sides, her face taut. 'It is no business of yours, but I was left a legacy, and I am quite able to afford the price of this "establishment". I may not look like the so-called "ladies" I've seen parading around the lobby, but I wouldn't care to dress like them anyway, not that my legacy would run to that height of fashion. I have no other motive but to help a man whom I believe is innocent. There is nothing sexual about my friendship with him, I am only interested in justice. I am sorry to have wasted your time but I took you to be a gentleman who could possibly guide me in what I should do. I can see I was wrong, excuse me.'

Ed Meadows rose to stop her, but Sir Charles laid his elegant hand on Ed's arm again. Evelyne reached the door, turned and thanked Sir Charles for the sherry and then turned abruptly and walked out.

'Why d'yer behave like that, sir? I fink she was a true 'un moment I hear her givin' that snotty lift-boy a bollockin'.'

Sir Charles smiled, raised his whisky glass. 'On the contrary, I would say she's magnificent, she's a tigress, Ed m'boy, but we have to be very sure, I'd say that gel will make a first-class witness, and from what I've read to date the boy will most certainly need that, plus a lot more. Go and check on a chap called Smethurst, he's a lawyer, we'll need the best there is – or the best Cardiff can provide.'

From the hotel lobby, Ed Meadows asked if Miss Jones would care to have dinner with him, as Sir Charles had suggested it. Evelyne said she had a previous engagement and Ed apologized for disturbing her, but thought he should mention to her that His Lordship had already set the wheels in motion. He was hiring a lawyer first thing in the morning to act on behalf of Freedom Stubbs. He was going to pay a visit to the prison himself, and Ed added that he hoped she was not affronted by his invitation to dinner. Evelyne felt awful and would have liked to change her mind, but she knew she had nothing suitable to wear so she thanked Ed again and said perhaps another time.

Miss Freda had taken Evelyne at her word. She had been round the second-hand shops, run-down tailor's shops, bespoke tailor's, pawn shops. With an eagle eye for a bargain she bartered and argued and scrimped, and saved a penny here, twopence there. There was a dreadful pink satin ball gown that she could pull the beads from and hand-stitch instead round the collar of a fawn suit, the pinkish beads setting off the fawn of the jacket.

Accustomed to rising early, Evelyne was sitting on the window-seat with her legs curled beneath her when Freda arrived at seven-fifteen. Poor Freda looked pale, with deep circles beneath her eyes, but she had brought four garments, all finished down to the buttons. She was able to double her money on each item, but she didn't feel she was cheating Evelyne, she had cut and sewn all night long and she would defy anyone to tell what or whose they had once been.

Freda hid in the bathroom when Evelyne called down for some coffee to be sent up to suite twenty-seven, and stayed there until the waiter delivered the steaming pots.

They discussed Evelyne's outfits and talked about what sort of hat she needed to go with each. Evelyne counted out the shillings and pennies, double-checked it and handed the money to Freda, then she went into the bathroom to brush her hair. Returning to the bedroom she found Freda curled up like a dormouse on the unmade bed, so deeply asleep, she didn't even stir when Evelyne slipped the eiderdown round her tiny shoulders.

The rest of the day was spent in shopping and carefully choosing material and one pair of shoes that would be suitable for all the outfits.

Ed Meadows was waiting in the lobby when Evelyne got back, and he rushed her up to Sir Charles' suite.

Freedom Stubbs had turned down Sir Charles' offer to take over his case, refusing point-blank, although thanking Sir Charles for his time and obvious expense. Sir Charles had pulled many strings and had his motorcar waiting to take Evelyne to the jail. She must talk to him, tell him he was being foolish and would hang for it unless he accepted their offer.

Ed Meadows sat in the front of the car with the chauffeur, and gave Evelyne details of the offer, making it sound simple and, of course, to Freedom's advantage. Sir Charles wanted Freedom to sign a contract to be under his sole management.

'We reckon he could be a contender, see Evie, me and the guv'nor want to train 'im, like, get 'im ready. It's a fair contract, all the money 'e laid out for the court case, legal fees and what 'ave you, would be comin' out of whatever 'e'd earn as a boxer.'

Evelyne, clutching the contract, was led through the jail to the visiting room. This time the prison officers were cordial and called her 'ma'am'. Freedom was brought into the small room in handcuffs, but he had bathed and shaved. His hair was shining, and was braided down his neck. He sat, head bowed, opposite her, and the officer told Evelyne quietly that she could stay as long as she wanted.

One officer was left on duty inside the room, as usual, and another outside the door, but this time the room was not locked.

'Well, what have you got to say for yourself, Freedom? You know how much trouble I've been to, and Sir Charles, you can't say no, you must be out of your mind.'

Freedom looked down at his hands and pursed his lips. Evelyne leaned over and whispered that no one was concerned about anyone else, nothing had been mentioned about anyone else's involvement, no names. All they were interested in was his innocence or guilt.

'You are innocent, I know it, I can stand up and prove it in Willie's case, but you'll have to say where you were on the days when the other lads were killed.'

Freedom shifted his weight but still he would not look up and meet her eyes. He remained silent, infuriating Evelyne.

'Sir Charles Wheeler's no ordinary man, he can help you in your boxing, all you've got to do is sign this contract an' he'll make you a contender.'

Having misunderstood what Ed Meadows had said, Evelyne had no idea what 'contender' meant. Freedom smiled, still with his head down, his eyes averted.

'You sign this and he'll take all the court costs out of what he's agreed to pay you. It's a chance for you, you can't throw it a way.'

Still he said nothing, and she tried cajoling and various other approaches.

'Do you not want to box, is that it?'

Freedom lifted his head and stared at her, then turned to face the prison officer. 'Aye, I want that, I just don't want no one else to be involved.'

She knew he was thinking of Rawnie and Jesse, and she couldn't believe it. Her temper got the better of her. 'You are a fool, you know that, a stubborn fool, I don't know why I'm wasting my breath on you!'

'And I don't know why, you tell me, I don't know why I deserve this, no one has ever fought for me before, why you, what do you want?'

'Because you're *innocent*, that's why, I'd do it for any man who was about to hang when I knew he shouldn't.'

She laid out the contract and read down the detailed, neatly typed pages. She turned it over, Sir Charles was guaranteeing Freedom a wage, and a fair one as far as she could see.

'Is there something here you don't agree with, is it too long a contract, is that it?'

Freedom rubbed his head, glanced at the attentive prison officer and then said in a barely audible voice, 'I can't read, I don't read.'

Evelyne could see his embarrassment, and she got up to ask the officer if she could move her chair round the table to discuss the contract with the prisoner.

They sat close and she whispered each clause of the contract, her finger tracing the lines. He sat, head bent, staring intently at the pages.

'He promises to give you accommodation at his estate outside London for the time you will be training until the time you desire to find your own establishment. These costs will be deducted from your wages together with the costs this case will incur. He also wants you to have a suit ordered for the trial, and ... ' Evelyne looked at him, his face close enough for her to touch. He was not paying any attention to the contract but looking at her closely, scrutinizing her face. She turned back to the papers, blushed, coughed, and started again.

'Clause four, this one down here, says you will be contracted to Sir Charles for five years, after that time you will be free either to renew your contract with him or not, as you choose. This contract is valid for all parts of the world.' As she turned the page her hand brushed against his, and he moved his handcuffed wrists further away.

'He, Sir Charles, that is, has the right to bring all contractual obligations here assigned to termination at any date he so wishes.'

She opened her bag, and the officer moved a step into the room. She held up a pen, then looked at Freedom. 'You going to sign it? You *have* to, it's the only chance you have, and I think it's a pretty fair deal.'

Freedom nodded, and with her hand guiding his he signed his initials, 'F. S.'

Evelyne promptly folded the contract and slipped it into her handbag. Freedom looked at her with a strange expression, then he looked away and kept his voice low as he said, 'You gimme your word they'll not try to bring in my friends.'

Evelyne snapped her bag shut and nodded her head. 'You have my word, and I want yours that you'll give Sir Charles any information not concerning your friends that'll help you, will you promise me that?'

Freedom promised, and she gave the officer a look to let him know the meeting was over. She went to walk straight out, but then she stopped, bent her head towards Freedom and lightly kissed his cheek. It was a friendly gesture, there was nothing sexual and no intention of it being so. As the door closed behind her she turned back and saw him through the small window. He held his handcuffed hands over his face, and he seemed defeated.

When Freedom took his hands away from his face the tears were wet on his cheeks. He was crying, without a tremor, without a sound. His dark eyes blinked, and with one gesture the tears were gone, and he rose and lifted his hands to the officer. He was ready to be returned to the cells.

Sir Charles Wheeler brought Ed sharply down to earth. The fact that Freedom had signed their contract was no reason for celebration. They still had to prove the boy innocent and that was not going to be easy. He turned to Evelyne, checking his watch, and told her that they had a meeting with the lawyers in one hour. He didn't exactly dismiss Evelyne, but he told her he had things to do, and Dewhurst hovered at the door to usher her out.

'Have you the finances to remain here, Miss Jones? As I recall, you had only booked in for three days. The case could take a considerable time to get to court and you are the star witness.'

Evelyne was in a bit of a dilemma. Basically, she did have the money, but that would mean dipping into her precious legacy, and she had always taken great pains not to touch it unless absolutely necessary. But if she said she didn't have it, would Sir Charles pay for her room, or would she be moved elsewhere?

Sir Charles took her silence to mean she did not have enough money, and with hardly a pause for breath he turned to Dewhurst and gave instructions to have Miss Jones' account at the hotel given to him. He did not even wait for her to thank him, but strode into the study with Ed at his heels.

Evelyne wanted to dance along the corridor, she could still stay here, and for free. She could have as many baths as she liked, as many cream cakes, and all paid for by Sir Charles.

*

The lawyer's office was dark, wood-panelled and lined with books. One whole wall was taken up with yellowing documents. The desk was claw-footed and covered in more of the same thick, yellowing documents. Smethurst swept into the room wearing his gown, having come directly from the court. His domed head was framed by a strange fringe of orange hair sprouting out at the sides, but the thickness of his eyebrows made up for the lack of hair on the top of his head. Mr Smethurst was a junior partner, but Evelyne decided that if he was a junior then the senior partners must all be really ancient.

Smethurst, Humphrey George, Esquire, had a booming voice, and his flabby hand gripped Sir Charles' in a pulverizing handshake. 'Charlie, well, Charlie, sit down, sit down old chap, you must be Miss Jones, seat, take a pew all of you, be back in a tick.'

They could hear his booming voice as he called for someone named Ethel to get the kettle on the boil for tea. He returned quickly, minus the gown and pulling on a Harris tweed jacket, almost the colour of his hair. His baggy trousers and heavy brogues were covered in mud. His Old Harrovian tie had worked its way around to the back of his neck, and the collar of his crumpled shirt stuck up. He and Sir Charles had been at school together.

'Right, I've done a bit of prelim on this, and I'm afraid things don't look too good, not good at all ... Ahh, Ethel, thank God, I'm parched ... tea, everyone? Oh, and Ethel some ginger nuts, there's a good gel.' He poured tea and talked constantly as it slopped into the saucers, then waved the milk liberally over the whole tray.

'Now, my gel, let's take a look at your statement, jolly well written and clear as a bell, but we have one problem the opposition will be on to like hawks ... How long have you known this fella? Two – no, don't interrupt me, tell me when I've finished. Right, point two, you state you were at a boxing match up on Highbury Hills, right? Yes, now I have to have witnesses to that fact, witnesses to say you were not, *not*, with the gypsy people, but there under your own steam, so to speak, and that before that date you had no connection with the ... the er ... chap, Freedom Stubbs. These two points are *extremely* important because what they will throw at you is that you were, you are, fabricating the whole story to enable us to get the chap free ... so I will have to ask you certain ... delicate questions, that will no doubt be asked by the prosecution counsel.'

Smethurst listened attentively to Evelyne as she stated clearly that until the time of the first boxing match she had never set eyes on Freedom Stubbs.

'So tell me, what does an attractive young woman like you want to take up with this gypsy for?'

Evelyne was up on her feet and banging on the desk in fury at Smethurst's insinuations. He leaned back and raised his eyebrows. 'So I am to take it that there is no romantic connection, purely a platonic friendship on your part with this gypsy, yes? Have you ever had any form of sexual relationship with him? And, further, do you intend to do so should this lad be set free?'

Evelyne banged the desk again, saying she had never ever had such thoughts and nothing was further from her mind. All she was interested in was Freedom's innocence. 'I saw that girl, I saw the girl the lads raped, and I believe in British justice, they will not let an innocent man hang.'

Smethurst gave her a slow hand-clap and pushed his chair back from his desk.

'I think, Charlie, she'll be wonderful, and as you said, like a tigress, but I'm afraid, Miss Jones, you'll have to control that temper of yours. In the witness stand it is imperative that you behave like a lady at all times, never raise your voice – never – just answer clearly and concisely, understand?'

Suddenly he threw a question, like a dart, towards Evelyne. 'So who do you think killed those miners, hum? Any ideas?'

She swallowed and looked down at her hands, licked her lips and lifted her head to stare straight into Smethurst's bright eyes. 'I have no idea, sir.'

He chucked the pencil down and opened a drawer, took out some toffees and unwrapped one. 'That was a lie, but don't . . . no, don't argue with me, I don't want to know, just tell me whether Freedom Stubbs himself is innocent.'

Evelyne kept her voice level, her eyes fixed firmly on Smethurst. 'He did not kill those lads.'

'Good, good, because I don't think he's guilty either. Right, let's get started, yes?' He flicked a look at Sir Charles who caught it like a tennis player and with a brief nod to Evelyne instructed her to wait in his car.

Smethurst waited until the door closed behind Evelyne before speaking. His manner changed slightly, he grew quieter, less expansive. He unwrapped another toffee. 'I think, Charlie, it's best that you let Miss Jones settle her own accounts at the hotel. By all means hand her the finances, but I don't want it known you are paying her way. Secondly, I shall check all the alibis the fellow has and then get back to you, leave the statements of Collins and Lord Carlton to her . . . Oh, and fix the gypsy up, you know, get him a suit, looks better if he's respectable, I think that's about it for now.'

As Sir Charles rose to leave, Smethurst rocked in his chair.

'You still see that chap you used to adore at school, Willough-by something-or-other? Still fond of him, are you?'

Sir Charles prodded the floor with his cane. 'Killed in action, Ypres.'

'Oh, sorry, nice fella ... so, Charlie, you think you'll have a champion, do you?'

Sir Charles smiled softly, leaned on his cane. 'When have I ever been wrong? So, what do you think our chances are?'

Smethurst sniffed, sucked at his toffee. 'Not good, but then I have never lost a case. I'd like to get Freddy Carlton's statement sewn up, and that other bloke, Collins. Push those through, they are rather important.'

Sir Charles already had the door open and his trilby sat on his head at a jaunty angle. He tapped his cane. 'Leave it to me ... Thank you, Ethel, for the delicious tea and ginger nuts, good afternoon.'

Smethurst rocked backwards, then swivelled round in his chair. He thought Sir Charles was still the unfathomable gent he had been at school. The question of fees hadn't even arisen, but he was sure he would make a fair amount.

'Ethel, I think, dear heart, we'd better get the press on our side for this one, start calling them, would you?'

The case was by no means easy, and if the truth be known Smethurst felt they didn't stand a chance in hell of acquittal. The gypsy was, after all, charged with not one murder but four ... but, by Christ, it would make headlines, and with the society mixture Smethurst knew he had a very potent cocktail.

Chapter 14

Evelyne could feel her whole body tense up. Her mouth went dry, but there was no turning back now. The operator was on the line, and with an encouraging nod from Miss Freda she went into her carefully rehearsed speech. 'Would you please put me through to Lord Frederick Carlton's residence, the number is Cardiff five-five-four . . .'

Miss Freda moved closer, listening. Evelyne covered the mouthpiece. 'It's going through, don't get so close, you make me nervous.'

Miss Freda edged away. Evelyne went red, swallowed. 'Hello, is that you? Er, you may not remember me, but my name is . . . oh . . . oh yes, I would like to speak with Lord Freddy Carlton please . . . Evelyne Jones . . .'

'What did he say? What, what?'

Evelyne hissed, 'It was the butler, shusssshhhhh . . .'

Freddy reached for the phone, irritated. These newfangled things were a dreadful intrusion on one's privacy. Even more so with a friend like David Collins. One was forced to accept calls from God knows who, and on reverse charges. He snapped into the phone. 'Yes, speaking . . . who is this? Who . . . ? No, I'm sorry . . .'

Freddy was about to replace the phone. 'Evelyne who? Who?'

Frantic, Evelyne looked at Miss Freda. 'Oh, please don't put your phone down, sir, not until you have heard what I have to say, it's very important.'

Miss Freda was gesticulating wildly. Evelyne covered the mouthpiece.

'You don't 'ave to shout, darlink, they can hear you as if you were in the same room, don't shout.'

Evelyne started again.

'Do you recall the boxing match? With the gypsies? The night there was a . . . hello? Hello, are you still there? Oh, Freda, I can't hear him now, there's no sound at all coming out.'

Freddy glanced across the hall towards the drawing-room, hoping his wife would not appear as usual to ask who was on the telephone. He spoke in hushed tones. 'Now listen, dearie, I don't like you calling my private number, firstly, and secondly I have absolutely no intention whatsoever of admitting to being at some wretched boxing match, is that clear? Now, please do not call me again.'

As he had expected, Heather came in from the garden, carrying a large bouquet of flowers. She paused, eyebrows lifted. 'Something wrong, dearest?'

Freddy covered the phone with his hand, smiling. 'No, no darling, just a call from the club, snooker game.'

Heather smiled, knowing perfectly well it had nothing to do with a snooker game. She went in to the drawing room where her mother, Lady Sybil, sat in her wheelchair, playing patience. 'Who's he talking to?'

'Just his club, Mother, nothing important.'

Freddy waited until the door closed behind his wife, then turned back to the phone. 'Are you still there? Hello?'

Miss Freda handed the telephone back to Evelyne, whispering that he was back on the line again. Evelyne started to shout again, but lowered her voice when Freda waved frantically.

'I said, sir, that perhaps David Collins will help, you see it is imperative that you act as my witness, my witness ... He is charged with murder, and he is an innocent man.'

Freddy tried to control his voice. 'And David Collins is sick, you must not at any cost disturb him. I won't allow it, do you hear me? And I think you have a nerve, yes, a bloody nerve, calling here. We want nothing to do with you. Is that perfectly clear?'

Poor Freddy sensed the drawing-room door opening behind him, heard a bang as his mother-in-law's wheelchair was wheeled out, and was almost beside himself. 'I am sorry, I really cannot discuss the matter any further, the answer is no, and please do not call again.'

He replaced the phone and strode along the hall.

'Going out, dear?'

'Yes, yes, I have to go to my club. If David calls, tell him I need to talk to him.'

Heather pushed her mother's chair into the hall, watching Freddy grab his trilby and slam out of the front door without a backward glance. Lady Sybil sniffed and rattled the vast array of beads on her chest. Her thin wrists clanked with rows of bangles.

'For someone who has never done a day's work in his life, he certainly does rush about, doesn't he? Really, always amazes me why you put up with him, dear, what on earth has he ever done for you?'

Heather sighed, sucking in her breath over her protruding teeth. 'He married me, Mother.'

Evelyne replaced the phone.

'Well, Freda, that was dreadful, he wouldn't even listen to me.'

Not one to give up, Miss Freda paced the room. 'Next we find this Tulip girl, she will also be a witness, yes? Come along, Bianco's still thrives, we will ask there.'

Tulip? Yes, the owner of Bianco's remembered her very well indeed, he could describe her in detail. He rolled his eyes lewdly and made clucking sounds as he talked.

'Do you know where we could find her?'

He sighed, sat down, and shook his head sorrowfully. 'I'm sorry, the lady is more than likely pushing up the tulips herself. She died, oh, one year, maybe less ... but I knew her well, many nights she was here, but ...'

They returned, crestfallen, to the hotel, and took the lift to Sir Charles' suite. As they knocked, Sir Charles swung the door open. 'Well, how did it go, dearie? You have good news?'

Evelyne sighed and shook her head. Far from it. She told him the bad news, that neither Freddy nor David would act as witnesses, and that Tulip was dead. She had never before seen Sir Charles angry. He muttered under his breath and swung his monocle about by its ribbon. He paced the room and asked her to tell him once more, right from the beginning, what had taken place. All through her story he drummed his fingers and wandered around the room.

'Freddy, or His Lordship, as he is now, wouldn't stand up in

304

court because of the possible scandal, but the gossipmongers would like to know just how familiar he is with David's wife. I saw him, saw him with Lady Primrose, she doesn't love David . . .'

Sir Charles replaced his monocle and sat down, interrupting Evelyne's bitter tirade. 'Lady Primrose Boyd-Carpenter? Getting me rather confused, my dear. Now repeat what you just said with a little logic so I can piece it all together.'

Evelyne felt as if Sir Charles' magnified eye was boring into her as she repeated her story yet again. He threw back his head and roared with laughter, which took her completely off guard.

Dewhurst carried in the telephone from the study, trailing the long cord. 'Mr Smethurst for you, sir, I apologize for interrupting but it is long distance and rather urgent.'

Smethurst was very pleased with himself, so far the story Freedom Stubbs had told him was checking out. The killings that had taken place in Cardiff could not have been committed by their client. In each case he was in another town, and in two instances he was actually in a boxing ring. Sir Charles replaced the receiver. It was more important than ever that Evelyne's story checked out one hundred per cent. 'Now you are sure, absolutely sure, that David Collins' wife is having some sort of liaison with Lord Freddy, yes? Am I right, yes?'

Evelyne bit her lip. Never one to gossip, she hated the sound of her own voice saying it. 'Lord Freddy was engaged to Lady Primrose before David. After the war, when David came home, they married and had a son, but David had changed, and Freddy and Primrose were friendly even then. Now, well, I have seen them being very familiar actually in the tea room here at the Grand.'

'Good God, the tea room, well, well.'

She felt he was laughing at her primness, but the next moment he opened his wallet. 'I want you to purchase a very special evening gown. It's essential that you look absolutely stunning. Off you go, and remember, a *stunning* creation, I think something green to go with your colouring.'

He didn't even look at the amount he had given her, just handed her three notes. They were five-pound notes, and Evelyne didn't know what to say. Dewhurst ushered her out of the suite, and Sir Charles got to work immediately, making calls to Lady Primrose and to Freddy Carlton.

Ed rushed in, looking crestfallen. 'Gor blimey, I just 'eard, not one of them toffs will admit to even being at the fight, that's our defence up the spout, ain't it?'

Sir Charles covered the telephone with his hand.

'Ed, my old chum, don't be such a defeatist, do you really think I would give up so easily? You know the Wheeler family has relatives all over England, rather distant, of course, but I intend to pull family strings.' He listened to the telephone. 'Yes, dearie, I'm still here ... oh, thank you.'

Ed sat on the edge of his seat.

'Hello, my dear gel, is that Primrose? Why, it's Charlie, yes, I am in town ... oh, only just arrived; goodness, it must be so many years ... how's your mother? Oh, she is? So sorry ...'

Sir Charles appeared to be in the throes of one of his usual social calls so Ed made for the door, but Sir Charles stopped him.

'Ed, pass the word to Miss Jones that she is to be here in my suite prompt at nine o'clock, not a minute before, thank you ... Hello, Primmy? You still there? Ah, now then, I know it's short notice, but could you make it this evening? Oh, splendid, splendid.'

Finding no answer at Evelyne's door, Ed went down to reception and left a message for her – nine o'clock sharp, not a minute earlier or later. They were to dine in Sir Charles' suite. Just as he was licking his lips at the thought of a nice, frothing beer, he was called back to the desk. Sir Charles wanted him to collect a small package from a local jewellery store.

Freda had not been one hundred per cent certain about the gown, and nearly fainted at the price tag, but Evelyne was sure, and she bought it.

'Oh, Evelyne, I could make it for a quarter, no a tenth of the price, I could, I really could.'

The pair returned to the hotel, exhausted, and Evelyne collected her keys. As she read the message she turned to Freda in horror. 'It's tonight, the dinner's *tonight*! Oh, Freda, I'll never be ready!'

As tired as she was, Miss Freda worked on Evelyne like a little beaver. She laid out the long satin gown, the white gloves and the tiny, embroidered handbag. Evelyne sat in front of the dressing-table mirror in a pure silk underslip, and Miss Freda began to brush her hair, which fell to below her waist. Freda had to get down on her knees to brush out the ends. They had shampooed and scrubbed the hair until, when dry, it shone like gold.

A tap on the door sent Evelyne rushing this way and that as she was nowhere near ready. 'Who is it? I'm not dressed!'

'Miss Jones, it's me, Ed, I got somefink for yer from Sir Charles, it's just for ternight, 'e says, but for you ter use it.'

At Evelyne's nod Miss Freda opened the door, peeked round it and took the parcel from Ed. As she shut the door he tapped again.

'It's Miss Freda, ain't it? Evelyne said you was helping her, like, are you available ternight for a few drinks, there's a good dance hall wiv a band?'

Blushing and tittering, Freda said she would be delighted.

'Oh, Evie, I have a date myself, now I have to rush ... Oh, my hair, oh, my dress ... Oh, can you manage without me, darling? Oh, he said to give you this, for tonight, from Sir Charles.'

Not two minutes ago Freda had been too exhausted to move. Now she leapt about like a young girl.

Evelyne was delighted to be left alone. She opened the brown paper and looked at the leather case, then inched open the lid and gasped. It contained a necklace of diamonds and emeralds with matching bracelet and drop earrings.

At eight o'clock sharp Dewhurst ushered Lord Frederick Carlton into Sir Charles' suite, accompanied by what Sir Charles at first presumed was his mother, only to discover it was his wife. The short, squat, dumpy woman wore a frightful dress, and more diamonds than the royal jewels.

'Freddy, old boy, how delightful to see you, come in, come in, and Dewhurst, champagne immediately.'

The champagne, well chilled and in tall, fluted crystal glasses, had just been served when Dewhurst announced David Collins and Lady Primrose. Freddy blushed, not expecting to see them, and quickly rose to his feet. David was obviously slightly drunk, but even so he looked as handsome as ever. He wore the new-style dinner jacket, but then he would, he had always been obsessed with fashion. Lady Primrose wore the latest fashion, a very short sequinned dress with a small cloche hat to match. The sequins on her dress were rose pink at the top, shading down to almost plum colour at the hem. She wore dark velvet slippers with a small heel, and fine silk stockings. She looked stunning, more beautiful than Freddy had ever seen her. His heart lurched inside his chest, and he had to gulp champagne to stop himself shaking.

Sir Charles went straight to Lady Primrose and called her 'Primmy', kissing her affectionately on the cheek, then took her hand and guided her into the room.

'Do you know my cousin Lady Primrose? Yes, I'm sure you do, and her husband, David Collins?'

Dewhurst slipped in and out serving champagne and then passed a trayful of tiny squares of crisp brown toast topped with caviar. He squeezed the lemon himself to ensure that none of the guests had to get their fingers sticky. Tiny lace napkins were placed on knees, everyone smiled and gradually the atmosphere relaxed.

Lady Primrose gave David a slight warning look as she saw him accepting another glass of champagne. They had had the most awful row earlier about his drinking. If it wasn't his drinking, it was his erratic, often violent moods. He had even accused her of telephoning Freddy when it was Sir Charles on the phone. He was jealous, and with such tantrums he exhausted himself. He had become more like a child than ever. She hoped he would behave himself this evening, Sir Charles being her mother's sister's son, and so immensely rich. She wanted at all costs to keep on the right side of his family. Their own finances were being depleted fast. One day she might have to turn to Sir Charles for assistance.

David leaned back on the velvet sofa and crossed his legs. He always felt a flicker of irritation when he was announced as Mister David Collins. He was, after all, a captain, not that anyone ever remembered or gave him his rank. How he would have loved a title; still, he hadn't done too badly, he was married to one. He gave Freddy a shifty look. Rather be married to Lady Primrose without a lot of cash than be married to the homely Heather, fortune or no. He could see that Heather was wearing a couple of hundred thousand pounds around her squat neck.

Sir Charles was the perfect host, giving his complete attention to his guests. He made each one feel like the most important person in the room, but somehow he seemed to ignore David, laughing and joking intimately with Primrose, chatting about the times they had met as children. 'Remember, Primmy, the day I beat up that stable lad? Gawd, it was funny, even funnier now to think I am so closely associated with boxing. Do you ever go to any of the matches? Jolly good sport, not that the ladies enjoy it of course, it's very much a man's game.'

Sir Charles caught a slight look of panic passing between David and Freddy. He gestured to Dewhurst to refill the glasses and stood with his back to the fireplace. Freddy still sat about ten inches away from his dumpy wife, his eyes constantly straying to Primrose, who was being delightful, telling a witty story about the time when she drove to London to be presented at court. As she spoke her head shimmered and glistened with sequins. She took a cigarette and placed it in a long holder, and Freddy leapt to his feet with his lighter. He touched her hand slightly and she quickly withdrew it, promptly moving across the room to stand closer to Sir Charles who took out his fob watch and told them they were waiting for his special guest and then they would dine. He had ordered dinner to be served in his rooms, if that suited everyone. They could adjourn to the ballroom for more champagne and a twirl round the dance floor after dinner. Lady Primrose began to giggle and display her new dance steps. Her movements were beautifully co-ordinated as she danced the Charleston.

Sir Charles took the opportunity to cross the room and stand by David looking down at him and murmuring that he must get his tailor's name, he liked the cut of David's trousers. He studied this handsome man, noticing the slight, nervous tremor of his hands. 'You were cavalry, weren't you, Captain? Yes?'

David's hand tightened on his champagne glass and he pursed his lips.

'Your chaps had a bad time of it, heard your regiment was one of the first up front, dreadful carnage. I was lucky, they started bringing in the vehicles by the time I made it over there. Bit of shrapnel in the eyes, that's why I have to wear this, but I was one of the lucky ones.'

Primrose could also see the signs – David's face had paled, and his whole body was shaking slightly. She danced over to Charles and tried to change the subject. 'When are you going to get yourself married, Charlie? You've been on the society lists as a catch from the early days.'

Sir Charles laughed his wonderful, infectious giggle. 'Never found the right one yet, but that doesn't mean I'm not still huntin', ya know.'

Primrose sat next to David and gripped his hands, whispering for him to hold on, not to start it here, not tonight.

'Good heavens, Charlie, aren't we ever going to dine?'

As if on cue there was a tap on the outer door, and Sir Charles checked his watch. Exactly nine o'clock.

'My last guest, and then dearest we will dine immediately.'

Dewhurst opened the door. The whole party turned expectantly. Sir Charles took a fraction of a second to realize that this really was his little Miss Jones before he leapt to attention and bowed, his hand out to draw Evelyne into the room.

Dewhurst had not given her a second glance when he opened the door, which deflated her a little.

'Miss Evelyne Jones, Sir Charles.'

Sir Charles greeted her with his arms open wide. 'Well, my dear, do come in, I am so thrilled you could come . . . now, let me introduce you . . . Lord and Lady Frederick Carlton . . . my cousin Lady Primrose . . . and her husband, Captain David Collins.'

Freddy had the most awful sick feeling in his stomach, but he swallowed, forcing a smile. He should have known something was up, but all he did was bow and gesture for his wife to step forward.

Heather was so nervous she didn't recognize Evelyne immediately, but as she came closer to shake hands her piggy eyes widened in amazement. 'Oh, but we've met before.'

Sir Charles gave one of his infectious laughs, and turned to Primrose and David. 'Isn't she stunning? Quite beautiful, absolutely beautiful, my dear. Now, give me your hand and I think if you don't mind Evelyne dearest, we shall go into dine straightaway.'

David bowed low over Evelyne's hand, she could smell his lavender perfume and his silky hair was the same as ever. He had not recognized her.

'Where on earth did you find this stunning gel, here in Cardiff?'

Already guiding Evelyne towards the dining room, Sir Charles was holding her hand tightly, giving her great comfort. 'Oh, I thought, dearest, you said you had once stayed with David, in his father's house, am I wrong?'

She looked directly at David and saw awareness dawning. For a moment he looked panic-stricken, flicking nervous eyes towards his wife, but she was laughing with delight at the elaborate dinner table.

'Oh, Charlie, you are so clever, what a delightful table ... oysters, too! Oh, you are *such* a delicious man, you really are.'

Sir Charles seated everyone, putting himself at the head of the table and David on Evelyne's left. He still held her hand. Suddenly Sir Charles leaned so close she could feel his breath. 'My dear, you have surpassed yourself, you look like a queen. I shall not leave your side. Quite, quite lovely.'

David could not take his eyes off Evelyne, he was confused, trying hard to collect the jagged pieces of the picture which were gathering like a storm in his head. She was dazzling; could it be that funny girl, could it really be that girl he had taken to the fight that night? Her cheeks were flushed, the rest of her pale skin translucent. Her dark eyes, like the sea, looked even more green because of the rich colour of her satin gown. The emeralds and diamonds glittered, but it was her hair that outshone everything, like gold, so simply done, a single braid to below her waist.

Freddy looked at Primrose with beseeching eyes, but she refused to look at him, afraid David would do something embarrassing. Under the table he felt for her foot, but she pulled her satin-clad feet back beneath her chair, giving him a cool, tight look of disapproval. She found it hard not to stare at the girl, who stood head and shoulders above her. It was obvious to everyone there that Sir Charles was smitten. Only Primrose knew how very strange this was, as she had heard family rumours about him ... well, she thought, they must be wrong.

'May I propose a toast to my dear friend Evelyne, ladies and gentlemen, will you raise your glasses?'

Dewhurst had filled their champagne glasses, and they all toasted Evelyne. Sir Charles gave the hovering waiters a discreet signal to begin serving then slipped an arm around Evelyne's shoulders and whispered in her ear, 'Don't be nervous, just follow me, do whatever I do.'

Again he was close to her, and she smiled into his piercing, unsettling eyes. He was a strange kettle of fish – she never knew where she stood with him. She would never have believed he could be so familiar, but it did give her confidence. At one point he made her turn her head so that he could straighten one of her earrings which had become entangled in a stray curl. His fingers brushed her neck and he allowed his hand to linger for a second too long, then he turned his attention back to his guests. They sat quietly, not sure how to react to Sir Charles' 'lady'. Seeing him so intimate with her made them even more uncomfortable.

Occasionally Evelyne shot a sidelong glance at David. He seemed oblivious to everything, even to his food now, and was staring, stony-faced, at the wallpaper. His only gesture was to lift his wine glass to his lips, his movements neat and delicate. When the next course arrived Evelyne had to pay close attention to Sir Charles, it was a thick lobster bisque. She watched as he used

the big, round spoon from the right-hand side of his place setting, and Evelyne followed suit, using the same outward strokes,
and did not once scrape the plate. The dinner seemed to go on
for ever, the conversation stilted and extremely strained, David's
withdrawn silence affecting them all. Lady Primrose battled on,
trying to encourage the party spirit, and told them funny little
stories about her two sons, Clarence and Charles, or Charlie, as
he was known.

'We named him after you, didn't we, David darling? David?'

Lady Primrose smiled, but her quiet voice had an edge to it.

'David, I just said we call him after cousin Charles ... you really
must come and see the boys, will you be here long enough?'

Ignoring her question, Sir Charles signalled to Dewhurst to
serve the main course. Primrose gave David a kick beneath the
table. She was trying so hard, and in their precarious financial
situation they really needed to keep on the right side of her rich,
if rather distant, relative.

When the main course was served, Evelyne had to hide her
smile as she saw Heather eating like a horse, everything before
her vanishing at great speed. She made unconscious little
'mmmm' sounds of appreciation, which irritated Freddy. He
frowned at her, making her peer around the table like a guilty
child. Freddy's fork clattered on to his plate when Sir Charles
spoke out of the blue.

'Any of you read about this gypsy chap, the one on the
murder rap? Very interesting case, I have a personal interest in it.'

This game was partly at Evelyne's instigation, although it saddened her. She was being used as a pawn, and she waited
expectantly to see what the outcome of the evening would be.

*

The port and brandy decanters were placed on the table, and the ladies withdrew to the sitting-room.

'Very nice dinner, Mother always says this is one of the *best* hotels . . . oh, coffee, and mints, *très bon*.' Heather gave a toothy smile as Evelyne poured the coffee. 'I didn't catch where you were staying? Evelyne?'

'I have a suite here.'

Primrose began a slow dance across the room, swaying, moving closer and closer until she stood directly before Evelyne.

'Can you do the Charleston? No? Want me to teach you? Come on, try it.'

She backed away flicking her heels out and humming the tune. Evelyne sensed that Primrose was laughing at her, the baby blue eyes were spiteful, glittering.

'Thought your sort of woman had to know the latest steps.'

Evelyne continued pouring the coffee, held a cup out to Lady Primrose, who waved her hand. 'No sugar, sweet enough, be-boop-be-doo.'

She danced past Evelyne, whose cup went over and spilt down the glittering, sequinned dress. Lady Primrose didn't shriek out, she didn't move; the coffee made a dark brown stain, spreading and dripping over the beads. Her little delicate hand shot out and slapped Evelyne's face. 'I believe my husband should have done that to you a long time ago.'

The port went round for the third time, the cigar smoke swirled around the men's heads. They were relaxed, enjoying the many witty anecdotes with which Sir Charles regaled them. He played the evening like a poker game, finally delivering his winning hand, card by card. He began by moving first the decanter, ash-tray and his port glass to one side, and with the table cleared he leaned on his elbows on the table. 'Gentlemen, now to the business of the evening, the reason I asked you both here.'

David leaned back, smiling, the drink had eased him. Freddy, sharper and more alert, had been waiting for something. His heart beat faster.

'I want you both to stand as witnesses to Miss Evelyne Jones' statement in court next week. You were, I am led to believe, both present at a certain boxing match on Highbury Hill. The fighter was a gypsy called Freedom Stubbs.'

Freddy leaned forward, pushing his glass away. 'I am aware of the case, a murder case, but perhaps I did not make myself clear to Miss Jones. I really feel that my presence in court, particularly in such an appalling case, would be most distasteful, I have already stated my feelings on this . . .'

Sir Charles interrupted, 'Rubbish, man, your word is essential. You both instigated the evening's outing, am I not right? Miss Jones had no prior knowledge of this boxing match?'

Freddy stubbed out his cigar. 'I really couldn't say, but judging by what I know of her she's a little tramp, and the public outcry surrounding these murders would be frightful. The gel is a blackmailer, David here can tell you more . . . David? How much money did she demand from you?'

Sir Charles banged the table. 'I don't call twenty pounds a large sum, especially as the girl was more than likely owed twice that from her share of the Collins' house.'

Nonplussed, Freddy turned to David.

'You told me she had demanded more than a hundred, good God, I gave you over fifty towards it, David?'

David downed the remains of his port. His manner changed, he became surly, giving Freddy a foul look. 'The way you carry on, old chap, I'd say you owe me a hell of a lot more, you think I'm blind as well as sick? Do you? *Do you?*' He rose to his feet and lurched against the table, glaring at Freddy. 'Not your money anyway, you don't have a penny to your name, so what are you bleating about?'

Sir Charles poured more port. He spoke in a calm, conversational voice that was not raised in the slightest. 'Now, now, let's not get into a nasty argument, let's just take things easy, shall we? Whatever marital problems you both may have they certainly wouldn't look good spread across the *Cardiff Herald* . . . all that is required of you both is a simple statement saying you escorted Miss Jones . . .'

David turned his anger on Sir Charles. 'Exactly what are you implying? None of your bloody business! What marital problems? Eh? What? What's he talking about?' He was on his feet, blazing, moving round to Freddy's chair with his fist up and looking foolish and inept.

'*Sit down, David*! Sit, please, let's not raise our voices, we don't want the ladies upset . . . and I really don't want to drag my cousin into any adverse publicity.'

David sat down again like a lamb, reached for his port and downed the remainder of the glass in one gulp. Freddy looked at Sir Charles. 'The girl was brought to the fair by David, that is all I know, I had nothing to do with her, but if David agrees, then . . . David?'

David simply stared at Freddy.

'If David agrees, I will go along with whatever he has to say. David?'

There was a short burst of humourless laughter from David, then he glared at Freddy. 'I'm sure you will, always such a friend, I am not going into a bloody court and that's final.'

Sir Charles smiled his thanks at Freddy and asked to be left alone with David. As Freddy closed the door Sir Charles picked up the decanter, carried it round the table and sat close to David, who reached for the port. Suddenly, Sir Charles' hand shot out and gripped David's wrist. 'No more, old fella, I want a private chat.'

'I've got a headache.'

'Dare say you have, this won't take long ... David, I would hate what I say ever to go beyond this room, but I want you, should I need you, in that courtroom.'

'I don't remember things, haven't you been told? You put me on a witness stand and I'll go to pieces.'

'All you have to do is sign a statement, that'll be good enough. I don't want to have to subpoena you, then you'd have to take the stand, don't make me do that ... You know, David, you were not the only officer to turn tail, you were in the front line for six months, and your reputation was unblemished ... I recall many officers – in particular poor old Ridgely – often spoke of you. Remember Ridgely, do you? Died of syphilis, I'm told.'

David went grey, his forehead puckered, and he turned terrible, pleading eyes to Sir Charles.

'Face it, don't be afraid, it's over, no one blames you. But sadly, there are those who can never understand. There was nightmare carnage, human carnage, to face day in, day out. It can destroy any man ...'

'I don't know what you are talking about.'

319

Sir Charles rose from the table and carefully replaced the chair. He felt deep disgust for this shell of a man, a captain who had turned tail on twenty-five of his men. Not one survived. His voice was little more than a whisper. 'Oh, I think you do.'

David stared at him, like a frightened child.

'My lawyer will contact you for the statement. Now shall we join the ladies, Captain?'

Freddy had already joined the ladies. The atmosphere was decidedly chilly. A bowl of water and a cloth were brought by Dewhurst, and Freddy helped Lady Primrose try to remove the coffee stain. In furtive whispers he told her what had taken place in the dining room. 'Charles knows about us, God knows how. David's been drinking, you'll have to get him home – he looks as if he's going to throw one of his fits.'

They were joined by an ebullient Sir Charles. He gave Evelyne a small wink to say all was well, then sat with Heather, offering her the remains of the chocolates with a flourish. They discussed the family chocolate and toffee business, and he made a mental note to check out the Warner shares, perhaps buy a few. The company would be at an all-time low after the war, so the shares would be cheap.

Lady Primrose went to the open dining-room doors, then turned with a sigh, saying that she felt she should take David home, he was obviously tired. Dewhurst fetched wraps and coats, and everyone thanked Sir Charles politely. Evelyne was ignored, left sitting with her empty coffee cup. David seemed in a world of his own, his eyes vacant and a soft smile on his lips, but as they all left he turned back to Evelyne, raised his hand as though he wanted to say something. Primrose slipped her arm about his waist. 'Come along, David, the car's waiting.'

When he returned from seeing them out, Sir Charles clapped his hands.

'All went as planned, dearie, we will have their statements first thing in the morning. Now, if you will excuse me, I'm away to my bed. Dewhurst, show the young lady out.'

Evelyne stared at her reflection in the dressing-table mirror, then she tried to do the Charleston, holding on to the back of the chair. A sad, silly gesture, and she immediately felt foolish.

She replaced the diamonds and emeralds in their leather case. Like the jewels, she felt as though she had been hired for the night.

Ed Meadows walked Miss Freda home through the damp night. He was flushed from all the beer he had drunk, and Miss Freda was equally pink in the face from her numerous port and lemons.

'Well, it's been ever such a nice evenin', Freda, perhaps we could do it again if you'd like, I mean, I don't wanna be too forward. Are you walkin' out wiv anyone?'

Tittering, Freda placed her hand over her mouth. Ed grinned.

'You're a lovely-looking woman, and I've thoroughly enjoyed meself ternight, been a good time.'

Lifting her tiny hand to his lips he gave it a resounding kiss. She smiled sweetly, very much the lady. 'I would like so much to see you again, I have had a wonderful time too.'

Ed rocked on his heels, he was so tickled. 'Well then, we'll do it again, g'night ... Oh, Freda, I'm not married or nuffink, are you available, like?'

She patted his barrel chest and he caught her to him and hugged her expertly. She giggled and pushed him away, gave him a coy, sexy flutter of the eyelids and hurried inside.

Ed tottered back to his bed–and–breakfast hotel, singing at the top of his voice, 'I'm 'Enery the eighth I am, 'Enery the eighth I am, I am ...'

In her cracked dressing-table mirror Freda studied her reflection. Well, she thought, he's not much, but then nor am I. She wished she hadn't lied about her age, though. She put her curlers in, creamed her face and lay down in her tiny, single bed. 'You're never too old, darling, but you'd better reel this fish in fast.'

The Rolls-Royce glided soundlessly along the dark, wet streets. David sat hunched in a corner, staring out into the night. Lady Primrose had tried to hold his hand, but he shrugged away from her. She remained close, trying not to let her thigh press against Freddy's as he, too, sat in the back of the Rolls. Heather was sitting in the front with the driver, and she spoke as if to the windscreen wiper. 'Thought it was a good meal, didn't you, dear?'

Freddy made no reply. He sighed, and Primrose looked at him. His face was haunted, he wanted her, loved her so dearly.

'I want to see a doctor, some kind of specialist, maybe it would help me,' said David, petulantly.

Primrose slipped her arm through David's and rested her

head on his shoulder. He was trembling, his whole body shaking.

'Yes, dearest, that is a good idea.' Tears came into her eyes. She couldn't bear to turn to Freddy, she wanted him so much, loved him so much.

They were silent as the car drove on, the only sound the 'swish, swish' of the tyres on the wet streets.

Evelyne lay wide awake in bed. She was finding sleep hard to come by. She tossed and turned, and began to think of the village, her Da, which made her keenly aware of her loneliness. She could see Hugh's big face, and would have liked more than anything to be wrapped in his strong arms. She was twenty-four years old, and had never known what it was like to be loved by a man.

Chapter 15

Smethurst and Sir Charles sat at a small corner table in the restaurant of the Feathers public house. Smethurst was slicing his cheese with delicate precision. The port was brought to the table. Smethurst wiped his mouth with his stained napkin, lifted his glass in a toast. 'Well, here's to this afternoon's proceedings.'

Sir Charles sipped his port, noting that Smethurst had downed his glass in one. He swivelled round in his seat as Smethurst made an expansive gesture to the doorway. Standing talking to the head waiter was a stern-faced man wearing a charcoal overcoat and carrying a homburg. 'That's the opposition, old chap.' Smethurst bellowed across the restaurant, '*Jeffrey*, will you join us?'

Jeffrey Henshaw crossed to their table and introductions were made. Shaking Sir Charles' outstretched hand, he politely refused to join them. He tapped his gold fob watch and cocked his head to one side, smiling at Smethurst, 'I'd say you should be on the move, proceedings are due to start in fifteen minutes.'

Smethurst laughed, stuffed another slice of cheese into his mouth, spattering Henshaw's overcoat with flecks of it. 'Just you remember you owe me more than one favour – *Ethel Patterson*, Jeffers, *Ethel Patterson*.'

Henshaw stepped sharply back from the table, pursed his lips and tapped his homburg against his thigh. 'Listen, you old devil, you know what these committal proceedings are like, ruddy magistrates dither around and I've got a very busy day, so get those flat feet on the trot.' He gave Sir Charles a stiff bow and strode off among the tables.

'What was all that about?' asked Sir Charles.

Smethurst picked up his battered briefcase. As he placed it on the table a cheese cracker crumbled under the weight.

'I got him out of a very sticky situation with one of his clients, a Miss Patterson – very naughty lady. Well, old chap, this is it, I'll call you soon as I have a result.' Suddenly his manner was more subdued.

'You sure you don't want me along?' asked Sir Charles.

'Good God no, it could take hours. There's a hellish lot of statements to be read and witnesses to call – no, no, I'll be in touch soon as I have any news. I'm confident, we'll get the lad off, be no problem . . . unless Henshaw plays a double hand, but I have a feeling he won't. He wants the rope for Stubbs, but has to concede there's no evidence on the first three charges. Won't be as easy on the fourth murder rap, you can take my word for that . . . He's got a long list of prosecution witnesses. Well, I'm off, thanks for a splendid lunch.'

Sir Charles watched Smethurst stride off, dropping his napkin on the floor as he squeezed among the diners. He wished he could feel as positive as his friend. Smethurst's bulging briefcase, stuffed with what he had described as 'hard evidence, old bean', did not, in Sir Charles' opinion, sound good enough to get

Freedom Stubbs off three of the four murder charges filed against him.

Sir Charles had underestimated his old friend. Even Henshaw was slightly taken aback at the amount of paperwork and obvious private detection Smethurst had managed to do. Henshaw, of course, had access to the statements, but still he was impressed, and still slightly in awe of the man he had learned so much from.

Smethurst held forth, resting his elbow on top of a mound of papers. More and more were produced and waved around. The row of magistrates listened intently as Smethurst proved without a doubt that Freedom Stubbs could not have committed the three murders that occurred in Cardiff. Statements from witnesses proved that Freedom Stubbs was not even in the vicinity of Cardiff when the killings took place. A humorous throwaway line clarified his point.

'Unless my client had an aeroplane, which I assure you he did not have, it would have been physically impossible for him to have been in Cardiff on the days in question. I therefore submit that there is no case against Freedom Stubbs on the first three counts of murder, and ask for those counts to be dismissed in view of the evidence I have laid before you. There is no case to answer, sir.'

Smethurst burst out of the court. Henshaw, close on his heels, held the door open to allow his colleague to exit without getting either his briefcase or coat caught. 'Round one to you, old chap ... but I guarantee your man will swing.'

Smethurst hailed a taxi and offered Henshaw a lift, but it was refused. The taxi passed him as he walked briskly down the street swinging his immaculate briefcase. Smethurst leaned back, patted his own bulging case and smiled. He had done his work for the dismissal of the first three counts, but Henshaw had established a *prima facie* case for the fourth murder. He was pleased with the dismissal and knew he had done well. He sucked in his breath. The contest between himself and Henshaw would certainly be interesting.

Sir Charles received the news of the dismissal by telephone. He wasn't elated, more relieved. Smethurst assured him he was confident the trial would prove Stubbs not guilty of the fourth murder, and confirmed that he was well ahead with his preparations. They discussed expenses – Smethurst did not come cheap. There was no question of it all being done on an 'old friends' basis, Smethurst was one of the best barristers in Wales, and his fees reflected the fact ... perhaps they were just a little higher than usual but it was, after all, a difficult case.

As Smethurst replaced the receiver he rested his feet on his untidy desk. The first three young miners had all been found with their hands tied behind their backs, their throats slit from right to left. In all three cases they had been marked with a cross on their foreheads made with their own blood. Willie Thomas had been killed in exactly the same way, the blood mark on his forehead. Smethurst chewed his lower lip. He had been able to prove without a doubt that Stubbs could not have committed the first three killings ... but Willie Thomas was different. Smethurst prowled his office's worn carpet, ruffled his hair. Freedom Stubbs had been there, in the village. He knew how very important a witness Evelyne Jones was. Maybe Freedom didn't knife Willie Thomas, but it was going to be a hell of a job proving he hadn't had *any* part at all in the horrific murder. Smethurst's strong evidence, Freedom's alibi, depended on the jury believing he was actually with Evelyne at the time of the boy's death. Miss Jones had a lot on her shoulders.

Evelyne tried to understand, but Sir Charles had to repeat himself twice and was losing patience. The first three charges of murder had been dropped, he explained. 'Quite simply, Smethurst was able to prove there was no case against him. But he has been committed for the murder of William Thomas.'

'When? Will it be soon? How long will he have to wait in gaol?'

'Until the trial, gel, until the trial. Now we don't want you going to see him, you must have no contact with him, is that clear?'

'Yes, sir.'

'You are a very important witness, and you must behave impeccably until the trial. You can spend the time getting yourself some nice dresses, subdued, nothing too flashy, gloves and what have you, perhaps a hat . . .'

Evelyne accepted the money His Lordship gave her, money to pay her hotel bill, and for her clothes. Left alone, she couldn't stop her hands shaking, she repeated over and over to herself that the charges had been dropped. What she couldn't understand was why, if they believed her evidence, was Freedom still having to go on trial at all.

*

Freedom was as confused as Evelyne. Smethurst spoke very slowly, sometimes repeating himself two or three times. By now he had discovered his client was illiterate.

'But I never killed the last lad, sir.'

About to leave, Smethurst gestured to the gaoler. He looked back as the strange, unfathomable eyes searched his face. Freedom seemed childlike in his confusion.

'I'll come in to see you again – until then, keep your chin up.'

'Thank you, sir, thank you for everything you're doing.'

The police officers and warders assigned to Freedom had nicknamed him the 'Queer Fish' because he was always so silent and unapproachable. They had segregated him very early on from the other prisoners awaiting trial. Many of the men were striking miners who had resorted to stealing and poaching to make ends meet. They knew he was being charged with the murders of their fellows and they constantly jeered and catcalled in the direction of Freedom's cell. Every officer had to agree that he was a model prisoner – too good – he said neither 'thank you' nor 'good morning'. He said nothing. His black eyes frightened some of the officers, and they had drawn lots to see who would be the ones to take him back and forth to court when the day came. No one wanted to start a fight with him. Even though he was handcuffed, he still looked as if he could be dangerous.

The exercise yard was cleared for Freedom's solitary morning walk. Only he didn't walk, he ran round and round and round, running until he was sweating and exhausted. He would then be taken back to solitary for a shower. One of the warders supervising him whispered that the man was 'built like a brick shit-house with muscles standing out all over his body like a marble statue'.

Freedom knew they watched him, talked about him, and like an animal he stared back with his dark brooding eyes, and said nothing. Here, silence was his only defence against the world. No one could understand what the cell, the high brick walls and the key turning in the lock, were doing to Freedom's mind. The cell closed in on him until his only relief was to pound his fists against the walls. He wrapped them in his blankets to muffle the sound. His morning run reminded him of his stallion, the way he used to toss his head and run round and round on the training rope. He was like a roped *gry*, an animal.

When the news leaked out that three charges of murder had been dropped, the prisoners banged on their cell doors with their tin mugs, screaming at the injustice. '*You bastard, you'll hang . . . They should hang yer, you gyppo scum!*'

The press also got to hear of the murder charges being withdrawn and a small article appeared in the paper. They mentioned Freedom Stubbs by name as the gypsy being held in custody, and that he was now only being charged with the murder of William Thomas. Smethurst was furious, knowing the damage this information could cause to a jury. They could be prejudiced against Freedom before the trial began.

Tension mounted as the date of the trial grew closer. Sir Charles had spent the time staying with friends or out shooting. Ed Meadows was courting Miss Freda and they held hands like two teenagers, gazing into each other's eyes and sighing. Ed was thinking about popping the question. Miss Freda was reeling in her fish, and had already made up her mind to accept if he proposed.

Evelyne spent her days wandering around the museums and art galleries. The trial was ever-present in her mind.

Smethurst worked on in preparation for the trial. This big, scruffy man was totally dedicated to his work. His scrupulous attention to every single detail was impressive. He knew he held a man's life in his hands and, although he appeared almost buffoonish, he was an exceptionally intelligent and honourable man. He was also a kind man, and very patient.

The trial was to begin the following morning. Smethurst found a brief moment to explain everything to Evelyne.

'We begin tomorrow morning. You must not be seen talking to anyone associated with the trial. You'll be called to the stand when I am ready . . . but we'll talk again before then, just remember all I've told you and don't let him ruffle you. Answer clearly and concisely . . .'

'How's he holding up, sir? Is he all right?'

'Well he's getting a lot of stick from the other inmates, naturally, and he'll more than likely have to take a lot more. Don't you worry yourself about him . . . I take it you've not seen him, made no contact?'

'No sir, His Lordship forbade it.'

'Quite right . . . well dearie, I'll take my weary body to bed, be refreshed for the battle.'

'*Will* it be a battle, sir?'

Smethurst gave her a small pat on her shoulder, and one of his lopsided smiles. 'Trust me . . . Goodnight.'

*

Evelyne tossed and turned all night long. Early the following morning, the first day of the trial, Miss Freda and Ed peeked round her door on their way to court.

'I'll come to see you later, tell you all about it,' whispered Freda.

'Now, now, Freda, yer know that's not legal. She's a witness, you gotta stay away – maybe I'll just pop in though, eh! Ta-ta, gel.'

Left alone, Evelyne tried to read, but she couldn't concentrate for wondering how the trial was going. She prayed it would be over soon. She ordered lunch but couldn't eat anything, and eventually she sat by the window, waiting for them all to return.

The gallery was packed with spectators. They were rowdy and jocular. As the court began to fill, Smethurst swept in, his wig already at a precarious angle. Henshaw, immaculate as ever, took his position at the bar, waiting for the judge to be seated. The courtroom became hushed. There was a silent moment while both defence and prosecuting counsels took out their papers. The tension could be felt by all as they heard the sounds of keys turning in locks, and Freedom Stubbs was led up from the cells.

He dwarfed the prison officers on each side of him. He wore a neat, single-breasted suit, white shirt and tie, courtesy of Sir Charles. His long hair, as Smethurst had instructed, was tied back off his face in a thong. He was handcuffed, and he kept his head bowed, looking neither right nor left. The clerk of the court stepped forward.

Henshaw began his opening speech for the prosecution. The

court listened attentively. No reference was made to any of the previous murder counts. Henshaw made a blistering verbal attack on the accused man. He then proceeded to call his witnesses; miners who had seen Freedom's fight with Dai 'Hammer' Thomas, men who had heard him threaten to take revenge. Evan Evans gave a stuttering, nervous statement regarding the arrest of the accused man. Smethurst didn't let a single thing slip by him. He was in and out of his seat like a bobbing buoy, consistently attacking Henshaw for leading his witnesses, particularly in Evan Evans' case. The man was so nervous he even had a problem remembering his own address. When it was time for Smethurst to cross-question Evan Evans he bellowed, and the poor man actually jumped.

'When you arrested Freedom Stubbs did you find anything?'

'Pardon?'

'When the prisoner was arrested, did you find anything on his person?'

'No sir, we did not, but we had a damned good look. We also searched the gypsy camp, found nothing.'

'And could you tell us how the prisoner behaved? When arrested?'

'He came along quiet like, after we'd got him.'

Smethurst smiled his thanks and resumed his seat.

The next witness was yet another miner who had witnessed Freedom Stubbs' threatening behaviour after the fight at Highbury Fair. Morgan Jones revelled in the fact he had been called to the witness stand. He gave lurid details of Freedom's prowess in the ring, drawing murmurs from the gallery as he lifted his voice theatrically. When Smethurst began his cross-questioning, he kept his voice low, hardly audible, to make the witness more attentive.

'So you saw the prisoner threatening to take revenge, could you elaborate?'

'Oh yes, sir, he pointed like this, and his face was terrible fierce. He said he would get each man there, I took it to mean he would kill 'em.'

'Thank you Mr Jones, but the fight was over, was it not?'

'Yes, Dai Thomas was lying out cold, had to be hospitalized, he did, they thought he had killed him he was so bad.'

Smethurst then asked Morgan if he knew anything of Dai Thomas' present state of health. Morgan elaborated, his fist raised in a boxer's stance, telling the court that 'Hammer' was alive and well and fighting in Brighton. Morgan beamed around the court, waved to his mother in the gallery.

'Tell me, Mr Jones, why, in your opinion, was the defendant still fighting after the bout with Thomas was over?'

'Ah well, there had been some hanky-panky with one of the gyppo girls, and a few of the lads ...'

'Hanky-panky ...? What exactly do you mean by hanky-panky?'

'Well there had been a lot of beer flowing.'

'Are you saying there was a certain amount of drunkenness?'

'Oh yes, I'd say so ... a few of the lads had got a bit excited ...'

'Excited? ... I am sorry Mr Jones, I am still not exactly clear ... What were these lads doing?'

'Well, there was one of the gypsy girls, you know what they're like, she must have encouraged them. They were ... having their way with her ...'

The court buzzed. Smethurst sighed ... 'Ahhhhhh, having their way with her! What, all of them? How many lads did you see with this gypsy girl?'

Morgan Jones huffed and puffed, rubbed his head, and coughed with embarrassment. 'Maybe it had got a bit out of hand, but those lads paid for it.'

Smethurst ignored the reference to the boys' killings. He bellowed, making Jones gulp, 'You call *raping an innocent girl "getting a bit out of hand"*?'

The court erupted in loud boos and hisses. The judge called an adjournment for lunch.

Evelyne sat on her bed while Miss Freda tried to relate all the day's happenings. Suddenly Freda burst into tears.

'What is it, Freda? ... Oh, for goodness' sake, tell me! Have you any idea what it's like for me, sitting here day after day, not knowing ... *why are you crying?*'

Miss Freda gulped and sniffed. 'Because ... because I feel so sorry for him – Oh Evie, they say he'll hang.'

Evelyne wanted to shake Freda, but she fought for control, told her that she mustn't even *think* like that.

'I've not been on the stand yet, Freda, just wait until I get my ten penn'orth in ...'

Freda calmed down and blew her nose, while Evelyne wished she felt as positive as she sounded. Freedom was to be called to the stand the following morning.

In the early hours she woke from a nightmare, a terrible nightmare of a man swinging on the end of a rope. The man was Freedom.

*

Smethurst kept his eyes on Freedom and his fingers crossed as he was sworn in. He knew he was going to have to handle the man carefully. He had told Freedom to concentrate on him, to answer clearly, and above all to take care not to incriminate himself. He must make no reference to the other murders; he was on trial for the killing of William Thomas, and Thomas only. The handcuffs were removed and Freedom rubbed his wrists before placing both hands on the rail of the dock. If he was nervous he didn't show it, but stood, head high, and looked directly at Smethurst, as instructed.

In the gallery the women whispered and nudged one another, and a woman's voice was heard gasping, 'It's Valentino.'

Smethurst's voice silenced the court. 'State your name and occupation.'

Freedom's voice rang out, sounding somehow incongruous when he said the word 'fighter'.

'You have been brought before this court charged with the murder of William Thomas. Are you guilty or not guilty?'

Freedom's 'not guilty' met with a low buzzing from the court as if a swarm of bees had been let loose. The judge lifted an eyebrow and the noise subsided.

'You are a Romany gypsy, is that true, Mr Stubbs? And you have been working as a booth boxer and fairground boxer for the past eight years?'

Freedom answered every question firmly. Miss Freda, in the gallery, leaned forward to catch every single word. She noted his strange unfathomable eyes, his face like a mask, no one could tell what he was thinking. Not until Smethurst mentioned Evelyne did she see a strange reaction. His hands gripped the dock bar tighter for a second and then relaxed.

'Would you tell the court how you met Miss Jones?'

'She helped one of the girls from my clan. The girl had been raped and beaten, and Miss Jones helped her, cleaned her wounds, she was gentle and kind.'

Freedom took Smethurst by surprise by continuing, without any encouragement, 'If I am to hang, even though I swear before God I did not kill the boy, I take this time to say that no woman could have behaved more kindly or with such good intentions. If there is any man in this court who says different, he is a liar.'

Smethurst could see that the judge was about to interrupt. Freedom's speech was irrelevant, and he coughed loudly. 'I am sure everyone understands. As you said, Miss Jones was very caring and . . .'

Freedom interrupted calmly, his voice as loud and clear as a bell. 'No sir, she was different. We have a word for non-Romanies, we call them "palefaces". We do not trust them, we do not want them near our camps or with our people. Because she showed us respect and was gentle to a girl that had been raped, it is not right for people to say the things I have heard outside in the streets. They are calling her a "gyppo woman" . . .'

This time the judge interrupted and told Smethurst to control his witness. Smethurst glared at Freedom. 'Please, Mr Stubbs, in your own words, tell us what happened, to the very best of your recollection. How you met Miss Evelyne Jones, and exactly what occurred on the night of the murder of William Thomas.'

Freedom explained in detail exactly how he had met Evelyne, what had happened afterwards. How, months later, he had been to the valleys for the boxing match. The spectators listened attentively. Freedom continued uninterrupted right up until the night of his arrest. Smethurst nodded, keeping a watchful eye on him, encouraging him to speak freely. Freedom finished by saying how he had been brought to Cardiff. Smethurst raised his hand to pull at his wig, a signal he had told Freedom to watch for – he was to remain silent.

Smethurst left a long pause before he raised his voice. 'Thank you, Mr Stubbs. Now, I ask you, in front of this court, knowing you have sworn on the Bible to tell the truth – did you, Freedom Stubbs, take the life of William Thomas?'

'No sir, I did not.'

Smethurst looked at the judge. 'No further questions, Your Honour.'

A low buzz went around the court as Henshaw, taking his time, stood up to begin his cross-examination. He looked with chilling eyes at Freedom. His voice was softer, quieter than Smethurst's, and the spectators all leaned slightly forward, afraid to miss a word.

'Mr Stubbs, would you please look at exhibit number four, a photograph, and tell me what the mark across the deceased's forehead means?'

Smethurst chewed his lips. Freedom was handed the blown-up photograph of William Thomas. 'Yes, sir, it's a *dukkerin*'s sign.'

'I'm sorry Mr Stubbs – *dukkerin*?'

'Romany sign, sir, a *dukkerin* is what you call a fortune-teller. It is a curse sign.'

The court murmured and hushed immediately. Smethurst sucked in his breath. His foot tapped, and he gave Freedom a hard glare. He had already said too much. Henshaw bided his time, the spectators giving him their rapt attention.

'Mr Stubbs, you say you did not kill William Thomas, a nineteen-year-old boy, a boy found with his hands tied behind his pitiful body, his throat slit, and a blood mark, a strange symbol daubed on his forehead, a Romany curse ...'

The spectators murmured. Henshaw held up his hand for silence. Freedom appeared about to speak ... but Henshaw continued. 'You say you did not kill William Thomas, you swear this on the Holy Bible – tell me, as a Romany, are you a Christian?'

Smethurst swore under his breath. The buzzing grew loud again, and the judge hammered with his gavel to quieten the court room. He warned that, unless the spectators controlled themselves and behaved according to court rules, they would be removed. But the noise persisted, and shouts began from the gallery ... 'Liar – hang him – give him the rope ... *The rope, the rope ...*'

Two ushers approached the judge's bench. He leaned down to listen for a moment, then gave a tight nod of his head as he agreed to the troublemakers being removed. Several men and three rowdy women were ejected. Their voices could still be heard arguing in the corridor. Henshaw raised an eyebrow to Smethurst as silence fell once more in the court.

'I did not hear an answer to my question, Mr Stubbs. Are you a Christian?'

Freedom looked at Smethurst then back to Henshaw. 'I believe in God, and the Devil, may he take my soul if I am lying.'

Henshaw stepped up the pressure. 'Tell me, Mr Stubbs, are you or are you not the lover of Miss Evelyne Jones? Miss Jones, the only witness to give you an alibi for the night of the murder of William Thomas? Please reply to my question, Mr Stubbs. Is Miss Evelyne Jones your mistress?'

Freedom's hands gripped the dock bar tightly. 'No sir, she is not my woman.'

Henshaw turned round, shrugged his shoulders, tapped his pencil on the rail before him. This tapping was to become familiar, first the sharp end of the pencil, then the blunt end, tap–tap–tap . . .

'So Miss Jones, a schoolteacher, is nothing more than a true friend to the gypsy people. Could you tell me why, if she was simply a friend, a woman you had met on only one occasion before, why, during a boxing match at Devil's Pit three days after the brutal murder of William Thomas – I am referring, Mr Stubbs, to the night you were trying to avoid arrest – why did you . . . one moment . . . 'Henshaw perched a pair of half-moon glasses on the end of his nose. He picked up his notes. 'If I may quote you, Mr Stubbs, "I drove my wagon through the crowd of people and helped Miss Jones up beside me" . . . end of quote. Do you recall saying that? So would you now please tell the court why you would take hold of a woman, by her waist I presume, and lift her into a moving wagon . . . ?'

Freedom was nonplussed, unable to follow Henshaw's train of thought, his complex questioning.

'Perhaps I should refresh your memory again, Mr Stubbs. We are talking, are we not, of the night the police arrested you. If she was *not* your "woman", *not* your mistress, why did you take hold of her in what I can only describe as a very familiar, if not barbaric, way?'

A woman waved from the gallery and screeched, 'He could get hold of my waist any time he likes, ducks!'

Henshaw stared at the blonde woman leaning over the gallery. The court broke into laughter and the judge again rapped his gavel sharply and called for silence. Henshaw pursed his lips, removed his glasses, and sighed. 'Again, Mr Stubbs, I have to ask you please to reply to my question. We are not here – although I must say, some appear to think so – we are not here for our own amusement. This is a court of law. I am waiting, Mr Stubbs.'

Smethurst carefully unwrapped a toffee. Henshaw had learned some of Smethurst's personal tricks, he was playing to the gallery, condoning their behaviour. It was obvious that Freedom was at a loss. He gazed helplessly at Smethurst.

Tapping his pencil with an air of martyred patience, Henshaw repeated 'Well, Mr Stubbs, we are waiting.'

'She stood by me again, sir, she said they were out to kill me because they – the villagers – believed I had done the killing. There were many men trying to push the wagon over, I took her aboard the wagon because I was a-feared for her life.'

'Are you saying Miss Jones' own people were turning against her?'

'Yes, sir, they knew she'd been with me, and that lad was dead, and in the Romany way . . .'

Smethurst closed his eyes and gritted his teeth. The court was in an uproar.

The judge called for a lunch break, and everyone filed out of the room. Freedom was led down to the cells. When he was brought back after lunch, Henshaw cross-examined him for the rest of the afternoon.

*

That evening Evelyne waited for Freda's usual visit. She came into the hotel room and promptly burst into tears. 'Oh, I feel so sorry for him, Evie, he looks so alone, so alone ... And that Mr Henshaw twisted him so, made everything he said sound so bad ... he asks one question and leads it into another, and gets Freedom confused.'

Evelyne grew more and more nervous as Miss Freda described how cold and arrogant Mr Henshaw was. They both jumped with fright as someone pounded on the door, and they heard Sir Charles' voice demanding admission.

'Now look here, this isn't on. You know you mustn't talk to the witness, Miss Freda. Now please leave instantly ... go along, out, out – and make sure no one sees you as you leave.'

With a fearful look at Evelyne, Freda hurried out. Sir Charles closed the door after her. 'I shouldn't be here either.'

'How do you think it's going, sir?'

'Not good, not good at all – they're making him look like an oaf. Er ... look here, gel, you and this fellow ... er, you *have* been telling us the truth, haven't you?'

'About what, sir?'

'Well, this chap Henshaw's pretty sharp, and he's picked up that perhaps there's more to your so-called "friendship" with this fella than meets the eye.'

Evelyne's hands tightened in her lap. She swallowed hard. 'If I had lied to you, I would not get on to that witness stand and swear on the Holy Bible to a lie. Everything I said to you, and Mr Smethurst, was God's truth.'

'Ah, yes, quite ... well, I think you'll be called soon. I suppose Smethurst will talk to you before then. I'd best be off ... Goodnight.'

'Goodnight, Sir Charles.'

Evelyne lay down, hardly able to believe that after all she had been through Sir Charles had to ask her again. Her heart pounded and she began to worry. Mr Henshaw sounded even more threatening than Miss Freda had made out. He had obviously sown a seed of doubt in Sir Charles' mind.

In the morning Freedom was led, handcuffed, from the jail to the waiting police wagon. A small crowd outside hurled rotting vegetables and abuse, and spat in Freedom's face as he stared at them between the wagon's bars. They raised their fists and gave chase as it moved off. Most of them then went to join the dole queues, satisfied that they were at least better off than the gyppo. Poor they may be, but they were free.

Freedom touched a slight swelling on his right cheek.

He had been taunted so much at breakfast – not by the prisoners but by the warders – that he had lost his temper and hurled his porridge at a particularly unpleasant warder who took delight in needling him constantly. He had made lewd gestures and implied that Freedom and his kind were up to no good. Freedom was beaten as he was dragged back to his cell. The warder, still dripping cold porridge, shouted, 'They'll hang you sure as I'm standing here, and, by Christ, I'll pull the rope meself, you bastard!'

The wagon bounced and rocked over the cobbled side streets on the way to court. Freedom closed his eyes, breathed the fresh air into his lungs. As they drove through the back gates of the court yet another small group of people pelted the wagon. But a few girls stood by the gates waving flowers, calling his name. One blew him a kiss, and got a severe wallop from a man for behaving like a 'gyppo bitch'.

*

Smethurst was very angry. Freedom was looking rough, his suit crumpled, and there was a bruise forming on his cheek. He handed Freedom his own greasy comb and told him to do something with his hair. Clean it might be, but long strands hung loose from the leather thong. Smethurst felt sorry for losing his temper. 'The women in the gallery are on your side, lad. I wish we had a few on the jury. They'll be tossing flowers at you before the trial's over. Apparently you resemble that film actor chappie, Valentino.'

'I never been to no picture house, sir.'

An usher gave Smethurst the nod that court was about to sit, and he rushed to his chambers to throw on his wig and gown. Henshaw was already waiting, spick and span, checking his appearance in the mirror. 'So it's the big day – your girl's on the stand? Should be interesting.'

'You get copies of those two statements? From Lord Carlton and Captain Collins?'

'I did, old chap, I did. Personally I doubt if they'll help, you'd need the prince himself to step on the stand to get your chap off this one.'

'We'll see, we'll see – don't count your eggs yet. Want a toffee?'

Henshaw smiled a refusal as the judge entered, muttering about the riff-raff outside the court. Smethurst joked with the judge. 'They say my client's the spitting image of this movie star, fella called Rudolph Valentino.'

The judge snorted, 'Well, for the Lord's sake I hope the press don't pick that up, the wife'll be here next. She's seen *Four Horsemen of the Apocalypse* twice.' Smethurst nearly swallowed his toffee the wrong way as the judge swept out. '*Four Horsemen of the* what?'

Henshaw laughed, checked he had his glasses and then winked at Smethurst. 'Old boy's wife's a bit of a lady, so I've heard. Well, come on, let's get on with the show.'

Evelyne was driven to court in Sir Charles' Rolls-Royce. She was shaking with nerves and kept licking her lips because her mouth felt so dry.

At the court they were surrounded by newspaper reporters pushing forward to speak to Sir Charles. The flashes and bangs of the photographers' lights made Evelyne jump.

'May I ask you, Sir Charles, what your interest in this case might be? Please, Sir Charles, just a few words?'

'I simply want justice done, that is all. Freedom Stubbs is an innocent man who has already spent too long in jail.'

Two police officers pushed the reporters back, allowing Evelyne and Sir Charles to enter. The massive marbled reception area of the Law Courts was daunting, and Evelyne would have found it awe-inspiring if she had not been so nervous. Voices echoed and people rushed hither and thither. She was thankful to see the familiar figure of Smethurst striding towards them.

'Ah, you're here, good, good – curtain up in about five minutes.'

'Good God, man, can't you afford a better wig, the tail's over your left ear, looks dreadful.'

Smethurst turned his wig round, only to leave the tail sticking out over his right ear. An usher was waiting to lead Evelyne round to the waiting area. Sir Charles went ahead into the courtroom as Smethurst, his gown floating around him, walked with Evelyne to a long bench.

'Now just keep calm, and remember, don't let Henshaw ruffle you. He'll try his damnedest. Shouldn't be too long a wait, and may I say you look charming.'

He strode off before she could reply or thank him for his compliment. She could see what looked like food stains down the back of his gown.

She became aware of a man scrutinizing her from the doorway. His cold eyes made her shiver, his drawn face was set and hard.

Henshaw detected how nervous she was, and knew instantly she would be putty in his hands. He followed Smethurst into the court.

One hour ticked by, then another. Evelyne paced up and down the marbled corridor. She walked to the far end and peered round the corner. There was another bench, with a number of men sitting on it, some with cigarettes in their cupped hands. Above them hung a 'No Smoking' sign in bold red letters. Evelyne returned to her bench and sat down again.

In the courtroom Smethurst was in fine form, his face flushed a deep red, his big hands waving in the air. He called for the defendant, Freedom Stubbs, to be brought into the dock.

The raised voices from the court made Evelyne's nerves even worse. Suddenly the double doors were thrown open and an usher called her name. She dropped her handbag in her haste to follow him into the court.

*

Evelyne's hand trembled visibly as she held up the Bible, standing ramrod straight in the witness box. 'I swear by Almighty God that the evidence I shall give shall be the truth, the whole truth and nothing but the truth, so help me God.'

Smethurst smiled at her. 'Would you state your name and occupation?'

Evelyne's voice wavered, and she got another encouraging smile from Smethurst as she answered, 'I am a schoolteacher.'

'So at the time of the murder of William Thomas you were a schoolteacher. Now then, would you, in your own time, please tell the court how you first came to meet the accused, Freedom Stubbs?'

Evelyne told the court how some friends had taken her to Highbury Hill for an evening's entertainment. At this point Smethurst interrupted her. 'I'd say that was a rather unusual evening's entertainment for a respectable schoolteacher, wouldn't you agree, Miss Jones? And just exactly *who* were these friends who suggested you go to this boxing match?' He directed a half-smile at Henshaw.

Evelyne replied, 'Lord Frederick Carlton and Captain David Collins.'

A murmur ran round the court at the mention of the high-society names. Sir Charles gasped and dropped his monocle. Smethurst had assured him that neither man's name would even be mentioned in court. He slapped his kid gloves against his hand in anger – this was really outrageous.

Evelyne was in the witness box for almost an hour before they broke for lunch. She had hardly looked at the dock, at Freedom – she couldn't. He had never taken his eyes from her face. As they led him back to his cell he tried to catch her eye, but she was being escorted from the stand by an usher.

The afternoon session began with Evelyne once more in the box. The court heard how she had helped Rawnie, but her name was not spoken. She had everyone's full attention as she explained how she had collected the newspaper cuttings, how she had seen Freedom in her village and recognized him from the boxing match. She told the court why she had gone to his camp to warn him the police were looking for him. As she stated that on the night William Thomas was killed in the picture house, Freedom had been with her, the spectators stirred and whispered. Her voice was strong, confident, as she said that Freedom could not have committed the murder. She was calm and concise throughout the ordeal, and above all spoke clearly, accurately recalling dates and times. Smethurst turned to the judge. 'At this point, Your Honour, may I say that both Lord Frederick Carlton and Captain David Collins have given statements to verify what Miss Jones has said, and they will both, if required, repeat their statements in court.'

Sir Charles gave Smethurst a furious look as he sat down.

Before Henshaw cross-examined Evelyne, he requested permission to approach the bench with Smethurst for a moment.

They spoke in whispers. Henshaw had picked up on the newspaper cuttings and he was going to find it impossible to avoid mentioning the previous murders. Smethurst gave Henshaw the go-ahead. He had been prepared for this, and it did not involve any change in tactics. He knew he could turn it to his own advantage.

Henshaw walked back to his seat and shuffled through his papers, waiting for the court to be brought to order once again. He took his time, lips pursed, carefully placing his glasses on his nose. He coughed lightly and appeared to be concentrating on his notes. In a blatantly sarcastic manner, he asked 'Miss Jones, could you please tell the court where you gained your diplomas to teach?'

Evelyne flushed and replied that she had not taken examinations, but had taught at the junior school in her village.

'So you are not, as you stated, a schoolteacher, is that correct? And at the time you visited Highbury Fair, what was your profession then?'

Smethurst jumped up and objected that the line of questioning was irrelevant and had no bearing whatsoever on the case. The judge dismissed his interruption.

'So, Miss Jones, we take it that you were not in fact a schoolteacher but a pupil, am I correct?'

Evelyne unwittingly fell into the carefully laid trap. She admitted that she had actually left school because her family needed her at home. Henshaw gave a sarcastic smirk. 'Ahhhh, I see, so now we have gone from being a schoolteacher to not even being at *school*. Dear, dear, this is all very confusing. Let us now take the reason why you were at the fair. As my learned friend stated, a boxing match is not really a fit place for a lady . . .'

Smethurst was on his feet, objecting in his booming voice. It was irrelevant whether or not a boxing match was a suitable place for a lady to be taken – indeed, if the great Ethel Barrymore frequented boxing matches he felt sure there could be no slur attached to his witness.

The judge had had enough and called Smethurst to the bar to reprimand him, saying that unless he curtailed his constant interruptions the court would be adjourned. Smethurst apologized and returned to his seat, then turned in astonishment as Evelyne blurted out, 'I may not be a lady in *your* opinion, sir, but I assure you I was invited to the fair, unaware that there was to be a boxing match. I trusted my companions and I had no reason to believe they were taking me to anything more than an innocent fair. My companions were Lord Frederick Carlton and Mr David – *Captain* David Collins. Both gentlemen, I believe. So, in your rudeness to me you are also accusing two respected men of being less than gentlemen.'

This speech caused the gallery to erupt in loud shouts and a spate of hand-clapping. The judge pounded with his gavel and called for order. Henshaw's mouth twitched with anger, he shuffled his papers and was about to move on to another tactic when Evelyne, after a glance at the judge, spoke again. 'I'd also like, if I may, sir, I mean Your Honour, I would like to explain my education. It was partly private, and from Captain Collins' aunt. Mrs Doris Evans was her name, sir, and it was Mrs Evans who first brought me to Cardiff, and that is where I met Captain Collins. Just so you don't think I met him for the first time on the night of the fair.'

Henshaw snapped, 'Thank you, Miss Jones. You are implying, I believe, that you were a friend of Captain Collins' family?'

Evelyne again had the court in uproar when she agreed that Henshaw was correct, that she was a family friend, albeit a poor one.

Smethurst coughed and smiled at Henshaw behind his hand.

He knew Evelyne had got him rattled, and it tickled him. Smethurst was also pleased to see the judge's obvious delight in the witness.

Henshaw was aware that he had to get the situation back under his control. 'Let us move on to Freedom Stubbs.'

From the public gallery a raucous female yelled that she'd move on to Freedom Stubbs any time they liked, and she threw down a single red rose. Again the judge resorted to his gavel to bring the court to order. He then announced a recess until the following morning and asked both Henshaw and Smethurst to come to his chambers.

Smethurst proffered a toffee to Henshaw just as the judge entered. 'Now look here, you two, tomorrow I want no more of your baiting each other out there. Just conduct yourselves and your questioning in an orderly fashion. Is it true? Ethel Barrymore goes to watch fights? Where on earth did you get hold of that?'

About to reply, Smethurst stopped short as Henshaw slammed out of the room. It was in some way an omen, a foretaste of what was to take place the following morning.

Evelyne had been in the witness box for more than an hour, answering question after mundane question, but although she was tiring she maintained her concentration throughout. Henshaw was unrelenting, eventually bringing up the fact that Evelyne had kept newspaper cuttings of the previous murders. 'You cut articles from the papers and kept them for no other reason than mere interest? I find that hard to believe, just as I find your statement that you went alone to the gypsy camp on the night William Thomas was murdered hard to believe. It was almost dark, it was, after all, almost eight o'clock.'

Smethurst had wanted Evelyne to watch every word. This time she made no reply. By not actually asking her a question, Henshaw had hoped to trip her up. He sighed, twisting his glasses around. 'We are expected to believe an awful lot, Miss Jones, that you, just an ordinary girl, climbed a mountain to a gypsy camp to warn, *warn*, a man you insist you did not know, but you go alone, taking with you newspaper cuttings regarding that man's possible association with certain murders . . .'

At this point the judge clarified that the defendant had been cleared of all charges relating to the aforementioned murders. He allowed Henshaw to ask again why Evelyne had collected the reports from the newspapers, and why she took them to Freedom Stubbs. Evelyne answered that Freedom was illiterate, he could neither read nor write, and he was not aware that he was wanted for questioning. Henshaw raised his arms and shook his head in disbelief. 'You expect us to believe this? This preposterous fairy-tale? Wouldn't the truth be rather that you were less than a stranger to the accused? I think, Miss Jones, you knew him well, more than well – he is illiterate, how did you know this? What I believe you *did* know was that the defendant was in your village for the sole purpose of killing William Thomas, is that not the real truth?'

Evelyne could hear Mr Henshaw's breathing, the court was so quiet. Smethurst leaned forward, tense now. She kept her voice to a low whisper. 'At the time I did not know whether or not Freedom Stubbs had any involvement with those other boys, but I had to find out . . .'

'Could you tell the court why?'

'I recognized Willie Thomas, and I knew there could be trouble. I wanted it to stop even though I felt he should pay in some way for what he did to that poor girl. I just wanted to warn Freedom Stubbs, that was all.'

Henshaw shouted over Evelyne's words, '*You approve of murder, is that what you are saying?*'

Evelyne's temper snapped and she pointed at Henshaw, her voice rising. 'I never said that! What I said was, that if anyone saw what they had done to that poor girl, I mean if anyone had seen Willie that night, like I saw him, on top of her, ripping at her clothes, they would believe he should be punished. I *never* said I approved of *murder*.' She gripped the edge of the witness stand. She was so angry, angry because tears were running down her cheeks. 'You keep putting words into my mouth, sir. I just went up to the camp because I wanted to warn him there could be trouble and there might be a fight.'

'Mr Stubbs was there that night to do precisely that – *fight*. Miss Jones, have you at any time had sexual relations with the accused?'

All the spectators craned forward for Freedom and Evelyne's reactions to this question. Evelyne picked up the Bible and held it high. 'I am here because at the time of the killing of Willie Thomas I was with Freedom Stubbs, that is the sole reason I am here.'

'I am sure it is, Miss Jones, but you have not answered my question. Did you and the accused have a sexual relationship?'

'*No!* No, as God is my witness, I have not,' Evelyne sobbed.

Women in the gallery blew their noses and shook their heads. To them breaking down was somehow confirmation of her love for Freedom.

There was a sudden commotion as Freedom tried to get out of the dock, pushing at the guards. He shouted, 'Leave her alone! *Leave her be!*'

He was dragged from the court. A scuffle broke out on the way to the cells. The judge broke off the day's session.

Evelyne was driven back to the hotel in the Rolls. She knew it had not gone well. She was unable to talk to Sir Charles, who appeared more concerned about Freddy and David's names having been, as he put it, 'bandied about'.

After bathing and dressing, Sir Charles swept out of the hotel to dine with the Carltons. Evelyne watched from her window as he left. She felt drained, totally exhausted. Miss Freda could sense that she didn't want company, and tried to cheer her up by saying she'd done well, but Evelyne knew she hadn't.

'Oh God, Freda, I was just dreadful. I went to pieces, I said things I was not to say . . . If he hangs, it's my fault, my fault.'

Miss Freda shook her finger at Evelyne. 'I watched, all through the trial. He sits with his head bowed, his eyes down . . . but for you, he held his head high, he didn't seem afraid. So, you have faith too.'

'I wish it was over, dear God how I wish it was over.'

Freda hugged her, kissed the top of her head and whispered that if it was bad for them, think what poor Freedom must be going through.

Freedom lay on his bunk. He could hear the other prisoners singing, 'Swing me just a little bit higher, la-de-la, de-la . . . ' He pulled his pillow over his head. It wasn't the rope he was afraid of, he didn't think of it, all he wanted was for the night to come down, for the silence. Only then, when it was quiet, when all was calm, could he believe that she had stood by him. He wrapped his arms around the pillow and whispered her name. The pillow stank of prison. A month ago he had been able to dream, even wonder what she would feel like, smell like, close to him in bed. This night he could not dream, could not even hope.

The following morning the papers were full of the society names connected with the murder case. There was a large photograph of Sir Charles Wheeler and Evelyne pushing through the crowds.

Today was to be the summing-up, and Evelyne sat with Sir Charles on one side of her and Freda and Ed on the other. The court was packed to capacity.

Everyone rose as the judge took his seat and declared the session open. Henshaw gathered his meticulous notes, rose to his feet, his face stern. His voice rang out, 'I ask you, ladies and gentlemen, to look closely at the man standing in the dock. The defendant, a man known for his prowess in the boxing ring, a Romany gypsy, a booth boxer, a fairground fighter. William Thomas was nineteen years old, a young boy ready to start out in life. His life was brutally cut off, as brutal a killing as I have ever known. His hands tied behind his back, his throat slit, and to add insult to injury he was marked with a sign of a cross, a cross of his own blood smeared on his forehead. That mark, as we have heard in this court, is the symbol of a Romany curse. The accused man was heard, by witnesses, men brought before you in this court, to threaten – threaten revenge for an attack on one of his own people. This girl has not come forward, and we cannot ask William Thomas whether or not he did in fact rape this gypsy girl. So what do we have? We have, gentlemen of the jury, a defendant who wanted revenge. Freedom Stubbs was in the village, seen close to the picture house where this unfortunate boy was slain – seen on the actual night of the murder, and recognized by Miss Evelyne Jones, a woman with whom he was already on familiar terms, a woman we are expected to believe tried to persuade him to leave because she knew, *knew*, there would be trouble . . .'

Evelyne's heart was pounding. She gripped Freda's hand tightly. She could see the row of witnesses for the prosecution nodding their heads in agreement with everything Henshaw said. She looked only once at Freedom, and it was as if he sensed she was looking – he lifted his head and gave her the faintest glimmer of a smile. She bit her lips and stared at the floor.

Henshaw continued. 'I beg you, consider the evidence that has been heard in this courtroom. This man is guilty, and he must pay the penalty. This is no Romany court, no eye for an eye or tooth for a tooth. I ask for nothing more than justice, and it is in your hands. You, the jury, must find this man guilty of murder in the first degree.'

Smethurst tossed his toffee-paper aside and began his speech in a low voice. 'Oh, my learned friend is very persuasive and, looking around this court now, right now, I feel many people have already made up their minds that the man standing there, the man in the dock, is guilty.' He swung his big, domed head from side to side, and gradually turned to look up into the gallery, not once directing his gaze at the jury. Instead, he looked over the assembled people with a faint look of disgust on his face.

'Freedom Stubbs is accused of killing Willie Thomas, a boy who, as you have heard, raped and beat one of his people. Looking around this court right now I would say that any man here, *any* man confronted with someone they loved in the state that young girl was in, would threaten revenge. That is not to say that any person would actually go through with the threatened act. The defendant was not alone when this girl was discovered. There were at least forty other gypsy men at the boxing fair that evening – perhaps one of those men *did* take revenge, but we have a witness to prove that this man did not – could not, because at the time Willie Thomas was murdered she was with the accused.

'My learned friend has taken pains to point out that the witness for the defence, Miss Evelyne Jones, was more than familiar with the accused man. Is there a woman here today who would not have gone to the aid of a raped girl? Who would not have felt a certain amount of disgust that William Thomas was not punished for this crime? We *know* he was scared, we *know* he went to the Cardiff police, terrified the gypsy people would take some kind of revenge. You have heard a statement made by William Thomas to the Cardiff Constabulary stating that he did indeed play some part in that poor girl's rape. Miss Jones saw this girl, and has said, under oath, that she was raped and beaten. And what is the outcome? Her name has been blackened, she has been accused of being this man's mistress, he her lover, and both have sworn on oath that this is not true ... I say she is a woman who showed nothing more than simple, decent

357

kindness to a group of travellers. Miss Evelyne Jones should be *held up as an example to us all*, instead of being belittled, her education sneered at because, as my learned friend pointed out, she had not the qualifications to teach at the school. We have had a witness stand in front of you and give glowing reports of her ability – a qualified man, a man with examinations, the present headmaster of that same school ... But more, her character is without blemish, she is a Christian, a deeply religious, honest woman. She has *not* lied to this court, and her evidence is of the utmost importance. She has stated on oath that on the night of the killing of William Thomas she talked with the accused, that at no time could he have returned to the village, to the picture house, and committed murder.'

Smethurst was building up steam, facing the jury, his voice growing louder and louder as he swung his arms around. His black gown billowed like a bird, a big, dangerous bird. 'Where is the witness to say the accused was at the picture house? Look at him, look at his face, the size of him – do you think you would forget that face? If this man paid over money for a ticket, don't you think *one* person would remember? Come forward?'

Evelyne swallowed hard, and took a sneaky look around the court. All the faces showed rapt attention. 'Dear God,' she prayed, 'let no one mention the back door, the other entrance to poor Billy's picture house, always better used than the main door.'

Smethurst was sweating, his hair sticking to his head, his face redder than ever. Now he banged hard on the bench, slapping it, punctuating his words, '*Where* is the murder weapon?' he demanded, bellowing, 'The police *questioned* every man in that gypsy camp, *searched* every wagon, and they found nothing, *nothing*! No *blood* on any of the accused man's clothes, and at *no time* after he was arrested did he try to escape. Is *this* the behaviour of a guilty man? *This man is innocent ...* he stands in the dock for one reason, and one reason alone – he is a gypsy. Can you really believe that Miss Evelyne Jones could have an ulterior motive for coming forward? She is one of you, *one of your kind, you in the gallery*, and she has been mocked and insulted because she dared, yes, *dared* to come forward on behalf of the accused. She gains nothing, she wants nothing more than to see justice done ... and you, the jury, if you have any reasonable doubt, then you have only one choice – only one – give this man justice, and pronounce him innocent. He is *not guilty.*'

Smethurst slumped into his seat. He had not referred to his notebook once. He sat back, exhausted.

The judge called for a recess until the following day, when he would give his summing-up. Evelyne wanted to weep – it was still, after all this time, not over.

The following morning, the judge spent two hours summing up the case. He then instructed the jury in their duty. His voice was chesty and hoarse as he patiently explained to them that they must digest all the evidence they had heard. That they must be unanimous in their verdict, and if there was any reasonable doubt in any of their minds they had no alternative but to find Freedom Stubbs innocent. The jury filed out, and the judge went for a glass of port with Smethurst and Henshaw.

Evelyne, Ed and Miss Freda waited in the corridor, afraid to leave in case the jury came back in. None of them felt like talking – they just sat with their eyes on the ushers standing quietly in a group by the entrance to the court. Evelyne wanted to scream. She clasped Freda. 'Oh God, Freda, they've been out over an hour, it must be a bad sign, it's a bad sign – Ed, do you think it's a bad sign? Oh . . .'

Ed saw the spectators streaming in through the main doors. The group of ushers broke up and began directing people back into court. 'Here we go, Evie love, this is it by the look of it. Come on, or we'll miss our seats.'

Evelyne sat down, trembling, expectant. The clerk stood waiting for the judge, the ushers closed the doors.

'Please be upstanding . . .'

The noisy clamour of everyone rising drowned the last words as Smethurst and Henshaw preceded the judge into the court. Smethurst did not so much as glance at Evelyne, or Sir Charles, who was standing at the back of the court.

The jury filed back into their seats, the foreman obviously nervous, twisting his cloth cap round and round in his hands.

The clerk of the court waited for the judge to settle himself, then stepped up to the jury foreman.

'You have made your decision?'

'Yes sir, Your Honour sir, we have, sir.'

'And is it the decision of all of you?'

'Yes, sir, it is.'

The clerk held out his hand for the slip of paper in the foreman's shaking hand. He licked his lips. 'Please tell the court your decision. Do you find the accused, Freedom Stubbs, guilty or not guilty of murder?'

'Not guilty.'

The court erupted in one enormous cheer. Evelyne covered her face, the relief was unbearable. She repeated, 'Not guilty, not guilty,' over and over as if she could hardly believe it.

Freedom, standing in the dock, lowered his head and wept. The noise of the court was like a drum beating in his brain. A whirlwind whooshed around him, he was floating above everything, no voice was clear, no face – just hands grabbing, shaking his. He realized his handcuffs had been removed without knowing how. It was all a blur of confusion which climaxed in Freedom, surrounded by Sir Charles, Smethurst, Freda and Ed, walking from the court. He was free.

The press clamoured around them, camera flashes popped, the babble of voices asking him to look this way and that way, people screamed at him, wanting to know how it felt to be free. Crowds of women threw flower petals like a wedding party as they stood on the courthouse steps.

Sir Charles waved and smiled to the people, his arm around Freedom, then he held up Freedom's right arm as if he was in the boxing ring. The crowd went wild, chanting 'Freedom, Freedom, Freedom . . . ' and still he kept feeling it was a dream, that he would wake up, at any moment he would wake up in his small cell.

Ed pushed the people away as they moved down to a cavalcade of cars drawing up outside the court. Evelyne put her hands over her face as the flashing cameras blinded her, and she was separated from the main group. In the excitement Ed turned to Miss Freda, who was crying one moment and laughing the next, and shouted to her above the din.

'Marry me, will you marry me?'

Freda flung herself into his arms and they were carried along by the crowd to the waiting cars.

Evelyne was helped into Ed and Freda's car. Sir Charles had taken Freedom in the first car, which was now drawing out of the driveway. People ran beside the car, cheering, and Sir Charles waved to them as though he were the Prince of Wales himself.

Smethurst bundled himself into the last car and leaned back, satisfied with himself.

At the hotel, reporters hung around the entrance, more hovered inside the tea-room, and the cameras popped and flashed. They clustered around Sir Charles and Freedom, all talking at once, demanding interviews with the boxer. Sir Charles dominated the proceedings, while Freedom stood at his side.

'Gentlemen, please, please stay back, we will give a press interview in the morning, please, please stay back.'

Freedom looked over the heads to see Evelyne standing to one side. She seemed as overawed by the whole experience as he was. He tried to catch her eye, but she was jostled by a group of women determined to touch Freedom.

Some large porters arrived on the scene and began to move the crowd out of the hotel. Sir Charles steered Freedom towards the lift, where the snooty bellhop, beside himself, bowed and flushed and smiled to the cameras at the same time. They were the first to get clear of the lobby.

The movement of the lift made Freedom's heart lurch, and he put out his hands to steady himself.

'Keep your hands off the sides, sir, or you'll get hurt.'

The bellhop swung the gates open and Sir Charles stood aside for Freedom to go ahead of him. Dewhurst was hovering at the door of the suite, delighted but trying very hard to remain aloof and cool, as was his place.

'Book a table for dinner, Dewhurst, take over the small private dining room. Tonight we will celebrate.'

The door to Sir Charles' suite closed as the second lift reached the third floor, and Freda, Ed and Evelyne stepped out. The pair were so brimming with happiness and excitement that Evelyne's quietness went unnoticed.

'You comin' in? We'll 'ave some champagne, double celebration, eh? You told 'er yet, Freda? Come on, let's get in there.'

Evelyne was at the door of her own suite before Freda gasped out that she and Ed were going to be married, then Ed pulled Freda's hand and led her towards Sir Charles' suite.

Evelyne let herself into her room and closed the door, welcoming the silence, the peace. She was exhausted. She threw her hat on to the bed. So much for Freda's creations, no one seemed to have noticed her, never mind her clothes.

The bath water was running as Evelyne lay on her bed. She realized then that it was all over, she had finally seen something right through from start to finish. Freedom had been proved innocent, he was free, and instead of feeling elated she felt empty. While the trial had been on, she had had somewhere to go, something to do, and now she had nothing. She knew Sir Charles would be returning to London and, if Freda and Ed married, more than likely her only friend would be gone, too. She was alone, once more she was Miss Evelyne Jones, but now there was no 'schoolteacher' after her name. She had nothing.

She closed her eyes and tried to think what she would do with her life. The truth was, she didn't know what she wanted. She hadn't thought much of home – her Da, yes, but not the village. The verdict would certainly make some of those bitches swallow their words. They all seemed so far away, it was hard for her to believe she had only been away for a matter of weeks. She made up her mind that she would put a call through to the post office, just to see how Da was.

Evelyne had no idea that while she was soaking in the bath the papers were streaming off the printing machines. Headlines declared Freedom Stubbs' innocence, and there was a large photograph of Freedom standing next to Sir Charles. Below it was a smaller, single photograph of Evelyne. She was called the heroine, the woman who had brought about the gypsy's release from jail.

Chapter 16

Evelyne may not have thought that anyone had noticed her clothes, but one person did, and was so bitterly angry she tore the newspaper to shreds.

Lizzie-Ann, with a charabanc full of miners' wives, was on a day trip to Swansea. They had scrubbed their best clothes, begged or borrowed their fares for the trip to listen to a political meeting organized by striking miners' wives.

The lecturer addressed the women, unaware that actually to be there some of them had spent their week's food money. Their clothes were clean, why shouldn't they be? They were proud women, women who would not in any circumstances plead poverty, and their men were proud too. They were there to prove that they encouraged their men to fight for their rights, to claim better wages, they were there to stand up for their striking men.

The naïveté of the women, their belief that, by standing up and showing others, they would be followed went sadly amiss. The report that eventually found its way back to the powers-that-be claimed that, judging by the women who had shown up at the meeting, there was not so much hardship as was believed. The women showed no signs of exceptional stress, they seemed clean and prosperous, and it was noted that since the strike the death rate in the villages had dropped. Articles were written by various people stating that the men and boys were benefiting from the open-air life. The women, free from coal dust, began actually to enjoy regular hours. Schoolchildren now had a decent meal provided by the school every day, in some cases eleven meals a week, at a cost to the government of three shillings and sixpence per child. Special supplies of clothes and boots were sent to mining villages.

The state of the women's minds was even harder to detect than their outward show of 'prosperous, middle-class women'. The papers reported that they all seemed to be in good spirits, hard-working and running relief funds, collecting money from whist drives, women's football matches, dances and socials.

None of the government officers seemed really to see these four hundred women or the miners for what they were, an embattled community fighting for its life. The more determined they were to win, the braver the face they showed to the world. As their fellows, the blacklegs, caved in under the strain of unemployment and returned to work, they were slowly breaking the fighting spirit. The ridiculous calculations of strike pay and poor relief screamed out by government propaganda nailed their coffins down.

The strike was almost over, but the women didn't know it yet. As they travelled back to their villages they had high hopes that they had accomplished much for their men. The year was 1926, and it was a sad year for almost all the families of the largest single body of workers in the country. They had lost their battle and returned to work, caps in hands, defeated.

The Rhondda contingent was on the last stage of the journey. Tired, happy and ignorant, they passed around a bottle of gin they had clubbed together to buy. As the bus careered and jolted over the rough roads, the women sang their hearts out. 'My Little Grey Home in the West ... ' For some who had never travelled beyond their village, it was a day out to remember for the rest of their lives.

Lizzie-Ann cavorted up and down the aisle, hanging on as the charabanc rounded the sharp mountain bends. She was doing her old music-hall turns. She flopped into one of the empty seats at the back and saw a clutter of newspapers, a couple of days old, crumpled up on the floor. They had been used to wrap sandwiches in Swansea. The photograph of Evelyne stared up from the floor.

'They only gone an' *freed* the bugger, he's been proved inno- cent ... will you look at 'er, all togged out for a dance an' mixin' with the posh people, an 'er a dirty gyppo lover.'

One skinny woman stood up and said that in her opinion if a man was proved innocent in a court then that was the Lord's word.

'You're only saying that, Agnes Morgan, because your old man's been inside more times than you've had hot dinners, so siddown and shuddup.'

The rain started pelting down, and the bus bumped and rolled its way to the valley. Lizzie-Ann held a shredded piece of the paper. She smoothed it out on her worn skirt and studied the picture in minute detail.

Evelyne looked like a lady, standing there with a titled gent and wearing her fancy clothes. Lizzie-Ann couldn't help but compare herself, her worn, red hands, her stockingless legs and her puffy feet encased in hand-me-down lace-up shoes with thick, unflattering soles. Lizzie-Ann couldn't contain herself, she started to sob, her whole body shook, and all the bitterness and jealousy rose to the surface. 'I hate her, I *hate her guts*! It should have been *me*, it should have been *me*!'

The rain was still bucketing down as the women made their way home. Depression hung over every house in the village, and none more so than at Hugh Jones'. He stared into the fire, shaking his head. He had failed, the men had trusted him and now they were to return to work for even lower wages. He pounded the mantelpiece with his fist. 'Bastards ... *Bastards ... You bloody bastards!*'

Lizzie-Ann pushed open the back door and chucked in the torn and muddy newspaper. 'Here, Hugh Jones, read what your own's doin', whilst we're stuck here fightin' for a livin' wage, you should be ashamed of her. She'll never step over my front sill again, that's for sure.'

She banged the door shut so loud the curtains along the street flickered and faces peered out into the dark, rainy night.

Hugh picked up the paper, pressed it out flat on the table and saw his daughter's beloved face crowned with a smart hat. She was staring arrogantly into the camera. Above her was a picture of Sir Charles Wheeler, one of them rich land-owning bastards, how could she? Hugh felt a shadow cross his grave, and slowly he picked the paper up and stared at the photograph of Sir Charles Wheeler. He was holding the arm of the boxer, Freedom Stubbs, above his head.

Hugh dropped the paper and grabbed his cap, the back door banged once more and the curtains along the street flickered. The neighbours watched the big, hunched figure of Hugh Jones walking down the street.

'Probably goin' to Gladys's.'

But Hugh went into the pub. The place was empty apart from a few old'uns, and they sat hunched with their fags stuck in the corners of their mouths, playing dominoes.

'Yaaalright, Hugh lad? I'll have a half if you're buyin', and if you're not, sod ya.'

Hugh paid them no attention. He carried his frothing pint to an empty table and sat down. The men's hacking coughs and mutterings were accompanied by dull thwacks from the dartboard. Jim, Lizzie-Ann's husband, with his skeletal frame, a cigarette hanging from his mouth, stole sly looks at Hugh, but Hugh seemed not to notice. He was drinking steadily, draining his glass and banging it down for a refill.

'Ya gel's gone off with a gyppo, we hear, Hugh boy. Like 'em big, does she?'

The toothless old domino players cackled and coughed and went silent as they fingered their empty mugs.

Eventually, Hugh lurched out of the pub, and one old boy creaked to his feet and pottered over to drain the very last dregs from Hugh's fifth pint.

'All right fer some buggers, course, she hadda legacy, that's wot's carryin' 'im.'

Gladys could smell the drink on Hugh's breath. She said nothing, but folded her arms. She'd not seen him this bad before. He had a tipple like the rest of the men, but he was well away tonight.

'Have you eaten, lovey?'

'The lad got off free, Gladys, the gypsy, they found him not guilty.'

Gladys pursed her lips.

'Well, we know who we've got to thank for that, so the least said the better.'

Gladys couldn't even say the girl's name. She shuddered as Hugh put out his big hand to her, not even looking at her. 'Come here, come here, whassamatter with you? Come here.'

Gladys wouldn't move, she muttered that he was drunk and that he knew how she hated it, the drink.

He stood up, almost stumbled, straightened up and put his cap on. 'I'll be away then, goodnight.'

Gladys bit her lip as Hugh tried clumsily to open the door. He swore, and kicked it.

'We're going to have to talk, Hugh, a proper talk, not now, when you're sober.'

He turned on her and glared, he wasn't drunk, that was what was wrong with him, he wasn't drunk. 'I don't belong here, Gladys, I never did.'

Gladys let rip, afraid of losing him, afraid of having him. She became hysterical, her voice shrieking, 'She's not coming back, Hugh, you've been waiting for her to come home. Well she's gone, and you walk out that door you'll not come over my doorstep again. She's no good, you're well rid of her.'

Hugh gave her such a look that her blood froze. 'You're not fit to clean her shoes, woman.'

Gladys burst into tears and Hugh strode out into the wet,

dark street. As he turned the corner into Aldergrove Street he quickened his pace, the lights were on in the house, the lights ... Evelyne had come home.

He ran the last fifty yards like a young man, round into the back alley, overturning milk cans, till he burst into the kitchen.

'Evie? Evie? *Evie* ... ?'

It was Hugh that had left the gaslights burning. He laboured for breath, realizing the house was empty. Pain shot up his left arm like a red-hot poker, shooting and burning.

'Evie? *Evie*? Oh God, gel, come home.'

He picked up the newspaper, his breath heaving in his chest. The gas lamps lit the picture like a Chinese lantern, the faces alive, looking at him, and it was the face of Freedom, with the black hair, the arrogant slanted eyes and high cheekbones that made the second burning, stabbing pain rip up his arm and across his chest. He felt his arm stiffening, he couldn't bend it, he couldn't bring the paper closer to his face, his mind couldn't control his limbs, couldn't make them work. Hugh felt himself falling, unable to stop himself. His outstretched hand, gripping the paper, crashing into the dying embers of the fire. He couldn't move his hand away from the coals, the paper caught light and still he couldn't move.

Freedom's face burnt in front of him, the paper curling and browning as the flame crept slowly, slowly, towards his daughter's face. Then they were both gone, small, black flecks of burnt paper fluttered from the fire. Hugh could see her, see her with her bangles and her beads standing at the pithead, her little parcel of clothes tucked under her arm. Dark, heavy slanting eyes, black hair – the gypsy girl and Freedom were one.

*

Gladys took over the funeral arrangements and buried Hugh. The whole village walked behind the coffin. The choir and the brass band sang and played their hearts out in their farewell to the Old Lion. No one even attempted to contact his daughter; Gladys had told them all that on the very night Hugh had died he had been with her, and had disowned Evelyne. He was ashamed of her and wouldn't have wanted her at his burial. Gladys did concede to having Hugh buried alongside his dead, she couldn't do otherwise. He was with his sons and his wife.

The small headstone bore just the family names and dates. All the fragility and hardships of life, the laughter, the love, all contained in the silent, sad grave. Summer was coming, and cornflowers were scattered across the fields beyond the cemetery, but no flowers lay on this plot of freshly dug earth, there had been no one who cared enough to place them there.

The owners of the mine had already taken over the house in Aldergrove Street. They made a half-hearted attempt at tracing Evelyne who was still unaware of her father's death. It was as if there was nothing, nothing left of the Jones family but a list of names on a grave. How the Old Lion would have roared one last time with rage, but he lay with his sons, his wife, in silence.

Sir Charles had installed Freedom in one of the rooms in his vast suite at the hotel until they were ready to depart for London. They had been very busy, signing release papers, giving press interviews, settling accounts. They were now ready to leave Cardiff first thing in the morning, and Sir Charles had arranged a small dinner.

Freedom had not spoken to Evelyne since the trial, even to thank her. He had asked about her many times, but was always dissuaded from calling on her personally.

'Wouldn't look right, Freedom, remember how they questioned your relationship with her in the courtroom, I don't want you ever to be seen together, is that clear? You will be able to thank her at dinner before we leave, that will have to suffice.'

When he was not being led around by Sir Charles, Freedom sat alone in his small servant's room. He was free, but he wondered if he had simply exchanged one cell for another; his life, he knew, was no longer his own. It had been accepted without question that he would accompany Sir Charles when he returned to London. He would miss his people, miss his life, but there was nothing he could do about it.

Evelyne had dressed and changed for the dinner. She wore the dress Sir Charles had bought for her, the green ribbons in her hair, but the diamond and emerald necklace had been returned to the jeweller's. She had been just about to leave her suite when the telephone rang. The receptionist had been trying to get a call through to the village post office for her. Evelyne had tried so many times, and had asked them to keep trying, but the line was always busy. It was the only one in the village apart from the doctor's and the police station.

She ran to the phone, excited, she wanted to hear her Da's

voice, knew he would make everything all right, she had decided to go home.

Sir Charles was flushed, his familiar laugh filled the room, and the champagne flowed freely. He congratulated Ed and Miss Freda, but he couldn't help thinking that Ed was making a mistake. As sweet as Miss Freda was, to Sir Charles' critical eye she was a bit of an 'old boiler'. Ed seemed overjoyed so Sir Charles assured him that of course there would be a place for Miss Freda on the estate.

Lady Primrose and David arrived. The fact that he had 'spoken up' for the gypsy had given David a new social standing. Society admired him for it, as they did Lord Frederick who was also expected. Sir Charles smiled to himself. No one would ever know how he had twisted their arms.

Lord Freddy arrived with a magnum of champagne. They had been photographed in the hotel lobby and Freddy had given a rousing speech about 'British Justice'. He enjoyed the limelight, and he shook Freedom's hand, congratulating him.

Miss Freda constantly turned to the doorway, expecting to see Evelyne, but still she didn't arrive. Sir Charles beckoned her and suggested perhaps she should fetch the heroine to share in the celebration. Freedom went to Miss Freda's side and suggested that he should go to her. She blushed, having to crane her head to look up into his face. She told him Evelyne's room number and sighed. It was all so romantic.

Freedom slipped from the room and leant on the thick, flocked wall-paper in the corridor. He felt hot and the shirt and tie made his neck hurt, as if he was still bound and cuffed. He appeared relaxed and able to take care of himself, even mixing with the people in Sir Charles' suite, but all the faces and voices, the handshakes and the pats on the back, combined with the camera flashes to make him feel like roaring.

Two housemaids in their black dresses with white caps and pinnies scuttled past Freedom with lowered glances and nudges. He blushed and walked down the corridor to Evelyne's door. He pulled at his collar, ran his fingers through his hair. When he knocked he found the door was slightly ajar. He was not sure what he would say to her, how he would say it, but it was to Evelyne that he owed so much, far more than to Sir Charles.

He tapped again and then pushed the door open. He had begun to think she wasn't there when he noticed the bathroom door. He moved silently across the room and pushed the door gently.

Evelyne was huddled in a corner on the marble floor, her face pressed against the tiles, pressing hard so the white, ice-cold tiles hurt her cheeks. She couldn't cry, couldn't speak, she just wanted to press her body so hard against the walls and floor that it would disappear. Freedom knelt beside her, reached for her hand. It was as cold as the tiles, and she withdrew it and hugged her arms around her. He reached to turn her face towards him, and felt her straining against him, trying to hide her face.

'What is it, *manushi*, what is it?'

He lifted her easily from the floor and held her in his arms, carried her into the bedroom like a child. She was so close, he could feel her cold cheek against his neck, and he sat down, cradling her in his arms. Cupping her chin in his hand, he looked into her face. She was like a mute, staring helplessly at him, and he didn't know what to do to help her. 'What is it? Tell me, tell me?'

Freda opened the door.

'Come, darlinks, Sir Charles is waiting, everyone has arrived.' Her face creased with worry as she saw Evelyne. 'My God, what is wrong? Evelyne ... Evie, are you sick?'

Firmly but gently, Freedom told her to leave them alone, he would take care of Evelyne. She went straight back to Ed and whispered that something had happened, Evelyne was sick. Sir Charles beckoned her to his side. He asked her quietly where Freedom and Evelyne were, and Freda told him that Evelyne was sick, but it was all right because Freedom was taking care of her. Sir Charles' monocle popped out as he straightened up, angry.

Striding down the corridor, Sir Charles burst into Evelyne's suite without knocking. Ed followed, with Miss Freda close on his heels. His voice rose in anger, 'I want you out of here this instant, you hear me? Out! Did anyone see you come in here? Did they? Answer me, man, did anyone see you enter?'

Freedom was standing by the bed on which Evelyne lay curled like a child, her face as white as the bathroom tiles. Her hands were clenched to her sides, her eyes staring, oblivious to everyone in the room. Freedom moved silently to Sir Charles and gripped him by the shoulder, blocking his way. He hissed. 'You treat me like I was a guilty man! I done nothing wrong – I came to bring her to you, I've not laid a hand on her.'

Frightened for Evelyne, Miss Freda went to her side. It was as if she were frozen. Freedom left Sir Charles rubbing his shoulder where the pain of that grip still burned, and walked softly to the bed. 'She has grief inside her, Miss Freda, let me talk to her.'

Sir Charles gave Freda a small nod, but did not move from the room. Ed still hovered behind him. They were all slightly in awe of Freedom's contained strength, his power.

Freedom moved close to Evelyne, placed his hand on her head, then bent low, crouching down to look into her vacant, faraway eyes. '*Manushi*, let it go, don't hold it inside you, it will hurt you more. Embrace it, love it, grow from it, release your pain.'

Evelyne did not move, but her mouth quivered and she formed the single word, 'Da'.

Freedom whispered, 'Is it your father? Then see him, hold him, kiss him goodbye.'

Sir Charles stepped closer, 'If the girl's father has died, really I think we should leave her alone. Come along, everyone, please.'

He waved Ed and Freda out, and then waited for Freedom. There was a fleeting moment when no one was sure how Freedom would react to being ordered from the room. The dark eyes flashed, but then he bowed to Sir Charles' wish and walked out.

It was not in Sir Charles' nature to show emotion. He coughed, then spoke from where he stood, 'Can you hear me, dear? You have a good cry, and then if you feel well enough, join us when you can.'

Evelyne neither moved nor spoke. Sir Charles sighed, 'We leave Cardiff first thing in the morning, you are welcome to join us, I am sure I will be able to find some employment for you ... Miss Jones? Ah, well, perhaps this is not the time to discuss it ... but, should you need anything, you only have to call.'

Evelyne couldn't hear him, only the soft words of Freedom

cut through her pain . . . She began to picture her beloved Da. He was standing on the mountain, his arms open wide, laughing his wonderful, deep, bellowing laugh. She did not hear the door close behind Sir Charles. She knew what she had to do, and she rose from the bed as if every limb was stiff. She began to pack her clothes.

Sir Charles bade everyone farewell and surveyed the debris of the party. He sighed, he was tired out. He instructed Dewhurst to leave everything for the hotel staff, they both needed a good night's sleep before the journey.

On his way to his bedroom he passed Freedom's door. He paused and tapped lightly, inched the door open. Freedom lay sprawled across the bed, naked apart from a sheet draped across him. His long hair splayed out across the pillow; he looked like a Greek god, his handsome face more beautiful in sleep than any man's Sir Charles had ever seen. He swallowed, embarrassed at his intrusion on the sleeping man, and closed the door softly. His skin felt hot; he owned that creature, owned him, at least for the next five years.

The following morning Sir Charles and his chauffeur were packed and ready by seven. They departed with Freedom for the railway station, leaving Ed to arrange transport for all their luggage.

Freda was waiting in the lobby with her few possessions when Ed came down. He looked harassed, mopping his brow with a bright red handkerchief. It took four porters to carry Sir Charles' luggage from his suite to the waiting taxi.

'Have you seen Evelyne, Ed? Have you seen Evie?'

'I just went into 'er suite, she must 'ave already left wiv Sir Charles ... now, don't get me muddled, love, I got a lot ter think about ... Gawd almighty, you see 'ow much luggage I got to take charge of? His Lordship's offered her work on the estate so don't you worry yerself none, Gor Blimey, thirty-four cases.'

Miss Freda sighed, relieved to hear Evelyne was coming with them. 'He is a good man, Sir Charles, and with all of us together it will be like a family, Ed. Just like a family, won't it?'

Ed paid no attention as he ticked each pair of suitcases off the list. Satisfied all was well, he picked up Miss Freda's case.

'Well, let's be on our way, love, don't want to miss the train.'

Sir Charles was already installed in his private first-class compartment with Freedom. Ed and Miss Freda, helped by Dewhurst, settled themselves into the third-class compartment at the far end of the train. Picnic hampers, luggage, tickets, all caused such comings and goings that no one missed Evelyne. Freda and Ed presumed that she was with Sir Charles and Freedom, and if Sir Charles gave it a thought at all, he believed she was in the third-class compartment.

Evelyne had caught the local steam train to the valley earlier that morning. She could not face goodbyes. She wanted the mountain, the clean air, it was as if she couldn't breathe properly, her whole body felt constricted, tight. Hugh floated in and out of her thoughts as if she was going through her life, year by year. She could not really remember who had said, 'Reach out and love him, hold him, release the pain', all she knew was that she had to go on up to the mountain one last time.

As the train wound its slow way through the valley she began to relax, as if Hugh would be waiting on the platform for her.

Her head was light and she felt dizzy. She had to make herself breathe deeply, knowing that if she didn't, she would come apart. 'Hold on,' she whispered to herself, 'you are almost home.'

The movement of the train rocked Freedom gently from side to side. He was sitting opposite Sir Charles, who had begun the journey in good spirits, pointing out views to Freedom but, receiving little or no response, he had fallen silent.

Freedom stared out of the window and chewed his lip. He wondered if he should ask about Evelyne. Sir Charles had been openly irritated when he had ventured to ask after her as they boarded the train. He had told Freedom she would be with the others.

'She's on the train then, sir?'

Sir Charles crossed his immaculately tailored legs. 'Let us get something quite clear, shall we? Miss Jones was your only witness, your only alibi. You swore in open court that there was nothing between the two of you but the desire to see justice done. If you lied, you make a mockery of everyone concerned in your release, even the verdict. Without her testimony you would, most assuredly, have been hanged. If it was ever to be discovered that you both lied, then I would feel it my duty to hand you over to the police. I don't want you seeing the woman.' He stared hard at Freedom, his eyes glinting, and was met with a black, unfathomable, hooded look.

Freedom leaned forward, but Sir Charles didn't flinch. 'All I asked was if she was on the train, I have not had time even to say thank you. I was innocent, I never cut no man's throat . . . sir.'

'Do not worry yourself over her, I shall find her work, I think we both owe her that much.'

Freedom nodded and again stared out of the window. The matter closed, Sir Charles opened his writing-case. Freedom waited, leaning back, and through half-closed eyes he studied Sir Charles, as if willing him to sleep. The pen scratched on the paper, dipped in the inkwell ... then the case was set aside and Sir Charles' eyes slowly drooped, his head lolled on his chest.

The moment he was asleep Freedom rose like a cat, stealthily slid the door back, and went silently out into the corridor. He made his way down the train, from compartment to compartment, until he reached the third-class section, searching for Evelyne.

Ed Meadows looked up as the door slid open and Freedom bent his head to enter. 'Hello, son, how's the toffs' section, then? Sit down, sit down, soon be time to take down the picnic hamper.'

Freedom looked at the sleeping Dewhurst, then Miss Freda. He remained standing.

'Sit down, lad, you'll get a crick in the neck.'

'I was wanting to pay my respects to Miss Evelyne, sir.'

'None of your "sirs", name's Ed ... Is she not wiv you?'

Miss Freda looked concerned. 'We thought she was with you ... Ed, you said she was on the train, is she not with Sir Charles?'

Ed went red, rubbed his balding head. 'I went to her rooms, like, an' she'd gone. I thought she was wiv you, ain't she wiv you? Hey, where you goin'? Just a minute ...'

Freedom strode to the rear end of the compartments, opened the door.

'She won't be back there, lad, that's the luggage ... Freedom?'

Ed stood up, then fell backwards as the train lurched. Miss Freda caught his arm. 'Oh, Ed, Ed, I feel terrible, I should have gone to her.'

Ed released her hand, about to follow Freedom, then turned. 'You don't fink 'e'll get off, do you? He wouldn't, would 'e?'

The train gathered speed, and Ed hung on to the strap above his head. 'He couldn't, could he? Freda, what do you fink?'

Miss Freda felt wretched, but she shook her head. The train thundered into a tunnel, and Ed felt his way along the corridor in the darkness, banging against the sides. He kept telling himself the lad was just looking for Evelyne, but his heart was pounding. God, he wouldn't run away, would he?

As the train sped out of the long tunnel into the light of day, Ed sighed with relief. He could see Freedom, way up ahead of him. He called out, but the noise of the train drowned his words. He ran on, bumping into the luggage piled high on both sides of the compartment. Freedom shouted back to him, 'She's not on the train!'

He was pulling at the stiff white collar and tie, courtesy of Sir Charles. In a panic, Ed reeled from side to side of the train, grabbing at the straps. 'Now, don't go doing anything silly, son, we can contact her when the train stops.'

Freedom slid open the big loading door in the side of the compartment, and Ed screamed at the top of his voice.

'Don't! *Don't, for God's sake!*'

Desperately, Ed ran to catch Freedom as he stood poised at the open door, but he was still just out of reach when the train lurched and Ed had to hang on again. He could see the ground flashing past, and then Freedom jumped. Ed clung on for dear life to the side of the door, the wind whipping his cheeks, his jacket billowing out. He saw Freedom land, roll away from the wheels of the train, and in seconds he was on his feet running like a wild stallion. Trailing from the door where it had caught was Freedom's tie.

'Dear God, Freda, 'e's jumped the train, what the hell are we goin' ter do?' But there was nothing they could do, and Ed slumped down into his seat. He was beside himself. 'I'll get a bollockin' for this, mark my words, 'is Lordship'll blame this on me. Gawd almighty, the bloody fool, what he go an' do a fing like that for? What are we goin' ter do? He's just thrown away the chance of a lifetime ... Gawd almighty, that's me out of a job, us out of a place ter stay ... Bloody hell, what a mess.'

'He will have gone to Evelyne, she'll make him see sense, you will see, Ed, he signed the contract, didn't he?'

'He's a gyppo, Freda, nobody ever knows what those buggers're thinking. We should 'ave tied 'im up, that contract don't mean nuffink to them ... it don't mean nuffink ... Oh, Freda, we just lost a champion, me 'eart's breakin' ... he's gone, he's gone.'

Dewhurst slipped his bookmark into the pages of *Crime* and *Punishment*. 'I think I'd better go and tell Sir Charles, he may want me to pull the communication cord.'

Near tears, Ed watched Dewhurst bounce his way down the corridor. He gripped Miss Freda's hand. 'You watch Sir Charles get the law on 'im, they'll 'ave 'im back in a cell, the bloody fool.'

*

From the opposite side of Aldergrove Road, Evelyne could see her house, the lines of washing billowing in the breeze. Two children sat playing on the doorstep. She turned, head bowed, to walk up the cobbled street towards the mountain. She had to pause, leaning against a wall to rest and give herself strength to continue. Looming high above her, high above the village, the mountain rose as if fighting through the thick mist of black coal dust.

Her feet echoing on the cobbles caused a few curtains to flutter, and someone whispered, 'Evelyne Jones is back'. She hurried on, passing Doris Evans' house. Lizzie-Ann was just opening her bedroom curtains, and almost called out, but she clamped her hand across her mouth. 'Oh God, please don't say she wants her house . . .'

But the hunched figure kept on walking, looking neither to right nor left.

'She's going up to the grave,' Mrs Pugh murmured as she peered from behind her back-yard wall. All around were the sounds of the village waking, preparing for the morning shift, buckets clanking, clogs clattering. The mine spewed forth its blackened men, doors opened and slammed closed as the miners set off for their day's work. Like a shadow, Evelyne quickened her pace towards the grassy slopes, as if the clean air drew her.

'Hurry, Evie, it's bath time, come on, gel, get the water on.'

The church organist began his morning practice, squeezing out 'Onward Christian Soldiers' from the old organ. Threading her way through the soot-stained tombs, she began to run. The grass, fresh with dew, glistened, the water drops holding small speckles of coal dust like black tears. Hugh Jones, Mary Jones, the stillborn baby, little Davey, all lay together in the shadow of the mountain. Will, Mike and Dicken, all gone. The grave, so tiny, so cold and grey. There was nothing for her to embrace, nothing tangible for her to hold and feel. Drained of all emotion, she stood staring at the names of her beloved family. Nothing to embrace.

High on the mountain peak the sun broke, piercing the grey like a shaft of gold. Evelyne looked up and, hardly aware of what she was doing, began to run, higher, higher. She scrambled over bracken, stumbling, falling, but pushing herself on, upwards, higher, to the clean air, to the sun.

Freedom knew she would make for home. He had no thought for himself. He hitched a ride, then, to the consternation of the driver, jumped from the moving car. He ran the five miles down to the village, along the small, winding footpath, keeping up the steady, strong pace until his lungs were bursting. He saw the village below, pushed himself on. At the far end of the valley the mountain rose.

The streets were thronging with miners. Freedom was no fool; he knew what would happen if any of them caught him. He kept to the back lanes, his jacket collar turned up, his breath catching in his throat. He reached the corner of Aldergrove Road and saw a woman with three children slam the front door. Had he got confused? Was it the wrong street? He felt a tug at his sleeve and spun around.

Lizzie-Ann hugged her worn cardigan to her and stared up into his face. Her voice was strained, hoarse, 'She's gone up the mountain, gone crazy like her Ma.' Backing away, she took a sly look over her shoulder, afraid to be seen talking to the gyppo. She was frightened of him.

'There's nothing here for her, nobody wants her back.' She couldn't meet his eyes.

Freedom gave her a small nod of thanks, but she turned on her heel and scuttled away before he could say a word.

Gladys Turtle was out of breath when she caught Lizzie-Ann at the water taps. 'They say she's back, Evie Jones, is that right?' she gasped. 'Have you seen her? And the gyppo? Well?'

'By Christ, yer a moaning Minnie, Gladys Turtle, if I hadn't two kids an' another on the way I'd be off, now bugger off and mind yer own business.' Lizzie-Ann watched as the water spurting from the tap overflowed the bucket, ran over her worn, down-at-heel shoes, and trickled away down the cobbles. She whispered a prayer. 'Don't come back, Evie, please, oh, please . . .'

Although near exhaustion, Evelyne was still climbing, but now she gasped clean air into her lungs, heaving for each breath. Not far, not far now – she was almost there.

Her hair had worked loose, tumbling around her shoulders. She unbuttoned her coat. Soon she would be on the very peak, high above the valley.

Far below, Freedom began to climb. He couldn't see her, but he had found her suitcase by the grave. Further on he found her scarf caught in a bramble bush and held it, standing poised and still, listening, shading his eyes to look up the mountain against the sun. He threw his jacket aside and moved on, his heart thudding in his chest. Alert as an animal he could sense her, knew she was not far. He climbed higher, and suddenly fear gripped him tight. He looked down – it was her coat, cast aside. For one terrible moment he thought it had been her, his *manushi*. He called for her, shouted. Her name echoed around emptily, no Evie answered back.

'Evelyne ... Evelyne ... *Evelyne!*'

Rounding a shelf covered in man-sized boulders, he saw her, way above him, standing like a statue, arms up, hair blowing in the clean wind. She was turning, slowly, dangerously, her head back and eyes closed. At any moment she could fall, lose her balance. She was dancing with death.

His voice was low and soft, a whisper. 'Is it a partner you're wanting, Evie?' He was terrified she would open her eyes and fall, but she smiled, head high, facing the sun. He inched towards her without a sound, closer, until he could reach out and catch her ... he grabbed her by her long hair and pulled her to him. She turned on him like a wildcat, eyes blazing, and struck out at him, but he held her, took the blows ... dragged her to safety, while she scratched and fought him every inch. When he had got her to a safe distance, he gripped her by the shoulders, trapping her arms at her sides ... 'Look, look, see how close you were, woman, you could have been killed.'

She struggled, kicked out at him. 'Maybe that's what I want, get off me, you bugger, let me alone, this is my business ... *It's my life, God damn you!*'

He didn't mean to hit her so hard, her head snapped back and her mouth started to bleed. The shock made her still, calmed her.

'You're my life too, you'll give yourself to no mountain.'

'I'll not give myself to you either, let me go!' But she didn't struggle any more, and he eased his hold until he simply held her in his arms. The wonder of the valley spread below them, as if only for them. He picked her up, gently, and carried her to a rock, sat her down.

'What was his name? Your Da's name?'

She turned her head away from him, touched her bleeding lip ... after a moment she whispered his name, 'Hugh, Hugh ...'

'Well, girl, call out to him, call as loud as you can, release it, release him ...'

She shook her head, and Freedom cupped his hands to his mouth and called her Da ... called for Hugh.

His voice came back with the name of her father, and she felt the tears inside. She threw her head back and, as if defying the mountain, she cried out for her father. 'Hugh ... *Da*! *Da* ... *Da* ...'

The echo thundered, boomed, the words meeting, joining, until the sound became a roar ...

Freedom watched her, her face like a child's as she cupped her hands to her mouth and called to the air. He let her rise, moving closer to the edge ... '*Mary ... Will ... Mike ... Daveyyyyyyyyyyyyyyyy* ...'

She reached out to her dead, arms spread, calling to them, and when her grief broke through he was there at her side. All the tears she had not shed when she was a child, the tears for Hugh, for her family, for all of them.

She would never remember how long she had wept, only that he was there. He cradled her, rocked her like a baby and she felt safe, secure, and slowly, gradually, she was quiet.

'I can feel your heart, *manushi*.' He laid his hand over her right breast. It felt as if it was burning through her ... then he took her hand and laid it against his own heart. He laughed, lying back in the grass.

'You laughing at me, man?'

He took her hand, kissed her fingers. 'No, *manushi*, I'm not laughing ... see, we gyppos, when we marry we don't need no church, no service. Some of 'em have 'em, but most place hands to hearts ... when they beat as one, well, then they're married.'

She didn't know whether he was serious or not, because he had such a strange smile on his face. But she could feel the imprint of his hand on her breast, as if her heart were on fire. She looked into his eyes, and he drew her gently to him. His kiss was so sweet, his lips hardly brushed hers, and it was Evelyne who reached for him, pulled him to her ... the burning in her heart spread through her whole body, and she clung to him.

He reached over and slowly undid each button of her blouse. She didn't resist, but lay still until it was undone completely, and he pulled it gently away from her breasts. Her skin was white, her breasts had the palest pink nipples he had ever seen ... He bent his dark head and kissed each nipple in turn, then lay his head on her breast and felt the pounding of her heart.

He whispered, '*Manushi*, my *manushi* ... ' Gently, unhurriedly, he slipped her boots off, untying each lace and easing them away from her feet, kissing her toes, light, featherweight kisses. He unhooked her skirt, and she did nothing to assist him, lying with one arm across her face, eyes closed. He lifted her in his arms and pulled the skirt from beneath her until she was naked, and then he laid her down on her skirt. She was frightened, afraid to open her eyes, to see him, see his face. He stood up and slipped out of his trousers until he too was naked, and stood looking down at her for a moment. Then he lay next to her, she could feel his heart and she waited, but he didn't touch her. Her whole body was burning, her mouth dry, her heart pounding as if it were going to burst through her breasts.

She lowered her hand from her face and let it rest at her side. She could feel his skin. Slowly turning her body to face him, looking into his eyes, she put her hand to his heart. He smiled and laid his hand on her heart.

He made love to her gently, guiding her, making sure he didn't hurt her or make her afraid, and when he was sure of her, knew by the movements of her body that she was ready, he let loose his passion. Evelyne rose with him, moved with him, and they were insatiable, their greed for each other consuming. She made love with a rage, until she was released by an explosion inside her body that in turn released her mind. It was such an exquisite emotion that she wanted it over and over again.

She slept safe in the crook of his arm. He studied her face. She sat at peace now, and she was his. He would never let her go, she was his *manushi*, his wife.

She was shy at first when she woke, covering her naked breasts with her hands. He made her take her hands away, telling her she was more beautiful than any wildflower they could see. To assure her of this, he gathered wild cornflowers till his arms were filled with them and laid them over her body.

'Oh, these were my Ma and Da's favourite.'

There was no pain when she said their names. Her grief had

gone as her loved ones had been embraced and kissed goodbye. Then together they laid cornflowers on the grave.

'Now, gel, which way would you say London was?'

'London?'

'Aye, I'm to be a champion boxer, I signed a contract. Sir Charles said he'd give thee work ... Come, give us yer hand, gel.'

Freedom had made a crown of cornflowers. She laughed when he set it gently on her head. Then arm in arm they walked down from the mountain, away from the grave. Evelyne's gentle, delighted laugh echoed back to them, like the soft whisper of Mary Jones ...

'Leave the valley, Evie, promise me ...'

BOOK THREE

Chapter 17

Sir Charles Wheeler's estate was twenty miles from Salisbury. After passing through Andover, the route then wound through mile upon mile of country lanes. Eventually, small, white, hand-painted wooden signposts directed the traveller towards 'The Grange' and along lanes only wide enough for a single vehicle, so that it seemed as though The Grange might be only one of the numerous farms buried among the fields and woods.

The arched stone entrance, with gates twenty feet high, set in six-foot stone walls, gave no indication of what lay beyond. The driveway was of gravel, raked smooth, and showed no tracks, but the hedgerows and the profusion of rhododendron bushes with their bright pink and purple blooms gave a hint of what lay beyond. The bushes gave way to a stretch of oak trees half a mile wide, their thick trunks and massive branches joining in an arch, and still the driveway continued.

After a further mile through the magical bower, The Grange itself was still not in sight until, rounding a curve, there it was, standing in such splendour it took the breath away. Hundreds of rose bushes covered immaculate sloping lawns which bordered the horseshoe drive. A vast fountain sprayed fans of water twenty feet from the open mouths of marble dolphins. Glittering mermaids rode on the creatures' backs, hands outstretched to welcome visitors. But dominating it all was The Grange, a majestic, overpoweringly beautiful house. Six white pillars flanked the fifteen marble steps to the arched entrance. Three storeys high, built in white sandstone, the house was awe-inspiring in its size and architectural proportions.

On each side were more lawns and gardens, with lily ponds and statues. Paths led to the outhouses, stables, barns and, hidden behind a bank of trees, a farm with sprawling, well-kept fields. Behind were more gardens, a man-made lake, and mile upon mile of forest and sloping hills. The Grange dominated the thousand acres surrounding it with such power that any onlooker bowed to its presence.

Also behind The Grange were staff quarters for those who worked the land. In comparison with the house, their cottages were like rows of dolls' houses. The stables were more splendid, with vast paddocks containing a herd of the finest hunters, groomed by a score of stable boys. The ground staff numbered thirty-five; gardeners, gamekeepers, huntsmen. In addition, there were more than twenty full-time staff employed to run the house. Cooks, butlers, footmen, pantry-maids, valets; all quartered on the very top floor of The Grange ... the personal estate of Sir Charles Wheeler.

Rawnie blew a circle of smoke from her hand-rolled cigarette. It drifted and curled above her head in a blue haze. She closed her eyes. She stood high on the brow of a hill overlooking The Grange. Next to her stood Jesse, chewing a long piece of grass, as handsome as ever. He shaded his eyes to look down into the paddocks below.

'Do ye see him?'

'Aye, it's him, cross the paddocks, running like a hare ... Mun runs for 'em like one of their *grys* ... look at 'im.'

Way below her Rawnie watched the running figure of Freedom. Behind him was a motorcar, and they could see a boy standing on the running board, shouting and waving his arms at Freedom.

With one eye on his stopwatch and the other on the road, Ed Meadows swerved the car, almost knocking the boy off the running board. He put his foot down on the accelerator, and closed the gap between the car and Freedom. 'Tell 'im to ease off, that's enough for today.'

The boy shouted, but Freedom continued to run. If anything, he picked up speed.

'Jesus God, 'e'll run 'imself ter death.'

Ed tooted the horn and drove alongside Freedom. 'Hey, hey, that's it, Freedom ... come on, lad, ease yerself down.'

Freedom turned his head towards Ed, but ran on. He had a look on his face that Ed had become accustomed to, a strange, defiant stare. Eventually Ed drove in front of Freedom and turned the car across the lane, got out and shouted at him in a fury, hands on hips. 'When I say you've 'ad enough I mean it. You've run more'n fifteen miles and we got to go an' work out, you tryin' ter kill yerself?'

Breath hissing, lungs heaving, Freedom faced him. His long hair was dripping, and his old, rough shirt was sodden with sweat. He laid his hands on the motor, and Ed quickly wrapped a towel around his shoulders and began rubbing him down. Freedom shrugged him away, flicked the towel out of his grasp, and stepped aside to wipe his own sweating body. 'Months I been here, mun, every day, runnin', sparrin', liftin' the weights, trainin' . . . and for what, when do I fight, mun?'

Ed's look told the young lad to move off. The boy was one of the sparring partners they had brought from London and he was standing staring at Freedom, hero-worship written all over his face.

Ed moved closer to Freedom. 'You don't talk ter me that way. You want a fight, I want a fight, but we do what 'is Lordship tells us to do, we wait. *I* tell *you* when we're ready for a bout, not you, *I'm* the bloody trainer.'

His breathing eased, Freedom tossed the towel to the boy and shrugged. His voice was quiet, his fist clenched.

'I'm ready, you know it. I been fighting years before I was brought here, I'm in the gym day in day out, an' for what? To entertain 'is Lordship's toffs when they come ta visit? I hate him always watchin' me, is that all I'm here fer? I want a fight.'

Ed knew all that Freedom was saying was right, but he could do nothing. He moved to Freedom and began to rub his shoulders, calming him as if he were an animal. 'I know, I know, lad . . . maybe we'll take it easy for a few days, huh? Maybe I pushed you too hard.'

Freedom laughed, rubbed Ed's balding head. 'I want a fight, Ed, that's all.'

As they were about to climb into the car there was the sound of an owl hooting. Neither the young boy nor Ed paid any attention, but Freedom turned, suddenly alert. Then came a whistle, soft but shrill, and Freedom shaded his eyes to look up into the woods. He cupped his hands and whistled, and again came the high-pitched, single note, like a bird.

'Gawd 'elp us, get in the car, what yer doin' now? Birdwatchin'? Come on, lad, let's have breakfast, I'm starvin' after all this exercise.'

Freedom jumped on to the running board of the car as Ed drove back to The Grange. He looked up to the woods and smiled, gave a small wave like a salute. Jesse and Rawnie knew he was aware that they were waiting, he had answered their call.

Evelyne had been up since six-thirty, eaten her breakfast in the kitchens and then begun her work in the library. Sir Charles had given her the job of repairing and cataloguing the vast collection of books. Since her arrival at The Grange, Evelyne had seen him only once, when he implied that he would employ her on condition that she have no contact with Freedom. Quietly and icily, he had told her he was prepared to make Freedom a champion, but if he discovered there was anything more in Freedom's run from the train than the desire to thank her for her part in his acquittal, he would have no option but to destroy Freedom's contract. He did not want any scandal, any repercussions or publicity in relation to the murder charges Freedom faced in Cardiff.

'He ran once, let him try it again and I will wash my hands of him, is that clear?'

Evelyne understood the veiled threat and assured Sir Charles that she would work in the house as instructed, nothing more.

She was given a small room in the servants' quarters at the top of the house. She spent her days in the musty library, ate her meals with the servants. The housekeeper, Miss Balfour, was loathed by all of them. She ran The Grange like a military camp and God help anyone who did not knuckle under her regime. Due to the nature of Evelyne's work, she was immediately set apart.

'I have always interviewed the staff in the past, Miss Jones ... However, as Sir Charles has already instructed you in your duties, make sure you carry them out to the letter.'

The housemaids' and parlour maids' gossip bored Evelyne, and the rules and regulations they all abided by frustrated her. The house revolved around the periods when Sir Charles was in residence, his weekend house parties. Evelyne had no chance to see any of his high-society guests. All servants, unless they were actually in attendance, were told to stay out of sight. Evelyne felt trapped. Even to enjoy the beauty of their surroundings was forbidden; they were not allowed to use the grounds or walk among the rose gardens. The gulf between 'them' and 'us' was brought home to Evelyne daily.

Her frustration mounted until she felt she would explode. This was not what she wanted, to be a servant. At least in the valley she had felt free, but here she was bound by such strict rules that even to be in the main hall was a sin. But her secret meetings with Freedom would have been judged a greater sin, were they discovered.

Freedom had also had the lecture from Sir Charles, but with a difference. Sir Charles had implied that Evelyne would be dismissed if he should hear so much as a whisper of an association between them.

*

Freda, now Mrs Ed Meadows, had tried to talk to Ed, tried to tell him that keeping the couple apart was asking for trouble. In his heart Ed knew she was right, but it was not only the cottage and his job that were at stake, there was the future champion's career. 'You got ter do what 'is Lordship wants, Freda love, there's no way round it.'

'Ed, this is our home, Sir Charles won't even know if they come and have a little supper with us now and then, just once a week, on her afternoon off . . .'

Ed huffed and puffed, but the suppers had become a regular weekly occurrence, and it was during these evenings that Evelyne had begun to teach Freedom to read and write.

They had been at The Grange almost four months, and tension lay close to the surface. Freda could feel it and it worried her. She hoped the four of them would discuss it today, it was Evelyne's half-day off. Freda always cooked a roast on these occasions, and she had already begun laying the table. Ed paced up and down, unable to relax enough to put his carpet slippers on.

'You know he's ready ter fight, and we ain't had a word from Sir Charles. He's gettin' hard ter handle, Freda, he knows 'e's ready an' all. I just don't know what else I can do . . .'

Evelyne arrived and tossed her coat aside. She sighed, and slumped into the fireside chair.

'I've had enough of that Miss Balfour. The library's nearly finished and she snoops after me, checking that I've done this or that. Well, she'll not get me lugging buckets of coal up and down them stairs like the maids. She caught me in the drawing room, I was just looking at the paintings and she tells me I have no right to be in there. "I'm just looking at the paintings, Miss

Balfour," I tell her. "You've no right to look," she says. Can you believe it, Freda? I said to her, "You don't mind if I look out of my window and see the woods, the countryside, he don't own *them*, does he?"'

Ed sighed, looking very glum. 'They do, love, they do, far as the eye can see – all his Lordship's land, he owns the lot.'

Evelyne turned to Ed with a furious look. 'Well, he doesn't own *me!*'

'As long as you are in his employ, he does.'

Evelyne paced the tiny cottage while Freda finished setting the table. Ed flicked the curtains aside, wondering where Freedom was and hoping no one would see him coming to the cottage.

'He's late, he's in a terrible mood, an' all, can't you talk to 'im, Evie? Settle 'im down, you know he's taken to sleeping outside, made hisself some kind of tent? The lads don't know what to make of him . . . where the hell is he? You got the time, Freda?'

Freda pointed to the clock, then checked to see how the chicken was cooking. Unlike everyone else, Freda was happy as a lark. The cottage, with its new curtains and loose covers, delighted her. 'Oh, he'll be here, he won't miss seeing his Evie.'

Ed sighed. That was another thing, if Sir Charles found out about those two, there would be real trouble. He was up and down, jumpy as a ferret, worried someone would find out about these weekly meetings.

Evelyne took out Freedom's exercise books, thumbed through the pages of looped, childish writing. 'He won't try half the time, you know. He should be able to read and write by now, but he won't concentrate for more than a minute . . .'

Freda tittered, waved her wooden spoon. 'His attention is too much on you, that's why, darlink.'

Ed flicked the curtains again, muttered, and sat down opposite Evelyne.

She was shaking her head, still turning the pages. 'Funny thing, he's completely ambidextrous, and he's no fool, got a wit about him, has me laughing . . .'

'What? What you say 'e's got? Ambi what? Ill, you fink 'e's ill?'

With a giggle, Evelyne explained to Ed that she meant he could write with either hand, right or left.

'Gawd 'elp me, I been assumin' he was a southpaw, but . . . Hey, wait 'til I get him in action termorrow, *ambidixious*, that what you call it? Well, I never . . . look, Freda love, I'll just go an' see what 'e's doin', all right, ducks?'

Freda raised her eyes to heaven. 'Well, at least that cheered him up . . . Evie?'

Evelyne was staring into the fire, Freedom's book still on her knee. Freda sat on the arm of her chair and hugged her.

'What is it, darlink, you want to tell me?'

Evelyne kissed Freda's hand. 'I'm thinking of leaving, Freda, I feel as if I'm being buried alive. There's a whole world out there, and I want . . . I want . . .'

'What, Evie? What do you think is so special out there?'

Confused, frustrated, Evelyne bit her lip. 'I won't know unless I try, but I want to teach, you know? And maybe I could get work that would fulfil me. Here, I'm just stifled.'

'What about Freedom?'

Tears pricked Evelyne's eyes, and she shook her head. 'There's no future for us, you must know that, and if Sir Charles knew we even saw each other ... well, I don't have to tell you what would happen.'

Freda kept quiet, knowing Evie had to talk, get it out of her system.

'We meet on Sundays, oh, far away from this place, up in the woods. We walk, and he's like a child. There's a wild deer, and he calls to it and it comes over, nuzzles him and takes food from his hand. He knows the name of every flower, every creature, and sometimes it's magic with him. He's so gentle, caring, and those times I love him ... He's like no other man I've ever known, and yet, he won't educate himself, he won't better himself ... I *have* to go away, Freda.'

Freda bent and kissed the top of Evelyne's head as Ed burst into the cottage. 'He's gone, no sign of 'im no place, the lads said they saw 'im crossin' the field at six, an' 'e had a bundle under 'is arm. He's run off ... you better go back to the house, Evie, I'm going ter 'ave ter get a search party out.'

'Oh, Ed, don't be stupid, he will be back! He will just have gone walking, you know the way he is – he knows it's Evie's supper with us.'

'There's a gypsy camp in the field behind the woods, I got to get to 'im first. If the estate manager finds out, they'll get the law on to 'em. If they're poachin', there'll be all hell let loose.'

Evelyne's hands clenched in anger. 'Ed, he came here of his own free will, he'll not run out on you ... for God's sake don't tell the game wardens, I'll go and find him.'

Ed gripped her by the shoulders, tight. 'You'll do no such thing, 'is Lordship's back, arrived half an hour ago wiv a whole party of society people, I don't want you gettin' involved. My job's on the line as it is, havin' you meetin' him here.'

It was Freda's turn to confront Ed. 'Ed, listen to her, she knows him better than anyone, he'll be back, you know he will.'

'*Will he*? Well, you go an' tell that bitch, Miss Balfour. He took a bundle under his arm all right, two hams, a chicken and a turkey what they was preparin' fer Sir Charles' bleedin' house guests. It ain't me settin' the gamekeepers on 'im, but Miss bloody Balfour.'

Evelyne grabbed her coat and was halfway to the door.

'Evie, darlin', I'm sorry, don't get me wrong, I trust him, Gawd 'elp me, I love the lad, but . . . I been worried sick these last few weeks. I knew somethin' was brewin', I didn't mean to sound off at you, you an' him are welcome here any time.'

Evelyne gave him a small smile, then hurried back to The Grange. From her tiny window high in the roof she could see the flare of torches as the gamekeepers prepared to search the woods. She was saddened by Freedom's foolishness, but at the same time it cemented her decision. She would have to leave.

The camp-fire was lit, piled high with logs stolen from The Grange's wood-house. There were only four wagons, belonging to travellers on their way back from the Ascot races. Sitting in a semicircle around the fire, they ate the food Freedom had brought. There was beer and Jesse had two bottles of whisky. They were all in good humour, and one of the men took out his fiddle and began to play. Strung up on one of the wagons were rabbits, poached from the estate.

Jesse was wearing a new, dark pin-striped suit, and he was proud of it, flaunting his waistcoat, amusing them all as he clicked his heels and danced to the fiddle. There were gold rings on his fingers, and his heavy earring was of gold. He clapped his hands, and his whiter-than-white teeth gleamed in the firelight. 'Will you *rokka* Romany, Freedom? Eh, ehe heyup yup?'

Freedom had been downing beer and whisky and now he lolled against the side of a wagon. He shook his head and waved for Jesse to continue. Jesse was making them all laugh at the fine man Freedom had turned into, living like a prince and being made to run each day to beat the motor vehicle . . .

Rawnie slipped to Freedom's side. She still wore her brightly coloured skirts, her bangles and beads. Her thick, coal-black hair was braided and threaded with gold. The kohl around her eyes made them seem huge, like the tame deer that fed from Freedom's hand. But she was thin, even gaunt, and she coughed constantly. 'Are thee well, mun?'

Freedom smiled up at her and nodded, held out his hand for her to come and sit with him. She looked back at the arrogant, dancing Jesse. She wouldn't come close.

'Does he care for thee?'

She drew on the ever-present hand-rolled cigarette, releasing a cloud of smoke that all but obscured her face as she spoke in her low, husky voice. 'He does . . . are thee with the paleface woman?'

Freedom smiled, tilting his head. 'Ay, she's my *manushi*.'

A small boy with dark, flashing eyes and thick, black curly hair appeared behind Rawnie's skirts. Freedom leaned forward and the child peeked around Rawnie and gave him a cheeky grin.

'He be called Johnny . . . Johnny Mask, he's a right bugger, we call him mask because you can belt the livin' daylights out of him an' he don't ever care none.'

Freedom looked up at her as she touched the young boy's head, gently. Then Johnny ran back to Jesse, clicked his heels, and the pair danced together.

'He be Jesse's boy, a pure *Tatchey*, then there are two more *doshas*, see them, on the *vargo* steps.'

Freedom looked over at the two little girls, hand in hand, watching the dancing. He stood up, watched Rawnie's sad eyes. They were not her own, she did not even have to tell him ... he held out his arms, wanting to hold her. She tossed her cigarette aside, stepping back so he could not touch her. 'We're moving to the races, north, we'll join the clans. Jesse is leader now, but we need a strong-armed man, the fights are where the money is ... livin' like a king, maybe ye don't need it.'

Her voice had become mocking. She rolled another cigarette, and as she lit it the flame illuminated her face, her haunted eyes. 'Will thee travel with us, Freedom? See, there's Chalida with no man beside her, she's Romanchilde.'

Chalida, sitting with the two *doshas*, was a beautiful girl with her hair unbraided to show she was unmarried. She looked up, and Freedom gave her a small bow, then turned to Rawnie and shook his head. Before he could say a word, two gypsies ran to the fire and began stamping out the flames. They shouted and pointed into the darkness, and everyone began to run this way and that.

Four gamekeepers with blazing torches were moving towards the camp through the woods. They carried shotguns, and their tracker dogs strained at their leashes. Jesse began shouting instructions. Pans and bottles and equipment were swiftly packed, and the horses were dragged from their roped pen to

407

harness to the wagons. The poached rabbits and pheasants were quickly hidden.

The children screamed in terror as the gamekeepers crashed into the camp and released their dogs. For a moment Freedom was frozen, he couldn't believe what was happening. One of the little *doshas* was hunched by a wagon, shrieking with fear as a dog snarled and snapped at her. In seconds Freedom was on his feet and at her side. He kicked the dog away and grabbed the child, lifted her into the wagon. 'Call your men off, you bastards, call the dogs back . . .'

Jesse was already fighting with one of the gamekeepers. Freedom ran to a man he recognized, grabbed him by his lapels. 'You call your men off or so help me God I'll have your throat wrung, hear me . . . look at me, mun, you know me.'

Little Johnny Mask was beating back one of the dogs with a stick. Jesse had wrested a shotgun from the hands of one of the gamekeepers, and had turned it on the man Freedom held. 'No . . . Jesse, no!'

He held the gun poised, finger on the trigger. Rawnie ran to his side and placed her hand over the barrel. 'Freedom, get them out of the camp, tell them we'll move out, we mean no harm . . .'

The gamekeepers, terrified, did not need to be asked twice. They backed off, calling their dogs to their sides. Freedom held the shotgun, keeping the men back, but he stood with them, not his own people.

It took only a short while before the wagons were ready. Jesse walked up to Freedom, carrying his son in his arms. 'Come with us, brother, leave with us.'

Past antagonisms forgotten, Freedom held Jesse close, and

they kissed each other on both cheeks. From his pocket Jesse took a gold coin, pressed it into Freedom's hand. '*Kushti rardi*, brother.'

The wagons moved out, and the gamekeepers made their way back down the hill to The Grange. The men were silent, their dogs under control. Freedom walked slightly ahead of them, his thoughts with his people. As they came out of the wood he saw below him, glistening like a mirage, The Grange, lit by a multitude of chandeliers. His anger rose up and he stiffened. They had treated his people no better than dogs.

'Come on, move on, bloody gyppo, get on back . . .'

In an instant Freedom swung around and knocked the man out, took his shotgun and broke it into pieces. Then he took off so fast none of them had a hope of keeping up with him . . . the night enveloped him, and he could no longer be seen or heard.

The gamekeepers ran into the courtyard and reported to the chief warden. 'Bastard took off after his people, bloody gyppo should never have been brought here in the first place.'

Evelyne could hear them and their dogs clearly. Watching from her little window, she saw the police wagon arrive, and she turned back to her cot bed. So Ed had been right, he had run. She was feeling queasy, and she reached for her dressing-gown, slipped quietly along the corridor to the bathroom she shared with the other servants. Fighting her dizziness, she was violently sick. More than ever she felt she must leave The Grange.

As she returned to her room, she found two housemaids whispering together near her bedroom door. One of them turned to Evelyne.

'Oh, Evie, they say the gyppo fighter's run off, half-killed the gamekeepers, tried to strangle one, and him what was almost hung afore ... *and* he stole the dinner cook was preparing for Sir Charles, what a to-do.'

Miss Balfour appeared, wearing a hairnet, tight-lipped, her skin wrinkled like a prune. 'Back to bed, all of you, now. This has nothing to do with you, back to bed this instant.'

The two maids shot into their rooms like rabbits bolting into their holes. Miss Balfour stared at Evelyne with such overt disgust on her face that Evelyne barred her way.

'If you have something to say to me, Miss Balfour, then say it to my face.'

Miss Balfour shrank back and scurried to her room, locking the door behind her. Evelyne entered her own bedroom and gasped. Freedom lay on her bed, smiling, his feet up on the iron bedrail. She closed the door fast. 'What are you doing here? Do you not know everyone's out searching for you, and now the police are called in – are you mad, man?'

Miss Balfour could have sworn she heard a man's voice. She slipped out of her room and crept along the corridor, listened at Evelyne's door. Afraid to confront them both, she tightened the cord of her dressing gown and hurried down the back stairs.

Freedom cocked his head to one side and placed his finger across his lips to remind Evelyne to speak softly.

'Will you come with me, you don't belong here, and they keep us like prisoners ... Come away with me? Is this the way you want to live your life? To be paid each month so they own you? So they can tell you when to eat and when to sleep?'

He began to undo his shirt, as if the sounds of the baying dogs below and the whistling of the searching policemen had nothing to do with him.

She whispered back, frantically, 'You're drunk, I can smell it, and you go back down right now. They think you've run, and poor Ed will get into terrible trouble.'

He threw his shirt aside and began to unbutton his trousers.

'Are you mad, man? What are you thinking of, here, in the house?'

His face changed, his eyes were so black they frightened her, 'They don't own me, they got a piece of paper says they do, but I'm no animal to be bought. No man sets his dogs on me.'

'You forget yourself, Freedom Stubbs. If it weren't for Sir Charles you'd be at the end of a hangman's rope and you well know it.'

'It's you that saved me, you, *manushi*, now come here.'

She backed away from him, pressed herself against the wall. 'I'm not your *manushi*, I am not your wife. You don't belong to them? Well, I don't belong to you. Now get out of here, go on, get out!'

His fist curled in rage, but she stood up to him, unafraid now.

She slapped his fist. 'That's all you know, isn't it – the fight? You don't want to better yourself – well, run back to your people, go on, run back, but don't expect me to be with you in some wretched wagon, chased off the land, run out of every town.'

In a fury he pulled her to him, but she slapped his face. He took it, smiled down at her, and she stepped back and slapped him again.

411

'Oh, *manushi*, is that all yer know, the fight? But my, my, you're *rinkeney* when you're angry . . . now come to me before you give me a *tatto yeck* . . . see, I got something for you.' He handed her the gold coin Jesse had pressed into his hand . . . she threw it across the room. He cocked his head to the side, then picked up his shirt and began to dress.

Suddenly she clung to his back . . . he turned in her arms and cupped her face in his hands. 'Eh, woman, you twist me so, ye don't know what thee wants, listen to your heart, *manushi*, listen.'

He kissed her, slipping her nightdress off, carried her to the bed and laid her down. He snuggled his head close to her and whispered, 'They'll have a long night ahead searching for me.'

'No they won't, you're going back, go and give yourself up to them before you cause any more trouble.'

'Is that what you want?'

Miss Balfour rapped on Evelyne's door.

'Open this door this instant, I know you've got a man in there, come along, I've got Mr Plath with me, open up.'

In a panic, Evelyne reached for her nightdress while Freedom pulled on his shirt and hopped around trying to get into his trousers. Miss Balfour threw the door open. She was carrying a policeman's truncheon, and was followed close behind by Mr Plath, the estate manager. They just caught Freedom slipping out of the window. Mr Plath made the mistake of grabbing Freedom's leg, and got a nasty kick in the groin. He rolled in agony on the floor while Miss Balfour screamed, 'Help, help . . . someone help!'

*

Sir Charles made a hurried exit from the house to talk to the police, who were there about the poachers. He had been playing an after-dinner game of rummy, and he was still clutching his cards. His house guests gathered at the windows.

Poor Ed was beside himself, he knew it had all got out of hand. The gamekeepers were embroidering their stories about the gypsy campers every time they retold it. They had been set upon, fired upon, punched and threatened with knives. 'Freedom, was 'e wiv 'em? Will someone tell me, was 'e wiv 'em?'

'Was 'e wiv 'em? Look at me throat, the bugger nearly throtled me.'

Sir Charles crossed the courtyard to speak to Ed, his cards still in his hand. 'I want him found, Ed, brought back, in handcuffs if need be. This is outrageous, do you have any idea of how much time and effort I have been putting in, trying to arrange a bout for him in London? So help me God, he can go back to jail, what on earth possessed him to . . .'

A screech from a gamekeeper interrupted him. 'Sir, oh, sir, there's a man on the roof, look, there he is!'

All eyes were raised to the roof of The Grange, and there he was dancing, singing at the top of his voice,

> *Oh, can you* rokka *Romany,*
> *can you play the* bosh,
> *Can you* jal adrey *the* staripen,
> *can you* chin the cosh . . .

Balancing, holding his arms out as if he were walking a tightrope, Freedom teetered on the roof's edge. The crowd grew silent.

'The man must be mad, or drunk, or both.'

Miss Balfour ran to join the crowd. Behind her, Mr Plath came limping, clutching his injured parts.

'This is her doing, sir, he was with her.'

Sir Charles turned to Ed. His voice was steely, and Ed's heart sank. 'When the fool comes down, give him to the law.'

'But, sir, he's done nuffink wrong, he's just 'ad a few too many.'

Sir Charles' face twitched, he was so furious. 'Don't play games with me, Meadows, I know exactly where he's been. His friends, so called, have been poaching on my land. He almost killed Fred Hutchins over there. Be in my study first thing in the morning, is that clear? And get all these people away, there has been enough disturbance for one night.'

As Sir Charles strode from the courtyard, there was a gasp from the onlookers. He looked up to see Freedom swinging down from ledge to ledge like a monkey. The police moved in to corner him, and he dodged and ducked as they chased him, then they surrounded him. As they dragged him away, he looked back and Sir Charles flushed as he gave him a dazzling smile.

Ed went into the barn. They had tied Freedom's hands to one of the posts. His shirt was torn, his face filthy.

'Why did you do it, lad, there's two coppers out back with black eyes, and to kick Mr Plath of all people, in the balls. He's the estate manager . . . I dunno, I don't, why in God's name did you do it? Why did you run?'

Freedom sighed, shook his head. 'If I'd wanted away, Ed, I'd not have been dancing on the roof, now would I? You tell me why they trussed me up like a chicken?'

'Sir Charles says he's through with you, you could even get sent to jail. Poachin's against the law, never mind what you done to the estate manager.'

With one movement Freedom wrenched the ropes away from the post, shaking the whole barn. He turned on Ed, and Ed backed away, terrified by the anger in those black eyes.

'You tell His Lordship I want to fight; I don't want to be kept here like one of his stallions. They're groomed, and brushed, but spend more time than they should in their stalls. You tell him I could have killed his gamekeepers, each one of 'em, and Mr Plath's lucky 'e still got anythin' between his legs.'

He swung a punch at the punchbag, splitting it in two. 'They set their dogs on children, that were wrong.'

Then he walked out, calm as ever. All Ed could think of was that punch, he had never seen one like it . . .

The following morning Ed went cap in hand to Sir Charles, beseeched him to listen before he launched into the speech he had obviously prepared.

'Last night I saw a punch, Sir, that would floor any champion in England. I saw it with me own eyes. He's wild, but he's trained every day, not put a foot out of line. Don't send 'im away, sir, find him a fight! 'E's yer champion, I swear it.'

Sir Charles listened, tapping his fingers on his mahogany desk. 'Ed, I'm a sportsman, you know that, I believe in him just as much as you, but I cannot have any scandal. Unless you control him, then I am afraid, champion or no, he'll have to go . . . if these riff-raff follow him around, then . . .'

'Your gamekeepers should not 'ave set the dogs on to the children, gyppos or not, sir.'

Sir Charles rose from his seat and stared out of the window, his back to Ed. 'How's your wife? Settled in, has she?'

'You bastard,' thought Ed. He knew exactly what Sir Charles was implying; his livelihood depended on Freedom. He and Freda didn't own their cottage, they owned nothing.

'I'd like to see how he's been doing, set up a bout in the barn, would you? Then we'll discuss it later . . . that's all for now.'

Evelyne sat on the edge of the leather chair. Sir Charles' study smelt of polish and cigars. She watched him carefully cut the end of his Havana with a gold clipper.

'I will, of course, give you references, but you must understand, under the circumstances your presence here is . . .'

Evelyne interrupted him. 'I have packed, sir, and Mr Plath has given me my wages. You see, I had already made up my mind to leave.'

Sir Charles studied her for a moment. Her composure unnerved him slightly. Sitting ramrod straight, her chin up, her green eyes never leaving his face, she was not apologetic in any way. Suddenly he leaned forward, and she could see a muscle twitch at the side of his jaw. 'Stay away from him, I shall clear everything with the police and my gamekeepers, he'll get every chance I can give him, but stay away from him.'

Evelyne stood, her mouth trembling slightly, but she held on to her emotions. Without shaking his outstretched hand she opened the oak-panelled door. She didn't look back, just closed the door silently behind her.

Freda was polishing her brass fender when a housemaid tapped on her door. She handed Freda a letter. 'She said be sure you get it, I got to rush now, I'm behind with me work ... you done this place up ever so nice, Mrs Meadows.'

Freda didn't hear the girl leave, she was turning the letter over in her hands. It was Evie's writing, she'd know it anywhere, with its fancy loops and curls.

Ed had warned Sir Charles to stand well back from the ring. The sweat from the boys might spray on to his grey suit.

Freedom was in high spirits, despite a slight hangover. The evening's drama appeared to have had little or no effect on him. He was unaware of how Sir Charles had settled everything, unaware how close he had been to losing his chance as a professional boxer.

Taking each boy in turn, even though he was only sparring, he gave such a good performance that Sir Charles gave Ed a wink, gestured for him to go to his side. Ed called out for the boxers to take a break, and he and Sir Charles waited for Freedom to join them.

Sir Charles leant on his silver-topped cane. 'Appears you don't think I've been pulling my weight? Not arranging a bout soon enough for you? Well, it's not as easy as that, old chap. You're unknown, a pit boxer, and they are, as you must be aware, two a penny. To gain a good rating in the game, why, you would more than likely have to take on twenty bouts before you could get any legitimate recognition.'

Freedom rolled his towel into a ball and chucked it aside. Sir Charles could smell him, like an animal, his sweating body was so close ... he stepped back, just a fraction. 'I have been masterminding a plan for you to hit the main circuits in one swoop. I have arranged for you to be the sparring partner for the present

Irish Heavyweight Champion. He will be arriving in England shortly for an attempt at the British title.'

Freedom was about to let rip, Ed could see it, so he put out a restraining hand. Sir Charles continued, uninterrupted.

'They will have all the sports writers there to see this Irish champion working out. And, Freedom, it will be up to you to show what you are worth – particularly when the press are in abundance – be your showcase, so to speak.'

'Sparring partner? But I been workin' for a professional bout, that's what Ed – what *you* promised me from the word go, sparrin' ain't no professional bout.'

Sir Charles checked his gold fob watch and pocketed it before he spoke, making Freedom wait, hanging on his every word. Then he smiled, such a rare occurrence with Sir Charles that it was rather off-putting. His voice was almost sexual in its softness, its humour. 'Ahhh, but what happens, old fella, if the sparring chappie knocks out the contender – leave a bit of a gap for the main event, wouldn't you say?'

Ed gave Freedom a warning look to keep his mouth shut. 'He'll beat that Irish git wivout a doubt, if you'll excuse the language, sir.'

Sir Charles strode to the barn doors, swinging his cane. 'Let us hope he can. Ed, we leave for London first thing in the morning . . . jolly good bout, lads, well done.'

It was a few moments before it dawned, then Freedom gave Ed such a hug it winded him and he had to sit down on a bench to get his breath back.

Freda could hear Ed singing, 'Oh, we got no bananas, we got no bananas today . . . tarrah!'

He opened the cottage door and threw his cloth cap in the air, then swung Freda round, wanting to dance, but she pushed him away. Behind him, Freedom bounded in, forgetting to stop so that he cracked his head on the top of the door, but he didn't care, he was in such high spirits. 'Get Evie for us, Freda, we got some news — we're off to London and we got a fight.'

It was Freedom's turn to twirl Freda round on her dumpy little legs. 'I got her this, picked it on the way over. She was in a fair temper with me last night, so put it between the sheets ... her book's sheets, Freda, no need to look so shocked!'

Freedom laughed and tossed the cornflower in the air, then tucked it into Freda's hand. She turned helpless eyes to Ed, but he was beaming from ear to ear. There on the table lay Evie's letter. Freda held it out to Freedom, then let her hand drop. She had forgotten Freedom couldn't read well enough yet. 'Evie's gone, Freedom, she left this morning ... Here, she wrote to us all. She says she couldn't come and say goodbye as ... well, I don't have to tell you, we'd all be crying. She wants to make her own way, better herself ... ' Freda couldn't go on, her face crumpled like a child's and she sobbed.

Freedom went to her, held her gently in his arms and whispered to her, 'It's all right, it's all right.'

Releasing her, he walked to the door like a man bereft. Ed tried to stop him leaving. 'Now, don't do nuffink you'll regret, son, we go to London and ...'

Like Freda, he couldn't continue. Freedom gave Ed a heartbreaking look, then a strange, soft half-smile. He seemed so calm, his voice so soft and gentle.

'We have a saying, if you love something, set it free, if it comes back to you it is yours, if it doesn't, it never was ...'

Freda opened her hand, and there was the cornflower. Freedom held her hand gently, then tucked the flower behind her ear. He smiled. 'Evie's favourite flower.'

Freda had never seen such open despair in a man's eyes, she wanted to wrap her arms around him and comfort him. She watched helplessly as he walked away.

'I'll go to him, go with him.'

'No, Ed, leave him, leave him a while.'

From the cottage window they watched him walk, straight-backed, across the courtyard. There was no spring in his step now, no high-stepping Romany saunter. As he reached the open fields he looked up and let out a single howl, like an animal caught in a trap. The cry chilled them both, the rooks screeched and flew from the trees like a black cloud, and then Freedom began to run, and run, until he was no more than a black spot on the horizon, as small as the birds he had disturbed.

Chapter 18

Ed became more expansive as the train pulled in to Victoria Station in London. He was getting back to his home territory, and he couldn't wait to get Freedom ready to meet the Irish champion.

From Victoria Station, Ed and Freedom took a taxi to Lambert's Gym in Bell Street, a run-down area of Soho. The city throbbed, noisy, crowded and dirty, and Freedom loathed it, was disgusted by it, but Ed was in his element, 'Oh, it's good to be back, you'll love it 'ere, Freedom, come on, down yer go, gym's in the basement.'

The gym was alive with the thudding sounds from punch-bags and ten boxers working out. The walls were covered with photographs and posters of famous boxers and bouts. Freedom looked around, feeling out of place in his suit and shirt. The boxers gave him only a cursory glance and carried on with what they were doing. Ed seemed to know everyone, waving across the gym, thumping a young boy on the shoulder. ''Ello, son, how ya doin'? 'Arry me boy, nice to see you, long time ... Jimbo, you still at it, thought you retired ...'

Ed passed through, beckoning Freedom to follow him, and they crossed the floor of the gym, skirted the ring in the centre and made their way to the small offices at the far end. Ed banged on the door and opened it, again gesturing for Freedom to follow.

'Jack, I just got in, any chance of a word in your shell-like? Want you to meet me new lad.'

An ex-boxer himself, with cauliflower ears and a flattened splodge of a nose, Jack Lambert was now a promoter. He wore a shirt that was minus its collar and wide red braces, and he was rarely seen without a huge cigar sticking out of his mouth. Freedom and Ed followed him into his small office at the back of the gym.

Freedom was aware of being given the once-over by the cigar-smoking man. The puffy eyes stared hard, examining him from the top of his head down to his feet. Freedom shifted uncomfortably and looked down at the floor.

'This your new lad then, Ed? He's a big'un, isn't he? He a half-caste, is he? Dark, isn't he?'

Freedom opened his mouth to speak, but Ed shut him up with a quick look, and launched into a speech that had Freedom listening intently, hardly able to believe his ears. Ed told Jack that Freedom was a fresh'un, straight out of the booths, not had a professional fight, but they wanted to try him out for starters, he was just a gypsy lad.

'You rate him, do you Ed? What weight's he carryin'?'

Ed shrugged, although he knew Freedom's weight down to the last ounce, muttered that he was around twelve, thirteen stone, so he'd have to be in the heavyweight class.

'That's my trouble, see Jack, I don't want 'im to go into a

professional bout yet, 'e's not ready, what I'm after is – until I've 'ad time to work on 'im, just for a few shillings, lad's gotta eat, know what I mean – I was wonderin' if you could see to a couple of sparrin' matches, anyone comin' in fer a big bout around his weight. You got a match ahead? One suitable, eh?'

Ed knew exactly which bout was due – it was Murphy, the Irish Heavyweight Champion, coming to fight the present holder of the British title. Jack scratched his head and then drummed his fingers on a page of his book. 'There is the Murphy crowd comin' in, but they'll be bringing their own spar. Doubt if they'll want a bum an' mouth round before the big bout. 'E's an Irish bog fighter, an' he's takin' on Sam Gold's boy. It's a big bout, Ed, whoever gets through will have a crack at the world title, take on Dempsey 'imself.'

Ed homed in on Jack, Murphy would be perfect. 'You got it all up 'ere, Jack, always said that, we can see how the lad fares with a champ, we'll know for sure what we got or what we 'aven't, you'll set it up then?'

Jack stubbed his cigar out, had another good look over Freedom and then nodded. As Freedom and Ed left, Jack wasn't sure if he'd been given the bum's rush himself. But then it had been his idea, so he asked the operator to put a call through to Ireland.

Ed skipped along the pavement, clapping his hands. 'The old bugger fell for it, hook, line an' sinker.'

Freedom strolled along beside him, still not knowing what the hell was going on.

'Look, son, we got you a sparring bout with the Irish title-holder, he's comin' over for a crack at the British title, right?

British Heavyweight, now then, you show what you can do and 'is Lordship's gonna make sure the press'll be there, with me?'

Freedom still hadn't cottoned on, and Ed began to think that his prize didn't have much 'upstairs'. 'This is your fight, you ain't gonna spar, you're gonna box 'im right outta the ring.'

Freedom was dubious, it was a short cut, but somehow it didn't seem right to him. It was dirty. Ed snapped at him that it was life, that was all, and the best fighter would win, who knows, the Irish fighter might wipe Freedom out.

'Don't you think for one minute Murphy's a pushover, he's a fighter, and 'e's desperate to get that title, you any idea how much Dempsey took at the gate last fight, one million dollars, mate, *one friggin' million dollars!*'

After crossing town to Tower Bridge, Freedom and Ed took a bus over the bridge to the dockland area. Freedom trailed after Ed as he walked down squalid streets, up alleys, until they arrived at a small, two-up, two-down house which was squashed into a seedy row of identical houses, the street alive with noisy children.

Ed led Freedom along the passage into a small back room with two cot beds. It was a far cry from The Grange. 'Right, lad, dump yer bags, toilet's out in the yard, an' by the stink of the place the drains is clogged up. Still, maybe we won't be here for long, eh?'

Freedom stared around the squalid room, at the cracked window, grey with dirt, that looked straight out on to a high brick wall.

Unperturbed as ever, Ed was checking the blankets for bed-bugs. He whistled, full of energy, and talked nineteen to the dozen. He told Freedom to unpack, but Freedom had only the clothes he stood up in and his training gear.

'I'll be two minutes, gotta ring 'is Lordship, tell 'im we're set-tled, like, then we'll get us some dinner . . . put yer feet up, get as much rest as yer can, want you fit for Murphy, eh?'

Left alone, Freedom sat down on his bed. He didn't open his bag, or even check the bed for bugs. He simply sat, hands cupped loosely in front of him. When Ed returned almost an hour later, Freedom was in exactly the same position.

'Right, Murphy's comin' into town, you're to meet him tomorrow. I'll fill you in on how you behave. These bog Irish need a bit of handlin', and you are going ter give a perform-ance . . . but you save the best for the press, are you wiv me? . . . like an actor? Yer know, rehearsin', savin' hisself for the open-ing night . . . Freedom? You listened to a word I said?'

'What happens if he don't want me to spar?'

'Leave that to me. It's sorted, now get off yer backside, I'm starvin' 'ungry.'

Ed pulled open the door and turned back, hesitating, then went to Freedom and gave him a hug, 'Eh, this place ain't much, I know that, but give us time? Best nobody knows nuffink about yer, understand? Sir Charles, he knows what he's doing.'

Freedom gave him that half-smile of his. 'Thing is, Ed, I don't think there's room in here for His Lordship . . .'

Ed cuffed him one, but didn't laugh. 'There's them an' us, that's life . . . now get a move on or I'll 'ave shockin' wind.'

Pat Murphy looked far from 'bog Irish'. He was wearing a long, camel-hair coat with a velvet collar, and a black felt hat, a satin band around the crown. He wore a carnation in his buttonhole and carried a silver-topped walking stick. Ed slithered around the edge of the room, wanting to get a good look at the Irish champion without him knowing. Two men, equally well dressed, stood beside Murphy, and he towered over them. His huge chest under the tailored suit and overcoat looked a lot wider than Freedom's.

Murphy was posing for a photograph, the photographer hidden under a black cloth.

'Mr Murphy, could you please hold that pose, thank you sir, and now would it be permissible to have one of you on your own for the *Evening Chronicle*?'

Murphy smiled as his two men departed to lean against the ropes. He wore a fine leather glove on his right hand, in which he also held its mate, leaving his bare left hand to rest on the ropes. Ed could see a heavy diamond ring on his little finger. More disconcerting was the size of the man's fists – they were like spades.

'Come on then, man, let's be done with this, the bars are open.' Murphy held his pose, his white teeth gleaming in a frozen smile. He was an exceptionally handsome man and his face bore little or no sign of his boxing career. His nose was straight, his hair, thick, black and curly, hid his ears so Ed could not see if they bore telltale marks. Murphy's eyes were small and china-blue, and they twinkled as he spoke in his thick Irish brogue.

Jack gave the photographer his marching orders, and was about to join Murphy when he spotted Ed. Murphy gave Ed no more than a cursory glance as he moved with his two men towards Jack's office.

'This is Ed Meadows, he's got a good sparring partner for you, Pat.'

Murphy turned to Ed and gave him his full attention. His twinkly eyes went icy-cold as he gave Ed the once-over.

'Well, they better get him over here, I'll be needing work outs before the match, your lad good, is he?'

At that point Murphy's trainer, O'Keefe, laughed and said that his boy needed the very best, and it was lucky they had offered a sparring partner as their own had been put into hospital the night before they left. Murphy looked at Ed.

'I never meant it, stray punch, poor man went down like a lead balloon, and that's just how I intend to put the champ down, isn't that right, Paddy?'

Paddy O'Keefe nodded, raised his fist and punched the padded, camel-hair shoulders of Murphy's coat.

'Oi, watch out for the coat, it's pure camelhair, this, have you ever felt such soft material, Jack, go on now, have a feel, is it not like a baby's arse?'

They moved into Jack's office, and Ed asked when they would like his boy brought round. Murphy flicked his gloves and said he'd work out first thing in the morning, around ten o'clock.

Ed met with Sir Charles at the Pelican Club, and they ate a big fry-up together. A boxing match was taking place while they ate, not that Ed paid any attention.

'He's a champ, and 'e's flash, must 'ave made a lot of money on the Irish circuits, his face looks unmarked and he's got fists the size of shovels. I wonder if we're not pushin' our lad too fast.'

Sir Charles picked at his steak and seemed more concerned with his tomato than with anything Ed had told him. Ed sighed and tapped Sir Charles on the arm to draw his attention to the entrance. Murphy, his camelhair coat and hat taken from him, stood at the grill-room bar. 'There 'e is now, sir, look at 'im, and 'e's got the confidence of Jove himself.'

They watched as Murphy shook hands with a group of well-dressed City gents and was shown to a table.

They made a great fuss of him, and many eyes were turned towards the ringside table where he sat.

The Pelican Club was half-full of regulars, and a strange bunch they were, a mixture of toffs and betting men. Titles rubbed shoulders with gamblers, bookies and sportsmen and, thankfully, there was not a woman in sight. The club was very much a man's world, reverberating with loud laughter and men calling to each other between the booths and tables.

'Man's a heavy drinker, by the look of it, and likes the social scene, wouldn't you say? Our boy'll take him, he's not our worry, old chap, take a look at the title holder.'

Ed looked around and leant across the table, 'He here, is 'e? I can't see 'im?'

Sir Charles pushed his plate away and signalled to a waiter, and at the same time he told Ed rather curtly that the champ was under wraps until the main bout, as it should be, he was not even in London.

'You just make sure Freedom knows what to do. I want *him* under wraps until I give the word, let Murphy think he's simply a sparring partner.'

Sir Charles tossed money to the waiter to hand to the boys in the ring. Some toffs came over to the table and Ed knew he was dismissed. He got up and put his hand in his pocket as a gesture, knowing the bill was taken care of.

If Ed Meadows had ever thought Freedom was in any way difficult to control, poor O'Keefe had his hands full with Murphy. He had remained at the Pelican Club all afternoon, drinking.

Eventually O'Keefe had poured him into a taxi and taken him back to the hotel, and after a few hours of rest Murphy was up again and raring to go. Fresh as a daisy now, he wanted to see the sights of London. No amount of persuasion from O'Keefe would keep the boxer resting. In exasperation he looked at Murphy prancing around the room in his evening suit, looking for his dancing pumps.

'For God's sake, you're supposed to be getting ready for the British title bout, you're not here to sightsee, and what you getting all fancied up for?'

Murphy beamed. 'Bejasus, I've got three weeks to get one night out of me system, an' I give you me word I'll not touch a drop after tonight, now come on man, let's get going.'

Poor O'Keefe was dragged off to the Hammersmith Palais to hear the Dixieland Jazz Band. Murphy beamed with delight, he clapped and sang along, 'Do-wack-a-do, boop-a-doop ... ' He was up doing the Black Bottom with a woman O'Keefe had first thought to be an old lady with white hair, but when she turned round he saw that it was the new ash-blonde colour, not white but silver. Murphy wouldn't come off the dance floor and O'Keefe sat subdued and wretched. At least he was exercising, even if it was the Black Bottom.

Ed pushed open the privy door, still buttoning up his trousers. His morning ritual had been disturbed by loud, childish sobs ... Freedom was standing in the yard with a small, ragged boy, who was clutching a rotting, dead pigeon to his chest.

'Go on, gerrout of it or I'll tan yer hide.'

Freedom frowned at Ed and gently eased the dead bird from the little boy's hands.

'It was me pet, I've tried everyfink ter make 'im eat.'

Freedom sat back on his haunches with the little corpse in his hands. The maggots were eating its eyes out, but Freedom stroked the bird's head gently. 'I tell thee what, I'll take him with me, maybe I'll have him right as rain.'

From within the crumbling house a woman called for 'Will', and the child ran off. Ed cringed with distaste.

'You'll get disease from that, chuck it in the canal, and never mind talkin' wiv the kids, you'll 'ave 'em hangin' round yer neck . . . an' get a move on, you're meeting Murphy today.'

Pat Murphy showered and O'Keefe rubbed him down, then gave him a heavy massage.

'My God, I couldn't believe my eyes, she was a dragon, boy, woke up next to a dragon, must have been near sixty, why d'you let me do it?'

O'Keefe thumped Murphy's back, hard. It wasn't for want of trying to prise his champion away from the woman. He'd almost got a back-hander as Murphy, drunk as a lord, insisted the woman was Gloria Swanson.

Soon Murphy was togged up and waiting, ready, in the gym. He was doing press-ups in a corner while two young lads watched in awe. Then he worked out on the weights, sweating, easing up his muscles. His body was very powerful, and he stood six-foot-two in his leather-soled boxing boots. Ed reckoned he was at least half a stone, maybe more, heavier than Freedom.

O'Keefe noticed the big fella immediately and crossed over to Ed, jerking his thumb in Freedom's direction.

'This the lad, is it? He's a big'un all right, let's hope he'll be able to give him a work out, he certainly needs one. Pat, Pat, come on, into the ring with you.'

Murphy danced his way towards the ring, and couldn't keep still while O'Keefe put on his gloves. He inserted his gumshield and put his leather head protector on, then Murphy began punching the sides of the ring. Freedom stepped into the ring, gloves tied, gumshield in, and his leather helmet strapped on. The two worked well, Freedom giving Murphy a run for his money. He also took a number of punches, and pulled back on his punches a little, and was stopped as Murphy spat out his shield.

'Bejasus, what they got here, a ballroom dancer? Can't you do anything better than this punk?'

Ed gave Freedom a tiny hooded nod, he could push a bit more. The men started again, this time Freedom was feeling Murphy's punches, fending them off, but they were like iron, the man had a lot of power behind him. Freedom stepped up his punching, gave a good body blow, only to be encouraged by Murphy himself.

'Thatta boy, come on, get your pecker up, come on, gimme a run for my money.'

O'Keefe nodded to Freedom, then talked out of the side of his mouth to Ed. 'Your lad's got promise, nice mover, needs to train up the power behind his punch but he's got promise, you're right.'

Throughout the bout Freedom was using his right fist, never giving his left space, he defended, defended, very rarely pushing Murphy. Murphy dominated the centre of the ring, moving Freedom around, on him, after him, and he didn't pull some of his punches. At the end they were both sweating profusely and

Murphy threw in the towel, he wanted to rest. Ed could have swiped Freedom, he just stood in the centre of the ring, unsure what to do next.

'For Chrissakes, man,' he whispered, 'look like yer out of bloody breath, heave yer chest up an' down a bit!'

The following day's sparring match was a little tougher. Murphy was working now, and not playing around. Freedom didn't have to act, he had his work cut out trying to fend off the body punches. Murphy concentrated on the body, even after the bout he went and worked on the punchbag for a further hour.

'Well, what you think, can you take him?'

Freedom mulled the question over for what seemed to Ed to be a very long time, then he said he didn't know. He didn't think Murphy was giving full power, he was holding back. The next spar Freedom would push a few punches, but Murphy had one hell of a right hook.

'But he opens up, I've been watchin' 'im, he goes to a format, right upper, right upper, an' then he's comin' in with a body left, but he double swings and in comes that right hook. You got to get into that opening, he's wide open for a moment each time.'

Freedom raised his eyes to heaven, shook his head. 'Ed, what you think I bin trying to do, mun, he's a dancer too, you know, light on his feet for his weight.'

Ed shoved his stubby finger into Freedom's chest, said that he, Freedom, was twice the mover, and lighter.

'I'm lighter, Ed, that's for sure, I'd say by about sixteen pounds.'

*

Jack came out of his office and went over to O'Keefe. He had a list of reporters requesting permission to photograph the Irish champion. He also had a lot of press photographs of the title-holder from the morning paper's sports edition. On the back page, Micky Morgan stood with his fists up. Unlike Murphy, his face showed war wounds, a flattened nose, crumpled ears. His eyes were slightly puffy, eyes that glared out of the newspaper.

'Eh, Murphy, wanna see how Micky's lookin' lately? Not good, that Scotch fella really gave him a going-over, see?'

Murphy took the paper and stared at the glowering man, adding up on his fingers how many weeks had gone by since Micky's last bout. 'He was cut, wasn't he? Right eye? Lemme see now ... I'd calculate the lad's only just got nice, clean, fresh skin over this right eye, what you say, boss? Oi, O'Keefe, what you say, doesn't look too dangerous to me?'

O'Keefe didn't even cross the room, he was winding bandages into rolls, concentrating on them. 'He's a real fighter, Pat, and he's hungry, they had a good "take" on the Scottish bout. I wouldn't think that eye worries him one jot, man's a boxer, know what I mean? That opponent was good, and dirty, thumb in the eye round one, he was also very handy with his head. Micky took him out in round five, they say the fella's still not sure what hit him. Mickey was a stoker on board HMS *Junnsanta*, word is the shovel's still attached to his hand.'

Through O'Keefe's slow assessment of his next opponent, Murphy stood with his arms folded. As O'Keefe wound down and finished rolling the bandages, Murphy turned to the assembled room.

'That's what I like to hear, man giving his boxer confidence, right, thanks a lot, an' where's that gyppo? You hear him?

Tomorrow, son, put a bit of energy into it, Jack, you get the press up here, I'll give 'em something to write about, and, O'Keefe, I'll have that stoker running.'

O'Keefe looked over to Ed and gave him a wink, then he went to Murphy and cuffed him over the head, flung an arm round his shoulder and said he loved him.

'Now you're talking, Pat, talking like a winner.' Freedom picked up his kit bag. He had not said more than a few words to Murphy or his trainer. He liked them both, liked them a lot. He was silent on the journey home on the crowded tram. He liked to sit up front on the open deck. He wore a cloth cap pulled down and a woollen scarf, his jacket collar turned up. Ed wondered what he was thinking, but he never could tell, it unnerved him.

The following morning the gym was crowded with reporters hanging around with their big cameras and tripods. They were setting up by the side of the ring. Jack, dressed in his Sunday suit, brought out all the old photographs of himself, but no one was interested.

O'Keefe had to restrain Murphy from wearing his best velvet shorts, telling him they should be kept for the fight. He couldn't, however, stop him wearing his new, hand-stitched, monogrammed robe. He was there, flaunting himself, swashbuckling up and down the gym, and he had the reporters roaring with laughter as he posed and danced about. Ed looked over to his two lads, who were standing at the far end of the gym. They looked uneasy and nervous, and he made his way over to them.

'Where in God's name is he?'

Ed threw up his hands, Freedom had gone to the toilet, what a time to go! All the press gathered and where was their man? On the throne. 'He gloved up?'

Freedom was standing in the dirty, broken-down toilet. His coat was round his shoulders, gloves on, and he was leaning against the brick wall. His eyes were closed and he was talking quietly to himself. 'Doing this for you, Evie, I get through this then it's the title, and you'll have all the dresses and hats you want, this is for you, Evie, I'm doing this for you.'

Ed sighed with relief when Freedom entered the gym, no one paying him any attention. Murphy was up in the ring, posing, swinging on the ropes, and yelling for Freedom to join him. 'I'm not wearing me helmet, man, I want me face to be seen in all its beauty.'

As Freedom stepped into the ring, Murphy pranced over and gave him a wink. 'Right, son, don't hold back, let's give 'em a show, get your face in the press with me, all right?'

The room was set up, all the cameras in position, and O'Keefe stepped into the ring, spouting a few words about this being just a taster for the championship. Freedom's name was not even mentioned, he sat in the corner while his two lads massaged his shoulders. Murphy was pounding the air, and was led into his corner for his gumshield to be fitted.

The bell sounded, and everyone in the room focused their attention on the ring. Murphy came out hunched and ready for the attack, gave Freedom a good pounding, flashy punching, and even while he was doing it he was still talking. 'Oh, wait 'til they see me in the papers, me mother'll throw a fit, me lovely face on every stand.'

Murphy's face altered as he felt a punch hit home hard, and this time he didn't mess around, he went back at Freedom, his eyes never leaving Freedom's face. Murphy was amused, he'd seen that look, so the boy wanted to make a show of himself, did he? Well now, he would have the lesson of his life.

The whole room picked up the new atmosphere in the ring – suddenly it wasn't a game. Ed could feel his right leg shaking all by itself, and he swallowed and looked at O'Keefe. The last thing he wanted was for him to step into the ring and stop the sparring match.

A murmur ran around the gym, people moved closer in, the cameras flashed. Ed was saying a silent prayer, over and over he was willing Freedom to find that break, that break in Murphy's defence. Murphy had Freedom up against the ropes, gave him a good left jab and was about to come in with a right, left, and his famous right, when he felt as if his stomach had been blown out. The punches came one after the other, three times the force of Freedom's punches in their previous sparring matches. Murphy couldn't believe it was happening, he gave back everything he had and his fists seemed to glance off the lad, eyes to eyes, the blue twinkle had gone, and the last thing Murphy remembered was the blackness, the blackness of those eyes staring into him, expressionless, masked, in a set, impassive face.

The room went silent as Murphy crashed, unconscious, to the canvas. Then the place was in an uproar, the reporters clamouring, fighting to get into the ring, shouting for the name, the boxer's name. Ed gave the signal and the two lads grabbed Freedom and hauled him to the ringside. Freedom shoved them aside and pushed his way through the men gathered around the still-unconscious Murphy. Ed was shouting, 'Freedom Stubbs, his name is Freedom Stubbs.' It was the name that went with the first face Murphy saw as he came round. O'Keefe was hemmed in by reporters already asking if his man would still fight. O'Keefe ignored them and tried to get to Murphy.

Freedom already had Murphy sitting up, leaning against his shoulder. Murphy's right eye was streaming blood, his face blotchy red and his lip cracked. He was dazed, but even in that condition he managed a joke, 'Well I'll be buggered, I've been beaten at me own game.'

He looked helplessly at O'Keefe, beseeching him to get him out somehow. Freedom helped the big man to his feet, he wanted to tell him he was sorry, but O'Keefe pushed him away with tears streaming down his face, and helped his man out of the ring, 'You bastard, Ed Meadows, you bastard!'

It was Murphy who broke up what looked as if it could become an ugly situation. He held his hand up and looked to Freedom. 'There's your champion, good luck, son, you certainly took all o' mine!'

Murphy's legs buckled beneath him and he was carried into the dressing room. The press surrounded Freedom.

Jack looked stunned, he stared at the departing group carrying poor Murphy out, then back to Freedom in the ring. He said it to no one in particular, to the air.

'I ain't ever seen a punch like that, not ever, Gawd almighty, what a punch.'

Chapter 19

Sir Charles swung into motion, the press had a field day, and Freedom was accepted as a contender for the British Heavyweight title. He was going to make sure his champion would be totally acceptable both socially and in the ring.

Freedom was removed from Ed's lodgings and installed in Sir Charles' small bachelor flat in Jermyn Street. He wanted to dress Freedom in the finest before he was taken to the Pelican Club or White's. Freedom went to Mr Poole, the famous tailor, for his sporting set, then to the equally famous trio of high priests of fashion – Mr Cundy, the general manager of the store, who waited on his every whim, Mr Dents, in the coat department, and Mr Allen, responsible for waistcoats and trousers. Mr Allen had to measure Freedom's inside leg twice as he couldn't quite believe how long it was, and the shirtmaker tutted and muttered as he measured and remeasured Freedom's arms and neck.

On all questions of cloth, texture and style, Freedom allowed Sir Charles to dominate him. He was unbelievably pernickety, feeling each piece of cloth and taking it to the daylight to examine it.

'Would it be possible, sir, to have a camelhair coat?'

Sir Charles didn't even reply to this, just let his monocle pop out in disgust. The fellow would be wanting a velvet collar next.

Freedom's feet were measured for boots and shoes, and Sir Charles put pressure on the makers to complete them as soon as possible.

The Jermyn Street flat consisted of a single bedroom, a valet's room, a dining room and a small sitting room. There was no kitchen, one either sent out for food or dined out. Dewhurst was installed in the flat and instructed to make sure Mr Stubbs never ate with a serving spoon again. He was to be shown how to eat like a gentleman with the correct tableware, and to be taught about wines.

Ed was amazed to see Freedom allowing himself to be carted around like a show-horse without a murmur. Not once did he complain, and only kicked up a fuss when it was suggested that he have his hair cut. This became a major argument, and eventually Sir Charles attempted a compromise.

'All right, old chap, we'll find a happy medium – won't have you sheared, just a trim, it's frightfully long and could do with a simple trim, what do you say?'

Freedom stared gloomily at his reflection and stubbornly refused to have it cut. They couldn't say it would get in the way when he was boxing, because it would be tied back with a leather thong. Ed knew what would happen if Freedom's temper was roused so he quietly suggested to Sir Charles that the long hair could be a unique advantage in being so unusual. At last Sir Charles acquiesced, and Freedom grinned. It wasn't that he minded taking care of it, he loved having it washed, loved his head being massaged, and loved choosing perfumes to use on it.

*

One week later Freedom stood looking at himself in the bedroom mirror. After three attempts to tie Freedom's tie, Dewhurst was finally satisfied, and stood back to admire his work. He had to admit the man looked splendid, apart from the hair, of course, which went without saying. With that hair and the colour of his skin Freedom could never be taken for a gentleman. Yet somehow he looked almost regal. He now had a complete wardrobe of suits, shirts, ties, overcoats, boots and underwear.

Sir Charles rested his chin on the top of his cane and looked up as Freedom entered, then beamed. Now they could dine at White's. Ed gaped and looked with renewed interest at Freedom. He was a fine looking fella, and Ed hid a smile. The lad was certainly a looker, just like the movie idol, Valentino, no doubt about it.

'I wonder, Sir Charles, if you've had any word from Miss Evelyne?'

Sir Charles was nonplussed for a moment, and Ed gave Freedom a shifty look. 'He means Miss Jones, yer know, sir, from Cardiff, she was stayin' at The Grange wiv us.'

'You see, she was my girl, an' I'm worried about her.'

Sir Charles pursed his lips. 'Miss Jones? Is that who you're referring to, Miss Jones? Good God, man, I've absolutely no idea where on earth she is, she left weeks ago. Besides, I don't like this "my girl" thing at all. If you recall your words on oath in the witness stand in Cardiff, you categorically denied any relationship with Miss Jones, are you now telling me you lied?'

Freedom's hands were clenched at his sides, and Ed began to sweat.

'I never lied, sir, it was the truth, but that didn't mean I didn't have no feelings for her. That came after the court case, she's my wife.'

Sir Charles' monocle popped out and he had to sit down. He repeated the word.

'Wife . . . ? Wife? Ed, did you know about this? I find it all very disturbing. When Miss Jones left, she made no mention of you being married.'

Ed was so perplexed he didn't know which way to turn and he could see Freedom's temper rising. 'Now, now, Freedom, that might be stretchin' it a bit far, they're not married, sir, not in a church, they did some Romany thing.'

In an icy voice Sir Charles reminded Freedom again of what he had said in court, on oath. He went on to inform him of the mounting costs of his new wardrobe, not to mention the lodgings, the training, wages for Ed and the two corner men, everything provided for Freedom on the simple condition that he box. Freedom was fighting to hold on to his temper as he faced Sir Charles.

'I reckon, sir, that I done that, and I am indebted to you, course I am — but that don't mean I am owned by you.'

This caused Sir Charles to throw his hands up in horror, it was all getting really out of hand. 'Your contract with myself is legal and binding. With reference to Miss Jones, she asked to leave The Grange the day before you yourself left. Surely if she had felt any overwhelming emotional tie to you she would have told you herself? Now, I think we really must forget all this nonsense, I have a table booked for nine-fifteen and I am looking forward to introducing you to my guests.'

He swept out, signalling for Ed to follow him. They walked a short way along the street together, Sir Charles' manner deathly cold. 'Make sure he's there, will you, old chap, maybe you should tell him what he'll be worth if he wins the title. He'll get a purse of near two hundred. Tell him that and we'll see how much this wretched woman means to him.'

Ed went slowly back up in the small, gilded lift. He sat down next to Freedom and patted his knee like a father. It was impossible to know what Freedom was thinking, his face was mask-like, the black eyes expressionless, he even seemed relaxed. He stared down at his big hands and he spoke softly, as if he was miles away. 'We have a saying, an old Romany saying, that if you love something, you must set it free; if it returns to you it is yours, if it doesn't then it never was ...'

Poor Ed didn't really know what to do. He couldn't afford to lose his job, and Sir Charles was such an odd man, Ed never knew which way he would turn. 'Freedom, lad, 'is Lordship's investin' a lot of money in you, and 'e don't want no dirty publicity 'bout you an' that murder investigation.'

Freedom protested his innocence, and Ed sighed. 'He's adamant about it, an' you know without 'im you would be swingin' fer that murder, you know that. See, you'll be meetin' all kinds of people now, society, like, perhaps even the prince himself, they can't 'ave no scandal.'

Freedom frightened Ed with his sly, strange smile. 'He won't want me, though, if I lose the title, mun, will he?'

Ed shouted at him that he would have two hundred pounds purse money if he won. 'Gawd 'elp me, two hundred pounds, you know how many years I gotta work ter make that much?'

Freedom still wore that smile and Ed was scared, not of what Freedom might do to him, but because he knew Freedom didn't really care about money.

'So what happens if we was to find 'er, and she not want you? Eh?'

Freedom moved his hands like a bird, she could fly away, do as she wanted, but he had to see her.

Evelyne had found work in a small bookshop in Charing Cross Road. The owner was an eccentric gentleman called Arnold Snodgrass. He wore a crumpled, stained suit, and was never without a cigarette hanging from the side of his mouth. His yellow teeth could be seen when he spoke in his strange, theatrical voice.

The shop was stacked from floor to ceiling with books, manuscripts and papers. The stench of cats and musty, ageing paper was at first nauseating. Evelyne was so dizzy at times she had to sit down on the stepladder.

Old Snoddy was unaware of her, as he was of the stench. 'Listen to this, dear heart, a little snippet of interest – did you know that Shakespeare, that wondrous bard, actually made up the word "lonely"? Imagine him sitting at his desk with his quill and thinking it up ... alone ... lone ... lonely ... now first play he used this new word was ... *Coriolanus*, fascinating, what? Wonderful play ... lonely ...'

Evelyne picked up a volume so heavy she could only just carry it from one side of the shop to the other. She sighed, her own loneliness taking precedence over Mr Snodgrass' snippet.

The next thing she knew Mrs Harris was standing over her burning one of Snoddy's own quill pens. Mrs Harris was a round, motherly woman who cleaned the shop and back room as best she could, and she also cleaned various other shops in the same area.

'She's comin' round now, sir. What 'appened, did she fall or what? It's them 'eavy volumes she's carrying round.'

Snoddy slurped his morning tea and shrugged, not interested in the slightest in the health of his assistant. He was buried in *Coriolanus*, still musing about his discovery.

'Come on, ducks, best get you home an' put yer feet up, 'e won't notice yer gorn, 'e don't know what day it is.'

Mrs Harris was shocked when she saw where Evelyne was living. 'Lord luv-a-duck, yer can't swing a cat in 'ere, and by the looks of it it's damp, shockin' ... have you no place even to boil a cup of tea?'

Evelyne lay on her bed, wanting to cry, but she shrugged off Mrs Harris' questions. 'I'm saving my money, I want to go to night classes, get my teacher's diploma, it's all right.'

Mrs Harris looked her over and then felt her forehead. 'You're running' a bit of a fever, ducks, maybe you should see a doctor.'

Evelyne buttoned her blouse, straightened her skirt and came out from behind the screen. The doctor was writing a prescription. She sat down and opened her purse, counted out the one shilling and sixpence her visit would cost.

'You must eat fresh vegetables, get your strength up, but there's nothing wrong that rest and a good diet won't put right. I wouldn't lift anything heavy, just in case ... this is a tonic, you should come back for regular check-ups until the birth.'

Evelyne blinked, swallowed hard. 'Beg pardon, sir, what did you say?'

*

When Evelyne came out into the waiting room, Mrs Harris rose to her feet, clutching her big cloth shopping bag, bulging with groceries. The girl looked worse now than when she had gone in. 'It's nuffink serious, is it, ducks?'

Evelyne shook her head, biting her lip so she wouldn't cry. Mrs Harris helped her into her coat, feeling sorry for her, 'You come round and 'ave supper at my place, no need to go back to yer work, Snoddy's got 'is brandy out so he won't know if you was workin' or not.'

Sitting beside Mrs Harris on the tram, Evelyne suddenly blurted it all out. 'I'm having a baby, that's what he told me, but I can't be, I just can't be . . .'

Mrs Harris sighed, she'd guessed as much, but Miss Jones was such a nice girl, very proper, and always so well dressed, so neat and tidy. 'Well, love, there's only one way to make one, have you been doing it? Have you got a young man?'

The floodgates opened, and Evelyne sobbed her heart out on top of the tram. She was still in floods of tears by the time they were sitting in Mrs Harris' kitchen.

'Yer see, ducks, in some cases yer can go on gettin' yer monthly bleedin' and still be carryin', how far gone are you, did he say?'

'He reckoned about five months, but I just can't be, I *can't*.'

Mrs Harris poured thick, strong tea, spooned in the sugar and eased her bulk into a fireside chair. 'Well, if yer that far gone there's no gettin' rid of it – mind you, there's some that would try . . . Drink yer tea now, don't go gettin' all upset again, we'll sort it all out . . . but yer won't be able to lift no more Shakespeare, that's fer sure.'

*

With seven children of her own, Mrs Harris needed Evelyne like a hole in the head. Her two-up-two-down was bursting at the seams. To help make ends meet her husband Ted worked nights at the gasworks, and during the day in a carpenter's shop. When he came home he found his missus stewing up a large pan of soup, the brood sitting round the kitchen table.

'We got a house guest, Ted. Now before you hit the roof, she's able to pay us threepence a week rent ... She's in the family way, and she's no one else to turn to. I've put her in the front room on the sofa.'

'Gawd 'elp us, woman, how we gonna fit in? Even with threepence extra?'

Covering the table with newspaper, Mrs Harris set out the cutlery. Ted sat down at the table, sighing. He was such a good-natured soul. 'You know, ducks, you'd take in a lame donkey if he was homeless, but we got to think of the kids ...'

His wife pulled up a chair and held his calloused hand. 'Remember our youngest, little Dora? Remember how I was all set to have a gin bath at Widow Smith's in the Hollow?'

Ted nodded, and kissed her big red cheek. Mrs Harris had been beside herself when she had discovered she was pregnant again, and had not said a word to Ted, but made up her mind to get rid of it. Ted had arrived home unexpectedly from work, knowing the kids were out, knowing she would be at home. 'Come here, you big old fool,' he had said, 'you fink after sixteen years of marriage I don't know when you're in the family way? Now, gel, it's gonna be tough on us, but we'll manage, and I've got a name, it'll be a girl if there's anything in the law of averages, and we'll call her Dora ... now give us a cuppa.'

'Evelyne's ever such a nice gel,' Mrs Harris went on, 'an' I can leave our Dora wiv her until her baby's born, that'll save us a few coppers, won't have ter farm her out whilst I do me cleanin'.'

Ted spooned up the hot soup, dipped a chunk of bread in the bowl and sucked on it. 'An' what 'appens when the baby's born, Ma? What's she gonna do then?'

'Oh, Ted, get on wiv yer, we'll face that when it comes, an' she can read an' write, she can teach the little 'uns their schoolin' . . .'

Evelyne entered the hot, stuffy kitchen, and Ted gave her a wide smile, held out his hand. 'Welcome to the family, gel, sit down, the missus'll take right care of yer, an' we'll all fit in somehow.'

Evelyne had never known such friendliness, such warmth and love, she was once more in the bosom of a family. The seven Harris children were rowdy, scruffy, and as open and friendly as their parents. Baby Dora, just eighteen months old, was left in Evelyne's care while Mrs Harris went out cleaning.

Exhausted from a long day's hard work, Mrs Harris sat by the fire while Evelyne changed Dora's nappy, cooing and making the baby gurgle with laughter. Evelyne's pregnancy had advanced quickly, and Mrs Harris began to think the doctor could have miscalculated. Evelyne was a big girl, and looking at her now Mrs Harris reckoned the baby was probably more like seven months.

Evelyne had not said one word about the father, or what she would do when the child was born.

'Will you keep the baby, Evie, ducks?'

Evelyne rocked little Dora in her arms. 'Oh, yes, I couldn't part with him, couldn't even think about it.'

'Well, it won't be easy yer know, love, woman on 'er own, you could have the baby adopted, there's many wivout that would give it a good home.'

Evelyne pursed her lips. 'There'll be no one bringing my son up but me, I'll find a way, I'll get work.'

'You never talk of the father, an' you're so sure it's a boy yer carryin' . . . does he know, lovey? About the baby?'

Whenever Mrs Harris mentioned the baby's father she saw Evelyne withdraw into herself. She had grown used to Evelyne, the way she could clam up. 'Do you love 'im still? Is 'e a society man, that what it is?'

Evelyne busied herself with Dora, but Mrs Harris battled on. 'Only, a first-born is important to a man, an' you seem so sure you've got a son inside you, d'yer not want ter contact 'im?'

She watched Evelyne put little Dora into her crib, an old orange box, and kiss the child lovingly. Her heart went out to the girl, especially when she turned with tears in her eyes. 'I just don't know what to do, I don't, but . . . feeling the baby inside me, well, I think more and more of him, but I just don't know what to do . . .'

Evelyne did think of Freedom; every night before she slept she saw his face. Leaving him the way she had was cruel, she knew it, and the more she thought of the way she had treated him the more ashamed she was. She decided to write to Freda, tell her about the baby, but ask her not to say anything to Freedom. She would want to tell him herself.

*

The Legacy

As soon as Freda received Evelyne's letter, she wrote back, knowing she shouldn't, giving Freedom's address in Jermyn Street. She also set about making baby clothes, but said nothing to Ed in her letter to him. She did as Evelyne asked, and kept the secret.

Evelyne opened Freda's letter in the park while little Dora was asleep in the pram. She read that Freedom was waiting for acceptance to fight the British Heavyweight Champion, Micky Morgan, how he had beaten the Irish contender, and that they were all on tenterhooks waiting for the promoters to give the word.

Seeing his name in writing, Evelyne's heart missed a beat. She knew she had been a fool. She touched her swollen belly, pictured Freedom's face. She could almost laugh at herself, she who had wanted a better life was now living in the slums, without a job, and wheeling someone else's baby around. Then she felt a bit guilty. Mrs Harris might be poor, but she was like a second mother to Evelyne. Poverty was all around them, but Evelyne had never said a word about her legacy. It had become an obsession with her, she scrimped and saved every farthing, and yet she had more money in the post office than the Harrises ever dreamed of. Originally it had been intended to pay for her own education, but now it would be for her son's. She blushed with shame, but then argued with herself that she paid her way, she wasn't taking the Harrises' charity, just their love.

Every single head turned as Freedom entered the Café Royal. Women particularly noticed him, towering over every other man, even the elegant Sir Charles went unnoticed. All eyes focused on Freedom.

Their table was very prominent, chosen for that specific reason, just as the table at White's had been the night before. The whispers spread as the diners recognized Sir Charles and knew that the handsome man with him must be his contender. The sporting sections had been full of coverage of the forthcoming British title fight, including Pat Murphy's unprecedented knockout. The venue had been changed from the National Sporting Club to the Albert Hall, and the fight delayed for two months as posters and tickets were altered and reprinted. The pre-fight sales were already the biggest in English history, and it was rumoured that tickets were scarce now and were becoming a 'must'. It was also rumoured that the Prince of Wales himself would be the guest of Sir Charles and Lord Livermore.

Much of the press coverage was down to Sir Charles negotiating long and hard with the promoters, who wanted to recoup their losses from the Pat Murphy knockout, which included billboards, posters, tickets, et cetera. With the larger showcase of the Albert Hall, the losses were soon made up. Sir Charles announced that a quarter of the profits would be given to charity, thus giving the match the seal of approval for society to be there.

The British Heavyweight Champion himself kept well out of the limelight. Sir Charles had no intention of keeping Freedom under wraps, and was betting heavily on the champion as well, intending to cover his losses should Freedom lose. He loved the fuss, the glamour and the attention, basked in it, and paraded Freedom as if he were a prize hunter on a rein. Freedom held up well, his dark eyes flashing, his smile captivating everyone. His romantic Romany origins were well publicized, and the women fluttered and pretended to swoon when he kissed their hands.

Tonight, at the Café Royal, Freedom had to stand for a round of applause as the band leader moved the spotlight on to Sir Charles' table.

Poor Ed shuddered with embarrassment as Sir Charles' generosity had not included him and he was self-conscious in his ill-fitting suits and old shirt. Realizing that the slight was intended, he stepped aside from now until the last stages of his training. He contented himself instead with reading about his golden boy in the society columns.

Freda was delighted when Ed sent for her to come to town. She had worked her fingers raw, sewing clothes for herself, hoping to be there on the big night. She set off from The Grange as excited as a child.

When Ed met her at the station she was a trifle disappointed to discover that they had to travel by public transport, and even further let down to find that they had to stay with Ed's family, who were waiting for them with tea all ready on the table. Ed's brother and his wife and kids greeted the new sister-in-law with suspicion at first, but then made her welcome. They were East Enders and, although Freda never said a word, they were obviously living from hand to mouth. She and Ed were given the front room to sleep in, and it was not until late evening that Freda had a chance to talk to Ed in privacy.

'Well, darlink, how is Freedom? Will we all have tickets for the fight?'

Ed was hesitant at first, not as enthusiastic as she had expected. In truth, his nose was very much out of joint.

Freedom seemed to have changed. Only a short while ago Ed couldn't have got him to put a tie round his neck, and now he was never without one. Freedom had also been very cold and aloof with Ed, and that hurt him. He didn't like to mention it to Freda, but she detected he was not too happy.

'You won't recognize 'im, Freda, 'e looks like a toff an' 'e's actin' like one, out every night gallivantin' around the town, showin' 'imself off to everybody. He should be trainin', night an' day. You don't see this Micky out in the clubs, no way, he'll be trainin' mornin', noon an' night.'

Freda made all the right noises and bided her time. She didn't like to mention Evelyne now.

'I'm worried, Freda, see, I know 'is Lordship, next minute the lad'll believe in 'is own publicity, believe that Sir's 'is closest friend, but if 'e loses he won't see 'im fer dust, an' 'e'll lose, Freda, mark my words 'e'll lose, 'e can't go on like this. I been round three times an' 'e's still in bed at twelve o'clock, him what was out at the crack of dawn at The Grange.'

Patting his hand and kissing his cheek, Freda assured him that she would have a word with Freedom when she saw him.

'You'll need an appointment, Freda, see if 'e can't fit you in between 'is barber an' 'is tailor.'

Often at night Freedom would walk along Jermyn Street and cross into St James's Park. Climbing over the railings he would run silently round and round, or sit for hours staring at the sleeping pelicans. Then when he had exhausted himself he would return to Jermyn Street. The running eased his restlessness, his feeling of being cooped up, of being on display, a fairground amusement. The women who pawed him only made him long for his Evie, and the pain inside him grew worse and worse instead of easing, but he said nothing, told no one.

Dewhurst woke Freedom to say that Mr Meadows and his wife had called, and would return later that afternoon for tea. Then he ran Freedom's bath and began to lay out his clothes to wear for luncheon.

Mrs Harris could tell something was up, Evie was as bright as a button. She had also washed her hair and let out her best coat. She kept on asking how she looked, did she look ugly?

'Lord love us, gel, there's nothing more beautiful than a woman with a baby in her, you got a glow ... are you off visitin'?'

Evelyne gave a tiny smile.

'Well, you tell 'im from me, ducks, he's got a special woman, you go to him, bring 'im back for supper an' all, go on wiv you, you've waited long enough as it is ...'

Evelyne caught the tram into London's West End. Winter was coming on fast, and she hugged her coat around her. She got off the tram outside the big store in Piccadilly, Swan and Edgar. The windows were all lit up, and one of them was filled with baby clothes and cradles. She peered into the brightly lit window. Such beautiful things, the toys, the clothes. She couldn't move away, she found herself smiling with pleasure, with excitement at the thought of seeing Freedom again. She could visualize him so clearly, in his old cap and baggy trousers, running across the fields, and she couldn't understand why she was crying, it was so foolish of her, and in a public place, too.

She bathed her face and checked her appearance in the ladies' powder room inside the store, then nervously enquired the way to Jermyn Street. She was surprised to find it in the heart of the West End, having expected it to be a tram journey away. She was directed across Piccadilly, past a very fashionable shop, and down a small alley alongside a church. So this was where Freedom was staying. Evelyne stood in Jermyn Street taking in the rows of small shops selling soap, the tailors, the barbers.

Freedom stepped down from the motorcar and held out his hand to help two women from the back of the car. Evelyne could hardly believe her eyes, was it Freedom? She inched further forward, trying to see round the open door of the car. He was wearing a long, charcoal-grey overcoat, with a wide fur collar slightly turned up around his neck, and a white silk scarf. He laughed, throwing his head back, as one of the women pulled at the scarf and stood on tiptoe to whisper in his ear.

Dodging through the shoppers, Evelyne huddled in a doorway and watched as he held out first one arm, then the other, for the women to take. They fought for his attention. Being so tall he had to bend down to listen to what one of them had to say, and she took the opportunity to kiss his cheek. Evelyne gasped and stepped forward for a better view, then dodged quickly back as the three moved towards the building. A uniformed doorman stepped out and doffed his cap to them, holding the door open wide. As they went inside and the glittering doors closed behind them, Evelyne ran the few yards to the entrance, and peered through the doors in time to see them standing by a lift.

*

Freedom pressed the lift button. His head was aching from drinking too much champagne, but Dewhurst would have coffee ready. He was supposed to be training, but he would make up for it in the morning. As the lift gates opened he had a strange tingling sensation like an icy hand down his spine, and he whipped round, his scarf flying, ran to the doors and pulled them open. 'Evie? Evie . . .?'

He stared along the crowded, fashionable street, then shook his head. He must be drunk. The door swung to and fro, and he returned to the women.

'Oh, Freedom, we simply must take you to tea at the Ritz, say you will? Pretty please?'

He gave her a nasty, cold stare, gritted his teeth.

'Pretty please, get in, let me show you *my* Ritz!'

The two of them giggled at his awful mood, and they cuddled close to him, clinging to his arms. They felt like a pair of monkeys to him, they loved to scratch him with their long, red-painted fingernails. Still, they helped him to forget, forget Evie.

Ted Harris heard Evelyne come in, and opened the kitchen door.

'Evie, that you, ducks? A cabbie came round wiv a parcel for you, here, see, cab all by itself, no one inside.'

Evelyne took the parcel but wouldn't meet his eyes.

'You all right, ducks? Feelin' poorly, are you?'

'I'm fine, I'll just rest, I'll see to the children's tea in a minute.'

Ted watched her hurry along the passage to her room. She was so pale, it worried him.

In the room Evelyne opened Miss Freda's gifts. The tiny baby clothes, so perfectly made, were perhaps not in the colours she would have chosen, but they were beautiful. There was a little note in the parcel, but the writing was so bad that it took Evelyne ages to decipher what Freda had written.

'In haste, darling, I will come and see you. God bless you and keep you well. Yours, Freda.'

Freda's mouth seemed to be out of control, it kept dropping open as she sat and watched Freedom lounging on the sofa opposite her. He wouldn't meet her eyes, she had noticed that right at the start, as soon as they had arrived. He was being flippant and amusing, and from his shoes to his shining hair he was so well-groomed she would never have known him.

'Lads reckon you'll be having to start work first thing Monday, Freedom?'

Freda knew what Ed was going on about, but Freedom seemed to pay him little attention. Suddenly he sprang to his feet and asked Ed if he would go down to the teashop and order something for them.

An extremely disgruntled Ed departed, leaving Freedom and Freda alone together. They sat in silence for a minute, Freedom staring down at his shiny boots and Freda looking at the curtains, reckoning the material would cost at least four or five shillings a yard. He wanted to talk to her, desperately needed to talk to someone, but he just didn't know how to begin.

Eventually he rose to his feet and picked up his walking stick, tossed it in the air and then showed Freda the silver handle. 'See, it's a boxing glove, Miss Freda.'

She looked, not that she was particularly interested. It was Freedom, he had changed, and she couldn't speak to him any more.

'Yes, Sir Charles give it to me, bought it for me, he likes buyin' things, yes he does, I reckon he got me cheap, though . . . Well ta-ra, Dewhurst'll see to your needs.'

He gave a low bow and was gone.

That night, Freda agreed with Ed that Freedom had changed. She couldn't talk to him, not in the old way, it was as if he was a stranger.

Poor Ed was at a loss, 'It's the way 'e 'as of making you not know what 'e's thinkin', what 'e's feelin' . . . 'e told me they was married, did I tell you that? Yes, 'e said Evie an' 'im was married, not a proper service like ours, some Romany thing they just did together – becomin' a real ladies' man now, though!'

This was Freda's moment to ask if Freedom was missing Evelyne, wanted to see her at all. 'Does he still ask after Evie, Ed?'

Ed replied in a mutter that Sir Charles had forbidden it, in case a scandal about the trial got out. ''E was on a murder charge. You think the prince an' all those society people'd be sittin' pawin' at 'im if they knew that? It's best Evie's name never crops up.'

Freda couldn't bring herself to tell Ed about Evie's letter, about the baby. If anything it would cause an even greater scandal.

Sir Charles was staying at the Savile Club, and Ed went to meet him there.

'He's not the same lad, guv, shows no interest, an' 'e's not comin' to the gym, I was wonderin' if you could 'ave a word wiv 'im, seein' as you're takin' 'im out an' about . . . Only, if we don't get 'im ter buckle down 'e'll lose the championship an' we'll both be left – if you'll pardon the expression – we'll both be left lookin' like bleedin' idiots.'

'Ed, what do you take me for, I've not seen him in over a week! Good God, man, I'm the first to know that a fighter mustn't, as you say, burn up his wick, tell him to come to the Pelican tonight, and you too, Ed.'

Freedom was late arriving at the club, which annoyed Sir Charles, who had checked his watch three times. There was a good snooker game going on in one of the annexes, and he saw Freedom strolling along, watching the players.

'Here he is now, Ed, leave it to me.'

When he joined them Freedom asked the waiter for a beer, then leaned back in his chair, rocking it on its back legs.

'Thinking of bringing in a sparring partner, just to work you up for the big day, what do you say?'

For a reply he got a shrug of the shoulders. Freedom seemed more interested in the snooker. Staring at him through his monocle, Sir Charles lit a cigar, puffed on it.

'Ed here tells me you're below par. That true, feeling off colour, are you?'

Again the annoying shrug of Freedom's shoulders as he murmured that if Ed had said it then it must be true. Sir Charles had had enough, he leaned forward and snapped at Freedom in icy tones, 'When you feel you can talk, please contact me. I'm afraid I have better things to do with my time than to sit here and be insulted. You may believe I own you, so be it, but I am not prepared to be treated like a pimp, pull yourself together, lad, or I will throw your contract back in your face, is that clear?'

He walked briskly away from the table without a backward glance.

Wanting to weep, Ed stared sorrowfully into his beer. How could Freedom do this to him after all the love and hard work Ed had put into him? 'You just kicked me down, you know that, lad? I dunno why you done this to me, you could be the next British champion, I know it, but not this way. You're breakin' my 'eart.'

Shoving Freedom's hand away he stumbled from the table, leaving Freedom sitting alone in the pit.

Outside the club an old, bent man was sweeping the pavement, where the sawdust had travelled on the gents' shoes into the road. The old chap didn't seem to notice Freedom, and almost ran the brush over his shoes.

'Aw, sorry about that, sir, here, allow me ... you a fightin' mun are ye?'

Taking a handkerchief from his pocket, he was about to bend down to dust Freedom's shoes. He looked up for a moment. His bruiser's face was wrinkled, and he had cauliflower ears, a broken nose.

'Hammer, it's you, isn't it? Dai Thomas, Hammerhead?'

The old boy chuckled and wagged his head, spat on his fists and held them up.

'Ay, lad, that's me all right.'

With a toothless grin he looked into Freedom's face with no sign of recognition. Freedom's heart went out to him, he looked at all the traffic heading towards Piccadilly. 'Where can a mun get a cup of tea this time of night?' Hammer waved his brush to a small alley, and accepted Freedom's offer to accompany him there. He also accepted the steaming bowl of soup Freedom placed before him. He sucked at the bread, making loud noises as he slurped the thick soup. He wiped the bowl with his crust until it glistened. He made no reply when Freedom asked how long he had been in London. But his face lit up when the ham and eggs followed, then he turned sly.

'What are you after? Why you buying all this for me, eh?'

He raised the fork and tucked into the ham, not waiting for a reply. At least, not until he had filled his belly.

'I'm Freedom Stubbs.'

Freedom stared at Hammer, did he remember? Know him? Hate him? He could clearly recall the man as he had been, arms up in the air, swaggering in his corner all those years ago in Cardiff. The café owner slapped his fat thigh and went behind the counter, delving underneath for newspapers. 'By Christ, I thought I recognized yer. Will yer look at this, this is the man that knocked out Pat Murphy just the other month.'

'Gawd almighty, I know you, this is him that knocked me teeth down me throat, remember me always talkin' of the bout, this is the mun that did it.' Hammer seemed flooded with renewed energy, he was up on his feet, prancing around on the sawdust floor. Freedom had expected the old man to go for him, but there was no animosity, more hero-worship. He thudded round to stand by Freedom's side, his big fist came down on the shoulder of Freedom's expensive overcoat and gripped it hard. 'Now then, mun, you'll have one hell of a bout with Micky, lemme tell you, I see 'im box, oh, must be four, five years ago. He was just a kid, but 'e's got hands like spades, and they hurt.'

Some old boxers sitting in the café began to take notice, pulling their chairs closer to listen. Hammer basked in

Freedom's glory. 'I went down so hard they never thought I'd be comin' round, three-quarters of an hour I was out, out for more than the count, eh?'

By the time Freedom and Hammer walked back towards the Pelican Club, they had their arms about each other's shoulders, the best of friends, buddies. Hammer collected his broom from the club's doorway.

'Handle yerself well, son, don't want to see you on the other end of one of these, well, not yet, anyway. Could you see your way to getting me a ticket for the Albert Hall? I'd like to be there to see you thrash the Liverpudlian. Be a proud day for me to say I went down to the British champ ...'

Freedom promised to send him a ticket, then he hesitated. 'Don't put yer money on me, Hammer.'

Hammer grabbed Freedom's arm, and his bent body straightened. Through globs of spittle at the side of his mouth he swore at Freedom, almost pushed him off his feet.

'That's not fighter's talk, what's the matter with you, lad? I'd have given me life for an opportunity like you got, any mun would – I know I would. What's up with ye?'

To Hammer, of all people, the man Freedom had sent sprawling, he opened up, near to tears. 'They own me, mun, own me, an' I'm through, there won't be no fight.'

Hammer's chin wobbled, and tears came into his already watery eyes. He looked at Freedom with disgust, thudded his fist into his own chest. 'Nobody owns a fighter's heart, mun, you throw the fight and you'll not live with yourself. Take the fancy clothes away and you're a gyppo. But win the title an' you're a champion.'

461

Hammer stepped aside as three gents came out of the club and slipped him a few coppers. He immediately started sweeping the sawdust-covered pavement again. Freedom walked away, he didn't look back, he couldn't.

Mrs Harris could hear Evie down in the kitchen. She pulled on her worn coat over her nightdress and went downstairs.

'All right, are you, lovey? Fancy a cup of tea?'

Evelyne turned her face away, not wanting her friend to see she had been crying. They had not spoken of what had happened in Jermyn Street, there had been no need. Evelyne had been so quiet that Mrs Harris knew something had gone wrong.

'There's nothing to say, just . . . I saw him, and, well, he's not the man I knew, and I know he wouldn't want me, I know.'

Mrs Harris put the kettle on and stoked up the fire, questioned her no further. She sighed, it looked as though they would have their guest to stay for a long time. 'Whatever 'appens, ducks, this is your home now, yours and the baby's, so put your mind at rest on that.'

Evelyne hugged the big, kind woman, and the strong arms held her tight.

'There's a good gel, you'll be all right, you'll see.'

In the cold light of dawn Freda woke to see Ed standing by the window. He was dressed, ready to go out, and she put out her hand, but he didn't take it. She watched his depressed, squat figure walking down the street. The milk cart began its round, the horse clip-clopping out of the dairy half-way down the road. She made up her mind then and there that she would go and see Evelyne. Not just for the girl, but for herself and Ed too, if Evelyne could make Freedom see sense then she would see him, whether Ed liked it or not.

Sir Charles laid a neat ledger in front of Freedom, with all the expenses calculated to date. Every item bought for Freedom was carefully listed in Ed's handwriting. Clothes in one column, food in another, lodgings, keep, train tickets – every item was accounted for. There were pages and pages of figures from Cardiff, the lawyer's and the barrister's bills from Smethurst's firm, Evelyne's hotel bills and receipts, even down to her satin dress and the rented jewellery. On the following pages were the wages paid to Ed and the two lads, their expenses and their keep. Freedom's head began to spin as Sir Charles flicked the pages over. 'Not done yet, take a look at these figures, this is just for the tickets, the posters, the press.'

Page after page was turned over, and the final amount was written in the last column. More than five thousand pounds.

'I'd say we've invested quite a large sum, wouldn't you? And I think Ed told you, you will be allowed two hundred from the purse, *if* you win the championship.'

Sir Charles flicked a small piece of thread from his trouser leg, held it aloft to inspect it.

'If you lose, the contract we have will be null and void, it's quite obvious why, and surely you must see why I have to have a contract in the first place. You win the British title and you'll have God knows how many promoters after you. Next stop America, and the fights there take ten times more money than they do here. All I have done, old chap, is to protect my investment.'

He couldn't determine what Freedom was thinking, but he assumed it was slowly sinking in. 'If I have made you feel anything less than a friend, I apologize, it certainly was not my intention. I have believed in you right from the very beginning, from Devil's Pit, you know I travelled up there to see *you*?'

Pacing the room, Freedom felt guilty, confused. He was all mixed inside.

'Ed will be waiting at the gym, what do you want to do? I am perfectly willing to listen to anything within reason ... I will be saddened if you want to walk away, but I can't stop you. You will, of course, have to repay all the costs, and I don't think it too unreasonable, not at this late stage.'

Freedom could hardly swallow, his tongue felt dry and seemed to be sticking in his throat.

'It's entirely your decision but we can't wait, not too long. If you want to back out I shall have to find another contender, won't be easy. Then again, fighters are two a penny, Freedom; sooner you learn that the better.'

Ed made both men jump as he slammed into the room, flushed with anger. 'Fighters, maybe, but not champions. You're a bloody fool, Freedom ... sorry, sir, ter barge in like this, but I been up all night long, an' I just can't, can't let 'im walk away.' He turned to Freedom. 'If it's Evie you want then we'll find 'er, if that's what all this is about. If it is 'er, then bugger the press, I say, and I'm sorry, sir, but sod the prince an' all. I put months of my time into this lad, an' I won't let 'im throw it away.'

Sir Charles was on his feet, his manner controlled but more angry than Freedom had ever seen him. 'One moment if you please, Ed, I am sure your theatrical entrance was meant well.'

His voice was chilling in its calmness as he glared at Freedom.

'I want the truth, Stubbs, you swore on oath on that witness stand. Tell me, it was a pack of lies, wasn't it? You killed that boy in the picture house, didn't you? *Didn't you? Tell me!*'

His control left him and he raised his stick, looking as though he would bring it down on Freedom's head. Ed gaped, but Freedom moved fast, wrenching the stick away from Sir Charles. Ed thought he would break it in two, but he held it calmly, tapping it into the palm of his hand.

'I did no killing, sir, an' what I said on that stand was the truth. I dunno why I'm acting the way I am, I can only say I'm sorry ... I love her, sir, I dunno why she went without sayin' nothin' to me, and it's eating me up inside.'

Tight-lipped, Sir Charles picked up his gloves and told Ed to take Freedom to his woman, he would see to the press personally.

'You'll fight, then?'

'I just need to see her, that's all, mun.'

Ed sighed with relief, grabbed Freedom's coat. 'Get yerself down ter the gym, I'll get Freda to bring her to you, go on, get out.'

Freedom didn't need to be told twice. He was out of the room like lightning. Ed hovered at the door.

'Well, sir, do we go on or not?'

Sir Charles shrugged. 'As you said, we've put a lot of time and money into him, why not?'

Ed ran after Freedom. Sir Charles could see them both from the apartment window, running along Jermyn Street, dodging the passers-by. The gypsy spring was back, all right.

Dewhurst coughed politely.

'Will you be wanting anything, sir?'

Still staring into the street, Sir Charles was carefully pulling on his gloves. When he spoke his voice was matter-of-fact, with hardly a trace of emotion. 'Appears our problems were to do with the gel, young fella loved her.'

Dewhurst raised his eyebrows. Sir Charles didn't look at him, could have been talking to himself. 'Funny, ya know, I have never known that sort of love, the sort he feels for this girl, never known it ... but I do understand. You see, somewhere in the darkened recesses of my mind, I have dreamed of him loving me – never known me treat one of my boxers with such lavish care, have you, eh?'

'No sir, I have not, sir.'

Sir Charles' monocled eye glistened with a magnified tear. He adjusted his cravat. 'Get my things sent over from the Savile, would you, shall be moving back here. Ed can arrange accommodation for him, and he will not be using my barber or my tailor again, is that clear?'

'Yes, sir, perfectly clear, I shall call them straightaway.'

Sir Charles smiled at his manservant, 'You're a jolly good fellow, Dewhurst, I appreciate you greatly ... still, I didn't embarrass myself, did I? Does no harm to have lascivious dreams ...'

Dewhurst bowed himself out of the room and went immediately to the bedroom where Freedom had been sleeping. Sir Charles followed him and stared at the crumpled sheets. 'Well, maybe we'll have a champion. Then again we may not, send everything here to the gym. Oh, and Dewhurst – throw the sheets out, would you?'

The door closed silently behind him, and his voice echoed from the corridor.

'I'll be at my club should anyone call.'

After folding Freedom's clothes carefully, Dewhurst got some brown paper and made a neat parcel.

Freedom worked out hard and well with his two sparring partners, but he constantly glanced at the doors, waiting. Finally, Ed reappeared. 'Freda's gone to get her, lad, now get on wiv it, we need all the time we can get ... Come on, get on with yer work out, the press is comin' fer an interview in 'alf an hour!'

All the neighbours were staring out of their windows, peering out of their doors. Freda had arrived in a horse-drawn cab, and she knocked and knocked on Mrs Harris' door.

'What's up, somebody die? Hey, darlin', you with the rat-catchers then, are you?'

A scruffy little boy answered the door.

'Is Evie here? Evelyne, is she here?'

He couldn't understand what the hysterical little woman was saying. Mrs Harris came to the door and opened it wider. She was carrying little Dora on her hip. 'Evie? Is it Evie yer want? Well, she's gorn ter the clinic, it's in Upper Lambeth Street.'

Freda was already rushing back to the cab. Mrs Harris called after her.

'If she ain't there, try Swan an' Edgar's, she winder-shops a lot.'

Freedom had changed into his best clothes for the photographers. He seemed not to care about posing, constantly glancing at Ed and then to the doors. 'Freda not called yet, Ed? You think she's found her?'

Ed began to panic, maybe Evie had moved, that would be all they needed. 'Just concentrate on puttin' on a good show fer the photographers, lad, I'll nip outside an' have a look, she'll be here.'

As Ed bustled out he offered a silent prayer that Freda would find Evie, and fast. They'd got Freedom back to work, but if she didn't show up Ed didn't know how long he would behave himself.

Evelyne had walked up Jermyn Street every day for the past five days, each time pausing outside the ornate building where she had seen Freedom, and the uniformed porter had begun to raise his hat to her and smile in recognition. Today she had been about to ask him if Mr Stubbs still lived in these apartments, but at the last moment she couldn't find the courage. She turned and hurried away.

Freda swiped the tram conductor with her handbag when he tried to prevent her jumping off, shouting to her that she would kill herself. She had seen Evelyne, staring into one of the windows of Swan and Edgar. Poor Freda ran round and round the building, calling Evelyne's name frantically, but she had disappeared.

'Get yourself thinking, Freda darlink, where would she 'ave gone from here, where? Please, dear God, tell me where she is?'

She scurried among the baby clothes and toys, diving among the shoppers, but Evelyne wasn't there. Disappointed, she turned back towards the stairs ... and caught sight of the familiar red hair. Her heart skipped a beat, and she hurried around the counter ... and lost her again ... no, she hadn't, there was Evelyne, bending over a cradle, touching it lovingly ...

'*Evie! Evieeeee ... Evie ...*'

The reporters and cameramen were just packing up when one of the boys fell down the steps into the gym. He rubbed his shin and gasped incoherently. 'They got her, she's found her, she's coming!'

Ed shouted for quiet and ran to the boy, grabbed him by the collar. 'What ... ? What ... !? Speak up, lad.'

Freedom seemed to cover the distance from the far end of the gym to Ed's side in one leap.

'Take it easy, mate, Freda's found her, we've found her.'

Freedom sprinted up the stairs to the street, looking this way and that, desperate, but there was no sign of anyone. Panic-stricken, he turned to Ed, who ran up and down the road shouting for Freda, for Evie. The lad joined them, saying he had just seen them in a cab, they were outside the gym not two minutes ago.

Freda held Evelyne's hand as the cabbie drove them once again around the block. Evelyne studied her face in Freda's small mirror.

'Oh, Freda, I can't, look at me, I look terrible, my hair's all down and I got my old coat on and shoes full of newspapers.'

Freda rummaged in her bag for a comb, waved her hand for the cabbie to go round the block yet again. 'Here, darlink, my comb, come, let me, let me.'

Freda tried frantically to drag the comb through Evelyne's hair, but it was a tiny comb and there was so much hair.

*

On the corner stood Ed, hopefully eyeing each vehicle that passed. He spotted the cab and jumped right in front of it, making the horses shy. Diving into the back he fell into Evie's arms, kissing her as if *he* were her long-lost lover, he was so excited. Freedom reappeared and Freda and Ed ran down the road to him, Freda's feet hardly touching the ground.

'She's in the cab, go on, she's in the cab.'

The look on his face made them both want to cry, he didn't know what to do with himself. He ran his hands through his hair and tried to straighten his tie while at the same time running as fast as he could to the cab. Fascinated, the cabbie looked down from his seat, this was better than the picture houses.

Freedom bent his head into the open carriage window. Evelyne had pressed herself shyly into the corner of the carriage, her cheeks flaming red and her wondrous hair tumbling over her shoulders. Standing staring at her, Freedom could find no words. His breath heaved in his chest, and try as he might he couldn't stop the sobs forcing their way into his throat, nor could he move.

Eventually he spoke, his voice strained. 'Can I ride a while with you, *manushi*?'

He climbed into the cab and sat by Evelyne's side. He could hear Ed shouting to the driver to just keep driving, drive anywhere. The carriage jolted forward.

Evelyne took Freedom's hand and placed it on her stomach, and he gasped as if he were about to explode. Immediately she let his hand go, and turned to stare out of the carriage.

She whispered, 'I'm sorry, he's yours, Freedom.' She felt his hand gently caress her swollen belly, and fraction by fraction she turned her head until she could look into his face. She placed her hand over his heart, felt it thudding, and he put his hand over her milk-filled breast. Heart to heart, they whispered each other's names.

'Never leave me, *manushi*. I died a little while you were gone.'

It was getting dark, and the cabbie began to wonder who would be paying his fare. They were still trotting round and round Regent's Park. The lovers whispered to each other, their fingers interlocked as they vowed they would never again be parted.

Chapter 20

Ed Meadows led Freedom into the weighing-room. It was full of reporters, promoters and officials, standing around the scale. Freedom wore shorts, boxing boots and a robe, the hood pulled over his head, hiding his face.

Micky Morgan, dressed in the same way as Freedom, stood with his corner men and trainer at the far end of the room. His back was to the entrance, but as the murmur of voices died down he knew his opponent had arrived. He didn't turn, but his back straightened, like an animal sensing danger.

'Gentlemen, to the scales, please.'

Micky turned slowly, eyes down, refusing to look at Freedom as they were led to the scales. Micky took off his robe first and stepped up. The two officials looked at the pointer, conferred with each other and pushed the weights along the scale bar as Ed tried to get a look over their shoulders to see what weight Morgan was carrying.

'The champion weighing in, gentlemen, at thirteen stone ten pounds, standing at six feet one and a half inches.'

Still without even a flicker of a glance at Freedom, Micky stepped down, and his trainer immediately replaced his robe around his shoulders. Ed gave him a clinical, professional appraisal. The man was in terrific shape, his skin taut, his body muscular, and his shoulders were slightly concave – good, hunched, boxer's shoulders. There was no sign of the cut he had taken over his eye in his last championship bout, it seemed completely healed. His nose was flat, eyes hooded, and there was a slight puffiness just below the brows. One of his front teeth was missing, and one of his ears was larger than the other. As he pulled his robe around his shoulders, Ed could see his massive hands, the flat, gnarled knuckles.

The fight was by no means going to be easy, Ed knew Micky looked confident, and Ed knew he was purposely refusing to look in Freedom's direction.

'Would the contender please step on the scales.'

It was Freedom's turn, and off came his robe as he stepped on to the scales. The officials moved the weights, checking carefully, and Micky now watched closely. Freedom was one hell of a size, and his skin was tawny, unlike Micky's which was whiter-than-white. As the marker on the measuring stick was lowered to Freedom's head, Micky could see he was well over six feet tall.

'The contender, gentlemen, weighs in at fourteen stone, one pound, eight ounces, standing at six feet four inches.'

'He's a ruddy Red Indian, look at the hair on 'im, halfway down 'is back.'

Both boxers were taken back to their dressing rooms, and an hour later they were called in to the conference room. The champion was applauded as he entered. He was wearing a cheap, brown pin-striped suit, a white shirt and tie, and he was carrying a brown trilby hat. He took his seat on the platform beside his trainer and promoter, Lord Livermore, who wore a black coat with an astrakhan collar and smoked a fat Havana cigar. Sir Charles, as immaculate as ever, was talking quietly to him, and shook Micky's hand when they were introduced.

Ed ushered Freedom into the room and everyone turned to look at him. He did not warrant applause, and Ed whispered for him to take the seat next to Sir Charles. He stepped on to the platform and sat down, fingering his collar and straightening the jacket of his new, single-breasted suit, tailored in soft dove grey. Carrying Freedom's fur-collared coat, Ed inched his way in behind them and sat down, worried about falling because the leg of his chair was precariously near the edge of the platform. Lord Livermore held his cigar in front of his face and smirked to Sir Charles about his snazzily dressed boxer.

'How many rounds do you think it'll go, Micky?'

Smiling, Morgan gave a jerk of his head at Freedom and said that maybe they should ask the contender how many rounds he reckoned he could stand up for. This got a roar of laughter, and Micky posed for a solo photograph. Freedom was asked if he wanted to answer the champ's question, but he stared blankly and remained silent.

The press requested a shot of Micky and Freedom together, and the two men rose and faced each other, Micky confident and brash, smiling his gap-toothed grin. He got no response from Freedom whose dark eyes stared back, expressionless. The photographers took their time preparing their cameras, and as they waited Micky whispered to Freedom, his voice inaudible to the rest of the room, 'Goin' to mark that pretty face, gyppo, goin' to mark you, break you, gyppo, hear me, take you out in five.'

Freedom stared impassively into the champion's face, as if he hadn't heard the threat.

Ed's brother had found a house for Evelyne and Freedom, further along the terrace in the same street, not five turnings away from Mrs Harris'. The previous occupants of number twelve had fallen behind with their rent, and the bailiffs had moved them out. The house had been infested with mice and bugs so they had had to scrub and disinfect everything, and call in the rat-catcher to put down poison. This was Evelyne's first home of her own and, to the concern of all the women in the street, she had worked herself into exhaustion. Seeing her, heavily pregnant, scrubbing at the steps, had earned her the acceptance of all her neighbours. Freda and several other local women had scrubbed and washed and helped hang curtains, nail down lino, and had even brought odd bits of china to help out. They all called her Evie.

Mrs Harris was Evelyne's first proper visitor. She came walking slowly up the road, carrying a big pot of stew. "Ello, lovey, I 'ad this on when one of the kids came round, so I didn't like to waste it . . . well, well, just think of it, you a neighbour! Well I never!'

Evelyne showed her round the scrubbed little house with pride. When she saw that Evie had got a gas stove, Mrs Harris went into raptures. There wasn't a stick of furniture yet, but the curtains were lovely, and the lino was a pretty shade of green.

'Oh, Evie love, it's a palace, a real palace, you've done wonders.'

A small crowd had gathered outside, and one of the women

yelled to Evelyne at the top of her voice, 'It's the bed arrived, yer bed's come!' A new bed in this street was something, and all the neighbours were agog. The mahogany headboard met with nods of approval. The bed was enormous, and the delivery men had to be helped getting it into the house.

Freedom and Evelyne went up the narrow staircase and stood looking into their bedroom. There it was in all its glory, the special-sized bed.

'Well, I never thought I'd be a *kairengo*!'

Lying down on the thick mattress, Evelyne patted it for him to lie beside her. 'What does that mean?'

He lay down and told her that a *kairengo* was a man who lived in a house. He stared up at the ceiling, and she picked up his hand, kissed it, 'Do you not like it?'

He turned and touched her face, kissed her softly, 'It's what you want that's my pleasure. Tell me, are you happy?'

She rolled over, rubbed her belly and stretched. She told him she had never been so happy in her entire life. Up she got and swished the curtains, showing him the wooden rail, then insisted that he see everything, pulling him by the hand until he got up off the bed.

'This is our home, Freedom, and here, in here, this is where the baby will be. Mr Harris said he'd make me a cradle . . . and come on down, let me show you how the gas stove lights up. You don't need to have the fire lit, see, you turn this tap here, and you light it like so, isn't it lovely?'

Delighted, he watched her as she touched the walls, the lino, and then brought him her notebook to show him what kind of furniture they would save for. 'We'll not get anything on tick, that way we won't get into debt, but we'll buy it piece by piece, it'll be so lovely.'

Freedom went back up to the bedroom. He didn't want to spoil her happiness, couldn't tell her the house was already weighing on him, closing in on him, and he hated it. Evelyne thought he was sleeping, but he was dreaming of the open air, the fields, riding on a wild pony. He felt her lie down beside him, and her body heat warmed him like a fire.

'Feel him, he's kicking, feel.'

He put his hand to her belly and felt the strange movements of his child inside her. He would fight for his very life in the ring, and he would give her everything she dreamed of, now he had something to fight for, his wife and his child.

Evelyne shifted to a more comfortable position, careful not to wake him, knowing he needed his sleep before the fight. Sweat broke out all over her, and the kicking, thudding, unborn child felt as if he was trying to punch his way through her backbone. 'Dear God, don't let him come now, not tonight. Stay put until after the fight.'

The morning of the fight was cold, and the snow was falling thick and fast. It was not yet five, but Evelyne could hear Freedom moving around downstairs, stoking up the kitchen fire. She felt the first spasm, it shook her body, and she bit hard on the blanket. He wasn't going to wait . . . She gasped, and the spasm subsided.

Ed banged on the front door, wrapped up and waiting to take Freedom over to the gym for a work out. Freedom was in high spirits, and raring to go. 'I done made a cup of tea on the stove, Ed, and it brought the kettle to the boil as fast as ever! You get me the tickets I asked for, Ed? I got to see they get their seats.'

Ed threw up his arms and said he'd given all the tickets out, they all had them, and he had taken one over to Hammer personally. 'You got more to worry about than ruddy tickets, mate, come on, I want you running in half an hour.'

As he put his coat on, Freedom noticed that Ed had trailed some mud in on his shoes so he fetched a cloth to wipe the lino.

'Now what you doin', Freedom?'

He could hardly believe it, there was his contender worrying about dirty lino.

'Ed? Ed, is that you? Will you come up for a minute?'

Freedom pushed Ed up the stairs and wiped the floor – he didn't want Evie getting down on her knees to do it. As Ed thudded up the stairs Freedom asked him if Evie's ticket was all right.

Exasperated, Ed leaned over the banister. 'Evie's ticket's all right, she'll be at the ringside, now will you stop maunderin' on an' get yer gear together. Gawd almighty, I don't know what's come over you.'

He tapped on the bedroom door and popped his head around, about to tell Evie she was married to a charlady, when she signalled to him to shut the door.

'The baby's coming, Ed, will you get Freda? But don't tell Freedom, I don't want him worrying.'

This was all they needed! Ed went dizzy, dear God, what a time for the baby to choose, the day of the fight! Panic-stricken, trying hard to look calm, he backed out of the room.

'I'll have to go back to the house, I've forgotten the liniment.' Freedom laughed and said he would start walking,

Ed could catch up with him. So much for all Ed's hurrying,

he was the one delaying them now. He was about to go up and say goodbye to Evelyne when Ed stopped him, pushed him down the stairs saying she was sleeping, he should let her rest. They tiptoed out, and Freedom closed the door quietly behind them as Ed sprinted down the street to his brother's house. The kids were in the middle of breakfast when he burst in, yelling for Freda. She hurried in with her hair still in curlers, already preparing herself for the big night.

'It's coming, you'd better get over there fast, it's coming.'

The children started to ask what was coming, but Freda understood immediatcly. 'What, now? But it's not due, not yet . . . oh my God, what a time to come!'

Still the kids asked who was coming, but no one answered. Freda rushed to get dressed.

Another contraction had Evelyne wailing with pain, wishing Freda would come. She was sweating, the hair on the nape of her neck damp, and the ache in her back agony. She felt the baby moving inside her.

Freda hurried along the street, carrying two big pots for boiling water. Evie opened the door to her, 'Will you get Mrs Harris? I want Mrs Harris here.'

Freda ordered Evie back into bed, then she fetched the pans and put them on the gas stove before rushing out to get Mrs Harris, leaving Evelyne writhing on the bed in agony.

Mrs Harris asked Evelyne how often her pains were coming, and Freda replied that it was immaterial how often – they were coming, that meant the baby was imminent. Although childless herself, Freda was suddenly an authority on childbirth. But Mrs

479

Harris, having had seven, knew exactly what it was all about, and she shouted upstairs to Evelyne, "Ave yer waters broke yet, love?'

Freda replied that they had two pans full, and they were just putting some more on. 'I know what to do, I read all about it for Evie. I got the water boilink,' she said proudly.

With a sigh, Mrs Harris shut the door, went to the bedroom and felt Evelyne's brow. Then she checked the sheets and shook her head. 'Yer water's not even broke yet, love, you're a long way off, when was yer last bellyache?'

Feeling better, Evelyne sat up and realized that she'd not had any contractions for quite a while.

'When they start joinin' into one, yer baby's on its way down the chute, so 'ow about a nice cup o'tea?'

On his morning run Freedom conserved his strength, running easily, relaxed, not taxing himself. Then he and Ed went to the café for a huge breakfast of steak and eggs. Freedom would not eat again until after the fight.

While Freedom was out of earshot, Ed sent one of the boys over to Freedom's to find out how Evelyne was and report back. He watched Freedom working out, holding back all the time, never pushing, and later gave him a rub down in the small massage room at the back of the gym, using his own concoction of olive oil mixed with a small amount of horse liniment and a spoonful of surgical spirit. He began on Freedom's calves and worked upwards to his back and shoulders.

'If I don't knock him out, Ed, I'll gas him!'

Ed thumped him on the back and told him to shut up and relax, he was to rest and prepare himself.

*

At four o'clock Freedom was sleeping in the back room, wrapped in blankets, while Ed paced the street outside the gym. This was the third trip the lad had made and still the baby had not arrived. It looked more as if Ed was the expectant father, he was so worried.

'It's not come yet, they was all drinking tea an' playin' rummy.'

Ed told him he could go to the house once more, and after that Freda could call them at the Albert Hall from the telephone in the local pub. The mere mention of the Albert Hall hit Ed like a brick on the back of his head. It was getting near the time, they would be leaving for the match in less than an hour.

'He's still fast asleep like a baby 'imself, Ed, you'd think he couldn't go out like that on the day of the fight.'

Evelyne had been in labour for most of the day, and the women were beginning to get anxious. It wasn't her they were worried about, she was strong and was taking the pains well. They were worried about not getting to the fight themselves. Ed's brother was beside himself, sitting drumming his fingers on the kitchen table and coming in every few minutes for news.

'Can you not push it out? She carries on like this an' you'll be too late ter get ter the fight.'

As cool as a cucumber, Mrs Harris replied, 'It'll come when it's ready and not before . . . now, Freda, you go an' get yerself dolled up. I'll sit wiv her.'

Freda came to the back door, wearing her hat and carrying her coat. One look told her nothing had happened yet. It was six o'clock, and they had to leave in half an hour, the fight was to start at half-past seven.

'They won't get into the ring prompt, like, but if we ain't there someone might get our seats, and then there's the build-up, that's all part of it, we'll miss that.'

Evelyne, the centre of everyone's problems, looked around her at the concerned faces. It was almost laughable, there they all were in their best clothes, hanging on her every utterance. Mrs Harris had tied a strip of sheeting around the mahogany bedpost for Evelyne to pull against when the pains came, but the pains hadn't been coming for the last hour.

'Go on, don't miss the fight for me, I'll be all right, and Mrs Harris'll stay with me, go on.'

Mrs Harris shooed everyone out, then went back to check on Evelyne. The rubber sheet was in place, the hot water ready, and there was a clean blanket for the baby. 'You all right, love? Just breathe easy, nice an' deep, won't be long now.'

Hammer paraded at the café wearing the proprietor's jacket, and a shirt, tie and a good pair of trousers given to him by the Salvation Army. 'I'm ringside, mun, did I tell you, look, see, ringside seat, and I'm not payin' a farthing.'

He had been displaying his ticket for days. He parted with it reluctantly at the box office, and proudly announced to everyone that he had once been knocked out by the contender.

He made his way to his seat, clutching his programme and making a great show of reading it, although he couldn't read a word. Inside the programme was a photograph of Freedom, and he pointed to it, turning to anyone close at hand. 'I'd put me money on this lad, he took me out once, bout in Cardiff.'

*

The clamour of the crowd in the pit seats and the glitter of the society people filling the boxes made the huge hall seem to vibrate. A match was in progress in the ring, but no one was paying much attention, and many seats were still empty, most of the people not bothering to claim their seats until the main event. A murmur went up as the news spread that Prince Edward's party had arrived at the entrance to the hall. The tiered boxes were almost full and still the stragglers made their way to their seats. The first match ended in a spattering of applause, and a brass band began to play a lively march. The audience clapped their hands along with the music.

The noise drifted down to the dressing-rooms, where Ed had barred everyone but Sir Charles and the two corner men. Freedom sat on a table, hands out, as Ed carefully wound his bandages. Despite eighteen years' experience of bandaging boxers' hands Ed was meticulous, constantly asking if it was all right. Freedom looked at him, 'You don't need me to tell you, just get on with it.'

The atmosphere was tense, electric. In the main dressing room Micky Morgan's hands were being bandaged. His trainer stood behind him, massaging his shoulders, soothing him, talking quietly. 'Big crowd, not a seat to be had, His Royal's arrived, there's touts outside selling tickets at five times the price, gonna be a night, Micky, your night, it's your night, Micky.'

Freedom's hands were ready, and they waited for the referee to come and check them over. He sat with his eyes closed, swinging his legs. Ed wished he knew what made Freedom tick, but he never had been able to fathom him out. He might be sitting waiting for his dinner, he seemed so relaxed.

Freda, her brother-in-law and his wife edged their way along the row to their seats. They waved to a few faces they knew, and sat down. Evelyne's empty seat was now more obvious in the crowded hall. Freda had tried to get round the back but hadn't been allowed in, they'd done all they could. The phones were all engaged. The operator had said she herself couldn't put any calls through, as there were so many people waiting.

A group of men in evening dress came walking along the passage from the dressing-rooms. The hall grew quiet as all eyes watched the ring. The band struck up a fanfare. Now they could see, way up by the entrance, the tight group of trainers and corner men, and behind them the hooded figure of Micky Morgan.

'This is it, gels, here they come.'

The corner men flanked Freedom as he progressed down the hall and up into the ring. The crowd went mad, cheering and yelling, but Freedom kept his head low, his gloved fists touching each other. Behind him came Ed, sweating, his face bright pink.

'There's Ed, there . . . see?'

The group entered the ring exactly opposite them, exactly opposite the empty seat, but for the moment it went unnoticed. The fanfare blasted again and the cheers grew even louder, nearly lifting the roof off as Micky entered. He wore a dark red velvet cape with the word 'Champion' written across the back.

He bent to climb through the ropes, then stood with his fists above his head, and the crowd went wild.

Carrying a microphone on a long, thick lead, a white-haired man in tails and top hat stepped into the ring. He walked to the centre.

'My lords, ladies and gentlemen, please rise for the King!'

The band played and everyone in the hall sang in unison, 'God Save the King'. Prince Edward and his party were all standing in the royal box, and he too sang the National Anthem. He gave a small wave and then he, like everyone else in the hall, took his seat.

In the ring stood Freedom, head bowed, and Micky stared straight ahead. As the audience settled in their seats again, the boxers went to their corners. The master of ceremonies called out their weights and announced twenty, two-minute rounds. The referee, Ron Hutchinson, was introduced and bowed in the centre of the ring. He had once been a middleweight champion boxer, and was now about to retire from the police force. He had iron-grey hair and a stern-looking, craggy face.

On a podium overlooking the ring were two men with a film camera, recording the match. Ron Hutchinson went first to the champion's corner and asked if everything was ready, then crossed the ring to Freedom's corner. He actually had to ask twice, as Freedom was more intent on looking across at Freda than on what was happening in the ring.

'Her seat's empty, Ed. Where's Evie, she's not here?'

Hutchinson spoke a few words to the corner men, then made a slow circuit of the ring instructing all those close to the canvas to keep their hands away from the ring itself.

'Ed, she's not in her seat, Evie's not here.'

Ed gritted his teeth and swore at Freedom, this was not the time to start worrying about Evie.

Back in the centre of the ring, Hutchinson signalled for both boxers to come forward. Freedom was staring, concerned and preoccupied, at the empty seat. Hutchinson hooked an arm around each boxer's shoulders, and above the roar of the crowd he could be heard clearly, his voice harsh. 'I want a good clean fight, no butting, no holding. You break on my word, understand? No low punches, let's keep this professional. An' above all, obey my voice. I don't want to have to say things twice, an' I don't want to disqualify either of you for dirty fighting . . . All right, then back to your corners and may the best man win.'

As the boxers' gum shields were fitted the crowd went quiet, knowing the bell would clang at any moment. Ed whispered in Freedom's right ear as he rubbed his shoulders, repeating it over and over, desperate to get through to him. 'Evie's all right, she's fit an' she's strong, and she wants you to win, understand me, are you listenin' ter me? Evie had to stay 'ome, the baby's coming sooner than expected.'

Beneath Ed's kneading fingers Freedom's shoulders froze. 'Why didn't Freda stay with her for God's sake, mun? Is she on her own?'

Out of the corner of his eye, Ed could see the bell being lifted, the stop-watch being shown to the referee. Any moment now they were going to begin, and here was his man worrying himself sick over his wife.

'Evie said if Freda didn't come to the fight she'd never forgive 'er. She's got Mrs Harris, a doctor an' a midwife an' a nurse, so she's being taken care of . . . Now, think of the fight, son, concentrate, Freedom, get in there and go fer it.'

The bell rang, the corner men whipped the stools out and jumped down from the ring.

Micky was out of his corner like a bullet, his hands up, moving towards Freedom, and Freedom took two punches before the pain brought him round. Micky's eyes were like steel, staring into Freedom's face, and his gum protector made him look as if he was leering.

Mrs Harris knew it was time, the pains were ripping through Evelyne, and she was heaving for breath. 'Grab hold of the sheet, love, pull down, come on, grab it an' pull.'

Evelyne held on grimly to the twisted sheet knotted round the bedpost. With every contraction she held on and yelled her head off. Just by feeling her belly Mrs Harris knew the baby was big, so she heaved Evelyne on to her side, knowing her spine would take too much strain if she lay on her back.

''E's a big'un, an' 'e's on 'is way, so grip hard and press down, press him out of you every time that pain comes, press down and hang on to the sheet . . .'

Mrs Smith brought up hot water, standing by and giving way to Mrs Harris' experience. The big woman was so calm, soothing Evelyne and rubbing her back, talking quietly to her and going through each spasm herself.

''Ere we go, love, 'ere comes another one . . . and push him, that's my girl, push.'

Freedom slumped into the corner, and Ed dipped his sponge and squeezed it over Freedom's face. One of the lads dipped the gumshield in the water to clean it, and the other held it ready and gave Freedom water. He gulped and spat into the bucket.

'Is there any way we can get word if she's all right, Ed?'

The lad watched as Ed lathered Vaseline over Freedom's eyebrows and cheeks.

'We got someone standing by in the pub, anyfink 'appens they'll call us, don't worry.'

All Freedom's concentration was on Evelyne, and he was sick with worry. On the other hand, Ed was sick that Freedom wasn't fighting, he was letting punch after punch penetrate his defence. Already there were deep red marks on his chest, Micky's glove prints were all over him.

'You're buggerin' around out there, hear me? If Evie knew what you was doin' she'd get into this ring herself. Your gel's a fighter, for God's sake, you gotta win for 'er.'

The bell rang again, and Micky was up and out of his corner. His trainer was satisfied, so far Micky was ahead on every round, and he began to think that Micky would take the gyppo out in five rounds as he had bragged. All through the break his trainer said, over and over, 'You've got him on the run, and he's got no punch, he's not landed one home. Take him, Micky, go on, take him.'

Round four, and Micky certainly looked as if he was beating the contender. He began to get cocky, hissing through his gumshield, 'Whassamatter, gyppo, scared, scared? Fight, come on, whassamatter, hit me, hit me.'

So cocksure was Micky that at one point he turned to the crowd so they could see him smile. The sounds of cheering were getting mixed now with booing, so Micky decided to go for it, and moved in. Bam, bam . . . he edged Freedom on to the ropes. Freedom ducked, sidestepped, ducked, sidestepped, then threw two punches so wild that Micky got in one hell of a crack. His right hook landed on Freedom's jaw.

The crowd gasped, Freedom was off balance . . . he staggered slightly then recovered. Micky was sure the punch would have knocked him down, and was surprised when the big lad came straight back at him. The bell rang, and it was yet another round to Micky. Ed had screamed himself hoarse from the corner, Freedom wasn't using his brains, he was dancing, to Ed's knowledge he hadn't thrown one decent punch, one that had landed. 'He's wiping the canvas with you, an' you're lettin' 'im do it, come on, come on, get your temper up, fight him!'

Ed eased the elastic on Freedom's trunks as the corner men sponged and towelled him. Freedom spat water and sniffed, and again Ed lathered the Vaseline on. Freedom's face was marked on the right side.

In the other corner the trainer barked into Micky's face that this was it – this was the round. Micky heaved for breath and said it was like doing the Charleston out there, but he was still heaving. The gyppo might be on the run but he was still tiring Micky. 'I'll take him this round.'

Clang! They were up again, Ed's screams going unheard beneath the roar of the crowd. Ed was screaming, '*Body! Body!*' as Micky was keeping his hands high, head down. He held Freedom and they both lurched over to the ropes. Micky still held on, leaning his whole weight on Freedom until the referee split them apart. Micky was no longer hissing insults, he was moving in for the kill, and he looked as if he would pull it off until Freedom caught him with a good left jab, straight on to his old cut. Micky swore and went after Freedom, hurting now, his eye smarting. He was also worried, he'd felt that jab – not that it could have cut him down, but it could be dangerous if the old wound were to open up.

When the bell clanged, round five was evens, leaving Micky a clear four rounds ahead.

'He's like an ox, I've been hitting him hard and he just takes it, I dunno where he's coming from.'

Micky's eyes were checked and greased, his trainer giving him instructions all the time, telling him to go for the head, Freedom was open 'upstairs'. The bell rang for round six, and one of the lads ran to the dressing room to get fresh water.

Mrs Harris soaked strips of cloth in hot water and laid them over Evelyne. The heat soothed her. Mrs Harris herself had never been this long in labour . . . Evelyne lay on her side, hands slightly above her head, gripping the rope. A sudden, terrible pain shot through her, as though she was being torn in two, and she screamed through clenched teeth, screamed that she'd had enough, she didn't want him, she couldn't take any more. The relief was so sudden it stunned her, and she gasped, her mouth open wide.

'Here 'e is, love, here 'e is, come on you little bugger, and about time, too.'

She was right, he *was* big, and she had to help him in the first few moments, but out he came, and she held him upside-down by his heels, one sharp slap and the next moment Evelyne's howl was joined by a lusty yell from her son.

'Here 'e is, come on, Evie love, let go of the rope, 'e's 'ere.'

Evelyne loosened her grip and eased herself over. Mrs Harris held the baby out to her and she saw the thick thatch of black hair. His lungs were working overtime, and as Evelyne held him to her, his fists punched the air.

'He's a boxer like 'is dad, eh? Will you look at 'im, Evie, I'd say he was a ten-pounder, more . . . My God he's strong.'

Round seven, and Micky slumped in his corner. As they eased out his gumshield he gasped, 'By Christ, when he gets a punch home it hurts, how's the eye?'

Micky was confident, he knew he was well ahead on points, but the corner men had their work cut out for them because his eye was opening up. They painted it, daubed him with Vaseline, and his eyes smarted and filled with tears. He gulped at the water and spat it out.

Freedom was panting and Ed was sponging him down, drenching him with the cold water. 'That was the first time you connected, the first, and you 'urt 'im.' Is eye's openin' up, keep on that eye, an' watch 'is right. He's got a nasty sneaky double punch, left-left-right, and then in he comes, watch out for it.'

Suddenly Freedom jerked his head away from Ed's greasy fingers and stared up at him with such an expression that Ed stepped back, 'I got a son, I got a son, Ed, my boy's born.'

Ed's jaw dropped, and one of the lads had to ram the gumshield in Freedom's mouth as the bell was raised. Freedom was up before it rang and prancing into the ring. The lads had to haul the amazed Ed out of the ring. He wasn't sure what to think, the look on Freedom's face had completely unnerved him. He checked his watch and almost gave himself whiplash as a huge cheer broke from the crowd.

Freedom was punching now, for the first time he was show-ing his colours, and Micky was taken off-balance. He took a punch to his left side that winded him, and he rocked. The crowd roared, but Micky paced back and gave himself a push off the ropes. For once he was on the run, the crowd knew it, and so did Micky. Freedom was jabbing, tough, hard, tight jabs, and they were hammering down on Micky's eye. He felt it splitting, and the blood began to drip down his face; he knew he would have to keep on the move for this round. This was Freedom's first clear round, and the crowd began to sense that the fight had only just begun. They were on their feet, throwing caps in the air, and when the bell rang it was hard to hear. The sound of it was sweet relief to Micky, and his men worked double time trying to close the cut. His eye was puffing up, and his vision on the left was blurred.

Freda's hat was over one ear, she had eaten her handkerchief, and shouted so much she'd lost her voice. Hammer jumped up from his seat and swung his fist as Freedom began to perk up. The poor elderly man sitting directly in front of him felt his false teeth shoot out as Hammer's fist connected with the back of his head. The pair scrabbled beneath the seat, Hammer shouting his apologies.

'Just get me teeth, twenty-five shillings' worth there, mate.'

But the teeth were forgotten as the bell clanged for round nine.

Ed was mopping his brow with the sponge, his shirt drenched, his bright red braces sticking to him.

'Come on lad, this is it, go for it. *Go for it!*'

Micky was tough and there was no way he was going to go down easily. He knew he was still ahead on points, and he took a breather, keeping on the move, letting Freedom do all the chasing.

'Fight, mun, go on, stop doing the dance, mun, *fight!*'

Having worked so hard in the earlier rounds, Micky was warned three times by the ref for holding. Round nine went to Freedom, and the ref went over to Micky's corner in the break. His men grouped tightly around him, swearing that everything was all right, and the ref had to pry their pressing hands from Micky's cut. Satisfied that the blood had been stemmed, he gave the signal for the fight to continue.

'It's yours, Freedom, keep on his eye, it's split like an orange, hear me, get his eye.'

Round ten, and Freedom was on his feet before the bell rang. The crowd was going crazy, and fights were breaking out as the people behind tried to make those in the ringside seats sit down so their view would not be blocked.

Freedom swigged the water and tried to get his breath as Ed flapped with the towel. 'I'm hitting him with all I've got, Ed, and he's still on his feet.'

Ed massaged him and kept up a steady flow of instructions. He knew Freedom was exhausted, Micky was holding on to him at every opportunity. Freedom's face was red, but there was no broken skin, and not even a hint of puffiness around the eyes.

'You got the Prince standin' up shouting for yer in that last round, take him this round, lad, you know you can.'

Freedom smiled and said that if he won this round his son would be called Edward. Again Ed felt a chill through his sweating body, and he shuddered. Freedom talked as if he knew something Ed didn't, but the bell clanged and he had to hurry down from the ring.

Micky got a second wind, God knows from where, and lambasted Freedom. Micky's nose was bleeding and his eye was swollen so he couldn't see . . . He was flaying the air, coming back for a right hook when the jab caught him, right on the jaw, clean-cut, like steel.

Micky crashed to the canvas, tried to get up, but his legs wouldn't hold him. He clung to the ropes, trying to haul himself up, but again his legs gave way.

'*Eight . . . nine . . . ten!*'

Freedom Stubbs was the British Heavyweight Boxing Champion.

Chapter 21

The local people took their new neighbours to their hearts, and Freedom became their hero. On the night he and Ed went to the Sporting Club dinner to collect the championship belt and the purse, everyone was at the door. The kids asked for his autograph, they wanted it five or six times to sell copies at school. With Edward in her arms, Evelyne waved them off like the rest. Freedom was dressed up, with a white silk scarf wrapped around his neck. The Christmas lights were twinkling and the few houses that could afford them already had trees in their windows.

When they arrived at the Sporting Club, the porters stopped them as they were about to hand their coats to the cloakroom attendant, and slowly checked their names in a register. Ed patted Freedom's shoulder, 'He's the champion, mate, what's the hold-up?'

Several evening-suited gents passing through the lobby looked curiously at them while they waited. The porter eventually gestured for Ed to go through, then he bent down beneath his desk and drew out a brown paper package which he handed to Freedom. 'I'm sorry, sir, this is for you, I can't let you go in.'

Ed, of course, puffed and huffed, said there must be some mistake, but the parcel contained the championship belt. In a temper Ed told Freedom to wait, there had to have been some mistake.

The dining room was already crowded with sporting gentlemen, drinking. Sir Charles was sitting at the top table with Lord Lonsdale himself, who had embarked on one of his long, rambling tales. The guests listened attentively as His Lordship regaled them with the story of when he had met Rasputin in Russia. Most of them had heard it many times, but the story had grown to outrageous proportions. When Sir Charles saw Ed he gestured with his arms, his cigar clamped between his teeth, and excused himself. Rising from the table he stared coldly as Ed approached him.

'I'm sorry to intrude, sir, but there must have been some mistake, they won't allow Freedom into the club.'

Sir Charles was totally unruffled and told Ed that in his opinion – and in the opinion of most of the other gentlemen present – Freedom had not acted in a sporting manner. He had insulted the Prince by not appearing at the Café Royal on the night of the championship. Ed could not believe his ears – he stared, speechless, and when Sir Charles offered him a chair he refused it and turned to walk out. Sir Charles tapped him on the shoulder, 'I think it would be a good idea if you were to commence training at The Grange during Christmas. I've arranged suitable accommodation.'

Tight-lipped and burning with anger, Ed murmured that he would relay the message to Freedom. He knew it was no message, it was an order, and he held his back very straight as he walked out through the tables full of so-called gentlemen.

He found Freedom standing outside in the snow, his prize belt stuffed in his pocket. Ed didn't know how to tell him, but he didn't have to. Freedom took one look at his face and began to walk along the pavement, 'I don't want anyone to know about this, Ed, keep it between us. It's Christmas, the markets are open, we'll go and get a few things, make it a celebration to remember.'

Near tears, Ed grinned at him, and fell into step beside his champion. He knew Freedom would not forget this treatment; he had that strange look on his face, the mask had dropped into place. Even though Ed tried to tell him it didn't matter, he knew that the insult had been taken to heart.

The market was full of last-minute Christmas shoppers and the yell of the thronging traders flogging their wares. Birds were strung up outside the butchers' shops, chilled by the snow. A man selling Christmas decorations recognized Freedom and cries of 'Champion!' went round the market. Freedom was a celebrity, and the warmth of their voices and good wishes lifted his gloom.

He stopped at a pet stall and examined the pigeons, bought one in a proper cage, then grinned at Ed, 'Get someone to take this over to that little lad from the lodgin's, tell him Father Christmas sent it.'

Freedom walked down the street followed by a costermonger's barrow piled so high with parcels the donkey could scarcely pull it. Up on top of the cart was a cradle and there were so many toys that Freedom kept stopping and handing them out to children running alongside. He had bought a table and chairs, lamps, and so much food he could have fed the whole street.

Evelyne stood at the bedroom window and stared at the strange-looking carnival as it came to a halt before the house. Freedom called up to her to look, and he stood grinning from ear to ear, his arms open wide. Ed, well-oiled and with whisky bottles sticking out of his pockets, reeled around with the lamp-lighter, singing at the top of his voice.

Evelyne watched from the stairs as the furniture was hauled in. It seemed there were people everywhere, yelling instructions on where to put everything, and the baby started screaming. It gave Evelyne a splitting headache. Freedom carried the cradle upstairs – it was made of carved wood with angels on each side. Evelyne had longed for the cradle from Swan and Edgar, with its modern mattress and frilled drapes. This was so old-fash-ioned.

'Put him in, gel, come along, let's have him.'

He stuffed a pillow into the cradle, took the baby from her arms and laid him in it. Edward howled, clenched his fists and punched at the sides. This made Freedom roar with laughter, and he dug in his pockets. He pulled out his championship belt and tossed it aside as if it were no more than a piece of wrap-ping paper. Then he took out a small leather case, beaming as he handed it to Evelyne.

The necklace was delicate, gold with pearl drops, and there were matching pearl drop earrings. 'Put it on, gel, let us see you. Want you to feel like a real lady, and this is just to start with, wait 'til you see what else I got for you.'

Picking up the bawling baby, Evelyne followed Freedom

downstairs. Rolls of carpet were stacked in the hallway, chairs and cupboards had been dumped everywhere. Her spotless kitchen was a mess of straw and china, crates and boxes, but there was not one thing she had imagined for furnishing her home. Freedom strolled around like a magician, opening boxes and displaying his purchases. Then he sat in a big velvet chair and lit a cigar.

'Where did you get all the money for this? It must have cost a bit.'

She eased her way among the boxes while he puffed on his cigar, still beaming. She could smell that he had been drinking, and she went around looking at price tags. When she reached the mountain of food, she got a terrible sinking feeling. 'Did you get the fight money, then?'

With a wide, sweeping gesture to the room he said he had, and here it all was. Evelyne had to support herself on the edge of the new table that was too big for the kitchen. Freedom had blown the lot – everything apart from odd notes he had stuffed into his various pockets. He had to vacate the chair as Evelyne looked as if she was about to faint.

All her careful saving and scrimping, and in one night he had spent nearly two hundred pounds. More than the remains of her legacy – more than all the months of saving. She was shaking with anger and frustration, and it was then she vowed to herself that he would never know about her savings. His reckless spending shocked her to the core – that he had not discussed the money with her infuriated her and she wanted to scream the place down.

'I did it all for you, gel, for Christmas.'

She couldn't be angry with him, he looked so unhappy, his

dark eyes like her baby son's. She went to him and kissed him, lied and said everything was perfect.

Later, lying next to him in their huge bed with the canopy he had chosen in a colour that clashed with the paint, she stared at the ceiling, sleepless. All she could think of was what she could have done with two hundred pounds, and she wept.

Evelyne had learned her lesson. Money meant nothing to Freedom, nor possessions. If he had a shilling in his pocket, he would spend it or hand it out to whoever asked for it. He was a soft touch, a spendthrift, and the whole street knew it. Evelyne was quite relieved to depart for The Grange as, with no money coming in, she would have had to dip into her savings. At least in the country they would be fed and Freedom would be paid for his training sessions there ... so her savings could remain intact. She made up her mind to tell Ed that any money must be given to her, and she would dole it out to Freedom.

Freda was glad to be back in her cottage at The Grange, and in no time at all she had the kettle sizzling and a pot of stewed rabbit on the stove by the fire. Ed had his feet up, his worn slippers on.

There had been a lot of changes since they were last there, a whole new stable complex had been erected and on the other side of the yard beyond the barn were kennels for the hunting hounds. The dogs could be heard baying and howling.

'Ask me 'e's tryin' ter be like 'is Lordship 'imself, there's been some money thrown about here, you see the new gardens and the shrubberies ... Course, it's not a patch on Lonsdale's place, but that's what Sir Charles is after.'

Freda dusted and swept, stirred the stew and told Ed to pop over to see if Freedom and Evelyne had everything they needed. Grumbling, he put on his heavy coat and went out, crossing the yard to the stables. Freedom, Evelyne and the baby had been installed in the new stable complex along with the stable hands and gamekeepers. Ed looked around the two rooms, sparsely furnished with just the bare essentials, and he could tell that Evelyne was upset. Freedom had gone out to the woods and from the small window Ed could see his figure like a small dot on the white fields, running flat out.

'Well, there's one of us glad to be back here. There he goes, like a hare, isn't he?'

Evelyne snapped that she could use him indoors as she had to make up a bed for the baby, and Freedom had not lifted a finger since they arrived. He'd already had a row with the head stableboy because he had not been allowed to ride one of Sir Charles' hunters.

Ed made soothing noises while he watched four gardeners hauling a massive Christmas tree that was to stand in front of the drawing-room windows of The Grange. Sir Charles had not arrived home yet, and from the number of lighted windows in the house Ed knew all hell would be let loose as Miss Balfour organized the servants in their preparations for Christmas.

Evelyne handed the baby to him, and he cooed and chucked him under the chin. Ed looked up to see Evie, neat and tidy as ever, putting on her coat. 'Yer not goin' out at this hour, Evie. You'll catch yer death.'

'I'm just going over to the kitchens to see everybody, say hello.'

The cook, the footmen, the housemaids whooped when Evelyne entered the kitchen.

'Well, let's have a look at you, well I never, so you're married, well, well, and he's back as the British Champion, well, well.'

They opened a bottle of cooking sherry to celebrate.

'So you're back, well don't expect no special treatment from me, Miss Jones,' Miss Balfour snapped, 'And I'll thank you not to keep everyone chatting in my kitchen when there's work to be done.'

'Will you not toast my good health, and my baby's, Miss Balfour?'

Begrudgingly, Miss Balfour sipped a sherry then spoke with thin, pursed lips, 'Here's good health to you, is it a boy you have? Well, that's very nice, now if you will excuse me . . . ' She left, ordering all of them to return to work. The housemaids sighed and looked at Evelyne as though she were a heroine, and she was delighted at being the centre of attention. She had two more sherries before she left with her cheeks flushed and rosy.

In the cold starlit December night with the thick carpet of snow, The Grange looked magical. Evelyne breathed in the clear air, maybe it was good that they'd all come here, away from the dirty London traffic.

'You look as pretty as a picture, I've been watching you.'

Freedom slipped his arm around her and she cuddled close. 'Happy, *manushi*?'

She looked up into his smiling, handsome face. 'I am, an' you're a *rinkeney* man all right, Freedom Stubbs.'

He roared with laughter at her use of the Romany word for 'handsome', and together they walked towards Ed and Freda's cottage. They peered like children into the kitchen and then giggled. Ed had their son on his lap and Freda was standing by giving him instructions on how to change a nappy.

'I don't think 'e needs one, love, 'e's just done it all over me best pants.'

The following morning there was bright sunshine and Ed talked the stableboys into allowing Freedom to ride. 'Yer know, lads, if 'e wasn't a champion boxer 'e could 'ave been a jockey, will you look at 'im with that animal, bloody marvel, my God 'e's a wonderful fella.' Ed glowed with pride and beamed at Mr Plath as he strode through the stableyard.

'Ah, Meadows, all the servants are to gather in the main hall for Christmas gift time, will you instruct your party to be in the hall on the dot of eight?'

'Now, Freda, there's no need to get all uppity, all they want is us all gathered, like. Sir Charles hands out 'is gifts to the servants, see, then we 'ave a shindig, a dance in the ballroom.'

Freda pursed her lips, furious to be classed with the servants.

Evelyne laughed, 'Oh, come on, Freda, it'll be fun, and you can get all dressed up. Of course we're not servants, well, not any more.'

Ed refrained from pointing out to the two women that while they might not be staff, both he and Freedom were employed by Sir Charles. He was too relieved that Evelyne had accepted it and even seemed bent on enjoying her stay at The Grange.

Promptly at eight, not a minute before or after, the staff lined up in the hall. It was impressive to watch, there were kitchen maids, scullery maids, ladies' maids, butlers, footmen, valets, cooks, gardeners, stableboys, dog handlers, gunsmiths. Miss Balfour stood at one end of the hall with the general house manager, the estate manager and two secretaries. In a small group slightly apart from the general household staff stood Ed, Freda, Freedom and Evelyne.

Everyone wore their Sunday best or their immaculate uniforms, and the line of more than forty people stood as though on parade. It dawned on Evelyne just how wealthy this household was, how could some have so much and others so little?

Miss Balfour shook hands with Freedom and congratulated him as if she was telling him he'd brought in muck from the stables, 'Sir Charles will be coming down any moment, he will wish you all a happy Christmas, and then you are to file past him one at a time ...'

At that moment he appeared on the staircase, and there was a sudden hush. In clipped tones he wished every one of them a happy Christmas and a prosperous New Year, thanked them for all their good work, and hoped they would remain one big family.

Sir Charles handed Ed and Freda their gifts, polite, charming, and then turned to Freedom, who received the same cordial handshake with his neatly wrapped gift. Evelyne felt humiliated, as if she was lined up in the poorhouse, and accepted her token gift with lowered eyes, not once looking into the monocle.

'Do hope you will enjoy the dance, thank you for your service.'

'Well, *manushi*, I suppose we should go an' perform for our lord and master.'

Evelyne muttered that Sir Charles might be *his* lord, but he certainly wasn't hers.

In the ballroom a small orchestra played a waltz. Evelyne removed the heavy coat she was wearing over the satin gown Sir Charles had bought her in Cardiff, and got many admiring glances. Freda had shortened it, sewn on a few sequins to freshen it up, and arranged Evelyne's hair the way Freedom liked it in a long braid down her back with ribbon threaded through, green to match her eyes. This was the only time of year that Sir Charles actually mixed with his servants so it was quite an occasion.

Tables were laid for Sir Charles and his guests at one end of the ballroom, with pristine white cloths, silver and crystal, but they were empty as yet. A long buffet at one side was covered with cloths, and tables were ranged round the other walls for the staff. Evelyne and Freedom sat with Freda and Ed and a group of the stableboys. Ed and Freedom were sitting with their heads close together, discussing boxing as usual, and Freda gave Evelyne a little shake of her head and a shrug.

The orchestra played on, and the evening began to liven up as they all did the hokey-cokey around the room. Everyone was in high spirits, singing at the tops of their voices, 'You put your right foot in, right foot out, in, out, in out, and shake it all about . . . and that's what it's all about . . . Oh, the hokey-cokey, oh, the hokey-cokey . . . Knees bend, arms stretch, *Ra! Ra! Ra!*'

During the dance Sir Charles and his guests arrived and crossed the floor to their reserved tables. When the music ended Freda flopped down in her chair, fanning herself with her hankie, 'Oh, I'm too old, too old for this kind of dance, darlink, I must have a long drink.'

Evelyne laughed. She was flushed, too, and she headed for the table where drinks were being served. She turned to look over at Sir Charles' table, and her heart stopped.

David Collins was standing staring across the ballroom. He was lighting a cigarette in a thin gold holder. She had forgotten how handsome he was, how refined. She was jostled along the queue for drinks, and asked for two lemonades. As she waited for them she saw Sir Charles gesturing to Freedom to join his table. Evelyne stood on tiptoe to watch as Freedom bent to kiss Lady Primrose's hand, then pulled out a chair to sit down. His back was to Evelyne and David was on his right. Freedom must have said something amusing, as the whole group laughed.

Taking a roundabout route Evelyne went back to her table, avoiding Sir Charles' group. She sat down as Freda brought two plates piled so high with food it was spilling on to the cloth. 'My darlink, eat, eat, I have never seen so much glorious food.'

Evelyne smiled, but her eyes strayed constantly to David as she sipped her drink. Lady Primrose stood up and pulled at Freedom's arm, dragging him on to the dance floor. Evelyne felt sorry for him, she didn't know if he could dance and wondered if she should go to his rescue, but that would mean meeting David.

Holding hands, Freedom and Lady Primrose walked over to the orchestra, and he tapped the conductor on the shoulder and spoke to him. Still waving his baton, the conductor nodded his head. Evelyne wondered what had been said and was fascinated to see how relaxed Freedom was, he seemed almost on intimate terms with Her Ladyship.

The orchestra struck up a tango, and on to the floor glided Freedom, his hand out for Lady Primrose to follow. She giggled

and looked towards her table, then stood as Freedom demonstrated a step. A few couples stood and watched as he waited for
the beat to begin the dance. He closed his eyes and stood quite
still, head up, then slowly began to dance, clicking his heels in
Romany style, putting the whole room to shame as he glided
elegantly across the floor. After a short solo he swept Lady
Primrose into his arms and she laughed, throwing her head
back. Then, the show over, he began to teach her the steps.

Evelyne was so astounded by Freedom's dancing that she was
unaware of David's approach until he was standing directly
behind her chair. 'I don't know if I can tango, but I'm willing
to try, would you do me the honour, Evie?'

Startled, she turned to him, then told him curtly that she
didn't tango. He promptly sat down, insisting he could wait for
a waltz. He glanced at his wife on the dance door, then back to
Evelyne. 'You've not changed, not at all.'

She saw his eyes flick over her dress and she bit her lip, she
knew he recognized it. He *had* changed. She could see the fine
lines around his eyes and mouth, and a slight gauntness. His blue
eyes were paler than ever. He still smelt of flowers, and was as
fresh and clean as his starched white collar. The orchestra began
a slow waltz and he held his hand out to her, smiling softly.
They stood up and began to dance, Evelyne overpowered by
David's closeness, his blond hair brushing her face as he held her
close, manoeuvring her around the polished floor.

Freda looked at them with a worried frown and swivelled in
her chair to see where Freedom was. Through the throng of
dancers she could see him leaning on the back of Lady
Primrose's chair. She watched him take the delicate hand and
began to read her palm and suddenly realized he was a bit of a

ladykiller, and by the look of Primrose she was responding to his charm.

Lady Primrose could smell Freedom's musky perfume – sweet, strange and exciting, as he was – and his touch on her hand was gentle as he traced the lines on her palm. Giggling, she told Sir Charles she didn't believe in all this mumbo-jumbo, and pulled her hand away, taken aback by the expression on her cousin's face. He was staring at Freedom, his eyes furious. When he caught Primrose looking at him, he turned away and blushed the scarlet of his monocle ribbon. It was obvious that the gypsy boxer had powers which were not necessarily confined to fortune-telling.

David didn't know what to say to Evelyne, he kept trying to think of some way to start a conversation, but then stopped before speaking. He could feel her in his arms, so close and yet so many miles away. There was so much he wanted to tell her – needed to tell her – but they danced on and he remained silent. Going back through the years in her mind, Evelyne turned around and came back again. Here she was, dancing close, very close, to the man she had believed she loved, so close that if she turned her cheek she could kiss his lips, and yet nothing could be further from her thoughts. He had shrunk, she was sure of it. She was taller than him now, and that cloyingly sweet perfume was surely not the one he used to wear. His eyes were so pale they seemed filled with tears, and as if he were reading her thoughts he suddenly stopped dancing and sighed, 'I need some air, which way should I go?'

*

Evelyne sat on the balcony steps, feeling cold, and David took off his jacket and wrapped it around her shoulders.

'Do you remember everything now, David? How I used to come and visit you? Do you remember?'

His head twitched, his mouth working. He reached for her hand and threaded his fingers through hers, pulled her closer, 'You are the most beautiful creature, that is what I remember most – and you have filled out to perfection, to perfection.'

His free hand traced her bosom, heavy with milk for her son. 'Please don't do that.'

He smiled, kissed her neck softly, and she gasped.

'You liked it once, you like it now: excite me, excite me, set me on fire.'

She looked around; he was holding her hand tightly, hurting her fingers, pulling her close, and he forced her head back, kissed her just as he had kissed her that night in his car, forcing her mouth open with his tongue.

'No, don't, please, please . . . Let go of me, please.'

He held her even tighter. 'What's the matter with you, you liked it once, I remember. I remember that, you liked it, you loved me.'

Evelyne looked at him, amazed. How could she have been so foolish? 'That was a long time ago, David, I think we should go back into the ballroom.'

He grasped her shoulders, tight. She didn't push him away, but neither did she encourage him. She whispered, 'What do you want from me?'

'You know, what's the matter? Not good enough for you now? Tell me, what have you set your sights on for tonight? My God, for a little slut you certainly have done well for yourself,

I have to hand it to you, wormed your way in here very nicely ...'

Evelyne drew back her right hand and slapped David's face so hard that he reeled.

'I am a married woman, with a son, how dare you make such insinuations, how dare you?'

He laughed, a humourless, barking sound, a sarcastic smile on his face. 'You are still for sale, Evie, and to the highest bidder, your type always are and you know it.'

He was about to move away when she gripped his arm. 'I've *never* been for sale, David, just poor. Is that a crime? You sicken me, for if there's anyone selling themselves it's been you ... I loved you with a passion, a childish, naive passion that you abused, just like you abused your own friend, Freddy ... How's your wife? You knew he loved her, and yet you had to have her. Why, David? Because she's titled? Because she had money? It's *you* who's been for sale, David, *you* ... you're nothing. Go back to your high society, your rich friends who laugh at you behind your back!'

He backed away from her, wringing his hands. 'You know, you're terribly wrong about one thing, my wife, I love her, I always have, but she makes a fool of me ... a public fool.' His voice was childish, pitiful, and to Evelyne's dismay he started to cry. His shoulders shook, and he stuttered through his sobs, 'We're stony broke, all my fault. I lost my way, Evie, so long ago, lost my way, you see ...'

He lifted his hands to Evelyne, a helpless gesture, then she saw the familiar habit he had of sweeping his hair back. His signet ring glinted. 'Damned wretched business, can't seem to hold on to anything ... my father short-changed me, ya know, should have given me a sharp rap across the knuckles, but instead he encouraged me, because ...'

He turned away from her, rested his hands on the balcony rail. ' ... Because he wanted me to succeed. Laughable, really – get in with the right set, Mother always used to say – and here I am, cap in hand, begging from Charles because we're penniless.'

'Why don't you work? You were studying to be a lawyer.'

His voice was soft, full of pain. 'I can't remember things, hardly the best credentials for the Law Society ... ' His eyes pleaded with her, 'I don't remember, Evie, I pretend I do, but so help me God, I don't, because ... because I'm scared. Sometimes when I have been with you I recall pictures – Mrs Darwin, my father ...'

She knew he was lying, she sensed it, lying like a guilty child. She moved closer, almost touching him, 'David, you *can* remember. What happened? What happened to you?'

He stared at her as if cornered, trapped. He shook his head and she inched even closer. 'What did you do that made you so afraid? Tell me? You can tell me.'

She held him in her arms, felt him trembling, smoothed his hair, patted the silky hair she had longed to touch all those years before. 'You know, David, in a way you don't belong here either, you are as much out of your depth as I am. Whatever you did surely can't make you hide for the rest of your life?'

His face altered, the child disappeared. His slender grasp of reality began to slip. His mouth turned down and his face twisted in fury at her assumption that he was no better than she, as if they were of the same class. When he spoke he had reverted to his usual, over-precise speech pattern. 'I'm not hiding,

duckie, what do you take me for? I know what you bloody are.'
He made a grab for her breast, ripping her gown.

Neither of them had heard Freedom's soft footstep, or were
aware that he had been standing close by. With one swift move
he gripped David's jacket and tossed him aside.

'It was that bitch's fault, don't hurt me, please don't hurt me.'

For one moment Evelyne would have liked Freedom to
throw David over the balcony, then she turned, looking for help
to stop him.

Ed had been searching for Freedom since Freda had told him
David and Evelyne had disappeared together. As he came
around the side of the house, he saw Freedom dragging David
along the balcony and ran as fast as his fat legs would carry him.

'Freedom ... *Freedom*! Evelyne, stop him, for God's sake. *Stop
him!*' He launched himself on to Freedom's back and tried to
pull him off the hysterical David. Freda and one of the stable
lads ran out on to the balcony and the boy tried to help Ed control Freedom, but they were no match for him, and it was not
until two more lads came running that they were able to haul
Freedom away from the weeping man.

David flailed his arms in the air, his voice a high-pitched
shriek. 'How dare you, how dare you manhandle me, *I'll have
you horsewhipped, you animal!*'

It was a grotesque, embarrassing scene, and Ed tried his
damnedest to calm everyone down. 'Show's over – it was nothing, just a bit of fun. Everybody go back inside, it's over ... You
all right, sir?'

He put his arm around David's shoulders, trying to smooth
his jacket, but David pushed him away.

'Don't touch me, get away from me, all of you, you rabble, *you common bastards!*'

Shaking he arranged his handkerchief in his breast pocket and smoothed his hair with the palm of his hand. 'I shall be a gentleman and forget this ever happened.'

He gave Evelyne a strange, disdainful look, turned, his head held high, and made a sad, foolish exit, still trying desperately to hold on to his dignity.

One of the stableboys looked at Ed, 'You need us, Mr Meadows?'

All eyes turned to Freedom and Evelyne. As if they were animals in a circus ring, they waited for the roar. The pair of them faced each other and the atmosphere was so highly-charged that no one dared speak. Then Evelyne walked away. She heard scuffling behind her and raised voices, but she hurried on, almost afraid to turn back and see what was happening.

Ed was trying to persuade Freedom not to ride, not at this hour of the night – it was dark and the horse could fall. The head stableboy stuttered that Sir Charles would hit the roof, and received the snarling reply, 'Bugger Sir Charles.' No one had the nerve to try to stop Freedom as he galloped off without a saddle, leaving Ed thinking, 'There's Freedom's best suit ruined,' and silently praying his champion wouldn't fall. He was doubly concerned because Freedom had taken Sir Charles' prize stallion. God help them all if anything happened to the horse, never mind Freedom.

If Ed had watched for another second he would have had a heart attack as Freedom and the horse jumped a five-foot wall and headed for the forest.

*

The baby was sleeping, his thumb stuck in his mouth, and his warmth and peacefulness touched Evelyne. She lifted him gently out of the bizarre cradle they had brought from London and sat by the fire, rocking him in her arms. She closed her eyes, vowing to herself that he would never have to endure the humiliation she had known. She hated being poor, being subjected to ridicule. Growing steadily inside her were seeds of loathing for the so-called aristocracy.

If only Freedom would educate himself, beat them at their own game, learn to use them as they were using him. She was even more determined that she would teach him to read and write, *make* him learn. She shuddered when David came into her thoughts. He'd called her a slut. Well, she would not waste her time on him any more, he was out of her life. She looked down into her son's face, touched his head.

'You see, Edward, David's trouble is that he got given all the opportunities a man could have, but he frittered them away. You know why? Because he won't face up to being who he is. It doesn't matter, Edward, where you come from. Titles? Half of them don't have two pennies to rub together ... You're going to be somebody, be successful, be powerful and not need anyone. You have to want it and fight for it – not with your fists, like your dad, that isn't good enough. No, you're going to have to fight for an education and I'll be right alongside you. I'll kill for you to have it, so help me God I will – you'll never be any man's servant.'

Hours later Freedom came home to find the curtain drawn across the window and Evelyne already in bed. She heard him kicking off his shoes and knew he would be scattering his clothes all over the room. She got up and pulled her cardigan round her shoulders, checked that the baby was asleep, and opened the curtain quietly so Freedom did not hear her.

He was sitting by the fire, staring into the coals, his bare chest gleaming in the firelight. Evelyne curled up at his feet, squeezing her body between his knees. He didn't speak and made no effort to hold her, but at the same time he did not push her away. For a few minutes they sat in silence, and then Evelyne began to tell him, softly, everything there was to know about her and David – how much she had loved him in a childish, romantic fantasy way, and how he had humiliated and hurt her . . . how even tonight he had made her feel like a second-class citizen, because of his background, his money. When Freedom had found them David was crying like a baby because he couldn't have what he wanted, she had refused his advances. Not that he really wanted her – he never had – she was poor, something that could be bought, and thrown away when he had tired of her.

'We may be poor, but our son will have everything, and you know what everything is, Freedom? Us, you and me beside him always. He's going to have what we never had, proper schooling, education. We can have that for free, but love costs a lot more, you know that?'

He didn't really understand what she was saying, but the fact that she had told him everything about David without his asking made him reach to hold her. He was so proud of her, the fight in her. He built up the fire until it blazed and brought the mattress from their bed, put it in front of the fire. Then he took off her long cotton nightdress and laid her down on the mattress, naked in the firelight. She loved him all the more. David's weakness emphasized his strength, and she lifted her arms to him. He knelt beside her and kissed her, and they made love as they had in the enchanted summer months out in the fields. Since the child's birth he had been gentle and caring, but now he loved her roughly, taking her time and time again until they lay sweating, their bodies close, so close, their love deepening, bonding them together.

'Don't ever betray me, *manushi*, not ever. It would set a demon loose inside me, and I wouldn't care what happened to me, do ye understand what I am saying, gel?'

Evelyne did, she too had felt that surge of jealousy when she had seen him dancing with Lady Primrose, and it was a new emotion. She felt she would kill if anyone ever tried to take him from her. She turned in his arms and stroked his long hair, placed her hand to his heart, 'And we must always talk, Freedom, be honest with each other, never pretend or lie.'

He lay back and thought about what she had said, about them being there for their son. It had never occurred to Freedom that he had never had a father, but then the elders of the camp acted in that role. Evelyne told him the difference, what it had been like with her Da, the closeness, the strong bond between them. She sat up and prodded the fire, snuggled down in his arms and asked him what he knew of the man who had fathered him. He could remember little, just that his mother had been very young, she was a *Tachey Romany chal*, of high blood, her father a prince and her mother the *dukkerin* of the camp. Her family had visited a village in the Rhondda and she had seen with her 'eye' the boy, tall as a tree, she said, and so *rinkeney* he had made her heart stop. She had known immediately that she wanted him. Freedom reverted to his Romany tongue as he described his mother, and the tall, wild man the village had nicknamed 'The Lion'.

During the telling Freedom sat up, slightly apart from Evelyne, and she suddenly clutched him, hugged him, desperately. She clamped her hand over his mouth to prevent him going any further, 'No, no, don't say any more. Dear God, don't say any more.'

He had to prise her away from him, she was that strong. He lifted her bodily, and from her face he knew something was terribly wrong, it frightened him.

'Oh, God, Freedom, what have we done?'

She wanted to scream, she covered her own mouth with her hands, afraid she would cry out and wake the child ... she bit her hand so hard he could see her teeth sinking into the flesh, her whole body trembling. When he pulled her hand away her sobs shook her, and she tried to push him away from her.

Holding him at arm's length she finished his story for him; her voice harsh, each word bringing her pain. She told him of his mother, how she had stood at the pithead and waited for her 'lion', how the man had laughed and she had cursed him. It was Freedom's turn to freeze, how did she know – how was she able to tell something he had never told another soul?

'Oh, don't you see, don't you understand ...'

Whatever reaction she anticipated, something akin to her own horror, never came. Instead Freedom lay back and started to laugh, a deep, throaty laugh. She stood up, stark naked, and kicked him, shouting. How could he laugh, how *could* he? He caught her foot and brought her crashing down beside him. She tried to fight him off, but he was so strong it was useless. He rolled on top of her, grasping her wrists above her head, holding them tightly, 'Tell me everything about him. Let me know everything. Am I like him? Tell me, tell me.'

'Are you not afraid – that we have the same blood?'

He released her arms, caught her to him so tightly she could hardly breathe, 'Blood to blood, Evie, we are closer, closer, do you not see that?'

His acceptance of the fact that they were even closer, bonded by blood, was at first frightening to Evelyne. Then his mood caught her, and to her amazement she found herself laughing with him.

'No one must know, Evie, they'd not understand.' He had no need to tell her that, she knew it, and even her fears for the child of such close blood were dispersed. They picked up their sleeping baby son and held him between them, and he opened his eyes and stared up into the two adoring faces.

'Our son is near pure *Tatchey*. He'll have the powers, Evie, and look at his strong body.'

To their delight, Edward gurgled and laughed up at them, and at that moment there was magic in the night, the red flames from the fire flickering on their naked bodies.

Later, while Evelyne slept, Freedom took out a hunting knife and made a cut on his forefinger. He squeezed it until the blood formed a heavy drop, then crept to the baby's cradle. He let the blood drip slowly on to the sleeping child's forehead. The stain spread, forming a cross, and Freedom's voice was a whisper as he buried the curse his mother, the clan's *dukkerin*, had laid on Hugh Jones.

BOOK FOUR

Chapter 22

Life moved at a fast pace after that Christmas at The Grange. Freedom was still the undefeated British Heavyweight Champion, and British Empire Heavyweight Champion . . . he fought in Liverpool, Birmingham, Porthcawl, Edinburgh, and Manchester. Evelyne did not accompany him on these travels, but stayed at home in the East End. Freedom was a celebrity, money was not short, and Evelyne kept a close watch on the purse strings. Their house was well furnished, and some items had been passed on to Ed and Miss Freda, even Ed's brother and sister-in-law Billy and Mary Meadows. The neighbours watched with avid interest as number twelve even had carpet laid all down the stairs. There was no jealousy, they were proud, and welcomed the distinction of having a champion living in their street.

Edward was almost two years old, a handsome child, tall for his age. He was very strong, and never still, so that it took all Evelyne's time to keep an eye on him. He had a terrible temper, and threw such tantrums that their neighbours would say, 'There goes that little bugger again.' But they would smile, as everyone knew how the little lad adored his father. As soon as he saw his dad coming down the road, Edward would run out, arms outstretched and shouting with delight. Proud as Punch, Freedom would swing the lad upon to his shoulders.

Sir Charles kept a close but discreet watch over Freedom's successful career. He was determined that 'The Gypsy' would try for the world championship. It was only a matter of time until a fight was arranged in America.

They were getting close when the news came that the great Dempsey, the man known as the 'Manassa Mauler', had lost his title to Gene Tunney. Sir Charles was delighted. Tunney now reigned as World Heavyweight Champion, and his reputation was on a par with Dempsey's at his peak. The new champion appeared invincible and was taking on all challengers.

Ed Meadows arrived at number twelve, his face alight with excitement. 'Where is he ... *Freedom*!'

The moment Freedom looked up from the table he was building and saw Ed, he knew something big was on. 'Is it America, Ed?'

Unable to speak, Ed clasped Freedom in his arms, and the two men danced around the kitchen.

Evelyne returned from shopping to find Freedom out and a dozen bottles of champagne on the table. When she took a quick look at the price, she had to sit down. She had to watch his spending all the time. When he went abroad, he always brought back lavish gifts and wouldn't hear a word from Evelyne about the cost. Neither did he discuss the fights themselves with her, avoiding her questions with shrugs and laughs. His face was still unmarked so Evelyne never really knew what it took for him to get into the ring or, for that matter, what punishment he had taken.

Freedom came back with his arms full of turkeys and fruit.

'Lord, man, what on earth have you been doing? I've already been to the shops.'

Putting everything down he caught her in his arms. 'Ah, well, this is a farewell dinner, for the street, then you'd best pack your things. We leave for America and this time you'll be with me, it'll be the trip of a lifetime.'

Evelyne hugged him. 'Is it the world championship?'

He swung her round, lifted her in the air. 'Aye, it is, and I'm going to take it from Tunney.'

'Well, you'd best put me down. Any more of this tossing me in the air and you'll hurt the baby.'

Freedom lowered her gently and cupped her face in his hands. 'We'll take Edward with us, and I'll take great care of thee . . . ' Suddenly what she had just said dawned on him . . . he yelped with joy. 'Are you sure?'

Evelyne laughed and said she was more than sure, she was three months gone.

The excitement of packing and arranging for their departure made the weeks pass so fast Evelyne could hardly believe it when they arrived at Southampton Docks with Freda, Ed and a pile of luggage. There was their ship, their home for the next three weeks, looming so large it took everyone's breath away. RMS *Aquitania* was majestic, dwarfing the small group at the dockside. It wasn't a ship, it was a floating city.

A steward led them to their cabins, pointing out various features along the way. The restaurant, with an oak-beamed ceiling and leaded windowpanes, seated seven hundred people. A long gallery led to what could only be described as a high street, with shops that included ladies' and gentlemen's outfitters displaying all the latest fashions in lighted window displays. There was a huge main lounge at the end of the gallery – a glorious, stunning room, as large as a concert hall, thickly carpeted and with a magnificent domed ceiling. All the chairs and settees were upholstered in the finest fabrics. There was even a post and telegraph office, unlike any the bemused group had ever seen. Adjoining it was the library, a big, square room with hundreds of books, and there was no charge for borrowing them.

Freedom had trailed around without much interest, but when he saw the gym his eyes lit up. There were parallel bars, horizontal bars, electric – yes, electric – cycling machines, and even a riding machine that rocked backwards and forwards as if you were on a real-life bucking bronco. There were also rowing machines, fencing masks and foils, boxing gloves and punchbags. Ed and Freedom stood and stared, awestruck.

The steward turned back the bedcovers and opened some of the many wardrobes and dressing-table drawers to show Evelyne. He also told them about the full-time nursery with a nanny to take care of the child at night if the passengers had not brought servants with them. He hovered for a while, then proffered a crumpled piece of paper and asked if Freedom would autograph it for him. He was so pleased, he didn't even wait for a tip.

Freedom lay back on the bed and smiled, 'Happy ...? You like it?'

From the massive funnels of the *Aquitania* the hooter

sounded, the ship was about to sail. They went upon deck and waved to no one, just the disappearing docks.

That evening, the dining room was a hubbub of noise as they took their seats, and Freda's mouth watered as she peered short sightedly at the menu. It was written in French and confused everyone else, but Freda prattled away, *'Turbot poché en sauce fenouil, épinards, pommes frites* ... oh, là là, *rouget grillé beurre diable* ... darlinks, it's just divine ... *noisettes d'agneau Maltaise, ris de veau, côtelettes de volaille aux haricots panachés* ... It is fantastic, darlinks.'

Ed settled for the lamb cutlets, Freedom a steak, and Evelyne, after a long explanation from Freda, chose fish. They started with caviare served on crisp toast with finely chopped onions and egg yolks. They were mightily impressed, and Freda's exuberance and obvious delight in everything was very infectious.

Freedom insisted Ed accompany him to the menswear shop where the pair of them were measured for black tie and tails. Ed did try to prevent the expenditure, but Freedom laughed, asked him how much Dempsey had received for a single fight. 'You know, lad, it were more than five hundred, and bugger me yer right. You're gonna take that title, so mister, bring that shirt with the nice pearl buttons and one for the champ here.' The more Ed talked of how much Dempsey had made, the more expansive he became, smoking a Havana cigar, flicking the ash on the assistant's head as he pinned up six inches on his new trousers.

They had all been invited to dine with Sir Charles, and Freedom and Ed cut quite a dash in their penguin suits as they strolled along the deck to Sir Charles' opulent stateroom. Seeing everyone shaking hands with his champion, admiring him as they sauntered along, rubbed off on Ed. He was having the time of his life.

Freda and Evelyne followed their men, arm-in-arm, laughing at the contrast between Ed with his waddle and Freedom with his cocksure stride, towering above Ed.

Sir Charles was equally enthusiastic, warmly welcoming them to his suite. 'Here he is, everyone, this is my champion.'

As usual, Sir Charles had invited a roomful of elegant guests. The dinner was very formal with four waiters hovering to look after them. Freda insisted on speaking French to the waiter who served her, which nonplussed him as he came from Bradford.

Freedom was being very attentive to the attractive blonde woman on his right. Evelyne excused herself, saying she must see to her child, and the gentlemen rose, half-heartedly. Freedom seemed unaware she had left.

On her way back to her cabin Evelyne stood for a while watching the dark sea. Strains of music drifted up from the ballroom and slowly she began to waltz along the deck – one, two three, one, two three ... she stopped to sit in a deckchair. Suddenly the lovely, balmy night was too good to miss.

She heard Freedom's voice and rushed to the rail to look over and call to him to come and sit with her. She could see him, with the blonde on his arm, strolling along the deck below her with some of the other dinner guests, towards the ballroom. Evelyne had never felt so jealous in her life. She wanted to go down and dance with him, but she couldn't. She was fat and ugly while the blonde was so beautiful and slim, not pregnant, not so tall.

She watched Freedom's progress, inching down the steps to get a better view. There was applause, and there he was, bowing and smiling. A waltz was being played and Evelyne could see him with his arms wrapped around a small woman. She was beginning to feel furious when the couple did a twirl and she could see that he was hugging Freda in his arms. They danced towards the open deck, and Evelyne stepped into the concealing shadows on the stairs. Their voices could be heard clearly below her.

'Oh, oh, I am so dizzy, darlink.'

'Aye, well, I had to have some excuse, Freda, that woman was hanging on my arm so I couldn't leave.' They leant on the rails, looking out at the sea. 'Does the sea not remind you of my Evie's eyes, Freda? Freda . . .?'

She had slithered down and was sitting on the deck, the champagne and wine too much for her. Freedom picked her up and put her over his shoulder. Evelyne put her hand over her mouth to stop herself giggling as the blonde lady appeared. 'Oh, Mr Stubbs, don't tell me you are leaving so early.'

'I'm afraid so, ma'am, my partner here has overexerted herself.'

'Oh, do come back, we are all going for a midnight swim.'

'Aye, well, it's a nice night for it.'

The blonde was joined by another woman and they watched Freedom stride off. 'Oh, he's so manly, Gertrude, and so strong, he really is.'

'Now, now, Mabel, he's a married man.'

The blonde giggled, twirled around. 'That's never stood in my way before, darling.'

Evelyne had heard enough. She bent over the railings and spoke to the astonished Mabel. 'It had better stand in your way when it comes to *my* husband, miss, or you'll get more than you bargain for.'

Mabel nearly fainted as Evelyne marched off down the deck.

When the time came to dock in New York, they stood together on the deck to watch as the huge ship eased its way into the harbour. Towering above them was the Statue of Liberty, and Freedom lifted Edward up on to his shoulders to see her. The ship's hooters screamed and streamers and confetti scattered from the top decks while a band played; everyone's excitement was at fever pitch. They had arrived in New York. Freedom slipped one arm around Evelyne, his face serious and his voice quiet.

'When we go home, Evie, I'll be world champion. I promise you.'

The wonders of America did not stop at the docks. A limousine was waiting to drive them to an airport, from which they were to fly by mail plane to Chicago. Even the garrulous Ed was stunned into silence. Sir Charles bent down to talk to them through the window of their car. 'I'll be flying with you, see you there ... Ed, you've got the itinerary, the hotel booking and the tickets. Have to get a move on, the plane leaves in two hours.'

As they sped through the streets, they stared at the towering buildings in awe, but their sightseeing tour was short and they soon arrived at the small airstrip.

They had accepted the fact that they would be flying as if Sir Charles had said they were going by train, but when they saw the fragile aircraft on the landing strip it really sank in.

'Oh, Ed, darlink, I think I am going to faint, I do. Are we really going up in that little thing?'

Freedom hugged Evelyne to him, 'You scared, *manushi*?'

She shook her head, trying to keep hold of Edward who jumped up and down in uncontrollable excitement.

Sir Charles was elated to be flying, and as soon as they climbed on board he sat next to the pilot. Freedom held Evelyne's hand, his son on his knee, and they looked out of the single, small window. They were a little frightened, and were not reassured by Sir Charles bellowing instructions to the pilot. The faithful old Dewhurst sat with his rosary in his hands, eyes closed and praying, all through the journey.

As they prepared to land, Sir Charles strapped himself into his seat, a glint in his monocled eye. 'This is thrilling, absolutely thrilling.'

The plane bounced on to the landing strip, and they all turned a little green, but were thankful to be down and in one piece. Dewhurst's knees gave way and he had to be helped down the stairs, constantly apologizing to Sir Charles.

'Freda, I think I'm dying, oh God, I'm dying, my heart it's my heart.' Freda gave Ed a big hug and told him he could open his eyes; they had landed, everyone else had already left the plane.

'Gawd 'elp us, Freda, I feel as if I was still up in the clouds.'

Sir Charles had been driven into Chicago, leaving the others to wait for Ed and Freda with the longest car any of them had ever seen. It was silver, and the chauffeur wore a blue uniform. They climbed into the Cadillac limousine, and Ed flipped through the itinerary and instructed the driver to take them to the Lexington Hotel. Sir Charles, he noticed, had 'The State' suite in The Sherman Hotel. He still as always kept his distance, and Ed knew it would be costing more than all their rooms put together ... but as His Lordship was footing the bill for the trip, it was his prerogative.

The journey into the city was almost as exciting as their voyage, once they had overcome their nervousness at travelling on the wrong side of the road. Immensely long cars whizzed by, drawing gasps of admiration. The chauffeur gazed at them through his mirror and when he spoke his accent made Freda giggle.

'You folks from England? Well, jeez, ain't that great, I never been outta Chicago myself; that's the state capitol we just passed.'

He asked them endless questions, while stealing glances at the 'black guy' with the long hair. He thought they looked pretty scruffy, but they must have dough to be staying at the Lexington.

When they arrived at the hotel, Ed realized he had no American dollars so he had to go to the hotel bank to change his English pound notes. Two porters carried their luggage into the hotel and the limousine drove off.

They pushed through the revolving doors after the porters, Freedom lagging behind as he struggled with several pieces of hand luggage, including his kitbag. The mahogany reception desk was immensely long and at least eight uniformed bellhops rushed around in the lobby, which was crowded with guests and potted palms.

The manager looked through the glass-fronted door of his office and pursed his lips. He could see the new guests checking in and didn't like what he saw. He made a quick call to the receptionist to tell the assistant manager to come to see him immediately.

Ed couldn't understand what was causing the delay. They were all very tired, and Edward had started to cry. Ed showed the receptionist the telegram confirming their rooms. He was beginning to get impatient as no one seemed in the slightest hurry to register them and hand over their keys.

The assistant manager, flushing beetroot red, hurried from the office, lifted the mahogany flap and slipped in behind the desk. 'I'm afraid there has been some mistake. We only have one room booked, Mr Meadows. I cannot apologize enough, but I'm afraid the rest of your party will have to find accommodation elsewhere.'

Ed was confused as he crossed the lobby to Freedom and Evelyne to tell them of the situation. The little boy was really beginning to scream now, so Ed suggested that Freedom and Evelyne take his room; he and Freda could find another hotel. He returned to the reception desk and asked for the key for his companions to take the room.

'I'm sorry, sir, that is not possible, I am afraid we cannot accept your companions, that is the hotel rule.'

What on earth was the man talking about? Ed's protests grew louder and then, to his astonishment, the assistant manager pushed a card across the counter. Neatly printed on it were the words, 'No coloureds or blacks to be allowed as guests of the Lexington Hotel.'

Ed stared at him, confused, then picked up the card and reread it. 'What's this got to do wiv us, for Gawd's sake?' Ed jabbed the manager with his finger and pushed the card forward, his voice rising as he demanded to know what was going on. He had personally sent a telegram to the hotel for two double rooms, one with a cot for a child, and now he was told there was only one room vacant and his friends couldn't move into it. Sensing an impending explosion, the manager drew Ed quietly aside and repeated the hotel policy that no coloureds and no couples of mixed race were allowed in the hotel.

'Mixed *what*? What you talkin' about, mate, we ain't black, what you think we are?'

The manager turned and flicked a look at Freedom, then turned back to Ed. Suddenly it was painfully clear, they thought Freedom was black. Indeed, because of the sunshine on the crossing, his dark skin was even darker. Ed spluttered and could hardly speak with rage. 'He's contender for the World Heavyweight boxing title, for Chrissake, he's not black, he's a gypsy! That don't make him black.'

Freedom handed his son to Evelyne and began to cross the lobby towards Ed. The next moment the place was in an uproar, as Ed knocked out the manager with one punch. Ten minutes later they were on the pavement outside the hotel, Freda in tears and Ed so angry he could hardly speak.

'We ain't stayin' in this dump, any of us, come on, we'll get a taxi an' see where there's a better hotel.'

Freedom pulled the still furious Ed aside and asked what on earth had happened in there. Ed wouldn't say, but he hailed a taxi and ushered them all into it.

They stopped at two more hotels and Ed went in alone to investigate, but at each one he was told, 'No coloureds'. While he was in the second one the cabbie, who had been staring at Freedom, realized what was going on. 'Most of da hotels around dis part of the city don't take blacks. I know a place where maybe they'll let you in, you want me to try there for ya?' He hooked his arm along the back of the seat and looked enquiringly at the party in the back. They stared at him, not understanding what he was saying. He pointed to Freedom and repeated that there was a rule in the best hotels, no coloureds and no Indians. Some even refused Mexicans. A defeated Ed returned to the cab, and now that they all understood the predicament he blushed in shame for them. 'I'm sorry, lad, I told 'em all you wasn't black, but they don't believe me.'

Evelyne was silent, but as they drove off she saw in the distance a huge hotel towering above the shops and apartment buildings. The Metropole Hotel, 2300 South Michigan Avenue.

'Driver, take us to that hotel, please, and, Ed, I want to go in this time.' She would hear no argument, even when the cab driver tried to dissuade her, implying that the Metropole, of all hotels, would most certainly refuse them. Freedom said nothing, he was so taken aback, but the driver went on ominously about the Metropole and that he would lay odds against their being allowed in, not just because of Freedom but for other reasons. Evelyne repeated her instruction to take them to the hotel and gripped Freedom's hand.

As they stopped, Ed made to get out, but Evelyne wouldn't let him move. She insisted on leaving them alone and, head high, she walked into the lobby.

'She'll get no joy in dere, pal, I'm tellin' ya, I know dis town an' I know dis hotel, ya tryin' the wrong place.'

All their eyes followed Evelyne as she walked from the cab through the revolving doors and into the ornate lobby.

Inside it was opulent, thickly carpeted, with massive ferns and palms in every corner. There was so much brass and so many chandeliers that the whole lobby seemed to glitter.

Evelyne strode to the reception desk, along, polished counter with racks of keys and pigeonholes for letters. She had to wait for a gentleman in front of her to sign the register, a burly, fat man smoking a cigar. The clouds of smoke rose up to form a ring around his head.

A clerk, seeing Evelyne waiting, hurried forward to attend to her.

'I wish to book two double rooms, one with a child's cot, and private bathrooms, please.'

The clerk reached for the register and thumbed through the pages.

'There will be a Mr and Mrs Ed Meadows, and Mr and Mrs Freedom Stubbs with the child. Mr Stubbs is here as a contender for the World Heavyweight Boxing Championship. I am his wife.'

The clerk murmured and leafed through his book, and the large man with the cigar turned to Evelyne and beamed. 'Excuse me, ma'am, but I couldn't help overhearing, there's more fighters comin' in for that title. The whole of Europe's after it so I wish you luck, and may I say your husband's a fortunate man to have such a beautiful wife.'

Evelyne smiled her thanks, but she was shaking. Aware that the clerk could hear her, she told the fat stranger that her husband was the British Heavyweight Champion. 'You may have heard of him, Freedom Stubbs, he's a Romany gypsy, a prince.'

Even to her the statement sounded childish, and the big man laughed. From his back pocket he took a roll of banknotes larger than his fist, turned back to the receptionist and began peeling some off. They were fifty-dollar bills, and he was paying for his room up front.

A doorman appeared outside and leaned on the window of the waiting cab. He told the cabbie to move on, go round the block – he could return in a few minutes but the forecourt had to be cleared. The cabbie started the engine and they did a slow crawl out of the forecourt. Coming in was a glittering Cadillac limousine, bright yellow and so highly polished that the lamps and wheels seemed to spark. The chauffeur rushed from his seat to the rear passenger door and two burly men in dark-grey suits and smart white shirts and ties hurried to the entrance. They stood like guards as the chauffeur stepped back, holding the car door open.

A square, stocky man stepped out of the limousine, wearing a pale lilac linen suit, a white fedora hat, and carrying white gloves and a silver-topped walking-stick. He didn't acknowledge the two men standing on guard, but strode past them into the hotel.

Evelyne was still waiting patiently at the desk, as the clerk took forever to flip through the register, and as the brass-framed doors swung open and the lilac clad gentleman entered, the whole lobby went quiet. The two bodyguards walked immediately ahead of him, and two more appeared from behind the potted palms, hemming the squat man between them.

'I'm sorry, ma'am, but we don't seem to have nothin' available right now ...'

Evelyne had hoped so hard it would be all right that she was bitterly disappointed. She was unaware that a porter had been sent outside to check on the occupants of the waiting cab, had taken one look at Freedom and given the thumbs down.

She had not noticed the flurry of excitement behind her, she had been so intent on the receptionist. The man wearing the flashy lilac suit was heading for the lifts, the two thickset men making a path for him. There was actually no need, as everyone stepped back quickly as soon as they saw the group. Evelyne clenched her teeth, trying hard not to cry. She knew that by now Edward would be starving and fretful, but she thanked the clerk, and her initial show of confidence ebbed fast as she hurried towards the exit.

She was so eager to leave that she bumped into one of the two bodyguards. She barely touched the man, even apologized, but the next minute she was shoved roughly aside, with such force that she fell against a pillar. This was the final straw and she turned on the man, catching him by the sleeve. 'There was no need to push me like that, it was an accident.'

She received no reply, but another shove. As she struck the pillar again, she dropped her handbag and all the contents spilled out on to the marble floor. As she scrabbled for her things, she missed seeing the boss give his protector a nasty crack on the shoulder with his walking stick. She only became aware of him when she saw, close to the handkerchief that had fallen from her bag, a pair of highly-polished, two-toned shoes. Her eyes travelled up the lilac pants to look into the dark eyes beneath the fedora hat.

'You okay, ma'am? Want me to give you a hand ... here, allow me.'

As he bent down, she could smell a heavy, sweet perfume. The perfectly manicured hand picked up Edward's well-chewed dummy and held it out. Evelyne stood up. She was a head taller than the man, and his chubby face beamed up at her as he asked about her accent.

'I'm from Britain, Wales.'

The fedora was lifted off, he made her a small, courtly bow. As he replaced his hat, he asked if she was a guest of the hotel. Evelyne bit her lip, her eyes filling with tears. He was so friendly, so charming ... he took out a clean white handkerchief and handed it to her. She was deeply embarrassed, and try as she might to stop them, her eyes kept filling with tears. She wiped her face and told him the hotel was full, she could not get rooms. She was unaware that the lobby had come to a complete standstill as she talked to him.

The man swept over to the counter, and now Evelyne could see the impact he made on the porters and desk staff. Every move he made was shadowed by his attendants, and now they seemed more than cordial, bowing and scraping as if the man were royalty. She watched him talk quietly to the clerk, then he gestured for her to join him at the desk.

'They tell me your husband's gonna be a contender – I tell you what, if you make sure I get a ringside seat, I'll make sure you get the best rooms in this hotel, whaddya say, pretty lady? Is it a deal?'

Evelyne was speechless as the clerk laid two keys on the counter.

'You got a kid with you? A boy, is it? I gotta boy, see, Sonny, I call him Sonny.' A photograph was taken from his wallet and displayed with great pride, then replaced carefully so as not to crease it.

The clerk coughed nervously, and looked at his ledger. 'Well, sir, there's forty-eight and fifty-eight.'

'How's that suit ya, Mrs Stubbs? Two suites next to each other?'

Evelyne flushed and managed to say 'thank you' several times.

A nearby bellhop was poised on his toes in his eagerness to please. At a wave from the fat, manicured hand he was at Evelyne's side.

'Boy'll help you carry your bags, ma'am, don't you forget my tickets, just leave them at the desk ...'

Evelyne almost curtsied with gratitude, and followed the bell-hop out to the waiting taxi. Behind her she missed a strange, chilling scene.

The gentleman in the lilac suit leaned across the polished mahogany desk, swiftly grabbed the clerk by the lapel and pulled him halfway over the counter. 'You treat a lady with discourtesy again and you'll be found with your balls stuffed down your goddam throat, you pint-sized prick.'

The terrified clerk, released, gabbled an apology, and found himself lightly shoved against his letter-rack. 'Make sure they get first-class treatment, flowers, fruit sent up, the whole bit, okay?'

'Yes sir, Mr Capone, sir. Right away, sir.'

Capone stuffed a twenty-dollar bill in the frightened man's pocket and moved off towards the bank of lifts. His bodyguard fell into step beside him, opened the lift doors and checked it over before Capone got in. As the last grey-suited man stepped inside, the folding gate was slammed on his hand. He gasped with pain, but made no other sound.

'Check 'em out. Who's with the broad, get me the whole low down on 'em.'

As the lift glided up to his private floor, Capone adjusted his silk cravat in his reflection in the polished brass control panel. He was in a good mood. He began to sing. His voice was strong, not quite Beniamino Gigli, but no one would dare say he wasn't at least on a par.

Chapter 23

A week after Freedom's arrival in Chicago there was still no fight arranged. Ed was beginning to think Sir Charles was out of his depth. He had to admit the influx of contenders for the heavyweight title didn't make bouts all that easy to organize. Sir Charles assured Ed that he was trying.

'I have to look after Freedom's interests — not quite so cut and dried as we had anticipated. There are a lot of contenders, and Freedom's nowhere near the top bracket. Thing I don't want is that he has to plough his way through every boxer arriving in the States.'

Ed sighed. Running up hotel bills, trying to keep Freedom happy, was getting him down. Sir Charles poured Ed a brandy. 'I have a meeting with two chaps who may be able to guide us. They *made* Dempsey — Jack Kearn and Tex Rickard.'

Ed's jaw dropped, his eyes sparkled. Together, these two men had taken boxing into million-dollar gates, and promoted Dempsey into that league. Word was out that they were both millionaires. Rickard had been a cowboy, a small town marshal, a prospector and a honky-tonk proprietor, and the ballyhoo he created around the fights earned Rickard, Kearn and Dempsey the nickname of the 'Golden Triangle'. Ed rubbed his hands excitedly.

If they could get those two on their side, they would be made.

Ed bounded into the hotel room. The women were out shopping, and Freedom had been left to babysit. He snapped, unpleasantly, 'Who am I going to fight? Sir Charles arranged a bout for me yet? You tell him if I have to travel for a fight, I need time to train, to prepare. You tell him this waitin's driving me spare, mun?'

Ed pulled up a chair, took out a crumpled piece of paper and began to read out the awesome list of fighters pouring into Chicago from all over the world – Knud Hansen of Denmark, Tom Heeney from New Zealand, Paolino of Spain, Luis Angel Firpo from Argentina – not counting all the American fighters who wanted a crack at the title. That list was even longer.

Ed scratched his head. Their only hope was to get Dempsey on their side and Dempsey's men in their corner. With such backing they could bypass more than twenty contenders because Sharkey or Schmeling had already beaten them. For Freedom to work his way through the list would be madness. Ed shoved the paper under Freedom's nose. 'Look at 'em, count the names ... But 'is Lordship's gonna get some help, see the three main contenders.'

Freedom interrupted, already over-eager, ready to take all three on. 'Who are they?'

'Johnny Risco is one, then there's the European titleholder, Max Schmeling, and, last but not least, the one they say will take the title, Jack Sharkey.'

Freedom paced the room. 'Can't Sir Charles get me a bout with one of them?'

Ed shook his head, becoming impatient with Freedom's impatience. 'That's what I'm tryin' ter tell yer. All these other boxers, they want a bout, but it can't be arranged. The top three have fought most of these geezers, can't I get it through yer brain? It's like a knockout competition, any of these names wot's listed 'ere gets through all the prelims – then, *then*, they can try for the big three.'

Freedom slumped into a chair. 'So what do I do? Sit here?'

'No, son, you get down to that gym an' work out like you never done before, 'cause you gotta be ready at all times. We get a chance of a good bout we grab it wiv both 'ands, an' we pray ter God a bit of the Golden Triangle gold rubs off on us.'

Freedom blinked. Ed could almost see the wheels turning in his head. He repeated, 'Golden Triangle', then looked at Ed. It was dawning on him exactly who Rickard and Kearn were.

'Yeah, my idols. An' Sir Charles is pullin' strings ter get 'em on our side, so do as I say an' we'll get yer a fight.'

A week went by without any news, and the hotel bills were mounting. Freedom was becoming restless, he had nothing but aggravation at the gym, where they referred to him as 'the black', and he had almost got into a street brawl. A car passed him and Evelyne as they strolled arm-in-arm, and the occupants had shouted 'white trash' at her. He had chased the car in hapless fury.

He felt caged in the hotel, and Ed worried himself sick. He recognized the signs and knew that Freedom needed a bout soon. He also needed a change of scenery.

*

At long last there was progress. Sir Charles received a cable from Tex Rickard, cordially inviting them to visit him at his villa in Miami. Freda, Evelyne, and Edward, along with all their luggage and a very disgruntled, moody Freedom, left Chicago to take up residence in a small, rented villa in Miami. The villa was right on the ocean front, and Freedom began to relax a little. Sir Charles had instructed Ed to stand by, hire a car and wait. Ed was on tenterhooks, practising driving the car up and down the drive. He almost ran his future champion down as he came out of the villa swinging his towel at the motor. 'How long, Ed? How long does he want us to wait here?'

Ed pulled on the handbrake. 'That was a bloody silly thing to do. I could 'ave run yer over.'

Freedom glowered. 'You tell me how long mun? eh?'

Ed went red in the face, shouting back, 'I dunno, do I? Why don't you get on the beach, run, spend yer time gettin' fit; just fer God's sake stop asking me when-when-when-when. It'll be *when* Sir Charles says, that's all I ruddy know.'

Freedom took off down the beach and Ed hit the steering wheel, shouting at himself now. 'When you bastard, when? . . . when?'

Ed rushed into the villa bellowing for Freedom at the top of his voice. Freda was inspecting the fridge with delight, having never seen one before. 'They're on the beach, Ed . . . Ed, just look at this, it makes cubes of ice for the drinks.'

Ed was already rushing out on the beach waving his arms in the air. Evelyne and Edward were at the water's edge, laughing at the little waves. Freedom was doing press-ups.

'Freedom ... come on, we got to go an' meet 'em all now ... *Now*, come on, lad ... Here, wrap this round yer neck, don't go gettin' cold.'

Freedom took the towel and flicked it at Ed. 'That'll take some doin', mun, it's blazing hot.' He went off at a fast run towards the villa, Ed following on his stubby little legs as quickly as he could.

By the time Ed collapsed on the stairs, Freedom was already taking a shower. He could hear Freedom whistling, taking his time. Ed puffed his way up the stairs and paced up and down outside the bathroom until Freedom came out, stark naked. He was deeply tanned, the outline of his shorts showing lighter. Ed hovered at the bedroom door while Freedom dressed. It never ceased to amaze him how beautiful his lad was, like a statue, every muscle clearly defined.

'What yer doin' now? We can't keep these fellas waitin'. Gawd almighty, you do nothin' but moan about wantin' a fight, now when we got to go an' talk about it, what you doin'?'

Freedom beamed at him as he pulled on a shirt. Ed heard Freda below mixing drinks in a new-fangled machine. 'Gawd love us, git yer pants on ... *Freda*? Don't you go cookin' nothin', we're on our way out, at least, we will be when this bloody lad gets his gear on. Now, come on ...'

At long last they were on their way.

Ed parked the rented car outside the ranch-style house, and he and Freedom were led on to a shaded patio by Kearn himself. There, already seated with Sir Charles and waiting to meet them, was the second point of the Golden Triangle, Tex Rickard. He rose to his feet and they were introduced. He was wearing a cowboy hat, tooled leather boots and a large silver and turquoise buckle on his belt. He was a big, expansive man, and a man who got immediately on to familiar terms. Ed loved him. Sir Charles was looking cool and suave in a white linen suit.

The men were drinking beer and their cigar smoke drifted up into the clear, bright sky. Ed and Tex Rickard were talking nineteen to the dozen, as they had been all afternoon, of boxers, of fights. Rickard gave a blow-by-blow account of the Tunney–Dempsey fight, the bout known as the 'fight of the long count'. The new rule was that when a boxer was knocked down, his opponent had to go straight to a neutral corner. Only then could the count begin. If he didn't move, the referee would not start the count.

'Ed, ma boy, that count must have been well over sixteen, I was out of ma goddam mind! I screamed for Jack to get into the corner – he'd forgotten, see, in the heat of the moment. Jeez, I'm tellin' ya, I wanted to get in the goddam ring myself . . . so of course, Tunney got a second wind, who wouldn't after sixteen seconds?'

Ed turned to Freedom and jerked his thumb towards Rickard, telling him to pay close attention to what the man, *the man*, was saying. Freedom leaned forward and listened as the two men began to discuss the last Tunney fight, then relaxed again. He had seen the film, knew the fight punch by punch. Freedom was beside himself. There was Ed with Rickard, apparently going over every detail of every fight that had ever taken place in the USA, and on his other side Sir Charles and Kearn talking non-stop about aeroplanes.

The real reason they had all gathered at Kearn's was to discuss

a bout for Freedom, to make him a contender for the championship, but so far no one had said a word about it. In fact, they
never brought the subject up at all.

Freedom was moody, his temper fraying. With a terrible grinding of gears they stopped at the villa, and as they climbed out
of the car, Freedom began to question Ed. 'So when do I fight,
Ed, what went on? They going to help me get a bout or not?'

Ed puffed on a Cuban cigar, a gift from his new friend, Tex,
and waved his hand majestically. 'These things take time, son,
got to be worked out, an' Sir Charles is going ter have ter give
them a percentage of the gate, see, so we don't want ter rush
fings. They want ter see you work out tomorrow at a friend's
place ... Anyway, did I tell you what Tex told me about when
he was gambling in Paris, France?'

'I don't give a bugger about his gambling, I want a fight and
I want it soon, Ed.'

That night, Freedom felt Evelyne's belly, and they both
agreed it was going to be another boy. They discussed names,
and Evelyne decided she would like to call him Alexander.
Freedom muttered that it was a name for a woman, and she
threw a pillow at him. He would have let her call the baby Freda
if she'd wanted to.

The sun had tanned Evelyne's pale skin and lightened her
long red hair. He had never seen her so beautiful. The good life
suited her, and he was determined it wouldn't stop – not now,
not ever.

He slipped from the bed and lifted the blind. The night
was dark and the sea was lit by a perfect, brilliant moon. He
clenched his hands, his frustration was building to bursting

point. He couldn't sleep at night, and he spent all day waiting, always waiting.

At breakfast the following morning, Freedom had already been up for hours, running himself into exhaustion. He ate in silence, and the atmosphere grew tense. Ed was eating the most enormous platter of sausage and pancakes, and his paunch was growing as fast as Evelyne's pregnancy.

'Be patient, fings is goin' just right.'

That was it. Freedom banged his fist on the table. 'Sittin' around eatin', mun, you call that going just right? I came here to fight, so far I done nothin' . . . maybe it's not just Sir Charles out of his depth, mun, maybe you don't know what *you're* doin' . . . Get me a fight, that's all I want.'

As if on cue, a Western union boy rang their bell and handed over a telegram. Rickard had requested another meeting.

Ed and Freedom departed with the usual crashing of gears, Ed refusing to speak to Freedom until he apologized. Evelyne sighed, Freedom's moods were getting to them all, apart from Freda, who spent most of her time with her nose in the fridge eating all the goodies she had discovered on their trips into town.

'I'll take Edward down to the beach.'

'Freda, what if he loses? If he gets a bout and loses, we are all here, living in luxury – who's paying for it?'

Freda sat down at the table with her raspberry ripple ice-cream. 'Don't talk that way. Of *course* he will win, don't ever speak like that.'

But Evelyne couldn't rid herself of her foreboding. She knew

Freedom was getting dangerously impatient. Freda waved her spoon at Evelyne. 'Maybe today they'll know about a fight, and you must not let Freedom see you are worried, promise me . . . have some raspberry ripple.'

Evelyne shook her head, collected the bucket and spade and, with Edward pulling excitedly at her hand, went down to the beach.

Ed drove through the gates of the luxurious ranch-style villa. This time Freedom hardly gave a second glance, already bored by Ed's non-stop description of all the Dempsey fights. Only when a servant led them into a gymnasium did he perk up. Everything was geared to boxing – a ring built in the centre of the vast, sprung floor. The servant showed them the dressing room, gesturing to Freedom to help himself, and then bowed out, leaving him to stare at the rows of gloves, robes and boots.

'Go on, get a work out, I'll take a stroll round the stables. I got a surprise for you, you wait. Go on, get dressed.'

Freedom was hammering hell out of a punch bag when the gym doors swung open. A tall, elegant man in a pale cream linen suit, his black hair slicked back, leaned on the doorframe. A large diamond ring glittered on his little finger.

'Carry on, son, let's have a look at you. Go on, hit that bag.'

Puzzled, Freedom blinked. Ed appeared behind the man and stared in adoration, near tears. As the man moved into the centre of the room, Freedom looked at him again and realized who he was. He wore a perfectly tailored suit and shirt with a silk tie, and a handkerchief placed just so in his breast pocket, but no amount of fancy tailoring could hide his muscular body. This was none other than Dempsey himself.

Dempsey's polished shoes made no sound on the pine floor. 'How ya doin', Freedom, glad to meet you.'

The hand was like a rock ... so this was the 'Manassa Mauler', the iron man. Ed clutched Dempsey's hand, and for one awful moment it looked as if he were going to kiss it. Dempsey began to peel off his jacket, his perfect white teeth gleaming. 'Let's go to it, son, I need a work out.'

It took quite a lot of persuasion for Dempsey to get Freedom into the sauna, as Freedom had never been in one and didn't like it at all.

'Sweats out all the impurities, all the rage over here, they'll get to England in about twenty years. America's the place, this is the land, here, I love this goddam country.'

He poured pine essence on to the bed of hot coals and sat on one of the benches. His body was flabby, but still in better shape than most men of his age. He thumped his belly and roared his deep, bellowing laugh.

'This is the good life, I earned it, I earned it and now I'm living, really living ... hey, you married?'

They both wore short white towels wrapped around their hips, and Dempsey seemed very proud of his 'manhood'. He snorted when Freedom told him he was married, and said marriage was the worst contract he had ever got himself into.

'An' that toff with the enlarged eyeball, your – what?'

Freedom smiled at his reference to Sir Charles, and said that he was his so-called promoter.

'They'll have him for dinner, you stayin' ta eat? Good, I'll make us a barbecue, one you won't forget, an' we'll have something wet to go with it.'

He was referring to the prohibition order, and when they were dressed they made their way to the patio for the barbecue, passing a very well-stocked bar. Prohibition hadn't, it appeared, affected the ex-world champion.

Ed was grinning like the Cheshire cat, his tête-à-tête with Tex Rickard had obviously lasted all afternoon. Dempsey made no reference to Freedom's fights, but they had worked out hard together in the afternoon and Freedom had been aware of the close scrutiny he had been under.

Dempsey heated the coals on the open grill, and some Mexican servants brought chops, steaks and sausages, already prepared for cooking.

'You ever eaten an American hamburger, Freedom? Hey, what kind of a hell of a name is that, Freedom?'

Tex poured drinks and said that it was a name that would look good in lights, on posters, and then Freedom knew that something must have been settled.

The whisky hit the back of the throat like a fireball, and Ed whistled. Dempsey grinned and said it was the best around these parts, he had the best contacts. The men lit cigars and watched as the food went on to the open grill, while Dempsey, in his shirt sleeves and with his cigar stuck in his mouth, wielded the fork like a fencer, jabbing and inspecting the meat. A table was set on the patio, and soon they were joined by Sir Charles and Jack Kearn. They were greeted with a bellow from Dempsey, who wanted to know where the hell they had been. Kearn poured himself a generous measure of whisky and, gesturing to Sir Charles, said that he was going to make a first-class pilot.

Suddenly there was a silence, the sort of silence they say means an angel is passing over, and Freedom knew instantly that something had definitely been decided. Rickard looked at him. 'Right, son, if all goes to plan – as you know, there are the big three, Risco, Schmeling and Sharkey. Right now you can't get a bout with any one of 'em, but we want you to start ploughing your way through a few smaller bouts – get some good publicity, get your name known. Then, if all goes well ... it's Risco first, then the German, then the main contender, Sharkey. We've seen all their managers and it will be up to you to show us your worth ... We want the Sharkey fight in Miami, that way Jack don't have to travel too far.' They roared with laughter, and more drinks were served. Freedom was beside himself. If they'd asked him to fight anyone then and there he would have been up on his feet.

Freedom was never to discover exactly what the financial arrangements were, he left that to Sir Charles. They were very relaxed, the conversation centred entirely on boxing, and Freedom ate like a horse while Dempsey held the floor. He was a great raconteur and made everyone roar with laughter at the stories of his days on the 'tank town' circuits. The subject of the forthcoming bout did not arise again and Freedom had no idea when it was to take place, but he was sure Ed would tell him everything on the journey home. In the meantime he enjoyed himself for what seemed the first time in months.

The following morning, Freedom and Ed received a visit from Sir Charles. He drove up to their villa in a car almost as long as the villa itself. The three men went into the front room and closed the door.

Ed was surprised to see Sir Charles was as hung over as himself and Freedom. His face was a greenish colour and he accepted black coffee gratefully. 'Right, now then, it's not quite as easy as those fellas made it out to be. They want you accepted as a real contender, so I have drawn up the eliminator bouts. If you come through, as I am sure you will, then they'll come in with their promotion for the last three – Risco first.'

Ed was sweating. He mopped his brow. 'Who does he take on first, sir, and where?'

Sir Charles paused a moment, then coughed. 'It's the Dane, Knud Hansen.'

Ed was tense, gripping his cup and saucer to stop them rattling. 'Next, who's after the Dane?'

'Monty Munn . . . first fight takes place in Cleveland, at the St Nicholas ring.'

'Where's Cleveland, local is it?'

'No, Ed, it's in Ohio, so get packing and be prepared to leave first thing in the morning.'

Freedom was beaming from ear to ear as Ed showed Sir Charles out.

'I don't know what you're so bleedin' 'appy about, you seen the size of this ruddy Dane? He's over six feet four, a fuckin' Viking.'

Freedom laughed and stood up, raising his arms. 'So am I, so what?'

'His bleedin' Lordship didn't mention yer might 'ave ter take on the friggin' French feller. Just two fights. Well, don't fink they're easy, you're up against it, and wivout much time in between bouts if yer do win . . .'

Freedom rumpled Ed's thin, frazzled hair. 'That's what I like about you, mun, give me confidence, encouragement . . .'

Ed grinned and punched Freedom good-naturedly on the arm. 'You'll take 'em easy, lad, just don't want yer finkin' yer don't 'ave ter train.'

Freedom went into the kitchen to give Evelyne and Freda the news. Left alone, Ed's good humour dropped like a stone, and he muttered to himself, 'Christ almighty, 'e's got 'is 'ands full.'

The following morning they were packed and ready. Ed wouldn't even hear of Freda or Evelyne accompanying them. 'You'll both be there for the championship fight, but in the meantime me an' my lad's got our work cut out. We don't want you two slowin' us down.'

Evelyne was relieved. The thought of travelling all over America with little Edward, and pregnant at the same time, was daunting. Freedom was happy, confident, and couldn't wait to get started. But when they had gone the villa felt empty without them, peaceful.

Freda carried two milk shakes on to the patio. 'Banana, try it – have you ever had a banana?'

Evelyne shook her head and sipped the milky yellow drink, then smiled approval. Edward clambered on to her knee and grabbed the drink with both hands while Evelyne struggled to prevent him spilling it all over the table. At the same time she asked Freda what she thought about the forthcoming fights.

'Oh, darlink, first it's just a little one, with Knoot somebody, then a few more to get the Americans familiar with Freedom's name. You don't worry, Ed's not worried, and he knows ... look, Edward – see, this is a straw, and you suck up your drink like so ...'

She demonstrated sucking through the straw. Edward couldn't quite get the hang of it and blew instead. Freda turned to Evelyne with banana milk shake dripping down her face. She laughed, saying it was for her sunburn.

Ed and Freedom travelled to Ohio by train, while Sir Charles flew there in a private plane owned by Jack Kearn. He was even allowed to take over the controls, and began to think about acquiring one himself.

The gate for Freedom's fight with Knud Hansen was only fair, about four hundred people. Ed was confident Freedom could take the Dane with ease; the man punched wildly, and used an open-armed swing. He was enormous, weighing in eight pounds heavier than Freedom.

The crowd cheered them both, and as the gong went for round one their cheers turned to loud boos. Freedom was moving around, trying to assess his man, and had hardly thrown a single punch when he caught a wild right and was knocked clean out, to the fury of the crowd.

This was Freedom's first defeat, and he was totally demoralized and dejected, stunned at his own stupidity. However, with Ed always close by and confident that it was a fluke, they arranged a second bout fast. Although the press had been there, the fight hardly caused a ripple in the papers as they were all carrying banner headlines about a brutal killing, a blood bath that had taken place in Chicago.

The headlines ran, 'St Valentine's Day Massacre'. Only a small article, a single paragraph in the sporting section, reported the English contender, Britain's only hope for the Heavyweight Championship, had lost. 'Stubbs KO'd Round One by the Great Dane.'

Evelyne's heart stopped when the rotund figure of Freda charged down the beach, kicking up sand behind her. Evelyne jumped to her feet, panic-stricken. 'What is it? Freedom? Is he all right?'

'Ohhhh, oh, oh . . . it was on the radio, you won't believe it, but . . . they were murdered, all of them gunned down.'

Freda saw the horror in Evelyne's face and quickly gasped out the Al Capone story. Evelyne flopped back on the hot sand. 'Freda . . . oh, Freda, I thought something terrible had happened.' She sat up suddenly, stared at Freda. 'Al Capone? No, are you sure? It couldn't be right, he was so nice! He wouldn't do anything so terrible as shooting people, you must have misheard it, Al Capone?'

Freda was adamant. It had been on the radio, so it had to be true. Evelyne let a handful of sand trickle through her fingers. 'Was there anything about the fight?'

Freda shook her head, then screamed as Edward brought his spade crashing down on her head. Evelyne jumped up and grabbed him, taking the spade from his chubby fist. 'That was naughty, you apologize this instant to Auntie Freda! Edward, I mean it, say you're sorry . . . *Edward*!'

Edward pursed his lips and glowered.

'Right back to the house you go, my lad, and no more sand-castles today.'

Edward screamed and kicked at the sand in fury, his eyes black with anger. Evelyne chased him in circles on the beach until she eventually caught hold of him and dragged him back to face Freda. He wriggled free, then hurled himself into Freda's arms. He kissed her cheek, holding her face in his small hands. 'Kiss it better, kiss you better.'

Freda wrapped him in her arms, laughing. 'Oh, Eddie, you have lady-killer eyes, you have . . . It's all right, Auntie Freda forgives you, and I'm sure Mama will let you build another castle . . . Evie?'

Edward turned big, dark, innocent eyes on Evelyne and she gave a brief nod, then sat down next to Freda. They both watched him digging frantically, then he turned and gave them a wicked grin. Evelyne sighed. 'You spoil him, you know, he gets away with too much – and don't call him Eddie, I don't like it, his name's Edward.'

'Okie-dokie, whatever you say, darlink. He had such a look of Freedom, the image of his father – the eyes, oh, what eyes.'

'Well he won't take after him, that's for sure, I'll not have him fighting, he'll not be a fighter.'

Evelyne was staring, stony-faced, out to sea. She was so beautiful, her long red hair blowing in the breeze. Freda thought to herself, 'With a mother and father so handsome, the world could be little Edward's oyster.'

Ed had his hands full trying to keep Freedom's spirit up, as well as frantically trying to arrange a bout he could go on to immediately. Then they had a stroke of luck – the massive Dane was knocked out by the French contender, Pierre Charles. This left the contender Monty Munn available, so the fight was arranged.

Freedom received a call from Dempsey, who gave him a talking-to. 'Listen to me, Stubbs, I been KO'd more times than I been balled. Pick ya self up, show us what you got, ya hear me? Go, boy *go!*'

Ed also kept up a steady, encouraging patter, assuring Freedom that if he won the Monty Munn fight he would take on the number three man, none other than Johnny Risco. 'They call him Rubber-legs. The man goes down and bounces back. Well, you get Monty down an' you'll bounce that Risco fella right outta the ring.'

Freedom went ten rounds with Munn, a tough fight, then got his famous punch in. Monty went down. Freedom's confidence was restored, and Kearn and Rickard were now convinced of his potential beyond doubt. They began to play a minor part in promoting Freedom, but they were still holding back. In a private meeting with Sir Charles they told him they both felt it was too early for Freedom to take on Risco, he was not ready. They also had an eye on the gates, wanting to build Freedom's name up.

The fight with Pierre Charles went ahead. This time Freedom had to go the full twenty rounds, and he won on points. Press reports began to feature Freedom Stubbs as a powerful contender for the title. The gates were also improving – money was coming in – and although deals had been set up between Sir Charles and the Golden Triangle, there was still a lot left in the purse for Freedom. But once again his hopes of getting closer to the championship were thwarted and another bout was arranged, this time in Chicago.

As always, Sir Charles kept his accounts with meticulous care, and all Freedom's expenses were deducted. The boat fares, the hotel, the train, the plane rides, nothing was left out. Then there were Ed's wages, taxes, the rent for the Miami villa, every dollar and cent was accounted for. Sir Charles, whose constant battles with the trustees of his estate made him only too aware of his cash flow, was miserly in many ways, but he astounded everyone by handing out huge tips. He would give with one hand and take with the other. Ed put it down to eccentricity, but Dempsey laughed, he put it down to his Lordship being 'just a goddam tight-ass'.

Whatever the outcome of the finances, Ed made sure Freedom's share was looked after, and to date they were, in his own word, 'flush'. Ed was holding more than five thousand dollars for Freedom, in large bills in a money-belt round his rotund stomach. Freedom never questioned Ed about finances. In truth, he didn't care. Being knocked out had marked him, and he was back in training with a vengeance. He never wanted to experience *that* humiliation again.

Ed had forgotten their problems in Chicago. In New York Freedom was accepted as a gypsy, but in Chicago they were again refused admission to any of the best hotels. Freedom grew moodier than ever, and twice Ed had to hold him back from physically assaulting hotel clerks.

Most blacks in Chicago resided in the area known as the South Side, ranging from 30th to 39th Street, and there was a famous hotel, the Du Sable, on the corner of 39th and Cottage Grove Avenue. The Du was one of the most popular hotels for the black élite, where great jazz musicians rubbed elbows with black politicians, judges and lawyers. Duke Ellington and Count

Basie often stayed there when playing theatres in downtown Chicago. The incongruous situation of being able to play there but not live there was a sore point. To Ed's shame, Freedom moved into the Du while he himself stayed at the Lexington with Sir Charles. Freedom had joked about it, saying he didn't give a damn what they wanted to think he was. Black or white, he was there to fight.

And he got a fight, not in the ring but outside a speakeasy. It started with Freedom and two black boxers he had met at the Du being barred from entering the speakeasy. The three boxers started slugging it out with the bouncers on the door, and the police were called. They were on a tough training schedule and Ed had assumed Freedom was resting, when he was summoned to the local police station. Along with his 'brothers', Freedom was put behind bars for the night. Sir Charles paid a heavy fine and made a large 'donation' to police funds to get Freedom released. Afraid of the bad press this situation was bound to cause, the venue was switched, and a hasty retreat to New York organized. In the end this proved beneficial because their luck was in. A contender removed from the running left an opening for Freedom in a fight scheduled to take place in Madison Square.

Freedom's arrest seemed at first to have no effect on him, but Ed detected a difference. He had often said that Freedom lacked the 'killer instinct'– now he saw an anger in Freedom that unleashed itself, but not necessarily in the ring. Ed warned him to keep his temper, at all cost they must avoid bad publicity. The old, familiar mask came down and he received that blank, hooded stare. Ed was told quietly but firmly that it was up to him to make sure that Freedom was never subjected to the insults his 'brothers' received.

Ed made a point of telling Sir Charles it was imperative to make the public aware of Freedom's Romany origins. If he were to be barred from any more hotels, there would be trouble and Ed doubted if he could control it.

From then on, Freedom made a point of mixing with black boxers in the gymnasiums and socializing with them in the bars and nightclubs. He felt an empathy with their segregation, and they in turn accepted him as one of them. They encouraged him and waited in line to act as sparring partners, and many of them should, by rights, have been put forward as contenders.

Ed sat in Freedom's sparse room in the run-down hotel. Freedom had pulled the mattress from his bed and laid it on the floor to sleep. He was stretched out on it now, his head resting on a grubby pillow. Ed knew he was exhausted, but all the attention he had been getting pumped him full of adrenalin.

Freedom felt Ed's eyes on him and turned with a smile. 'You got a big paunch on you, Ed. Want to run round the clubs with me, do the Black Bottom. That'll slim you down.'

'No I don't, and you shouldn't be out gallivantin' wiv all sorts. I'm not a stickler, I know you gotta let off a bit of steam now an' then, but keep it to a minimum. This isn't all belly, neither – this is our cash, son. I don't let it out of me sight fer a minute.'

Freedom laughed and told Ed he should take care on his way back to that posh hotel, joking that Ed might be robbed by some of his 'black brothers'.

'Never mind me, it's you I'm bothered about, you need to rest up.'

Freedom stretched his arms above his head and sighed. 'How

many more times do they want me to show how good I am? I want Risco – I done my part, I've proved myself, I want Risco. So you get that fat body round to his Lordship and tell him I'm through waiting.'

'I hear you, lad, but you remember I'm the trainer, don't get too big fer yer boots or you'll be leavin' 'em on the canvas ... An' stay in ternight, all right? No bloody Black Bottomin'.'

Ed clutched his belly all the way back to the hotel. He decided that perhaps it would be better if the winnings were put in the hotel safe. He counted all the dollar bills and stacked them in a neat pile. As always, Sir Charles had made Ed sign for the money when it was given to him. Ed now decided to ask him to arrange for its safekeeping.

That evening, Sir Charles watched as the money was put into the hotel safe. He suggested to Ed that he open a bank account, but Ed wouldn't hear of it. He had never had much to do with banks, he didn't even have an account back in England, having rarely had more than a pocketful of loose change to his name. Besides, most of the money belonged to Freedom. Another reason, which Ed did not mention to Sir Charles, was that Freedom was still barely able to write more than his own name. To give him a cheque book would only confuse the issue, and knowing his spendthrift ways it was better all round for the money to be kept out of generous hands.

Ed cabled Freda and Evelyne that all was well – more than well, they were inching closer and closer to the title. He did not mention that Freedom was becoming hard to handle. He wanted to get Freedom out of New York. Even though he still worked out in the gyms, he was hitting the booze, and many a morning he was too hung over to train. At last Ed got a call to meet with the Golden Triangle. It seemed they had some good news for him.

The fight with Johnny 'Rubber-legs' Risco was on. Ed wanted Freedom to rest for at least a month, but Dempsey laughed at him, saying that in the days when he was in the booths he fought three or four fights a week, and he knew Freedom was raring to go. Against his better judgement, Ed agreed. The publicity campaign for the Risco–Stubbs fight was under way.

Freedom was working out when Ed told him the Risco fight was going ahead. He belted hell out of the punch-bag, then clasped Ed joyfully to his sweating body. Ed did not mention the hours he had spent arguing with Sir Charles that it was too soon, that Freedom needed more rest.

Sir Charles had organized Freedom's match with Risco only three weeks after his win on points at Madison Square, but Ed gave Freedom no hint of his misgivings. Right now, Freedom was confident, even over-confident. 'This is it, I get through with Risco, there's just Sharkey and the German to go, that title's getting closer.'

'Yeah, yeah, I hear you. Just remember Sharkey's still number two contender. He's already wiped out Risco, so he'll be watching you like a hawk.'

Freedom went back to the punchbag with renewed energy. Ed sized him up. He reckoned Freedom could take Risco, but Sharkey would be another matter. Sharkey was lighter than

Freedom, but he was said to be unstoppable. He would fight the winner of the Stubbs–Risco bout and, if Freedom won, he would be a very tired boxer.

Sharkey's only obstacle to the vacant throne was the big German, Max Schmeling. He was Germany's international champion and a formidable contender. Schmeling was already at the top in the betting. He and Sharkey had noted the meteoric rise of the gypsy fighter and, as Ed suspected, both men calculated that Freedom would be a very tired man. They booked ringside seats for the bout, which was to take place in Chicago and was already a sell-out. Rumours began to circulate; the Golden Triangle had an interest in the gypsy – tired he might be, but he was beginning to draw crowds. Freedom, at first a rank outsider, now featured in the last lap for the vacant throne. The running was still Schmeling first, Sharkey second, Risco third. Having done extremely well, Freedom was now placed fourth.

Freda and Evelyne felt cut off, waiting for the results. Both understood the importance of Freedom's fight against Johnny 'Rubber-legs' Risco. Evelyne would stand at the gate of the villa for hours on end hoping the Western Union boy would bring her a message. She couldn't sleep for worry.

Freda, who usually tried to keep Evelyne calm, almost induced a miscarriage by screaming at the top of her voice. 'He's here? He's coming! *Evie, Evie, he's got a telegram*!'

Evelyne's hands were shaking as she tore open the envelope. She read it, then closed her eyes. 'He's won, Freda, he's *won*!'

It had taken sixteen rounds for Freedom to get Risco down on the canvas. Down and unable to bounce back. Freedom was tired but jubilant, and Ed was beside himself. The throne was closer – his boy was now placed third.

Sharkey and Schmeling were impressed, but Sharkey was still more than confident. If the gyppo was tired before the Risco fight, now he would be exhausted. He put pressure on his promoters to push his fight with Freedom forward.

Dempsey and his partners celebrated when they received the news. Rickard increased the publicity with Sir Charles right alongside him and not afraid, as Dempsey joked, 'to get his hand outta his pocket'. Having been unsure to begin with, they now all believed there was a chance. They brought out the 'big guns' and set about designing posters. Their boy, they were sure, had the 'Golden Glove'.

Chapter 24

Ed was unusually quiet on the flight back to Miami. Freedom sat next to him, wearing dark glasses, his head resting on the back of his seat. He was exhausted.

Poor Ed had lost even more hair during their travels, forever worrying, and now he believed he had a gastric ulcer. Out of the corner of his eye, Freedom watched him take out a cigar, roll it in his fingers, put it back in his pocket and then take it out again. Fidget, fidget . . . Freedom laid his hand on Ed's arm and quietly asked him the important question, 'How long have I got, Ed?'

Ed stared out of the window, his stomach churning. He wasn't sure whether it was the fight that caused it, or the realization that they had barely a month to prepare. Freedom hesitated only a moment when told. 'Well, I said I wanted to fight, looks like Kearn and Rickard are coming up trumps.'

Ed was too much the professional to get excited. He knew it was too soon. Freedom needed more time to rest. 'I think those two think they're goin' ter make another Golden Triangle with you at the apex instead of Dempsey. They'll be behind this razzmatazz. You think you'll be fit enough, lad?'

Freedom laughed, punched Ed's shoulder and said he was

ready. 'Sir Charles'd step in if I wasn't, wouldn't he? He wouldn't let me fight if I wasn't up to it, don't worry, Ed.'

'Sir Charles, lad, blows with the wind, that's all I know. Right now he's all over those two big Americans, talking of buying his own plane, God help us if he wants to take the controls.'

They strapped themselves into their seat belts as the pilot shouted that they were about to land. Ed's face turned green. 'Gawd, this is the bit I hate. S'all right getting up, an' while yer up there, but comin' down's horrible.'

'Yeah, it's like fighting, Ed, no fun when you're down.'

They landed safely and Ed fussed about their bags, worried they would lose the precious sets of gloves. Freedom shouted, 'Ed! Ed, look, will you look at that, well I'll be goddamned if that ain't a sonofabitch!'

He was pointing to a huge billboard God only knew how many feet high. 'STUBBS VERSUS SHARKEY.' 'Jeez, ain't that a goddam thing?' He had already picked up a lot of American slang and everything was 'Jeez, Ed' this and 'Jeez, Ed' that. Ed muttered that he'd got it wrong, it wasn't 'Jeez' but 'gee', like in 'gee whizz'. Freedom continued to get it wrong, and in the end Ed also found himself saying, 'Jeez, will you look at that goddam billboard, you could be a movie star.'

Tex played on Freedom's uncanny likeness to the film star Rudolph Valentino to the hilt. He also made much of Freedom's long hair and gypsy blood. On many of the boards, in huge red letters, were the words, 'The Gypsy King'; another favourite was 'The Wild Man'. All of them, like circus posters, were in brilliant colours, showing Freedom with his gloved hands held up, his hair flying out behind him.

*

The hired limousine was piled to the roof with gifts, many of them toys for Edward. Ed had tried hard, but in the end he had given way and let Freedom have some of his winnings, more than he would dare tell Evelyne. Freedom had gone on one of his wild spending sprees – suits, hats, coats, dresses, jewels, and, of course, a rocking horse, a drum and miniature boxing gloves for his son. For once, Ed had also been spending money like water and was loaded down with gifts for Freda. Also, both of them had bought the lightweight, light-coloured suits that were all the rage.

The elegance and superb tailoring of the clothes Sir Charles had had made for him were rejected for the flashy style favoured by their idol, Dempsey. They both sported loud floral silk ties with matching handkerchiefs and dark glasses.

Sir Charles' new-found friend, Jack Kearn, had taken him to an airstrip, where they inspected a second-hand light plane. Kearn was amazed to hear the usually thrifty Englishman giving instructions for the plane to be elaborately fitted out in red leather. He also wanted certain improvements on the control panel. Kearn paled when he heard how much it would cost, but Sir Charles was ecstatic, and they departed in high spirits. Kearn puzzled over the Englishman's eccentric behaviour, one moment fussing over five or ten dollars and the next spending thirty thousand as if it were no more than a couple of bucks.

All day Evelyne and Freda had waited, running to the gate every few minutes, eager to see their men. The car eventually drew up outside at five in the afternoon, and Ed and Freedom hopped out with all their bags and boxes of gifts.

The reunion was feverish, everyone talking at once, unwrapping their presents with shrieks of delight, and Freedom throwing his son up in the air and catching him.

Evelyne sensed that Freedom was slightly evasive, kissing her lightly without removing his dark glasses. She felt uneasy with him, knew there was something wrong.

When Freda and Ed went for a walk on the beach, Evelyne said, 'I think the boxing gloves are a bit big, we'll put them away until he gets bigger.' She was reluctant to tell Freedom that she didn't want Edward to be encouraged to fight.

'I see you're bigger now, how you been, all right?' Freedom asked.

She felt a distance between them. She was aware of how fat she had become with the baby, and felt unattractive, even ugly. She always forgot how tall he was, how handsome. His presence filled the room and made her self-conscious. She picked up all her gifts and thanked him.

'You see all the posters of me, then, love?'

Evelyne hadn't; as neither she nor Freda could drive they had hardly left the villa. She studied Freedom. The pale linen suit, she thought, was not too bad, but the silk tie with the painted flowers was utterly tasteless. 'You look very fancy.'

She could have bitten off her tongue as he looked into the mirror with a hurt expression and examined his tie.

'Not to your liking? Well, you can use it as a bandanna.'

She wished he would take the glasses off, not seeing his face unnerved her. She reached out to take them off, but he backed abruptly away from her. She withdrew her hand, her feelings hurt, but as he slowly removed them himself she understood why.

Both his eyes were bruised and swollen, and beneath his left eye was a gash with fresh stitches. The bridge of his nose was swollen and his cheek was puffy. The sight of him made her feel faint, and she steadied herself on the edge of the table. She knew she mustn't let him see the effect his injuries had on her, and she forced a smile. 'I'd better see if we've got some steak in the icebox, that's what they use, isn't it? Now, come here and let me have a good look at you.'

She could feel the relief in him, feel him relax, and as she took his face gently between her hands she couldn't stop the tears coming into her eyes. She kissed his bruised, hurt face softly.

Freedom gathered her into his arms and returned her kisses, murmuring that his face was fine, and he was just desperate for her. He laid her down on the bed and loosened his flowered tie. She unbuttoned her blouse, and he could see her breasts, swollen but still beautiful. He pulled his shirt open to reveal heavily strapped ribs. His body, like his face, was marked with deep, dark bruises. He sat close to her and helped her off with her blouse, and she kissed his chest, touched the tape.

'It's nothing, just to keep me standing straight.'

He oiled Evelyne's belly and asked if it was all right for him to make love to her. She smiled up at him, loving him for his consideration, and held him tightly. She felt him flinch slightly as she touched his bruised ribs.

He treated her so gently that it was she who urged him on. Again and again he took her until they lay back, sweating and exhausted. Leaning on his elbow he touched her face, brushed a strand of her wonderful long hair aside and kissed her neck, his voice husky and shy. 'There's never been a woman like you, *manushi*, you take me to a place so high up I'm flying. No woman but you can ever take me there, you know that? I love thee, worship thee, and to know you're here waiting for me, fills my soul.'

She looked up into his adoring face, and in her shyness could not tell him that he made her clumsy body feel as light as the day they first made love on the mountain. She felt beautiful again under his gaze, and she glowed.

That night the four of them ate a celebration dinner. Freedom was in high spirits, laughing and playing the fool, showing Freda some new dance steps. Ed put his arm around Evelyne, his eyes shining as he watched Freedom with total adoration. He just loved the lad to death. 'He's done well, Evie love, not just fighting, and he's near nine thousand dollars richer – you're looking at a wealthy gent.'

Evelyne gasped with astonishment. 'Nine thousand? But that's ... why, Ed, that's ...'

Ed laughed as she tried to translate dollars into pounds. 'Why, Ed, we're millionaires!' Suddenly she looked at Freedom, who was grinning broadly. He danced around the table with Freda, pausing briefly to turn the radio up even louder as he swung her in his arms.

'Ed, can I have a little word?' Evelyne asked quietly.

Puffing on his cigar, Ed walked with her to the verandah. She looked over her shoulder and whispered, 'Ed, he's not got it all, has he? You know what a spend thrift he is ...'

Ed chortled, 'There's no need to tell me, Evie love. Sir Charles keeps it in the hotel safes for us. 'E'll take care of it, 'cause we'll have taxes an' fings to work out before we leave.'

They could hear Freda insisting that Freedom try her banana and raspberry milk shake. She had taken to making elaborate concoctions in her new blender and, of course, feasting on them herself. She had gained at least eight pounds since they had arrived.

Ed turned his adoring expression on his little wife. 'My Gawd, she can certainly put the food away, what a woman.'

'Ed . . . will he win? Tell me, please – I can see his face, his body's all bruised, will he win?'

Ed assured her that, with rest and preparation, Freedom would win. There was nothing to worry about. 'He's goin' ter beat Sharkey, love, I know it.'

Evelyne planted a kiss on his shiny nose, then went into Freedom's arms. They danced around the room.

Ed's good-humoured expression faded quickly. Even from where he was standing, he could see Freedom's swollen face. He knew there would barely be time for it to go down before he went into the ring again. Ed didn't like it at all, especially with Freedom's bruised ribs. He sighed, turned to stare out at the ocean. He tossed his cigar away – it tasted bitter, he felt bitter. He muttered under his breath, 'Bastards, you bastards . . . some rest he's gonna get . . . bastards.'

Freedom took himself off to bed carrying his son high on his shoulders. Tired as he was, he wanted to bath the little fellow and spend some time with him because he had been away so long.

Freda and Evelyne washed up the dishes. By the time Evelyne went to bed Freedom was sleeping. In the crook of his arm lay Edward, who had crawled out of his cot and into the double bed. The child was fast asleep. With his thatch of dark hair and suntanned body he looked like a miniature of his father. Evelyne stood looking at them both, not wanting to disturb them, then slipped downstairs to lie on the settee. She felt her belly and knew that this time she would be there at the ringside, he would not be coming for another two months.

She slept fitfully, Freedom's bruised face floating in her mind's eye. She woke in the early dawn, cold, her body stiff. All around her lay the gifts, the child's toys, and she picked up the tiny boxing gloves. She would hide these, Edward would never have them, never have his face bruised and cut like his father's. Now they had the money she would be able to send him to a good school.

Evelyne smiled, hugging herself with pleasure. She could picture the house they would buy with the money, maybe even a pony for Edward. She would also take herself back to school – yes, she would pick up her studies. When she was qualified and the boys were grown, she could start teaching again. As the sun came up, Evelyne made notes on all the things she would do with the money, using one of the drawing books she had bought for Edward. She enjoyed writing and it had been a long time since she had written anything. She sighed as she looked at her handwriting. Perhaps with their new-found fortune she could persuade Freedom to learn too. Suddenly the thought of how much more they would take home when Freedom won the title made her gasp. She laughed out loud, then put her hand over her mouth, realizing how silly she must look.

She placed the notebook carefully in a dressing-table drawer, inching it open silently so as not to wake Freedom, then slipped into the warm bed beside him and their son. She sighed with happiness and found, to her amazement, that she could recall word for word Christina Rossetti's *The Dream*.

She laid her hand on Freedom's thigh. He turned towards her and, still asleep, pulled her to him. Cradled in his arms, with Edward asleep at Freedom's side, Evelyne felt happier than she had in her whole life. The future was rosy, glowing, and financially secure at long last. She fell into a deep, contented sleep.

Chapter 25

The fight was now only days away, and prefight fever made the villa a target for reporters. They photographed Freedom running along the beach, they tried to get to see him at the gym, and he was photographed with Dempsey. Ed finally had to ban the press completely so his fighter could concentrate on training.

Tension mounted in the house. Meals were worked around when Freedom was ready to eat, when he finished, when he slept. He kept himself apart from them all as much as possible, and had been sleeping in the spare room, as little Edward woke often in the night, and Freedom had to rise at the crack of dawn to train.

There was not a mark left on his face from his previous bouts. The small scar under his left eye had healed and he was in peak condition. As the day drew closer and closer, they read in the papers about the arrival of Jack Sharkey.

Every day Freda read the papers avidly, as there were so many articles about Freedom. She cut each one out and put them into a scrapbook. She would then display her cuttings and hand-written notes at breakfast. Evelyne started one, too, and the women would discuss the layout of their books together.

On a recent trip into town for groceries, Evelyne had bought two books and had taken to reading each afternoon on the porch. She loved the gentle, romantic, beautifully structured stories of Jane Austen.

Edward and Freda were making sandcastles on the beach. Evelyne could hear Freda screeching, 'Eddie! Eddie, that's far enough in the water . . . Eddie!' No matter how often Evelyne corrected her, she still called him Eddie. Evelyne sighed and tutted. Jane Austen would not have approved.

Far along the beach she could see Freedom running, no more than a small black dot. Ed drove the hired motorcar alongside, the exhaust leaving a trail of blue smoke in the warm air. Evelyne checked the time – she still had a few precious moments alone before the house would again revolve around Freedom. He ate early, a large steak, salad and fresh fruit, and drank a strange mixture that Freda spent ages mixing in her treasured blender. It consisted of raw eggs, milk, honey, and a vitamin powder Ed had been given by Dempsey. Freedom's training schedule ruled their lives, and now that Evelyne knew what was at stake financially, she made every effort not to disturb his rigorous routine. Mealtime and exercise charts hung all over the kitchen. The lounge was now used for Freedom's massage and as a place to discuss tactics, and the two of them spent hours closeted in there. In the afternoons Freedom went to Dempsey's gymnasium to work out on the proper equipment, returning for his long run, his massage, dinner and bed. The fight was drawing closer and closer, but if Freedom was nervous he took pains not to show it in front of the women. Ed was sharp-tempered if they were a minute off schedule, but neither Freda nor Evelyne argued. The fight was all-important.

Ed had taken Evelyne aside for one of their private chats. Flushing with embarrassment, he forced himself to say what had to be said, 'Now, love, I know he won't tell you, so it's up to me – yer not to 'ave it away, not 'til after the fight.'

Evelyne smothered her smile and stared, poker-faced, at Ed, 'Have what away? I don't follow you, Ed.'

'Now, now, yer know what I mean! He's in the spare room and, well, yer see, one night's love-makin', Evie, is equivalent to about a six-mile run – d'yer understand me now? Conserve 'is energy.'

Evelyne repeated what Ed had said to Miss Freda. She patted her hair looking at her dumpy little husband, 'Well, I wish he'd do a bit of training. I don't know what's come over him of late, I think it's nerves, either that or he's been taking your Freedom's vitamins.' Ed, unaware that they were whispering about him, paced up and down. Evelyne kept her face straight as she looked back at Freda. 'I don't think it's vitamins, Freda. It's that float-ing nightdress with all the swansdown he brought you from New York, makes you look the image of Fay Wray.'

Freda giggled as Ed gave them a grunt, and walked out. 'Well darlink, if that's true, he's King Kong. Tonight I'll put my flan-nel nightie on, that'll finish him off, always has before ...'

The two women giggled and looked through all the film magazines Ed had bought. Evelyne had to put her hand over her mouth as she caught Freda looking at herself in the mirror. She had made up her mouth with a cupid's bow and obviously thought she really did look like Fay Wray, or Clara Bow. She pursed her lips and batted her thickly mascara'd eyelashes. 'Oh, I just don't know what I am going to wear for the fight, have you thought about your outfit, Evie?'

Evelyne's good humour evaporated. Her stomach turned over – just for a few moments she had forgotten about the fight. There were only three days to go ... 'Oh God, Freda, it's not long now, not long.'

They both turned to the calendar where the dates were marked with crosses. Those few days slipped by fast.

On the day of the big fight Freedom left early with Ed. They all hugged him and wished him well. He kissed his son, and waved to them all as the car disappeared down the drive. The villa felt very quiet without him and Ed, and the day seemed to stretch endlessly ahead for Freda and Evelyne.

Jack Sharkey and Freedom faced each other at the weighing-in. Freedom had learnt fast – he out-stared Sharkey, glared for the press cameras and whispered that he was going to wipe the floor with Sharkey. He held up his fist for the photographers.

In the stiflingly hot dressing room, the thunder of the crowd could be heard. Ed bandaged Freedom's fists, and Dempsey came in, raising his clenched fist to Freedom in salute. Sir Charles, Tex and Kearn also made an appearance, Sir Charles bringing a crowd of visiting English aristocracy who all wanted to meet Freedom. Finally, Ed ordered everybody out and banged the door shut.

The seconds were sweating with nerves as they checked their equipment – the buckets, sponges, gum-shield, plasters and towels.

Having finished bandaging Freedom's right hand, Ed gestured for him to lift his left. When he was wrapping the cloth tightly between Freedom's fingers, Freedom asked. 'They in their seats yet, Ed? Is she here?'

Ed gave the nod to one of the seconds to check that the women were there, and he came back saying they were, and that the excited Edward was standing up in his seat waving a rattle. Having finished the bandaging, Ed started to massage Freedom's shoulders. He could feel the tension and kept up a steady flow of chatter, easing the stiffness from the muscles. 'Now remember the rules, Freedom. Make sure if 'e goes down you get over to the neutral corner fast as your legs'll carry yer. That's the law, they won't start the count until you're in the neutral.'

Freedom cuffed Ed good-naturedly on the chin. Before every single bout Ed went on like this, as if Freedom didn't know. Ed was keeping an eye on the clock – it was almost time. They waited for the referee to come in and inspect the bandages. At last he arrived and checked each hand meticulously, then patted Freedom's shoulder. 'I'll go over it in the ring, but I like to have a private word before the bout, understand me? Okay, you break when I tell you, no low punches, no holding. And remember, if either man goes down, you must return to the neutral corner for the count. I will not count until the fighter is in the corner – understand? We got judges each side of the ring, their decision is based on the effectiveness of your punches, they want nice, clean, forceful punches ... Okay, right, we go in ten minutes, and good luck.'

Ed began to tie on the gloves, still talking in his soft, non-stop way. 'Remember yer get points for aggression, so go in there ter win. Sustain the rounds, don't pussyfoot up there, get in an' take 'im. This is the big one and the most important to date, so I want you in there ter win, you wiv me? You wiv me? Yer goin' ter knock 'im out, and yer goin' ter get that title, yes? Yes, yes?'

Freedom slapped Ed's open palm and yelled back, '*Yes yes yes!*'

There was a knock on the door and they were told to stand by. Ed pulled the robe around Freedom's shoulders and double-checked that the corner men had everything ready. After one last look, he winked and they went out through the door.

The stadium was packed to capacity and the thunder of the crowd's noise drowned out Ed's pep talk. At the opposite entrance stood Sharkey, hopping from one leg to the other, waiting for the signal to enter the ring. A fanfare started up and the audience rose to their feet as the band played the 'Victory March'.

Edward was jumping up and down in his seat, not really understanding what was going on but loving every minute of it. Evelyne's heart was thudding, and she felt the baby kicking inside her. The heat in the stadium was overpowering and the noise like thunderclaps overhead. Freda held Evelyne's hand tight, both their palms sticky from nerves.

The crowd roared as Freedom entered the ring, hemmed in by Ed and the seconds, with eight attendants to keep back the well-wishers' outstretched hands.

'Ladies and gentlemennnn ... in the left-hand corner, the British Heavyweight Champion *Freedom Stubbs*, wearing the black shorts. Weighing in at two hundred and two pounds. In the right-hand corner, Jack Sharkey, from New York City, weighing in at one hundred and ninety pounds!'

Not a single one of the ringmaster's words about Sharkey was heard, the crowd rose with a deafening cheer, flowers were thrown and feet thudded on the wooden stands.

The two boxers met in the centre of the ring, while the band played first the 'Stars and Stripes', then 'God Save the King'. The referee was introduced, to whistles and cheers, and the boxers retired to their corners.

'Ladies and gentlemen, there will be twenty rounds of two minutes each round.'

The judges took their bows and went to their seats, flowers and streamers were removed from the ring, and the gong was held up for display. Slowly the stadium grew quieter and quieter as they waited expectantly for the bout to begin.

Freedom glanced quickly over at Evelyne and smiled. She wanted to cry out, reach out to him and touch him. His hair, oiled to keep it off his face, was tied back in a leather thong, and his eyes, brows and cheeks were smeared with Vaseline. The gumshield was put into place and he sat poised and ready.

Sharkey delayed getting his gumshield in, talking to his trainer. The gong clanged loudly, and both men were up and moving to the centre of the ring. The seconds were out, taking the stools with them. Freda was shouting, 'Come on Freedom, come on Freedom . . .'

The boxers were well-matched, and it was not until round four that the crowd began to settle down. The two men were in close, jabbing, punching, trying to find each other's weaknesses. It was a good, clean fight when suddenly a punch that Evelyne didn't even see made Freedom's whole body buckle, and he fell to his knees. The crowd went wild. Ed waved his towel, screaming at the top of his voice, and climbed into the ring. There was almost a fight between Ed and the referee, two judges conferred and Freda was on her feet screaming along with everyone else in the front rows.

'*Foul . . . Foul . . . Foul . . .* !'

Freedom was helped to his feet by the ref, who looked into his face and turned, holding off Sharkey with his right hand. He was not counting. Sharkey, panicking, thought he had been disqualified, and turned to his seconds, who now got into the ring. The chant of 'foul' was taken up by a vast group at the back of the stadium, and the sing-song of 'low punch, low punch . . .'

The referee was holding Ed off, and Freedom backed, bent over slightly and shook his head. To everyone's amazement, the referee held up his hand and gave a two-minute respite to Freedom, throughout which Sharkey fumed and raged like a madman. Ed had to be hauled out of the ring, still insisting it was a foul, but the ref gave the signal for the round to continue.

The muscles in Freedom's left leg were seizing up, and it felt as if it were paralysed. For the duration of the round he fended off Sharkey's punches as best he could and at the end he limped back to his corner, which drew a series of loud boos and catcalls from the spectators.

Evelyne sat huddled in her seat. She couldn't understand what was going on, he was in pain and she knew it. 'He's hurt, Freda, he's hurt, he can hardly walk.'

In desperation Ed massaged Freedom's leg, at the same time yelling above the noise to Freedom, 'You want me to stop the fight? Tell me, shall I stop the fight, can you move it, Jesus God, can you move your leg?'

The seconds could see that Freedom's old cut was an angry red, and they plastered it with grease . . . Ed had actually reached for the towel to throw it into the ring when the gong sounded for the round to begin. Ed knew his boy was hurt, it was obvious from his stance. This wasn't Freedom's style, he was a mover, and a fast one.

Freedom took a series of short, fast jabs to his face and keeled over backwards, lost his balance and fell heavily out of the ring. Evelyne was on her feet, tears rolling down her cheeks. She couldn't stand to see it, see him hurt, she wanted him never to get back into the ring. The crowd around her were screaming like wild animals.

The referee started the count, holding Sharkey back as Freedom hauled himself back into the ring. The fall had cut him just above his left ear, and blood was trickling down on to his shoulder. Ed was at breaking point, but held back by the seconds. He wanted to throw in the towel; it was obvious Freedom couldn't stand properly. His left leg was dragging, useless. Freedom was taking his punishment, gritting his teeth to hold on until the round ended. It was taking everything he had just to stand with the agonizing pain in his left leg and the feeling that someone was hacking into his spine ... Every movement made it worse.

Sharkey took every opportunity, spurred on by relief at not getting disqualified, and came on to Freedom with punch after punch. He was a short jab man, and Freedom was on the end of his hard rights time and time again. He felt his nose split open and stood dazed as the bell rang for the end of the round.

Ed concentrated on Freedom's face and begged him to throw in the towel. Blood was pouring from his nose, and the cut above his ear wouldn't stay shut. 'It's over, Freedom, it's over, he's mauling you.'

Sir Charles sat stiffly through the next round, not making a sound, and his companions went quiet as they saw his champion beaten. There was nothing anyone could say, the ring said it all, the crowds bayed for a knockout and Sir Charles knew they would get it at any moment. There was a flash of Freedom's old brilliance, but he stumbled and took a left hook to his jaw that lifted him off the canvas. No one could believe he would get up from it, but he did. It was tragic to see him swaying, blinded by his own blood, and for Evelyne and Freda it was a nightmare. Edward shouted, 'Daddy, Daddy,' and waved his rattle, thinking it was all a game. Evelyne hugged the child to her and sobbed; she couldn't bear to look into the ring.

At long last Freedom was down and out for the count, but there was none of the hysterical cheering. The crowd went quiet as they saw Freedom's terrible injuries and the pitiful attempts of his seconds to bring him round. His blood was all over the canvas, all over his opponent.

The referee held up Sharkey's hand as Ed was still trying to bring Freedom to. He lay face down, breathing in the resin, and eventually the two seconds managed to lift him back to his seat. From then on it was a blur to all those close to Freedom – the ride in the ambulance, the wait outside the hospital room for news. Ed wept unashamedly, but Freda had strength enough for them all. She chided Ed, saying he must put on a brave face for Freedom, Freedom mustn't see him like this. Evelyne cradled the sleeping child and was so exhausted she couldn't even cry.

The doctors took Ed aside and said that Freedom was going to be all right. He was semi-paralysed down his left side. They doubted that the paralysis would be permanent, and hoped he would recover the use of his leg completely. The blow to the side of Freedom's head caused much more worry, and although he had regained a semblance of consciousness he wasn't lucid. So they had taken X-rays of his skull and he was under sedation.

Ed went into the private room. Unable to speak he just stood looking at the still figure with the terribly swollen face and broken nose plastered up, and his heart broke. The room was silent except for Freedom's shallow breathing, and Ed touched his hand and had to hurry out before he broke down.

Ed tried to persuade Evelyne to go home with Freda, but he hadn't counted on her strength of will. She refused point-blank to move, insisting that Freda and Ed take the child home and return in the morning. Evelyne sat outside the room, quiet, alone, her eyes closed. She prayed for him, hand to her heart, and whispered his name over and over again.

Sir Charles was led past the waiting room. He could see her, her anguished face, as she waited. He followed the nurse down the corridor and into Freedom's room. The nurse hovered at the door.

'Thank you, I won't be a moment.' Left alone with the shrouded figure in the bed, surrounded by machines and intravenous drips, Sir Charles stood as if frozen. Slowly, without making a sound, he inched towards the bed, peered down into the distorted face with the swollen eyes and the thick bandages over the broken nose. He removed his monocle and his mouth twitched.

Freedom's hands were unmarked, his long, tapering fingers resting peacefully on the white sheet, making Sir Charles want to weep. Such fine hands, he had never really noticed them before. He looked towards the door, then reached out and touched Freedom's hand, as if afraid, then bent and kissed the tips of the fingers. Then he slipped from the room and walked back along the corridor to where Evelyne waited.

He looked embarrassed, he didn't know what to say to her, and he tapped his walking stick on the blue lino, making small indentations. She said not one word, but stared at him, her face tight and angry, her eyes cold.

'I'll make sure all the hospital bills are taken care of, and, well, any expenses will, of course, be paid. I'm sorry.'

She wanted to strike him, smash his arrogant, stiff face, hit him so hard that his monocle would shatter on the floor. 'That's very kind of you, sir, what about his heart, can you pay for that, too? He'll not get over this and you know it.'

He coughed, shuffled his feet and said he would be flying to Chicago the following morning, and would no doubt see them on their return to England.

'He's just like one of your thoroughbreds really, isn't he, sir? Except when they break a leg you shoot them. Where's your gun? You're finished with him now, aren't you? Just like that, because he didn't win.'

Sir Charles went white with anger at her rudeness. 'Your husband never did anything he didn't want to. You of all people should know that. No one forced him into the ring and no one is to blame. He is a sportsman.'

Evelyne moved closer to him and her fists clenched. '*You* forced him and you know it, you never let him off the hook, did you? Because you owned him, from the day you first met him, you bought him.'

Sir Charles snapped that perhaps she would have preferred him to hang, as he most assuredly could have done without him.

'He repaid you, every penny you spent on that court case. How much have you made out of him?'

He pushed her away from him, his face ashen. His fury, usually so controlled, burst out. 'If there was anyone to blame, my dear, it was you, you who never let him be, you hung on to your meal ticket as he would have hanged from a rope. Do you think I don't know that?'

Evelyne slapped his face so hard that he reeled backwards. Taking out a silk handkerchief he dabbed at the corners of his mouth, then replaced his monocle and reached for the door handle. He froze for a moment, his back to her, his voice choked, 'Forgive me, I should never, never have said those things to you. I cannot say how deeply sorry I am, I can only say that I am as distraught about what has happened as you are. You won't believe me, but it is the truth.'

Evelyne gave him a bitter smile, and he wouldn't meet her eyes, but he did turn towards her. 'I remember him from those early days, at Devil's Pit. I had such hopes for him, and they did not include you. I am sorry, perhaps I had a reason – you may call it jealousy, whatever you wish. But you have him now, he's all yours, and I feel sure your love for each other will be strong enough to overcome this sad situation.'

He wanted to leave but Evelyne caught his arm, and only his icy stare made her release him.

'They say he'll never fight again, do you know that? And I don't want him to, ever. Stay out of our lives, stay away from him, we don't need you.'

He gave her a brief nod, said his contract with Freedom was void as of that day. He opened the door, holding his back ramrod-stiff, and walked out. He said his last words to the corridor, not even directing them at Evelyne, 'You never needed me, my dear, never.'

Sir Charles walked slowly out of the hospital. His car drew up and he stepped in and leaned his head on the soft leather. He had a clear picture of the very first time he had seen Freedom, there at Devil's Pit, with his flowing hair and perfect body. How could those foolish people know, understand anything? No other man had had such care and attention lavished on him, but they believed it had been purely business.

'I wanted him, I wanted him.'

The chauffeur turned a puzzled look to Sir Charles, they were still outside the hospital and he was not sure where he was supposed to take his passenger. Sir Charles opened his eyes and snapped that they were going to his hotel immediately; he had already made the decision not to return to Chicago, there was nothing there for him. He decided to go to Hollywood. Perhaps there he would find what he was always searching for but so afraid to make happen. Hollywood beckoned, the decadence, the freedom to love whom he chose.

Evelyne saw the limousine drive away and knew that an episode in her life, in all their lives, had closed.

At three o'clock the nurse came out with some hot tea for Evelyne and told her Freedom was asking for her. The nurse was worried, the woman looked heavily pregnant, and quietly warned her that he was not lucid, still under the effects of the drugs.

Evelyne walked to the bedside, and sat in the chair the nurse had placed there for her. Freedom's hands were still, lying on top of the folded white sheet. His face, so bruised and beaten, looked grotesque with the bandages over his nose.

'That you, *manushi*, that you?'

She took his hand and kissed it, whispering that she was there, she was there, and to go to sleep.

'I'm sorry, so sorry, *manushi*, sorry . . .'

The tears she thought had dried up flowed freely, dripping on to his hand, and he slept, holding her tight, afraid to let her go. In his sleep he was running through the fields, he was dragging the wild horse towards him and riding bareback through the clean, sweet, fresh air.

In the morning Ed came to find her still holding Freedom's hand, her head resting on the bed. He eased her away and she tried to argue, but he said it was not for her but for the baby, she must eat.

The villa's shutters were closed; Evelyne didn't want the sunlight, she wanted the dark to wrap around her and comfort her. Freda came and sat beside her, held her hand.

'Sir Charles was at the hospital. He said Freedom's contract was cancelled.'

Freda wanted to cry, but she kept herself under control. 'We'll go home, Ed says, as soon as Freedom's well.'

'How did Sir Charles come to have all that money? It doesn't seem right, the way he can pick people up, then drop them.'

Freda sighed and patted Evelyne's hand. 'Well, darlink, he never even met any of his miners, but he treats them the same way.'

'What do you mean?'

Surprised she didn't know, Freda told her Sir Charles' family money was made from coal mining. She was taken aback when

Evelyne laughed, a bitter, humourless laugh. 'My God, I should have known it. I hate him, Freda, I hate him so.'

'He has troubles, too, Evie. His trustees, so Ed tells me, always keep him short of money, he has to fight them all the time.'

'Keep him short? He wouldn't know the meaning of the word. My brothers worked the mines, their knees cut and their elbows bent, their backs torn to shreds. He wouldn't know what it felt like to go short, to beg for a crust of bread. I hate him.'

Freda saw the rage in Evelyne, the deep anger, unleash itself. The violent movements of her hands emphasized what she was saying, 'I wonder how much he made out of him, how much? It'll be more than we have coming to us. Dear God, Freda, I hate that man so much I could go and . . . and . . .'

Suddenly Evelyne was sobbing, her shoulders heaving. Freda stroked her hair, knowing it was best Evie should cry, to release her anger. It wasn't really hatred for Sir Charles, it was her pain for Freedom.

Ed came home from the hospital, heavy-hearted. He laid his straw hat down. 'I dunno what's goin' ter 'appen, Freda, they tell me he's still paralysed down 'is left side. It must've 'appened when he fell outta the ring. I should've stopped 'im, Freda, I 'ad the chance first time 'e went down. I should've made 'im quit. But I wanted 'im ter win so bad . . . wanted 'im ter win, an' I failed 'im, I failed my boy, Freda.' He rubbed his head, held his hand out to Freda. He clung to her and sobbed, and she rocked him in her arms. Ed wasn't weeping for a fighter, the loss of the championship – he was heartbroken for his 'golden boy', his 'son'.

They could hear Evelyne moving around upstairs; she came down with her face set, pale and drawn from crying. 'Ed, will you drive me to the cab stand. I'll go back to the hospital, sit with him until morning.'

Ed wiped his tears with the back of his hand, afraid Evelyne had seen. He put his straw hat on at a jaunty angle.

'Right, then, let's be 'avin' yer.'

Sir Charles had been so silent, so preoccupied that Dewhurst crept around the hotel suite. 'I've packed everything, sir, and we are ready whenever you wish to leave.'

Sir Charles gave him a small smile. 'Jolly good. I'll be flying, I know how you feel about planes, if you would prefer to travel straight back to The Grange I can arrange your passage.'

'Oh, that's very good of you, sir, but I have a great inclination to see Hollywood. They say there's a guided tour of the film stars' homes that's rather special.'

Sir Charles nodded, but seemed loath to leave.

'Will you be wanting to drive to the hospital before we depart, sir?'

He received no answer. 'May I ask how Mr Stubbs is, sir?'

Sir Charles stood up, straight as an arrow. He placed along finger on the centre of his forehead as if he were in pain, and his voice sounded strangled, ''Fraid he's not too good, old chap, will you make sure they have their passages arranged, the boat, will you do that?'

He swallowed, still pressing his finger to his head, then took out a silk handkerchief and blew his nose.

'Will you be looking for a new fighter, sir?'

Sir Charles tucked his handkerchief back into his top pocket, making sure the folds were sitting exactly as they should. 'No, there'll be no more fighters, Dewhurst. Er! Well, hurry along and I'll meet you at the car.'

As the door closed behind Dewhurst, Sir Charles stared around the room. Crumpled in the waste basket was the fight programme, Freedom's face twisted and torn. The wondrous face, the long, flying hair, the 'Gypsy King' ... He picked it up, took it to the table and tried to press out the creases, but they would not be smoothed. The beautiful face was cracked, crumpled, and Sir Charles tore it into tiny fragments. But the face was still there, in front of him on the polished table. He felt as if Freedom were in the room with him and it frightened him.

Freedom lay still, his breathing shallow, and Evelyne sat beside him. For a moment his eyes opened, and he murmured, 'Sir Charles? Did he come, Evie?'

'He's gone, darling, we're free of him now. There'll be no more fighting, it's over.'

Freedom's body trembled, he moaned softly. His lips moved as if he were saying something she couldn't quite hear. She leaned closer, but the words were in his own language, jumbled, strange, sighing words. The trembling grew stronger, his whole body shaking. He gripped her hand tightly, and the tremor ran through her, making her body feel electrified. He gripped tighter, tighter, until her hand hurt, but she couldn't release it. Then, just as it had started, the shaking ceased. Freedom sighed, a long, soft moan that continued for almost half a minute. Evelyne drew back her hand, afraid, but now he was relaxed, a sweet smile on his lips. The time was exactly twelve o'clock,

Evelyne knew it was exactly on the hour because her wrist watch had stopped.

Sir Charles looked at the dials, the needles were swinging round and round, and the engine cut ... without power, they were dropping from the sky, a dead weight. Dewhurst tried to unbuckle his seat belt to get to his master, but there was no time. It was over in seconds, the plane spiralling as it made its terrifying journey to the ground. Sir Charles tried desperately to regain power, and then he gave up. A face, blurred, floated in the clouds like a hand-coloured photograph, but it was cracked and torn. In the seconds before the plane crashed into the Nevada desert, Sir Charles Wheeler saw the face of Freedom Stubbs, not as he had been when Sir Charles had first seen him in the ring, like a wild animal at Devil's Pit, but bloody, beaten, crumpled like the programme in the hotel waste paper basket.

The search party found the wreckage from the sky. The black smoke curling up in a spiral, thick grey and red smoke clouding the air with black specks of charred dollar bills. All Freedom Stubbs' winnings, all Ed Meadows' hard-earned wages, all gone. The plane was no more than a shell when the rescuers came on the scene.

They knew exactly what time the plane had crashed. Sir Charles' fob watch had stopped at precisely twelve o'clock. The dials on the plane's control panel were cracked and broken from the heat and the impact of the crash. The clock on the panel had also stopped at twelve o'clock.

BOOK FIVE

Chapter 26

The Stubbs family returned to England with the Meadows. The news of Freedom's terrible defeat arrived ahead of them. The British Champion limped, and his face still bore tell-tale marks of the beating. He felt he had let everyone down, and was ashamed to look anyone in the face. He could not defend his British title; his boxing days were, as Evelyne had said, over.

News of Sir Charles Wheeler's death also preceded them, as well as the two bodies, which were flown from Nevada. Ed did not understand the full implications of Sir Charles' death until he contacted the Wheeler trustees. Freedom's earnings and his own had been in Sir Charles' keeping, and it seemed to Ed a simple matter. The solicitors replied to his letter cordially enough, but in legal language that took along time to decipher. The gist of it was accounted for, and there was no indication that anything was due to the fighter or his trainer – quite the contrary. The receipts were there to prove it – Ed had signed for all the money he had received on his own and Freedom's behalf. Ed wrote back stating that he had given the money back to Sir Charles for safekeeping, after signing for it.

The letters passed back and forth, until Ed became frantic. He visited the solicitors personally, only to be told again that there was no record of any outstanding debts, either to him or Freedom. He was even shown the notification from Sir Charles that the hospital bills and the fares for their return journey were to be paid, but there was no mention of any cash. They could only suggest that Sir Charles had taken it with him to Nevada and it was destroyed with the plane, but they could do nothing.

Evelyne wrote copious letters to the trustees and received similar, cordial replies. The Wheeler estate was in financial difficulties. Death duties had taken their toll, and The Grange was to be sold in order to meet the heirs' interests.

She took legal advice. They could, if they wished, take the Wheeler estate to court over the matter, but they would have to be prepared to meet heavy legal costs, and there was very little hope of success.

Only Freedom appeared to have very little inclination to recover what was rightfully his. His attitude infuriated Evelyne. One morning, after receiving yet another letter of refusal from the trustees, she flew into a rage. 'They're saying the estate has no money? My God, what do they take us for? What's no money to them is millions to us. Freedom, will you go to them, in person?'

Freedom shook his head. 'No, I'll not go begging. We've no need of them, best we forget it. Besides, he paid for our passage home, all the hospital bills.'

'And so he should have, it was him put you in there! Can you not see how our lives would be if we had what was ours? Oh, Freedom, *will you not fight?*'

The look on his face made her want to weep. He picked up

his cloth cap, his face twisted with emotion. 'I did fight, Evie, but I lost. I wasn't good enough. I've no fight left in me now, so just let things be. I mean it, girl, I want no more of these letters – it's over, let us get on with our lives, or what life I've got left.'

Evelyne wept as he limped out. He didn't even slam the front door, but closed it gently, as if he were closing an episode in their lives. In a way, he was.

The new baby was born in the winter of 1926, the same year the film star, Rudolph Valentino, died. They called him Alex, as Evelyne had wanted. He was not as heavy as Edward had been, but he was perfect. His hair was sandy-coloured, his eyes blue. Evelyne touched a dimple that had already formed on his chin. 'Well, if it's not Hugh Jones himself.'

Edward was led to the old cradle where his new brother lay, and he peeked over the edge. Mrs Harris had warned Evelyne that, with only two years between the boys, there could be trouble. Edward might well be jealous of the 'intruder'. So it was a touching sight when the small boy, clinging to the side of the cradle, looked with adoration into the big blue eyes. Gently, he reached out and touched the baby's face, then ran out of the room, returning in moments with his arms full of toys. 'For Alex, for my bruvver.'

Edward showed not a hint of jealousy where Alex was concerned. He was very protective, and even at two and a half he insisted on taking care of his brother. He helped to bath and dress him, and watched while he was breast-fed.

Freedom went out and got work at the docks, without any encouragement from anyone. When he came back he said simply that with another mouth to feed he had to work. But there was one moment of his old glory when he handed over his British Championship to the new titleholder. He received a standing ovation at the Albert Hall, wearing his expensive clothes and looking as handsome as ever, and no one noticed the way he dragged his foot.

Somehow Ed knew he would be feeling low, so after the occasion he took Freedom to the pub and they got well and truly drunk. At long last the locals were able to talk about the American bout and Freedom opened up, describing the United States and each of his fights. He had an avid, attentive audience, and he enjoyed himself. He felt more confident, less defeated. The other dockers had nicknamed him 'Champ', and Freedom began to adjust to everyday life.

Money was short, unemployment was at a terrifying level, and the mere fact that both Ed and Freedom were working was in itself a feat. Ed was now taking work as a trainer wherever he could get it, and he asked Freedom if he would help out at the gym. Freedom refused and Ed never pushed it, knowing intuitively not to ask again, and kept quiet about what he was up to until Freedom asked him.

Ed never forgave Sir Charles, even though he was dead. He wept privately when he read of the championship match between Jack Sharkey and the German Max Schmeling. Against Freedom, Ed knew, Sharkey had punched low, and should have been disqualified. Ed read with satisfaction that he had lost the world title because of another foul. Max Schmeling won the title on a foul – the title Ed still believed should have been Freedom's.

*

Out in the back yard of number twelve, the small square that backed on to the canal, the ex-heavyweight contender held a small white rabbit aloft. He shouted for his boys to come and see what he had brought them, and they ran to his side. 'That's it, be gentle – see, you two are a lot bigger'n 'im, and we don't want him afeared of you, now do we? So, gently does it, an' he'll get to know you and not be afeared, see his little pink tongue, and his wonderful eyes? Now then, his whiskers, lads, they're like his ears, and they tell him when danger is close. They're very sensitive.'

The two brothers, so different, one as dark as his father, with black eyes, the other with a shock of sandy hair and big blue eyes, listened to every word their beloved father said. In turn, they touched the small, white bundle of fur.

Both boys were big for their ages, both had big hands, and they would take after Freedom in build. They were usually dressed in similar clothes, and there was rarely a time when they were not together. When Evelyne took them out, there was always someone who remarked how handsome they were. Edward would always answer, proudly, 'We are brothers.'

By 1931 unemployment in Britain had reached over two million. It was a time of crisis. The Labour Government was split over how to deal with the economic situation and a caucus led by J. Ramsay Macdonald joined the Conservatives and Liberals. The result of the ensuing election in October 1931 was a disaster for the Labour movement, and the most hated of all measures introduced by the First National Government was the means test. After twenty-six weeks on the dole, no money was given until the relieving officer, commonly known as the 'RO' man, had visited your house to see what could be sold. In this way many treasured possessions went in order to buy food. Pianos and wireless sets, considered luxuries, were always high on the 'hit list'.

The Stubbs family lived at number twelve, then there was Ed's brother and his big family at number sixteen, and Freda and Ed had moved into a house two doors the other way. They were always in and out of each other's houses, and even though money was scarce and there was terrible unemployment, they still felt like a family unit. Mrs Harris, living only a few streets away, was a frequent visitor. They would all gossip, moan about shortages and their menfolk, their doors always open to visitors.

Beer was cheap and it was used like aspirin. The pubs were warm, and with others in the same predicament they found companionship, but often kids, sent by mothers, would be seen trying to haul their menfolk home.

Monday mornings were days of reckoning, when the publicans counted their profits and tallied up the 'tick'. Mondays would see the wives carrying bundles to the pawnbrokers to get a few shillings, and their men's Sunday suits were constantly in and out of hock. They even took their blankets off the beds to get a few coppers in the constant battle to cover debts simply to feed their children.

You could always tell the widows, who would suddenly appear in black from head to toe, and remain in black for the rest of their lives. Sometimes, however, the fact that they had lost their loved ones changed their circumstances for the better, because of insurance. Realizing that this would more than likely

be the one time in her life when she would have an accumula-
tion of money, the widow would set herself up as a
moneylender. The interest was very small, but it still proved
profitable, and often these widows became more than merry, for
the first time in their lives better off than they had been with
their 'other halves'.

Funerals were a common sight, the black horse draped in
mauve velvet. The mortality rate was high, mostly due to pneu-
monia, and survival was down to the fittest. Somehow, God
knows how, every family was able to raise money for their dead,
as if having been so unimportant in life they had to be noticed
in death.

The Stubbs family was surviving, and better than most, partly
due to Freedom's work on the docks, but also due to Evelyne's
frugal household economy. She bought well, and wasted nothing; she counted every penny, and would traipse miles to a
market-stall butcher with fresh cheap meat rather than buy in
the shops. She always went to market late on Friday nights,
when the stall-holders flogged off their wares cheaply. There
were no fridges or iceboxes, so food had to be kept cooled in
larders or meat-safes outside in the yard.

Evelyne sewed, making most of the boys' clothes, cutting
down Freedom's trousers, knitting, her watchful eye on the
purse strings, and she wasted nothing. Twice a week she would
go to two bakeries to do their accounts, for which she was paid
one pound fifteen shillings. She never used this money, but put
it in her post office savings account. Freedom had never so
much as seen her treasured, small, folded book, he didn't even
know of its existence. She was obsessive about it, forever

totalling the figures. She had saved more than one hundred and twenty-five pounds over the years, which was a lot of money, but she wouldn't touch it. She would use it for her sons' education when the time came, although she kept a small float and had become the 'widow' in her street. She lent out a shilling here, half-a-crown there, and would make neat notes on exactly how long her customers took to repay the small loans, with interest. She had begun with five pounds, and after four years she still had her original stake, all the money she had earned having gone straight into the post office.

Of course, Evelyne was lucky to have Freedom. If anyone was late in paying it took only one visit from him for the money to be handed over. Freedom hated it and would do anything to get out of having to pay these visits, but Evelyne would fold her arms and ask him if he thought they were a charity, they needed the money as much as anyone else did, and as he was the man of the house he had to pull his weight. He would look at her as she stood there, tall as ever and neat as a new pin, her hair coiled in a tight bun, and shrug his shoulders. He often wondered who really was the man of the house, she was a right devil with her temper.

The whole street respected Mrs Stubbs. Nothing defeated her, nothing got on top of her, and everyone had to admit she kept her house spotless and her two boys immaculate. She was not a great mixer, although she would have the odd schooner of sweet sherry at the pub, but she never stayed long and didn't like to gossip. They all knew she had some stories to tell, about her time in America, about her husband when he was boxing champion, but she rarely if ever spoke of these times. Freda, on the other hand, regaled everyone with stories of when they had travelled on the boat across the Atlantic, and of Miami. Freda was very popular and would feed back all the gossip to Evelyne whenever she called round for a cup of tea. She soon learned that Evelyne didn't want to discuss the past or even remember.

Freda always recognized the signs in Evelyne. Her face would tighten up, her mouth clamp shut whenever Freda tried to talk of the past, of the days in America. Freedom's agonizing headaches were a strong enough reminder. Evelyne would make a vinegar and brown paper compress to put on his brow, and he would lie in a darkened room for hours. Freda eventually gave up mentioning America, she kept her stories for the snug bar at the local pub.

Freda had seen change slowly creep up on Evelyne. She was still handsome, but her face had thinned, the prominent cheek-bones making her look gaunt, though not haggard. They ate too well for that. It was just a strange hardening. She was obsessively clean and neat, her kitchen spotless. Her small row of leather-bound books was dusted and treasured. Hers was still the only house in the street with carpet, still the only house with good furniture and a bed that had been brand-new when they first arrived. Evelyne Stubbs was certainly very houseproud.

No matter how Evelyne had tried to make everyone use Edward's full name, he was always known as Eddie. He had a thick cockney accent and was a handful for anyone, always up to something, and she had discovered that smacking him had no effect at all. The only way she could control him was by showing more affection towards Alex, his younger brother. That always brought him to attention. Eddie adored his little brother, so long as he remained just that. Any sign that Alex was considered more special would result in moody tantrums. Alex, on the other hand, was easy-going, always cheerful, and did whatever his brother told him to do. Seeing them go off to school, hand-in-hand, wearing their matching grey sweaters and shorts, made Evelyne feel that all the hard work was worthwhile. They were different from the rest of their school-fellows.

Their tea was ready on the table, and Evelyne stood on the front step, waiting for them. They were more than half an hour late so she wrapped her shawl around her and went down the road to search for them. As she turned the corner near the patch of waste ground, she saw a tight group of boys cheering and shouting. Eddie, his fists flying, was on top of another boy, holding him by the hair and banging his head on the ground. Evelyne rolled up her sleeves and dragged him off, boxed his ears and picked the howling child up from the ground. The other children ran like hell, leaving Eddie and Alex with their mother, and the weeping boy still in Evelyne's tight grip.

'What's all this about then? Come on, I want to know ... Fighting in the street like common nothings— what's it all about?'

Alex shuffled and looked away, and the little boy with the bloody nose wriggled out of Evelyne's grasp and ran off. Eddie yelled after him, his fist in the air, and turned defiantly to his mother. 'The little bastard hit me and me.' He pointed first to his brother and then to himself, referring to Alex as 'me', as if they were one.

'Why did he hit you? Come on then, why?'

Eddie picked up his school books and glared at his brother to keep quiet, but Evelyne was adamant.

'I want to know what it was about. I'll be down at the school first thing tomorrow morning if you don't speak up.'

Alex burst into tears, and stuttered out that Johnny Rigg had called them 'gyppos'.

Mrs Rigg couldn't believe her eyes when she opened her front door. There was Mrs Stubbs, arms folded, and with such a furious look on her face that Mrs Rigg was scared stiff.

'I want a word with you and your son, and I want it now.'

Eddie and Alex flushed with embarrassment as Mrs Rigg made her son apologize to the Stubbs family. When the door shut behind them she belted the boy, which caused her husband, who was just arriving home, to ask what the hell was going on. Poor Johnny got another thrashing from his father, as the last thing any of them wanted was that bloody gyppo coming round. The Stubbs boys' father was a champion boxer, and the family lived in fear of repercussions for weeks afterwards. But Freedom's reaction was a roar of laughter, and he pointed his fork at Alex and told him that after tea he would take him out in the yard and teach him a few punches.

Evelyne banged on the table. 'There will be *no more fighting!*'

Behind her back, Freedom winked at his sons, knowing she would soon be going off to do her accounting at the bakeries. So that night, in the small yard with the rabbits and the two hens, Freedom made Alex put up his fists. Eddie sat on the wall and watched, then it was his turn. They often had these secret lessons, Freedom sparring with his boys, jabbing short punches at their heads. His light taps hurt like hell, but Eddie loved it, and was showing signs of becoming a fighter like his Dad.

They were all sweating when they went back in, and Freedom saw the fire had gone out so he ordered Eddie to bring in the coal to stoke it up. 'She'll be after me, lads, if she knows what we been doin', so let's keep it our secret. When she's out at her work, we'll have our boxing nights.'

The boys were sleeping when Evelyne came home to find Freedom sitting by the blazing fire, staring into space.

'You stoked up the fire, I see. Do you think we have money to burn?'

He sighed and looked at her, held out his hand for her to sit on his knee, but she was too busy checking a pile of socks and stockings, putting aside the ones that needed darning. 'I'll go up to the school in the morning. I want a word with the teacher anyway — are you coming to bed?'

He shook his head, and again stared vacantly into the fire.

'Your head all right, is it?'

He got up and slammed out of the kitchen, shouting that his head was just fine. He loved his boys, of course he did, but she seemed to think of nobody else but them. It was as if he was a lodger in his own house. Her penny-pinching and her constant scrubbing and cleaning got on his nerves.

He walked along the canal towpath and sat on an old crate, tossing pebbles into the murky water. The alley cats screeched, and in the distance he could hear voices laughing, floating out of the pubs. They didn't seem to laugh all that much nowadays, it was all work, but he supposed he should thank God that he was still getting it. His strength usually made him one of the first to be called. Even with his bad leg he could do the work of two men, and the management at the docks knew it.

Evelyne was tired, her eyes aching from the darning. She rubbed them, looked at the clock on the mantle. Freedom had still not returned. She stood up to prod the fire with the poker and became aware of Alex. He was hovering by the kitchen door, his teeth chattering with the cold. 'Mum, I can't sleep, Dad not come back yet?'

Evelyne shook her head, then gestured for Alex to come into the kitchen. She smiled at his hair, which was ruffled and standing on end. 'You look as though you could do with the basin round your head – I'll have a go at it tomorrow. It's all right, you can sit with me a while. Let me rub those feet, they look blue.'

'Where's me Dad gone? I heard him go out.'

'Not *me* lovey, *my* . . . he'll have gone walking – now don't you worry about him. Do you want a biscuit? Well, shush, you know what that brother of yours is like, he can hear the biscuit tin opening a mile away.'

Alex sat beside her and nibbled one of her homemade biscuits. She stared into the fire, gently stroking his thick, blond curls. She was almost surprised when he spoke, she was so immersed in her own thoughts. His voice was soft, 'Will you read to me, Ma? Not my school work, one of your books.'

'My books, are they? Now, you know everything here is ours, just that you're not quite old enough yet and they're well . . . they're special. That is real leather they're bound in, did you know that?'

She watched him as he solemnly chose one from the row of books and brought it back to her. She laughed softly, 'Well, well, it's my favourite writer you've picked out. Her name was Christina Georgina Rossetti, now there's a name for you.'

Alex opened the book, traced the inscription with his finger. '"To Evie, from Doris . . . " Who's that, Mum? Is she related to us?'

'No, lovey, she's no relation, but she was a very special friend to me. A long, long time ago now.' She told Alex about Doris, about the valley, and he listened without saying a word. His mother looked so beautiful, caught in the firelight, he was almost afraid to move.

'Oh, Alex, she opened up a world to me, a world that was out of my reach. And, for a while, just a short while, I almost . . .'

Alex hung on her every word. She looked down at his upturned face and cupped his chin in her big, worn hands. 'You know, sweetheart, there's a world open to you if you want it. It's all there, but you have to work hard, because you'll only be able to find it if you get qualifications.'

'Eddie's clever, Ma. He's always top.'

'So you're clever too, it takes all sorts. You're not Edward, you're Alex, and you're top in some subjects, too.'

He smiled and nodded, then laughed softly. 'Tell you one thing he's not, Ma – tidy! Never puts a thing back in its place.'

'Well, he's like his father. The pair of them think I'm just here to pick up after them. Now, my lad, you should be in bed.'

Alex hugged her, whispering in her ear, 'Can I come and sit with you another night, just you and me?'

Kissing him, she whispered back, as if they were playing a game, 'I'd like that, and maybe, no promises, I'll read my books to you. Would you like that?'

Beaming, Alex went off to bed like a lamb. Evelyne yawned and stretched her arms. The book fell to the floor, and she picked it up, looked again at the flyleaf.

Lovingly, she replaced it and drew her hand along the row of books, taking down a thick volume of Ibsen. It opened naturally in the middle, and there between the pages were sheets of her own handwriting. Leaves from a child's drawing book. The colouring book she had bought for Edward in America. Slowly, she read her own work, placing each page on the fire as she finished it, letting the flames eat her memories. Tears trickled down her cheeks, and she sighed. What would Doris think if she saw her now?

Freedom sighed, pulled his coat collar up, and wondered how he had come to this. He felt tied, bound to that spotless house. He had almost forgotten his old life – not the boxing times, but before that – the caravans, the wagons. He decided it was time to show his sons where their roots were, and the more he thought about it the happier he felt. Come Saturday he would take them on a trip, no matter what Evelyne said, they could spare a few shillings. He walked on along the towpath and decided he would take them on a trip to Brighton, to the sea.

The schoolteacher, Miss Thomas, was relieved to see Mrs Stubbs. She had been hoping for a word with her but didn't like the thought of going down their street. The Stubbs family lived in one of the toughest districts, and she was not sure how they would react to her paying a house call.

They sat in the headmaster's office and Miss Thomas poured tea. She couldn't help but notice how clean and well turned out Mrs Stubbs looked. At one time she must have been a beauty. 'I'm glad you came in, Mrs Stubbs, I've been wanting to talk to you.' She paused briefly, then went on, 'Edward is far in advance of the other children in his class, Mrs Stubbs. I would like to put him into the class above. It will mean he's with boys two years older and he may find it difficult to adapt so I wanted to talk to you first.'

The pleasure in Mrs Stubbs' face when she smiled softened her whole appearance. Miss Thomas warmed to her, and continued, 'I think Edward is clever enough to win a scholarship to a good grammar school. I have a couple of schools in mind, but there could be a slight financial problem. The best schools require the uniform to be bought by the student's family, and it would mean Edward would have to take the bus every day.'

Interrupting her, Evelyne assured her very firmly that there would be no financial problems. Her son's education was of the highest importance and if he gained a scholarship he would have his uniform.

'There is another reason, Mrs Stubbs. I think it would be beneficial for Alex. He is dominated by his older brother, and I think he would find his own personality if they were split up into different schools. They are unusually close, Edward is very protective.'

This observation met with a stiff reply. They were brothers and that was just how it should be.

Evelyne dropped in on Freda to tell her the news. Freda hadn't seen her so happy in a long time.

'He'll be the first lad from these parts ever to get a scholarship to that grammar school, and I know he'll do it, I just know it.'

Freda had been suffering with rheumatism, and had gained a lot of weight. Evelyne noted her frizzy hair, with the assistance of henna powder, was a rather strange orange colour, but even without the grey she was beginning to look her age. She gave

Evelyne two jumpers she had knitted for the boys, identical as always, and Evelyne paid her for her work. Freda would have liked to have given them, but times were hard and Ed was making nothing at the gymnasium. They were mostly charitable institutes and his earnings were a mere gesture.

'Your boys never go to the gyms, Evie, and Ed'd love to see them there. Why don't you let them go, just to see what a boxing ring's like?'

Evelyne jumped up, that tight, pursed look on her face, and put her coat on. 'My sons are not going into any boxing ring, Freda, and that's final.'

Freedom fetched the tin bath and began to boil water for the boys' bath. He whistled, and Evelyne looked up from rolling the pastry. 'It's not Saturday, love, you've got the days muddled.'

He came up behind her, gave her a hug, and said they were having a bath early, because on Saturday they were going on a trip.

'Oh, we are, are we? And where's this trip to, then?'

Freedom tapped his nose and concentrated on the stove. He was in a good mood for a change so she continued with the pastry.

'An' I want you all decked out tomorrow an' all, we're all goin' and I won't have a word against it.'

She trimmed the edges of the pastry and when he slipped his arms round her waist she gave him a quick peck on the cheek.

'I've got some good news. It seems our Eddie's doing well at school.'

Freedom seemed not to hear, but continued pottering around the kitchen.

'He could get into the posh grammar school, his teacher told me. What do you think of that?'

Freedom shook his head and asked where on earth they would get the money to send him to one of the posh schools.

'If he wins the scholarship, they pay for everything.'

Bath time was always fun for the boys, sitting in the tin tub in front of the roaring fire. Evelyne would scrub them both with a pumice stone and a big bar of carbolic soap. She scrubbed until their bodies were bright red, then rubbed them dry with a big towel. When they were dry they ate their tea in the cosy, warm kitchen.

'Your Dad's got a surprise for you both – we're going on an outing tomorrow, all of us.'

They looked up in glee, and when she told them they would be going on a train to the seaside, they were so excited that neither of them could sleep.

Sandwiches were made, lemonade bottles filled, and the family rode into the West End on a tram. The boys had never been out of the East End, and they sat spellbound by the sights and the traffic. On the train, they ran from window to window in their excitement. Freedom sat holding Evelyne's hand, tickled that he had arranged it all and as excited as the boys. Evelyne talked of the old times, of how she had been shopping in Swan and Edgar, how they had found each other again, and they behaved like young lovers.

As the train pulled into Brighton Station, the boys let out such screams of delight that some of the other passengers frowned, but nothing could dampen their spirits. When he saw the beach, Edward ran like a wild pony towards the water and he had both feet in the sea before Freedom could haul him away.

Alex, riding on his father's shoulders, pointed hysterically at a big Ferris wheel and the lights of the fairground, the music drifting across the beach towards them. Up ahead, Edward climbed over a small wall and disappeared among the rides as Freedom shouted to him to wait.

The two sticky-faced boys wandered around with their candy-floss, open-mouthed with amazement. They went from booth to booth, and Freedom won a teddy bear on a shooting range, which Alex cuddled. They stopped at a punching machine.

'Punch the bell, mate, punch the bell and win a prize, come along now, punch the bell . . . lovely prizes, take your pick, all you gotta do is ring the bell . . .'

Freedom stepped back and punched, the bell clanged and the man almost fell over. He'd not had anyone ring the bell in ten years and he reluctantly offered a prize. Edward jumped up and down as Freedom led him towards the display, and he pointed to a tin of soap bubbles with a small wire hoop. The fairground man handed the boy the prize and nudged Freedom, saying with a wink that he would bet a shilling that he couldn't do it again.

Evelyne pulled at Freedom's arm, she wanted to move on, there was a small crowd gathering.

'Go on, Dad, do it again!'

Freedom looked at the man and asked if he was serious about the shilling, then rolled up his sleeves and belted the punchbag. The bell clanged again, drawing a ripple of applause from the crowd, and Freedom turned and gave them a mock bow.

Evelyne went to choose a prize and after surveying the array of cheap gifts, she pointed to a doll. She would give it to Mrs Harris' little girl.

'You not lost your touch, mun.'

Freedom turned, and there, lolling against the side of a booth, was Jesse. He wore a flashy suit and a red polka-dot neckerchief. His long, dark eyelashes were as thick as ever. He still wore his earring, but now he had a big gold watch and heavy gold rings on his fingers.

The pair sized each other up, and slowly they moved closer. '*Auv acoi.*'

Jesse held out his arms. 'It's *buddigur duvus*, a good time for us, but you *jinned* we'd be here, mun, more likely in the fairground than furniture sellin'.'

Jesse felt the muscles of Freedom's arms, their eyes locked. Then they kissed each other's cheeks. Freedom held Jesse's head in his hands and kissed his lips. Evelyne felt chilled, and drew her shawl closer around her shoulders.

'Eh, boys, come and meet Uncle Jesse, say hello to your Uncle Jesse.'

Evelyne stared, wanting to call the boys to her side, but she said nothing. The two of them hung back slightly, but then Jesse reached forward and took a coin from behind Edward's ear, and the child gasped. Jesse kept finding coins all over Edward and the boy was completely hooked. Alex, who had drawn back to cling to his mother's skirt, moved forward.

'Well, now, lemme see if this young 'un's got the magic ... Ohhh, yes, will you look at this, the money's just falling from him. Come and see this boy, he's got the Midas touch.'

Evelyne smiled but remained aloof and watchful as Jesse

patted the punching-machine man's shoulder and told him Freedom was a boxing champion so no need to worry, his machine wasn't out of kilter.

'Will you come to the wagon?'

Evelyne opened her mouth to say no, but Freedom was already following Jesse. The boys hung on every word Jesse said, looking up into his face with adoring eyes.

'You like my fair, then, do ye? Well, there's a fine thing, I'm doin' all right, mun, am I not? Come on, come on.'

He strode among the booths, waving and smiling to everyone, and they made their way to the far end of the fairground. On a large square of wasteland was a line of caravans. He went to the door of the first one and opened it, calling to someone inside that he had a surprise. He lifted first Edward and then Alex up into the wagon. As they went inside, Evelyne caught hold of Freedom's sleeve.

'We should be going, the train leaves in half an hour.'

Freedom shrugged and said they would catch the later one, and gestured for her to go inside. It took Evelyne by surprise. A lot had changed with the years, and it was like a real house inside. The walls were draped, the place was filled with ornaments, and there were two parrots in a cage.

'Rawnie? Rawnie, come on out and see what I've found.'

The curtains at the far end of the caravan were drawn aside, and Rawnie, like a ghost from the past, stood staring at them all. Evelyne was shocked at her appearance, she was so thin her skin hung loose on her bones. Her thick hair was greying at the temples and, although she still wore it in two long braids, there was nothing youthful about her; she had to hold on to the sides of the wagon to move towards them.

'Freedom, mun, *auv acoi, acoi acoi*, it's been *bershor*.'

He held his arms out to her and she went to him, touching his face. She kissed him and then held her hand out to Edward.

'Well, *chavo chiv*, ishenot *rinkeney*, then, will you gimme a *choom*?'

Edward went straight to her and kissed her as if he understood every word she'd said. She held his face and looked into his eyes, then laughed, giving Freedom a look. She held on to the table and eased herself into a chair, tapped her knee and held out a hand to Alex.

'Eh, eh, eh, they're real *tatchey* Romany, and dressed like a *rye*.'

Alex was more wary of her, but in the end he sat on her knee and played with all the gold bangles along her thin arms. The two men spoke Romany together, sitting on a velvet settee with their arms around each other. Rawnie stared at Evelyne, nodding for her to sit down. 'The eldest has Romany *yocks*, looks like his Da – big 'n' strong, the pair of them. Yer little 'un's gentle, and yer got one wild, ain't that right?' She began to cough, and her whole body shook so that Alex had to get off her knee. Evelyne moved closer, put her hand on Rawnie's shoulder and could feel the sharp shoulder blades heaving beneath her clothes as she tried to catch her breath. Jesse stood up and clapped his beringed hands together, said he would take his brother around the fair, they'd be back shortly. The two boys ran to Jesse, and after a moment he gave way and they were allowed to go with the men. Evelyne tried to catch Freedom's eye to tell him they must leave, but he was out of the caravan too quickly.

Rawnie rolled herself a cigarette, a *tuv*, and began to smoke, then pulled herself up and put the kettle on, showing Evelyne the gas taps which were linked to a cylinder outside. She said that, like Freedom, they were almost *kairengos* now, the caravan staying at the fair all year round.

'Your eldest, he has the *dukkerin* look. He could read well, I can feel it, and you, me love, you look well-fed.'

While Evelyne sipped the thick, spicy, hot tea, Rawnie was twice seized by such spasms of coughing that it frightened her. Someone tapped on the caravan door and two little girls peeped in, but Rawnie shooed them outside.

'They're Jesse's babes from Martilda, she lives yonder. He's got a fine boy up in Scotland and one down in Cornwall, both fine boys.'

Evelyne didn't wish to appear shocked, and Rawnie's obvious acceptance of Jesse's other women made it seem almost natural.

As Evelyne finished her tea, Rawnie reached over for the cup and stared into the tea leaves. She put the cup down and sighed, she frightened Evelyne. 'What did you see? Rawnie . . . ? What is it?'

Rawnie would not meet her eyes, she sucked in her hollow cheeks.

'Remember all those years ago, that terrible night at the fair, you saw something in my hand then, is it the same?'

Rawnie kept her head bowed. 'Do I remember that night? Now there's a question, do you think I would forget? 'Tis not something you forget, bein' defiled, torn inside. Don't heal like a cut on the outside.'

'I'm sorry, that was thoughtless, but will you tell me? You see,

I always remember your words – you said "Beware of the birds in the sky", but I don't understand . . .'

Rawnie coughed again, her body shaking, her bangles tinkling and jangling. 'Ye'll know when they come, I can't say when, but they're big, big birds.'

Rawnie did not finish telling Evelyne what she could see, could not tell her that when the birds flew over Evelyne's head they would take everything from her, all that she loved. Evelyne would have persisted, but the caravan door was flung open by Edward. He demanded that Evelyne come with him, the fair was closing and they were going to have chicken cooked over a real fire.

All the men from the fairground had gathered around the wagons and a fire had been built in the centre. Behind them the Ferris wheel was still lit up, but the organ that piped out the music was silent. A fiddler was sitting on a beer crate, tuning up.

'Well, gel, it's a night to celebrate, is it not, we're all brothers here, and we're going to put on some entertainment for you.'

Evelyne could see Edward and Alex, their shoes and socks discarded, running like wild things round and round the caravan. The fiddler started playing and the girls began to dance and sing.

Rawnie sat at her caravan door, tapping her foot and clapping to the music. Evelyne sat with a group of women who were peeling potatoes for a big pot of stew. She knew the last train would have gone by now. There was nothing she could do or say – Freedom was standing drinking with a group of his brothers and had no intention of leaving.

Evelyne wished the night would end. They had eaten, and

the men were getting drunker and drunker. The girls still danced and the fiddler still played, and the fire had been constantly fed so that it still blazed. The two boys were curled up beside three other children on a large straw mattress dragged from one of the wagons, their arms wrapped around each other in exhausted sleep. Rawnie beckoned Evelyne to her caravan and pointed to a bed she had made up. Evelyne was as tired as her sons so she didn't refuse.

'He looks happy, a happy mun, will you see?'

Evelyne looked out of the door. Freedom was the centre of attention. Someone had given him a bandanna, which he had tied around his head, and he was roaring with laughter. He was well drunk, and they were trying to pull him to the fireside to dance. He made excuses about his bad leg, but they would not hear and he gave in to the young girls that pulled him. The fiddler began anew tune and they all watched as Freedom stood, straight backed, heels together, slowly lifting his hands above his head. He began to clap, short, sharp slaps, then clicked his heels, and there was no sign of his limp. The alcohol and the atmosphere made him unaware of the pain in his leg, and he danced to his heart's content, soon joined by three other men.

At one point Jesse looked over to where Evelyne sat with Rawnie and gave her a cold stare. She was an outsider tonight, not her children nor her husband, but she was and she knew it. She got up and went to lie on the bed. The heavy, oily perfume that Freedom had always worn swamped her, but this time it was Rawnie's perfume, it was oil from her hair on the pillows.

Evelyne fell into a deep sleep, and when she woke it was fully dark, the blackness lit only by a warm, glowing light from the fire. No candles, no blinking lights from the fairground, nothing but the fire.

The voice was beautiful, clear, singing such a sweet, sad song, and she lay back on the pillows and listened. There was no fiddle this time, but a guitar being played well.

> *Can you* rokka *Romany,*
> *Can you play the* bosh*,*
> *Can you* jal adrey the staripen
> *Can you* chin the cosh . . .

The singing lulled her, the voice deep and soft. She felt the caravan rock slightly as Rawnie moved, and she opened her eyes.

Rawnie gestured for Evelyne to come to the door, and she crept forward. She wanted to weep – the singer was Freedom, and he was playing the guitar. She had never heard him sing like this, had not known he could play. 'Oh, Rawnie, sometimes he is like a stranger. I've never seen him play, heard him sing . . . he does it so well.'

Rawnie patted the step for Evelyne to sit beside her. She too was moved by Freedom. That wondrous face, singing with his eyes closed, his whole body seeming to shimmer in the firelight. All the people around him were hushed. His voice rose and fell, emotional but clear, with such ease that it reached their souls.

'I loved that mun, but you know, I loved him so.'

Evelyne was touched by the dying woman, and she slipped her arm around the wasted shoulders. She did know, perhaps she always had. 'He loved you too, Rawnie, he would have hanged for you.'

Rawnie's gnarled hand reached out, gripped Evelyne's chin, and she looked into her face. 'So would every mun around the fire. It were not love fer me, gel, but honour. Gringos don't understand, cannot understand our ways, our love of the stars, the air, the land . . . But we can hate, and we believe in revenge, an eye for an eye, a tooth for a tooth. This is our way, our law.'

Evelyne bit her lip. Rawnie knew revenge, hadn't she slit every one of those boys' throats? Or had it been Jesse? As if Rawnie had read her mind, she gave a chuckle. 'It were me, gel, me used the knife. Now I'll tell yer what yer man is singing.'

She whispered the meaning of the song to Evelyne. Freedom was asking if they understood the Romany tongue, asking if they could hold their own in a *laychingarpen*, an argument or a fight; he was asking if they could play the fiddle, if they were men enough to fight the music, to hear a prison sentence and do their bit without flinching: last of all the song was asking if they were qualified to earn their living as gypsies. If they could not in one way or another *chin the cosh*, they would never be successful on the road.

Evelyne clung to Rawnie. Now she could see her boys, the two little brothers, standing naked by the fire, hand in hand, looking at their father, their eyes fixed as though hypnotized by him. An elder knelt down beside them, and she saw the knife. Rawnie gripped her tightly so she could not move. The sick woman had more strength than Evelyne had given her credit for.

'Let him make their blood our blood, their father's blood, it is right, they are Romany.'

Neither child made a murmur as his thumb was cut, and the blood kissed by their father. Then they were wrapped in blankets and taken back to sleep on the mattress. Evelyne now knew that Freedom had planned this – not necessarily with Jesse and Rawnie – but she remembered that bank holidays were their big days for fairs right across England. He had known all along that some of his people would be at Brighton – his brothers as he called them. She returned to Rawnie's bed.

When the morning came, Rawnie gave each child a golden sovereign. They kissed her, eager to get on to the train, not to get away, but just because it was a train. Their night's initiation had had no obvious after-effects, and Freedom was preparing to leave. 'I'll come again to you, sister, we won't be parted as long again.'

Rawnie touched his face, tracing it with her fingers; it was still handsome, even with his battle scars. She traced his lips, and then stood at her caravan door to wave their farewell. Rawnie knew she would never see him again, she would be dead within months.

'Well, gel, it looks like our brother's come back into the fold, eh?'

Rawnie smiled. Jesse had never had the powers, he couldn't read what was in the air. The woman still had Freedom, and she was stronger than they were.

The train journey home was as exciting for the brothers as the one to Brighton, and they wanted to go back again as soon as they got to London.

'We're going home, and you've got to go to school tomorrow.'

Eddie started sulking, and had to be dragged along to the

tram stop. He wanted to go back to the fair, he didn't want to go to school. Evelyne slapped him hard, pushed him ahead of her up the tram stairs.

'You'll go to school, my lad, and what's more you'll get that scholarship or you'll end up on a fairground with no education and no place else to go. Now get up these stairs this instant.'

Evelyne received a mask-like glare from Edward, and he stomped up the stairs to the top deck. Alex, close behind him, slipped his hand into his brother's, and they went to the very front seats.

Evelyne and Freedom sat at the back, looking at the busy traffic below as they headed across London. Evelyne took out the doll for Mrs Harris' youngest, and checked that she had all their things. She looked up sharply when she heard two small voices singing from the front seats,

> *Can you* rokka *Romany,*
> *Can you play the* bosh*,*
> *Can you* jal adrey the staripen
> *Can you* chin the cosh . . .

Freedom smiled and nodded to his sons, slipped an arm around her shoulders.

'Well, gel, looks like we gotta pair of gyppos up front.'

Chapter 27

Edward Stubbs was awarded a scholarship to a grammar school, the first boy ever from his area. For one son to gain a scholarship was a cause for celebration, but for a second son also to pass gave rise to suspicion and jealousy, and set both boys apart from the children of the neighbourhood.

In their identical uniforms the boys travelled to school together, always together. Already closer than most brothers, they grew even more so. Eddie and Alex were both tall for their ages, well-built and athletic, excelling at all sports. In the classroom, however, although Alex was bright, he fell short of his brother's academic brilliance. Edward was the dominant one, and Alex accepted life in his brother's shadow without jealousy. Edward was his hero.

Unemployment was as high as ever. Dole queues were long and money short, and for the workers and their families times were hard in the reign of King George.

Proud of her boys, Evelyne Stubbs worked constantly, and kept her head above water while all around her others sank. Freedom worked at the docks most weeks, and when he was laid off he busied himself making rabbit hutches in the back yard and selling them.

Occasionally he would disappear for a few days to visit his friends, and those were the times Evelyne dreaded. He would return surly and bad-tempered, and found it difficult to get back into the day-to-day routine.

Rawnie had died of consumption, and Jesse had lost his fairground through gambling. He was serving a sentence for robbery in Durham gaol.

Miss Freda and Ed were in financial trouble and had taken in more lodgers. They now had a married couple and two single girls. The girls, it was suspected, were 'on the game', but Freda wouldn't hear of it. To her they were simply youngsters trying to make their way.

Ed's brother's family were even worse off, and although their kids were working they still lived on the breadline, always in debt. They invariably owed money to Evelyne, whose money lending business was growing. Freedom collected the debts for her, and the boys helped him at weekends. The Stubbs family was secure, and the brothers went from strength to strength with their school work.

Evelyne later tried to pinpoint the turn of events, to recall exactly why things went wrong. She had to try to blame someone, but she knew in her heart that the trouble was within her own home.

Freedom was the perfect father when the boys were small, attentive and fair, and they obeyed him. But he couldn't make head or tail of their homework, he was so far removed from them academically that his frustration turned to anger, and they in turn realized that their father – the man they had always

looked up to – was illiterate. They were too young to be understanding about it, to help him, and they turned against him and
looked increasingly to their mother for guidance. The resulting
bitter arguments usually ended with Freedom storming out to
the pub.

Evelyne had cleared the table, tidied away the boys' books, and
was about to start on the weekly wash when there was a hard rap-
ping on the door. A policeman informed Evelyne that Freedom
had been arrested for brawling outside the docks. He had
knocked out the manager who was pressing charges for assault.

Ed and Evelyne hurried to the police station and found
Freedom sitting gloomily in a cell. The fight had started because
Freedom, who always expected to be given work, had been
rejected for three days running. He had not told Evelyne, pre-
tending he had been taken on. But on the fourth day he *had*
been offered work, and that was the cause of it. One man who
was turned away muttered something in Freedom's hearing
about black bastards getting work before whites, and when the
manager had tried to break up the fight Freedom had knocked
him senseless.

At the hearing the magistrate reprimanded Freedom
severely – a man with a history of professional boxing should
never resort to fighting in the streets. Freedom was given a
three-month suspended sentence. Evelyne never said anything,
but her reproachful looks and above all her silence tormented
him. If he had felt inadequate before, now things were far
worse. Evelyne had arranged for a lawyer and paid him, and the
more Freedom thought about it the more frustration he felt.

*

The appearance of Jesse on their doorstep was the kiss of doom. Recently released from prison, he was as cocksure as ever, with rings on his fingers and gold chains around his neck. He offered Freedom the chance to go into business with him, buying and selling furniture. Evelyne tried to persuade Freedom to have nothing to do with him. They were sitting at the kitchen table where the two boys were doing their homework. Evelyne tried to keep her voice calm, not wanting to get into an argument in front of them. 'He's no good, Freedom, he never was. You and I know just how far he will go. Don't go with him, please, you can do my debt-collecting full-time, we could do it together.'

Freedom banged his fist on the table and Edward's inkwell tipped over, spilling its contents on his exercise books. The boys scrabbled to pick them up and mop them, fussing around.

Freedom couldn't take it any more and he roared, 'Will you get out from under ma feet, mun, take yer readin' out of here, better still, go get work like the other lads around here.'

Edward stood up to his father, just as hot-tempered, but cocky and self-assured. He gathered his schoolbooks up and hurled them across the room. 'Right, I'll go out now and join the dole queue, just like you and every other sucker round 'ere. You call that work, do yer?'

Freedom struck him so hard that he sprawled on the floor. Alex sprang between them, trying to protect Edward. 'Dad, no, don't, don't hit 'im no more.'

Freedom lashed out at Alex in fury, trying to grab Edward, and now Evelyne pushed between her sons and Freedom. With her arms out she faced her husband.

'You'll have to hit me first, Freedom, I mean it. Just stop this nonsense right now or so help me God I'll take the rolling pin to you, I will.'

Freedom backed away. The three of them were against him, and he knew then that Evelyne would choose her sons before him. She was like a lioness with her cubs, glaring at him so fiercely ... He turned and beat his fist against the fireplace.

Evelyne shooed the boys from the room, but Edward held on to her. She shook her hand free. 'Get out, the pair of you, leave us alone. Go on, nothing's going to happen.'

They slunk out and closed the door behind them. Freedom gave her such a helpless look, filled with guilt and remorse. It was the first time he had ever struck his sons, and his voice sounded choked in his throat. 'I'd never have struck thee, Evie, God help me, never.'

She held him in her arms and comforted him, whispering over and over that she knew, she knew it. She felt remorseful herself, it was becoming obvious that she put the boys before Freedom. 'I'm sorry too, Freedom. I should never have gone against you. Sometimes Eddie needs a firm hand. Will you forgive me?'

They kissed, it had been a long time since they kissed as lovers, and she sat on his knee by the fire. 'What is it, my love, what's hurting you so?'

He buried his face in her chest, and she stroked his hair.

'It's the debt-collecting, Evie. It's hard for me to face them that owes you, going to them with me hand out for their shillin's. Some of 'em have nothin', and to stand there frightening the life out of them, wantin' money paid over, knowing they've not got it to give – it's no job for a mun, I can't do it no more.'

Evelyne forced herself to keep her mouth shut, although she could have asked how he thought she felt. How did he think they could have lived so well for so long without her money-lending business?

'Just don't do anything against the law, the boys are doing so well and I don't want people talking.'

That did it. He pushed her away from him and grabbed his coat.

'Always the boys, always them, when do you ever think of *me*? When it's *too late!*'

He slammed out of the kitchen.

Eddie came downstairs and slipped his arms around his mother, kissed her and patted her head. 'Maybe he's right, Ma, I'm fourteen, I could get work.'

She grabbed him and held him, shook him roughly. He was shocked by her tone, her expression. 'You think I *like* collecting money I lend out? Do you? Why do you think I'm doing it, working myself into an early grave, why?'

Edward backed away from her, and Alex came to stand at his side, as their mother marched around the kitchen, rolling up her sleeves as if she was ready for a fight.

'Both of you are going places, getting out of this slum, and you won't do it like your father, with your fists. You'll do it with your brains. So help me God I'll go out on the streets if need be, to make sure you both stay at school, now is that clear, clear to both of you?'

They nodded solemnly.

'Right now, get your work and I'll fix us tea.'

Alex ran into the hallway, but as Edward turned to follow him he felt his hair tugged, and Evelyne kicked the door closed. She hit him so hard on his right ear that his head spun.

'If I ever hear you talk to your Dad in that tone of voice again I'll beat the living daylights out of you. Now hop it.'

Freedom was gone for more than two weeks, longer than he had ever stayed away from home before. At the weekend the brothers went around collecting the debts, and a couple of times they had to get tough in order to be paid. When they returned, they got out the books and began to tally up as Evelyne was out shopping. Edward fiddled the figures and pocketed sixpence, and Alex saw him do it. He wouldn't eat the toffee bar Edward offered him later.

Evelyne went to Ed's brother's house. There was a showdown on the cards as they owed her two pounds fifteen shillings, which was long overdue. There was no way around it – she couldn't run her home and support the Meadows family. But the rent-collector had got there before her, and two bailiffs waited outside with a cart. The Meadows owed six months' back rent at eighteen shillings a week.

'We're on the street, nothing we can do.'

Evelyne didn't like the way the rent-collector shouldered her aside. The bailiffs hammered on the door and shouted that the Meadows had better pay up or get out, otherwise they would break the door down. They couldn't wait all day, they had another call to make.

Again Evelyne was thrust aside and the two bailiff's men forced their way into the house. She barred their entrance. 'Out, the pair of you, there's no one moving a stick of furniture from here. Bugger off, or I'll get my boys ...'

They hesitated, looking for guidance from the rent-collector. Evelyne siezed her chance. 'Now, it's Mr Simms, isn't it?'

Mr Simms, the most hated man in the district, pursed his chalk-white lips and adjusted his bowler. 'Yes it is, and I know who you are – Mrs Stubbs from number twelve. Now I've never had any trouble from you, so let's not start now. I am within the law, so I suggest you just leave well alone. The only way round this situation is for the back rent to be paid.'

Half an hour later in the kitchen of number twelve, the situation was more than resolved, and the bailiffs left with the cart to call on their next poor victim.

Evelyne Stubbs bought the Meadows' house, and they now had to pay their rent to her. She calculated that the rent would cover the cost of the house by the time Edward was in his final year at school. Knowing Ed's brother's financial state better than anyone, she offered him a job. He would collect the debts, and she would deduct the rent from his wages.

Edward looked up from his homework, threw down his pencil and picked up his mother's accounts book. 'You know, Ma, if you could, it might be a good thing to get hold of Auntie Freda and Uncle Ed's place. It'd be about the same price.'

Evelyne smiled and told him she'd already looked into it, and liked the fact that he was taking an interest. 'You just do your homework, lovey, and I'll think about it.'

Alex came in with a box, saying the rabbit looked poorly. He sat the box down in front of the fire. The rabbit was panting, its eyes glazed. 'He misses Dad. When do you think he'll be coming home, Ma?'

Alex really meant that he himself was missing Freedom, but

he didn't like to admit it. He was closer to Freedom than Edward was, and night after night he stood by the front window watching for his father. Evelyne sighed, put down her sewing and brought some water for the rabbit. She had no idea where Freedom was – she had had no word. She was worried, of course, but at the same time the house was running like clockwork without him. 'He's working with Jesse, he'll be home when the time is right. Don't fret yourself, Alex. Done your homework, have you?'

The next day, at school assembly, the headmaster announced that the King was dead. Rows of small faces looked up in awe, and some of the juniors whispered 'what king?', but the whole school cheered when they were told they were being given the day off. This was not the effect the headmaster had desired, but shouts for quiet went unheard as the boys streamed out gleefully.

Edward and Alex took the tram home, and finding the house locked they went down the alley and along the canal to climb over the back wall. It was January 1936, and King George was to be replaced on the throne by his eldest son Edward VIII. England went into mourning, but the Stubbs boys were thrilled that they had a whole afternoon to themselves.

Alex stood on Edward's hands and climbed over into the yard, while Edward stood on an old crate and followed. He found Alex in tears by his rabbit hutch. Not only had the King died, so had his beloved rabbit.

Evelyne was out working, collecting her rents and doing her bakery accounts. Freedom had still not come back, and when she let herself into the house she called his name, thinking he had

632

returned. She was surprised to find the boys waiting for her. 'There's nothing wrong, is there? Why aren't you both at school?'

Edward searched through her shopping bag for something to eat. 'King's dead, we all got the day off – I'm starvin', Ma!'

She took the bag away from him, muttering that no one had told her about the King, but that must be why the traffic was so bad. 'You'd best both sit at the table and do your school work, then. And no moaning, you're both old enough to know better. Lads your age were already working down the mines . . . You all right, Alex, you're a bit quiet?'

Eddie told her that the rabbit had died, that they had buried it by the canal. 'I got a shillin' for its cage, Ma, here's sixpence for you to buy yourself something.'

Alex glanced at his brother. He could lie so well, not a flicker on his face, and Alex was ashamed.

Touched by Edward's gift, Evelyne kissed him and said that they could have threepence each, but no more rabbits.

Later that night, as Evelyne brushed her hair, she heard soft, muffled sobs. She peeked into the boys' room.

Edward was sprawled across his bed. The blankets were tumbled, and the bed was surrounded by books, football boots, and the clothes he had taken off and dropped on the floor. On the opposite side of the room was Alex's neat bed, with the sheets and blankets just so. His school satchel and books were stacked neatly on his bedside box. It was Alex who was weeping, holding his pillow over his face.

Evelyne crept over to him and gently lifted the pillow. His eyes were red-rimmed from crying. She put her finger to her lips, pulled the bedclothes aside and gestured for him to follow her to her own room.

'Now, my love, what's all this about? Nothing wrong at school, is there? You want to tell me about it?'

Alex gulped his tears, bit his trembling lip.

'Is it the rabbit? Come on, get into bed with me ... come on, Edward won't know. And it's not cissy, you're still only ten.'

'Nearly eleven.'

'So you are, so you are.'

Alex snuggled close to his mother, and she kissed the top of his head. She asked again what was wrong.

'I miss him, every day I look for him. Eddie says he might never come back ... Oh, Ma ... where's me Dad?'

'Now, now, it's not *me*, it's *my*, and your Dad is just away working. Don't you pay any attention to Edward. I'll give him a piece of my mind tomorrow for telling you such things.'

'Oh, no, please don't. He'll know I've said something.'

'All right, I won't. Now snuggle up, and I'll read to you. I'll read my favourite poem, how's that?'

Alex was delighted, and with his arms wrapped around her he listened to her soft, lilting Welsh voice. She had tried so hard not to pick up the East End accent. It had been difficult – everyone she worked and mixed with spoke the local dialect – but she prided herself that she spoke well.

'Remember me when I am gone away, Gone far into the silent land, When you can no more hold me by the hand ...' Evelyne knew the poem by heart.

Alex sighed, slowly his eyelids drooped, and he slept curled up beside his beloved mother. Evelyne lay, unable to sleep, staring at the ceiling. Her eyes filled with tears as she wondered where Freedom was ...

From then on, Alex often came to her bed after Edward was asleep. Evelyne found herself waiting for him, and over the weeks she read through her small library until he slept in her arms.

Months had passed with no word from Freedom. Freda seemed more concerned about it than the Stubbs family, she was worried that something had happened to him. 'He's with that Jesse, Freda, so the least said the better. How's Ed doing? All right, is he?'

Freda nodded. Now that he was working for Evelyne it made the world of difference to Ed, bringing in that bit extra every week.

'Darlink, we owe you so much. Poor Ed was getting so upset about the money troubles. It is easier now, thanks to you.'

Evelyne shrugged it off, and said she never wanted to hear a word about it. 'We're a family, Freda, and we should help each other out, that's all that has to be said ... now, how are your legs?'

Freedom still had not returned when the street began to prepare for the coronation of Edward, hanging memorabilia in their windows for the big occasion.

On 1 December 1936, the Crystal Palace burnt down. It was the most spectacular conflagration ever seen in London in peacetime. The flames lit the sky, and many gloomy speculations buzzed round the streets and in the newspapers that the fire was a disaster, a portent that boded ill for the monarchy. The new king, Edward, was not long in proving them right. Sitting around the radio, Evelyne, the boys, Freda and Ed listened to the abdication speech at one fifty-two on the afternoon of 10 December. Edward VIII, forced to choose between the woman he loved and his country, opted for his lady.

That night Ed sat in the local pub with Freda and Evelyne. It was a hive of gossip. He downed his pint, shook his head. 'Hard to believe, ain't it, I mean, fancy givin' up the throne fer a woman what's been married twice, I mean, it's not on, is it? She don't even 'ave no 'igh society connections, beats me.'

Someone shouted across the bar, asking if Freda knew the American woman.

'When I was in Florida I passed this close, within inches, and I didn't think much of her looks. Small, piggy eyes, and a very large nose, and so thin! Oh, she is so *thin!*'

Evelyne couldn't help but smile, and the more port and lemons that came Freda's way, the more intimate details of the royal couple she remembered. 'Mind you, what worries me, darlinks, and I am sure it will worry everyone – his brother, George ... Well, he's always been in his shadow, always the quieter one. I hear he has a stammer, too. Well, darlinks, a younger brother always suffers if he has such a charming and handsome elder brother, it is always the way.'

Royalty forgotten, Evelyne went home. She wasn't thinking of King Edward but of her own Edward, and Alex. She considered what Freda had said. In a way Alex did suffer from Edward's dominance – he was quiet, easily led.

Alex was still pining for Freedom. Every afternoon he would sit on the front doorstep, looking up and down the road, and his little face would be crestfallen when eventually he came indoors to do his homework. She continued to allow him into her bed, enjoying the closeness and looking forward to reading to him. For the first time in years, she had begun to take odd spare moments to read for herself.

One night she read Alex one of her own stories, and his astonishment when she told him that she had written it herself filled her with pleasure.

Evelyne had begun to feel angry with Freedom, angry at the way he had disappeared without even a letter. Then she would sigh to herself – she knew Freedom's writing ability was confined to little more than his own name.

Coming home from the bakeries one day, she opened the door and knew he was home, without even seeing him. She rushed into the kitchen, and had to put her hand over her mouth to stop herself screaming. She thought he was an intruder and it wasn't until he turned to face her that she knew it was Freedom. His hair had been cut short, shaved round his ears, and he was thin, almost gaunt. 'Dear God, man, what happened?'

The two boys were sitting watching their parents, wide-eyed, and Evelyne told them to go up to their room. She closed the door behind them, then opened it again to give Edward his marching orders, as he was listening at the door.

'They tell me the rabbit's gone. I'll get 'em another.'

Evelyne was trying to control her anger. 'Bugger the rabbit, where have you been all these months?'

The haircut told her all, of course, but she wanted him to say it, and she stood with arms folded, looking at him as if he were a child.

Freedom had served six months in Durham gaol for handling stolen property. Evelyne threw up her hands in despair. How could he do something like that, how could he be so stupid? 'Jesse got you into this, didn't he? You might as well tell me, did he get you involved in this?'

Freedom gazed into the fire and shrugged. He wore that mask-like expression, and he didn't even have to tell her, she knew.

'Jesse go to prison with you, did he? Don't even tell me, I can see by the look of you. He left you to take the rap just like he did all those years ago! My God, Freedom, sometimes you behave like a child. Had you no thought for us, for the boys? What do you think they'll say at their school if they find out about this?'

Freedom wanted her to hold him, give him comfort, he felt so ashamed, but he could do nothing because she was so strong, so far out of his reach. He felt helpless, and he sat with his head in his hands. She put her arms around him as if he were just as she'd said, a child. She told him everything would be all right, at least he was home for Christmas.

'We'll make it the best Christmas since that time you came back with your Championship belt – remember all those years ago, Freedom, the way you came home with a cartful of furniture? Well, it'll be just like that again.'

He held her and kissed her neck, and the smell of soap and her clean, scrubbed hands moved him so that he couldn't speak. They went up the stairs together, arm in arm, to their bedroom, to the big bed they had bought all those years ago.

Edward sat up in bed, listening, wondering what Freedom was doing to his Ma, she moaned so. He wanted to hit his father. It was better when he was away. Edward put his head under the covers to block out the sound of his mother's moaning.

Alex slept like an angel, a wooden carving Freedom had made for him clasped in his hand. He was happy now, his Dad was back.

Christmas fever was all around, and in number twelve they looked forward to it with as much happiness as the two Meadows' households. They were all out of debt because of Evelyne, and they were closer and more like a family than ever before.

Evelyne had told them all that they were never to let on to Freedom about how she had covered their rent, or that they were working for her. It was bad enough for him to lose his job at the docks and serve a prison sentence, let alone to have his manhood taken away from him in his own home. But Evelyne underestimated Freedom's intelligence. He knew she was the provider and at first he was distraught, then deeply ashamed. He could still get no legitimate work, but he bought and sold odd pieces of furniture, among them the cradle he had bought all those Christmases ago. Evelyne wasn't sad to see it go, she was glad of the space. She prepared the food for Christmas Day and went shopping in the markets with Freedom to choose the boys' presents.

On Christmas Eve Freedom was very cheerful. He had a fistful of pound notes, and told Evelyne that he had done well on a couple of pieces of furniture. He was going out to buy Evelyne's gift and a surprise for the boys. Evelyne was thrilled that he had accomplished something, but when she went to her wardrobe she saw that her hatbox had been disturbed. Something was missing. She searched the chest of drawers, but she knew what Freedom had done. He had taken her pearl and gold necklace – that was where his new-found wealth had come from. She sat on the bed, wondering what to do, and decided to say nothing, at least until Christmas was over.

When the boys were asleep, she filled their stockings with oranges, apples, sweets – and a volume of Dickens and a book of poetry for Alex. Freedom had bought some cheap, bright toys from the market and she slipped them in as well. Hearing him come into the house, she crept down to the kitchen. He was grinning from ear to ear, and gestured for her to come into the yard to see the present he'd got for the boys.

Tethered to the gate was a bull terrier, white, snipe-nosed with pink eyes. At first she thought it was a pig, but on closer inspection she was so angry that she swore. 'Just take that bugger back where you got it from. I'll not have it in the house. Is it not enough with four mouths to feed, and you go and get another? Go on, take it back where you found it.'

Freedom's fists curled and he felt like hitting her. He'd chosen the dog so carefully, he'd even given him a name. Standing his ground, he said the dog would stay – he couldn't even take it back if he wanted to, the kennels were closed for Christmas. She knew she'd been hard on him, but the last thing she wanted was a dog. He would go back after Christmas she said, and walked into the house.

Edward was up at the crack of dawn, delving into his stocking, and when he had eaten everything he started on Alex's presents. Evelyne woke to hear them fighting and yelled for quiet.

Freedom had not slept with her, he was in the kitchen. From the back window she saw Alex run into his father's arms and kiss him, and the joy on the boy's face as he saw the dog made her regret what she had said the night before. By the time she was dressed and in the kitchen, Rex was sitting eating sausages by the blazing fire.

'Ma, he's mine, Dad give him to me! He's mine an' we're calling 'im Rex – ain't he just lovely, will you look at his face, and watch, Ma, he's as clever as anything . . . Sit!'

Rex promptly sat, and he even held out his paw on command. Freedom looked at Evelyne over the ecstatic Alex's head, and said that he thought a moneylender ought to have some protection, especially if there was cash in the house.

Christmas went by without any further arguments, and Rex became part of the household. He guarded the front door with a vengeance, and no one could get in or out unless he allowed them to. Alex adored Rex and made it his job to feed him. The dog slept curled upon the end of his bed. But Edward was not interested, he was more studious than ever and, as he was taking exams, the house revolved around his hours of study.

Edward came to his mother's side and slipped a note into her hand. The school prize giving and sports day was coming up, and Edward whispered in her ear, 'Don't let him come, Ma, please, I don't want him there.'

Evelyne slapped him, and told him he was not to talk about his father like that.

'He's done time, Ma, I know it, everyone in the street knows

641

it, and he's always in the pub. You earn our keep, not him, he's no use to us.'

Edward got another box on his ear, and was sent out. He hadn't noticed his father standing at the kitchen door.

'His report all right then, is it?'

It was more than all right, he was top of his class in every subject, and the headmaster had requested a meeting with Edward's parents on the prize giving day. They were invited for tea in the headmaster's study.

'I'll not go with you, I've business to do.'

Evelyne put down the report and took his hand, held him close. She said that he was their father, and by God they were going to be proud of him, he was going at her side no matter what. 'Besides, your hair's grown now, you look like everyone else, so you're coming.'

The headmaster rose to his feet as Evelyne and Freedom entered his study, and gestured for them to sit down in the two chairs opposite his desk. He could see where the Stubbs boys got their size from, and he remarked that they were fine, big lads.

'My husband was Heavyweight Boxing Champion of Great Britain. I don't suppose the boys told you?'

He was surprised that they had never mentioned it. He shook Freedom's hand and asked him if he would be good enough to give the sports prizes in assembly. Freedom was tickled pink, and he gave such a dazzling smile to Evelyne that she gave his hand a quick pat.

'Now then, Mr and Mrs Stubbs – about Edward. It must be obvious to you that he is a more than excellent pupil – he is our star pupil really, not that we like him to know that, but if it is permissible I want him to go into the sixth form.' He paused, peered at them for a moment, 'I am fully aware of how hard these times are for us all, but I think Edward might be a suitable candidate for Cambridge University. He cannot take the entrance examination until he is sixteen, more likely seventeen. I shouldn't be surprised, with the state the country is in, if war were declared. However, in special cases, and I believe your son is a special case, enlistment can be deferred.'

The headmaster was really feeling his way around the Stubbs family's financial situation. It was rare, nowadays, for families to be able to afford to keep their boys at school for the sixth form. However, Mrs Stubbs' reaction was immediate. She smiled, brimming with pride. 'He'll stay on, sir, and thank you very much.'

Freedom, not fully comprehending what the headmaster was saying, said nothing. He knew, as did everyone else, that war was imminent, so he presumed it was some sort of military training the head was referring to.

The assembly hall was filled to capacity, the boys lined up for their prizes and the school choir sang on the platform. Edward was up and down like a yo-yo as he collected prize after prize. Alex, in the lower class, had gained a special prize for endeavour, and one in maths. Evelyne applauded so often her hands were red. She couldn't help but turn to the parents sitting next to her to say, 'That's my son.'

The majority of the parents were very middle class, but the Stubbs couple only stood out because of their height. Evelyne wore a new hat and coat, and Freedom was in one of his American suits, altered for the occasion by Freda.

'Now, ladies and gentlemen, as you know, the school boxing team has done well this year, and the school's senior boxing champion has become the overall grammar school champion. We are very fortunate to have an honoured guest to present the medal. I ask to join me on the platform, Freedom Stubbs, the ex-British Heavyweight Boxing Champion.'

They met Freda and Ed as they arrived home with the prizes, and they listened as Freedom told them about how he had gone up on the platform to present the boxing prize to the school champion. Alex wanted photographs of Freedom's boxing days to show the boys at school, and Ed had them enthralled with stories of Freedom's boxing matches. When they left, the boys went along to bring Freda's scrapbook home.

Freda had saved all the newspaper cuttings and photographs taken in America. The boys were fascinated, and Alex wouldn't let Evelyne turn a single page until he had asked every possible question. He wanted to know who was who and where all the places were.

'Freedom, come and sit with us, you know all these people better than I do . . . come on.'

Freedom pulled up a chair. He had not seen many of the photographs himself, had tried to forget that part of his life. Now, after his success at the school, he was almost as eager as the boys to go over old times. He drew the book towards him. 'Now then, lemmesee . . . ah, see this fella here, on the side of the picture, that's Jack Dempsey, the greatest boxer I've ever seen.'

Alex hung on his father's every word, and clung to him. Edward had read the article and tried to turn the page. Alex stopped him. 'Did you fight him, Dad?'

'No, son, he'd retired when I met him ... Now, then, this man on his right was Jack Kearn, a promoter, and this was Ted Rickard, they were a famous team, known as the "Golden Triangle" ... An' look, see, this is Dempsey's thoroughbred stallion, ain't it just lovely?'

Evelyne had relinquished her place at the table to Freedom, and she looked up from her sewing and smiled at the boys hanging onto their father's arms, shouting and clapping.

'Now, lads, this is a great fighter, Gene Tunney. I was to fight him for the title, but then he stepped down and left his throne vacant, see. So fighters from all over the world came to try for the belt. See this, it's a picture of the belt, an' it's solid gold, pictures hand-painted round the sides, see? Oh! An' will you look at this, this was the Danish contender, name of Knud Hansen, big fella, eh?' He turned the pages, animated, eager, 'And Monty Munn ... this chap's a Frenchman, can't remember his name. Here ... here's the villa where we stayed in Miami, Florida. You wasn't born then, Alex, an' you was just a toddler, Eddie.'

Evelyne came back into the kitchen, clutching her own scrapbook. It was immaculate; all these years it had been carefully wrapped in brown paper. Beneath each article was the name of the newspaper and the date, in her neat handwriting.

'I notice your Dad is not showing you himself. Now, you've not seen this, it's a really big occasion.'

The book was such a contrast to Ed and Freda's, as theirs was full of their own memorabilia, and very well-thumbed as Ed had taken it down to the gym at every opportunity.

'Now then, you're going to learn something tonight, boys. Take a look at this – it's a programme, but see the front. There were posters, twenty, maybe twenty-five feet high. As you came in on the plane, your Dad's face was the first thing you saw.'

The two boys gaped as she turned the page. Freedom had to swallow tears. He reached for Evelyne's hand and she gave him such a look it made his heart swell. He had never known about the book. It was so precious it touched his soul.

'See, he was surrounded by autograph hunters, he was more famous than a film star. There was not a street in Miami he could walk down without crowds gathering.'

Freedom laughed and said she was exaggerating.

'Oh, no I'm not, and this should be a lesson to you both. Your father was a champion, a very famous man, but you don't see him pushing it down people's throats like some people from around these parts who have never gone further afield than Brighton.'

The boys were agog, holding the book between them, shouting, vying with each other to turn the pages. And then there was the programme for the match between Freedom and Sharkey.

The boys fell silent, their eyes popping out of their heads. This was a man they scarcely recognized. The handsome face stared back at them, the hair long, the fists raised. Alex was close to tears of pride, touching the pictures, patting them. Edward looked at his father, then his mother. They were so close to the boys, had their arms around them, and yet it was as if they were alone. Evelyne bent to kiss Freedom, their eyes hungry for each other.

'What happened then? At the big fight, Dad, what happened?'

Freedom turned the pages, trying to change the subject.

'This man was Sir Charles Wheeler, he was my promoter, an English knight he was ...'

Edward turned the pages back to look at the fight programme. 'Well, did yer beat 'im, Dad? Jack Sharkey?'

Freedom gave him a sad smile. 'No, son, he beat me, wiped the floor with me, knocked me out of the ring.'

Evelyne leaned over and pointed to the picture of Jack Sharkey. 'He punched foul, that's why, he punched low, and your Dad's leg got paralysed. Sharkey was never world champion either, because he fouled again at his next fight. You shouldn't run yourself down like that, Freedom! Your Dad would have won, but he had so many fights and not enough rest before the big bout ... Your face had to have time to heal – there were cuts around his eyes, his ribs broken. No man in that condition should have been allowed to go into the ring. You ask your Uncle Ed about it.'

Again, Freedom reached out and held her hand. 'I dunno, suddenly your mother's an authority on boxing, she who hated the very thought of it, now will you listen to her?'

Evelyne laughed, and sat on his knee. 'Ah, well, I hate it, and that's the truth, but I'll not hear you tell of everyone else. You were a champion, not many can say that. But neither of you two lads will ever have to go through what your Dad had to, fighting for money is a terrible way to earn a living ... Have you never wondered why your father limps the way he does? That's fighting for you ...'

Edward leafed through the book and then opened a folded page of newspaper. 'What's this? Dad, what's this?'

Freedom glanced at it and flushed, looked up at Evelyne. He couldn't read it. Evelyne took it from Edward, bit her lip.

'It's the headline about Al Capone, Freedom.'

Freedom laughed and jigged Evelyne up and down on his knee. The boys whistled and started in amazement as Freedom told them about the St Valentine's Day massacre. Alex started jumping up and down. 'Dad, Dad, there's films about him, they have guns, bab–bab–bab–b–b–b–b, real machine-guns that kill hundreds 'n' thousands at the same time.'

Edward continued to read the article, but Alex was beside himself. 'Tell us more, Dad, tell us more, Ma, make him tell us more.'

Evelyne slid off Freedom's knee and picked up the paper. Clearing her throat theatrically, she acted out her scene with the bell hop in the Chicago hotel. She did not mention that the trouble they had getting rooms was due to Freedom's dark skin, but went on to tell how she had met the man in the lilac suit. She switched to a heavy Chicago accent, '"Well, Ma'am," he said ...,' and mimed smoking a huge cigar. The boys clapped their hands. They had never seen their mother behave in this way. Freedom roared with laughter and applauded. 'We got sent flowers and fruit, and we'd never even heard of him. Then when Ed saw his name, well, he almost shit himself.'

Evelyne cuffed Freedom's head. 'And we'll not use any language like that! Well, come on now, let's clear the table. Who's hungry?'

Edward held up a photograph of Evelyne, dressed in all her finery, on board the *Aquitania*, 'Ma, is this you? This you?'

Freedom took it from him and turned to Evelyne. 'Yes, it's your mother, and she turned every man's head on the ship. Wearing her real pearls, she was.'

The boys stared from the photo to Evelyne and back again. 'Is that necklace real, Ma? The jewels, are they real?'

Evelyne ruffled Alex's hair and said they were, and she had to get on with the tea. Edward gave her a sly look, then a hooded glance at his father. 'You still got yer necklace, have you, Ma?'

Evelyne looked hard at Edward, but he had the masked look on his face so similar to his father's. Edward, who pried into everything, did he know? Had he seen her frantic search for her necklace that day? She couldn't tell. Freedom, uncomfortable, tried to change the subject, but Edward persisted, asking again and again to see his mother's jewels. Freedom stood up. 'Why don't you show 'em, Evie, go on.' He left the room, and came back downstairs a few moments later to show the necklace to the boys.

'Here you go, Alex, look at this. See, that was the time when I bought your Ma the very best.'

How had Freedom got it back? When? She didn't know, but Edward's frown told her for certain that somehow the boy had known something.

Chapter 28

3 September 1940 – England had been at war for a year and the effect was shattering as the young men enlisted and went off to fight. Not that they noticed much difference in their streets, just that many faces were missing. Times were still hard, but as so many men were employed in the forces it left opportunities for work open to women. Hundreds of children were evacuated to safety in the country, but not Edward and Alex. Evelyne was adamant. They would remain in London and at school – they were not babes in arms and she and Freedom would keep their eyes on them. Edward, nearly eighteen years old now, was in the sixth form at the grammar school, taking his entrance exams for Cambridge University.

Freedom had been turned down when he tried to enlist, because of his age and his bad leg. He was furious and felt slighted, but he got a job as a warden patrolling the streets.

The bombs were hitting the East End and the dock areas worst of all, and blackouts every night was the rule. Buckingham Palace was hit in the same month, and the Queen announced publicly that she was glad, it made her feel she could look the East End in the face. The Royal Family committed itself to the needs of war with a zeal and conscientiousness that won the respect of the people.

Jesse made an appearance and roped Freedom into black market activities, and although Evelyne was against it from the start she had to admit that the food they obtained helped their meagre rations to go round. She still did the accounting at the bakeries and still lent money, but she also went to work in a factory on the morning shift. Planes flying overhead and bombs dropping became an everyday occurrence, which left gaps in the rows of houses like blackened skeletons. There was hardly a family that hadn't lost a relative in the fighting, and now they were being hit themselves they lived in constant fear of air-raid warnings. The raids usually took place under cover of night. Evelyne had seen families lose everything they possessed, and, always one to take care, she carried her savings book with her at all times, strapped around her waist under her clothes.

At the factory Evelyne hemmed army blankets on a machine, and one day when the sirens sounded during work, they all ran for the shelter. As they crossed the yard, one of the foremen looked up into the sky. 'Dear God, look at 'em, they're like big, black birds, the bastards. In broad daylight an' all.'

Evelyne was in the shelter before his words struck home, and she remembered Rawnie's words so many years ago. She screamed at one of the workers, shook the women. 'What day is it? What day is it?'

Thursday was the boys' half-day at school, where they had a good shelter, but on Thursdays they came home. She ran from the shelter, forcing her way past the boss, who tried to hold her back. She yelled to them that it was Thursday, then she was gone. She couldn't get a bus, they had come to a halt, and the whole area was bedlam. The planes were coming closer and closer, and looking up she could see them like big, black birds flying she knew, towards the city, towards number twelve.

She ran until she was so exhausted that she had to lean against a wall. She looked up as the drone of the planes passed overhead. There was pandemonium as people screamed and ran. The glue factory took a direct hit, and the overpowering smell of glue and the black smoke choked the few workers who escaped, and the firemen alike. Evelyne gasped for breath but pushed herself on and on, towards home. Twice she was held back by firemen but dragged herself away. 'My boys, my boys, lemme go.'

At long last she reached the corner of the street to find it a nightmare of flames and charred buildings. Fire engines were trying to get through the rubble. Stumbling and crying, calling her boys' names, Evelyne stopped in horror. Ed's brother's house was no more than a heap of rubble, and fire gushed from next door's wooden window frames. Screams echoed around, the thick black smoke filled the street, and Evelyne pushed her way through the dazed people wandering around calling for their loved ones. One of Freda's lodgers, one of the tarts, was sitting on the pavement sobbing, repeating over and over in a shocked, hysterical voice, 'Me new dress, me new dress, I just got it, me new dress.'

Evelyne could see Ed and Freda's house burning, the roof on fire, and as she pressed on she prayed over and over again that her boys were safe.

She saw Edward first, he was scrambling over the rubble calling out for Auntie Freda, Uncle Ed, his hands bleeding as he clawed at the bricks. A fireman tried to haul him away as burning timbers came crashing down. Evelyne ran towards him, and Alex appeared, black from head to foot, his tear-stained face hysterical with fear as he pointed back to number twelve, still gabbling as Evelyne held him tight, tried to calm him down. An unexploded incendiary bomb was sticking through the roof of their house, and the firemen were trying to clear the street. It could go off at any time.

'Where's your father, *Alex? Alex?*'

Evelyne had to slap his face, he didn't even seem to know that he was in her arms.

'Get the bloody fool outta there, it's going up at any time.'

Knowing both her boys were safe, Evelyne headed for number twelve. A fireman grabbed her, shouting that the house would blow at any minute, everyone had to get back.

'He's inside, Ma, he went in for Rex, he's gone to get Rex.'

The hoses drenched her as she screamed out for Freedom. The smoke was so thick now that their eyes were red and smarting, and the fumes from the glue factory hung in the air like an overpowering cloud.

'Freedom ... *Freedom?*'

As the roof blew, Freedom hurtled out of the house, clutching the terrified, snarling dog to his chest. Evelyne, her arms wrapped around her boys, almost collapsed with relief. They all stood together and watched the house blaze. Alex clung to her, holding his beloved dog at the same time. The hoses sprayed them as they stood in the debris of their street. Freedom went back to help with the fire.

*

Freda had been at her sewing machine, and Ed had obviously tried to warn her – his body was found in the passageway between the rooms. Ed's brother and sister-in-law and two of their children had been trapped in the kitchen. They had not stood a chance.

The realization of how lucky they were did not dawn until later that night as they lay in the underground shelter. They huddled together, clinging to each other. Alex whispered to his mother that Edward had known it would happen, he had known.

'What are you talking about, love, how did he know?'

Edward was sleeping, his filthy face resting on his arms. Evelyne wrapped the blanket closer around him, tried not to cry.

'He knew, Ma. We were out in the yard and there was no sound of the planes, nothing – no sirens even, an' as it was day we didn't worry, like – an' suddenly he grabbed hold of me and said go and warn Auntie an' Uncle Ed. The planes weren't even overhead.'

Freedom left the shelter and went off to do his warden's duties, and in the morning he was back and said they could return to their house. The roof was badly damaged and they didn't have a single window left, but at least it was still standing.

The sad, bedraggled group made its way home. The street was full of rubble, and the ambulances were still taking the bodies of the dead away. Firemen were digging in the bombed-out buildings looking for survivors, for bodies. The family kept their eyes down, not wanting to see Freda's frilly curtains, charred and sodden, lying in the gutter. They stepped over puddles, charred furniture, shattered glass, until they stood outside their house. Evelyne shuddered, it looked so derelict, so black, so deathly.

'Freedom, I don't want to go in, is there anywhere else we could go?'

He was carrying Rex in his arms, and he paused. Was she reading his mind? 'It's our home, and the way you look at it is, they hit us once, be a miracle if they get us again . . . Come on, lads, let's make some tea and get the place cleaned up.'

Freedom could feel the horror, the house closing in on him, and he gasped for breath. The acrid stench from the glue factory hung in the air, burning his nostrils. He put his shoulder to the door and it crashed open.

The impact of bombs all round had made the house subside. The passageway was waterlogged and strewn with broken glass, and over everything was thick, black dust. It broke Evelyne's heart. Ordering the boys to search for what could be salvaged, Freedom began to clear away the ruined furniture. In the centre of the room was the scrapbook – not one page was left intact. He picked it up, and all he could think of was Ed, how he had looked with his warden's tin hat on the back of his head. He gritted his teeth and threw the remains of the book out of the back door along with everything else. But he couldn't get Ed's voice out of his mind, heard again the last words Ed had said to him, 'Now, look, lad, I'm not one wiv words, but I want you ter know somefink should anyfink ever happen . . . I love you, like you was me own son, an' I'm depending on you ter take care of Freda. I've not much, but what I 'ave is yours, that includes all me memorabilia.'

Freedom felt the loss swamping him, overpowering him, and he hurled a chair out through the broken window with all his might. Edward started screaming, and Freedom's heart lurched. He turned in panic, to see Edward waving a telegram, his face shining.

'Ma, Ma, it's come, I've won a scholarship to Cambridge. I've won a place at Cambridge University . . . I've done it!'

Before Evelyne could congratulate him, Freedom slammed his fist into the last intact pane of glass, shattering it into the yard. His fist bleeding, he turned on Edward, his face dark with rage.

'Don't you ever think of anyone but yerself, boy? There's Freda an' Ed dead, an' all you can scream about is that *you won a bloody scholarship! I'll knock that smile off your face!*'

Edward was taken aback for a moment, then he glared. 'You just try it – come on then, try it.' He threw a wild punch at his father, and Freedom blocked it with a swift movement of his arm. Edward tottered backwards, off balance.

'You better stay away from me, Eddie, I mean it.'

Edward charged, head down, and butted Freedom in the stomach, then swung his fists like windmills, but again Freedom threw him off as though he were a small child. This time Edward lurched backwards, striking his head on the mantelpiece. His face red, his mouth tight, he picked himself up. 'That's the last time you'll ever hit me, you bastard, you bastard.'

Reaching out, Freedom grabbed Edward and pulled him closer, slapping his face, the blows jerking his head back and forth. 'Don't try fighting me, sonny, you don't stand a chance. Go and join the army like the rest of the lads, like a man, instead of a nancy boy tied to your mother's apron strings.'

Edward dodged behind the table. 'Only nancy boy round this place is you, the great champion fighter, an' the army wouldn't even take yer.'

Alex ran from the room into the hallway, calling for his mother, 'Ma, Ma, come quick, Dad and Eddie are fighting!'

Panic-stricken, he ran up the stairs. Freedom kicked the door shut, and began to roll up his sleeves. 'You'll not have your Ma to help you now, son, you've been asking for this for a long time.'

Evelyne ran down the stairs, screaming at the top of her voice. 'Freedom, Edward, what's going on?'

Freedom stood with his back against the door and shouted for her to stay out of it. She tried to push the door open, but he slammed it shut. Rex ran to Freedom, whimpering, but he kicked out at the dog.

'That's right, kick the dog, he can't kick you back, can he? I can and I will. What you ever done for us, you with your big mouth an' even bigger fists? Ma's provided for this family, not you, it's never been you. *Go back to prison an' leave us alone!*'

Freedom clenched his fists, fighting for self-control, trying to keep his blind fury in check. Suddenly he was pushed forward as Alex forced his way into the kitchen. He grabbed Freedom's arm. 'Dad, Dad, don't, he doesn't mean it! Tell him you didn't mean it, Eddie, please, Dad, don't!'

'I meant every word, we were better off when he was in jail, at least Ma didn't have an extra mouth to feed.'

Evelyne came in and moved right between Edward and Freedom. 'I'll talk to him, just don't fight, let me talk to him.'

Freedom pushed her aside. 'No, Evie, not this time, you've always protected them, protected him. He's going to have to learn.' Freedom's voice was icy calm. He moved closer and closer to Edward. 'You're going down to that recruiting office right now, if I have to drag you there meself.'

Edward spat at him and ran round the room, ducking behind Evelyne. She put her arms out, pleading, 'Don't, Freedom, ah, don't, don't do something you'll be sorry for, please, please, don't.'

The belt slithered from Freedom's trousers and he wound it around his hand. Edward shrieked, suddenly afraid. 'I'm going to university, tell him Ma, tell him.'

'You're going to work, lad, we can't afford no university, not with the house burnt down round our ears. You are gonna earn your keep like every other lad around here.'

Evelyne made a grab for Freedom, shouting, 'That's for me to say, Freedom, it's *my* savings, *mine!*'

Deflated, Freedom turned a beseeching look on her. She ran out of the house, shouting for help. Heartbroken, Freedom watched her go. Once again she had taken her son's side.

Edward took that moment to open the kitchen drawer and take out the carving knife. 'Satisfied, are you? You bloody satisfied, you bastard?' He was hysterical, shaking, holding the knife like a dagger. Alex was the one to move towards his brother to try and take the knife, but Rex ran to him and he tripped over the dog, sprawled on to the floor. Freedom's face terrified Edward, the mask in place, no expression, the eyes black ... He kept moving, coming closer and closer, unafraid, menacing, daring Edward to use the knife.

Evelyne was out in the street. Police and firemen were

everywhere, clearing the debris. She screamed. 'Dear God, stop them, *someone stop them!*'

Freedom reached out to grip his son by the hair, and Edward brought the knife down in one single, stabbing thrust. Freedom remained standing. He looked into his son's face, his mask dropped, and his eyes full of anguish. Edward stepped back, stared first at his empty hand, then back at his father. Freedom made no attempt to remove the knife. He lifted his arms as if to embrace his son, then he fell forward, fell on to the knife, pushing it further into his heart.

There was a terrible silence in the room. No one moved. The colour drained from Edward's face and he swayed. Alex still held Rex's collar as the dog howled, trying to get to Freedom. Two policemen rushed in, kicking the door wide open, and took the situation in immediately. Rex barked furiously, his claws scrabbling on the lino to get to Freedom, Edward stood, stupefied, staring at his father. One of the policemen knelt down, slowly turned the body over. The blood had already formed a thick, dark pool, the knife in Freedom's heart right up to the hilt.

'Oh, Jesus God . . . right, you two lads, up against the wall, the pair of you, against the wall, now.'

Like terrified children, Edward and Alex stood with their backs against the wall. They watched in horror as their mother looked from the open kitchen door at the body. Her legs were shaking, the tremor running right through her . . . she pushed the policeman's helping hand away, stumbled to kneel beside Freedom. She cradled him to her, the blood oozing over her chest as she rocked him in her arms. She made not a sound. They could see the blood spreading over her pinafore, his blood,

blood to blood, heart to heart. Without looking at his brother, Alex put out his hand, and they grasped each other tight, but made no move towards their mother.

The drone of fighter planes coming closer made one of the policemen swear out loud, 'Dear God, the bastards are coming again, and in broad daylight.'

The air-raid warning sounded for everyone to take cover. Edward's black eyes clung to his mother, never leaving her face as he watched her cradle the body. He had never seen such raw agony. His body felt chilled, icy, as if his own life were draining steadily away. The grasp of his brother's hand gave him assurance, but the voices of the police became distorted, unreal. 'There's an ambulance outside, we'll get him outside later, best get to the shelter. There's nothing we can do here until after the bombing. You two lads come with us, come on, move it.'

Alex and Edward were herded roughly out of the door by one of the policemen, and the other bent down to Evelyne. 'Come on, come on Missus, the bombs'll be dropping any minute. There's nothing you can do for him now ...'

Evelyne looked up and told him quietly that there was no need for the ambulance, he was dead ... 'Leave me, please, leave me with him, please.'

The policeman realized it was pointless to argue. She was so calm, like ice, and he didn't want to waste any more time. The unearthly wail of the sirens continued, and he followed the others out. As he hurried to the shelter, he looked up. Broad daylight, the bastards had the audacity to come in broad daylight, like big, black birds in the sky.

The deadly bombs fell all around number twelve, but Evelyne couldn't hear them. She sat on the floor cradling

The Legacy

Freedom's body in her arms, unable to cry. Her body felt wounded as if the blood were slowly dripping from her. Rex whimpered, crawling on his belly to lie beside her, licking the outstretched, lifeless hand.

Under the watchful eyes of the policemen, the brothers huddled in the shelter. Alex held Edward in his arms, and whispered to him, softly so the police couldn't hear. 'Edward? Listen to me, I'll say that I did it. No one saw, no one will know, can you hear me?'

Holding his brother tight, needing his warmth, Edward listened.

'I'm two years younger, they can't do nothin' to me, I'm a juvenile, they'll not send me to jail. You can go to Cambridge, you can still go.'

Edward shuddered and clung even closer, feeling the softness of his brother's skin. He kissed Alex's neck.

'See, it's what Ma wants, what she's dreamed of, so I'll do it, I'll say it was me that knifed him.'

Edward whispered close to Alex's ear. 'I didn't mean it, you know that, I didn't mean to do it ... I'll make it up to you, I will, I give you my word I'll make it up to you.'

Alex seemed satisfied, patting his brother as if he were the younger of the two. Edward gave him a small thankful smile. 'You won't go back on your word, will you? I mean, you won't ever tell anyone, will you?'

Alex blinked back his tears. 'No, Eddie, I'll never tell no one else, not even Ma if you don't want me to.'

Edward gave him a hug, then peeked out of the shelter, said he thought the bombing was almost over. Alex looked at

661

Edward, who no longer seemed to be distressed, no longer clung to him. Alex was shocked, confused, but it was too late, he had given his word.

The bombing had ceased and the all-clear sounded. Edward's voice was calm. 'Will you have to take my brother to the police station, sir? I should get back to our mother.'

The people who had sheltered with them lingered to watch, but they were moved on by another officer. Alex was taken away from Edward, and was led to the front of the house. The police officer took Edward aside. 'Now, lad, best take care of your mother. We'll have to take him into custody, understand? Tell her she can come down the station any time, but we have to get your brother's statement.'

'What'll happen to him, sir? It was an accident, he didn't mean it.'

That was not for the officer to say, but he gave Edward permission to have a few words with Alex before they took him away.

Some of the neighbours stood on their front steps, whispering and nodding at the ambulance and the police. Two air-raid wardens joined the gathering, and they all watched with interest, but the police kept them at a distance.

Edward went over to the silent Alex, standing between two police officers. He looked unafraid, his chin up and managing not to cry. Edward couldn't say what he wanted, not with the officers standing so close . . . He caught Alex's hand and tried to hug him, but the sergeant broke them apart, and pushed Edward roughly aside. 'Don't start anything, sonny, go to your mother, there's a good lad. Let's get this over with as quietly as we can. The whole street's watching.'

Alex was led to a police wagon and helped up into the back of it. Edward called out to him that everything would be all right. He watched the white face staring from the back of the van as they drove off.

The policeman and the ambulance attendant stood talking at the front door, and Edward went to pass them to enter the house, but the policeman put a hand on his arm. 'She's in a bad state, and she won't let anyone touch him. We've been waiting for a doctor so they can take him up to the morgue.'

Edward couldn't face her. She sat in exactly the same position, with Freedom still in her arms. Rex still licked the lifeless hand.

'Ma, Ma, you'll have to let him go. They have to take him away.'

Slowly she turned vacant eyes towards him, and as if in slow motion she blinked. Prising her rigid arms from his father's body, he held her. She was covered in blood, and it had dried, hard. The police and an attendant moved in, wrapped the body in a blanket and carried it outside to the ambulance, where the doctor was waiting. Several people watched the body being lifted into the ambulance, and the doctor examined it briefly and told the ambulance crew to take it straight to the morgue, the hospital could do nothing. One of the spectators asked if bombs had dropped on this side of the street, if they had he hadn't heard them. 'I've got so that I don't hear 'em any more, was it a bomb done it?'

The policeman shook his head, said quietly that this was a murder. They shut the back of the ambulance, not noticing the white dog standing by the closed doors.

The truck drove off, the dog followed, followed until his

paws were bloody from running on the broken glass and rubble. He knew his master was inside the wagon, and he wouldn't stop following it. In his exhaustion and the confusion of the traffic he began to follow the wrong vehicle, becoming more bewildered and confused, unable to find the scent, unable to find Freedom. In the end he lay in the gutter, chest heaving, tongue lolling, and his pink eyes closed as his heart gradually stopped.

Evelyne felt as if her heart had broken, it was so painful, she kept her hand pressed to her chest, to the dark, crusted stain. Edward made her some tea. She didn't speak, but she sipped it, slowly. At long last she appeared to thaw out, the hand that had remained pressed to her chest moved, and she stared at her stained fingers. 'Where's Alex, where's Alex?'

Edward bit his nails, looking guilty. 'They took him down the station, Ma, just to give a statement.'

Evelyne was puzzled, she rubbed her head. 'Why Alex, Eddie? Why have they taken Alex?'

Edward chewed his thumbnail down to the quick, he couldn't face her. 'Because he did it. They said you can see him any time.'

She knew it was a lie and she felt sick. She had to hold the table-top tightly, or she would have fainted. 'Alex would never have touched him, Eddie, he worshipped the ground he walked on ... *Don't ever lie to me, don't lie to me!*' She gripped his hand so tight it was like a vice on his wrist.

He sobbed, 'He said that he would say it was him, then I could go to Cambridge. He said it was what you wanted, Ma, what you dreamed of, you always said that.'

She stared at him, as if he were a stranger. He had sent his own brother to jail.

'He's still a juvenile, Ma, they can't do anything to him, but they could to me. I'm two years older . . . It's what you always wanted, isn't it? You want me to go to university.'

She walked out into the hall, feeling her way along the walls, clinging to the banister as she walked up the stairs. Edward followed and stood at the foot of the stairs. 'It's what you want, isn't it?'

She looked down at him, her eyes as cold as the North Sea. 'It's what *you* want. Well, you go, if Alex doesn't mind, you go.'

'I'll show you, Ma, I'll be somebody for you, I will, I'll not stop until I prove it was the right thing to do . . . *Ma? Ma?*'

The bedroom door had slammed, and he banged on the banister rail with his fist.

Evelyne undressed, carefully folding each garment, the blood-stained apron, the blouse. She sat on the bed, touching it, running her fingers along the carved posts. One son at university, one in jail, Freda and Ed gone . . . this was what Rawnie had seen in the palm of her hand. 'Beware the black birds in the sky. You will lose all you love.' They were the planes, the German bombers, and it was true, she had lost Freedom, she had lost her love.

The scream echoed down through the derelict house. In the kitchen, Edward raised his head, looked up towards the bedroom. She frightened him, the terrible sound of her screaming, calling his father's name over and over. At long last the screams stopped, and he heard sobbing, it reverberated through the whole house. He put his hands over his ears to try to block out the noise, but it went on and on. He rocked in his chair. 'Stop it, stop it, stop it . . .'

When he took his hands away the house was silent. He didn't

know when he had fallen asleep, but he sat up sharply as he heard her calling for him.

'Edward, bring me up some hot water, I have to wash.'

He carried up the big kettle, poured the water into her bowl. 'I'll be down in a minute.'

He had a pot of tea ready for her in the kitchen, and two slices of buttered toast. She was dressed in her best clothes. 'I'll go to the police station, poor Alex must think we've forgotten him. We'll have a lot to be getting on with, there's everything to arrange for you to go up to Cambridge, and then we'll need the best lawyer there is.'

Edward was stunned – she was as calm as ever, but when he went to kiss her she pushed him away. She didn't touch his tea or the toast, just counted the change in her purse. Edward would never forget the way she looked at him, it released him, released him from her. Her eyes were filled with such loathing – as if he were no more than an animal. She never let him touch her again, never held him in her arms, and never spoke of Freedom. She even removed the photograph of Freedom from the mantelpiece, along with those of her two sons.

Evelyne buried Freedom, and the local people showed their love and respect for their dead champion, walking in silence behind the hearse. Ten high-stepping men wearing dark pinstriped suits, bright neckerchiefs and gold earrings appeared as if from nowhere. Somehow news had reached them that their fighter was dead. They kept a few yards back from the rest of the mourners, their heads held high – arrogant, black-haired men.

When the ceremony was over, Evelyne remained beside the

grave. There was an air of aloofness about her, an untouchable grief that made it difficult for her friends and neighbours to comfort her. Even Mrs Harris couldn't take her in her arms. It was strange, but it was Jesse, who had brought the men from the clans, who stood alone with her when everyone else had gone. It was Jesse who sensed her need, her devastating loss. He held her gently, and she could smell the same musky oil that Freedom used to wear.

'We burn our dead's possessions so they take them with them, and in that way they rest and will not haunt the living.'

'They've already gone, Jesse, went in the Blitz.'

'Have you nothing he were proud of? He's a Prince, he cannot lie without a treasure, with no talisman.'

Evelyne remembered the necklace, how proud Freedom had been the day he gave it to her. She hesitated.

It was all she had left of him, all she had to remember the good times. Jesse seemed to know instinctively that there was something and his black eyes went darker than dark as he whispered,

'He loved thee, woman, more'n ye may know, but he was the son of a *dukkerin*, his blood was royal. He has strong powers. No church, no service will give him peace. You bury the gold tonight, place it at the foot of the cross and he'll rest quiet.'

Evelyne knew now, more than ever, how much of his past Freedom had given up for her, how much of his life she knew nothing of, as if in death he had returned to the wild, returned to his people.

'Will you sing that song for me. He loved it so.'

Jesse straightened his waistcoat, and in a clear voice that rang out across the graveyard, he sang,

Can you rokka *Romany,*
Can you play the bosh,
Can you jal adrey the staripen,
Can you chin the cosh . . .

Evelyne stared at her reflection, her face worn and pale, her naked shoulders as white as her shift. She carefully clasped on the gold and pearl necklace and then each earring. She searched her own face, her own sad eyes for the past, eyes brimming with glistening tears; they once again sparkled with youth and vitality. In the half-light of the small bedside lamp she was sure, sure he had entered the room. A small china figure was placed in front of the lamp and, caught at that moment, held in the beam of the light, it formed a lifesize shadow. Evelyne carefully inched the tiny figure forward until the shadow seemed to stand over her bed. She then lay down and lifted her arms and the shadow kissed and enveloped her, and she knew he would never leave her.

The police constable took Alex a mug of hot tea. The boy had hardly had a bit of food since his arrest. As the key turned in the lock, Alex looked up with a pitiful expression of expectancy on his face.

'Here, lad, get this down you, you'll feel better for it.'

Alex's hands shook as he cupped the tin mug. His teeth chattered against the rim, and his face crumpled. The constable felt sorry for him, and sat down on the bunk. 'He was buried today. Streets of people walked behind him to say goodbye. They gave him a champion's . . .'

He broke off to grab the mug from Alex. He had begun sobbing, his whole body shaking, and he was spilling the scalding tea on himself. All night he sobbed for his father, until he was exhausted, totally drained. The police officers heaved sighs of relief when at last the boy in their charge was silent.

Edward walked across the cobbled courtyard towards the main hall. Hundreds of black-gowned students milled around, shouting and calling to each other, joyously reunited with old pals. Cycles wobbled past, bells rang and everywhere the eye fell there were students. The excitement was contagious and exhilarating, even for the nervous first-timers, the freshmen who looked shyly to one another with small embarrassed smiles. Edward wanted to touch the stone of the walls, wanted to get down on his knees to kiss the cobbled quadrangle, he still could not quite believe he was here, he had done it, he was at Cambridge. He could not contain the feeling of achievement. It was bubbling inside him, bursting from his brain. He had made it. As he crossed the threshold into the main hall for his first assembly, he noticed the stone was worn, curving at the centre from hundreds of years and thousands of students' hurried steps. Now it was his turn, his time, and he would use every second, every moment. Edward knew that there would be many students who could match him academically, but doubted if anyone, bar himself, would have committed murder to cross this worn, hallowed step. This would be one accomplishment he would never think or speak of; if he did it would destroy him.

As Edward crossed the threshold into his new life he left behind the East End, his mother and his brother. He could not lose or forget as easily the last image of his father. This memory, like a clearly painted picture, was not of when he had seen his dead father cradled in his mother's arms, it was not of when he had turned to threaten him, it was not even of the smile he had on his face when Edward had felt the knife cut into his heart. The image, the clear, brilliantly painted picture that swept into his dreams and often into his waking hours, was of a man with flowing black hair – a handsome wild man with black angry eyes. The man was Freedom holding his bare knuckled fist up ready to fight, Freedom, the fighter from Devil's Pit, Freedom alive in the days before Edward had even been born, before he had married Evelyne.

Alex would dream of him too, and in his dream was a surreal mountainside where the grass grew green, the sky was a brilliant blue and the sun sparkled, glinting rainbow colours like a child's picture story book.

Alex saw himself, running towards the peak of the mountain. There came a thunder of hooves, ringing and echoing around the mountainside, and still he ran on, breathing the sweet, clean air as he jumped for joy . . .

Breaking through clouds with his raised hooves came a black, shining stallion. Astride him sat a man of magical ethereal beauty. A wild man, with flowing, blue-black hair, barechested, at one with the beast. Alex lifted his arms, crying, 'Don't go! Don't go!' But the rider passed him by, as if leaping over the very mountain. The thunder of hooves merged into a thunderclap, and the clouds closed like a grey curtain. Alex screamed, struggling to run those last few yards up the mountain, 'Freedom! Freedom! Freedom!'

He was too late, he was too tired. He collapsed to the ground, and from the earth came the last, faint sounds of the still-gal-loping horse, fainter, fainter . . . The skies opened and rain began to fall.

Alex woke, drenched in his own sweat, his body stiff and cold. He pulled the worn blanket around his aching body and closed his eyes again, hoping to conjure up one more glimpse of the rider. Unable to sleep, he comforted himself with the thought that one day he would reach the top of the mountain.

Romany Curse

He must lie with his treasures, be they tin or gold,
Resting in finery, his back to the soil.
One wheel of his *vargon* must light up with fire,
In the flame is his evil, his pain and his soul.
But beware of his *taelizman* (talisman) carved out of stone,
If not in his palm, then a curse is foretold.

For who steals the charm of this *dukkerin*'s son,
Will walk in his shadow, bleed with his blood,
Cry loud with his anguish and suffer his pain.
His unquiet spirit will rise up again,
His footsteps will echo unseen on the ground
Until the curse is fulfilled, his talisman found.

Epilogue

The Talisman follows the lives of the two brothers: Edward's meteoric rise to vast wealth, Alex's prison sentence and release.

To ensure they were never to forget their origins, Edward took from his mother's grave the necklace his father had given to her the night he had claimed his championship belt. He melted the gold to make two medallions, and had their names inscribed, so they would never forget. Unknowingly he had committed a Romany sin. By opening the grave he had taken from his father and his mother their treasure. He had taken his father's life, and now he ransacked his soul, ignorant of the old customs and the curses. Edward evoked the unquiet dead.

The Talisman introduces the brothers' women, their wives and their children, all of them inexplicably bound by ghosts from the past. The murder of their father, Freedom Stubbs, the Champion fighter, constantly draws them back to their Romany origins . . . they have his blood in their veins, and his death on their consciences. They have inherited the Romany second sight and, as they reach a phenomenally high pinnacle of both material wealth and power, attained deviously and violently, one of them must now pay the debt. One must pay at last for the murder. It is the law of the Romanies, be it sons or daughters, wives or mothers, fathers or brothers, a debt must be paid. A tear for a tear, a heart for a heart, blood to blood, soul to soul . . .

SIMON &
SCHUSTER

Lynda La Plante
Prime Suspect

Coming soon from Simon & Schuster ...

When a prostitute is found murdered in her bedsit,
the Metropolitan police set to work finding the perpetrator
of this brutal attack. DNA samples lead them straight to
George Marlow, a man previously convicted of attempted
rape. Everything appears to add up and the police think
they've found their man, but things aren't
quite what they seem ...

Detective Chief Inspector Jane Tennison came through
the ranks the hard way, opposed and resented at every step
by her male colleagues. So when DCI Shefford falls ill,
the opportunity for Tennison to get herself noticed finally
arrives. But the boys are not happy and every one
of her colleagues is willing her to trip up.

Desperate to remove all doubt around her suspect,
Tennison struggles to make the charges stick. And then
a second body turns up. With the team against her, and a
dangerous criminal still on the loose, DCI Jane Tennison
must fight to prove herself, now or never.

Paperback ISBN 978-1-47110-021-5
Ebook ISBN 978-1-47110-023-9

**SIMON &
SCHUSTER**

Lynda La Plante
She's Out

**They locked her up in Holloway for murder . . . but
now she's out, she has unfinished business to attend to.**

After serving a lengthy sentence for shooting her husband
at point blank range, Dolly Rawlins is set free from prison,
with only one thing on her mind – the six million in
diamonds she stashed prior to her imprisonment.

Waiting for Dolly is a group of women who all served time
with her. They know about the diamonds and they want a
cut. Also waiting is a detective sergeant in the Metropolitan
Police. He holds her personally responsible for the death
of his sister in the diamond raid ten years earlier.
And now he wants her back inside.

Dolly Rawlins has other plans: to realise the dream that
kept her going for years in prison. But against such
determined opposition, the fantasy soon turns into
a very different, tragic and violent reality …

**Paperback ISBN 978-1-47110-027-7
Ebook ISBN 978-1-47110-029-1**